REBELS OF RUSHMORE

THE COMPLETE SERIES

MICHELLE HERCULES

INFINITE SKY PUBLISHING

Rebels of Rushmore: The Complete Series © 2023 by Michelle Hercules

This book is a work of fiction. Names, characters, places, and incidents either are products of the author's imagination or are used fictitiously. Any resemblance to actual persons, living or dead, events, or locales is entirely coincidental.

Photography: Michelle Lancaster
Models: Lochie Carey & Meika Woollard

Paperback ISBN: 978-1-959167-21-1

HEART STOPPER

REBELS OF RUSHMORE BOOK ONE

Troy Alexander is sex on a stick and every girl's dream at John Rushmore University. He's also the bane of my existence.

Our meet-cute wasn't exactly cute. He called me a nerd, and I accused him of slacking off on the field. Now, we have to live together.

I'm supposed to try to play nice to keep a roof over my head. Not in my nature. Our arrangement could be a living hell, but slowly, I realize the worst thing he ever did wasn't calling me names. It was making me see there's more to him under the surface. And now, I'm screwed.

ONE

CHARLIE

I'm already on my second cup of coffee and still no sign of Troy Alexander, the star of the Rushmore Rebels football team, who I have to interview for the school newspaper. I almost strangled Blake when he gave me the last-minute assignment. It was only his promise to be my bitch in next week's LARP event that convinced me to step in for Ludwig, the dude who usually covers the sports section of the paper.

Football and jocks are not in my orbit, so I spent the last twenty minutes learning as much as I could about the Rushmore Rebels' quarterback. People seem to regard him like a god, and honestly, no one deserves to be treated as such. He has an okay average, winning more games than losing them. This year is different though. He's a senior, and most of the time, that's when the players really try to give their all. But Troy seems to have lost his steam, not really going the extra mile when he should. That's according to the notes I got from Ludwig, of course. I wouldn't be able to tell the difference if I watched a game, which I haven't.

Since the jerkface is late, I snoop his social media profiles. I can't gather much from Facebook unless I'm friends with him, and there's no chance I'll send a request, not when his Instagram feed has plenty of photos that paint a picture of who Troy Alexander is. It's clear the guy has acquired a taste for high-adrenaline sports, from skydiving to mountain climbing. Some are quite intense and dangerous, such as extreme snowboarding. I wonder what his coach has to say about his quarterback's new hobby.

I swallow the last drops of my coffee, already debating if I should go for a third cup, but when I can't stop bouncing my legs up and down, I have my answer. I'm already jittery as hell; inhaling more caffeine is definitely a bad idea.

The coffee shop's doorbell chimes, earning my attention. But it's not Troy coming in, only a couple of sorority girls wearing their matching pink hoodies with their house's emblem embroidered on them.

Clenching my teeth, I check the time. *Fuck.* He's forty minutes late. It's safe to assume he stood me up. I lost track of time, or I wouldn't have waited so long. *Great.*

I'm busy texting Blake, telling him he owes me big time, when someone drops onto the chair opposite mine. It's Troy, looking hotter than Hades in casual jeans and a T-shirt. Golden hair, golden skin, and a face that belongs on the cover of a magazine. He's sex on a stick, something I wasn't prepared for. His Instagram pictures don't really do him justice.

"Hi, you must be Ludwig's replacement. Have you been waiting long?" He smiles as if he didn't already know the answer to that.

I pick my jaw up from the floor, hoping he didn't catch me drooling, and frown. "How did you know who I was?"

"You look like the type who works for the paper." He shrugs, then eyes the two girls who entered the coffee shop earlier, giving them a wolfish grin. They were already ogling him, but Troy's attention sends them into a fit of giggles.

Really?

"What's that supposed to mean?" I snap.

Troy faces me again, sporting an innocent expression. "Are you that unaware of the vibe you give off?"

I lean back, crossing my arms over my chest. "Enlighten me."

His lips curl into a smirk while his eyes dance with glee. "Your T-shirt with the paper's logo. That's how I knew."

Heat rushes to my cheeks. I had completely forgotten I was wearing it.

"But you also have the nerd look about you," he continues, renewing my irritation with him.

"Nerd look, huh? Could it be my glasses?" I push the frames back up my nose using my middle finger.

Troy quirks an eyebrow. "Probably. Can we please make this a quickie? I have places to be."

I scoff. "You have some nerve. You're the one who was forty minutes late!"

He flinches as if my outburst surprised him. "Gee, I'm sorry, okay? I had to deal with a situation. I'm here now, so fire away."

Flaring my nostrils, I grab my phone. "Is it okay if I record this?"

"Sure. Go ahead."

"So, Troy, when did you decide not to give a fuck about football anymore?"

He doesn't answer for a couple of beats, narrowing his eyes. "Excuse me?"

"I mean, your performance in the last game was half-assed at best, and you only won because the other team was awful."

A humorless laugh escapes his lips. "So, this is how it's going to be, huh? I'm late a few minutes, and you're going to pull the heinous bitch card."

I try not to wince at his name-calling, but if I'm going to succeed in this profession, I can't let assholes get under my skin. "Oh, sweetie. It's cute that you think I'm asking tough questions because I'm mad at you. But we both know the truth. You messed up royally in the previous game. What was your excuse? Did you also have to deal with a *situation* then?"

Troy's face turns ashen, and his jaw clenches tight as he shoots daggers from his eyes. I notice his balled fists on the table and how his breathing is shallow now. Boy, I got to him good. I feel kind of guilty. You never know what issues people are dealing with.

He stands up suddenly, almost toppling his chair over. "We're done."

Shit. Maybe I went too far.

TROY

Fuck. I knew today was going to be hell. I can always count on everything going wrong whenever I have to meet my mother. Sometimes I suspect she's a witch because she sure as shit can hex my life. We had our monthly lunch at an upscale private club, during which she spent the hour downing martinis and picking on my sister, Jane, and me. Well, she mostly enjoys criticizing Jane. It's her feeble attempt to act motherly.

I can handle Mommy Dearest's harsh words, but poor Jane takes everything to heart. The more Mom talks, the more my sister shrinks into herself. It pisses me off. I was late for my interview with that shrew from the paper because I'd had to undo all the damage Mom had done to Jane.

I can't believe I let that Lois Lane wannabe get under my skin. To be fair, I had already been on edge. I should have just rescheduled the damn meeting. What I shouldn't have done is storm out of the coffee shop like a coward. No wonder my blood is still boiling.

Who does she think she is to judge me like that? I doubt she knows anything about football or even attended the last game. She'd have been with Ludwig, and I'd have remembered a face like hers. Too fucking pretty and doesn't even know it. *Damn it.* She had to go and be a bitch.

Coach Clarkson already gave me a tongue-lashing for sucking last Saturday. I had fucked up. My head wasn't in the game, but explaining why wasn't an option. Sure, if the coach knew the truth, he wouldn't have given me such a hard time. Only I'd rather people believe I slacked off for no good reason than them know it was the anniversary of Robbie's death. No one knows, not even my closest friends. What would they think if they knew I'd let my brother die?

I can't go back to the mausoleum I call home in this state. I don't want to be alone right now, and I have too much pent-up aggression that needs to go somewhere, so I shoot a quick text to Andreas, telling him I'm headed to the gym. He's always game for a workout. The guy has an infinite supply of energy. He's like the Energizer Bunny, a comparison that suits him well in more ways than one. The fucker is a damn Casanova and has probably banged his way to New Zealand and back.

When I park in front of the upscale warehouse-style gym, my anger has decreased by half. I spot Andreas's Bronco two spots to my left. No surprise he's already here. He, unlike me, lives right on campus in a shared apartment with Danny Hudson, a freshman who will probably take my place as the new QB next year.

I grab my duffel bag from the trunk and head inside the building. It's the middle of the afternoon, and the place is pretty packed. It annoys me to work out in a full house, but beggars can't be choosers.

I quickly change and then head to the gym's main room. Andreas is spotting Danny at the bench press when I find them.

"Dude, who stole your cookie?" he asks.

I roll my eyes. Everything out of the guy's mouth is related to food or girls. "It's one of those days. I had lunch with my mother and Jane earlier. You know how those events usually go."

"Like eating sawdust?" Danny chimes in.

"Pretty much."

"How is Jane doing? I haven't seen her in months," Andreas asks casually, not even glancing in my direction.

He knows he's not allowed to get near my sister or entertain any ideas about her. She's still in high school, for starters. Also, she doesn't need to get her heart broken by the most notorious manwhore on campus.

"Jane is fine," I reply through clenched teeth.

"Whoa. You don't need to bite my head off. I was just asking."

"You look pissed," Danny pipes up. "Are you still sour about your talk with the coach?"

"Nah. I'm over that," I lie. I hate that I screwed up, but wallowing in it won't help either. "He had the right to chew my ass. My current mood is in part to blame on a fucking nosy reporter from the school paper."

"Wait. I thought Ludwig was a buddy of yours." Andreas arches his eyebrows.

"He couldn't make it, and his replacement was a fucking bitch. She dared to ask when I stopped giving a fuck about football."

"Wow. That's savage." Danny chuckles. "Your charming skills didn't work on her?"

"I wasn't myself."

"Please tell me you put the bitch back in her place," Andreas retorts angrily.

I take Danny's spot on the bench. "That's what I should have done. Instead, I left."

Andreas whistles. "Troy Alexander avoiding a confrontation. That's new. Are you sure you didn't sleep with her and forget to call the next day?"

"Unlike yours, my bedroom doesn't have a revolving door. I remember my hookups."

He shrugs. "If you say so."

"Can we drop the subject? I didn't come here to gossip like a fucking sorority girl."

A wicked grin appears on Andreas's face. "Speaking of sorority girls...."

He proceeds to tell us about his latest sexual escapade, not sparing us any details, but I tune him out. No matter how much I want to forget what happened in the coffee shop, I can't get the Lois Lane wannabe out of my head.

Damn it.

TWO

CHARLIE

I'm in the zone, my fingers flying over the keyboard, when Blake sits on the edge of my desk. I ignore him. It took forever for me to get a good flow going, and he's not going to mess it up.

Wishful thinking.

Blake is a pest and clears his throat, as if his butt occupying precious space on my workstation wasn't obvious enough.

With a sigh, I lean back in my chair and glance at him. "What?"

"What the hell did you just send me?"

I fake an air of innocence. "You have to be more specific than that."

"Cut the bullshit, Charlie. You know I can't publish that article about Troy. You destroyed him. Shit, I've seen movie critics be kinder to *The Phantom Menace*."

"I only wrote what was presented to me. It's not my fault Troy bailed from the interview when I asked the tough questions."

"Come on, Charlie. I know you. You can't fool me with your

angelic face. I've seen your dark side, and it's mean as fuck. You got mad at Troy because he was late, and you decided to get revenge. You can do that on your own time, not in my paper." He jumps off the desk, fixing his tweed jacket in the process.

Blake is the poster child for the dress-for-the-job-you-want mentality, hence the stupid jacket and slacks. His dark hair is combed back, highlighting his widow's peak and pale complexion. It's not by chance that he plays a vampire in our ongoing LARP game.

We've known each other since kindergarten, and we dated in high school. Most exes can't remain friends, but Blake and I had a solid friendship before, which helped. And the decision to break up was mutual.

"Whatever. I'm not rewriting it." I turn to my screen.

"We can't simply not run the interview!"

I shrug. "Get Ludwig to write one for you. He's buddies with Troy. I'm sure he can come up with a bullshit article that highlights all of Troy's assets."

"You can be such a bitch sometimes," he mumbles.

"Heinous bitch. That's what Troy said." I smirk.

"Did he really call you that?"

I look at Blake, noticing the deep frown. He can call me names—*sometimes*, when I deserve it—but we have the relationship for that. He won't tolerate any jerk disrespecting me.

"Chill, okay? Technically, he said I was pulling the heinous bitch card, which, to be fair, I was. You can put away your knight in shining armor outfit for now."

He clamps his jaw shut, but he'll ruminate on that for hours. "If you were trying to get me to publish your interview, it won't work. I'll think of something to fill that spot."

"Whatever."

I don't care one way or another. I wrote the article, which served as a way to get rid of the anger. I might also have tweeted about it, but no one in Troy's circle follows me, so the chances he'll read it are slim.

I'm fine if my article never gets published. I have bigger fish to fry. I'm writing the storyline for next weekend's LARP event, and it needs to be finished today. Most of the time I don't mind this side job. It's fun to come up with crazy stories that will be acted out, but I've had to work on several assignments for school as well, which has made my schedule this week hell.

A text message pops on my screen. It's from Ben, my baby brother. I see it's a picture, so I click on it. A smile blossoms on my lips. Ben finally finished his costume for this weekend. His character is a troll hunter and, as such, needs several props. He's been working on that project for months. I reply with a heart emoji.

Growing up, Ben and I shared our love for fantasy worlds and grand quest stories, so it's not a surprise we both got into LARPing. He found it first, a suggestion from the school counselor to help him with his social anxiety.

"Wow, did you see that? Ben is looking badass," Blake says from across the room.

No surprise Ben also texted Blake. They're close.

"Yeah. I can't wait for this weekend."

"Me neither. How is that storyline coming along?"

"I'm almost done."

"If you make me look good, I'll forgive you for the Troy mishap." He winks at me.

"You're out of your mind. You've already agreed to be my bitch. No backsies."

"Ugh. You're the worst."

"I'm going to ask again. Why aren't you two dating?" Angelica, the newest member of the *Rushmore Gazette*, asks.

"Been there, done that, bought the T-shirt," I reply with a shake of my head.

"But you have great chemistry."

Blake and I trade glances, then burst out laughing.

"What's so funny?" The poor girl alternates looking between us.

"Maybe one day we'll tell you," I say.

Unlikely.

Blake and I are the perfect match on paper. We like the same movies, the same books, are into similar hobbies, and mesh really well intellectually. But chemistry, the stuff that makes my knees go weak and my stomach turn into knots, is what we never had or will.

"Are you going to the Pike party tonight?" She changes the subject, thankfully.

Blake snorts. "Not in this lifetime."

Angelica gets the dumbfounded look again, so I'm quick to explain, "Blake doesn't do Greek Row."

"Why not?"

"Because they're all fucking assholes," he replies angrily.

She glances at me for further explanation, but I just shrug. That's Blake's issue. It's up to him to elaborate.

"We also have a LARP meeting tonight," I add.

"Oh, that's the Live Action Role Playing thingy, right?"

"Yep."

"I've always thought people who were into those things were a bunch of weirdos, but you guys aren't."

My spine goes taut, and I see Blake has a similar reaction to mine. Angelica's comment wasn't malicious, but it's hard not to get defensive.

"How do you know we aren't weirdos?" Blake raises an eyebrow.

Angelica's cheeks turn bright pink, and she drops her gaze to her laptop, avoiding eye contact. "I have to finish this article before my English Lit class."

Blake and I share a what-can-you-do glance. A second later, he sends me a message through Facebook.

> I'm kind of tired of people's bullshit. Aren't you?

Since when do you care about what people think?

I don't.

Hmm. It sounds like you do, or is it Angelica's opinion that you care about?

Ha-ha. She's too vapid for my taste.

Oh, look who's judging now.

Shut up. What time are you picking me up?

Excuse me? Why do I have to drive?

Because my car is being serviced.

What about Fred?

He's going straight from the store. He said he has a surprise for us.

Oh, I love Fred's surprises.

Samesies.

I chuckle out loud.

Samesies? What are you now, a thirteen-year-old girl?

I'm practicing being your bitch for this weekend. LOL.

Right. I'll pick you up at five.

Sounds good.

F red is one of my best friends, but he's also a lunatic with mad convincing skills. If the guy wasn't an artist, he'd be a fantastic salesman. It's the only explanation for what's happening just outside of Zuko's Diner in the pouring rain.

The California sky decided to drop on us with all its fury as we were taking pictures, wearing Fred's surprise. His father owns one of the biggest movie prop companies in LA, and he scored us some sick postapocalyptic costumes. It won't work for our current LARP theme since we're not doing the *Mad Max* thing, but it was too badass to resist trying them on.

"I think we're ruining the pictures with our umbrellas," I joke.

"I'm not getting this baby wet," Blake replies.

"Just take the damn picture already," Fred shouts at Sylvana, the coordinator of our LARP group, who also happens to be his cousin.

"Stop talking and strike a pose, dumbasses," she fires back.

We have fun for about ten seconds until Sylvana demands to be in the pictures too. I remove my headgear and then trade places with her. Despite the rain, the sun hasn't set yet, and the clouds are scattered, so it's not as dark as it could be. I wait for them to get in position, aiming the phone in their direction. I only manage to take one photo before a splash of cold water drenches the back of my pants.

I yell and then turn around to curse at the driver who sped over the puddle near the curb. The four-wheel-drive truck stops not too far from us at a red light. I can't see his face, but the license plate says it all—ALXNDR7. It's Troy's fucking truck.

Son of a bitch.

He lowers his window and waves at me before speeding off as the light turns green.

"Who was that?" Sylvana asks.

"Troy Alexander, Rushmore Rebels' quarterback," I reply.

"Did he run over that puddle on purpose?" Fred asks.

"Sure looks like it." I pat my butt, confirming that it's soaking wet, underwear included.

Shit. I have to go home.

"What an ass," Fred replies.

"You know what?" Blake chimes in. "Fuck him and the football team. I'm running the article you wrote."

"What about not using the paper for revenge?"

He looks straight into my eyes. "That fucker just made it personal. No one messes with my staff."

THREE

"**D**ude! I can't believe you did that. Ruthless!" Andreas laughs from shotgun.

"Shit, man. Remind me never to get on your bad side," Danny pipes up from the back.

I tighten my hold on the steering wheel while I wrestle with the immediate guilt that followed my impulsive act. I'm not an asshole, and I usually don't hold on to grudges. I thought I was past my anger with the little reporter until I found her tweet about me. She called the experience of meeting me akin to attempting a conversation with a Neanderthal and said she'd have more luck with the caveman from the Geico commercial.

Once again, I let her get under my skin, and the result was me acting exactly like she'd said I did. It's my fault for cyberstalking her. I learned her full name from the email Ludwig had sent me. Charlie Fontaine. I was quick to find all her social media profiles, and that included her tweet about me. She didn't mention me again, but that one judgmental paragraph was enough to set me on edge.

"Accidents happen. It's her fault for standing near a puddle."

"Sure, like you didn't accelerate on purpose." Andreas chuckles.

"Can we drop this? Charlie is taking too much airtime."

"Charlie? So, you learned her name finally?" Danny makes that annoying remark.

"You'd better shut your piehole before I make you walk back to campus."

"Gee, relax."

"Are you coming to the Pike party?" Andreas finally changes the subject.

"A frat party? Not in the mood to hang out with that crowd. Besides, I have plans."

"Oh yeah? A hot date, or are you back to eating old porridge?"

"Man, you have to stop with the bad food analogies," Danny retorts.

"I couldn't agree more," I grumble. "And no, I don't have a date."

"It's old porridge. I knew it. You have to stop sleeping with your ex, man. It's not healthy."

"For the thousandth time, I'm not sleeping with Brooke," I grit out. "We just chatted after that one game when she came to visit—that's all. Besides, she lives in New York, remember?"

"Okay then. If you say so," Andreas replies sarcastically.

"Whatever. Believe what you want. I promised Grandma I'd have dinner with her. That's my hot date."

"Ah, cool. Is Jane going too?" Andreas looks out the window casually, but his left leg begins to bounce nervously.

What's up with him?

"Yeah. I have to pick her up in thirty."

"Where are you heading for dinner? I could eat."

I peel my gaze from the road for a second to glower at him. "Did you just ask to tag along to a family dinner? Are you for real?"

He shrugs. "What? We're friends, and your grandma loves me."

"Sorry, buddy, but I have to get back home," Danny interjects. "I have a major test tomorrow that I have to study for."

"No worries. I'm dropping *both* of you off first."

"Wow, really? You're terrified that your grandma loves me more than you, huh?"

I roll my eyes. "Yeah, that's it."

I wouldn't mind Andreas tagging along if it was only me. But Jane is in the mix, and I really don't want him near her. My sister is shy and completely different than the girls Andreas goes for, but she's a knockout, and bro code or not, I won't risk getting her on his radar.

CHARLIE

Things couldn't get any worse. On my way back to the house I share with three other girls, I receive a text from Vivian, one of my roommates, telling me there's been a fire at our place. When I get there, the firemen have already put it out—it was concentrated in the kitchen, thankfully—but we can't stay there. They discovered what we'd already known all along—the house is a freaking hazard and in violation of several housing codes. Long story short, I'm homeless.

"Shit. Where are we going to live?" I ask Vivian while we wait outside for the firemen to allow us in to collect our things.

"My boyfriend said I can move in with him, so this has turned out great for me." She smiles from ear to ear.

"Wasn't he totally against commitment?"

"Yeah. This fire was divine intervention."

"More like cheapskate-landlord neglect." I pull up my phone to text my parents. They'll tell me to stay with them until I find a new place, but they live an hour from campus. The commute will kill me.

"What are you wearing anyway? I thought your LARP deal was this weekend," Vivian asks.

"Oh, this was a gift from Fred."

She gives me an elevator glance, arching her eyebrows. "Interesting gift. It'd be great for Halloween, although it's not very sexy."

"Hmm, I don't know. I guess if I forgo the pants, I can be a slutty Imperator Furiosa."

"Who?"

"*Mad Max: Fury Road*?" I reply. Vivian gives me a blank stare, earning a shake of the head from me. "Never mind."

I also text Blake and Fred.

Almost immediately, Blake calls me back. "Please tell me you were joking about your place."

"I wish I were. At least it's stopped raining."

"What happened?"

"Who knows? No one was home, so we're assuming a fuse blew. That house was a disaster waiting to happen."

"When can you go back?"

"It's going to be months."

"Do you need a place to stay?"

I knew he was going to offer, but Blake lives with two other guys, and their place isn't that big. I'd have to sleep on the couch for sure.

"Thanks, but I'll just head to my parents' tonight and then start looking for another room to rent ASAP."

"It's going to be brutal finding something now that school has already started."

I pinch the bridge of my nose. "I know, but I can't worry about that now. I just need to get out of these damn wet clothes."

My fury with Troy returns, and I don't think it will go away that easily. Even knowing my article will be published isn't helping me feel better. Why am I allowing that smug bastard to control my emotions? I'm better than this.

"Are you still up for LARPing this weekend?" Blake asks.

"Yeah, Ben will be disappointed if I don't go. Besides, I'm in dire need of some fun."

One of the firemen approaches us, so I end the call quickly.

"You can go in to pack up your personal belongings now," he says.

"Thank you, sir," I reply.

"Nice outfit, by the way. Very authentic."

Heat creeps up my cheeks. "Uh, thanks."

I quicken my steps, trying to hide my embarrassment.

Vivian catches up with me, and once we're inside, she asks, "Why did you run away? He was cute."

"I didn't run away." I make a beeline to my room. What's up with all the girls I know trying to set me up with random guys? Do I look desperate to them?

I pack a duffel bag with clothes that will last me a week, and also my costume and props for the weekend. Then comes the difficult decision to select only a few beloved books to bring with me. I'm not against e-books, but there's something to be said about holding a real book in your hands. Plus, you don't own e-books; you just buy the license to view the content. It can be erased from your digital library without warning. No, thank you.

In the end, I choose my Tolkien collection. I have to come back here Sunday to pack the rest of my stuff. I'll do that after my volunteering job. As busy as I am, I can't miss it. It's Gladys's ninetieth birthday party, and I have to be there.

I'm heading out the door when text messages and notifications start to blow up my phone.

What the hell? This can't be about the fire.

I click on a random message, which turns out to be hate mail.

Shit on toast. The article about Troy is out.

FOUR

CHARLIE

I skipped class on Friday—though not because I was afraid to deal with my article's repercussion. I don't give a flying fuck about Troy's fan club outrage. No, thanks to that idiot, I caught a cold—one more item for my list of grievances against him. I was still all sniffles and coughs during LARP, which made for a rough event. Thankfully, I'm feeling better today, so it didn't completely ruin my weekend, only half of it.

It's 9:00 a.m., and the parking lot at Golden Oaks is still relatively empty. Sunday is prime visitation day for the assisted living part of the complex, and I'm glad I got here before the crowd. Gladys's party is not until noon, but I promised the administrator I'd help set it up.

It was sheer luck that I kept the décor for the party in my trunk. I'd have stored it near the kitchen if I had unloaded it last week. I hoist the two extra-large bags over my shoulders and then head inside the building. Cheyenne Benson, the administrator, is behind the reception desk today. Her face splits into a wide grin when she sees me coming through the door.

"Charlie! You're here early. Nice dress." Her smile broadens.

"Thanks. I wanted to beat the traffic. I'm staying at my folks' in Littleton."

"Oh no. You had to brave the freeway? That beast never slows down."

"Perks of living near LA." I wink at her.

"For sure." She walks around the desk. "Let me help you with that."

I give her one of the bags. "How many people are we expecting today?"

"The usual number for a Sunday. I'm not sure if Gladys's grandkids will be here. I couldn't get a confirmation from her son."

"That's too bad."

"Yeah. Between you and me, I don't think the grandkids want to be here. She doesn't remember them, and it's just hard."

Gladys has Alzheimer's, and the disease is progressing fast now. The birthday party is more for the residents in the independent living wing of Golden Oaks than her.

We head to the entertainment area where tables have already been set up. I'm not surprised when I spot Ophelia Holland, the coolest lady I've ever met, giving orders to Jack Morris and Louis Romano, her boyfriends.

She's already dressed to the nines, wearing a pink Chanel suit and her pearls. Her chin-length hair is curly and currently baby blue. Every week it's a different color. She turns around and smirks when she sees my outfit. I lost a bet last weekend, and this is my penance—I have to wear a Sailor Moon costume today. I'm all for cosplaying, but there's a time and place for it, and it's definitely not at a ninety-year-old's birthday party.

"Looking good, Charlie," Louis says, not hiding his amusement. "Jon-Jon would have loved it."

"Yeah, right. He'd probably think I'd lost my senses completely."

Jon-Jon was my grandpa. He lived here for five years before he passed away last year. It's how I got to know the place and their residents. I became so attached to them that I kept coming back every weekend. Cheyenne was the one who suggested I list my time here as volunteer work to make my résumé look good. But that's not the reason I come. I love everyone.

I set the bag near the table before I hug Ophelia. She won't reveal her age, but even so, I can tell her body is becoming frailer. She looks healthy though, and she's full of energy as usual.

"Why are you here so early, Charlie? Didn't you have your LARP event yesterday?"

"Yeah, but I'm staying at my folks' temporarily, and it's a drive."

She furrows her white eyebrows. "Why are you staying there? Is everything all right?"

"There was a small fire at my place, and now I have to find another room to rent."

"Oh no. That's dreadful. Was there a lot of damage?"

"Mainly in the kitchen. Still, it's going to be a pain in the butt finding a room that's not out of my price range or a complete dump."

A light bulb seems to flash above her blue head as she widens her eyes. "I have the perfect place for you. You can rent a room from me."

"What do you mean?"

"I own a house fairly near your school's campus. My grandson goes to John Rushmore too, and he's currently living there."

"And he won't mind getting a roommate?"

"No, of course not. He's such an angel. You'll love him. Besides, the house is big enough that you won't be in each other's hair."

I begin to feel hopeful. I'd rather rent a room from Ophelia than deal with another sleazeball like my previous landlord.

"What's your grandson's name? Maybe I know him."

"Wolfgang, but I call him Wolfie."

I chuckle. "Love it."

"How about I give him a call and tell him you'll be coming by to check out the house? When can you stop by?"

"I guess as soon as I leave here."

"Sounds good. He should be home later today."

Something heavy crashes on the floor, earning our attention. The bottom of the box Louis and Jack were trying to move gave out, and now the karaoke machine is in two parts.

"What have you done?" Ophelia strides in their direction, ready to give them a good old tongue-lashing.

I shake my head, trying not to laugh at the scene. There's never a dull moment when the trio is involved, that's for sure. I'll have to remind Ophelia to call her grandson later. I've noticed she's become forgetful, and she's also been confusing names.

My chest becomes tight. I don't want to think about losing Ophelia. It was hard enough when Grandpa died. I can't bear the thought of her leaving me too.

TROY

Karma is a bitch. My stunt in front of Zuko's Diner earned me Charlie's prompt retaliation. She published a scathing article about me, but it backfired royally. She was destroyed on social media, #canceled being used everywhere in association with her and the paper. Even the dean got involved and forced the article to be retracted immediately.

I should feel vindicated, but oddly, I don't. I was an ass to her in the coffee shop. I should have apologized for being so late. I also shouldn't have splashed her on purpose. Now all I have is an annoying sense of guilt swirling in my chest.

There's nothing worse nowadays than to become a social pariah. Keyboard warriors and their digital pitchforks are a bunch of fucking bullies. But man, that article... she didn't hold back. And it was all bullshit. I'm not an entitled rich boy who doesn't respect their teammates. Yes, I do practice extreme sports, but they aren't life-threatening. At least not all of them. Besides, I know what I'm doing.

Damn it. I really shouldn't feel bad about what happened to her. She dug her own grave.

I've just gotten out of the shower when I see there's a missed call from Grandma. She left a voice mail. I listen to it immediately because you never know what kind of shenanigans she's involved in. Mom thought we wouldn't have to worry about Grandma when she decided to move in at Golden Oaks. *Yeah, right.*

There's a lot of noise in the background, so I can barely understand what she's saying. It doesn't help that Thing One and Thing Two—aka her boyfriends—are talking over her. They sound drunk, which means they probably are. What I can make out from their slurred speeches is that Sailor Moon is going to come by the house later to check out a room to rent.

I rub my forehead. Knowing Grandma, I can't simply discard her message as nonsensical. She's probably decided to rent a room to some stranger. But she wouldn't let my friends move in. Typical Ophelia Holland move. I'm not even annoyed. That's how Grandma rolls. I hope the girl isn't a fucking groupie. The last thing I want is to room with a football fan.

I doubt the girl's name is Sailor Moon, but I can't get hold of Grandma to ask for more details, such as when she's coming by.

I glance at the clock. I was planning to head to the grocery store now because I'll be too lazy to go later.

Ah fuck it. I'll just leave a message at the front door in case "Sailor Moon" decides to stop by before I get back.

FIVE

CHARLIE

I go check out Ophelia's house straight from Golden Oaks, which unfortunately means I'm still wearing my Sailor Moon costume. I wasn't planning on stopping by anywhere after the party, but it would be insane to go home and change considering the drive. I hope her grandson doesn't think I'm a lunatic.

I park in front of the Spanish-style house and stare at the construction for a minute. It's in a nice area, quiet, and the best part, it's only five minutes away from campus. It's closer to school than my old place was. And Ophelia wasn't kidding when she said the house was big. Judging from the outside, it must have at least four bedrooms. I wonder why Wolfie never got any roommates.

Maybe he likes to live alone. *Shit. Am I imposing?* It's Ophelia's house and she can do whatever she wants, but the last thing I want is to feel unwelcome.

I fix the skirt of my dress first to make sure my ass isn't showing and then stride toward the front door. Taking a deep breath, I look for the doorbell. My eyes catch a note taped next to it. It's addressed to Sailor Moon.

What the hell? How does he know? I groan internally. Ophelia must have said something. I don't know if I should be relieved or mortified.

I grab the folded paper and read the note.

Hey, sorry I missed you. I had to run a quick errand. Feel free to go in and check out the house. The key is under the welcome mat. I'll be back shortly.

P.S. In case you're not Sailor Moon but a regular burglar, I have hidden cameras everywhere. Steal from me, and your ass is mine.

A chuckle escapes my lips. I think Wolfie and I will get along fabulously.

I retrieve the key from under the mat and let myself in. A faint old-house smell reaches my nose, and as I walk farther inside, it mixes with a delicious lemony aftershave scent. Goose bumps break out on my arms. I'm a sucker for good smells.

The living room is large, but even so, the L-shaped leather couch almost looks too big for the space. There's also a brand-new flat-screen TV that takes up most of the wall, and tucked neatly in the storage unit below it, I spot several video game consoles. I shake my head. Boys and their toys.

I veer for the kitchen, and my excitement grows by leaps and bounds. It's been remodeled recently with top-of-the-line appliances. I like to bake when I have the time, but my old kitchen offered me zero motivation. It was small and too old. This is heaven.

It's a two-story house, and I quickly head to the second floor. I wish Wolfie had told me which room would be mine if I decide to stay, but he's not here, so that means I can explore the entire house.

I open the first door I come to, which leads to a big, airy room with large windows. It's almost empty except for some boxes that are stacked up in a corner. I walk in, guessing this one would be my room. There's an en suite bathroom, and the walk-in closet would fit all my clothes and costumes. This is a dream-come-true bedroom. I really have to make sure Wolfie likes me because I'm already in love with this place.

I continue my perusal of the second floor. The next door I try opens to a room that's currently being used as a home gym. There's a bench press, several dumbbell weights, elastic bands, and a treadmill. Apparently, Wolfie likes to work out. I wonder if he'll let me use this space too. I have a gym membership, but if I go there twice a week, I consider it a win. Working out from home would be much easier.

There's another door at the end of the hallway. That must be Wolfie's bedroom. I debate opening the door to peer inside, but then I remember his threat on the note to the potential burglar. He said there were several hidden cameras in the house. Was that a bluff or the truth?

The sound of the front door opening makes the decision for me. Curiosity killed the cat, but that won't happen today.

"Hello? Sailor Moon, are you still here?" Wolfie's baritone voice echoes from downstairs.

"Yeah, I'm coming down."

Suddenly, butterflies take residence in my stomach. I'm in love with this house, and I want Ophelia's grandson to like me. When I reach the living room, he's in the kitchen, putting away groceries in the fridge. His back is to me, and he's wearing a hoodie, so I can't really see his face.

"This house is amazing," I say as I approach the kitchen counter.

"Yeah, it's not too bad."

He turns then, and my stomach bottoms out.

Troy fucking Alexander is standing in front of me.

His eyes widen in surprise, and for a moment, neither of us speaks. My brain is going a hundred miles an hour.

This can't be happening. It must be a sick joke. Troy can't possibly be Ophelia's grandson.

"What the hell are you doing here?" he asks finally, narrowing his eyes.

"I came to see about the room," I reply automatically. I'm still in shock at Troy's presence here.

His eyes take in my ensemble. "*You're* Sailor Moon?"

Like an idiot, I drop my chin and look at my clothes for a second. "I guess I am for today. She told me your name was Wolfgang."

"That's my middle name. She never calls me Troy." He threads his fingers through his long bangs, pushing them back. "I can't believe this. How the hell do you know my grandmother?"

"She lives in Golden Oaks. My grandfather was also a resident before he passed. I've known Ophelia since she moved in. I still visit every weekend."

His eyebrows arch. "Why?"

"Why?" My voice rises. "Do I need a reason to visit friends?"

Troy stares at me with his mouth hanging open. He doesn't speak for several beats, but I bet his mind is whirling just like mine is.

"You're friends with my grandmother?"

"Yes. Is that a surprise to you? She's awesome."

His expression softens a tad, and I notice a faint twitch of his lips. "Yeah, she is."

"Well, I guess I should go."

I turn toward the front door. There's no sense in lingering. Troy would never agree to me moving in. I can't even blame the guy, not after the shitty article I wrote about him.

Mom was right. Sometimes it's better to just forget stuff and move on.

"Wait. What did you think?" he asks, making me pause.

Slowly, I turn back and look at him. "Are you asking me about the house?"

"Yeah. Do you like it?"

I don't detect sarcasm in his tone, and his eyes are devoid of deceit.

"I love it."

"Yeah. It's pretty nice. Why do you need to rent a room?"

I let out a heavy sigh. "There was a small fire incident where I used to live. No major damage, but the house was a dump to begin with. Now my landlord has to fix all the problems before we can move back in."

"I'm sorry to hear that. Well, if you like the house, I suppose you can move in. That is, if you don't mind sharing it with me."

My jaw drops to the floor. "Are you serious?"

He shrugs in a boyish way, making my heart skip a beat.

"Sure. I can't simply say no. Grandma likes you. That counts for something. Plus, you're wearing that." He pulls his cell phone from his back pocket and snaps a picture. "I can't send Sailor Moon away."

I cross my arms over my chest, feeling uber self-conscious. "Why did you take my picture?"

"Leverage." He shoves his phone back in his pocket.

I roll my eyes. "Dude, do you think I'm embarrassed to be wearing a costume? I LARP, for crying out loud."

"You what?" His eyebrows shoot to the heavens.

"Never mind." I step closer to the kitchen counter. "Okay, here's the gist. If you're saying I can move in only to get back at me for writing that article, just tell me now. I don't have time to engage in childish games."

"Wait. Do you think this is all part of a retaliation plan?"

"I'm not discounting anything."

He scoffs. "Girl, you're too conceited for your own good. I don't need to retaliate. Besides, your article has already been pulled down, and you're currently the most hated person on campus. I think that's plenty."

I ball my hands into fists, trying to hide how much his offhanded comment aggravates me. Several choice words get lodged in my throat, but I bite my tongue and keep them bottled inside. I need a place to live, and this is the best I'll get.

"Most hated person, huh?"

He shoves his hands into his hoodie pockets. "Do you want the room or not?"

"I'm assuming I'd get the one with the boxes."

"Yep."

"I do want it, but if you're not doing this as some kind of sick joke, then why?"

"Unlike you, I don't opt for below-the-belt retribution."

"Oh my God. You're so full of…." I trail off, almost forgetting that I can't antagonize Troy.

"So full of what?" He quirks an eyebrow, smirking at me.

I purse my lips, hating fate for putting me in this situation. "You know what? Forget it. When can I move in?"

"Whenever you want. We have an away game next weekend, so I'll be gone Friday."

I don't move from my spot as I keep watching Troy through slits, trying to sniff out the lie. But either he has a perfect poker face or he's truly moved on from our feud. If that's the case, he's a better person than I am.

Anger is still simmering in my gut. I don't care about all the bullies who came out to defend his honor. I'm pissed that he got the dean involved, which resulted in my article being removed from the paper's site.

What happened to free fucking speech?

SIX

Coach Clarkson went hard on us during training, so now we're licking our wounds at Tailgaters, a college bar two blocks from my place. I just told Andreas and Danny about my new roommate, and now they're staring at me with matching stunned expressions.

"You're joking, right?" Andreas finally snaps out of his stupor.

I take a sip of my beer before I reply, "Nope. It turns out Charlie is best friends with my grandmother. I didn't think it was worth upsetting her over that girl."

"Yeah, but she was horrible to you," Danny argues. "What if she's a bitch 24-7?"

"Then I'll kick her out, and Grandma won't be able to say a thing. Besides, she needs this room badly. She'll be on her best behavior."

"That doesn't mean *you* have to behave." Andreas raises an eyebrow.

"I'm not going to be an ass on purpose."

He shrugs. "Whatevs. It'd be the easiest way to get rid of her."

"Nah. She'll move back to her old place once the landlord finishes renovations."

I sense the lie as soon as it leaves my mouth. Charlie said her old place was a dump. She'll never move out of her own accord. But I won't resort to douche tactics. Maybe it won't be as bad as everyone thinks.

Or maybe you're just thinking with your dick, Troy. She sure looked hot in that Sailor Moon costume. Fuck.

My cock stirs in my jeans as I remember Charlie's getup. It's not helping my case that I took a picture of her… and I might have jerked off to it as well.

"Uh-oh. Troy has gotten the look," Danny pipes up, bringing me back to the present.

My erection is now straining against my jeans, but if I try to find a better sitting position, the guys will immediately know about my situation.

"What the hell are you talking about?" I take a large gulp of my beer, hoping the alcohol will give me some relief.

"Oh yeah. The look. I think our friend is not telling us the whole story. Come on, Troy. Spill it already. Why did you agree to let Miss Stick Up Her Ass move in with you?"

I shake my head. "There's nothing going on. I'm just helping her out."

Andreas watches me through slits. "Right." He turns his attention to his phone, and after a moment, a victorious grin splits his face. "Aha. Mystery solved."

"What?" Danny leans closer to look at Andreas's screen. "Oh. You didn't say Charlie was hot."

"She's not hot. She photographs well." I chug the rest of my beer, dropping the glass back down with excessive force. "I'm going home."

"We just got here." Danny glances at me.

Andreas elbows his arm. "He has a reason to hurry back. There's a sexy nerd waiting for him."

I get up and throw some money on the table. "You can be a real dick sometimes, Andy."

With a knowing smile, he leans back in the chair, linking his fingers behind his head. "Don't hate me because I'm right."

"Whatever."

I stride out of the bar, ignoring the hungry glances I receive from the girls I pass. If they're looking for cock fun, Andreas and Danny will gladly provide that. I love sports, but banging as many chicks as I can is not one I care for. That's Andreas's department. I'm not a saint, of course. I do hook up; I just don't make a game out of it.

When I turn on my street, I don't see a moving truck. Charlie told me she'd bring all her stuff today. Maybe she's done moving in. We don't have a garage, and to my annoyance, Charlie took my usual spot in front of the house. Grinding my teeth, I drive a little farther until I find another parking space. The walk back to the house serves to turn my irritation down a notch. If I tell her not to park in my usual space, it'd be a dick move. Besides, it's not reserved for me. Any of our neighbors can park there. They simply don't out of courtesy.

I'm looking forward to chilling out and playing a video game, but when I walk into the house, I realize that's not happening tonight. Charlie didn't simply move in. She took over my entire living room. There are a bunch of boxes spread in the area, some still shut but others with spilling contents. Loud music is pouring from her room upstairs.

"Charlie?" I call out.

I hear her hurried footsteps on the wooden floor, and then she appears at the top of the stairs wearing an oversize T-shirt and nothing else that I can see. Her legs are long, tan, and lean, and they're making my life seriously difficult at the moment.

Fuck me.

"Hi, Troy. Sorry about the mess. I didn't know you'd be home early." She runs down the stairs, pulling her hair back in a ponytail. The action lifts her shirt, revealing tiny jean shorts that barely cover her sweet ass.

"We have a six-hour bus drive tomorrow and a game on Saturday. Can't really stay out late." I stare at all the costumes and props that are covering my couch at the moment. "What happened here?"

She starts to collect the dresses that are draped over the back of the couch. "Oh, since I have so much more space, I decided to bring my stuff out of the storage unit. But I was doing a triage, and things kind of got out of hand."

"No kidding. If you don't mind, I'd like to have my couch back."

Charlie winces, and that's when I realize my words came out a little too harsh.

"Yeah, sure. I'll get this cleaned up right away. I'm not a messy girl, I promise." She quickens her pace, grabbing a load of clothes and tossing them back into boxes.

"Let me help you." I bend over to grab one of the closed boxes to bring up to her room when the bottom gives out. A myriad of clothes and objects falls out but luckily nothing breakable. "Okay, who did the packing?" I stare at the mess at my feet.

"I did, and don't give me that look. Some of those boxes got damp in storage."

I set the damaged box aside and bend over to retrieve one specific item that caught my attention. "What kind of cosplay are you into?" I show her a wooden dildo the size of my forearm.

Her blue eyes widen behind her glasses, and her plump lips make a perfect O. "Oh my God. Give me that." She snatches the dildo from my hand and hides it behind her back.

Her face is now brighter than a tomato, which makes me laugh.

"Hey, I'm not judging. But seriously."

"This wasn't part of a cosplay. This was a gag gift."

"That you decided to keep."

"Of course I did. It's an antique."

"If you say so."

"Oh, shut up and help me clean up this mess."

I arch both eyebrows. I can't believe Charlie just gave me an order. "Excuse me?"

"You're the one who dropped everything on the floor."

"I was just trying to help. It's not my fault you have terrible packing skills."

"I don't have terrible packing skills." She throws her hands up in the air—one still clutching the megalodon of all dildos.

A burst of laughter hits me again.

"What's so funny now?"

I stare at the object in her hand, making her roll her eyes.

"Oh, grow up."

"That's rich coming from the girl who still dresses up as fairies and princesses."

Her eyes narrow as she throws me a death glare. "Are you calling me a child?"

I shrug, shoving my hands in my pockets. "If the shoe fits."

"I knew things were too good to be true."

"What's that supposed to mean?" My good humor vanishes in a flash.

I sense she's about to blow a fuse, but whatever she was planning to blurt out gets stuck in her throat.

She shakes her head and says, "Never mind. Give me ten minutes. I'll get everything packed."

I was still willing to help, which is fucking crazy. But I sense that if I try, it'll only make matters worse.

Damn it. It's our first day as official roommates, and we've already argued over nothing. This will only lead to a bitter coexistence or angry sex.

My cock is totally on board for the latter.

SEVEN

CHARLIE

It's been a week since I moved in with Troy, and we've managed to avoid each other. Our schedules have been chaotic, and we're barely home. The beginning of our living arrangements was rocky, to say the least. It seems we can't be in the same room for more than five minutes before we start to argue. I've never met anyone who can push my buttons without even trying.

Troy had a game yesterday and didn't come home until the early hours of the morning. I only know the exact time because the jackass made a ruckus when he came in. At least he didn't bring a girl with him. We don't share a wall, but I'm sure I'd hear them getting it on.

I bet he's good in bed.

Whoa. Where did that thought come from?

You probably need to get laid, Charlie. It's been months.

Shut up, whore!

Ugh, my conscience is being such a bitch this morning. I'd better get my mind out of the gutter pronto.

I went to Golden Oaks yesterday, so I have Sunday all to

myself. I hit the gym first—I still haven't asked Troy if I can use his home workout room. Honestly, I don't think I'll ever ask. I'm in total avoidance mode.

The next stop is the grocery store. I load up, so I don't have to make another run in the middle of the week.

When I get home around noon, Troy is still sound asleep. I can hear him snoring from the hallway.

I haven't decided yet what I'm going to do the rest of the day, but a shower is the first order of business. I'm in the middle of washing my hair when the hot jets turn into drips, followed by nothing.

I glare at the showerhead while turning the knobs. "Are you kidding me?"

Cursing, I wrap myself in a towel and test the faucet. Dry. The toilet won't flush. Did the water company cut our water supply on a Sunday? *Fuck.* It can't be for lack of payment, and they warn you when they need to cut supply for maintenance work. I bet they did send a notice, and Troy simply forgot to tell me. *Son of a bitch.* I'm going to kill him.

Still dripping wet, I march to his bedroom. I don't barge in, but I do knock hard on his door.

"Troy! Get up!"

He groans, then says, "Go away!"

"No. Get your ass out here."

I hear the sound of sheets being tossed aside, then heavy steps stomping closer. He opens the door with a yank. "For fuck's sake! Wha—" His eyes widen. "Why are you naked and covered in soap?"

"Because I was taking a shower when suddenly the water cut off," I grit out.

"And how is it my fault that you forgot they were going to turn off the water for a couple hours?"

"I didn't forget! You never told me." I gesture widely with my hands, and the towel almost comes undone.

Troy notices, and his smirk is infuriating. "I attached the

notice on the kitchen board. It's really not my fault you missed it."

"Ugh! You're so annoying." I turn around and stride down the hallway. Instead of returning to my room, I run downstairs.

I have to get the shampoo out of my hair, and the only water we have in the house is Troy's sparkling shit. I grab a few bottles, then lean over the sink to rinse my hair with his fancy bubbly crap.

"What are you doing?" he asks.

Fuck. I didn't know he'd followed me.

"What does it look like?" I pour fizzing, ice-cold water over my head and hair, getting goose bumps immediately. Maybe I should have warmed it up in the microwave first.

"You'd better replace my Perrier," he says.

"Yeah, sure."

A throaty chuckle follows.

"What's so funny?" I ask.

"Do you realize that bent over like that, you're giving me quite a view?"

I snap back into a straight position, wincing as my now cold hair slaps against my back. "Were you ogling me?" I turn to glare at him.

He's not smiling now, and his hungry eyes make my mouth go dry. My pulse skyrockets as I wrestle with feelings of anger and desire. I was too pissed when I banged on his door to notice Troy was only wearing boxer shorts. Now his shredded abs and chest are all I can see.

My eyes have a will of their own. They travel south... and hot tamales. My lady parts turn into flames. Troy is aroused—big time. Emphasis on *big*.

Damn it. I can't fall for the trap that's Troy's godlike body.

"I couldn't help but look. You were flashing your... *goods*."

Heat creeps up my cheeks as I hug my middle, feeling completely exposed. "Well, don't get any ideas. That's all the view you'll get."

Summoning all the dignity I have left, I walk around him with my chin raised high. I purposely keep my pace normal, fighting the urge to run. Once in my bedroom, I begin to form a plan to protect myself from Troy's charms. I text Vivian, asking if her offer to set me up with one of her friends still stands. It's high time I get back into the dating scene.

TROY

Damn Charlie.

Why does she have to be so fucking hot? Now I'm sporting a raging boner, fantasizing about plunging my cock into her sweet pussy while she's bent over the sink like before. It's a sin for someone who I loathe so much to be that irresistible. And the worst part is that she wants me too. I saw the craving reflected in her blue eyes when she noticed my erection.

I. Cannot. Go. There.

She left a mess on the kitchen counter and on the floor. I focus on that, which helps dissolve any desire I had left. I clean up and then decide to head out for lunch. I didn't sleep nearly enough, but I can't go back to bed now.

After I put some clothes on, I go to one of my favorite joints, Zuko's Diner. It's an automatic decision. I always come here after a night of partying since they serve breakfast all day. But being here reminds me of Charlie again.

Hell. I need to get her out of my head.

I keep my sunglasses on as I stride to my usual booth; my head is pounding, so if I have to look like a douche, so be it.

"Troy?" a familiar voice calls out.

I turn slowly, and then my jaw drops. "Brooke? Holy shit. What are you doing here?" I change direction and stop next to her booth.

"I transferred to Rushmore," she replies excitedly.

"Really? Couldn't handle those New Yorkers, huh?"

She makes a face, furrowing her eyebrows and scrunching her nose as if she smelled something bad. "Ugh, no. They got two years of my life that I'll never get back. I'm a California girl through and through, no matter how much my old man wants me not to be. Are you meeting someone?"

"No. I'm solo today. I have the worst hangover."

She giggles. "I was gonna say, you do look rough. Sit with me. I can't believe I bumped into you here."

I slide into the seat opposite hers. "When did you get back?"

"Last week."

"And you didn't call me? I'm wounded." I press my hand against my chest, pretending to be hurt.

She waves her hand dismissively. "Stop. I was going to. I had to get situated."

"Where are you staying?"

"At a friend's condo for now. It's fifteen minutes from campus, but I'm hoping to find something closer. Is your grandmother still against you having roommates?"

She smiles in a persuasive way, making me uncomfortable. Like I'd ever want to live with my ex. Charlie is bad enough.

"Actually, I just got one."

Her eyebrows shoot up. "Oh, really? Let me guess. Andy?"

I snort. "Yeah, right. Grandma would never allow him to move in. Actually, my new roommate is a girl."

The easygoing smile wilts from her face. "Oh, you have a new girlfriend?"

Brooke seems hurt, which makes me uneasy.

We started dating in high school. She was a junior, and I, a senior. When she went to NYU, we tried the long-distance thing for six months. In the end, we decided to break up and remain friends. I hope she didn't transfer to Rushmore, wanting to rekindle our relationship. The spark is gone. I'm not sure if it was even there to begin with.

I laugh. "No, nothing like that. She's Grandma's friend, and she needed to rent a room last minute."

Brooke leans against the booth, looking relieved. "Oh, so you didn't even know her?"

"Nope. Total stranger."

"Is she nice?" Brooke asks casually, but I hear the double meaning of her question nonetheless.

Alarm bells sound in my head.

"Brooke, please tell me you didn't move back to Cali for me."

Her eyebrows shoot to the heavens. "What? Of course not. Gee, aren't you conceited?"

I shrug. "Just checking. I'm stoked that you're back, but we're just friends."

She narrows her eyes, flattening her lips. "Keep acting like an ass, and that friendship card might be revoked."

"Okay, okay." I flash her a dazzling smile. "Did you order already?"

"Yeah."

I flag the waitress and put my usual order in. She returns a moment later with a big cup of steaming coffee.

Brooke waits until she's gone to speak again. "So, you didn't answer my question. Is your roommate nice?"

I debate telling Brooke the truth about Charlie. The answer that comes out of my mouth surprises me. "Yeah, I think so."

Why did I lie?

"Well, I can't wait to meet her."

EIGHT

Another week passes, and I barely see Charlie. I should consider myself lucky, but at the same time, I secretly want to bump into her. Each one of our encounters has given me a perverted rush, and the adrenaline junkie in me craves that kind of stuff.

I just got home from the game, which we'd almost lost. If it wasn't for that field goal near the end, we might have. I'm pissed even though I did everything I could. I love football, but lately, extreme sports have been giving me the type of satisfaction I need. I can't stop; I have to keep moving, or bad memories will take over.

Charlie's accusation comes to the forefront of my mind, darkening my mood. If I'm honest with myself, my anger stems from the fact that she guessed about my inner conflict. It's not like I don't care about football anymore; it's just not my favorite pastime. I'd never jeopardize the team on purpose though. For her to assume that based off one game was bullshit.

Distracted, I open the small closet under the stairs to stash my duffel bag when a tower of boxes collapses on top of me.

"What the hell!"

This wasn't here this morning. I don't need to look inside to know this is Charlie's cosplay crap; she's written it neatly in block letters on top. She has a huge closet in her room. Why did she store her shit here?

Son of a bitch. It's bad enough that she's taken over my thoughts—I can't stop thinking about her—but now she's taken over my entire house.

I shove the boxes back into the closet, then go grab a beer from the fridge. I don't want to get into an argument with her now. The boys are coming in a few, so we can chill out and plan our next trip in December when our season is over. I'm jonesing for adventure and also to get Charlie out of my system. Too bad it's only the beginning of October.

The door opens with a bang, and Andreas comes in, carrying a case of beer. Danny follows, holding two bags full of snacks. Andreas wanted to throw a party, but I'm completely destroyed. The idea of cleaning up tomorrow makes the idea even less appealing.

"So, is your roomie home?" He sets the beer on the kitchen counter.

"Her car is parked in front of the house, so I'm assuming yes."

"Excellent. I can't wait to meet her." He rubs his hands together.

"Don't even think about it," I warn him.

He widens his eyes innocently. "Since when can you read my mind?"

"I know you."

"Should we order pizza now? I'm starving." Danny opens a can of potato chips and shoves a handful in his mouth.

"Yeah, go ahead," I tell him.

"Wait. It's your house. Why do *I* have to order? I got the chips."

Groaning, I reach for my phone. "Fine."

The doorbell rings then, and I glare at Andreas. "You'd better not have invited anyone here."

He raises both hands. "I didn't. I swear."

Suspicious, I jump off the couch and check the door through the window. There's a guy standing outside, and judging by his posture and fidgeting, he seems nervous. He'd better not be a salesman.

I open the door. "Can I help you?"

His eyes snap to mine, and a second later, his jaw drops. "You're Troy Alexander."

"Yes… and you are?"

"Ah, sorry. My name is Jacob Mueller. I'm here to pick up Charlie?"

Ugh, I hate people who end a statement as if they're asking a question. I keep my expression neutral, but my mind is whirling. *Charlie is going on a date with this guy?*

I open the door wider and let him through. "I don't think she's ready yet."

"Oh yeah, I'm a bit early. She didn't mention her roommate was you."

I shut the door hard. I'm aggravated, and I don't know why. Who cares if Charlie is going out on a date?

"Who's the preppy boy?" Andreas asks from the kitchen.

"I'm Jacob Mueller, Charlie's date. You're Andreas Rossi," he says in awe.

"Sure am. Are you a football fan?"

The guy chuckles. "Am I a fan? Yeah, you can say that. Great game today, by the way."

"What the fuck are you talking about? We almost lost," I retort angrily.

The guy's face goes paler. "I mean, yeah, but you didn't."

The sound of Charlie's hurried footsteps down the stairs makes me turn. *Fuck me.* She's wearing a burgundy bodycon dress that leaves nothing to the imagination. It's a dress that screams she wants to get laid. My cock immediately reacts, but it's fury that's coursing through my veins now. She wants to bang a loser like Jacob Mueller?

Why do I care? Damn it!

Andreas wolf-whistles, adding fuel to my anger. I'll never hear the end of it.

"Hi, Jacob." Charlie smiles at the guy, completely ignoring me. "Am I late? I lost track of time."

"You're not late. Romeo was so nervous, he got here early," I reply bitterly.

Charlie throws me a questioning glance, and then I see she's wearing makeup. She went all out for this guy. An ugly emotion swirls in my chest, and it feels like jealousy. I must have suffered a head injury on the field today because that's the only explanation for my reaction.

"He's not lying. I was a bit nervous," Jacob confesses.

Charlie smiles. "That's sweet. Well, we should head out then."

"Hold on." Andreas walks around the kitchen counter. "Introductions are in order."

I suppress a groan, pressing a fist against my forehead. He already knew Charlie was good-looking, but she's fucking gorgeous tonight. He'll be all over her, date or no date. I bet he already forgot we're supposed to dislike her.

"Let me guess. You're on the team," Charlie deadpans.

"Running back, babe. The name is Andreas, but you can call me Andy."

She narrows her eyes. "Right. Well, nice to meet you, *Andreas*." She glances at Danny, who hasn't moved from his spot. "And you too, Pringles Boy."

Danny arches his eyebrows, but since he's chewing, he doesn't reply.

As soon as Charlie and Jacob leave, Andreas whirls on me. "Dude, Charlie is way hotter than I thought."

"Don't let all that makeup fool you." I let the venom drip from my tongue.

Damn it. I am jealous.

"I know a beautiful woman when I see one. Since she's your roommate, I'm going to ask, are you planning to tap that? Because if you aren't, then I'm game."

I glower at him. "Don't even think about it."

His eyes become rounder. He lifts his hands, palms facing me, and steps back. "Okay, okay. Just checking. I won't get in your way."

"That's not why—you know what? Forget it."

"Is it wise to hook up with your roommate though?" Danny asks.

"I'm not going to hook up with her," I grit out.

"Then why were you acting like that Jacob guy stole your candy from under your nose?" Andreas quirks an eyebrow.

"I wasn't." I return to the couch to grab my phone.

"Sorry, bro. Your head might know Charlie is the enemy, but your dick sure doesn't."

"Fuck off, Andy." I keep my attention on the phone.

"Are you finally ordering food?" Danny asks.

"No. Change of plans. We're having a party."

***

CHARLIE

This has been the worst date of my life. Jacob spent the entire dinner yapping about football and how Troy is a god among us. How could Vivian set me up with a football fanatic? And if he's such a fan, doesn't he know I was the one who wrote the nasty article about Troy?

Jacob seems oblivious that I want to gag him with a chain saw as he drives me back home. I'm ready to bail as soon as he parks the car in front of my house, but it isn't to be. The house is packed with random people. Some are outside, chatting animatedly, and loud music can be heard, even from inside the car.

I can't believe this. Troy decided to throw a party without telling me? That's fucking wrong.

"Whoa. I didn't know you were having a party tonight." Jacob drives past our house instead of stopping, so I can get out.

"Where are you going?"

"Uh, I'm going to look for a place to park."

Shit. Of course he wants to come in.

Angry doesn't begin to cover my feelings right now. I'm going to throttle Troy when I get the chance.

Jacob manages to park his car two blocks away, which means the asshole is forcing me to walk all the way back to the house in high heels. If the date hadn't already been a bust, the lack of gentlemanly conduct would seal his fate.

I stride ahead in silence, not hiding the fact that I'm pissed. On the front porch, a stupid drunk girl almost spills beer all over me as she misses a step. Patience is not a virtue I possess. Troy had better stay the fuck out of my way tonight.

I have every intention to disappear into my room, but the sight I encounter as I walk through the front door raises my blood to the boiling point. Strangers are wearing the cosplay outfits I had separated to donate to my brother's high school. Some of those costumes cost hundreds of dollars and are now being ruined by monster football players who are too big for them. I'm going to lose my shit in front of all these people.

Fuming, I search for Troy in the crowd, finding him in the kitchen, surrounded by his adoring fans. Curling my hands into fists, I march in his direction. He doesn't notice my presence until I push one of the girls to the side.

"Hey!" she complains. "What the hell!"

I ignore her, keeping my murderous stare on Troy.

His lips curl into a lazy, drunken smile. "Hey, roomie. You're home. How was your date?"

"Why are your friends wearing my costumes?"

"Oh, I didn't think you'd mind. They were marked as donation."

"You ass! You had no right to go through my stuff!"

His bloodshot eyes narrow. "If you don't want me to mess with your personal belongings, don't leave them lying everywhere."

"So, the gloves have finally come off."

"Who is this bitch?" a random redhead asks.

I turn my ire on her. "What did you call me?"

Troy suddenly jumps in between his guest and me. "Whoa. Everyone, calm down. Charlie, why don't you grab a beer and chill? This is a party, for fuck's sake. Relax." He reaches for my arm, but I quickly pull away.

"Don't touch me."

I whirl around and make a dramatic exit, stomping with the fury of a stampede. I could call the cops and end the party, but everyone already hates me, and I don't need to give them more reason. Besides, my beef isn't with them; it's with Troy.

But if he thinks I'm going to simply forget his assholery, he's sorely mistaken.

He wants war? I'll give him war.

NINE

Trying to sleep while the party was raging downstairs was pointless. Eventually, the guests left at around four in the morning, but I was too angry to fall asleep. Now it's six o'clock, and I'm out of bed, showered, and ready to go.

The living room and kitchen are completely trashed. There are empty beer bottles, discarded cups, and leftover food everywhere. I wrinkle my nose in disgust. If Ophelia could see the condition of her house, she'd flip out. Troy had better clean this mess by the time I get back.

I search for the costumes I was going to bring to Littleton today. I find none scattered with the trash, and my heart sinks. It's possible Troy's teammates simply went home with them. I open the closet below the stairs, hoping they might have left something untouched. To my surprise, most of the stuff is back in boxes. Unfortunately, they stink of beer and other unsavory smells. And I'm pretty sure most are damaged.

With a sigh, I pull the boxes out of the closet and carry them to my car. I'll sort them out when I get to my parents'. Ben will be so disappointed when he sees what happened to the costumes.

A new surge of anger erupts from the pit of my stomach. I can't let Troy get away with this without retaliation. I'm a fair person, but I won't sit back and let people do bad things without retribution.

The hour drive serves to calm me down, and when I park in my parents' driveway, my anger is almost gone. The garage door is open, but only Mom's car is inside. It's still fairly early. I wonder where Dad is.

I bring all the boxes to the garage, and then I follow the smell of Sunday breakfast—pancakes, eggs, and bacon. Mom is behind the stove, cooking more food, while Ben is sitting at the table in the kitchen nook. Bailey, our golden retriever, is the first to come greet me.

I lean forward to rub behind her ear. "Hey, girl. How are you?"

She wags her tail and then licks my hand, making me laugh. Like a miracle, the dark cloud above my head dissipates. That's the power of Bailey. She's been part of our family for fourteen years. Her muzzle fur has already turned gray. There's no denying her age, and the certainty that she'll be leaving us soon brings a pang to my chest. I hate aging. I wish we were all immortal.

"Hi, Charlie. How was your drive?" Ben asks me.

"Not too bad. It's early."

I step close to Mom to give her a kiss. "Where's Dad?"

Her eyebrows furrow, and her lips become nothing but a thin flat line. "He went to the warehouse before we even woke up."

"On a Sunday?" I wash my hands at the sink, eyeing the rows of bacon. My stomach grumbles.

"Dad has been really busy lately," Ben pipes up. "We barely see him."

I frown. "Really? I thought he was going to slow down."

"Well, that's what we all thought. He put Roger in charge of daily operations, so I really don't know why he spends most of the time in the warehouse now."

Mom's bitterness is clear. I've been so busy lately that our phone conversations have been superficial. I didn't realize this was going on.

Dad has a successful carpentry business. He designs luxurious furniture for the rich and famous in LA and other parts of the country. His beginnings were humble though, working out of the garage at our old house. It wasn't until ten years ago that he sold a piece to a celebrity and his business boomed.

"Oh, before I forget, my boss is throwing a barbeque for his employees and family," my mom says. "It's two weeks from now. I hope you can make it."

"Is it on Saturday or Sunday?" I grab a plate and begin to fill it with delicious food. I didn't realize I was this hungry until I got here.

"It's Saturday, and don't worry, Charlie. We don't have LARP that weekend," Ben chimes in.

I sit across from him at the table, noticing his new hairdo. His blond hair is sticking out at odd angles, but it was done by design.

Pointing with my fork, I ask, "What's up with the porcupine look?"

"Oh, do you like it? This is for when Sir Lorenzo gets hit by lightning and gains new powers."

That's his LARP character, and we usually drop them in conversation as if they were real people.

I furrow my eyebrows. "When does that happen? I didn't write it."

"Oh, Tammara did. I have to show it to you." Ben gets a goofy grin on his face.

"Who is Tammara?"

Redness sneaks up Ben's cheeks, and he lowers his gaze to the plate before answering, "My girlfriend."

I hit the table with an open palm. "Shut up! You have a girlfriend? When did this happen?"

Ben just turned sixteen, so I shouldn't be too surprised by the development. But he's my baby brother, and I'm very protective of him. He was bullied when he was younger on account of his Down syndrome. I got into many fistfights to defend him. It wasn't until we moved and he enrolled in a private school that things improved. Understandably, I really want to know who this Tammara person is.

"Relax, Charlie. Tammara is nice. I've met her," Mom butts in.

"She's like me." Ben smiles from ear to ear.

I glance at Mom, and she confirms with a nod. When Ben says she's like him, he means, she has Down syndrome too.

"All right. Does she want to be a writer then?"

"Well, she likes writing stories for LARP. She's coming to the next event too. Isn't it great?"

"Yeah, that's awesome. Where did you meet?"

"Online."

My jaw drops.

I glance at Mom, and she simply shrugs. "It's how it is these days."

I shake my head and smile. "Man, look at you. All grown up. I can't believe my baby brother has a girlfriend, and I'm still single."

"You're only single by choice, sis."

"You got that right," I reply.

I tell Ben and Mom about my fiasco date, which leads to me also talking about my roommate from hell. Mom pulls up a chair and takes a seat with a cup of coffee in her hand.

"To sum up, most of the costumes are dirty or completely ruined, all thanks to Troy."

"I think you should look for a new place to stay, Charlie. That roommate of yours sounds like an ass."

"Mom! Language." Ben laughs.

She rolls her eyes.

"The house is pretty nice though, and the rent is cheap." I sigh. "I don't know. The problems only arise when we bump into each other, which doesn't happen often."

"I think Charlie should stay, but she can't let him get away with that. Raven the Sorceress would never let that slide."

Ben loves to bring up my LARP character into conversation. To be fair, I do the same to him.

Mom frowns. "Revenge should never be the answer, Ben."

"Okay, maybe not revenge, but a little prank never hurt anyone," he replies.

I sit straighter, resting my forearms on the table. "Oh, I like the sound of that. What do you have in mind?"

Mom stands. "Okay, if you're not going to listen to me, I'm out of here."

We ignore her remark. Mom has her convictions, but she never tries to impose them on us. She believes we're old enough to make our own decisions. But she *will* tell us *I told you so* when we—*I*—fuck up. Ben never does, so I'm intrigued by his remark.

"I saw on YouTube the other day that some guy pranked his roommate by filling his room with chickens. They shat everywhere. It was hilarious."

"That sounds like a fit punishment, but where am I going to find dozens of chickens?"

Ben's blue eyes light up. "Tammara's parents own a farm. They have a chicken coop. I'm sure we can borrow them."

I nibble on my bottom lip. It's one thing for me to do something outrageous on my own. I can take the repercussions of my actions. I'm not sure if I want to involve Ben in my shenanigans.

"I don't know. Maybe I should come up with something easier."

His shoulders sag in disappointment. "Oh, okay. Let me know if you change your mind."

TEN

TROY

My head is pounding when I get up. And don't get me started with my mouth. It tastes like something died in it. I need a shower and a shave, but I only use the bathroom to relieve myself before I drag my feet downstairs for a damage report. I don't know what time everyone finally left, but I'm glad I made it to my room alone. Waking up next to a random girl would have made this hellish morning even worse.

I stop halfway down the stairs and stare at the mess. It looks like a hurricane passed through. This will take hours to clean.

Fuck.

I sit on a step and text Andreas, cursing him for putting the idea of a party in my head. Technically, this isn't his fault—I was the one who changed my mind—but I need a scapegoat, and I'm choosing him.

He asks for a picture of the chaos. Apparently, he left with two girls way before the party was over. Typical. I do as he said, and a minute later, he texts that he'll come over to help. My bullshit alarm immediately rings. Andreas is not one to volunteer to do anything, especially a cleanup, but I'm too tired and hungover to question him.

I get my ass off the stairs and head to the kitchen. Coffee is in order and probably several painkillers. While I wait for it to brew, I investigate my fridge. As suspected, there's nothing appealing inside. Not even Charlie's food. *Damn it.* I text Andreas again, asking him to bring me something greasy.

He takes his sweet time, finally showing up forty minutes later. I've showered and changed already and just finished cleaning the kitchen when he opens the front door, wearing his leather jacket and sunglasses like he's Tom Cruise in *Top Gun*.

"Help has arrived," he announces, removing his glasses in a dramatic fashion.

"I didn't think you'd show up," I grumble.

"I said I'd come." He looks over his shoulder. "Come on, guys. This place won't clean itself."

Five freshmen come through and immediately get to work. They don't even ask where the cleaning supplies are, guessing their location.

"Who the hell are they?"

"New Pike pledges." Andreas grins, taking a seat on a high stool by the kitchen counter. "Am I good or what?"

"How did you get these guys?"

He shrugs. "Unlike you, I cultivate relationships off the football field. I promised Leo tickets to the next game and a date with the head cheerleader."

"You got Heather Castro to go out with him?" I quirk an eyebrow. "The Ice Queen of Rushmore?"

"Let's say, I can be very persuasive." He wiggles his eyebrows up and down.

I narrow my eyes. "You didn't fuck her, did you?"

Andreas looks surprised. "Are you crazy? She's not my type."

"She has a vagina. She *is* your type."

He shakes his head. "No, I draw the line at colder-than-Siberia chicks."

I pinch the bridge of my nose. This conversation is making my headache worse. I need to load up on carbs to soak up all the alcohol that's still in my system.

"Fine. You can tell me the details of your deal later. Where's my food?"

Andreas widens his eyes. "Oops. I forgot."

"Dude! Come on."

He jumps off the chair. "No worries. Let's get some grub while the guys clean."

"I'm not leaving them here alone."

The dude closest to me pipes up, "It's okay, Troy. We won't break anything. Promise."

Clenching my jaw, I debate between taking Andreas up on his offer and staying to supervise these guys. But in the end, the hole in my stomach wins. I need food, pronto.

"Fine. We'll be back soon. Stay off the second floor," I warn them.

CHARLIE

On the way back home, I think about Ben's chicken idea. As complicated as it would be to pull off, that would be an awesome prank. But no, I really need to learn to let go even though, last night, I promised war. Ben and I went through the boxes, and besides the beer stains, the costumes aren't completely ruined. After a wash, they'll be wearable again.

I make a pit stop at the grocery store first because, most likely, the little bit of food I had left in the fridge and pantry are long gone. I know how ravenous drunk people get.

It takes great effort on my part to keep my irritation to a

minimum when I think about last night's party. One of my flaws is the inability to forget and forgive.

I park just behind Troy's car and wonder if he managed to clean up the mess already. Boy, if he didn't, there will be hell to pay.

No, Charlie, you can't get mad all over again.

After a mental pep talk inside the car, I finally get out, bringing all the grocery bags with me in one trip. I prepared myself to deal with Troy, not the four strangers who are currently cleaning the living room, and it takes me by surprise.

"Who the hell are you?"

I would have dropped the bags and reached for the pepper spray can in my purse if it weren't for the fact that these guys are on their hands and knees, scrubbing.

"Uh, we're Pike pledges," one of them answers.

Like that's supposed to make me feel better. Fuckers.

"Okay, *pledge*. Why are you cleaning my house? Where's Troy?"

"He left with Andreas to grab food," a second dude replies.

"Of course he did."

I head for the kitchen, which is spotless. They did a good job here, I'll give them that, but my anger has come back with a vengeance nonetheless. Who leaves four strangers in the house and goes out? Nimrods like Troy. *Damn.* He didn't even stop to consider what I would think. Like that's every girl's dream—to walk into her house and find four strangers in it.

I put away my groceries and then head to my room, locking the door for good measure. I'm seriously considering Ben's chicken idea now. Still obsessing about Troy and my aggravation with him, I begin to take off my clothes. Absentminded, I open the bathroom door, half-dressed, only to find another pledge taking a shit in my toilet.

With a scream, I slam the door shut and quickly put my jeans back on.

"What the hell! Why are you in my fucking bathroom?" I yell.

"Sorry. I didn't want to go downstairs."

Fuming, I storm out of my room, almost colliding with Troy.

"What happened?" He looks at me, worried.

"What happened?" I shriek. "You're a fucking asshole!"

I don't think twice, just lift my knee, hitting Troy's crown jewels with all my might. He groans, folding forward as he covers his crotch with his hands.

"What the fuck? Are you insane?" His face is contorted in agony as he stares at me as if I'm crazy.

Poop Boy comes out of my room, sporting a guilty expression on his pale face. "I'm so, so sorry."

"Get the hell out of my sight," I grit out.

Giving me a wide berth, he hurries down the stairs.

Troy is standing straighter again, but his expression is no longer contorted in pain. Fury flashes from his eyes instead.

"You are one crazy bitch," he says.

"That's typical male behavior. You screw up, and when I retaliate, I'm the bitch."

"How in the world did I screw up this time?"

"Really? You don't know?" I gesture wildly. "How about you throwing a party last night without the courtesy of letting me know first? Never mind letting your friends tear through my things. And now I come home to find a bunch of strangers in my house with you nowhere in sight. But the cherry on top was to walk into my bathroom and find a dude taking a big dump in my toilet."

My breathing is coming out in bursts by the time I'm done with my tirade.

Troy is no longer shooting daggers from his eyes. What I see shining from those hazel depths is much worse than hate. It's desire. The realization that he wants me serves to awaken a fire in the pit of my stomach that quickly travels through my body.

"I'm sorry," he says in a husky voice.

My bones melt, and my pussy throbs as if getting it on with Troy is actually an option. Hell to the fucking no. He's an asshole. I don't fall for those, no matter how good-looking they are. Heart-stopper as he may be, I'm not going to succumb.

"Right," I say, hating how feeble I sound.

My knees are weak, and if he keeps staring at me with that hungry gaze, I might combust on the spot.

I run back to my room and lock the door. I have to do something to make Troy forget any ideas about me. I'm not sleeping with him, and he needs to stop wanting that.

Chickens in his bedroom it is.

ELEVEN

TROY

Rooted to the floor, I run a nervous hand through my hair. My heart is beating furiously inside my chest as I stare at Charlie's closed door. My junk still hurts like a mother, but that didn't stop my cock from standing at attention. I got a hard-on watching Charlie vent her frustrations. I must have gone insane. But her furious red face and wild arm gestures made me want to pin her back to the wall and crush my lips to hers.

"Oi, Troy. Everything okay up there?" Andreas asks from the bottom of the stairs.

His voice brings me back to the situation at hand. And then I get fucking angry. I practically run down the stairs just in time to catch the idiot who used Charlie's bathroom before he can sneak out.

I grab him by the back of his shirt and yank him away from the front door. "What the hell were you doing in my roommate's bedroom?"

His pale face turns ashen, and sweat dots his forehead. "I-I had the shits and didn't want anyone to know."

His friends snicker, but one pissed-off glance from me has them shutting their pieholes in an instant.

"I warned you to stay clear off the second floor, didn't I?" I glower at the guy in my hold.

"Y-yes. I'm so sorry."

"Troy, come on. He didn't do it on purpose." Andreas tries to help, but I'm not having it.

"You shut your mouth too. I should never have listened to you."

"Man, all that fuss because Charlie is pissed at you again. If I didn't know you any better, I'd say you have a major crush on the nerd."

His statement makes me see redder.

I shove the pledge forward. "Get out of my house. All of you!"

The guys don't waste any time, hurrying out the front door. Andreas doesn't move a muscle, just keeps staring at me with a knowing smile on his stupid face.

"You're wrong about me. I don't have a crush on Charlie."

He raises his hands. "Sure you don't. It's cool, man. I'm not judging."

"The hell you aren't."

He holds my stare for a couple more beats before turning his attention to the living room. "At least they finished cleaning the place."

I fleetingly look at the living room before my cell phone pings in my pocket. I welcome the interruption; if I continue the conversation with Andreas, I might use him as a punching bag for my frustrations. It's a text from Jane, asking if I want to hang out this afternoon. Damn, if she'd asked me an hour ago, my answer would have probably been no, but considering my mood and the situation with Charlie, I could use the distraction.

"So, what do you want to do?" Andreas asks.

"I don't know about you, but I have plans." I veer for the door.

"Really? I thought you said you wanted to do nothing but veg out in front of the TV."

"Well, that was before the clusterfuck with the pledges and Charlie."

"Who texted you?" He nods at my phone.

"Jane. She wants to hang out. And no, you can't come."

Andreas flattens his lips. "Charlie was right. You're an ass."

He strides out the front door with his shoulders tense and a storm of bad emotions hanging over his head. I pissed him off—something that's almost impossible to do. Whatever. I'm too wired already; I don't want to worry about Andreas flirting with my sister on top of it. Even if he swears he'd never cross that line, it's in his DNA to chase pretty girls.

A fter Jane tricked me into going shopping with her, we headed to our favorite restaurant in Manhattan Beach. The sun is shining, and the temperature is mild, so we grab a table outside. Perks of living in California. I'm almost over my hangover, but I still order a beer. I need to take the edge off.

"Are you finally going to tell me what was eating you when you picked me up?" Jane plays with the straw in her drink, watching me closely.

"I already told you. I was hungover. That's all."

Like I'm going to tell her about Charlie. I don't need another busybody on my case about that she-devil.

"All right then. I want to ask you something."

"Shoot." I relax against the back of my chair.

"Mom is on my case about school next year. She doesn't want me to attend Rushmore."

"Why the hell not?" I frown.

Jane twists her face into a grimace. "She wants me to go to an Ivy League school. Barf."

"Hmm, you're smart enough to get into one. What about Stanford? It's not Ivy, but it's a top school, and you'd still be in California."

"I don't want to move to Northern California. I like it here. Besides, John Rushmore is an excellent school. Why aren't you taking my side?"

I pause for a couple seconds. I'm always on my sister's side, especially where our mother is concerned. So why the hell am I not rebelling against the Ivy League idea?

"Because we're talking about your future here, Jane. If you can go to a better school, why not?"

Pursing her lips, she crosses her arms over her chest and glowers at me. "I'm not moving. If you're not going to help me convince Mom, then please don't gang up with her against me. It's bad enough that Dad is with Mom on that front."

He would be, considering he's a Stanford alumnus. Maybe I am being an ass by not supporting Jane with her decision.

"Sorry. I won't join the Stanford team. I'm on your side."

Her serious expression softens. "Thank you."

"You're welcome."

I glance to my right, trying to catch the attention of the waiter, when I spot a familiar face on the other side of the restaurant. *Son of a bitch.*

"Speaking of the devil, Mom is here."

Jane turns to look. Our mother is sitting alone at a table, but then a man approaches her. She glances at the stranger, and her face splits into a radiating smile. The man leans down to kiss her on the lips.

"Whoa. Mom has a new boyfriend?" Jane says in awe.

"It looks like it."

We watch the scene unfold in silence. Mom's new guy sits across from her and then covers her hand with his. The way they keep staring at each other tells me the relationship is new. They're in the honeymoon phase.

"I don't feel comfortable staying here. Should we go?" Jane asks.

"Sure, but not before I introduce myself." I get out of my seat. "Troy…."

Ignoring Jane, I make a beeline toward Mom's table. She doesn't notice me until I'm hovering over them.

Her boyfriend glances at me, frowning. "Can I help you?"

"No, just came by to say hello to my mother."

The guy's face becomes pale in an instant. He looks at Mom, who has a deer-in-headlights gaze. It's clear my interruption is soiling their romantic mood. Ah, something is finally going my way today.

"Troy, what are you doing here?" she asks finally.

"I could ask you the same thing." I turn to her companion, extending my hand. "I'm Troy Alexander. And you are?"

"Bill. My name is Bill."

We shake hands, and then an uncomfortable silence follows. Not for me though. I'm having a great time making Mom squirm for a change. This is too much fun.

"So, how long have you kids been seeing each other?" I ask.

"Uh, your mother and I are just friends."

The lie confuses me. Why would he say that when a second ago, they were gazing at each other like two teenagers in love? They both look extremely uncomfortable now.

"Is everything all right here?" a newcomer asks.

Glancing at his button-down shirt and slacks, I guess him to be the manager. Man, he's good if he noticed the discomfort at this table from afar.

"Everything is peachy. I was just saying hello to my mother." I flash the guy a dazzling smile.

He glances at my mother and her boyfriend as if to get confirmation that I'm truly not bothering them. Mom remains frozen, but her date nods ever so slightly.

I clap my hands together. "Well, I'd better get back to Jane. It was really nice meeting you, Bill."

"Yeah, same," he mumbles, still dazed.

I'm smiling from ear to ear when I return to my table.

Jane's green eyes are as round as saucers. "I can't believe you went there."

"I would never pass up the chance to annoy Mom. You should have come."

"Who is the guy?"

"Some schmuck called Bill. He didn't give me a last name."

"Odd. Maybe he was afraid you'd come after him." She laughs.

"Or he's a gigolo and Bill is his code name."

Jane glances over her shoulder. "Oh look. They're leaving. What did you say to them?"

My eyes are widely innocent when I answer, "Nothing."

TWELVE

CHARLIE

I have to wait until Saturday to exact my revenge since I don't know Troy's schedule. During the week, he tried to apologize again for what had happened, but I really didn't want to hear his excuses. The reason was simple: I didn't want him to convince me to forget about the prank. I can't afford to fall for his charm. A beautiful, cocky football player like him would crush me and obliterate my heart if I let my guard down. Then, I'd have to move out.

My accomplices today are Ben, Tammara, and Fred. Blake vehemently refused to help, citing his aversion to birds as an excuse. I would have preferred to not involve Ben in my schemes, but since he's the one with access to the animals, I couldn't leave him out. He and his girlfriend were like kids on Christmas morning as they helped load the birds in the van Fred had borrowed from work.

Troy left the house before the sun was up, and he won't be back until the end of the day. Enough time for our aviary friends to get comfy in his room. We brought only a dozen chickens with us, which should be plenty to get the job done.

Right before we release the animals in Troy's room, hesitation grips me. Maybe this prank is a little too extreme. But then I remember everything Troy has done to me since we met, the lack of respect and common courtesy, and the guilt takes a back seat.

I've never been in his room before today. He keeps it in immaculate condition. There isn't a thing out of order. No dirty clothes on the floor, no dust covering the furniture.

Man, he's going to blow a fuse when he comes home.

"Wow, look at this room. Who knew homeboy Troy was such an organized freak," Fred pipes up. "Are you sure you want to do this, Charlie?"

"I found a guy taking a shit in my bathroom last weekend. Yeah, I want to do this."

He shrugs. "Okay. You're the boss."

"Too bad we won't see his reaction," Ben says. "We should have bought a hidden camera."

"I thought about it, but I think the chickens are punishment enough. We don't need to add invasion of privacy on top of it," I reply.

"Oh, glad to hear there *is* a line you won't cross." Fred chuckles.

"Ha-ha. Shut up and help me release the birds."

"Release the Kraken!" Ben shouts.

"Make sure Troy doesn't harm the chickens, okay, Charlie?" Tammara glances at me.

"Yeah, of course. Besides, I don't think Troy is the type of person who hurts animals."

Once all the chickens are free, we close the door and head downstairs. We hang out for a little bit before Fred has to return the van and Ben and Tammara go to the movies.

It'll be hours until Troy comes home, and without company, I begin to worry about the birds loose in his room. What if they eat something they shouldn't? *Shit.* Maybe I should have waited longer to let them out of their cages. The lengthy wait makes me paranoid, and during the day, I check on them several times.

I'm in the kitchen making a sandwich when I hear a car door bang shut outside. My heart skips a beat, and then it accelerates to a hundred. I'm suddenly nervous about Troy's reaction. It's one thing to lash out in the heat of the moment; it's quite another to plan retribution. I realize then that serving revenge cold is not my game.

Troy comes in carrying his huge duffel bag over his shoulder. His hair is damp, pushed back off his forehead in a messy way. A wisp of desire curls around the base of my spine, an odd contrast to the twisted ball of nerves in my belly. I wish I weren't attracted to the guy. It would make my life so much easier.

He glances in my direction and hesitates for a second before he says, "Hello."

"Hi," I croak.

Shit. Okay, Charlie, you can still stop this. There's time to avoid Armageddon.

But as much as my conscience urges me to do something, I don't move from my spot. Instead, I watch in frozen terror as Troy heads up the stairs. I'm literally shivering.

Ugh. This is fucking madness, Charlie. Snap out of it. Raven the Sorceress would never second-guess herself.

I turn toward the fridge and pull a bowl of strawberries and a can of whipped cream from it, setting both on the counter.

A moment later, Troy curses so loudly that I'm sure it can be heard from miles away. I wince and then glance at the front door. I can make a run for it.

"Charlie! I'm going to kill you!"

Fuck. I don't think he's joking. But he's already at the stairs, so running now would be pointless. He'd be able to catch me.

"What? Didn't like my surprise?" I ask innocently.

His hazel eyes are dark with fury, and his body is coiled tight with tension. He strides in my direction and then walks around the counter like a lion that's about to attack. I lose my bravado then and stagger backward until my back presses against the fridge.

"My room is a fucking mess! There's shit and feathers everywhere," he screams, invading my personal space.

I've never experienced this kind of wrath aimed at me from this close, but all I can think about is how delicious Troy's aftershave smells.

What the hell is wrong with me?

"That's payback for the party, my ruined costumes, and Poop Boy in my bathroom. Now you know how it feels."

"Are you fucking kidding me? I said I was sorry."

"Well, excuse me for not taking your apologies to heart. Now, get out of my way. You're smothering me." I press my palms against his chest and push back. He barely moves. "Troy, I'm fucking serious. Do you want me to crush your balls again?"

He narrows his eyes. "You wouldn't dare. Besides, you won't catch me by surprise this time."

"Try me."

He watches me for a couple more seconds before he finally moves away. I let out a breath of relief when he turns his back to me, but it's too soon. A second later, he whirls around, can of whipped cream in hand, and the next thing I know, I have white foam all over my face.

I let out a shriek and then blindly try to find a towel near the sink to clean my eyes. They burn. Behind me, Troy laughs, making my blood boil. I finally find a dish towel and quickly wipe my face. I still have whipped cream everywhere, but at least now I can open my eyes.

Troy is doubled over, cackling like a madman. Him laughing at my expense snaps something in me. I see he no longer has the can in his hand, so I lunge for it. Before he can stop me, I squirt what's left of the whipped cream on his face.

Take that, sucker!

His amusement ceases immediately. He wipes his face with the back of his forearm, but I don't wait for him to attack again. I bolt for the stairs.

"Oh no. You're not escaping now. It's on."

He tackles me, wrapping his steely arms around my body and keeping me from moving.

"Let go of me." I struggle against his hold, though I know I won't be able to break from his boa constrictor embrace.

"No. I won't let you go until you apologize for all the headaches you've caused me since we met."

"You're crazy! You're the one who's acted like a jackass from the beginning."

I try to stomp on his instep, missing it. However, my effort makes Troy lose his balance, and we both end up on the floor. The fall would have hurt me if Troy hadn't taken the brunt of it.

"Fuck," he grits out.

His hold slackens, allowing me to slide away from him. It's not until I'm on my knees, ready to get back onto my feet, that I see he's clutching his right arm and his face is twisted in agony.

"Are you okay?"

"No. I think I dislocated my shoulder."

Shit. His shoulder does look weird now.

"Can you get up?"

He opens his eyes and peers at me. "Yeah. Can you call Andreas? I probably need to go to the emergency room."

"What? Are you crazy? We're not waiting for your friend to pick you up. I'll take you."

"You?" His surprised tone is obvious.

"I'm not a heartless bitch." I crawl to his left side and help him to a sitting position.

He winces when I move him, making me feel horrible. I'm responsible for his pain. I wanted to make him suffer but not like this.

"I'm so sorry," I say. "How bad does it hurt?"

"Not too bad. It's not the first time it's happened."

Our eyes lock. His are bloodshot thanks to the whipped cream. We don't speak for several beats. The air between us seems to be charged with electricity despite our situation. His gaze drops to my lips, making my breath catch. My heart drums a staccato beat in my chest, the sound so loud, I'm afraid he can hear it.

"We should go. I'll help you up." I clutch his left arm, then drag him up with me as I rise from the messy floor.

He steps closer to me, which sets my face aflame. My entire body is humming thanks to his proximity. He's like a beacon and I'm a moth, drawn to his light. I keep my eyes glued to his chest, but I don't step back.

Good grief. What the hell is happening to me? Troy is the enemy, and our war probably just took him out of commission. If he didn't hate me before, he does now.

"Charlie? You can let go." His voice is low, strained, *sexy*.

Not sexy, you fool. He's in pain.

At once, I let go of him and step back. Still not making eye contact, I return to the kitchen sink to wash my face properly. The small hairs on the back of my neck stand on end when I sense Troy's approach. I reach for a towel, stepping aside to let him use the sink as well.

"Can you help me?"

I freeze mid-motion, then slowly lower the towel from my face. He's watching me expectantly, but I also notice the tension around his mouth. He's trying to hide his discomfort.

"Sure."

I grab a clean towel from the drawer, and after dampening it with lukewarm water, I offer it to him.

He glances at the offering, then back at me. "Do you mind? It hurts when I move."

"Oh, okay. Sure."

I try my best to focus on the task and not on the fact that Troy's eyes are glued to my face. Neither of us speaks as I drag the towel across his cheeks, nose, chin, and forehead. When I'm done, I move away quickly, afraid my body will betray me further and I'll do something stupid, like lick his damn lips. I bet they taste sweet now.

Gee, Charlie, get your mind out of the gutter already.

"I should change," I say.

"Oh no. If I have to wear a whipped-creamed T-shirt to the ER, so do you."

"Really, Troy? Are you that petty?"

"Petty?" He arches both eyebrows. "There are a dozen chickens in my bedroom, and I have a dislocated shoulder."

Remorse sneaks into my chest, making me lose my misplaced annoyance. "I'm sorry. Let's go."

THIRTEEN

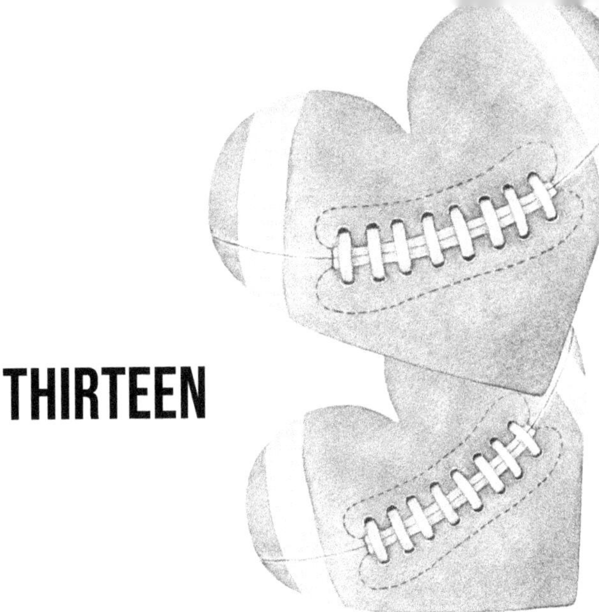

CHARLIE

Afugfter three hours in the ER, we're finally home. The doctor gave Troy a strong painkiller, and he's now a little out of it. I have to help him out of the car and hold on to him as we walk into the house for fear he'll stumble and fall again.

I haven't stopped feeling awkward thanks to my proximity to him. My heartbeat is still accelerated, and radioactive butterflies are having a rave in my stomach.

"I'm hungry. Are you hungry?" he asks.

"Yeah, sure. Let's get you to bed, and I'll make us a couple of sandwiches."

"Oh shit. We can't get to bed. My room is now a chicken coop." He chuckles.

Damn it. I had completely forgotten about those stupid birds.

"Ugh. Karma is indeed a bitch," I mumble.

"Sure is. Look at me. Coach is going to skin me alive."

"It was an accident. I'm sure he'll understand that."

"Are you coming to my defense? The journalist who roasted me for not caring about football anymore?"

I sigh. "I thought you were supposed to be loopy."

"I am or I wouldn't be so nice to you."

There's nothing I can say to that. He has every reason to be furious with me.

Clamping my jaw shut, I veer for the stairs, my hand firmly clasped around Troy's bicep.

"Where did you find them?"

"What? The chickens?"

"No, the alien babies doing the cha-cha in my room. Yes, the chickens."

I ignore his remark. "Someone I know owns a farm."

"Man, aren't you resourceful?"

I steer Troy to my bedroom because he needs to lie down and rest. "Okay, it's time for you to take it easy."

He smirks lazily. "Charlie, if you wanted to get me into your bed, you didn't have to go through all that trouble."

"Ha-ha. The doctor said you need to sleep, and thanks to me, you can't use your own bed."

"And where are you going to sleep? With me?" He grins.

"Not in this lifetime, pal. The couch will do."

I let go of him to pull the duvet out of the way. Troy crawls onto the mattress, shoes still on and everything.

"Hold on. Let me take off your dirty sneakers first, dummy." I drop into a crouch to get to them.

He laughs again. "You called me dummy. That's cute."

No, you are. Fucker. Even acting like a moron thanks to the drugs, he manages to be irresistible. Maybe it's because he's not acting like an ass now.

"You should take my jeans off too."

Heat spreads through my cheeks. "Not going to happen."

I unfurl from my crouch, meeting Troy's gaze. He has a lopsided grin on his face, which matches his up-to-no-good stare.

"Are you afraid you won't be able to resist me once you see what I'm packing?"

"Please. You think too much of yourself."

Before he can see the truth in my eyes, I escape to the kitchen. Hopefully, he'll fall asleep after his belly is full and stop tormenting me with his flirtatious comments.

My appetite is gone thanks to the knots of worry in my belly. Troy is acting carefree now because he's as high as a kite, but tomorrow will be another story. Maybe he'll kick me out, and I'll have no one to blame but me.

Knowing I can't eat right this second, I only make one sandwich. When I return to my bedroom, Troy is fast asleep. Okay then. I set the plate on my nightstand, then go take care of the chickens that are still loose in his room.

The place reeks of bird shit, making me wrinkle my nose. I'm definitely not eating anything tonight.

Getting the chickens back into their cages takes forever, but the worst part is definitely the cleanup.

Why did I agree to Ben's idea?

Since I'm not calling Fred to collect the birds now, I bring them all to the living room. We never made arrangements for after the prank, but the chickens have to be returned to the farm, obviously.

I feel disgusting, so I head back to my room to shower. Troy is still out to the world, but I don't want to risk waking him up. I cross my room on my tiptoes and then turn on the bathroom light, keeping the door open only a sliver. In the semidarkness, I quickly grab a change of clothes, then lock myself in the bathroom.

A quick glimpse at the mirror makes me wince. I look dreadful. My hair is hard and matted thanks to the dried whipped cream, and today's stress has given me dark circles under my eyes. I take my time in the shower, washing my hair twice. A sweet strawberry scent wafts from the bottle, and yet I can still smell chicken poop. Yuck.

I've almost reached pruny state when I finally step out of the stall. The bathroom is warm and foggy like a sauna. I brush my hair and teeth first before I put on my clothes.

"Wait. Where are the pajama bottoms?" I glance at the clothes I grabbed.

Crap. I took two T-shirts instead of a T-shirt and a pair of pants. At least I didn't forget my underwear.

The T-shirt is long enough and covers my butt, so I head back into my room like that.

"Charlie?" Troy calls from the bed.

Ugh. Of course he would wake up to witness me prancing around without pants on.

"What are you doing up? Go back to sleep."

He sits up instead, turning on the nightstand light. "What are you doing, skulking in the dark?"

"I wasn't skulking," I grit out.

"I'm really uncomfortable. Can you please help me out of my jeans?"

With a sigh, I head over to the bed. I wouldn't want to sleep wearing jeans either. "Fine. Just promise you won't make stupid comments."

"Cross my heart and hope to die."

I roll my eyes. "Please." Focusing on my irritation and not that I'm about to see Troy in his underwear, I unzip his jeans and try to get them off. "You have to help me. Lift your butt."

He does as I said, but even so, it's hard to remove someone's pants when they're sitting down. I force my gaze away from his crotch, but my eyes have a will of their own. They stray, giving me a glimpse of his package.

Shit. It's as big as I suspected.

"See something you like?" he asks in a dangerous tone.

"You wish."

I finally get his jeans off, but Troy doesn't do anything to cover himself. I fold his pants and set them on the chair by my desk, knowing I have to escape soon.

"Charlie?"

"Yeah?"

"Can you fix my pillow, please?"

With a groan, I glance at the ceiling. "Really, Troy? Now you're just milking it."

"I'm not. I'm in agony, and it's your fault. The least you can do is—"

"Cater to all your whims?" I quirk an eyebrow.

He smirks. "I wouldn't call them whims."

"Fine." I stomp back to his side.

As I lean closer to adjust the pillows behind his back, Troy's good arm snakes around me, pulling me in bed with him.

"What the hell, Troy? What do you think you're doing?"

He reaches for the back of my head, tangling his fingers in my hair. Damn, it feels good.

Too good.

"You smell like strawberries, Charlie. Do you taste sweet too?"

Grabbing a fistful of my hair, he pulls me to him and covers my lips with his. I should resist, but the moment we touch, a current of electricity spreads through my veins, sending tingles down my spine. His tongue teases my lips, prying them open. I don't fight, just completely surrender to the moment, to the fire that ignites in the pit of my stomach. I'm kissing the enemy, the bane of my existence, and it feels fucking amazing. It's a toe-curling, knee-buckling, panty-melting kind of kiss, and it's short-circuiting my brain.

A needy moan escapes my mouth, eliciting a throaty chuckle from Troy. My mind finally snaps into action, reminding me that this is a mistake of epic proportions. I pull back, ending the kiss abruptly, and jump off the bed as if I'd been electrocuted. My lips tingle, and my entire body is humming with desire.

Damn everything to hell. I can't believe I let this happen.

"You taste delicious, Charlie," he says lazily, right before he lies back down and closes his eyes.

I don't move from my spot, too stunned about what just

happened. Troy kissed me, and I let him. Even though the kiss was a product of his medication, I still loved it. What does that say about my sanity? We don't like each other, we don't get along, and worse, we're roommates. That's a recipe for disaster.

He's high on drugs, but what was my excuse?

You have none, Charlie.

All I can do now is pray he doesn't remember a thing about tonight.

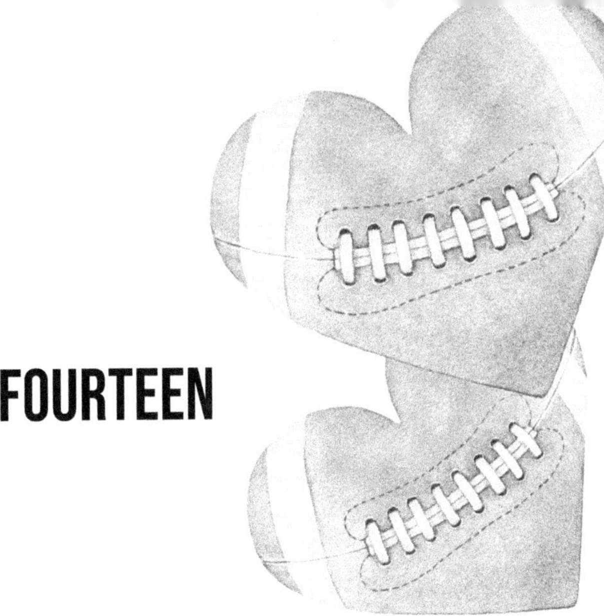

FOURTEEN

TROY

I wake up early thanks to my burning shoulder. My head feels like it's filled with cotton candy though, and I don't recognize where I am right away. This is definitely not my bedroom. When my nose catches the faint scent of strawberries, I remember that I slept in Charlie's room. Then the memories begin to trickle down.

Son of a bitch. I kissed Charlie last night.

Groaning, I press a closed fist to my forehead. I had to go and do something stupid besides getting my shoulder dislocated. I can't believe she let me get near her. Maybe she doesn't hate me as much as I thought.

A plate on the nightstand catches my attention. Instead of finding the sandwich I didn't eat last night, there are pieces of oranges and grapes on it. My prescribed painkillers and a bottle of water are next to it. A strange warmness spreads through my chest. It seems I like the fact that Charlie is taking care of me. I must be the stupidest moron on campus.

The ping of an incoming text sounds in the quiet room. I try to pinpoint its location, but it's only after a second text comes in that I discover where it's coming from. My phone is on Charlie's desk. I'm not sure how it ended up there. It's not until I get out of bed and come closer that I see it's connected to a charger. She must have done that since I have zero recollection of doing it last night.

The texts are from Andreas and Danny, asking if I'm meeting them at the gym. I said I would yesterday, but that was before my accident. I have to call the coach and tell him what happened. He's not going to be happy about it, but Danny is ready to take my place. I won't be letting the team down, only myself. I can't go back in time and not dislocate my shoulder though, so there's no sense in worrying about it now.

I take another pill and then eat a couple grapes before I head to my room. Bracing for the stench of chicken poop, I'm surprised when I smell vanilla instead. There's a scented candle burning on my dresser. Charlie cleaned the whole place, and she opened the windows to let fresh air in as well. Once again, a fuzzy feeling spreads through my chest, though I'm not sure why I'm so pleased that she cleaned her own mess.

I put on a pair of sweatpants and then head downstairs. The couch is empty, and the only signs that she slept there last night are the pillow and folded blanket.

Sitting on a stool, I bite the bullet and call Coach Clarkson.

He answers on the second ring in his usual grumpy voice. "Troy, if you're calling me this early, it means you have bad news for me."

"You know me too well, Coach."

"Out with it already."

"I dislocated my shoulder last night."

"What the hell did you do, son?"

"I fell in my living room."

"You fell, huh? That's it?"

"Yep."

"You expect me to believe that an elite athlete like yourself simply lost his balance over nothing?"

Ah shit. Yeah, that'd be pretty hard to believe.

"Actually, my roommate was mopping the floor, and I didn't notice. It was one of those stupid moments of distraction."

I pinch the bridge of my nose, realizing too late that I should have thought of a better story before I called the coach.

"Right. There's nothing for it now. I want you to come in and see the team's physician anyway."

"Sure thing. I'll drop by later."

Coach ends the call without another word. I should be glad he didn't chew me out over the phone, but that didn't make me feel any better.

It's my fucking fault that I got hurt. I should have never tackled Charlie. It wasn't only anger that propelled me to do so. I wanted to touch her, to wrap my arms around her body. If I hadn't lost my balance, I might have kissed her right then and there. Though she probably would have ripped my nut sack off in that moment.

But later, on her bed, she kissed me back. I'm sure of it.

I text Andreas and Danny, telling them I'll be out of commission for a while. I should have known Andreas would want an explanation in person. Ten minutes later, he and Danny are knocking on my door and calling my name.

With a sigh, I let them in, then veer back to the kitchen. I need coffee, stat.

"Dude, how the fuck did you dislocate your shoulder?" Andreas asks as he follows me.

"I told you, I fell." I reach for the coffee jar, but opening it with one hand is a struggle.

"Jesus, give me that." He pries the jar from my hand and then proceeds to fill the coffeemaker.

"That must have been a pretty epic fall. What did you do?" Danny asks.

"I tackled the wrong person," I mumble, immediately regretting my slipup.

Andreas whips his face to mine. "Come again?"

I walk around the counter, turning my back to him on purpose. "Nothing."

"Bullshit. I knew your accident had something to do with your roommate. Was it another prank?" Andreas is angry, which is never a good thing. I definitely don't want him gunning for Charlie when she's not at fault.

"Relax. She didn't do this. If she had, she wouldn't still be living here." I sit down on the high stool, facing him again.

He's staring at me through slits, trying to sniff out a lie. There isn't one though.

"Okay, fine. Charlie didn't do this, but I don't get your comment. Who did you tackle if not her?" Danny pipes up.

I pinch the bridge of my nose. "I *did* tackle her. We got into a whipped-cream fight, and things got out of hand."

Andreas's jaw drops, and he's looking at me with a goofy expression now. I stunned him into silence.

"A whipped-cream fight? That sounds like foreplay, buddy." Danny chuckles.

Hell, I don't want them to know how close his comment is to the truth. It would have been foreplay if I hadn't gotten hurt.

"Trust me, it wasn't."

Andreas crosses his arms and continues to scrutinize me. "Whatever. If you're not going to fuck her, then why keep her around? Even if she didn't plan what happened to you, she's still partially responsible. Please tell me you're going to retaliate."

"What the fuck are you talking about? I'm not going to punish Charlie because of this."

The sound of a key turning interrupts our conversation. Charlie comes in wearing skintight gym clothes that serve as a shot of desire straight down my crotch.

Shit. Why does she have to be so stunning?

She glances apprehensively at Danny and Andreas, maybe catching the tense vibe in the air, and then looks at me. "Oh, hey. You're up."

"Yeah. Where did you go so early?"

From the corner of my eye, I see Andreas shaking his head.

"I had to return the chickens."

"Uh, what?" Danny looks at me.

Ah fuck. I had forgotten about them. If I tell the guys what Charlie did to my room, Andreas will have my balls for not doing something about it.

The thing is, I'm tired of this bullshit war between Charlie and me. I'm more interested in getting to know her than getting revenge.

"Troy didn't tell you?" she asks.

"No, Troy seems to be tight-lipped these days when it comes to you," Andreas retorts angrily.

Charlie's eyes widen a bit, but that's the only sign that Andreas's comment caught her by surprise.

"Oh, well, never mind then." She veers for the stairs but stops before she takes the first step and glances at me. "I don't have class until later, but I can drive you to school if you need a ride."

"Uh...." I turn to Andreas, who is watching everything with rapt attention. "I'll let you know."

"Okay. I'm headed for the shower."

Why is she telling me that? Does she want me to imagine her naked? My cock twitches in my pants. *Son of a bitch. I have a hard-on. What am I, fifteen?*

She goes up the stairs two steps at a time, almost as if she's running away from me. I don't blame her. This was an awkward conversation. It would probably have gone better if we didn't have an audience.

"Okay, what was that?" Andreas asks.

"What was what?" I look at him innocently.

"Something happened between you and that girl." He points accusingly.

"Nothing happened," I grit out.

"Bullshit," Danny replies. "Even I noticed."

"You fucked her, didn't you?" Andreas says.

"No, I didn't. And since when are you a gossipy old fart?"

"Since that girl just cost us our QB!" He throws his hands up in the air.

"Danny is more than capable of holding down the fort until I'm better."

"That's not the point, Troy. Yeah, I know Danny will do an amazing job, but this is your senior year. It's the last time we're going to play together."

Ah hell. Now I get why Andreas is upset.

"What do you want me to do? I fucked up. Don't go blaming Charlie for something that was totally my fault. Besides, the doctor said I could be back in four weeks."

"Okay, that's not too bad," Danny chimes in, trying to defuse the tension. "That means our ski trip isn't canceled."

"Yeah, thank fuck for that." Andrea snorts. "Seriously, Troy, you have to get your head straight. Fine, I get it. Charlie is a hot piece of ass. But she's also a fucking menace. If you need to screw her to get over whatever it is you have going on, do it. And then kick her to the curb and out of your life."

Danny whistles. "Things escalated fast."

I curl my left hand into a fist, fighting the sudden anger that's bubbled up my throat. "You'd better watch your tongue, Andy. I'm not a fucking pussy who needs to be rescued by his friends."

His face remains closed off, but the storm has vanished from his green eyes. He knows he went too far. "Good. I'm glad you're not completely whipped."

"Don't worry, man. There's zero chance of that happening."

The biggest fucking lie I ever told.

FIFTEEN

CHARLIE

Maybe Troy doesn't remember our kiss. Yesterday, when I came home from the gym and found him with his teammates in the kitchen, he sure acted like he'd forgotten. I didn't want to linger to find out, especially when Andreas kept glowering at me. Troy must have told him that I was to blame for his accident. I'd be pretty pissed at me too if I were him. Their quarterback won't return to the game for a month.

Damn. I wonder if Troy is angry with me. He didn't show any indication, but he also didn't take me up on my offer to drive him to class yesterday or today. I only offered because it was the right thing to do.

You live in a house of lies, Charlie.

Ugh. Shut up, conscience!

It doesn't matter. My schedule is already busy enough as it is. I'm low on cash, so I decided to take more editing jobs. I have a two-hundred-page novel to start tonight. I'm glad I stopped by my favorite Tex-Mex restaurant and grabbed dinner. I was running all day and barely had time to eat a handful of nuts.

Troy is watching TV when I come home. He glances over his shoulder, and his eyes give me a quick once-over before he says, "Hi."

"Hey," I croak.

What the hell? Where is my damn voice? Oh yeah, it's being squeezed by the tightness in my throat. One single glance from him makes me as nervous as a schoolgirl in front of her first crush.

What was that look all about anyway? Was he checking me out?
Oh God. Maybe he didn't forget about the kiss after all.

I veer for the kitchen, angling my face in a way so my hair covers half of it. I'm acting like an idiot, but it seems that kiss shattered my protective shield, revealing the bumbling mess that I am. It was so much easier to pretend I wasn't attracted to him when I had all that hate going on.

"What you got there? It smells good."

"Tex-Mex. I got plenty if you're hungry."

He jumps from the couch. "Yeah, I'm starving."

Great. There goes my plan to make a plate and eat in my room. If I do so now, he'll know I'm avoiding him. I can't give Troy that kind of leverage. *Never show weakness.*

"All right then." I grab plates and utensils. While I'm unpacking all the food, I feel his gaze staring a hole through my face. "What's up, Troy? Got something on your mind?"

"You've been living here for three weeks, and this is the first time we're going to sit down to have a meal together."

"We have busy schedules. And there's also the fact that we don't like each other very much." I give him a lunatic grin, but Troy's face remains serious.

"Yeah, I don't think that's the case anymore," he says casually as if his words don't make my heart skip a beat.

"You can't possibly tell me that after everything I've done, you like me now. Come on. You had a chicken run in your room all thanks to me."

He finally cracks a smile, making my erratic heart go

haywire. It doesn't know if it should speed up or stop beating altogether.

"The room looks perfect though. I think you've made up for your mistakes."

"Well, you sure haven't made up for yours. I can't open my bathroom door anymore without a slight degree of apprehension."

He twists his face into something like remorse. "I'm truly sorry about that. I specifically told those pledges to stay clear off the second floor."

"You can't trust frat boys, that's for sure."

"Where is that comment coming from? Do you have a feud with someone from Greek Row as well?" He quirks an eyebrow.

"Not me per se. A friend of mine does."

He narrows his eyes. "Hmm. And you're the type of person who lets others' opinions sway yours?"

"If you're implying that I'm a sheep without a mind of my own, you're mistaken," I snap.

"Ah, there's the Charlie I know. I was beginning to worry you'd left me for good."

That makes me pause a beat. "What? You like when I'm mean to you?"

"Oh yeah, I live for your testy barks." He chuckles.

"You're crazy."

I pull up a chair, making sure I skip one so there's plenty of space between Troy and me. We eat in silence for a moment, and I begin to relax. He doesn't remember the kiss, or if he does, he wants to forget it happened too.

"This is pretty good," he says.

"Yep."

"Not as good as your kiss though."

I choke on my food as it goes down the wrong pipe.

"Are you okay there?" Troy glances at me, half-amused, half-worried.

Lost in a fit of coughing, I reach for the glass of water. When the danger of suffocating on fajitas is gone, I dare to look at him. "You remember we kissed?"

He turns in his chair, leaning his good elbow on the counter. "Charlie, no drug on earth would make me forget that."

Oh my God. What the hell does he mean?

"Is this a joke?" I ask.

He sits straighter, furrowing his eyebrows. "What?"

The doorbell rings, interrupting our conversation. Damn it, I wanted him to answer that. The butterflies in my stomach are wide awake now and wreaking havoc in my belly.

"Don't go anywhere," he tells me.

I stare at my plate, suddenly no longer hungry. My mind is spinning like a top. What the hell is going on here? Troy must be concocting something. It's the only explanation for why he would say he would never forget our kiss.

I mean, I know he's attracted to me. I've seen plenty evidence of that. That must be it then. He just wants to get me to sleep with him before he gives me the boot.

A female voice jars me from my inner thoughts. I turn in my seat to find a beautiful Barbie in our home. Her attention is one hundred percent on Troy, but I don't need to have a good look at her face to recognize her. She was in a few photos with Troy on his Instagram account. They seemed close in them.

"I can't believe the Pied Piper of all daredevils got injured at home. Are you sure you weren't doing tricks with your skateboard?" she asks.

Troy chuckles. "No. I wish that were the case."

He glances in my direction, catching me staring at the duo like an idiot. The girl follows his line of sight, and for a couple beats, her expression darkens.

"You must be Troy's new roommate," she says with a tight smile. "I'm Brooke."

"Nice to meet you." I get up from my seat with my plate in hand.

Troy arches his eyebrows. "Where are you going?"

"Now that you have company, I won't feel bad for eating dinner in my room. I have lots to do before hitting the sack."

He seems disappointed, but my eyes don't linger on his face long enough to be sure that's the case. Besides, why would he want to hang around me when there's a Victoria's Secret model standing in front of him?

Ugh, I sound like all those loser heroines with too much low self-esteem. When did I become that person?

SIXTEEN

CHARLIE

The drawback of bringing fajitas to my bedroom is that it stunk up the place. Food smells don't belong where you sleep.

It was all for nothing anyway. Troy's comment about our kiss and then seeing him with Brooke stole my appetite. I ended up having to throw the food away because I refused to return to the kitchen while they were still in the living room.

It was hard to concentrate on my work while their voices and laughter carried upstairs. The noise-canceling headphones helped, but then my imagination took over. I kept imagining Brooke smiling and touching Troy in an intimate way, and that kept my mind trapped in an endless torture loop. In the end, I gave up trying to work and called it a night.

I snuck out of the house pretty early, all in the hopes of avoiding Troy. My plan was a success, but that meant I was a zombie, and staying awake during classes could only be accomplished with copious amounts of coffee.

The good thing about today is that I'll escape a Troy ambush again. There's a game night at Fred's, and those usually run late.

Funny how yesterday I wanted Troy to answer my question, but today my bravado is gone. I don't want to know if he was serious or not because if he was, I have no idea what I'll do. Even if Troy is no longer acting like an asshole to me, he and I don't mesh well together. We're from different worlds. He's a jock who enjoys extreme sports; I'm a nerd who gets excited by pretending to be a magical being on the weekends. There's nothing wrong with our life choices, but we have nothing in common.

I'm on my way home to shower and get ready for tonight when Fred texts me.

> Hey, it seems my place is double-booked. My roommate planned a special evening with his lady, and he's begging me to postpone game night.

Crap on toast. I call him right away. "Hey, so what are you thinking? I was looking forward to tonight."

"Me too. Do you think we can go to your house instead? It's big enough."

I groan. "I don't know. I was hoping to avoid my roommate."

"Oh shit. Is he still super mad about the chicken incident?"

"Yeah, something like that," I lie.

I can't tell Fred the reason I'm avoiding Troy is because we kissed. Fred has a big mouth, and he'd tell everyone he knows.

"Ah, don't worry, Charlie. We'll be there to defend you in case he decides to be a prick."

"I don't think he will. Let me check with him first, and then I'll get back to you."

"Okeydokey."

Damn it. There goes my plan to avoid Troy for one more day.

I wait until I get to the house to text him. His reply comes a minute later. He doesn't mind. I didn't think he would even though I was kind of hoping for a negative answer.

An hour later, Fred and Blake are at my door, carrying all the food for tonight's sustenance. It's only Tuesday, and while the board games we play usually run for hours, none of us have classes in the morning, so it works perfectly. It's the only day of the week we can make it happen since we're usually too busy on the weekends.

We're just about to start when someone rings the doorbell.

"Are you expecting anyone else?" Blake asks.

"Nope."

I hope it's not Brooke paying another surprise visit. When I open the door, I do find a girl standing in front of it, holding a box with a pie if I were to guess, but it's not Brooke.

Great, another member of Troy's fan club.

"Can I help you?"

"Hi, you must be Charlie. I'm Jane, Troy's sister. Is he home?"

My ill attitude changes in an instant and shame takes over. I was already consumed by ugly thoughts. Jealousy is a monster.

"Not yet. Come on in. I'm sure he'll be here soon."

I open the door wider and let her pass. She freezes for a second when she notices Blake and Fred on the couch.

"Oh, I didn't know you had guests."

I chuckle. "I wouldn't call them guests. Those are Blake and Fred, my partners in crime."

"Hello." Blake waves.

Fred jumps from the couch and reaches the poor girl in three long strides. "Hi, I'm Fred."

"Nice to meet you, Fred." Jane smiles shyly while he stares at her with a goofy grin.

I watch them, waiting for her eyes to either focus on his spiky green hair or the vintage Scooby-Doo T-shirt he's wearing. She doesn't do either.

Instead, she turns to me. "I brought cherry pie. It's Troy's favorite."

"I'm sure he'll love it. Let me make room in the fridge for it."

"We're about to play Betrayal at House on the Hill if you want to join us," Fred tells Jane.

"I've never played that before. What's the learning curve like?"

"Steep," Blake replies from the couch.

I'm not surprised by his grumpy reply. He hates explaining game rules to newcomers.

"Be nice," I say. "Besides, it's not that complicated."

"If you don't mind, I'd like to join. I've always wanted to play board games, but none of my friends are into them."

"Awesome. The more, the merrier." Fred steps closer to Jane and, as if they were old friends, throws his arm over her shoulders. "Don't worry. I'll be your guide this evening. By the time it's over, you'll be a pro."

I expect the girl to shove him off her, but she simply laughs.

My eyes meet Blake's. He gives me a what-the-hell look before shaking his head. I respond with a what-can-you-do shrug and join everyone on the couch. For a brief moment, all thoughts of Troy recede to the back of my mind.

TROY

My shoulder is bothering me again, but I keep the discomfort to myself. I got a ride with Andreas, and I don't need him to get angry all over again over my accident. He hasn't brought up Charlie at all today, but despite his easygoing personality, he also has a mean streak. Mess with him or his friends, and he's out to get you.

We stopped by Zuko's Diner to grab dinner, and during the entire time, Andreas blabbered about a set of twins he'd been screwing—not at the same time, he made sure to point that out. In fact, it seems they don't know he's been tapping them both. He plans to propose a ménage soon, but I told him it would backfire royally. In his usual fashion, he wasn't worried about it.

We're ten minutes from the house when I receive a text

from Charlie. A surge of excitement runs through me just seeing her name pop up on my screen. We're no longer fighting like cats and dogs, which means my previous assessment that I enjoyed my fights with her because of the rush was false. It's her that gives me the high. And I have no clue what to do about it. If it's only a physical thing, then it should go away as soon as we bang. If it doesn't, then that's a problem.

"Who texted you?" Andreas asks.

"Charlie."

"What does she want?" His tone turns dark. Yeah, he's still not over Charlie's part in my accident.

"She wants to know if she can host a game night at our place."

"And what did you say?"

"I haven't texted her back yet."

"Say no just out of spite."

"How old are you? I'm not going to say no."

I text her back with a **No problem**, then look out the window, thinking about the conversation Brooke interrupted. Where was I going with it?

"Fine. I'm curious to see who her friends are. It'll probably be fun crashing her party."

"You're not coming in unless you promise to behave."

"Don't worry. I won't treat Charlie bad or anything. In fact, I'll be so sweet to her, she'll get a toothache."

I glance at him, narrowing my eyes. "Yeah, that's what I'm afraid of."

He doesn't offer another comment during the rest of the drive, and when we park in front of the house, his grin makes me suspect he's up to no good. I get out and head to the front, not bothering to wait for him. He doesn't follow me right away, but when he catches up with me, he's whistling. I notice the backpack strap hoisted over his shoulder.

"What are you doing with that?"

"I missed my gym session this morning. I figured I could lift some weights."

"I thought you said you wanted to crash Charlie's party."

"That too."

I'm not sure what he's planning, but he'd better not pull some crap tonight. I throw him a meaningful glance before opening the front door.

The scene I walk in on makes my steps falter. I see Charlie with two guys I've never met, plus my sister, Jane, animatedly speaking at the same time. They're so into their conversation that they don't notice we just walked through the door.

"Jane?" Andreas says.

The conversation ceases in an instant.

She looks at us, smiling broadly. "Hey, you're home. Hi, Andy."

"What's going on here?" he asks as if he lives here and not me.

"Dude, chill out," I tell him.

"I came by to see how Troy was doing, and then Charlie invited me to play a game while I waited," Jane explains.

"Oh, cool. What are you playing?" I ask.

"Betrayal at House on the Hill," she replies.

"I didn't know you were into board games." I walk closer, not glancing at Charlie on purpose. I'm afraid if I do, it'll show on my face what she's doing to me.

"I've always wanted to play, but no one in my circle cares for them."

"It's because your friends are all lame." The dude with spiked green hair bumps my sister's arm with his elbow, making me frown. A bit too familiar there.

"Who are you?" Andreas asks, not hiding the aggression in his tone.

I whip my face to his, hoping he can see the warning in my eyes, but he's not paying any attention to me. He's staring at Charlie's friend.

Shit. His beast mode is activated.

"You just got here. Shouldn't you be introducing yourself first?" the guy sitting next to Charlie retorts.

Andreas snorts. "Like you don't know who I am."

"Why should they? You're not a celebrity," Jane replies, making my jaw slacken. Ten minutes of hanging out with Charlie has put sass in my sister. I'll be damned.

Andreas seems to be at a loss for words as well. He simply stares at Jane, bug-eyed.

Charlie points at her green-haired friend. "That's Fred, and this is Blake."

I don't miss when she touches the dude's arm. She's standing way too fucking close to him, and I don't like it.

"How do you know Charlie?" I ask.

"I met Charlie through LARPing," Fred replies. "But she and Blake have known each other for like forever."

Crossing my arms, I look at her. "Is that so?"

"Yeah, I've known Blake since we were in kindergarten."

I sense the guy staring a hole through my face, so I move my attention to him. Looking closely, I realize he seems familiar. "I've met you before."

"Sure have. Ludwig dragged me to one of your games. He introduced us." I try to rescue the memory from the depths of my brain, but before I can, he continues, "I'm the editor of the *Rushmore Gazette.* Let me tell you, I loved getting censored by the school administration because of you."

Ah fuck. That explains why he's shooting daggers at me.

"You shouldn't publish garbage then," Andreas pipes up.

Charlie whips her head around so fast, her ponytail slashes across the air. "My article wasn't garbage."

"What's going on?" Jane asks, confused.

"Nothing is going on," I butt in before things get out of hand. "Charlie and I have settled our differences. Let's just keep the past in the past."

My remark seems to mollify Charlie.

When she looks at me, her eyes aren't crackling fire anymore. "Right. We're no longer archenemies, unless Troy decides to join us for game night. Then all bets are off."

Her lips curl into a mischievous smile that sets my body ablaze. I'm lusting for this girl badly.

"That's an unfair challenge. I've never played that before."

"And you're not going to. I'm not about to waste another twenty minutes explaining the rules," Blake grumbles.

"Hey. It didn't take me twenty minutes to learn," Jane complains.

"I know, but I'm going out on a limb here and guessing your brother will be a more challenging case."

"Blake! Stop it." Charlie hits him on the chest with the back of her hand.

I wave her off. "Nah, it's okay, roomie. Cheap insults like that don't bother me. But if you want to beat me in a game, I have Monopoly lying around somewhere."

Blake makes a face of disgust, but his friend perks up in his seat. "Oh, I haven't played Monopoly in ages. Let's do it."

I glance at Charlie. "What do you say?"

She smirks. "Oh, it's on. And so you know, you're going down."

SEVENTEEN

TROY

Andreas corners me as soon as I enter my bedroom. "What the hell are you doing?"

"I'm looking for my Monopoly game, in case you haven't noticed," I reply, annoyed. He's pissing me off with his attitude.

"Right. I'm talking about the little foreplay between you and Charlie. When did you flip, man?"

"Foreplay? Are you crazy?"

"I know what I saw."

"Uh-huh. Yeah, only your depraved mind would think anything dirty from a polite conversation."

"Whatever. Well, while you look for your game, I'm going to work out." He disappears through the door.

I don't stop him. It's better if Andreas doesn't join us downstairs. He's in an antagonizing mood and needs to chill out on his own.

It takes me five minutes to find the old board game. The box is falling apart, held together by tape. It belonged to Dad. I found it in a donation bin in his garage, though I'm not sure what prompted me to rescue it. I don't think we've ever played it as a family before my parents split up when I was fairly young, soon after Robbie died.

I run my hand over the top, getting sentimental over nothing.

Screw this. I'd better get back to the living room before I fall into a dark hole of memories and can't get out.

When I pass in front of the gym room, I glance inside. Andreas isn't there.

Where the hell did he go?

I get my answer right away when I hear his booming voice coming from downstairs. *Son of a bitch.* He must have changed his mind about working out. I wish Danny were here to serve as a buffer. Usually, the two of us can keep Andreas's mercurial mood in check much easier.

"I found the game," I announce from the top of the stairs.

"Oh goodie," Blake replies sardonically.

His rude comments are beginning to get to me. I can't fall for his goading though. I'm trying to stay on Charlie's good side. Fighting with her no longer appeals to me—unless we're sparring in the bedroom.

Jesus. I think Andreas's way of thinking has rubbed off on me.

We get ready to play the game. The L-shaped couch can't fit all of us, so I grab a folding chair from the closet beneath the stairs and set it right across from Charlie. I want to look at her all night. I hope my cock behaves. She's not even all dolled up tonight. Her clothes are casual and cover most of her body. Her hair is in a ponytail, and she's wearing her big glasses. Still sexy as hell.

The first few rounds of the game are fairly uneventful, everyone busy trying to acquire as many properties as possible. It's only when a few of us start to build houses and hotels that things get interesting. Andreas is currently spending time in jail. It's Charlie's turn now, and she's about to pass through my side of the board. I have three properties, all with hotels, and a mode of transport. Basically, it's a minefield.

I lean back in my chair, grinning like an idiot.

"Come on, roomie. Daddy needs more money for his empire," I say.

"Daddy?" She quirks an eyebrow.

I shrug a shoulder.

Charlie rolls the dice, then lifts her fist in the air when she gets double sixes. "Yes! Take that, sucker."

She blows past my properties, not landing on any of them, to my utter disappointment.

"I'll get you next time."

"I'm happy in jail. I never want to get out." Andreas chuckles, looking pointedly at Jane. He almost went bankrupt after he landed on one of her properties with two hotels.

"Sorry." She chuckles.

He holds her gaze for a moment, almost as if he's in a trance.

Ah shit. My worst fear is happening before my eyes. Jane is totally on his radar now.

I toss a handful of peanuts at him. "It's your turn."

"Hey, I'm not cleaning that mess." Charlie points at me, furrowing her eyebrows as if she were mad. But her eyes dance with glee.

Something has definitely changed between us since that kiss. I wouldn't call our banter foreplay, but it's definitely toeing the line of flirtation territory. I hate to concede that Andreas was right. I should stop, erect a barrier between us, but I don't want to. Deep down, I know if anything happens between Charlie and me, it won't end well. But I'm a fucking glutton for punishment.

"Sorry, darling. I can't do any housework." I point at my arm in the sling.

"But you sure can make a mess." Jane shakes her head. "Typical."

"I know, right?" Charlie piles on.

I snort. "That's rich coming from you. Have you already

forgotten that time I came home and it looked like a Halloween truck had exploded in my living room?"

She rolls her eyes. "Please, I was in the middle of moving. You can't use that as an example."

"Yeah, yeah. Whose turn is it now?" Blake asks, glowering at the board.

"Oopsie. It's mine," Fred pipes up. He reaches for the dice, then leans closer to Jane. "Blow on them for good luck?"

I sit straighter in my chair, ready to put the green-haired idiot back in his place, but Andreas beats me to the punch. "What the hell, dude? She's in high school. Stop putting the moves on her."

Jane's eyes turn as round as saucers. Her cheeks flush.

"Why? So *you* can take his place?" Blake retorts.

"Excuse me?" Andreas stands up, body coiled tight with tension.

I do the same, ready to get in between him and Charlie's friend.

"I should go. It's getting late," Jane announces, looking embarrassed as hell.

I turn to her. "Good idea. I'll walk you out."

"Hold on. I'm coming too." Andreas follows us. Of course he would.

I'm almost certain he only decided to stick around because of Jane.

"Finally," Blake mumbles.

"Blake, stop being such an ass," Charlie replies.

It's an effort to bite my tongue, but I do so because I'm not in the mood to start another argument. My shoulder is suddenly throbbing. I need to stop obsessing about Charlie and worry about my recovery.

"There's cherry pie in the fridge," Jane tells me outside.

"Thanks. I'm sorry the evening turned out sour." I glare at Andreas.

He scoffs. "What's with the look? I didn't do anything wrong.

That punk with green hair, on the other hand, is a fucking perv. Jane is barely eighteen."

"Fred is not a perv." She crosses her arms. "I don't need another big brother protecting me, Andy. Troy is plenty."

Andreas opens and shuts his mouth without making a sound, like a fish out of water.

Ha! It seems I don't need to worry about Jane after all. Thank fuck.

I pull her into a side hug. "Thanks for coming. We'll do something fun this weekend."

"We have Dad's barbeque on Saturday. Now that you can't play, you're coming."

"Ah hell. I forgot about that. Do we need to go?"

"Yes. I already said we would. I'm not going alone."

"That sounds like a lot of fun," Andreas pipes up. "I wish I were off. Maybe I could get the twins to come."

Jane wrinkles her nose. "Ew."

The consternated look on his face makes me chuckle.

He rolls his eyes at me. "Ha-ha. Laugh all you want. At least I'm getting booty. Meanwhile, you're pining for a girl who hates your guts."

His comment kills my amusement in a flash. "Get the hell out of here before I punch you in the throat, jackass."

He flips me off, then strides to his car.

"What's up with him?" Jane asks. "He used to be nicer."

"No, he's always been an ass. He just hid it from you."

"Hmm." She keeps her gaze trained on him until he gets in his Bronco. Then, as if she just finished processing Andreas's comment, she glances at me. "You have a thing for Charlie?"

Thanks a lot, Andy.

"No. That's all in Andy's dirty imagination."

Jane narrows her eyes. "I'm not sure if he's making stuff up. You guys were pretty flirtatious tonight."

I step away from her. "Not you too, Jane."

"What's the big deal if you like her?"

"For starters, we live together. Have you ever heard the saying, *Don't shit where you eat?*"

She rolls her eyes, followed by a sigh. "Okay, fine. I'm not going to bug you about it. But if you want to explore the possibility, I'd say the path is clear."

"What's that supposed to mean?"

"I'm saying Charlie is into you too."

I keep my expression neutral, but I can't ignore how Jane's comment sends a thrill down my spine.

EIGHTEEN

CHARLIE

With Troy unable to play football, we're constantly home at the same time. However, I go out of my way to not spend too much time in his company. It's not only that I'm afraid to explore whatever is going on between us, but I also legit have a ton of work to do.

It's Friday night, and I don't foresee going to bed until the early hours of the morning. I have to finish my editing job. It's a romance novel, and to be fair, I've been procrastinating finishing the assignment. Romance is not something I read for fun, but that's not the issue. The hero reminds me too much of Troy, even down to his description. That leads my mind to wander to him instead of focusing on correcting the grammar in the book. But I'm determined to finish it tonight.

I don't see Troy when I arrive home from class, so I quickly make a sandwich, grab a couple cans of Red Bull, and head to my room. To really keep my mind on the task at hand, I put on noise-canceling headphones and get to work. I'm making good progress until I notice a pattern in the manuscript that begins to irritate me. The author has a crutch phrase that she's already repeated a dozen times throughout the story, and I've only read half of it. Curious, I do a quick document search and get the exact number of offenses. She's used the same phrase twenty-two times. Worst of all, it's not even a good one.

"Oh my God. *My eyelids pressed together*? It's called closing your fucking eyes, damn it!" I yell at my computer screen.

Shit, I'm tired.

"Is everything okay in here?" Troy's voice sounds from the door, making me jump in my seat.

Pressing a hand against my chest, I swivel the chair around. "What the hell, Troy? Don't you knock?"

"I did. You didn't reply." He smirks. "What's making you so angry?"

"Ugh, nothing. It's just this book I'm editing. Bad writing gives me hives."

"Can't you make it better?"

"No. That's not my job. I was hired to fix grammar mistakes and point out glaring plot issues. If I mess with the manuscript too much, I'd be changing the author's voice."

"Gotcha. Anyway, I was going to watch a movie if you're interested in joining me."

My heart skips a beat, and my mouth turns suddenly dry. "What movie?" I ask when, instead, I should have told him I have work to do.

"*It.*"

"Oh, the horror movie?"

"Yeah."

"No, thanks. I don't do horror."

He curls his lips into a grin. "Why not? Are you scared?"

"Fuck yeah. I'm not ashamed to admit it. I once tried to watch *The Exorcist* on a dare, and I couldn't sleep for weeks unless the lights were on."

He chuckles. "We can pick something else. What's your favorite movie?"

Why is he being so nice to me? Immediately, suspicion sneaks into my brain. *"Lord of the Rings.* More specifically, *The Two Towers.* Why?"

"We could watch that. I confess I've never seen the whole trilogy."

"What? Are you serious?" My voice rises to a pitch.

"I might have fallen asleep during the first movie." He rubs the back of his neck, looking sheepish.

"Oh my God, Troy. Take that back. It's sacrilege."

He laughs. "Come on and help me atone for my sins then. Maybe you can turn me into a fan."

A fuzzy feeling spreads through my chest. I've never seen him so open, unguarded. Damn it, I don't know why girls prefer bad boys. Troy's nice version is much more irresistible.

I'm about to cave when a text message catches my attention. It's from the author of the book, asking when I'll be done.

I let out a heavy sigh. "As much as I'd love to indoctrinate you in the ways of Tolkien, I'm afraid I have to finish this job. Rain check?"

"Sure thing. I can't wait to be indoctrinated by you."

I don't know if it's the way he replies that sounds like a sex proposition or how his eyes turn to molten lava, but I'm most definitely hot and bothered now.

***

It goes without saying that after my convo with Troy, it took forever to get my groove back. I kept staring at the computer screen, seeing nothing, as my mind kept replaying his visit. But I had to push through, which resulted in burning the midnight oil and acquiring a bad kink in my back.

The pain doesn't improve after roughly four hours of sleep. My alarm blares at 8:00 a.m. like a banshee from hell. I'm tempted to shut it off, but unfortunately, I have Mom's work thing, and I'd like to drop by Golden Oaks first.

Resigned, I drag my ass out of bed, bleary-eyed and

annoyed. I have to learn not to overcommit to things. I can't remember the last time I wasn't juggling a million balls in the air.

As I brush my teeth, I eye the bathtub. I won't be able to survive the long day if I can't alleviate my back pain. I think I can spare thirty minutes to soak my sore muscles in a bubble bath. I turn on the water, and when the tub is half-full, I toss in one of my bath bombs.

A moan escapes my lips when I sink into the water. This is exactly what I need. Using a folded towel as a pillow, I lean my head back and close my eyes.

Immediately, Troy's image pops in my head. The memory of our kiss comes to the forefront of my mind, making my lips and other parts of my body tingle. My nipples turn into pebbles, and there's a new ache between my legs. *Ah hell*. This need won't go away until I get some relief.

I glide my hand down my belly, then flick my clit with my fingers. A zing of pleasure unfurls in my core, making me arch my back. Damn, I'm so horny, this won't take long. I imagine it's Troy's fingers playing with my sex, probing and teasing. I slide two fingers inside while I apply pressure on my bundle of nerves with my thumb.

"Fuck," I whisper.

I pump my fingers in and out, imagining it's Troy's cock pushing in, filling and stretching me. The pressure keeps building and building, but I don't want to climax just yet. My toes curl, my legs tense as I fight the wave of pleasure that's on the horizon and fast approaching. I slow my movements, but I've already passed the point of no return. There's no stopping this from happening now.

A strangled moan escapes my lips when the orgasm hits me. My hips buckle from the intensity of it. I'm not a fool to give credit to my hand for this; it's all Troy's fault for invading my thoughts, for making me crave him as if he were a drug I was addicted to after one single taste.

I'm uber relaxed now, and if I keep my eyes closed, I run the serious risk of falling asleep.

Fuck it. I guess I'm skipping my visit to Golden Oaks today. I'm too tired to even feel guilty about it.

I'm not sure how long I've napped in the tub, but when I blink my eyes open, the water is no longer warm. It's nippy actually. With a groan, I brace against the edge and stand up. Then I notice something alarming. *Oh my God. I've turned into a Smurf.*

"What the hell!"

I jump out of the tub and look at the mirror. My skin is blue from the neck down. I glance at the bathwater, which looks like raspberry Kool-Aid. I didn't notice before thanks to the bubbles. How is that possible? I grab a towel and begin to scrub. The white fabric quickly becomes blue too, but the stain doesn't vanish from my skin.

Realization hits me then. This was a fucking prank.

A roar comes from deep in my throat. I can't believe I was that stupid. Troy played me. He let me believe all was fine between us when in fact he was plotting his revenge. And I fell for it.

Propelled by anger, I wrap myself in a towel and march out of the bathroom. I don't stop until I barge into his room. I find him coming out of his closet, wearing nothing but boxer shorts. Of course he has to be half-naked.

"You ass! I can't believe I fell for your good-guy act."

His eyebrows shoot to the heavens as his eyes widen. "Charlie, what the hell are you talking about?"

"Quit the act already. You won. Look at me!" I open my arms wide, not caring if the towel stays in place or not.

"Why do you look like Smurfette?"

I breach the distance between us, then poke his chest with my finger. "I'm like this because you exchanged one of my bath bombs for something with blue dye in it. Don't even try to deny it."

He shakes his head, still keeping the innocent façade in place. "I swear, Charlie, I didn't do this."

My nostrils flare, a sign that I'm about to go savage on his ass. But what would kicking him in the nuts or punching him in the face accomplish? Nothing. He got me, just like I'd gotten him with the chickens. Now we're even.

I step back. "I should have known you wouldn't simply forget everything. Congratulations, Troy. You really got me."

My eyes prickle, surprising me. I haven't cried in anger since I was a kid. Not wanting him to see me bawl my eyes out, I whirl around and leave his room as fast as I can. By the time I slam my door shut, the first tears have already rolled down my cheeks.

The big hole in my chest tells me these aren't angry tears. They're the broken kind.

When the fuck did Troy get hold of my heart in order to stomp all over it?

NINETEEN

CHARLIE

No amount of soap or scrubbing gets rid of the blue tinge from my skin. Running late, I give up on trying to find a solution to my problem. The alternative is to wear a long-sleeved turtleneck and jeans. There's nothing I can do about my hands. I can't wear gloves to a barbecue. It's not that cold.

And to think I masturbated to Troy's image while marinating in blue dye. That added insult to injury. He made me cry, something no boy has ever been able to claim until him. That's what I get for lowering my defenses. Lust played keep-away with my intelligence. It made me forget what type of person Troy is—an egomaniacal asshole.

I don't have time to stop by Golden Oaks. It's the second weekend in a row that I haven't gone. I miss Ophelia and the rest of the gang, but I have to drive to Littleton first because Mom wants to go together as a family. Never mind that the party is halfway between where I live and Littleton.

When I arrive, the garage door is open, but only Mom's car is in it. Shit, did Dad have to work on a weekend again?

When I walk in, I get my answer right away. Mom is in a bad mood, sporting a glower as she finishes getting ready. Ben is on the couch, playing a video game, while Bailey naps by his feet.

"About time you showed up, Charlie. We're already running late."

"Sorry. I had a late night."

She stops in her tracks and takes in my clothes. "What are you wearing? It's going to be a lovely day today. You'll get hot."

I glance at Ben and debate if I should tell Mom about Troy's latest prank. In the end, I decide against it. She's already acting like a dragon; I don't need to give her more reason to be aggravated.

I plop on the couch next to Ben and bend over to rub Bailey's head. She doesn't even stir. Poor thing must be tired.

"What's up with Mom?" I ask softly so she doesn't hear.

"Dad said he couldn't make it to the barbecue. They had a big argument last night."

"Really? Ah, man. I'm sorry, Ben."

He shrugs, keeping his eyes on the game. "It's okay. I had my noise-canceling headphones on."

"Why didn't you call me?"

"I didn't want to bother you. I know how busy you are with school and your side jobs."

"What are you two doing, sitting around?" Mom stands at the edge of the living room with her hands braced on her hips. "Come on. Let's go!"

I jump off the couch, walking fast to meet Mom in the garage. She already has the car on.

The drive to her boss's party is tense as hell. I try to put on a radio station, but Mom barks that she isn't in the mood for music. Considering the shitty beginning of my day, it's fitting that I have to endure a party with Mom in a hellish disposition. I hope Ben and I can escape at the party and not interact with her at all.

Her boss's house is in Malibu, not a usual spot for a

technology mogul. He's a genius who built a company out of nothing, and he's now one of the wealthiest businessmen in the country. Mom has been working for his company for over six years, and this is the first time he's hosted a barbecue for his employees and their families. Any company event has been only for the employees and their significant others in the past.

Several cars are parked outside the beachfront mansion, but if we're indeed late, that's another story. Mom asked me to drop by the house at a certain time, and I was only ten minutes late. We didn't encounter a lot of traffic coming here, so it's possible she blew the situation out of proportion because she's in a funk.

Well, that makes two of us, but you don't see me acting out on it.

An attractive man in his fifties greets us when we come in. A beer bottle is in his hand. He's wearing a casual linen button-down shirt and pants. I can tell with only a cursory glance that he likes to work out.

"Tara, welcome! I'm so glad you could come." He gives Mom a casual hug that lasts a second. "Where's Jason?"

Her expression darkens for a moment, but she's quick to put on a phony smile. "He couldn't come. He feels awful, but he had an emergency at the warehouse."

"That's too bad." He switches his attention to us. "And who do we have here?"

"This is my daughter, Charlie, and my son, Ben."

"Hi." I smile feebly, keeping my hands hidden behind my back.

"I'm Jonathan. Nice to meet you, Charlie." He extends his hand, which I was afraid of. I have no choice but to shake it.

"Nice to meet you too."

Mercifully, he's one of those people who maintains eye contact—probably something to do with being a successful CEO —and he never glances at my blue hand. He shakes hands with Ben next and then returns his attention to Mom.

They're talking shop now, which allows me to observe him

more. His dark blond hair is peppered with gray, and expression marks deepen when he smiles, but other than that, he looks quite young. There's no wedding ring on his finger. I remember Mom saying he was divorced, but a guy who looks like him and with all this money must have a young-looking girlfriend.

Charlie, you're being judgmental. He could be single or dating someone his age.

I realize that with Mom distracted by her boss, this is the best opportunity for Ben and me to escape. I pull on his sleeve and point at the outdoor area where several people are mingling near the pool. He nods silently, and together, we slink away from Mom.

Most of the female guests are wearing summer dresses, which makes me stick out like a sore thumb. My turtleneck has to be black to boot. It's not like I don't own brighter colored sweaters. Maybe I was going for something that represented my mood, but now I'm regretting it.

"Let's get something to drink," Ben says.

I follow him to the bar, where a lanky ginger is prepping drinks like a pro. He moves so fast, I'm afraid he's going to drop one of the bottles he's handling.

When it's our turn, I ask him, "Are you training for something?"

"What do you mean?"

"I've never seen someone move that fast behind a bar, not even at a nightclub."

He laughs. "I *am* actually practicing. I'm auditioning for the lead role in the remake of *Cocktail* next week."

I raise an eyebrow. "Is *Cocktail* that eighties movie with Tom Cruise?"

"Yep." He bobs his head up and down. "So, what can I get you?"

"I'll have a dry martini, please." Ben casually leans his forearm against the bar, acting like he's a leery thirty-year-old man, not sixteen.

The bartender chuckles. "Sure, pal. How about a Sprite?"

Ben steps away from the bar, returning to his old self. "Nah. I'll have root beer if you have it."

"Sure thing. And how about you, sugar?"

"Sugar?" I laugh.

"She'll have a Blue Lagoon cocktail," a hateful and familiar voice answers for me. "I think it'll match her… *suit*."

The bartender gives me a quizzical look, but I'm no longer interested in him.

Curling my hands into fists, I turn around. "What the hell are you doing here?"

Troy crosses his left arm over the sling and stares at me with eyes that are cold and ruthless. Gone is the good-guy persona. "I could ask you the same thing."

"Charlie!" Jane walks over. "What are you doing here? Did Troy invite you?"

Oh my God. One of their parents must work for the same company Mom does. This is like a nightmare that will never end.

"No. I'm here with my mother. She works for Slate Corp."

Troy's eyebrows almost meet his hairline. "Your mother works for our father?"

"Wait. Jonathan is your dad?"

"Yeah," Jane replies. "What a small world."

"You don't say," I mumble.

"Hi, I'm Ben, Charlie's brother." He waves in Troy and Jane's direction. "This is a really nice house."

"Yeah, it's cool." She shrugs while Troy keeps glaring at me. "I'm Jane, by the way, Troy's sister."

"Are you in high school?"

"Yeah, it's my senior year."

"Uh, miss? Do you still want a drink?" the bartender asks.

I glance over my shoulder. "Just some water, please."

"Right away."

When I turn around, Troy is already going back to the house.

He goes out of his way to not come near the pool, glancing at it as if some danger lurks in the crystalline water.

"What's the deal with your brother and pools?" I ask, interrupting Ben and Jane's chatter.

"Oh, Troy can't handle pools. Not since the accident."

"What accident?"

Jane's expression clouds. Her mouth tenses, giving me a clue that it's not a subject she likes to talk about.

"It's okay. You don't need to tell me."

"It's fine. Our family doesn't really speak much about it, so it's weird to do so. But I guess since you're Troy's roommate, you should know. It would help you understand my brother."

I'm sensing it's something that irrevocably changed Troy. My heart clenches a little in expectation. Despite my animosity toward him, I'm already suffering in sympathy without even knowing what his trauma is.

"What happened?" Ben asks.

"Our younger brother drowned in a pool when he was three. Troy was eight when it happened."

"I'm so sorry," I say.

"Yeah, it was rough. I don't remember much about it. I was only four then, but Troy took it really hard. He doesn't do pools now."

As angry as I am with Troy, I can't help the guilt that sneaks into my heart. The sentiment is strange and not exactly logical. There's no correlation to Troy's prank and his early childhood ordeal.

"Well, I'm afraid of heights," Ben shares. "Probably because I fell from the neighbor's tree house when I was younger."

"Oh, I was the same way until Troy took me bungee jumping. You should try it."

Ben scrunches his eyebrows together. "Eh, I don't know."

"I'm sure if you ask Troy, he'll take you too."

I'm ready to put the kibosh on that idea, but Ben is quicker in replying, "I don't think so. He's mean."

Mental facepalm. Ben can be so blunt sometimes.

Jane furrows her eyebrows together. "Troy is mean? That's news to me. He can be a pain in the butt, especially when he enters protective mode, but I've never seen him act mean on purpose."

Ben opens his mouth to offer a retort, but I cut in before he says too much. "I never got a chance to ask the last time we hung out. Do you already know where you're going next year?"

"Ugh, don't even get me started on that. I want to stay here and go to Rushmore, but my father is pushing Stanford."

"Stanford is a great school," Ben pipes up.

"I know, but that's not my dream, you know?"

I turn my gaze to the house once more. Jane and Ben continue the conversation, but my thoughts are not in the here and now. They're with Troy.

Was he telling the truth when he said he didn't prank me? My head is telling me he's full of shit. Who else would have done it? But my heart is torn.

Shit. I'm a mess. That's a plot twist I didn't see coming.

TWENTY

TROY

I left the party as soon as I realized I couldn't hang out with Charlie and pretend I wasn't furious with her for accusing me of something I didn't do. That prank had Andreas's hands all over it, and he had plenty of time to plant a fake bath bomb when he came over on game night. He didn't pick up the phone when I called earlier, but as I drive without direction back from the party, I try the jerkface again.

"Troy? What's up?" he shouts over the phone. There's a lot of noise in the background. Considering the time, he's most likely in the locker room, getting ready for the game.

"Did you put a fake bath bomb in Charlie's stuff?" I ask.

"Oh yeah." I can hear the smile in his voice. "Why? Did Charlie take a bath?"

"Yes, asshole. And now she thinks I'm responsible for it."

He laughs, making me grind my teeth. "Please tell me you snapped some pictures for me. I'd love to see the look on her face."

"No, I didn't. I didn't call to congratulate you. I told you I was done fighting with her. Why the fuck did you have to take matters into your own hands?"

"Ah, quit the whining, man. It was just a harmless prank. Get over it."

"I'll get over it when you stop being a fucking meddler."

"Yeah, yeah. You sound like a whipped pussy. Just fuck the girl already and move on. This beta shit you have going on doesn't suit you. I want my friend back."

Coach Clarkson's booming voice echoes in the background. It's time for the pregame talk.

"I have to go," Andreas tells me. "I'll call you later."

He ends the call, which means I have to swallow all my angry retorts as if they were a bitter pill.

In hindsight, it's better this way. I don't want to get into a fight with Andreas over Charlie. We've been friends for years, whereas Charlie is just an annoying brat I have to put up with.

Do you, Troy? Really?

I've given her a chance, and if the last month has proven anything, it's that we're too different to get along. Grandma can't say I didn't try. However, I can't live with a person who doesn't trust me. Who's to say Charlie isn't plotting another bit of revenge right now? Fuck that. I don't want to be looking over my shoulder in my own house.

I make the decision to ask Charlie to move out, but I don't return home until hours later. Instead, I head to the private beach club where Dad has a membership for all of us and chill by the beach. I can't handle pools, but the sea has always captivated me. I love surfing, and if it weren't for football, I might have dedicated more time to it. The idea of traveling the world, chasing the perfect wave, sounds epic.

But as much as the ocean usually calms me, it isn't having the desired effect today. My chest feels unbearably heavy. I thought that after I made up my mind, I'd feel better. Not the case.

There's no sense in postponing what I have to do. It's time to go home.

CHARLIE

I didn't see Troy at the party again. Not that I was looking. *Yeah, right.*

We didn't stay long. No surprise there, considering Mom's mood. On the way back to my parents', I wonder why Mom wanted Ben and me to come. To put on a show? I just know this is the first and last time I agree to a company family event. I'm in college, for crying out loud. There should be a rule that exempts me from bore-fest gatherings like those.

All I know is I can't wait to go back home and try to get rid of the blue dye. I also want to speak with Troy. Jane's comment that her brother isn't mean made me second-guess myself. If I intend to keep sharing a roof with him, I should give him the benefit of the doubt at least. The other times he retaliated, he didn't hide. Why would he lie about this one?

I'm surprised that when we arrive, my dad's car is in the garage. Maybe he didn't really have to work; he simply didn't feel like going to the party. I can tell by Mom's face that she's gearing up for another major fight. I have to get Ben out of the house. Maybe he can stay over. But I erase that idea right away. I don't want Ben around when I have my talk with Troy, and I certainly don't want to avoid that conversation. *Crap.*

Mom is pulling into the driveway when Dad bursts through the garage door, holding Bailey in his arms. Something is wrong.

Mom presses on the brakes, and a second later, I'm out of the car.

"Dad! What happened?"

"Bailey is unresponsive. We need to get her to the vet immediately."

Mom lowers her window and shouts, "Get in here!"

Dad slides into the back seat, and I get back in the front. I'm not even done putting my seat belt on when Mom puts the car in

Reverse and burns rubber. All our problems become irrelevant. Bailey is our girl; we can't let her die.

There's a huge lump in my throat, and my eyes are beginning to burn. I turn in my seat to look at her.

"What happened?" I ask through a choke.

"I don't know. I came home and found her passed out in the kitchen next to a vomit puddle."

"She hasn't been herself since yesterday. We should have taken her to the vet, damn it!" Mom hits the steering wheel hard, right before she takes a sharp curve without slowing down.

I don't comment that they probably would have done that if they hadn't been busy fighting. But it's a petty remark and it would help no one. I can guess they must have come to the same conclusion because neither of them speaks again.

We arrive at the vet in five minutes—a drive that usually takes ten. Dad jumps out of the car and takes off to the entrance with me close on his heels. The vet's assistant immediately tells Dad to bring Bailey to the examination room but forbids the rest of us from going after him. Dejected, I sit in the waiting room with Ben while Mom fills out the forms.

Ben rests his head on my shoulder, and with a tearful voice, he asks, "Do you think Bailey will be okay?"

The "Yes" gets stuck in my throat. I can't bring myself to lie to him. Bailey is old, and even if the vet is able to treat her today, it's only a matter of time before she leaves us forever.

"I don't know, Ben. We should prepare for the worst." Fat tears roll down my cheeks. I wipe them away with the back of my blue hand. My fight with Troy becomes small, unimportant in the grand scheme of things.

"I don't want Bailey to die," Ben whines right before his body starts to shake.

I lace my hand with his. "I don't want to lose her either."

The wait is torturous but not long. Fifteen minutes later, Dad joins us in the waiting room. His slumped shoulders and teary eyes say it all.

"Dad?" I jump to my feet.

He shakes his head. "I'm sorry, honey. Our girl is gone. There was nothing Dr. Harper could have done."

Mom stands too and gives Dad a hug. Ben breaks into an ugly cry, so for his sake, I keep my tears at bay, even though I was crying before. There's a big hole in my chest now. I don't want to think what it'll be like to walk into my parents' house and not see that golden fur ball run to greet me. Bailey was a staple of my childhood. There are so many wonderful memories, it's impossible to count them all.

We wait a bit longer for Dad to fill out more paperwork. When we finally get back to the house, Mom wants me to spend the night. But I can't face the house knowing Bailey won't be there. I have to get out of here. It's selfish of me when I think of Ben, but at the same time, that's what my parents are for. Maybe what happened will finally force them to make up.

"I can't stay. I have to study for a test tomorrow," I lie.

"How can you think about tests when Bailey is dead?" Ben cries out.

I open my mouth to defend myself, even though I'm not being truthful, but Dad speaks first, "We all deal with grief differently, buddy. Your sister's way is losing herself in books."

His defense feels backhanded, but I won't complain. He's giving me a free pass.

"Thanks, Dad."

"Please drive safely, Charlie," Mom says.

"I will."

Despite my promise, I barely notice the road on the way back to my house. Everything is a blur. I thought that by putting distance between myself and my parents' house, the pain would diminish, but it works the other way around. By the time I park in front of my place, the choke in my throat is so immense, it's making it impossible to breathe. With quick steps, I approach the front porch. My hands are shaking as I try to unlock the door. I veer for the kitchen in desperate need of something strong to alleviate my pain.

I search each cabinet for the bottle of tequila I saw the other day. It isn't mine, but considering what I'm going through, I don't think Troy will mind. I finally find it pushed all the way back behind some tortilla chips bags. It's almost empty, maybe one shot left in it. I'm about to throw it back when Troy comes down the stairs.

His face is solemn when he says, "Charlie, we need to talk."

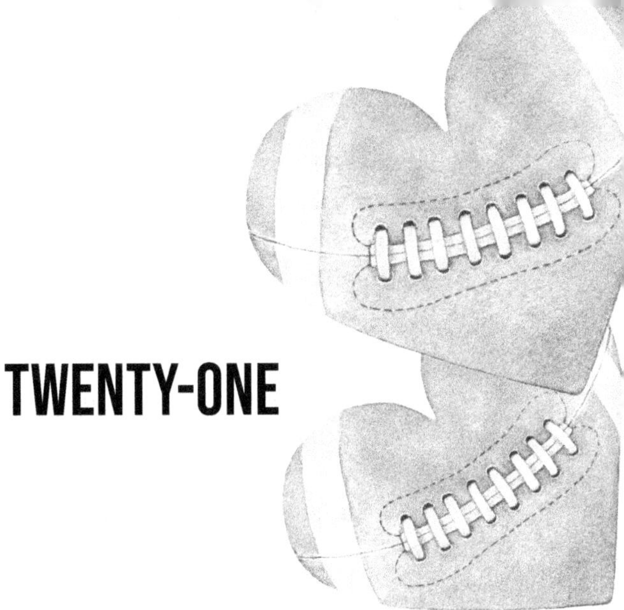

TWENTY-ONE

TROY

The moment Charlie whirls around, I see something is terribly wrong. Her eyes are bloodshot, her face tearstained. She's clutching an almost empty bottle of tequila as if it were her lifeline.

"What's wrong?" I breach the distance between us in three long strides.

"What do you want to talk about?" she asks in a small voice.

"It's not important right now." I take the bottle from her and set it on the counter. "Tell me what happened."

She can't hold my gaze. Her lips quiver as she lowers her eyes to my chest. "It's…. My dog died today." She tries to hide a sob by covering her mouth with her hand.

I pull her to me without a second thought, crushing her body to mine in an awkward hug. The sling is in the way. "I'm so sorry, Charlie."

"I knew she was old, but it was still a shock. She wasn't sick or anything."

Charlie steps back, easing out of my embrace. I want to hold on to her longer but catch myself in time.

"How old was she?" I ask.

"Fourteen. I can't imagine life without her. Bailey was the sweetest dog." She wipes a tear away, but more keep falling.

I take her hand in mine, then kiss her fingers. She gasps loudly, widening her eyes in surprise. I let go of her, just so I can cup her cheek, rubbing away another tear with my thumb. We don't speak for a moment, but our eyes remain locked. I'm keenly aware of how fast my heart is beating, how shallow my breathing is.

Before I can stop myself, I lean down and capture her lips with mine. There's no trace of tequila on them; she didn't drink a single drop. The kiss is soft, tentative, but when she doesn't resist, I tease at the seam, prying her lips open with my tongue. I can taste her tears, the saltiness on her lips, but also her effervescent passion that seems to grow at the speed of light.

I step closer, sliding my hand behind her head so she can't escape. Her hands find my T-shirt, her fingers curling around the fabric while a moan escapes her mouth. The sound sends a shot of desire straight to my cock. With a groan, I spin her around, pressing her ass to the counter.

"Troy," she murmurs.

"Yes, Charlie?"

"What are we doing?"

I ease off just a little so I can look into her eyes. "I don't know. Is this not okay?"

She doesn't answer right away, which tells me everything I need to know. I try to take a step back, but Charlie holds on to my T-shirt.

"This is more than okay."

She invades my space this time, rising on the tips of her toes to crash her lips to mine. There's nothing slow or easy about this kiss. It's fervid, urgent, and sexy as hell. It sets my body ablaze, it melts my bones, and it vanquishes any doubt I had that this was only a matter of physical attraction. I don't want only her body. I want everything.

If I wasn't injured, I'd take her in my arms and make a beeline to my room because the things I want to do to her require a bed. Cursing my recovering shoulder, I say between kisses, "Let's head upstairs."

"The couch is closer." She steps back, releasing my shirt to take my hand.

I let her steer me to the living room, and then we're on the couch, making out like two horny teenagers. There's only so much I can do with one hand though, but I'm glad Charlie is as eager to explore as I am.

She kisses my neck, sending goose bumps down my spine. "How is your shoulder?" she whispers in my ear.

"It's fine."

"Is it okay if I remove the sling?"

"Yeah."

While she's busy helping me out of it, my hand disappears under her sweater. Her skin is taut and warm to the touch, and I can't wait to taste it. Her lips return to mine when the sling is off. I always feel a tension when I move my shoulder, but I'm too busy exploring Charlie's body to notice. When I brush the underside of her breast, she slides onto my lap, sitting astride me.

"Take off your top," I tell her.

She pouts. "But I'm blue."

"So what? I've always had a thing for Smurfette."

She watches me through slits. "Was that the reason you put blue dye in my bath bomb?"

"No, that wasn't me. Andreas is the culprit. I'm sorry I have stupid friends." She doesn't seem angry anymore, so I press. "I'll take a bath in blue dye to make things even if you want."

"Do you mean, there are more booby traps in my bathroom?" Her eyebrows arch.

"To be honest, I don't know. To be safe, I'd get rid of all your bath supplies."

"Would you really turn blue for me?" She bites her lower lip, driving me further insane with need.

I kiss her again, unable to resist the temptation, while I slide my hand up, cupping her breast over her bra. She doesn't stop me, so I push the fabric aside to play with her nipple. It's as hard as a pebble and begging for attention.

"Damn it, Troy. You're really working your case."

I chuckle. "I'm very motivated. You smell so good, Charlie." I trace her jawline with my tongue, moving along to the side of her neck.

She grabs my arms, digging her fingers in while arching her back.

"Fine. You win," she breathes out.

I lean back and search her eyes. There's redness in them, which makes me feel guilty for a second. Charlie is dealing with grief, and here I am, taking advantage of her.

"As much as I want you, maybe we shouldn't continue."

She frowns. "Why not?"

I trace her hairline with the tips of my fingers, then tuck a loose strand of hair behind her ear. "You've been through a lot today, sweetheart."

Regret immediately takes hold of me when her eyes well with tears. *Fuck.* I shouldn't have said anything.

"Is that the only reason you want to stop? Because you believe I'm not thinking straight?"

I nod, afraid if I open my mouth, I'll say another stupid thing.

She captures my face between her hands. "I've never been more certain about anything, Troy. I'm tired of fighting my feelings. If anything, what happened today has made things clearer to me."

I see nothing but determination and sincerity in her gaze.

"Then fucking kiss me like there's no tomorrow. Don't hold back."

She heeds my words, covering my mouth with hers. I tangle my fingers in her hair, pulling her even closer to me. Risking pain, I reach for her waist with my right arm. I want her pinned to my body until she's molded to me. I'm about to combust on the spot, but when Charlie begins to grind her pelvis against mine, I lose my mind completely.

"These clothes need to go," she says before I can.

"Fuck yeah."

Thanks to my injured shoulder, the process of getting rid of our clothes takes longer than I'd like. She helps me first, pulling my T-shirt off carefully and then lobbing it aside. She stops for a moment to take in my naked chest, staring with hunger in her eyes.

"You can touch if you want," I tease.

"Oh, I will." She traces her fingers over my pecs, then leans down to run her warm tongue over them, making me hiss.

I grab a handful of her hair to bring her devious mouth to mine. I don't kiss her; I brand her with my tongue and teeth before pulling back. "You're not playing fair. I thought you wanted our clothes gone."

"What's the hurry? I'm not going anywhere."

What's the hurry, she asks. Woman, I'm dying here. I need to see you. All I had to hold me over for these past weeks was a little sneak peek of your pussy."

She gasps as if she were offended, then hits my shoulder—my *injured* shoulder.

"Ouch!"

"Oops. Sorry, I forgot," she apologizes sheepishly.

"Let me see your tits and I'll forgive you." I smirk.

"Patience is a virtue, you know?"

"Never had any, ain't gonna start now."

With a shake of her head, she helps me take off my jeans but keeps my boxer shorts on. Her eyes linger on my erection straining against the fabric, and I can guess what she has in mind.

"I do want your mouth on my cock, sweetheart, but let's level the playing field first. Clothes be gone."

She pouts. "You're no fun."

My lips curl into a grin. "Oh, I'm loads of fun. You'll see."

She reaches for the edge of her turtleneck, but before she takes it off, she says, "If you laugh, it's game over."

I'd believe her if she could keep a straight face, but I indulge her. "I won't laugh. Promise."

She finally pulls her sweater off, sitting in front of me in her panties and bra only. Even blue, there's nothing laughable about her appearance.

"Damn, you're breathtaking."

"Really? You dig the *Avatar* look?"

I don't reply right away, too busy thinking of the ways I plan to worship her body.

"Troy?" she asks.

I bring my eyes to her face. "Sorry. What was the question?"

She shakes her head. "Never mind. I got my answer."

I snake my left arm around her back, and with deft fingers, I unhook her bra. Her glorious tits spill free from their restraint, and before the scrap of fabric drops to Charlie's lap, my mouth and hands are on her. I circle one of her nipples with my tongue, teasing the nub mercilessly while I knead her other breast. I don't care about the pain in my shoulder—this is an all-hands-on-deck situation.

Charlie's fingers thread through my hair, and then she yanks at the strands while arching her back. I let go of her breast for a second to pull her onto my lap again. A deep groan escapes from deep in my throat when her pussy rubs against my shaft. She's already soaking wet, and her heat combined with the friction of our underwear grinding together, is sending me careening to the edge faster than I want. *Shit*. I can't pull a quick-draw move on her.

I let go of her nipple with a soft pop, then kiss her lips again, fast and deep. "I'm going to eat your pussy now, darling," I murmur against her lips.

"I want a taste of you too."

I grow harder at the idea of a sixty-nine, but I stomp on it for now. There's a real danger here that the moment Charlie's lips touch my cock, I'll explode in her mouth.

"In good time. Patience is a virtue, remember? Your words." I push her off my lap. "Now lie down and let me feast on you for a bit."

Her cheeks turn an adorable pink shade. I don't comment on it, not when she does what I asked without a fight. She's not as blue as before, but it'll take several washes to get rid of the dye. It doesn't bother me in the least. She's beautiful no matter what.

I peel her panties off with eagerness, almost tearing them in the process.

Charlie chuckles. "Are you that hungry?"

"For you? I'm starving." I sprawl my fingers across her hips, taking a moment to admire her pussy. My mouth waters at the sight.

"What's wrong?" she asks, a hint of insecurity in her tone.

"Babe, there's nothing wrong."

Then I dive in, going straight for the kill. My tongue sweeps over her clit, eliciting a cry from Charlie. Her hips buck toward me, but I keep her in place as I eat her like candy. She tastes like peaches, velvety on my tongue, sweet in the back of my throat. I've never had anything better.

"Oh my God," she moans.

I pull back to insert two fingers inside her while pressing my thumb against her bundle of nerves. I've barely started finger-fucking her when she cries out, and her pussy clenches around me. I increase the tempo, trying to prolong her climax and not think about the tightness in my balls.

"That's it, babe. Come for me."

Her tremors cease, and then she goes utterly still save for the rise and fall of her chest. "Holy fuck," she breathes.

I laugh, then jump off the couch.

She leans on her elbows. "Where are you going?"

"I need something." I run back to the kitchen and look for the extra box of condoms I keep there. It takes me a few seconds to find it and then run back to Charlie.

"You keep condoms in the kitchen?" She raises an eyebrow.

"I lived alone before. Any room in the house was fair game."

I only realize my error when Charlie's gaze darkens. "I see."

"Fuck. That made me sound like a horndog, didn't it? I swear that wasn't the case."

She sits up and takes the box from my hand. "I don't care." Without breaking eye contact, she retrieves a foil packet from the box. "As long as you fuck me like one now."

"Yes, ma'am."

My boxer shorts disappear in the blink of an eye, and the condom goes in place just as fast. Charlie then pulls the same move I did before, making me lie down and then straddling me.

"You've already abused your shoulder too much. Let me take over now."

I reach for her hips, guiding her pussy to my erection. "I can't make any promises."

Bracing one hand on my chest and the other against the back of the couch, Charlie slowly impales herself on me. I clench my jaw, fighting my body. A desperate groan escapes my lips.

"You were saying?" she asks.

"Damn. You're tight."

She begins to move, slowly at first, which works for me. But instinct takes over, and then I'm moving in sync with her hips. We don't speak, and the only sounds in the room are of our labored breathing and the slapping of flesh against flesh.

Getting closer to climax, I sit up to claim Charlie's mouth again. Our tongues mingle in the same rhythm as our bodies. She's getting tighter around me, or maybe I'm growing larger. All train of thought shatters when the release hits me like a cannonball. Charlie lets go of my mouth to bite my left shoulder. The sharp pain only serves to amplify my pleasure. Her body is shaking too, but her whimpers are muffled now that her face is hidden in the crook of my neck.

Eventually, our movements slow down. I relax against the couch, keeping my arms wrapped around Charlie. She rests her face against my chest with a content sigh.

"Are you okay?" I ask.

"More than okay."

"Good."

We don't speak for another minute, but I'm the one who breaks the silence again. "Can I ask you something?"

"Sure."

"Is your character in LARP a vampire by any chance?"

She becomes tense in my arms, then pulls back. Her eyes dart to my shoulder, which no doubt has her teeth mark now.

"Oh my God, Troy. I'm so sorry."

I chuckle. "Why? I can't say I was ever bitten before, but damn, it was hot."

Her face is bright red now. "You must think I'm a psycho."

"Not at all. And, sweetheart, you can make a snack out of me anytime you want."

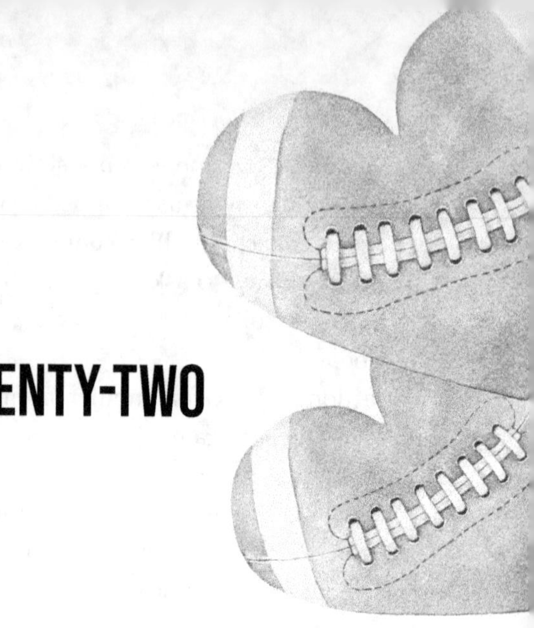

TWENTY-TWO

CHARLIE

I stare at Troy's beautiful, sexed-up face without blinking. Did I hear him right? He wants to keep doing this? My heart and my lady parts shout in excitement, but my head has to come in and ruin everything. I don't regret hooking up with him, but I'm not sure how to progress from here.

"Charlie? Why are you staring at me like that?" he asks through an amused smile.

"Like what?"

"With that deep V between your brows as if you were trying to solve an algebra equation."

"Not algebra, but—"

"Ah, the *but*. Is this when we have the talk? Can't we bask a little longer in the post-sex bliss?"

"I can't. I'm sorry. My mind is already spinning like a top. I don't know what will happen next."

He runs his fingers up and down my arm, giving me goose bumps. "What do you want to happen?"

Oh fuck. He did not just put me on the spot. "That's an unfair question."

"Why?"

"Fine. You tell me what you want to happen."

He leans forward and kisses me tenderly. My toes curl, and tingles run down my spine. My body ignites again, pushing my worrisome thoughts out of the way for now.

"I want to keep doing this," he whispers, then kisses me again right under my ear. "And this."

I swallow hard, hating how his answer has wreaked havoc on my body already. Reluctantly, I push him back. "So you want to keep hooking up casually."

He frowns. "Not casually. I've done that for the longest time. But it's different with you, Charlie. I could never be casual with you."

Sweet baby llamas. I'm about to turn into flames while my heart goes to a hundred. "What do we do then? You understand we live together, right? Talk about adding pressure to things."

He leans against the couch, narrowing his eyes. "How about this? We keep acting like roommates in the common areas and save the fun parts to the bedroom."

"Well, we kind of already ruined that." I pointedly glance at the couch.

"True, but that didn't count."

I nibble on my lower lip, still doubting Troy's proposal will work.

"Of course, if you keep doing that to your lip, I might have no choice but to ravish you where you stand."

My face feels hot. I'm not used to being on the receiving end of such raw sexual energy. And that's what Troy is—sex on a stick.

"Let's take things slow," he continues. "We won't have sex until we go on at least three dates."

I cross my arms, covering my breasts from his view. "Really? You want to go without sex until we've had three dates?"

"What are you saying, Charlie? You can't be in the same room with me without trying to jump my bones?" He chuckles, a sound that's quickly becoming one of my favorite things about him.

Who would have thought that I'd actually find positive traits in Troy to appreciate besides his looks? Is this the same guy who's pushed my buttons and made me see red on multiple occasions?

"I can resist your charms. The question is, can you resist me?" I reply.

He watches me through slits. "Are you challenging me?"

I shrug. "Maybe."

He keeps watching me with his smoldering gaze while the corners of his lips twitch upward. "Roomie, you don't know what you're doing. I never lose a bet."

Feeling sassy, I lean forward until my boobs press gently against his chest. "Me neither. Let's make it more interesting, shall we?"

"What do you have in mind?" he asks in a tight voice.

"How about we don't stipulate a set number of dates before we have sex again? Whoever caves first must pay a price."

"What kind of price?"

"That's to be decided by the winner."

"And what are the terms of the challenge? Is doing this allowed?" He licks my neck, making my eyes flutter closed.

"Yes," I hiss.

"How about this?" He reaches for my breast and pinches my nipple, sending a zing of pleasure down to my core.

"That's… gray area. It depends on the situation."

"What kind of situation, Charlie?" He flicks my nipple again while peppering my neck with open kisses.

"I don't know."

He chuckles against my ear, then tangles his fingers in my hair and turns my mouth to his. The kiss is deep, long, and so fucking delicious. I don't even know what we're talking about anymore.

"When do we start the challenge, babe?" he whispers against my mouth.

"Tomorrow. We'll begin tomorrow."

"Thank fuck." He pushes me down on the couch and then covers his body with mine.

When his erection teases at my entrance, I know I made the right call by postponing the start of our ridiculous bet. Why in the world would I suggest that? I hate losing, and Troy seems to suffer from the same malady. But I won't worry about that now. I have to take my fill of him and hope I manage to curb my sexual hunger later.

Troy finds a new condom and then slams into me without preamble. I cry out, loving the feel of him inside me, stretching me, completing me. We keep our mouths fused together while he thrusts in and out as if he's trying to bottle up every drop of pleasure. He tried to give me some control before, but now he's one hundred percent in charge. He grunts, then leans back to hoist my leg over his good shoulder. My hips rise off the couch, and in this new angle, he can get much deeper. I close my eyes, moaning like a cat in heat as he hits my G-spot.

"Open your eyes, Charlie," he commands.

I look at his flushed face, at the veins bulging in his neck, and I can't help but feel a little nudge in my heart. But the pressure inside keeps building, making it harder to think straight.

Good, I don't need to overanalyze my crazy feelings right now.

When Troy presses his thumb over my clit, I surrender to the wave of pleasure that sends me tumbling into an ocean of oblivion.

"Damn it, babe. You feel too fucking good," he says before he tosses his head back and shouts a string of curses.

He doesn't slow down during his climax, almost as if he wants to stretch the moment for as long as possible. Another mini orgasm hits me then, not as intense as the first one but a surprise nonetheless. I've never climaxed twice during sex before.

Son of a bitch. How am I going to deny myself this much fun?

TROY

I collapse on top of Charlie, spent. In any other circumstance, I'd hit the sack to recover. But since we're starting our ridiculous bet tomorrow, I have no intention of resting. A sex marathon tonight it is.

"Troy, you're crushing me."

"Oops, sorry."

I get off her, standing up to get rid of the condom. When I return, Charlie is already sitting down and, to my disappointment, putting her sweater back on.

"What do you think you're doing?"

"Getting dressed."

"Wait. Do you think I'm done with you?"

She arches her eyebrows and makes an O with her mouth. "Are you serious? How about your shoulder?"

I rotate it backward, wincing as pain flares up. It's not as bad as before, but I'm definitely not recovered. "It's okay. Maybe I can take a bath to relax my muscles. Do you want to join?"

She wrinkles her nose. "Uh, no. I won't be taking a bath until I buy new products. I don't trust that Andreas didn't leave us more surprises."

"Nah, he wouldn't prank me. But I think we should retaliate."

Charlie perks up in her seat. "Really? You want to prank that bastard with me?"

The way her voice rises in excitement is cute as hell. If I'm not careful, I might fall for her.

"Damn straight. I told him I was done fighting with you, but he didn't listen."

Charlie taps her lips with her index finger as her eyes become unfocused. I'm witnessing firsthand her devious mind at work.

"I might have an idea, but I need to check with my sources first."

"Wait. You're not going to tell me?"

"Not yet. Let me find out first if it's possible. I don't want to disappoint you if it doesn't work out."

"He's throwing a Halloween party at his place in two weeks. That would be the best time to prank his ass."

"Really? You want to do it at his party?" She laughs. "That's ruthless, Troy. And Jane said you weren't mean."

"Oh, she did, huh? What else did she say about me?" A grin tugs at the corners of my mouth.

The smile on Charlie's face wilts a little, and her gaze seems troubled. The change is fleeting, making me wonder if I imagined it.

"She mentioned you helped her with her fear of heights."

"Yeah, that was fun. We should do it sometime." I put my boxer shorts on, then my jeans.

"What are you doing?" she asks.

"If I can't ogle your hot bod, you can't ogle mine." I wink at her.

"Fine. I guess that's fair."

"Are you hungry? I could… eat." My eyes linger on Charlie's long legs as she pulls her panties up.

"Will you quit for a second?" She laughs. "I already know who's going to cave first."

"Ha-ha. We still have to establish the ground rules. And one of them is not parading naked in front of me."

"Fine. But that goes both ways, which means no walking shirtless in the house."

Damn it. I was totally banking on my six-pack to win me this bet. But it's okay, I have other ways to make myself irresistible.

"All right. So, food?"

"Yeah. Should we order in?"

"I think we have to. Unless you can whip up a miracle dinner with whatever is in the fridge."

"There's nothing there. I didn't have a chance to go grocery shopping."

"We'll go tomorrow."

She chuckles. "Look at us, planning to hit the store together."

"What? Roommates do that." I smile, knowing very well that we're way past being just roommates with benefits.

The crazy way my heart is beating now is proof of that.

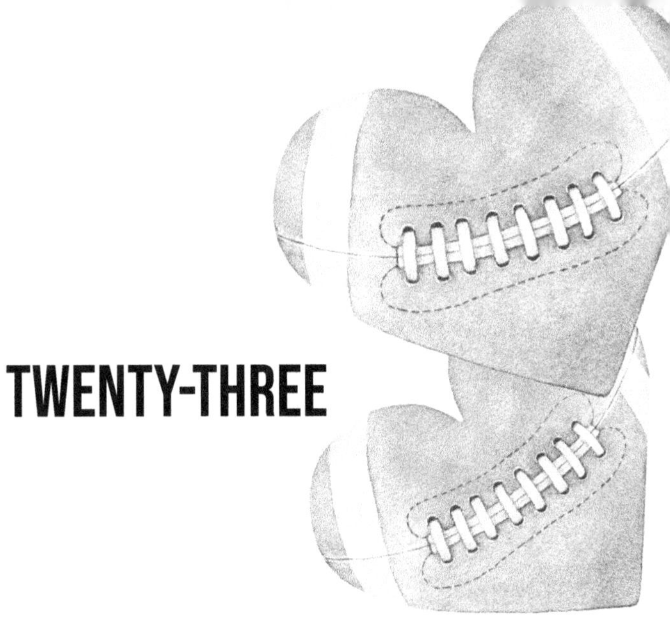

TWENTY-THREE

CHARLIE

Can women get blue balls? I feel like that's what I have. After the sex marathon of Saturday night, followed by the exact opposite on Sunday, I'm going through withdrawals. My pussy is in pain and missing Troy's magical wand. He might have ruined me for other men, and at the same time turned me into a nymphomaniac.

I haven't seen him this morning. He did say he had an early appointment with the team's physio. To be honest, I'm glad I missed him. I'm not used to the idea yet that I'm dating Troy. The situation is too surreal. But I can't keep obsessing about him. It's Monday, and I have to focus on the myriad of projects and tasks I've lined up for this week. I'm glad I finished my last editing job. The last thing I need is to read about a fictional character's sex life when I'm purposely denying myself the best sex I've ever had.

I spent an hour talking to Ben yesterday. He was still pretty sad about Bailey, just like me. But thankfully, his girlfriend was there to support him when I couldn't. I still feel guilty as hell for ditching him last weekend. I have to make it up to him.

My first class on Monday is two hours of Italian, which to everyone else seems like a curse. It never bothered me until today. My concentration is shot no matter how hard I try to pay attention to Professor Mantuano. I should be thankful he didn't give us a quiz today. But two hours later, I have a headache that could bring down an elephant. I would have taken painkillers when it started, but I had no water with me, and I'm not one of those people who can swallow pills dry. I'd probably end up throwing up.

As soon as the class is over, I make a beeline for the nearest cafeteria. I get distracted at the checkout line and hardly pay attention to the noise surrounding me. It's not until the girl in front of me mentions the name Troy to her friend that my attention piques. I follow their line of sight and see that the ruckus was caused by the football team, who is taking up three tables in the middle of the room.

My eyes immediately find Troy in the group, still wearing the sling. Andreas is sitting next to him, laughing at something someone said. Danny, the freshman who's temporarily replaced Troy as the quarterback, is on Troy's other side. He doesn't seem to be into whatever it is that sent the entire table into a fit of roaring laughter.

I can't keep my eyes off Troy. He's so fucking beautiful and sexy, more so now that I know what he's capable of in the sack. Suddenly, he turns his head in my direction, and our gazes connect. The amusement vanishes from his face, replaced by pure heat.

Fuck me. Even with the distance, I'm falling prey to his come-hither look.

Someone taps me on the shoulder. "Hello? Do you mind moving along?"

I realize then that the line has moved, and I've just been standing there like a moron, drooling over the quarterback like a football groupie.

"Sorry," I mumble.

It's my turn to pay, so I do so as quickly as possible, then hurry out of the cafeteria. I purposely avoid looking in Troy's direction even if it's hard. I'm glad he didn't come talk to me. We haven't discussed how we should behave in public. We agreed to date, but is he my boyfriend? *Shit*. Why didn't we talk about that beforehand?

I stop under a tree to finally take the painkillers, hoping they'll start to work right away before I have to suffer through the next class. After that, I have to stop by the newspaper and then ho—

A strong arm wraps around my waist, interrupting my train of thought and scaring the crap out of me. I shout, but a second later, Troy's aftershave scent reaches my nose.

"Troy, what the hell!"

He laughs but doesn't let go. "Sorry. I couldn't resist. You looked pretty distracted."

"I was." I turn in his hold so I can properly glare at him. "What are you doing?"

"You left the cafeteria so quickly. You didn't even give me the chance to say hi."

"I have class in five minutes."

His eyes take on a mischievous gleam. "Good. Plenty of time for a proper greeting."

He pins me against the tree and then kisses me long and deep, melting me on the spot. His entire body presses against mine as his right leg nudges mine apart. We would be melded together if the sling wasn't in the way. I should put a stop to it. We're pretty much engaging in foreplay in front of everyone, and my panties are already soaked through. But I'm too weak to stop. I want more. I'm not sure if I'll be able to win our bet after all.

"Get a room!" a random guy yells.

Troy chuckles against my lips and then steps back, leaving me breathless. At least my headache is gone, and I don't think it was the painkillers' doing.

"Why are you laughing?" I ask, caught between arousal and embarrassment.

"Because your face is redder than a tomato."

"Of course it is. You were dry-humping me against a tree!"

He places a hand over his heart and makes a phony expression of indignation. "I was not. My, my, Charlie. You have one dirty mind. I guess you should declare defeat now because it's clear to me who is going to lose the challenge."

I narrow my eyes to slits. "Aha! I see what you're doing. You might have gotten me hot and bothered, Troy, but I'm not the one who has to return to my friends sporting a major boner."

The mirth vanishes from his face in an instant. He glances down, then puts his hand on his hip. "Shit. I guess I didn't really think things through." He looks up again. "That's what I get for having such a sexy girlfriend." He rewards me with a toothy grin. "You'd better hurry up or you'll be late for your next class."

Crap. I lost track of time.

I run across the quad, forgetting to give Troy a smartass retort for making me late. It's okay. I can give him grief later at home. Maybe. Right now, I'm still processing the fact that he called me his girlfriend like it was the most obvious thing. Never mind that I had been agonizing about it not too long ago. How can he make everything so easy?

Because he's not overthinking everything like you, Charlie.

A necessity because I'm traveling in uncharted territory. I like adventure and quests in fiction. In real life, I'm content to remain in my safe zone. And Troy is the opposite of that. In fact, I should probably program "Danger Zone" by Kenny Loggins as the ringtone for him.

Troy is my boyfriend.

A smile blossoms on my lips despite the fact that I hate being late.

When I finally arrive to class—breathless and sporting a sheen of sweat on my forehead thanks to running here—I don't care. Not even when Professor Ross glowers at me and calls me out for my tardiness in front of the entire lecture hall. I quickly take my usual seat and pretend to give a damn about the class, but I've already accepted the fact that I'm getting nothing done today.

***

It was easy to blow off my classes, but newspaper time is a different matter. Blake will never allow me to skate by and not do actual work.

On my way to the office, Fred finds me, which is good because I do need to ask him for a favor.

"Hey, Charlie. What's the crack?"

I snort. "*What's the crack?* Are you Irish now?"

"Ha, sorry. We have a new hire at the shop straight from Ireland. I've picked up a few things from him."

"That explains it. What did he have to say about your green hair? I bet he dug it, huh?"

Fred quirks a brow. "Why? Because he's Irish? Gee, Charlie, that was weak. You're losing your mojo. That doesn't have anything to do with a certain jock you were spotted sucking face with earlier, does it?"

I stop in my tracks. "What? Where did you hear that?"

"Through the grapevine. You're trending on Twitter. Someone shot a video. Wanna see?"

"No, I don't want to see."

I turn around and continue toward the office. My face is in flames now. Curse Troy for kissing me like that in public.

"So, you and Troy, huh? When did that happen? I thought you hated his guts."

"I never hated his guts. I had an intense dislike for the guy."

"You have clearly moved on from that." He chuckles.

"Clearly."

The newspaper office finally looms closer. I was hoping Fred would just go on his way and leave me alone, but the pest follows me in. I should have known. He's a dog with a bone and he won't stop teasing me until something else catches his attention.

Blake is already at his desk, typing away with determination, but he stops to glance at us. I can't tell if he knows about my *faux pas* or not. He's pretty good at keeping his expression guarded.

"Are you two dating now?" Fred asks loudly in front of him. *Great.*

"Who is Charlie dating?" Blake asks.

I groan, rolling my eyes as I take my seat. "Why are you two being such busybodies today?"

"If you didn't want anyone butting in your business, you should have kept your affairs private," Fred retorts with a smirk.

The last thing I want is to tell Blake I'm dating Troy, but keeping it secret will be impossible considering the biggest gossiper in our group already knows. Besides, if it's on Twitter, it's only a matter of time until Blake stumbles across that.

I open my mouth to give him the news when Angelica comes into the office and blurts, "You're dating Troy Alexander?" Her voice is high-pitched, and she has manic eyes, like a small dog that just spotted a ball.

I rest my head in my hand, sighing loudly. "Fantastic."

"What the hell are you talking about?" Blake asks her.

"Oh my God. What kind of newspaper editor are you? Charlie's make-out session with Troy in front of the cafeteria building is trending like crazy on Twitter."

"That doesn't make any sense," he replies.

I glance at him. "It's true. Troy and I are together."

Blake's eyebrows shoot to the heavens. "Since when?"

"Since this weekend."

"But he's an asshole. You hate him."

"Why do you guys keep saying I hate him? That's not true. I had a deep dislike for him. It's different."

"Not really," Fred pipes up. "But what made you change your mind?"

"Several things. I don't want to get into it now."

Blake shakes his head, then returns to his computer screen. "I could tell you that dating Troy is a big mistake, but you're a smart woman. You know that already."

His snide remark does what he intended. It pisses me off. Not because he thinks I'm making a mistake, but because he knows I do believe that. That's what happens when your friend knows you inside and out.

"Why is she making a mistake?" Angelica asks. "Troy is hot as hell. Any girl on campus would die to go out with him."

"And yet he's a senior and has never dated anyone," Blake points out.

"Are you implying he's a player? If so, you're dead wrong. That's his best friend, Andreas Rossi," Angelica replies.

"Oh yeah, that Neanderthal who almost punched Fred for just talking to Troy's sister. You can tell a lot about a person simply by the company they keep."

For fuck's sake. I'm done with Blake's bad attitude. "Really? So what does that say about me? Because you're being a real jerk right now," I snap.

"He must be jealous," Angelica chimes in.

"Oh, that's not it," Blake refutes.

"Ignore him, Charlie." Fred sits on the edge of my desk. "I don't think Troy is that bad. He was pretty friendly at game night. His hothead friend was the one who kind of ruined the evening."

I nod. "Yeah, Andreas can be a prick. Speaking of which, I need your help with putting him in his place."

His eyes widen. "Oh? I'm all ears."

"I was wondering if I could get a custom prop from you."

"You mean a freebie?" He smirks knowingly.

I've hit him up before for free stuff for our LARP events. He's usually pretty chill about it since he also benefits from it.

"Yeah, you know I can't afford to pay. I wouldn't want to

spend hundreds of dollars only to prank Andreas either. He's not worth that much trouble."

"It really depends on what kind of prop you have in mind."

"Nothing major. I just need a head."

"A head?"

"Yeah, a severed head." I smile wickedly.

"Oh my God. You want to pull the severed head in the fridge stunt on him. Awesome!"

"Yep. So, can you help?"

"You bet I can, girlie. But on one condition."

"Name it."

"You have to record the whole thing."

I lean back in my chair, smiling from ear to ear. "That goes without saying. If it's not caught on film, it didn't happen. We're pulling the prank at his Halloween party."

"Awesome! Man, I wish I could come, but I already have plans."

"You can't possibly mean that after that douche Andreas almost punched you in the face for talking to Jane." Blake glowers at Fred.

He scoffs. "I'm not afraid of him."

"Oh, I want to come. Andy is such a dreamboat." Angelica makes googly eyes.

Oh crap. I forgot she was in the room. I shouldn't have talked about the prank in front of her.

"Sure, you can come, but on the condition that you won't say a word to anyone about the prank."

"Yeah, Angie. Don't be a party pooper," Fred adds.

She widens her innocent eyes. "I won't say a word. Promise."

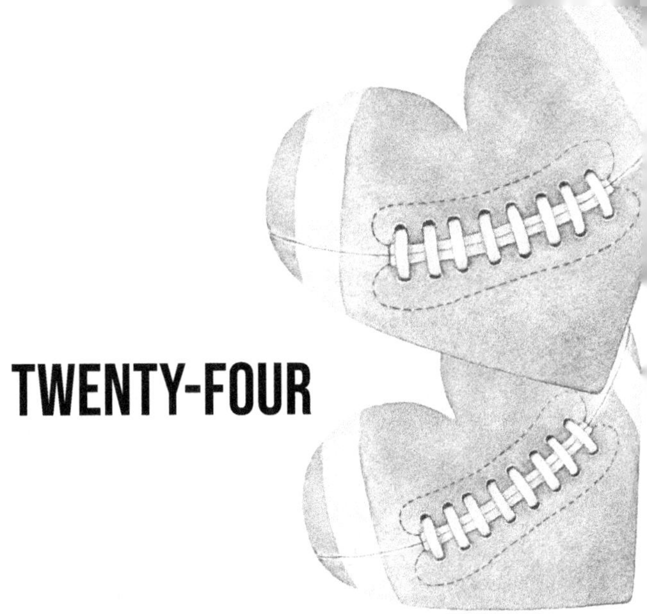

TWENTY-FOUR

TROY

"You have gone fucking mad." Andreas shakes his head. "You literally have dozens of hot girls throwing themselves at your feet and you pick Charlie to date? Madness."

I narrow my eyes at him. "Why the hell do you care who I do or don't date? I like her. She's different."

"Why? Because she wants to castrate you when you're sleeping?"

"What's with the drama? You've been watching too many daytime soap operas."

"More like those dark series with serial killers," Danny pipes up from the back seat. "Charlie seems cool."

"She called you Pringles Boy," Andreas retorts.

"Well, I *was* destroying that tube of Pringles." He laughs.

"Trust me, guys. Charlie is awesome."

"Oh my God. Please don't tell me you've gone and fallen in love with her. That's not you, bro." The indignation in Andreas's tone rubs me the wrong way.

"Don't be ridiculous. I'm not in love with her. Like I said, she's different than any of the hot chicks you mentioned. She's… exciting."

And that's what I crave the most in anything I do. Excitement, adrenaline. I can't do calm, quiet, boring. I can't let my mind have time to think about the shit I've done, the lives I've destroyed.

"Who are you, and what did you do with my friend? Are you sure you didn't hit your head when you had your accident?" Andreas peels his eyes off the road for a second to look at me.

"I can't believe she didn't seek revenge after the blue-dye incident," Danny chimes in.

"Oh, she was livid about it. But now she knows who the responsible party is." I glower at Andreas.

"Great. Now she's going to turn her psycho act on me. Fantastic."

"Hey, you brought that on yourself." I glance out the window, trying to hide my half-smile.

Charlie sent me a message earlier saying her prank idea was on. She's going to tell me in person tonight.

"Enough about the sexy nerd. You're coming to the next game, right? Coach wasn't happy that you didn't come last Saturday."

"I had a family function I couldn't escape from. But yeah, I'll be there this weekend. I miss the field too much. I can't wait to get rid of this damn sling."

"What did the physio say?" Danny asks.

"That I could potentially return in three weeks instead of four. Coach wants me back to training next week already."

"That's awesome news. Well, not for Danny boy though. Sorry, buddy. Your time will come." Andreas glances at him through the rearview mirror.

"No worries. It's Troy's senior year. It'd be a shame if he didn't finish the season."

"We're doing well. We have a chance at winning the championship," Andreas continues.

"As long as none of us gets injured during winter break," I joke even though I know it's a possibility with us.

"Before I forget, we're going to a party after the game. Your fans miss you."

And by fans, he means the football groupies who are only concerned with screwing one of us. Andreas is more than happy to oblige, but I value quality over quantity.

"I can't wait." I roll my eyes.

"Sarcasm? Really? Come on, man. It's your senior year." He turns onto my street, and I've never been happier for a ride to end. Maybe I can get Charlie to drive me instead from now on.

"I didn't say I wasn't coming."

"Good. For a second, I thought that was your train of thought."

"Are you bringing Charlie?" Danny asks.

"I don't know. I'll ask her."

Andreas parks the car right behind mine and then turns to me. "Are you serious about dating this chick? I mean, I understand fucking around. Psycho or not, she's a hot piece of ass."

I glare at him through slits. "Tread carefully, buddy."

He gives me a droll stare. "Please. Like I'd ever go after a girl you were seeing. I have plenty at my beck and call. I don't need to go through your leftovers."

"I was wondering when the food reference would come up." Danny laughs.

"Whatever. I'm serious, Troy," Andreas presses.

"I'm serious too, Andy. You'd better drop the Charlie subject. You're starting to piss me off. I don't fucking meddle in your affairs, so stay out of mine."

"Fine. I won't say another word about her. But don't come crying to me when she rips your nut sack off and feeds it to the sharks."

"I'm telling you, he's been watching too many serial killer shows," Danny chimes in.

"Thanks for the ride. I'll see you later," I say, annoyed.

I get out of the car as fast as I can. Andreas managed to put me in a foul mood during the short drive from campus to here. Maybe I should walk from now on if Charlie can't give me rides. Andreas has always been a pain in the ass, but as long as he annoyed other people and not me, I was fine with it.

I'm almost at my door when someone calls my name. I turn around and find Charlie's obnoxious friend Blake Ford coming my way.

Gee, what does he want?

"What's up?" I ask cautiously.

"Can I have a word with you?"

"Sure. Do you want to come in?"

"No. What I have to say won't take long."

His attitude immediately puts me in defense mode. "Okay?"

"I don't know what games you think you're playing with Charlie, but she's a nice girl and doesn't need a cocky jock to break her heart."

"Whoa. Hold on. Who the fuck do you think you are to come here and assume I'm going to hurt her?"

"I know your type. Charlie does too. But I guess she must have fallen prey to her physical needs."

I stare at the guy without blinking. *Is he for real?*

Shaking my head, I laugh without humor. "Dude, you know nothing about me, and clearly you know nothing about Charlie either."

He scoffs. "I know nothing about her? I've been friends with her since kindergarten. We dated for a year. Don't tell me I don't know her. I know her better than she knows herself."

A spear of jealousy pierces my chest and then quickly morphs into anger. *Charlie dated this tool? No wonder he's here playing the concerned friend to hide the fact that he's fucking envious. Why the hell didn't she tell me?*

I don't want to let him know his revelation bothers me, so, making a Herculean effort to control my rage, I reply, "If you know her so well, what do you think her reaction will be when she finds out you came here to warn me away from her?"

His condescending expression changes into one of worry, but it only lasts a moment before a cold mask takes its place.

"I don't care how angry she'll be. I did what I had to. If you hurt one single hair on Charlie's head, I'll destroy you, pretty boy. The dean won't be able to help you then."

Fuck. Why would he think I'd hurt Charlie? He doesn't know me, but he's quick to assume the worst because I play football.

What a load of crap.

My nostrils flare as I curl my hands into fists. This asshole is cruising for a bruising, but if I punch him in the face, Charlie will probably take his side.

He turns on his self-righteous heels and strides away with shoulders squared and chin high. I stay rooted to the spot, still pissed at his words. I don't know why I let him get to me like that. I've been judged my whole life; what's one more asshole doing it?

I was right, dating Charlie is definitely something new, and it even comes with knights in shining armor, ready to defend her honor. I wonder what Blake would do if he knew all the kinky stuff I've done to her already. The thought helps me shake off my irritation.

I try to forget the encounter when I get into the house, but his pesky comments are still in the back of my head, tormenting me. Why are my friends and hers all of a sudden shitting on our parade? Andreas thinks Charlie is responsible for my busted shoulder, and even though he acts like a dick, I know he has good intentions. But Blake is an asshole through and through who seems to still have feelings for Charlie. He'd better forget about her. I'm not letting her go.

Jesus, where is this possessiveness coming from?

I have a ton of work to do for school, but I can't concentrate to save my life. My relationship with Charlie has barely begun, yet it's already turning sour all thanks to outside forces. That's not what I intended when I cornered her in front of the cafeteria building earlier. I was only thinking with my dick, and that's my punishment. I should have kept things private a while longer.

It's getting late, and I keep anxiously looking at the clock and wondering when Charlie will get home. I have to stop myself from sending her a message. I don't want her to think I'm needy or controlling her. I wouldn't text her if she were only my roommate, and that's what we agreed to be.

At a little past six o'clock, the sound of her key in the lock has me perking up in my seat. I look over my shoulder and try to keep a straight face. I don't want to look too eager, but hell if a smile doesn't break through anyway.

"Hey," I say.

"Hi. Have you been home long?" She shuts the door with her foot since her hands are occupied with two huge bags.

I jump up from the couch and run to help her out. "I got home a couple hours ago." I take the bags from her hands, frowning at their weight. "What do you have here?"

"Fabric and other materials to make props."

"Oh, is there another LARP event coming soon?"

"Yeah, in a few weeks."

I set the bags down and then pull her to me for a kiss. She melts into my embrace, clutching my left arm as if she needs help keeping upright. Quicker than wildfire, our breathing becomes heavy, and I want nothing more than to peel her clothes off and lose the bet.

She breaks the kiss before I succumb and steps back. "Is this how you usually greet all your roommates?"

"Only the ones who drive me crazy with need. Besides, you're the only roommate I've ever had."

"Really?" She arches her eyebrows.

"Grandma was adamant when she let me stay here that I wouldn't have roommates, so I was surprised when she told me she'd be renting a room to you. You made quite an impression on her. She doesn't like a lot of people."

"Well, I'm very likeable. Only you thought otherwise." She smirks.

"Because you had a bad attitude when we met."

She puts her hands on her hips and glares at me. "And whose fault was that? You made me wait forty minutes and never apologized."

Guilt takes over me. She's not lying.

I rub the back of my neck. "I was a jerk to you. I shouldn't have agreed to the interview that day knowing I'd have to meet my mother right before. She has the ability to suck the joy out of everyone."

"I'm sorry. Your parents are divorced, right?"

"Yeah, for a while."

A shadow crosses Charlie's eyes, but she turns away and veers for the kitchen, almost as if she's hoping I didn't notice her change in demeanor.

"Is there something wrong?"

"No, nothing is wrong. I'm just sad about Bailey."

"I'm sorry. I never had a pet, so I don't know what you must be feeling," I lie.

I know exactly how painful the grip of grief is. But I don't tell her that. I have no intention of ever telling Charlie about Robbie. That's my biggest shame, and I'll take it to the grave.

When she looks at me, I have the feeling she knows I'm lying. She doesn't make a comment, only smiles sadly before looking away again.

"Are you hungry? I can make dinner."

"Yeah, I'm hungry." I hug her from behind as she peruses inside the fridge.

She leans against me, pressing her sweet ass against my cock. Instant erection. "Hmm. You know all you have to do is admit defeat."

"Tempting," I whisper before biting her earlobe. "But I definitely do not want to be at your mercy if I lose."

"You might like what I have in mind."

I dig my fingers in her hip, pulling her closer to me. "Maybe, but I don't want to risk it. Besides, I want to see you beg for me."

She frees herself from my grasp and pushes me off. "You'd better sit and wait. That's not likely to happen."

Since I'm not going to make her cave tonight, I might as well change the subject before I end up begging *her*. "Guess who came by earlier to have a chat with me?"

She looks over her shoulder. "I haven't the faintest idea."

"Your buddy Blake, or should I say, ex-boyfriend?" I try my best to keep the venom from my tongue. I don't think I succeeded.

She whirls around, shutting the fridge door hard. "Blake came here? I can't believe him. What did he say?"

"Basically, he came to warn me that if I broke your heart, he would make me pay." I shrug to hide that I'm jealous as fuck. "The usual empty threat stuff."

"Those aren't empty threats. When Blake says shit like that, he means it." Charlie pulls her hair back. "I can't believe him. He's never pulled a stunt like that before."

"Maybe because he was never threatened by another guy before." I lean against the counter, trying to convey a relaxed stance, when in fact I'm anything but.

"Blake isn't threatened by you. Why would he be?" She pulls a tray of chicken wings out of the fridge.

"He's your ex-boyfriend, isn't he? Maybe he's still harboring feelings for you."

"Please. There are no lingering feelings there. Trust me."

"I don't know. The way he was acting sure sounded like he was jealous."

Charlie narrows her eyes. "Where are you going with this? Do you want Blake to have a thing for me?"

I stand straighter. "No. I just want you to be aware of the possibility. You guys do spend a lot of time together."

The frown disappears from her forehead while the faint hint of a smile appears on her lips. She steps closer to me, wrapping her arms around my waist. "Well, Troy, it sounds like *you* are jealous."

"What if I am?" I grab her ass, squeezing it.

"I'd say you have nothing to worry about." She rises on her tiptoes and presses her lips to mine.

She meant it to be a quick peck, but I keep her in place and devour her mouth. My body turns into a furnace immediately, and my rock-hard erection presses against her belly. She moans against my lips, making me forget dinner, the bet, everything. I just want to rip her clothes off and fuck her on the counter.

I'm breaking all the rules, and I don't care. We're supposed to keep things strictly platonic in the common areas, roommate stuff only. But it seems whenever she's near me, I can't resist having a taste of her sweet lips, of feeling her body against mine.

I'm about to say to hell with the challenge when my phone rings. I'd be tempted to let it go to voice mail if it wasn't Grandma's ringtone.

Reluctantly, I end the kiss and go look for the device.

"Saved by the bell," Charlie murmurs.

"Too bad I didn't want to be saved."

I finally locate the phone under one of the couch cushions. "Hello?"

"Wolfie, I thought I was going to miss you."

"Is everything okay, Grandma?"

"Oh yeah. I'm fine. I'm just calling to see how everything is going."

"Everything is going great." I glance at Charlie.

"How are you and Charlie getting along? I haven't seen her in ages."

"Fine. She's nice." I wink at her.

Charlie smirks.

"Oh good. I was afraid you'd be mad at me for imposing her on you when I forbade you to have any roommates."

"It's your house. I'm lucky you let me live here rent free."

"Yeah, yeah. When can I expect to see you?"

"Uh, I don't know." I love Grandma, but I confess that seeing her with her two boyfriends freaks me out. That's why I prefer to take her out somewhere without them. "Grandma is asking when we're coming by."

"Oh, she is, huh?" Charlie shakes her head. "I heard what she said. I think she meant you specifically."

Fine. She caught me. "Well, you haven't shown your face in a while either. So, when?"

"We can come on Sunday."

I think of the party Andreas wants to drag me to on Saturday. If I manage to convince Charlie to come with me, we might actually stay late.

"How early are we talking?"

"Why? Do you have any late-night plans for Saturday?"

I cover the phone with my hand and smile. "No, sweetheart. *We* do."

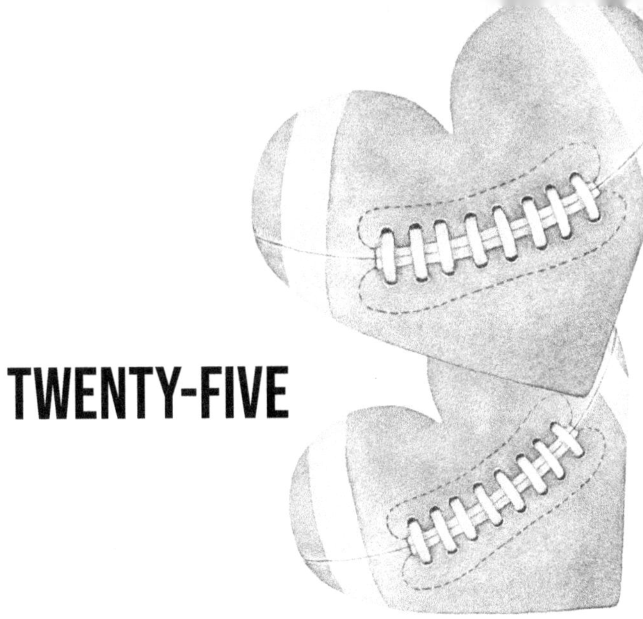

TWENTY-FIVE

CHARLIE

I call Sylvana the next day because she's the only close girlfriend I have. It's not because I have a dislike for my gender; it's just one of those things that happened. I need some advice, and since my best friend is being an idiot about Troy, and Fred can't be trusted to give a sound opinion about anything, she's all I've got.

Troy wants me to go to a football party with him. I reminded him that, not too long ago, I trashed him in the paper and all his teammates must hate me. But besides being the sexiest man alive, Troy also has killer persuasion skills. In the end, he got me to agree, and now I'm panicking. Going to a party with him is definitely something out of my comfort zone.

After I pour out all my worries over the phone, Sylvana asks, "Do you know what you're going to wear?"

"No. I have a cute dress that I wore to the last date I went on, but I don't want to wear that again."

"You can't go wrong with some tight jeans and a sexy top. Don't overthink it. And definitely leave the glasses at home. It's not like you need to wear them all the time."

"Sure, sure. The problem is, I don't think I own any sexy tops. You know if I'm in jeans, I'm wearing a T-shirt."

"Get your act together, girlie. I can't go shopping with you this week, but I can send you links of stuff I think will look good on you."

"But the party is Saturday. If I order online, will it get here in time?"

"Heck yeah. Don't worry. I'm sending some links now. Let me know which one you decide to buy."

"Okay."

"I gotta go. Late for my spinning class."

Before I open any of the links she sent, I finish getting ready, then head downstairs to grab breakfast. Troy is catching a ride to school with me today. He got into an argument with Andreas, but he didn't tell me the details, which means their fight was about me. It seems our closest friends have zero faith that what we're doing is going to work, which is really a kick in the shin. I already have enough doubt; I don't need people piling it on.

It's tempting to go check on Troy, but I fight the urge. If he's still in bed or in the shower, I'll probably want to join him. Hell, we might not even manage to go on a single date before one of us puts their hands up and surrenders.

I begin obsessing about the party. Does that count as a first date? I hope not.

While I wait for the coffee to brew, I check the links Sylvana sent me. Some of the tops are uber tight and with a deep plunge in the front that are a Janet Jackson accident waiting to happen. I don't like any of them, to be honest. They're not me.

Engrossed in my online shopping, I don't notice Troy's approach until he hugs me from behind and rests his chin on my shoulder.

"What are you looking at?"

"Clothes. It seems I need to update my wardrobe."

"Oh, I like that one." He points at a black cropped style that's closer to a bra than a top.

"Of course you do."

"I'm teasing. But why do you think you need new clothes?"

"Uh, in case you haven't noticed, my social activities require different types of ensembles."

"I can't wait to see you in cosplay." He kisses my cheek, waking the butterflies in my belly.

"Only because you think I dress slutty."

He circles around the counter and then glances at me with an eyebrow raised. "Do you?"

I clamp my jaw because unfortunately, Raven the Sorceress likes provocative attire. "Maybe."

His jaw drops. "Are you serious? Damn. I was only joking. When is your next LARP event? Because I'm coming."

"You want to come to LARP?" I fight the smirk blossoming on my lips.

"Well, I don't want to participate."

And the smile wilts before it can bloom.

"Sorry, buddy. LARP is not a show. You can't come and not be a part of it."

Troy wrinkles his nose as if the idea smelled funky. "I'm not sure. I was in a play once and I sucked."

I shrug, trying to downplay my disappointment. Troy doesn't need to love everything I do. I wish he'd be more open-minded though.

"You can create your own character. I can help you with that."

"Hmm, what would be a cool character?" His gaze seems to go inward.

Please don't say something cliché, like a knight.

"Oh, I know. Do you have trolls in your game?" he asks.

"You want to be a troll?" I arch my eyebrows, not expecting that answer.

"Yeah. A cool one, like Shrek."

"Technically, Shrek was an ogre. But I suppose we could use a troll who's not evil. Ben's character is a troll hunter. I'm sure he would get a kick out of hunting you. But I have to check with the other writers first."

"All right."

Well, that's something. He might not be super enthusiastic about LARP, but at least he agreed to try.

He gets distracted by the coffee machine, and I return to my search. Unfortunately, it seems all the clothes on this particular website are on the super slutty side. Not my style at all.

"What's with the frown, babe?"

I sit straighter. "I was frowning?"

"Big time. Does this sudden need to buy new clothes have anything to do with the party on Saturday?"

I twist my face into a scowl. "Yeah. Don't laugh, but I've never been to one of those infamous football parties."

"You have nothing to worry about. Just wear whatever you're most comfortable in. It's not like there's a dress code or anything."

"I'm most comfortable in my pajamas. Should I wear them?" I laugh.

"That depends. Are they the sexy kind?" His lips curl into a wolfish grin.

I throw my hands up in the air. "Oh my God. What's with you and sexy outfits?"

"I'm a guy."

My eyes drop to his crotch. Troy is wearing a snug shirt and sweatpants, which means there's no hiding his erection. My mouth suddenly goes dry while a wisp of desire curls around the base of my spine.

He snaps his fingers, getting me out of my trance. "Hey, eyes up here, Charlie."

Heat creeps up my cheeks. "You're breaking the rules."

"Am I now?"

"Those pants cover nothing."

"I'm dressed. Those are the rules. We never specified clothes that weren't allowed."

I watch him through slits, already concocting payback. "Fine. But you're not going out like that, are you?"

"What's wrong with my clothes?"

"For starters, you're not wearing any underwear."

That devilish grin appears once again. "My, my, Charlie. Aren't you observant?"

I ignore his quip. "So unless your plan is to make every single female on campus stare at your package, then I suggest you change."

"And what if I don't? Are you going to make me?" His eyes gleam with mischief. I hear the challenge loud and clear.

"No. But I can't be held responsible for gouging their eyes out if they dare to stare."

Troy doesn't move a muscle for a couple seconds. Then he throws his head back and laughs out loud.

"I'm serious!" I say, exasperated.

"Sure you are."

"In case you haven't noticed, I'm short-tempered with revenge tendencies." I cross my arms over my chest, aggravated that he's laughing at me.

He walks around the counter and then pulls me into a hug. "You're so darn cute when you're angry, babe."

"How cute are we talking?"

"Cute enough to make me want to do this." He kisses my neck, drawing his hot tongue up to my ear.

My reaction is immediate. My nipples become hard, my breathing turns shallow, and my clit throbs in anticipation even if my head is telling it to cool off. Not willing to simply stand there and take Troy's torture, I turn my face so I can kiss him hard and deep. He responds in kind, grunting like a savage and grinding his pelvis against mine.

I bet I could make him cave right now, but we don't have a lot of time, and there's no quickie with Troy. Reluctantly, I step back. His half-hooded eyes drop to my lips, and he would have followed them if I hadn't pressed my palm against his chest.

"If you want to catch a ride with me, then you have to finish getting ready. And before you complain, underwear is mandatory."

"You're so bossy."

"When it comes to punctuality, yes I am."

Grumbling, he veers toward the stairs. "Fine. I'll put decent clothes on. Don't want you gouging anyone's eyes out on my account."

I shake my head, then go grab a cup of coffee.

"Charlie?" he calls from the middle of the stairs.

"Yeah?"

"Are you free on Friday?"

"I think so. Why?"

"Would you like to have dinner with me?"

The butterflies in my stomach explode in a crazy fluttering while my heart takes off. "Are you asking me out on a date?"

"Yes I am."

The thumping inside my chest becomes louder. *Settle down, damn muscle!*

"That's so sweet." I smirk, trying to hide my excitement.

"Is that a yes?"

I shrug. "Sure. Why not?"

Troy watches me through narrowed eyes for a second, probably catching on to my false casualness, before he says, "It's a date then."

TWENTY-SIX

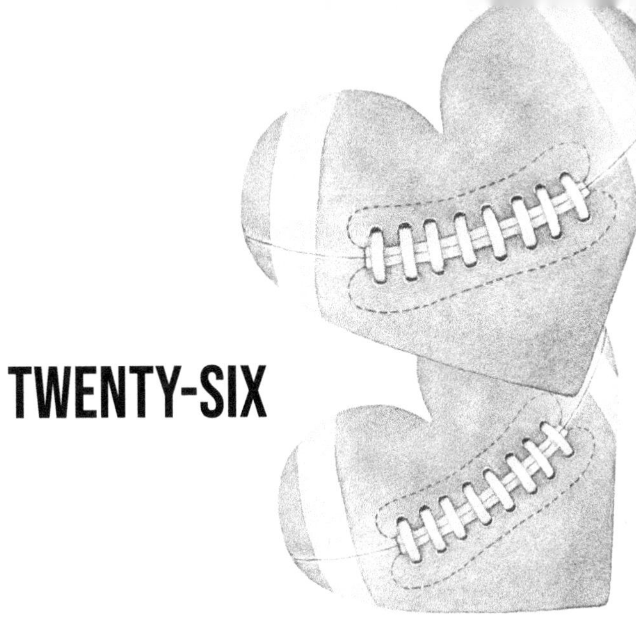

TROY

Keeping my hands off Charlie for the rest of the week is the hardest thing I've had to do. If I could go back in time and stop myself from making the stupid bet, I would. Too late now. The only thing I can do is make Charlie lose, and I plan to do that tonight.

I haven't gone out on a date since I was seeing Brooke, which means it's been ages and I'm rusty. However, I know that to impress Charlie, I can't simply do the usual. She's into LARPing, for crying out loud. Creativity is in her blood. I've agonized about it since Tuesday when I asked her out. I considered taking her to an experimental cuisine restaurant, but Jane convinced me to stick to a place I was familiar with. The last thing I want is to ruin the evening by giving Charlie food poisoning.

I decide on Le Gone, one of my favorite restaurants. You can't go wrong with French food unless you're lactose intolerant, which isn't the case with Charlie. She goes through gallons of milk a week. I also suspect she was a mouse in her previous life, judging by the amount of cheese she eats. My secret weapon to break through her defenses will come later when we get back to the house.

I haven't really spoken to Andreas since our argument, even though I've seen him during practice. I can't throw balls, but I can do everything else that doesn't require the use of my arms. Saturday's game is against our rival school, and it'll be a pain to warm the bench. At least I can give Danny pointers. I'd be lying if I said I wasn't disappointed that I'm not playing. I do miss football. But for now, the game with Charlie is keeping my excitement level high, which means I don't have time to deal with my inner demons.

As I'm heading to the locker room, Andreas stops me.

"Hey, Troy. Got a minute?"

"Yeah."

"Listen, I want to apologize about Charlie. It was an asshole move to interfere."

"Yeah, it was. But no worries, man. Apology accepted."

My statement is true. I won't hold a grudge against him, especially now that he realizes his error in judgment. But that doesn't mean I'm not pranking him later. Charlie told me about her idea, and it's genius. I can't wait to pull that one on him.

"What's the deal with you two? Is it serious?"

"I don't know if it's serious, but we're having fun."

He smirks. "Having fun, huh? I knew you wouldn't be able to resist the sexy nerd. Have you talked to Brooke since you and Charlie got together?"

Andreas, being my best friend, knows I got a weird vibe from Brooke when she got back to LA.

"Not yet. I haven't really talked to her at all in weeks. The last time was when she came by after my accident."

"She's probably nursing a broken heart." He chuckles.

"I hope not."

I know people say it's impossible to stay friends with your ex, but I'd like to believe it's possible with Brooke. She's into high-adrenaline sports like me, and she's fun to hang out with.

In a different scenario, we would be perfect for each other, but because we're so much alike, we were boring together.

"Hey, I'm going to meet the guys later for a quick beer. Do you wanna come?" Andreas asks.

"Ah sorry. Can't. I have a date." I smile even though I didn't mean to.

"Holy fuck. Look at your face. Dude! You got it bad for the sexy nerd."

I school my face into a neutral expression, but I'm not fooling anyone, especially not Andreas. "As usual, you're blowing things way out of proportion."

"Yeah, yeah." He shakes his head, then continues on into the locker room.

Damn him. He knows me too well.

I do have it bad for Charlie, and if I'm honest with myself, it's terrifying, and probably the reason going out with her is a thrill.

***

I'm pacing in the living room as I wait for Charlie. She's not late, I just got ready too early. I let Jane get into my head, and now I'm feeling like a fool. I have a bottle of champagne chilling in the ice bucket, and I bought a rose bouquet. Jesus, it looks like I'm going to propose, not going on a first date. *Hell.* I can't get rid of the flowers because Charlie will see them in the trash can and think I'm nuts. But I can put the champagne away.

As the world would have it, she catches me in the act. "You got me bubbles?"

I turn around and freeze. Charlie is wearing the same snug-fit burgundy dress she wore when she went out with whatever his name was. That was the first time I realized I was in deep trouble. I fucking love that dress on her, and she must be aware of it, because she's sporting a smug smile now.

"What do you think?" She twirls when she reaches the bottom of the stairs.

"Stunning."

With a bounce to her step, she comes to my side. "You look good enough to eat." She gives me a quick peck on the cheek and then takes a whiff of my neck. "Hmm, I love the way you smell."

"Thanks, babe. Remember, you can have the whole thing; all you have to do is ask."

"Tempting." She steps back. "But I'd rather you ask me."

I watch her for a moment, drinking her in. "We'll see."

She turns her attention to the ice bucket I'm still holding. "Are we having some or what?"

"I guess."

I feel my face getting warmer, so I quickly turn around to hide it from Charlie.

"And those flowers?"

Ah shit. What's wrong with me? I'm acting like an idiot.

I grab the bouquet and give it to her. "For you, sweetheart."

She brings the roses to her nose and takes a deep breath. "They smell lovely. Not as good as you though. Thank you."

"You're welcome."

"Why don't you pop that bottle while I go put these in a vase?"

"All right."

"How are we on time? How long until we need to be at the restaurant?"

"Half an hour. It's not that far from here." I open the champagne bottle with a loud pop—at least I didn't screw this part up.

"We probably should call an Uber soon. You never know how long it'll take to find a ride."

I smile to myself, remembering her comment about punctuality. "I have one request for tonight." I turn around, holding two flutes of champagne.

"And what is it?" She takes one.

"That you don't stress about anything. Cheers."

We clink our glasses together, and then, with our gazes locked, we take a sip of the champagne. I'm not particularly fond of it, but Jane said it was a must.

"Okay, I'll try." She takes another sip and then sets the glass down.

"You don't like it?"

"I do. It's not something I drink often though."

Shit, Jane. I shouldn't have listened to you.

I must have shown my disappointment on my face, as she's quick to add. "I love that you thought about it though. Super romantic. You're definitely trying to get lucky tonight."

"Yep. But you know how men live in hope—"

"And die in despair," she finishes for me.

We don't speak for several beats, and I'm highly aware of the stupid smile I'm sporting now. The air between us crackles with electricity and sexual tension. It won't take long until one of us caves to the pressure. My cock stirs in my pants, and I know it might be me tonight.

"So, where are we going?" she asks, breaking the silence.

"It's a surprise."

Her eyes twinkle with excitement. "I can't wait."

TWENTY-SEVEN

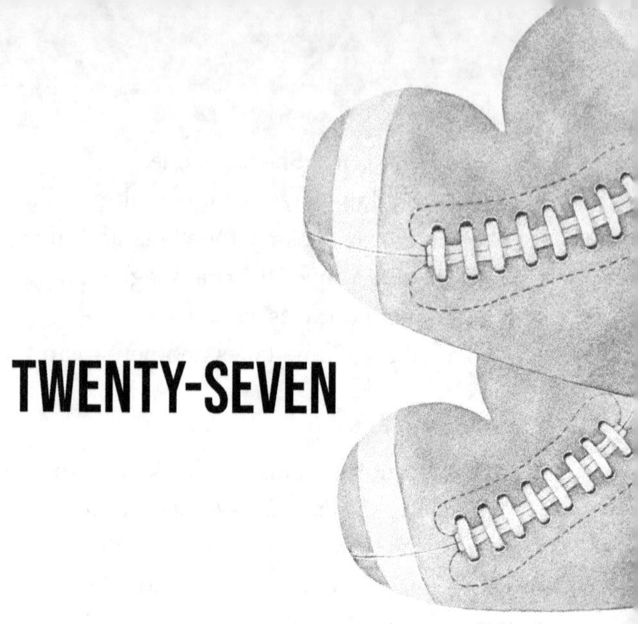

CHARLIE

Troy picked a small, intimate French restaurant located in an unpretentious open mall just twenty minutes from the house. The décor is rustic with a whimsical touch thanks to the exposed brick walls and twinkling lights hanging from them.

There's no hostess; we're greeted by the chef himself as we come through the door. He ushers us to our table in a flurry of excited comments.

"*Monsieur* Alexander. It's so good to see you. Oh, and you brought a lovely *mademoiselle* tonight."

"Yes. This is our first date."

"Is that so? Oh, then you need our very best table. Come this way."

Not long after we're seated at a cozy table in the corner, our waiter comes with the menu. "Can I interest you in something to drink?" he asks.

"Would you like a cocktail first, or straight to wine?" Troy asks me.

I can't answer. I'm too awestruck at the moment. "Hmm, I don't know. Maybe just sparkling water for now."

"Same," he tells the waiter.

When he leaves, Troy turns his attention to me. "I have to ask you this because I feel like I've already messed up royally. What are your favorite drinks?"

"You didn't mess up. The champagne was a nice touch."

He narrows his eyes. "Was it though? You barely touched it."

"Because I didn't want to get wasted before we even left the house."

"Oh. Okay then. Are you saying you're a lightweight?"

"To certain alcoholic beverages, yes. Champagne is one that goes to my head quicker than others. But I'm fine with drinking tequila shots or Duck Farts, for instance."

Troy's eyebrows shoot to the heavens. "Duck Farts? What in the world is that?"

"It's a combination of Kahlúa, Irish cream, and whiskey. But I prefer it without the Kahlúa. It's delicious."

"Noted. Would you like to have that instead of wine? I'm sure they can make it for you."

"Oh no. I don't think it goes with French cuisine. Wine is fine."

"Does it also go to your head faster?" His lips curl into a mischievous smile.

I watch him through slits. "Why do you want to know, Troy? Are you planning on getting me drunk so I can lose the bet?"

He widens his eyes innocently. "Me? Of course not. Are you implying you turn into a nympho under the influence?"

My face bursts into flames. *No, you've turned me into one, Troy.*

"I'm not saying that at all," I lie.

I'm already hanging on by a thread. Sitting across from him in his suit jacket that makes him look like he just sprang from a fashion magazine, plus being under the allure of his intoxicating scent, is already doing crazy things to my body. I really don't need to add alcohol to my system; it'll shut my brain down, and then my body will take control.

"Okay. Just checking." He opens the wine list and does a quick perusal of the menu. "Do you have any preference in mind?"

"Oh please. I know nothing about wine. You go ahead and pick."

He looks up. "What gives you the idea that I know about wine?"

"Aren't you a regular here?"

"Kind of. This is Grandma's favorite restaurant. I always come with her, and she chooses the wine."

"I guess we'll just have to gamble then." I wink at him.

He scrunches his nose. "Maybe we'll let the waiter suggest something."

"Sounds like a plan."

The server returns with our water, and after we tell him we have no clue about wine, he's more than happy to suggest a bottle. We turn our attention to the dinner menu, and I'm faced with the impossible choice of selecting what I want. Everything looks delicious.

"Besides your unusual reaction to alcohol, anything else I should know beforehand?" Troy asks.

I chuckle. "What do you mean by unusual?"

"I've never met someone before who would get drunk from a glass of champagne but could handle copious amounts of tequila and whiskey with no problem."

"What can I say? I'm special."

"Oh, I know that." He smirks.

I watch him through slitted eyes. "Somehow I feel your statement has a double meaning."

"Maybe, but nothing bad. I promise."

I open my mouth to ask him to elaborate, but the waiter returns to take our orders, and when he leaves, I decide to let the subject drop.

"How long have we been living together?" Troy leans back, obviously comfortable. Even though I pegged him to be a rowdy jock when we met, he fits perfectly in this sophisticated environment. He's like a rogue prince from a fairy tale.

"I don't know. Almost two months?"

"Right. And yet I only know that you're into LARP and board games, and you want to be a journalist. Is that correct?"

"Partially. I don't want to be a journalist. I want to write fiction."

"Oh, that's cool. Are we talking books or maybe a screenplay?"

No one has ever asked me that before. Whenever I mention I want to write fiction, all I get is a pitiful glance. I get it, making a living as a fiction writer isn't the easiest career path. Even with the growth of indie publishing, it takes dedication and long working hours to succeed. And even so, many people never do.

"Both? I don't know." I reach for my water.

"Have you written anything that I can read?"

I take a sip and then answer, "Yes and no. I have written plenty of stuff, but it's not ready for the public eye yet."

"Oh come on. Why not?"

"Because... I don't think I'm ready to open myself to criticism."

"You write for the newspaper. Aren't people reading that?"

"Yeah, but it's different."

"Different how?"

"I don't know."

I sense my barriers going up. My muscles are tense, and I can't wait to change the subject. As different as Troy and I are, he's the only one who seems to know exactly where my weak points are.

"I'm sorry. I didn't mean to push you into a corner," he says. "How about you ask me the tough questions?"

I'm not sure if his comment was meant to remind me of when

we first met, but his eyes are devoid of mirth, so maybe it was just a coincidence.

The waiter comes with our wine, and I'm thankful for the interruption.

Wine is poured and tasted. Not surprising, it's amazing.

After I take a couple of sips, I glance at Troy. "Where were we? Oh, it was my turn to grill you."

"Oh boy." He smiles casually, unaware of what it does to me. He's so beautiful that it makes my heart ache with the need to be close to him.

"What do you want to do when you graduate?"

Troy hangs his head low. "Ugh. You had to go there."

"Come on. It's not a hard question. You're a senior!" I say, trying to suppress my laughter, knowing Troy is being dramatic on purpose.

"I know. I'm a business major, but while most of my classmates are all set with internships or actively looking for a job, I haven't done any of that."

"You can always work for your father."

"Are you suggesting nepotism, Charlie?" He grins.

I shrug. "I mean, it makes sense."

"Nah. It's bad enough that he pushed me into that direction. I have no desire of actually working for him. I'm thinking about taking a year off to go travel, see the world."

"With all expenses paid by your parents," I note and then regret it immediately. That was a judgmental comment. "I'm sorry. I shouldn't have said that."

"No, I get it. Easy assumption, but no, they wouldn't pay for it. It's actually a job opportunity of sorts."

"Oh, how so?"

"I was approached by a digital media company a few months back. They have a YouTube channel, and they're looking for athletes to create content for them. The pay is minimum—it'd only cover basic traveling expenses—but the experience would be priceless."

I can see the excitement shining in his eyes. He's eager to do it, and that brings a sudden pang to my chest. It's ridiculous. We've only known each other for a couple months, and I'm not even sure the status of our relationship yet. It's definitely too new for me to be feeling sad about the possibility of Troy leaving.

"It sounds like you've already made up your mind."

"Not yet. I have time. Besides, many things can happen between now and then." He pierces me with one of his intense stares, completely messing with my ability to breathe properly.

"True." I take another sip of wine, trying to hide the effect he has on me. "A while back, I looked into the possibility of participating in an exchange program."

"You mean, studying abroad for a semester?"

"Yeah. I was looking into partner schools in Europe."

"I take it you didn't apply?"

Sadness takes over me, and I regret opening my big mouth. "No, I didn't." I glance at my plate.

"Why not?"

With a sigh, I look at Troy again. "You're going to think it's stupid."

"No I won't."

"I didn't want to leave Ben for that long. I know he has my parents, but... I don't know. Told you it was a stupid reason." I reach for the glass of water.

"It's not stupid. You're very protective of him. I get it. I'm also like that with Jane."

"But you're not letting that keep you from going places."

Damn it, Charlie. This conversation is getting too heavy and depressing. It's time to change the subject.

"Can we talk about something else?"

"Sure, like what?"

"Tell me your thoughts on Ophelia having two boyfriends."

Troy scrunches his face up as if he's in pain and groans. "God, I try my best to pretend they're just friends."

The appetizers arrive, and we take a break from the ten-thousand-questions game. I don't know how our conversation got deep so quickly. Maybe because we're not really complete strangers. I worry for a bit that we'll end up messing up, such as saying something thoughtless and going back to bickering and arguing. But once the food arrives, we keep our chitchat light.

The evening goes by in a flash, and before I know it, the Uber driver is dropping us off in front of the house. I was a little apprehensive about going out with Troy, but in the end, my worries were unjustified. Dinner was lovely. Troy was attentive, funny, and uber sexy—a dangerous combination to me. A cynic would think that was his master plan—to be charming and irresistible so he could win the bet. But he was too nervous in the beginning for that to be true. Poor thing even forgot to give me the flowers he'd bought.

As we walk side by side toward the front door, my stomach is suddenly tied in knots, as if this were indeed a first date and I didn't know what was going to happen. *Is he going to kiss me? Should I invite him in for a nightcap?*

Those thoughts are ridiculous, of course. We've already fucked like bunnies, and we live together.

Instead of unlocking the door, Troy turns to me and links his hand with mine. "So, here we are." He smiles at me, revealing the twinkle in his eyes that I've quickly come to love.

"Here we are." I smile back.

"I had a wonderful evening."

"Me too."

He doesn't say another word, just stares at me. Blush is slowly spreading through my cheeks. The intensity in his gaze is making me a little uncomfortable. I don't know what to say or do. The sexual tension between us is palpable. There seems to be a magnetic field pulling me to him. I have to fight the urge to jump into his arms and have my way with him right here on our front porch.

"Well, would you like to come in?" I ask to break the silence.

He chuckles. "I thought you'd never ask."

It seems we're keeping up with the charade that this is really a first date. If that's the case, who's going to make the first move? My hand is shaking a bit as I try to find the keyhole.

Gee, Charlie. Take it easy.

"Need some help there?" Troy asks, clearly amused.

Finally, I manage to unlock the door. "No. I got it."

I let Troy walk in first, and then I close the door behind me. My idea is to head to the kitchen to grab a drink, but he turns around fast and pins me against the wall, covering my body with his. His lips find mine, branding me with an urgent kiss. I melt against him, drowning in his scent, his presence. I clutch his arms, pulling him closer to me, needing to feel every inch of his frame pressed against mine. I've never felt this need, this ice-cold fever for anyone before. It gives me chills and burns me up at the same time.

When I think he's going to take things further, he stops, stepping back and leaving me feeling bereft.

"What?" I ask, a little dazed.

"I'm sorry. I couldn't resist. I've been dying to kiss you like that all night long."

"Why did you stop?" I pout.

He shakes his head. "Because I haven't crossed the point of no return yet. Why? Do you want me to continue, babe? Are you waving your white flag?" he says with a smirk.

"No." I walk around him—almost running really—to the kitchen. I need something cold to soothe the ache in my loins.

Loins? Oh God. Who am I? Amy Farrah Fowler?

I don't want to drink more alcohol because I think I've had plenty. If I'm to survive the rest of the evening without succumbing to Troy's charm, I have to be clearheaded. The only thing I see in the fridge is a can of Coke and Troy's sparkling water. If I drink soda now, I won't be able to sleep, so water it is. I press the cool bottle against my forehead.

"Poor babe. Are you hurting that bad?" He chuckles.

I whirl around, mortified to be caught in the act. "Shut up. I bet you need an ice pack to place over your groin."

His eyes take on a dangerous glint as they narrow. "Woman, do not remind me of the worst case of blue balls I've ever had."

"If it's that bad, why don't you use your hand?" I quirk an eyebrow.

He points at me. "You'd better stop that right now. I'm onto you, Charlie Alice Fontaine."

"Wait. How do you know my middle name? I never told you."

"I have a copy of your rent contract and ID." He gives me a toothy, victorious grin.

"Fine, *Wolfie*. I'll stop."

"If I could hate Grandma for telling you that odious nickname, I would."

"Well, I'd better go to be—"

"Oh no. You're not going to sleep yet. Our date is not over."

I put a hand on my hip. "Is that so? What else do you have planned?"

"If you'll follow me to the living room, I've prepared an evening of excellent entertainment."

"Oh, are we doing a Lord of the Rings marathon?"

"No. We can do that when *you* invite me on a date."

I tilt my head with a pitying frown. "Aww, and you were doing so well."

I sit down on the couch, pulling the blanket to me so I can create a barrier against Troy. It's a pathetic effort, but valid. "What are we watching?"

"One of my favorite TV shows of all times. You're probably a fan, actually."

"Oh? What is it?"

"*Supernatural*."

"What? Are you crazy? I'm not watching that."

Troy's expression falls. "Why not?"

"Because it's fucking scary. I told you I don't do horror."

"You're joking, right?"

"Do you think this is the face of someone who's joking?" I draw a circle in the air to emphasize my point.

"Charlie, *Supernatural* is not a horror series. Where did you get that idea?"

"From watching the first episode. I was freaked out."

"Okay, fine. I concede that the first season is a little spooky, but it gets better after that. Trust me, you'll love it."

"I don't know." I nibble on my lower lip.

Everyone I know has been bugging me to watch the damn series for years. Maybe I should try again. Besides, if it gets too scary, I can always jump in Troy's arms and hide my face against his chest. Maybe that's what he's banking on. But I can't refuse him when he's giving me those puppy eyes.

"Fine. But if I have nightmares, it's on you."

"If you have nightmares, you're more than welcome to sleep with me." He laughs.

"Oh, I bet that's exactly what you want."

"Charlie, you really have the worst ideas about me."

"Yeah, yeah. Put it on already before I change my mind."

He chuckles. "That's what she said."

"I said put it on, not in."

"Sure, sure."

TWENTY-EIGHT

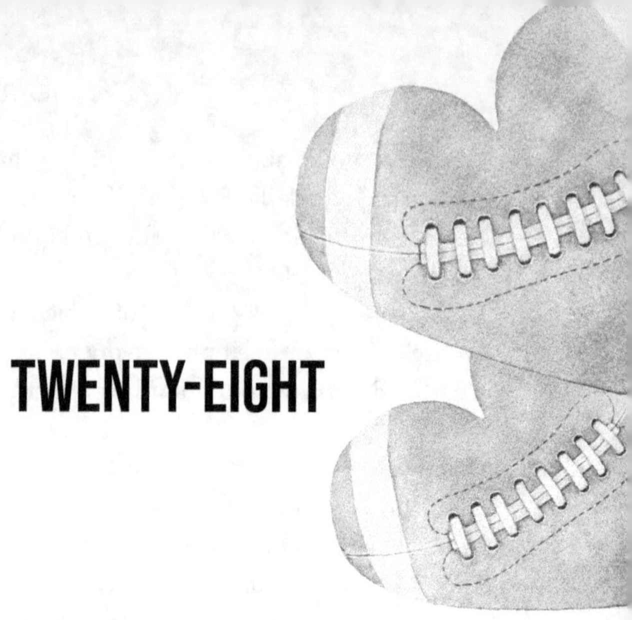

TROY

I can't believe how close I came to screwing up the evening. Why did I think watching *Supernatural* would be a good idea? Even if Charlie wasn't scared, there's the little issue that the TV show features two attractive dudes.

We're about to start episode five, and the wine is finally catching up with me. My eyelids are getting heavy, but Charlie doesn't seem tired in the least. She's tense, however, clutching the blanket in a tight grip.

"Charlie?"

"Yeah?" She turns to me.

"You know, it's okay if you want to scooch closer."

She hesitates, not moving for a couple beats, and I'm sure she's going to say no. To my surprise, she does shorten the distance between us, and when I throw my arm over her shoulders, she leans against my chest and lets me cradle her.

Unable to resist, I run lazy circles over her exposed skin with the tips of my fingers. She doesn't stop me; if anything, she gets nearer, making my blood pump faster. I don't want to make a move too soon, so I force my attention to the screen. The first two minutes of the episodes are always intense and scary, and this one is no different. Sam and Dean are facing Bloody Mary.

Charlie is rigid against me, and when the scary part comes, she hides her face against my chest, making me laugh.

"Stop laughing. I hate horror shit."

"I'm sorry, but you're too funny."

She eases out of my embrace, lifting her chin to glare at me. "I'm not too funny."

Her eyebrows are furrowed into a scowl, and her plump lips are set in a severe line. Right now, she's not funny at all. She's a sexy, pissed-off vixen.

"You're right. You're not funny." My voice comes out strained. "You're Venus personified."

I kiss her before she looks away, pulling her flush against my body once more. Her lips taste like chocolate, a trace of the lava cake she had for dessert. It awakens the hunger in me that was already hovering just below the surface. I try to move us to a horizontal position, but my right arm is trapped by the sling.

I pull back. "This thing has got to go."

Quickly, I release the clasp behind my neck, freeing my arm so I can better appreciate Charlie.

"Are you sure you should be doing this?" she asks.

"I'm okay." I push her back on the couch and then yank the blanket from her grasp.

Her dark hair fans around her lovely face. Her lips are partly open, her cheeks are flushed, and her blue eyes are laced with desire. *Fuck.* I'm going to lose this bet in an epic fashion, and I don't care. All my blood has converged in my cock, leaving my brain at its mercy.

"Do you have something to say, Troy?" she asks in a dangerous, husky tone.

Her velvety voice is like a caress, a prelude of what's to come. She knows she has me exactly where she wants me.

"I do. I—"

The shrill ringtone of her phone interrupts my speech of

defeat. I expect her to ignore it, but her hazy eyes become lucid in a flash. She jerks to a sitting position and then jumps off the couch to get to her purse on the kitchen counter.

"Hello?" she answers.

I watch her, keenly aware of the sudden tension in her body. Her eyebrows furrow as she listens.

"Slow down, Ben," she says.

I get off the couch too, any trace of my erection gone. I don't need to hear what her brother is saying to know things aren't okay.

"Okay, I'm coming," she replies before she ends the call, promptly shoving her phone back in her purse. "I have to go to Littleton," she tells me.

"What happened?"

"My parents had a huge fight. Ben said my father packed an overnight bag and left. Mom is locked in her room, crying. Ben is freaking out."

I don't know much about people with Down syndrome, but my guess is they're more sensitive than most. Even if that wasn't the case, he's only a teenager. He shouldn't be alone to deal with his parents' marriage problems. I was young when my parents divorced, but I remember their fights as if they happened yesterday.

When Charlie reaches for her car keys, I say, "You can't drive."

"You don't understand. I have to go now."

I touch her arm, needing to show my support through actions. "I do understand, but doing something reckless won't help anyone. It's a long drive to Littleton, and we've been drinking. Let's call an Uber."

She looks into my eyes for a moment, torn, but finally she relents. "Okay."

I order a ride. "I'm coming with you."

Her eyes become rounder, surprise shining in them, but then her expression turns into relief. "Thank you. I can't believe this.

My parents should know better than to fight when Ben is around. He can't handle shouting and arguments. It really gets to him."

"Can he call someone to stay with him until we get there?"

"The only person he could call is his girlfriend, but it's late, and she's like him. I'm not sure if she would be much help."

I don't understand Charlie's remark about her brother's girlfriend, but it's unimportant right now.

"Okay. How about we call him back when we're on our way? We can keep him on the phone; it might help with his anxiety."

"Good idea."

The Uber driver won't arrive for ten minutes, and while we wait, Charlie almost digs a hole in the floor with the way she's pacing. Nothing I could tell her would make her feel better, so I just let her be.

In all honesty, if it weren't for my busted shoulder, I could probably drive. I didn't drink as much, and I'm as sober as a rock now. But after the speech I gave her, it would be hypocritical to suggest I get behind the wheel.

Charlie calls her brother again as soon as we slide in the back seat of our ride. Judging by the conversation, I get the gist that Ben is somewhat calmer. I don't know what his mother is doing though.

The ride to Littleton seems to take longer than an hour even though there isn't much traffic at this time of night. When the driver stops in front of her parents' house, she almost jumps out and runs to the front door.

I follow her, feeling a little bit awkward for being here. I'm a stranger to them, and I'm about to witness some major family drama. Charlie makes a beeline for what I guess is Ben's room. I'm correct, so I hang back by the door, not wanting to intrude. The teen is on his bed, clutching a pillow. His tear-streaked face and red eyes tell me he's been crying a lot.

Shit. This is bad.

I hover by the door while Charlie sits on the edge of his bed and engulfs him in a bear hug.

"What happened, Ben?" she asks.

"I don't know. I was playing a video game with my headset on when their shouting made it through. I didn't want to hear them, but it was impossible."

"I'm so sorry. Is Mom still in her room?"

"I think so."

"I'm gonna talk to her."

"Okay."

On her way out, she stops next to me and whispers, "Do you mind keeping him company?"

"Not at all."

She squeezes my arm and then heads down the corridor.

I finally dare to walk into Ben's room, unsure about what to say or do.

"What game were you playing before?" I ask, feeling stupid the moment the question comes out of my mouth.

"The Witcher."

"Oh, cool. It's one of my favorites."

"Yeah, mine too."

I glance around his room, noticing Ben shares Charlie's enthusiasm for fantasy realms, board games, and comics.

"Charlie tells me you also participate in LARP. She's convinced me to come next time."

Ben's eyes widen. "Really? That's cool. What character are you going to play?"

"A troll."

A smile appears on his flushed face. "That's awesome. I'm a troll hunter. You're going to need a costume."

I make a face, which results in Ben laughing. "What?"

"Your expression of horror was priceless. I wish Charlie had seen it."

I rub the back of my neck. "She's seen it already."

"What's the deal between you and her? Are you dating now?"

I'm taken aback by his question, which is stupid. I told Jane about Charlie and me, so why wouldn't she have told her brother?

"Yes we are."

Ben's expression becomes serious. "If you're Charlie's boyfriend now, then I have to come clean about something."

Gee, what could he possibly want to tell me?

"Okay."

"The prank with the chickens was my idea. My girlfriend's parents own a farm."

I stare at him without blinking for a moment, trying to keep my laughter bottled in, but it bubbles up my throat anyway. Charlie returns, finding me in such a state of amusement that I have tears in my eyes.

"What's going on?" she asks.

"I told Troy the chickens were my idea. I think he lost it," Ben deadpans.

Swallowing my laughter, I wipe the moisture from underneath my eyes. "I'm sorry. Your brother gave me the giggles."

With a half-smile that doesn't reach her eyes, Charlie shakes her head. Her reaction sobers me up. They're dealing with a shitty family situation, and here I am, laughing like an idiot.

She turns to her brother. "I talked to Mom briefly. She's a mess, so you're coming home with me." As an afterthought, she glances my way. "That's okay, right?"

Why would she think I wouldn't be okay with that?

"Of course, babe."

"That might mean I won't be able to come to the party with you."

I'm disappointed by this turn of events—I was looking forward to introducing Charlie to my friends—but I keep my face neutral. "Hey, there are parties every weekend. It's no big deal if we miss this one."

I'd go and wait in the living room while Charlie helps Ben pack a bag for the weekend, but I'm afraid to bump into her mother. To avoid a possible awkward encounter, I stand in a corner and start looking for troll costumes on my phone.

This is definitely not how I envisioned my first date with Charlie would end.

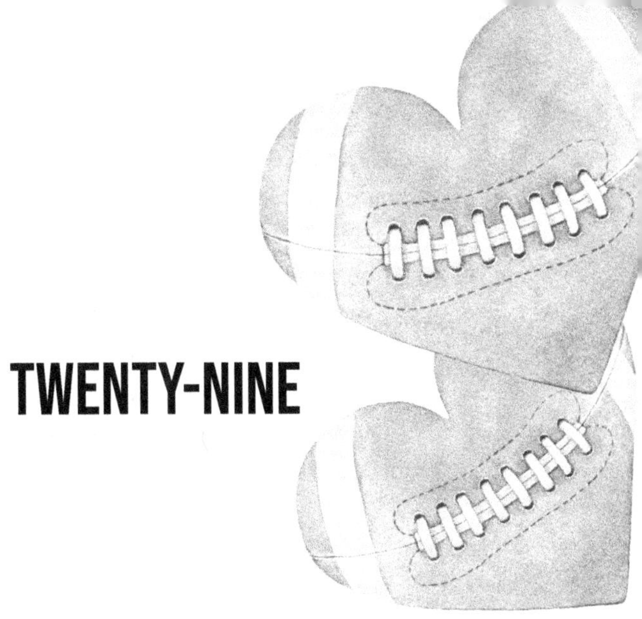

TWENTY-NINE

CHARLIE

I wake up before sunrise, feeling wretched about what happened last night. My back is sore from sleeping on the air mattress, but stiffness is the least of my worries. I couldn't get Mom to talk to me, which means I still don't know exactly what prompted my parents' fight, only what Ben told me he overheard.

Mom accused Dad of having an affair.

The idea brings bile to my mouth. I always believed my parents had a happy marriage. Growing up, it was rare for me to see them argue, and even when it happened, they made up quickly. I'm devastated by the possibility that Mom is correct in her suspicions.

Ben is still sound asleep in my bed. I tiptoe to the bathroom, and after I take care of my morning business, I head downstairs. My heart is heavy as I prepare coffee like a robot. Tears gather in my eyes, burning them. A few rogue ones manage to escape, rolling down my cheeks. I hastily wipe them dry, refusing to succumb to the sadness. Ben might be mistaken, or Mom could be wrong. It's too soon for me to fall into despair.

The wooden boards on the stairs creak, alerting me that my solitude is over. Troy is the one who woke early, like me. His hair is a mess, sticking out at odd angles, and he seems to be half asleep as he trudges to the kitchen, rubbing his eyes. He's also breaking our rules by only wearing sweatpants that hide nothing and no T-shirt. His pants hang low, emphasizing his delicious V that immediately turns me on. I'd complain, but he's offering me distraction on a platter, and I desperately need that.

"Morning, babe." He pulls me to him and kisses me softly on the lips.

Hmm, minty toothpaste flavor.

"Good morning," I whisper against his mouth, glad I brushed my teeth before coming down.

"Why are you up so early?" we both ask at the same time.

"Jinx," I say, making him chuckle.

"I couldn't sleep. And you?"

"Same." I step back, looking away.

"How are you feeling?"

I take a deep breath before answering, "Awful. I can't say I'm surprised about my parents' fight. They've been arguing for a while."

The coffee has finished brewing, so to keep me from going too deep into my grief, I focus on pouring Troy and me some. I know he's a caffeine addict like me.

"I'm really sorry, Charlie," he says, and I know he means it wholeheartedly.

"Thanks."

He understands better than anyone. His parents divorced, so I can imagine there was a lot of fighting as well before they finally called it quits. I hate to think my parents are going in that direction, but if there's no saving their marriage, then it's better for everyone if they go their separate ways.

I prepare our drinks, putting enough hazelnut creamer in mine that you could call it dessert and not coffee. Troy drinks his with just a splash of milk.

I offer him a mug. "Here."

He takes a whiff of the coffee, making a humming sound. "Thank you, babe."

We don't speak for a while, getting lost in our drinks and thoughts.

Troy is the one who breaks the silence first. "Do you know what you're going to do today?"

"No clue. I have to keep Ben distracted."

"Come to the game with me. It'll be fun."

"It's too late to get tickets."

Troy gives me a droll stare. "Charlie, I'm on the team. I have season tickets for family. They're pretty good seats."

I'm not a sports person, but I'm sure going to a game would be fun, even if Ben and I don't know much about football. "All right. What time does the game start?"

"At two. We have time to do other stuff, like find me a troll costume."

I give him a small smile. "Oh yeah. We have to do that. I totally forgot about it."

"If I don't have a costume, then I can't participate. Works for me." He shrugs.

Narrowing my eyes, I reply, "I'll get you a costume. Don't worry. And it's too late now. I've already signed you up."

He sets his mug on the counter and approaches me, caging me in against the fridge. His right arm is sling free, and he circles it around my waist while he cups my cheek with his left hand. "Fine. Now I want to make your knees go weak and set your body ablaze."

Good on his word, he kisses me hard, plunging his tongue into my mouth in a deliciously possessive way. I reach for his biceps, needing the support since he has turned my legs into jelly. The temperature in the kitchen goes up, creating a little inferno where clothes aren't mandatory. He parts my legs with his muscled thigh, creating a crazy good friction between them. His erection presses against my belly, and I want to free his cock and wrap my mouth around his girth, bet be damned.

I'm about to beg Troy to take me right here on the kitchen counter when a throat clearing douses the fire faster than having an ice bucket poured over my head. Troy jumps back, covering his crotch with both hands. He doesn't turn, just pretends to look for something on the shelf above the counter.

"Ben, you're up," I state the obvious.

"Yeah. The smell of coffee was like a beacon to me."

"Would you like a cup?" I ask, pretending my face isn't burning up.

I should have known better than to make out with Troy out in the open when Ben could walk in on us anytime.

"Sure, I'll have some." He pulls up a stool and then leans his elbows on the counter. "What's for breakfast? I'm starving."

I give him a cup of coffee, then go investigate our food situation. Peering inside the fridge tells me what I already guessed—we're low on food. "We have eggs, but we're out of bread."

"Do you have any cereal?" he asks.

"No, I finished the last box yesterday," Troy replies. "Let's go out for breakfast. My treat."

"Oh, we could go to Zuko's Diner," I suggest.

Troy cuts me a glance, and I don't understand his peculiar look until I remember what happened in front of the restaurant. The splash that ignited our feud. It feels like eons ago.

"It'll be good to reminisce," I add.

"For the record, I felt awful immediately after I did that."

"It's okay, Troy. I'm not mad about it anymore. And I have my share of regrettable acts when it comes to you."

His eyebrows scrunch together. "I hope not recent acts."

My lady parts clench, reminding me of those past performances. I glance at Ben, but he doesn't seem to be following the conversation. Thank heavens.

"No. I have zero regrets about those," I tell Troy honestly.

His eyes turn to molten lava in a split second, and a small tent appears in the front of his pants. I'd laugh if Ben wasn't around.

No, Charlie, you wouldn't laugh. You would be down on your knees, having a different kind of breakfast.

Oh my God. My conscience can be such a whore.

"Can you please stop with the sexual innuendos? It was bad enough to witness you in an act of foreplay a minute ago."

My eyes turn as round as saucers. "Ben! What the hell?"

"What? It's true." He shrugs.

"You can be such a brat sometimes." I storm out of the kitchen, running to the stairs.

"Charlie, where are you going?" Troy asks me.

"To change." And that's all I say before I disappear into my room.

I'm so fucking embarrassed, it's not even funny. And there I was, naively thinking Ben wasn't aware of the context of my conversation with Troy. Stupid me.

THIRTY

Besides getting caught by Ben in the kitchen, I'd say the rest of the morning went smoothly. I wasn't able to find a troll costume that I liked though, so that's something I'll need to sort in the coming week. It's bad enough that my curiosity got me roped into participating; I'm not going to wear something embarrassing.

We're now just outside the stadium in line to get in. It's surreal to be with the fans and not in the locker room with my teammates. Technically, I have to head there and get ready with them, even if I'm sitting on the bench, but I want to make sure Charlie and Ben are situated before I have to leave them.

We missed tailgating, but I'm not sure if Charlie would have enjoyed it anyway. I still have hopes I can persuade her to come to the party tonight, and I didn't want her turned off to the idea beforehand. The issue is Ben. He's a teen, so technically, he could stay home alone, but I'm sure Charlie wouldn't want that. And we can't bring him with us since he's a minor and it would be bad form to bring a kid to a party where booze was running freely.

As we stand in line, I'm recognized by some people, including fans of the opposing team. They're our rival school after all; they know my face and hate my guts. The assholes attempt to get me riled up, but their taunts can't find their mark. They're on my turf, and soon the Rushmore crowd drowns out their stupid shit. Charlie becomes tense next to me, and with just a glance, I can tell she's gearing up to defend my honor.

"Relax, babe. It's okay. They're gone now."

"They were awful and so rude." She seethes.

"I'm used to that. It's no big deal."

"Yeah, sis. If Troy cared about what others thought of him, he wouldn't be dating you." Ben laughs.

She hits him upside the head. "Quit being a brat."

"Ouch." He massages his head, glaring at Charlie. "I definitely shouldn't have interrupted you two this morning. Now you're in a mood."

I chuckle, but when I catch her glowering at me, I try to cover my slipup with a cough.

We're finally inside, and I make sure Charlie and Ben have everything they want from the concession stand before I escort them to their seats.

On our way down to the front row, I hear my name being called by someone in the crowd. I search the seats until I see Brooke waving animatedly at me. I wave back, but I don't stop or change course. I can't talk to her right now, nor do I want to.

"Was that your friend who came by the house when you got hurt?" Charlie asks.

"Yeah."

"I'm surprised she hasn't come by again," Charlie adds.

"We're not that close." I almost add "anymore" but that would no doubt result in a string of questions, and now is not the time to go down memory lane.

Eventually, I'll have to tell Charlie that Brooke is my ex. It was a punch to the gut to find out Blake was her ex from the douche canoe himself. I don't want that to happen to her.

"Here we are," I say when we reach our row.

Ben continues along until he finds his seat, but Charlie hangs back. "I wish you could stay with us. We're bound to not understand a thing and cheer at the wrong times."

"I highly doubt that's going to happen."

I reach for a strand of her hair and tuck it behind her ear. Almost immediately, her cheeks become pinker. I love how Charlie blushes when she's embarrassed or excited.

"Well, you'd better make sure your teammates don't lose to those assholes."

"They won't. Andreas knows that if they mess up, they won't hear the end of it from me."

"Good."

I swing my arm around Charlie's shoulders, pulling her to me for another scorching kiss. I swear I try to do sweet and easy, but I can't when it comes to her. She's a spark that always ignites me. I'm aware that we're putting on quite a show for all the cameras surrounding us. In less than a minute, our kiss will be all over social media. It's for that reason alone that I pull away faster than I want.

"Okay, I really have to go before I kidnap you," I say.

"Oh, we wouldn't want that," she says with a smirk, but then it turns into a frown. "I'm sorry you can't play today."

"It's okay. I needed a break. Besides, Danny is kicking ass. It'll be good for the team next year to know their new quarterback can handle the pressure."

"Tell them to break some bones."

"What?" I laugh.

"Not the right thing to say? In performing arts, we say break a leg, but I didn't think it would apply here, and 'good luck' felt lame."

I shake my head, fighting the urge to kiss her again. "I love how your mind works."

Immediately, I realize that was the wrong thing to say.

Charlie is now staring at me like a deer caught in headlights, and her lips are making a little O.

To downplay my slip of the tongue, I continue on like nothing is amiss. "I'll see you later, babe. Have fun."

My head is whirling as I dissect why I said that. I didn't say I loved her, but it was pretty close. Regardless, I used the damn L-word in a sentence, and that always gets girls in a tizzy. I hope it doesn't change anything between us. I like Charlie, but we're just beginning to get to know each other. There's no way in hell I've fallen in love with her already. I'm not one to get swept up by feelings.

I force those worries to the corner of my mind, and when I enter the locker room and hear the ruckus my teammates are making, my relationship doubts are so far back, they might as well not exist anymore.

"My, my. Look what we got here. Troy fucking Alexander is in the house," Puck, our giant linebacker, announces.

He walks over and pats me on my back so hard that it jostles my shoulder, making me wince.

"Gee, careful there. I do want to come back sooner rather than later."

Puck cringes. "Oops. Sorry."

Andreas comes over, watching me with a thousand questions in his eyes. He wants to know how my date went, and knowing the perv, he'll ask for all the details.

"So?" he starts.

"I have nothing to report."

"Come on, man. Maybe if you paint me a good picture, I'll consider sticking to one girl for a while."

Puck scoffs. "Yeah, right. When hell freezes over." He turns to me. "Is your girl watching the game?"

"Yeah. She brought her brother too."

"Cool, man. Nice to see Andy's heathen ways haven't rubbed off on you."

Puck comes from a super religious family and has been with the same girl since high school. He loves to pick on Andreas's amoral ways.

"Shut your piehole, altar boy," he rebuffs.

"Make me." Puck seems to grow in size, towering over Andreas.

Their banter is harmless, so I just head to my locker to put my uniform on.

A few minutes later, Coach Clarkson's booming voice cuts through the room, commanding everyone's attention.

His determined gaze finds mine, but all he does to acknowledge my presence is nod slightly. He proceeds to give the team a pep talk, and I usually hang on his every word, but I'm having a hard time getting focused since I'm not playing. I spot Danny next to Andreas, and a pang hits my chest that he's going in my place. I told Charlie I was fine with not playing, but being here with my teammates makes it harder to pretend that's true.

I hear my phone's text tone inside my duffel bag. Since I'm not invested in the coach's speech, I fish the device out. It's a message from Brooke.

When were you going to tell me you had a new girlfriend?

What the hell? Is she mad at me? It sure as shit sounds like it. *Damn it.* She picked the wrong time to annoy me with her bullshit.

I didn't think I had to.

I click Send, even knowing my reply is harsh. Her reply comes through a few seconds later.

Wow. Just wow.

It's pointless to continue the convo, so I just shove my phone back in the duffel bag and try to forget my ex is acting like we just broke up yesterday and not two years ago.

THIRTY-ONE

CHARLIE

I take back everything I've ever said about football. Being in the stadium, feeling the contagious energy of the crowd, made me understand why people love it so much. I still don't know most of the rules, but in the end, it didn't matter.

There was also the added bonus that I wanted the opposing team to lose badly all thanks to the encounter with those bullies earlier, and the Rushmore Rebels delivered. It was a hard game, and the score remained tight throughout the entire three and a half hours, but in the end, the Rebels won. My voice is hoarse from screaming.

Troy texts me that he might not be able to sneak out to ride with us. I totally understand. This victory was amazing, and I'm sure the celebration in the locker room is crazy right now. I tell him not to worry. His reply is to let him know when we're in the food court and he'll try to make it.

The crowd is slow to leave, and since we're all the way down, it takes at least ten minutes for our row to move. Ben and I file out, and then we trudge along with the rest of the people. It feels like an eternity before we finally reach the top of the stairs. I get out of the traffic headed for the exit and look for a quieter spot to text Troy back.

He'll be here in a few minutes, so I wait, keeping my eyes peeled and searching for him in the crowd. But I find someone else first, and I wish I'd missed her altogether. Brooke, Troy's beautiful friend, is coming in my direction. It's too late now to pretend I didn't see her, and it's clear she's making a beeline in my direction. She's with a friend, a brunette just as tall as she is but not as pretty.

"Hey. Charlie, right?" Brooke asks me with a phony smile plastered on her face.

"Yep. How's it going?"

"Oh, pretty good. So, you and Troy, huh?"

I knew she had ulterior motives for coming to speak to me. Thanks to my snooping of Troy's Instagram profile before my interview with him, I know they're close, probably dated at some point. But he's never mentioned her, so I wasn't going to ask. Judging by Brooke's fake friendliness, my assumption was correct. If they didn't date, then she has a major crush on him.

Too fucking bad.

"Yeah."

"I don't get it," the friend says. "Weren't you the girl who wrote that nasty article about him? Why would he date *you*?"

I narrow my eyes for a second, but when I reply, it's with a saccharine smile. "You know what they say: there's a fine line between love and hate. I guess we were just bound to cross it."

"Oh, so now you think Troy is in love with you?" She scoffs. "In your dreams."

"Tammy, please." Brooke touches her friend's arm as her face twists into an expression of discomfort.

Yeah, I'm not buying it.

The ugly brunette takes a sip of her soda first before replying, "What? I was just saying what everyone knows. Troy doesn't love anyone but himself."

Whoa. Maybe we have more than one scorned woman here, not only Brooke.

"I'm pretty sure his only problem is that he has high standards," Ben says before I can.

"Oh my God. The retarded boy speaks." The bitch looks at Ben with disdain, an expression I know too well. What she doesn't know is that every bully who has taunted my brother because of his Down syndrome has paid the price.

Brooke gasps, looking genuinely shocked by her friend's comment. It doesn't matter. My vision has already turned red, and before anyone can stop me, I pull my arm back and punch the bitch in the nose.

Her head jerks back right before she screeches, creating a commotion. "What the hell! You broke my nose."

Unlikely, since I didn't hear anything crack.

My pulse is pumping in my ears when I reply through clenched teeth, "Be glad that's all I broke."

Troy appears suddenly, breaking through the crowd to get to us. "What happened?"

"That filthy whore broke my nose." The girl points at me.

"You called her brother the R-word," a lady I hadn't noticed until then cuts in. "It's because of disgusting, prejudiced people like you that there's still a stigma today if people are different."

Wow. I didn't expect anyone to stand up for me. Her defense brings tears to my eyes.

She glances at me and smiles as a way to say she has my back.

Troy turns to Brooke. "That's the company you keep nowadays?"

"They were both out of line," she retorts, crossing her arms.

"I want to go. Can we go, Charlie?" Ben asks, clutching the sleeve of my jacket. His small voice breaks me.

I pull him into a side hug, ignoring the throbbing in my hand. "Yeah, let's go."

I'm too angry to check if Troy is following me. I just want to get out of here. The onlookers are smothering me.

A second later, he places his hand on my lower back and, using his body, makes way for us to pass. I never considered myself a damsel in need of a savior, but Troy's protectiveness feels nice.

We continue in silence until we get to my car. When I grab the door handle, I realize I'm still shaking and in no condition to drive.

Troy circles my wrist, keeping me from opening the door. "I'll drive."

"Don't be ridiculous. You can't drive with your shoulder like that."

"You're still reeling from what happened." He frowns. "Your arm is shaking."

"I can drive," Ben pipes up.

I glance at him with a refusal on the tip of my tongue. He can drive in Littleton, which is much quieter than here.

"I can do it, Charlie. Trust me," he insists.

"You have your driver's license?" Troy asks.

"Yes. I've had it for four months already." Ben puffs his chest out proudly.

Troy turns back to me, concern in his eyes. "Let him drive, babe."

I want to argue, but if I say anything, it might do more harm than good. I know my brother—he's putting up a tough front, but he's a mess inside. Growing up, he fought depression among other things because of assholes who treated him badly.

"Okay," I say. "But I'm sitting shotgun." I walk around the car, leaving Troy no choice but to slide across the back seat.

During the drive, I expect him to ask for details about what happened, but he keeps quiet. The silence becomes a heavy blanket of discomfort, and I eventually can't take it anymore.

"The game was amazing," I pipe up, turning to face Troy in the back seat.

He nods. "It was, but hell, I was a wreck the whole time. I thought I was going to lose my voice with the way I was shouting."

"I kind of lost mine," I say.

Troy smirks. "Hmm, I did notice a new sexiness to it."

"Dude, I'm right here," Ben complains.

"Oops. Sorry."

I laugh despite the horrible way the day ended.

"Is there any chance you would consider going to the party with me tonight?" Troy asks softly. "It's going to be epic."

I bite my lower lip, torn between a straight "No" and a "Maybe". After the altercation with Brooke's friend, and the way the blonde was acting all shady, I do want to show up at the party as Troy's date. Call it vanity or whatever with a pinch of possessiveness. But there's Ben to consider.

"I don't know. Are there going to be more people like that airless bimbo who name-called Ben?"

Troy winces. "Honestly, I don't know."

"You should go, Charlie," Ben says. "I think I'm ready to go home if Mom is feeling better."

My stomach bottoms out, and my chest, which was already tight as hell, constricts further. Ben staying with me was a way to distract him from the turmoil back at my folks'. I feel guilty, even though it's irrational. I can't control what ignorant people say or do.

"If that's what you want."

Ben nods. "Yeah, it is. I had fun today though."

I watch his profile, trying to sniff out the lie. His expression is serene, but Ben's always had a better poker face than me.

If he spirals down a dark tunnel again because of that bitch, I will break her nose for real the next time I see her.

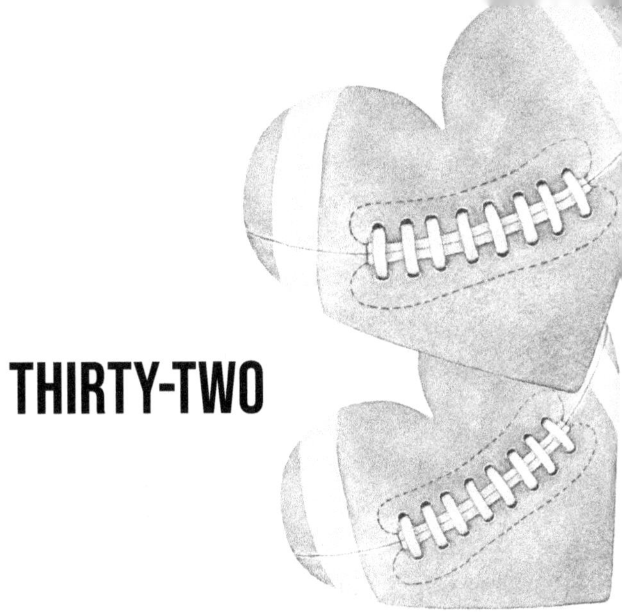

THIRTY-TWO

TROY

I confess that knowing Charlie went *Million Dollar Baby* on Brooke's friend made my admiration for her grow. I'd already known she was fearless and short-tempered, but her fierce protection of her brother moved me more than she could have known.

It also opened up old wounds that have never fully healed. I failed Robbie by not paying attention, and he drowned a few feet from me. Erroneously, I thought that was my parents' job, but they made it abundantly clear that I should have kept an eye on him. I was his big brother, after all. They weren't wrong, and the guilt has consumed me ever since.

Their mother came by to pick up Ben earlier, and with that, Charlie had no valid excuse not to come to the party with me. Regardless, I thought I'd have to use my convincing skills, but she surprised me by agreeing to come without me having to ask twice.

We had an early dinner, and now I'm waiting for her to get ready. I never asked if she'd bought any of those sexy tops she was looking at. They were nice, but I'd prefer if she wore a dress again. I love her legs; plus, a dress would give me easier access. I'm already over our bet. Life is too short, and I'm not going to keep punishing myself over nothing. God knows I already do that plenty with reason.

I'm nursing a beer while I wait. The only good thing about not being able to drive until the sling is off is that I don't have to worry about my alcohol intake.

I turn when I hear Charlie come down the stairs. Those old wooden boards creak so loudly that even the neighbors must hear when one of us goes up and down.

My jaw drops as I drink her in. She's not wearing jeans—thank fuck—but a short black pleated skirt with a spiked belt looped around her hips. Her top is a vintage *Highlander* T-shirt with the movie's catch phrase "There can be only one" typed across it. There are a bunch of headless dude icons and one with his head still attached, holding a sword. Man, I need to get me one. It's awesome. But what really completes the look and causes a stir in my jeans is the leather jacket and the over-the-knee fuck-me boots she's wearing. I won't be able to leave her alone tonight, or jackasses will be all over her.

"Hi. What do you think?" she asks with a cheeky smile. She knows perfectly well she looks hot as sin.

"Okay, I changed my mind. Let's stay home so I can get you out of those clothes stat."

She chuckles, shaking her head. "No way, Jose. I didn't spend an hour getting ready for you to destroy my look with your caveman urges."

I cross the distance between us in two long strides and pull Charlie flush to my body. "Oh, babe. You'll know how caveman I can be when I bend you over that couch and fuck you until you can't remember your own name."

"What are you saying, Troy? Is that your declaration of defeat?"

The "Yes" is on the tip of my tongue, but when I do say it out loud, I'm going to make good on my promise and pound her into oblivion. *Damn it.* Thinking about it is making my cock rock hard in a painful way.

"Hmm, no. This is my declaration of victory when you come to your senses and admit you can't resist this sexy machine."

A bubble of laughter escapes her throat, dousing the furnace inside me.

"Okay, Mr. Sexy Machine. We'll see how the evening goes."

I step back and then hold up her right hand for inspection. It's still a bit red, but the swelling has gone down. "Does it hurt?"

"Not so much. It was a good call putting ice on it when we got back."

"I can't believe I missed the punch. I would have loved to have seen that."

She pulls her hand back as her face twists into a scowl. "It felt good punching her in the moment, but it doesn't erase the ugliness that came out of her mouth. Words can't be unsaid."

"I know. I'm so fucking mad about what happened. I can't believe Brooke would be friends with someone like that."

Charlie tilts her head to the side as if she's scrutinizing me. This is the moment when I should tell her about my past with Brooke, but I really don't want to get into it right now.

"She's your ex, isn't she?"

Well, damn. So much for not talking about it. "Yeah. We dated in high school and through my first year of college."

"Why did you break up?"

"She went to school in New York, and the relationship fizzled with the distance."

"She's back now."

"Charlie, Brooke and I broke up over two years ago. There's nothing going on between us. We remained friends while she was away, but since she came back, we haven't really talked."

"Besides when she came over to check on you." She quirks an eyebrow.

"Yeah, and that was the last time. Why are you asking me all these questions? Please tell me you're not jealous." I smirk, guessing she is.

She snorts. "No. But if I'm asking all these questions, it's because you haven't provided the information yourself."

"Didn't think it mattered. I mean, I don't hang out with her all the time, unlike you and your ex Blake."

She throws her hands up in the air. "Oh God. Please don't be one of those possessive boyfriends who doesn't tolerate their girlfriends being friends with guys."

"Let me make myself clear. I'm only a caveman in the bedroom, and trust me, you'll like it."

She narrows her eyes. "I'm beginning to suspect you're referring to the tweet I wrote."

"Oh, when you called me a Neanderthal?"

"Yeah."

"I swear that wasn't the case." And I'm not lying. I had forgotten about that stupid tweet. "Grab a drink before I call an Uber. We're supposed to be celebrating tonight."

She sighs. "Okay. You're right. Let's leave the past in the past."

"Cheers to that."

CHARLIE

I don't know why I decided to ask about Brooke right before we left the house. I'd sworn to myself that I wouldn't broach the subject, and then bang, my tongue got the better of me.

He asked if I'm jealous. Of course I am. Any girl would be if Brooke had dated their boyfriend in the past. She's a freaking cover model.

I hate that I'm feeling so insecure about myself. I'm not blind. I clean up cute. And Troy has shown me time and time again that he likes what he sees. But it still manages to get to me.

Damn it, Charlie. Shake it off. You're Raven, the hottest sorceress in all the land.

"Our ride is here," Troy tells me, bringing me back to the here and now.

I glance at the beer in my hand, then chug it, taking several large gulps in one go before setting the bottle back on the counter.

"Thirsty?" Troy smirks.

"Not anymore."

The ride is short, only ten minutes. The party is being held at a frat house. Troy told me which one, but I already forgot. I texted Blake earlier to ask if he wanted to join us as a joke. His reply came swiftly—a string of angry and barfing emojis. I also extended the invite to Fred and Sylvana, but both already had plans. It would have been nice to see familiar faces here, but on the other hand, venturing out of my comfort zone is something I have to do from time to time.

The party is already in full swing when we get there. Everyone we pass greets Troy as if he were a celebrity. It's all high fives and shouting. People don't seem to care that he had no part in the game's outcome today since he didn't play.

Despite all the attention on him, he doesn't let go of my hand for a second, and when he stops to chat with some people, he introduces me as his girlfriend. Not a single person mentions I'm the girl who wrote the nasty article about him. I'm guessing no one knows or cares except Brooke and her nasty friend.

We finally reach the core of the party, the open kitchen where most of the team is gathered. Andreas is on top of the counter with red Solo cups in both hands. He tilts one of the cups back and then the next before he glances in our direction. Even from where I stand, I can see his eyes are glassy. He must have started drinking as soon as he left the stadium.

"Hallelujah, Troy Alexander is finally here. Someone give him a fucking drink already."

Danny, the young quarterback, gets to us first. Instead of

speaking to Troy, his attention is on me. "Hey, Charlie. I'm glad you could come. What do you want to drink?"

"I'll have a beer, thanks."

Bending over, he fishes a bottle from the cooler on the floor next to the counter. He twists the cap off before passing the bottle to me. "Here, you'd better drink the good stuff. I can't vouch for what's in those plastic cups."

"I'll have a beer too. Thanks for asking," Troy pipes up.

"Get one yourself," Danny replies with a good-humored laugh.

Troy shakes his head and then glances at me. "See the shit I get from this rookie here?"

Before I can reply, Troy slings his arm around Danny's neck and brings him to the level of his right hand so he can mess with the guy's curly hair.

"Hey, cut it out," Danny complains.

Two of Troy's teammates see the scene and join in the wrestling or whatever this is. I step back, not wanting to get my beer knocked out of my hand. I only stop when my back presses against the wall.

It doesn't take long for Troy to be engulfed by his teammates, out of my reach. He hasn't hung out with them in a while, and this is an important evening for the team. I'm fine with just watching and hoping no one bothers me.

But of course, my solitude doesn't last long. Wherever those guys are, a flock of giggling girls follows. It's easy to spot what kind of clique they belong to. The sorority girls are all dressed to the nines as if they were going to a wedding reception instead of a football party. They're all wearing cocktail dresses, and their hair's styled to perfection. Then there are the cheerleaders, wearing jeans and sexy tops like the ones Sylvana wanted me to wear. And finally, I see some girls who are clearly athletes judging by the confident way they move and talk. Their attire is less sexual, and they make me look puny next to their top-notch physiques.

One of them catches me staring and walks over. She looks familiar. "Hey, I haven't seen you at any of these parties before. I'm Vanessa."

"Hi, Vanessa. I'm Charlie. Yeah, it's my first time here."

"Are you a freshman?"

"Oh no, I'm a junior. And you?"

"Sophomore. Did you go to the game?"

"Which one?"

She smiles. "The football game, obviously. No one here would ever go to one of our games."

Finally, it dawns on me where I know her from. Ludwig has a major crush on her and keeps her picture by his desk. "You're on the soccer team."

"Yeah."

Someone shrieks, drawing our attention to the noise. It's one of the cheerleaders losing her shit over a spilled drink.

"Oh crap. Better see what my evil twin is crying about now."

"That's your sister?" The question slips from my mouth before I can stop it.

Vanessa gives me a pitiful smile. "Yep. Heather Castro, the Ice Queen of Rushmore, is my twin. There are worse fates; we could be identical."

She pushes her way through the crowd to get to her sister.

I search for Troy and see he's still busy socializing with his friends. It'd be fine to wait for him, but my bladder has other ideas. I shouldn't have guzzled down all that beer before coming here. I go in search of a bathroom, but the house is so crowded, it's impossible to get to anything. Finally, I ask a girl next to me.

"Oh, you don't want to use the bathroom downstairs," she tells me. "It's disgusting." She staggers forward, tripping over nothing.

Great. Drunk as a skunk.

"Use the one upstairs," a different girl chimes in. She looks more lucid, so I follow her advice.

I head for the stairs, and I'm actually surprised it's not off-limits. In fact, traffic is pretty heavy going up and down. Soon I find out that there's a second party going on in some of the rooms. Yeah, this is definitely party central. I'm about to ask again where the damn bathroom is when I see two girls stumble out of a room. They leave the door ajar, and with a quick peek inside, I spot the door to a bathroom. This is someone's bedroom, but my bladder is about to fail.

Fuck it. If they wanted to keep people out, they should have kept it locked.

I walk in, closing the door behind me, and then hurry to the bathroom. I try not to look at anything too closely; this is a guy's bathroom, after all, and it's also been turned into a Grand Central Station restroom. I pee standing up, even though it takes me ages to get it going in this position. Guys are so fucking lucky. In moments like this, I have serious penis envy. After a minute in a squat position that has my thighs burning, relief comes, but also the knowledge that after this first piss, I'll need to go every fifteen minutes. *Oh joy.* I should have gone straight to tequila.

I'm washing my hands when I hear a noise outside the bathroom—a drunk girl, judging by her slurred speech, and someone else. My hand is on the door handle when I hear Troy's voice.

What the fucking hell?

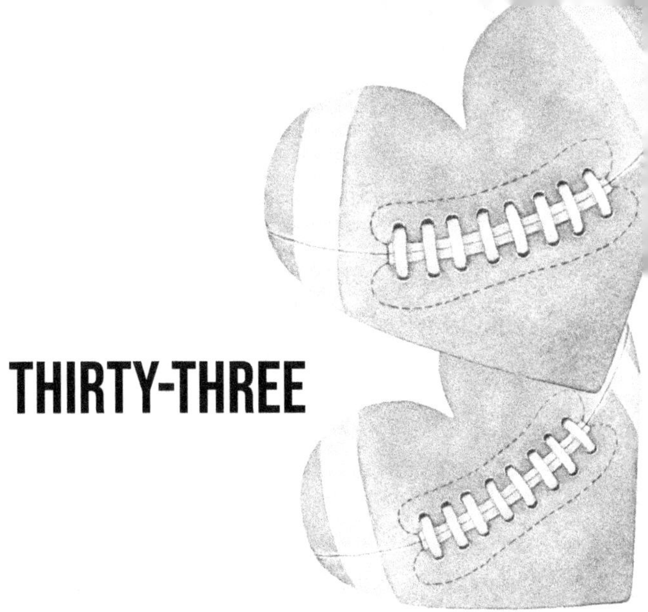

THIRTY-THREE

TROY

I lose track of time goofing around with the guys, and when I look for Charlie, she's no longer chatting with Vanessa Castro, the midfielder of the girls' soccer team. Afraid she got upset that I ignored her and left the party, I text her. When she doesn't answer, I go looking for her.

There seems to be more people now than fifteen minutes ago, and getting anywhere in the house takes a lot of shoving and pushing. I stretch my neck, trying to find her on the makeshift dance floor. I do find Vanessa with her teammates, but no sign of Charlie. I decide to talk to Vanessa and ask if she knows where Charlie went when I'm intercepted by Brooke, who pretty much throws herself into my arms.

Her makeup is smeared, and her eyes are bloodshot. Even if those weren't clues enough, she's wasted; her breath smells like tequila.

"Troy, the person I've been looking for the whole night." She hiccups.

I straighten her and then push her back. "What's the matter with you?"

"What's the matter with me? I'll tell you what's the matter with me. I shouldn't have ever let my parents convince me to go to New York. If I had stayed, we'd still be together."

Fuck me. I knew it. She came back because of me. I wasn't crazy when I got that vibe from her at the diner.

"Come on, Brooke. Don't do this now. You're drunk."

"I know I'm drunk. I had to. It's the only way I can tell you the truth. Liquid courage, right?"

I sense the crowd around us is staring. Not everyone is shitfaced out of their minds yet, and I'm sure some are hanging on to every word we say. I have to get Brooke out of here.

"Come on. Let's talk somewhere in private."

As much as I'm pissed that she's causing a scene, I can't leave her alone in this current state. For starters, it's not safe. There are a lot of weirdos on campus. Plus, I do owe it to our shared past to hear her out and explain that I'm with Charlie, and that's not going to change. There isn't any chance Brooke and I will ever get back together.

I steer her toward the stairs. There must be a quiet room where we can talk. In the back of my mind, I know this will look bad. I hope Charlie doesn't believe the gossip when she hears about it. Once on the second floor, I try every door until I find an unoccupied room.

"I'm such an idiot. I hate New York. Always have. Why did I go?" she whines.

"Come on, Brooke. Sit down." I push her onto the bed, stepping back quickly before she drags me with her.

I don't want this situation to get more awkward than it already is.

"You were right, Troy. I did come back because of you. Seeing you during the holidays made me realize I missed you terribly. Every single guy I dated after you didn't compare."

I listen to Brooke pour her heart out, but the only feeling she can summon from me is pity. There isn't a single spark left of what we had before.

"Aren't you going to say anything?" she asks.

"What do you want me to say?"

Her shoulders sag forward as she laughs without humor. "That you feel the same way."

"I can't do that."

"Why? Because of Charlie?"

"No. She has nothing to do with this."

Brooke sits up straighter, and a new glimmer of hope shines in her bloodshot eyes. "So you're not in love with her?"

"I didn't say that."

"Fuck, Troy. You're not making any sense."

I run a hand over my hair. "I don't want you to think that if Charlie wasn't in the picture, then I'd be with you. That's what I'm getting at. I care about you, Brooke, as a friend. Nothing more."

Her face twists in agony, and more tears gather in her eyes. "It would have been kinder if you told me we couldn't be together because you were madly in love with your roommate."

"That wouldn't be fair. I can't compare what we had with what Charlie and I have."

"What do you mean?" She wipes her face with the back of her hand.

"You were my first girlfriend, Brooke, and that's something no one can take away. You'll always be a cherished memory. Well, besides this one."

She snorts. "Gee, thanks."

"But Charlie is...." I struggle to put into words what she means to me. She drives me insane, whether with desire or grievance. She pushes my buttons like no other, but she also makes me feel alive. She's a high I never want to come down from.

"She's what?" Brooke asks.

"She's endgame," I say, not knowing it to be true until the words come out of my mouth.

Brooke's eyes turn rounder. "Oh my God. You *are* in love with her."

Maybe she's right, but I don't want to admit that out loud.

Like saying Charlie is endgame wasn't a big enough declaration of love, Troy.

I pass a hand over my face, giving my back to Brooke. "I have to find her. Do you need me to call you an Uber?"

"No, Troy. I can find my own way home. I'm not as hopeless as you think I am." She walks around me and out of the bedroom with her chin raised high.

Fuck. This conversation could have gone a million times better.

I pull my cell phone out of my pocket, and seeing Charlie hasn't texted me back, I call her. A second later, I hear her ringtone coming from nearby.

I whirl on the spot, noticing then that the light in the bathroom is on. When Charlie pushes the door open, holding her phone in her hand, I'm slammed by a wave of anger and disappointment.

"You've been there the whole time?" My question is rhetorical. Obviously, she didn't fly into the bathroom through the window.

"I'm so sorry. I didn't mean to eavesdrop."

"Really? Could have fooled me. You had plenty of time to make yourself known. Why didn't you, Charlie?" I raise my voice, expecting her to get riled up immediately. She's a firecracker, after all. But instead, she winces and stares at me with guilt-ridden eyes.

"I don't know. As soon as I heard you, I panicked and froze. Then she started spilling her guts out, and I had to see where it was going."

"You mean, you had to find out what I would do," I retort, still angry as hell, but at least I didn't shout.

She nods, crossing her arms over her chest. I've never seen her so subdued and small. I'm filled with the impulse to engulf her into a hug and tell her everything will be fine, but I'm still riding on the anger. I don't know what I resent the most, the fact that she felt the need to spy on me or that she overheard my heartfelt confession.

Fuck!

"I don't expect you to forgive me. What I did was pretty shitty."

"Yeah, it was."

I catch a quiver of her lips, but she clamps her jaw tight, then lowers her gaze to her phone and begins to type.

"What are you doing?" I ask.

"Ordering an Uber. I don't expect you to come home with me. You should stay and party with your friends."

"The hell I'm going to let you go home alone," I shout again, but this time, I'm frustrated with myself and I don't know why.

"It's fine, Troy." She won't meet my gaze.

Ah hell. I walk over and cave, bringing her close. "It's not fine. We came together, and we'll go home together." I kiss her forehead before I step back, lacing my hand with hers. "Come on. We have to brave a sea of drunk people to get to the front door."

CHARLIE

I've never felt more wretched in my entire life, not even when I accidentally set Blake's five-hundred-dollar costume on fire two years ago. I knew eavesdropping on Troy's conversation was wrong, but jealousy and insecurity clouded my judgment for a moment. I had to know what he would do upon hearing his ex's confession. I had no idea he would say what he did in the end. And now I don't know what I'm going to do with that information.

He said I'm endgame. How does he know? It hasn't been that

long since we were at each other's throats. It's too soon for him to be making those types of declarations—at least that's what my mind is telling me. My heart, on the other hand, skipped a beat when he said that.

The ride back home is quiet. Troy is sitting as far away from me as possible. The distance feels like a chasm. We both thank the driver when he drops us off, but no words are exchanged between us as we walk side by side to the front door.

The urge to cry returns. I messed up royally, and my heart is now twisted in agony. I don't want him to see me like this. I'm too full of pride for that, so as soon as he opens the door, I say good night and make a beeline for the stairs without looking back.

I'm two steps shy from it when Troy circles his free arm around my waist and pins my back to his chiseled chest. "Don't go," he whispers in my ear.

Butterflies flutter in my stomach as I melt against his body. I close my eyes for a second and allow myself to get lost in the feel of his arm keeping me in place, on the way his warm breath turns my already overheated skin into molten lava.

"I don't want to go, but…."

He turns me around, keeping me trapped against him. "I didn't mean to get so angry."

"You had every right to. I broke your trust."

"You didn't break my trust, not exactly. You didn't hide in that bathroom on purpose with the intent of spying on me."

"No. It was a matter of too many beers and a too small bladder."

He chuckles. "I can't stay mad at you when you say stuff like that, babe."

His eyes drop to my lips and stay there. He doesn't make a move, maybe because he's still gung ho on not losing the bet. I couldn't care less about that anymore.

"You win," I breathe.

He brings his eyes back to mine. "What?"

Oh for fuck's sake. Lack of sex has clearly addled his brain.

I rise on my tiptoes and kiss him hard and deep, leaving no room for doubt.

This is my surrender.

THIRTY-FOUR

CHARLIE

Troy responds in kind, matching my passionate tempo stroke for stroke. I don't know what to do with my hands; I want to touch him everywhere, but I also want him to touch *me* everywhere.

The arm in a sling is a hindrance. I reach behind his neck and open the clasp. His response is a deep groan that I can feel all the way down to my core. He makes quick use of both hands; they disappear underneath my skirt to grab my ass. I'd jump in his arms if it weren't for his injured shoulder. I'm sure he could lift me, but I won't be responsible for prolonging his recovery.

I hold his face between my hands and tilt my head to the side, trying to deepen the kiss. His tongue darts into my mouth, fiery, possessive, and then he does what I wanted him to do all along—he picks me up, lifting me off the floor. I wrap my legs around his hips, hooking them at the ankles and trying my best to be as light as a feather—if that's even possible. I half expect Troy to bring me to the couch. He did say he was going to bend me over it and fuck me into oblivion. But instead, he veers for the stairs, going up two at a time.

Our mouths stay fused together, trying to compensate for all the days we denied ourselves the taste of the other. We did make out, but always with restraint, never with this mind-numbing abandon.

Troy takes me to his room, even though my bedroom is closer to the stairs. The door is semi shut, so he kicks it open with a bang before almost running across the room, aiming for his king-size bed.

He tries to break the kiss to put me down at the edge of the mattress, but I'm not having any of it. We fall together on the bed, and our limbs quickly twist together. We stay in that lovers' embrace for a while, exploring each other with our tongues and hands. With each passing second, my body burns for him brighter, and the overwhelming yearning is agony, but the sweetest kind. I don't know how long we stay like that, but eventually, he slides off me, keeping one leg firmly between mine.

"What's wrong?" I ask against his mouth.

"Tired of getting poked by your belt."

Oh shit. The spikes. I completely forgot about them.

"Sorry."

I have to move away from his mouth to rotate the belt until I find the clasp, but Troy is intent on distracting me. His mouth strays to my neck, peppering my skin with delicious open-mouthed kisses that leave me panting like I've just run a marathon.

I finally locate the damn clasp and manage to pull my belt off just in time before Troy rolls over me again and nestles between my legs. His erection pushes against me through our layers of clothing, and now I want nothing more than to see them gone. I reach for the back of his shirt and yank the fabric until he finally decides to cooperate. He leans back, sitting on the balls of his feet, and finishes the job, pulling the T-shirt off fast like a ninja and mussing his hair in the process. The sexy look combined with the lust in his eyes makes my clit throb so hard that if he wasn't blocking access, I'd take care of the problem myself.

"Fuck, you're so beautiful," he says.

I know I should say thank you, or at least return the compliment, but I'm suddenly consumed with a voracious need that can only be satiated by Troy on top of me, fulfilling the promise he made earlier before we left for the party. I want him inside me, pounding into me so hard that I leave an imprint on the mattress.

"Yeah, yeah, clothes off." I reach for his jeans' button and then the zipper. But I can't do more while he's sitting in that position, watching me with a Cheshire cat smile. "Troy, help here."

"What's the matter, babe? Are you in a hurry?"

"Yes," I hiss. "Don't tell me you aren't. These past few days have been torture."

"Oh, but the torture is only about to begin, sweetheart."

He jumps off me—*finally*—and removes his jeans and boxers. I forget about his ominous comment in an instant at the sight of all his naked glory. Damn it, he looks like a golden Greek god. *Every. Single. Part. Of. Him.* I could spend all eternity staring at him and never get my fill.

He returns to the mattress and runs his fingers over one of my boots. "You know, I think we should keep these on." He continues his exploration, and now his fingers are running over my skin, leaving a trail of goose bumps in their wake.

I open my mouth to protest, but he silences me by pressing his index finger over my lips. Undeterred, I grab his wrist and suck that offending finger into my mouth. Troy hisses, narrowing his eyes. If he wants to torture me, well, two can play that game.

With his free hand, he lifts my skirt and pauses, his eyes widening a fraction.

That's right, babe. I dressed to kill tonight. I knew he would try to get a peek under my skirt, and I was hoping the little black lingerie number would bring him to his knees. I couldn't have foreseen that I'd be the one gladly losing the battle.

I'm his endgame.

Those were the words that obliterated the barriers I had erected around my heart. The memory of his confession makes my chest warm. My heart seems to overflow with emotion. Is Troy my endgame? As I take him in, I'm blasted with a mix of pure joy and euphoria that makes my entire body tingle. When I look into his eyes, something clicks into place. I feel light and whole, and I never want this feeling to go away.

I let go of his finger with a soft pop, and that seems to unfreeze him from his lustful daze. He rubs a rough thumb over my swollen lips, then reaches for both sides of my panties, curling his fingers around the fabric. He rolls them painfully slow down my legs, and now I get his meaning that the torture is just beginning. How can he stand this when I know he's about to blow?

I lower my eyes to his erection, and it's almost like it's daring me to touch it. I move toward it, but Troy captures my arm and lifts it above my head, then does the same with my other one, and finally, the meaning of his words penetrates my brain. He uses my panties to bind my wrists together and secure them to the headboard.

"Troy, what are you doing?"

His lips curl up. "You surrendered. Now I must make you pay."

There goes my clit, throbbing again in anticipation. I have no idea what Troy plans to do now that I'm immobile, but whatever it is, I know it's going to be earth-shattering.

His eyes drop to my exposed sex, and he licks his lower lip. "As much as I want to taste you, I'm hanging by a thread here."

He reaches over to the nightstand and pulls a condom packet from the drawer. I follow his every move while I try to break my hands free.

"Don't even try, babe. You lost the war. Now you're at my mercy."

"Is that so?" My voice is husky.

Troy doesn't reply as he finishes rolling the condom down his length. Still silent, he spreads my legs farther apart and then lifts one of them over his good shoulder before lowering his body to mine. The tip of his erection rubs against my entrance, making both of us moan.

He rests his forehead against mine and lets out a shaky breath. "Hell, whose idea was it to go without sex for so long?"

"Probably yours." I laugh, but in fact, I don't know anymore.

And when he pushes inside, sheathing himself in me, there's no chance I can remember. My brain takes a vacation, and all I can process is the intense pleasure that's making my body go haywire.

I forget that I'm bound and jerk my arms forward, needing to touch Troy as well. Frustration seeps into me when I can't. "Ugh, this is so un—"

Troy crushes his mouth over mine, cutting off my tirade at the same time that he plunges into me fully. He swallows my moans, taking control of the kiss, of the pace, of everything. Pulling back slowly he then slams into me again. He tries to keep the rhythm steady, but after a few more pumps, his movements become frantic, out of control. I can feel the pleasure building below, and I want to do something—grab on to his shoulders, sink my nails in his back. I'm miserable that I can't do any of those things, and yet I can't deny that being bound while Troy fucks me is the most erotic thing I've ever done.

He abandons my lips for a moment to kiss my neck and my shoulders.

I arch my back and beg, "Troy, please. Let me touch you."

"No," he replies gruffly.

As I near climax, I bring my legs closer together, even though one is secured over Troy's shoulder. He grunts again, louder, and then, taking a cue from my playbook, he bites me. Pain and pleasure mix, sending me spiraling over the edge. I cry out, uncaring how loud I am. He pumps into me faster, almost in a frenzy. It's not much longer until he finds his release. His body shudders on top of me, slowing down. Breathing hard, he hides his face in the crook of my neck, blowing hot air against my already burning skin.

I move my leg, sliding it off his shoulder. It falls numb on the mattress, but everything else in my body is alive.

THIRTY-FIVE

TROY

I can't move. My right shoulder is burning, but fuck it, it was totally worth it. This was the hottest sex move I've ever pulled with anyone. Beneath me, Charlie's breathing is out of whack, just like mine.

"Troy?"

"Hmm?"

"Are you still alive?"

"Barely."

"Thank God. I thought I was going to live through *Gerald's Game*."

Laughter ripples through me. Only Charlie would make such a comment. I roll off her but keep her cocooned within my embrace. "Are you telling me you couldn't rip those panties?"

She pouts. "I could, but I'd hate to ruin them. They're so pretty."

I bring my lips to hers, unable to resist the temptation she dangled in front of me. Anything she does that brings my attention to her mouth makes me want to kiss her.

I'd keep savoring her, but Charlie turns her face away.

"You're not starting this again while I'm still bound. I can't feel my hands."

Remorse pierces my chest. I didn't stop to consider what staying in this position for too long would do to her. "Does it hurt?" I ask as I untie her from the headboard.

"A little." She rubs her wrists, then opens and shuts her hands. "The bite on my shoulder hurt more."

Shit. I glance at the mark, feeling really bad about it. "I'm so sorry. I got carried away." I shake my head. "Ah hell. I'm an idiot."

Charlie laughs as she reaches for my face. "Relax, babe. I was just teasing you. It only hurt a little."

Relief washes over me. "Thank God. I really liked when you bit me, so I wanted to return the favor."

Her eyebrows pinch together as she narrows her eyes. "What are we now, a couple of vampires?"

"Hey, you started it." I kiss her nose and then jump out of bed to get rid of the condom.

I could toss it in the trash bin in my room, but I need something from the bathroom—painkillers. Now that the heat of the moment has passed, I can feel the consequence of my reckless decision. The pain isn't as sharp as when I returned from the hospital, but it's not great either. I hope I didn't buy myself another week on the bench.

"I knew I shouldn't have removed the sling," Charlie says from the door.

She's leaning against the frame with her arms crossed, still fully naked save for the boots. My cock stirs awake again at the sight.

"If you hadn't, I would have done it myself." I turn around, ready to go for round two.

Charlie's gaze slowly travels down my body until she sees I'm locked and loaded once more. Her lips curl into a satisfied grin. Wordlessly, she unfolds her arms and walks over. I swallow hard, my pulse already accelerating at the promise of more good times. She stops in front of me, not breaking eye contact.

"What do you have in store for me now, my dear lord conqueror?"

"What?" I try not to laugh, but how can I when my crazy girl keeps saying stuff like that?

"I'm on the losing side. I'm at your mercy, remember?"

"Oh, that. Hmm. I have a few ideas." I kiss her shoulder where the love bite is still red.

She shivers beneath my caress.

"Are you going to share them?" she whispers.

"Yes, dear, I will. Let's get back to bed. The night is young, and we have a lot of catching up to do."

An annoying blaring sound wakes me from a pleasant dream. Still refusing to acknowledge the noise, I drag a pillow over my head. Charlie moves next to me, and a moment later, the noise ceases. I sense a shift on the mattress, so I blindly reach for her, curling my arm over her stomach.

She snuggles against me, and I begin to drift once more into dreamland.

"Troy," she whispers.

"Hmm?"

"We have to get up." She traces circles over my chest, pebbling my skin.

"No we don't. It's Sunday."

"Exactly. Your grandma is expecting us."

Ah hell. I had completely forgotten about it. We did promise to visit, and I can't say I'm not coming now. Charlie will go without me, and that will earn me the title of the shittiest grandson alive.

"Ten more minutes."

She makes a tsking sound and then frees herself from my

hold. I'm too tired to fight to keep her in bed with me. I expect her to get up right away, but instead, I feel her body slinking lower on the mattress. The hand that was playing with my chest also moves down until it wraps around my cock. I hadn't even noticed I was already sporting morning wood.

"Charlie," I moan against the pillow.

She doesn't answer with words; she licks me from base to tip before her mouth covers my shaft.

"Fuck." My hips buck ever so slightly, but then I relax against the mattress and let Charlie do her thing.

My God, my girl has an expert tongue. I swear it feels like I'm inside her pussy and not her mouth. But she has a mean streak too. She keeps bringing me close to the edge and then slowing down right before I'm about to come. I'm close to flipping her over and taking control of the situation.

"Babe, you're killing me. Also, we're going to be late."

She lets go of my erection with a wet pop but keeps her hand wrapped around the base. "No we're not. Watch me."

I pull the pillow off my face and place it under my head so I can better do as she commanded. "I'm watching."

She smiles wickedly at me before resuming her task. It doesn't take long for her to bring me to the point of no return. Her ministrations combined with the visual of the most beautiful girl in the world sucking me into oblivion do the trick. I throw my head back and let out a guttural sound as I come into her mouth. Charlie keeps sucking me while pumping me with her hand until I have nothing left to give. With a shudder, I sink back into the mattress utterly spent. Honestly, I didn't think I had it in me to have an orgasm this morning after the all-nighter we pulled.

"All right. That was your ten minutes," she says.

I open my eyes to glare at her. "There's no chance those ten minutes are gone."

"It doesn't matter. You're awake now."

I sit up, grabbing her by the waist to drag her back to me. "Yes, but I'm hungry."

"Fine. Let's get breakfast, then."

She still doesn't get what I have in mind. "I have all the sustenance I need right here. Come on, babe. Sit on my face."

Her cheeks go from pink to tomato red in a split second. "Really?"

"Yeah. Don't make me beg."

She grins. "Like I would."

<hr>

Twenty minutes later—we showered first, it didn't take me twenty fucking minutes to make my girl come—we head down to the kitchen for a quick breakfast. I sit on the stool and watch Charlie work her way around the kitchen like she's racing.

"What's the hurry, sweetheart? It's not like we told Grandma a specific time."

"I want to beat traffic."

"There's no traffic on Sunday."

She pauses to give me a droll look. "You've clearly never visited Ophelia on a Sunday. It's prime visitation day. The place will be packed, and we might not even find a parking space if we arrive there late."

"Wow, I didn't realize families visited the residents that often."

"They don't, only on Sundays. I'm not sure why."

"Maybe they go after Sunday mass because they feel hella guilty."

She chuckles. "Maybe."

"Do you think Grandma knows about us?" I ask.

"How could she? Unless your sister told her."

"I doubt it. Jane is discreet. She wouldn't blabber about my love life to anyone."

"We should invite her to come to LARP next weekend. I'm sure Fred would love the surprise." She smirks.

"Yeah, I'm sure he would." Suddenly, my good mood turns sour.

"You don't have to worry about Fred. He's harmless," she assures me.

"No guy is harmless unless he has no dick."

Charlie rolls her eyes and resumes making coffee. A minute later, she sets a cup in front of me and then leans against the counter with a mug of her own.

We don't speak for a moment as we blow into our hot beverages. I bring the cup to my lips and take a tentative sip.

"You know Andreas has a thing for your sister, right?"

I choke on my drink and also manage to spill some on my jeans. Shit, it's hot. Charlie laughs at my clumsiness.

"How do you know?" I ask, not hiding my annoyance.

"It was obvious. At game night, he couldn't take his eyes off her. And let's not forget that he almost beat Fred up for asking her to blow on the dice for luck."

I run a hand through my hair. I was hoping I had misread the signs. "Fuck. I was afraid that would happen."

"She's eighteen, right? You can't keep all the guys away from her. She's gorgeous."

"Watch me," I retort angrily.

She shakes her head and takes another sip of her coffee.

"You think I'm being ridiculous." I square my shoulders, too tense for someone who just had the best blow job ever.

"Only a little. I mean, I get it. You're protective of your sister, especially considering what hap—" She stops abruptly, her face going ashen as she realizes she said too much.

Edgier than before, I ask, "Considering what, Charlie? What were you going to say?"

I can't mistake the sudden tension on her face or the guilt shining in her pretty blue eyes.

"Jane told me about your brother."

A bucket of ice-cold water pours over my head. I can't breathe. I can't move. I can only stare at Charlie while my heart gasps for air.

"Troy?" She sets the mug down and moves closer.

I put my coffee down with a jerky movement, spilling it all over the counter, and then stand up. "She had no right to tell you that."

"I'm sorry."

"Why are you apologizing? You weren't the one who gossiped." I look at the ceiling, laughing without humor. "I can't believe I just said Jane was discreet a minute ago. I guess I don't know my own sister."

"She didn't mean to gossip. She was trying to make me understand you." Charlie walks around the counter and stops in front of me.

"Why?" I frown, crossing my arm over the sling.

"So I wouldn't smother you to death in your sleep." She gives me a tentative smile, and damn it, it almost works. *Almost.*

"I don't know why she would tell you that. I never speak about Robbie. Not even Andreas and Danny know."

"Why is that?"

I look away, unable to hold her stare when the guilt of my fuckup comes back with a vengeance. I don't want Charlie to see the monster rearing its ugly head.

"Can we drop the subject? Please?"

She touches my lower back and then rests her forehead between my shoulder blades. "Okay. But know that I'll be here for you when you're ready to talk. Always."

The "always" gets to me. It makes me so thankful and yet undeserving of her. I let my brother die. What would she think if she learned that? I swallow the lump in my throat, vowing to never let her know.

"We should go. It's getting late."

I step forward and away from Charlie's touch, missing the contact at once.

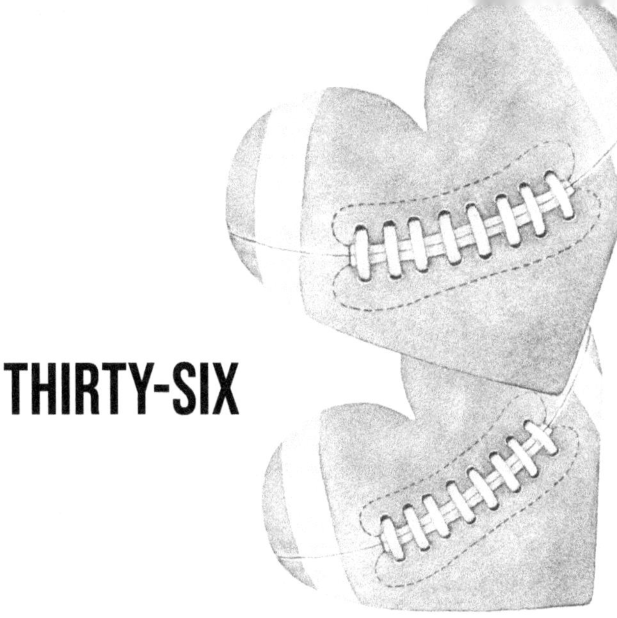

THIRTY-SIX

CHARLIE

I can't believe I let it slip that Jane had told me about their brother's death. It's obviously a forbidden subject, yet I went and blurted it out. *Fuck me.*

Now Troy is acting cagey and moody. His sullen disposition is not only ruining what I was hoping would be an awesome day, but it's also making me feel horrible.

My chest is tight as I imagine what it must have been like for him to lose his brother at such a young age. My thoughts predictably wander to Ben and how I spent my entire life terrified something would happen to him. My concerns haven't lessened as we've grown older—if anything, they've increased—but I'm better at hiding my protectiveness for Ben's benefit. What I confessed to Troy on our date—my crippling fear that prevented me from applying for the exchange program—is something I've never told anyone, not even Blake.

When the sign for Golden Oaks comes into view, I let out a breath of relief. Hopefully, Ophelia, with her quirky sense of humor and no-bullshit attitude, will be able to get Troy out of his funk.

As I predicted, the place is full, but we're not so late that we can't find a parking space. I snag a spot as far away as possible from the main entrance. It's tight, and if my car were any bigger, it wouldn't fit. I turn off the engine and glance at Troy with a small smile on my lips.

"Ready?"

He looks at me, his expression unreadable. My grin wilts as I'm blasted by his cold stare. I begin to turn, but he swings his arm around my shoulders, pulling me to him. His mouth slams over mine, rough and desperate. Wow, the boy is intense. I'm swept away by the passion of his kiss, melting against him. When it seems I'm about to combust on the spot, he pulls back suddenly, leaving me bereft and also so aroused.

Ah shit.

"Okay, now I'm ready." He smirks and then opens the passenger door.

Sweet baby llamas. I can barely think straight after that kiss, and he expects me to get out of the car and walk? I don't even know if I can move my legs.

I pull the vanity mirror down and check my reflection. My lips are swollen, and my light pink lipstick is smeared. I can't go in like this. I search for tissues in the glove compartment, but before I can actually fix my makeup, Troy opens my door.

"What are you doing, babe?"

I whip my face to his. "Fixing this." I point at my mouth.

He chuckles, and immediately, my irritation dissipates. I love when he laughs. My heart does a cartwheel, and a fuzziness in my tummy makes me feel strange. All because I used "love" in a thought about Troy. Does that mean I'm in love with him? My heart skips another beat as an answer. My brain freezes, and a gasp escapes my lips.

"What's wrong?" he asks, his tone filled with concern.

Like a moron, I shake my head. "It's nothing."

Troy keeps staring intensely at me. It doesn't help that my face feels warm, which means my cheeks are giving away my embarrassment. I quickly wipe off the lipstick and slide out of the car. He immediately places his hand on my lower back, sending ripples of heat up my spine and through the rest of my body.

Charlie, control yourself. You spent the night and morning fucking his brains out.

My inner pep talk does little to help me. It actually makes me even more hot and bothered. It won't do to walk into Golden Oaks like this. I have to start thinking of something completely unsexy to rescue my mind from the gutter.

I can't think of anything.

"I forgot to ask, what's going on with the prank we're going to pull on Andy? You didn't forget, did you?" Troy asks, saving me from myself.

"Shit. I kinda did. Let me text Fred real quick." I fish my phone out of my purse and send him a message.

I don't expect him to reply right away—it's too early for him —so when my phone pings with a reply, I'm shocked.

"What did he say?" Troy leans closer, peering at my screen.

"Hey! Stop peeking at my private messages." I push him off, pretending to be offended.

"Do you want me to start developing jealous boyfriend tendencies? Because I will if you start sending private messages to your buddies."

I glance at him, dreading to read truth in his statement. But Troy's eyes are dancing with amusement, and his lips are upturned.

"I like some possessiveness… in the bedroom."

Ah hell. I had to open my big mouth and put me right back into crazy nympho mode.

Troy groans. "Why did you have to say that? Now you've woken Junior." He points at his crotch. There's definitely a bulge there.

"Junior?" I snort. "I didn't know you named it."

"Babe, all guys name their dicks."

"Oh yeah? What do Andreas and Danny call theirs?"

"Excuse me?" He arches his eyebrows. "I'm not going to discuss my friends' penises with you."

This moment is too surreal. I can't believe we're talking about male anatomy when we're a minute away from meeting his grandmother.

We're right in front of the entrance, so I have to school my features. "Okay, okay. Let's try to behave."

"You're the one who started it," he replies tartly.

"You're the one who had to kiss me like you wanted to bang me right there in the car." I poke his chest.

"Keep up with the sassy attitude and that's exactly what I'm going to do."

Heat rushes through my face, especially when I belatedly notice a family right behind us. They must have heard the tail end of our conversation, judging by the wife's horrified expression and the husband's smirk. I let them go in first and won't budge from my spot until I can't see them in the lobby anymore.

Troy seems to have guessed why I'm stalling and doesn't rush me. I take the lead when I'm ready, saying hello to the receptionist working today.

She smiles and then tells us that Ophelia is waiting for us in the gardens. We continue down the corridor in silence. Troy refrains from touching me. I'm glad he's keeping his distance, but I can't help but wonder if he's acting nonchalant now because he doesn't want his grandma to know about us. Not willing to have a repeat of this morning and say what I shouldn't, I stop in my tracks right before we're about to walk out the back door.

"Do you want your grandma to know about us?"

He gives me a quizzical look. "Of course. Unless you don't want her to know."

"I have no reason to hide from her that we're dating."

"Good. Me neither." His eyes seem to twinkle with mischief.

"What?" I ask, immediately suspicious that he's up to no good.

"What if we don't tell her right away, just pretend we're nothing but friends until I sweep you off your feet and kiss you senseless in front of her?"

I stare at him without blinking for several beats until I finally say, "No."

His expression falls. "Why not?"

"Because I don't want to make out in front of your grandmother," I whisper-shout.

He sticks his tongue out. "You're no fun."

Heavens above, why do guys have to act like toddlers sometimes?

We find Ophelia chilling in a lounge chair, sipping a drink that could be regular iced tea or a Long Island. Hard to tell. Her boyfriends aren't around, which surprises me. She smiles when she notices our approach and sits up straighter, pushing her oversize sunglasses over her now pink head.

"Charlie, Wolfie. I was afraid you weren't going to make it."

I give her a hug and then Troy follows me, kissing Ophelia on her cheeks.

"Well, we almost didn't make it," he says.

"Why is that? Partied all night long?"

He gives me a naughty glance. "Something like that."

Ophelia, who is the sharpest lady I've ever known, doesn't miss the gesture. "Oh my. Have I inadvertently played Cupid?"

Hell. I'm blushing so hard now that it's a miracle steam isn't coming out of my ears.

"Gram, you're making Charlie uncomfortable." Troy sits on the lounge chair next to her, leaving me standing there to suffer my humiliation alone.

Jerk.

"What did I say? You're young and attractive. You should be going at each other like ferocious bunnies. I know I would with my boys if my joints allowed."

Kill me now.

Troy makes a face that clearly tells me he's regretting putting me on the spot. *Ha!*

I pull up a chair on the other side of Ophelia.

"Speaking of which, where are Jack and Louis?" I ask.

"Oh, they're out, running errands. I had to send them away because—"

"Jane? What are you doing here?" Troy sits straighter in his seat.

"You didn't know I was coming?" She glances at Ophelia.

"Must have slipped my mind to mention it."

Troy's gaze travels over his sister's shoulder, and he becomes visibly tense. "Oh great."

Curious, I turn around, and see the source of his irritation is an attractive, middle-aged woman who is sashaying in our direction. Her hair is bleached white-blonde, and her sunglasses are even bigger than Ophelia's. She's way too overdressed for a visit at Golden Oaks. She must be Troy's mother.

My spine goes taut, and sudden nervousness takes hold of me. I'm usually not bad with parents—Blake's folks adore me—but I sense it's going to take more than a sincere smile to win this lady over.

"Good morning. I see you beat me here, son," she deadpans.

"Yeah, Charlie got me out of bed early."

Gee, thanks, Troy, for throwing me at the shark without a warning.

She turns to me, and even behind the sunglasses, I can sense her eyes assessing me. I try not to squirm in my chair. If I had known I'd be meeting her, I'd have picked something nicer to wear instead of my faded jeans, Chucks, and a vintage T-shirt. At least my hair isn't in a messy bun, and I put makeup on to hide the dark circles.

"Oh, is that your new roommate?" she asks him as if I wasn't sitting right there.

I jump from my seat and extend a hand to her. "Yes, I'm the roommate."

"Actually, she's no longer my roommate. She's my girlfriend," Troy pipes up.

I swear the woman's handshake tightens when she learns that, and then she drops my hand as if touching me burned her. I wonder if anyone noticed that or if it was just my imagination.

"Is that so? Does that mean you moved out?"

"Uh, no," I say, looking at Troy for help.

Finally, he notices I'm floundering and jumps off his chair to come stand next to me. "Why would she move out?"

"Do you think it's a good idea to live with a girl you just started dating? Living together is a commitment, not a whim." She turns to me. "No offense, darling."

Yikes. Tell us how you really feel, why don't you?

"Oh, sit down, Elaine, and stop raining on everyone's parade," Ophelia butts in. "Just because you couldn't make your marriage work doesn't mean your son can't live with his girlfriend without causing the Rapture."

She twists her face into a scowl. "I'm sorry. I felt it was my duty to point out the obvious. But you're right; it's not my place to comment. Kids are so independent nowadays." She glances at Jane. "But don't you get any ideas. You're not going to move in with any boy while you're still living on my dime."

"Gee, Mother, double standards much?" Troy retorts angrily.

"Oh, honey, society is full of double standards. I'm merely protecting my daughter."

The small hairs on the back of my neck stand on end. Did she just insinuate that my parents don't care about me because they didn't say I couldn't live with Troy? To be fair, they don't know I'm dating him, and I doubt they would bat an eye, considering their marriage is hanging by a thread.

Immediately, my anger dissipates, and it's replaced by an overwhelming sadness.

If I knew how this day would toy with my emotions, I wouldn't have left the bed.

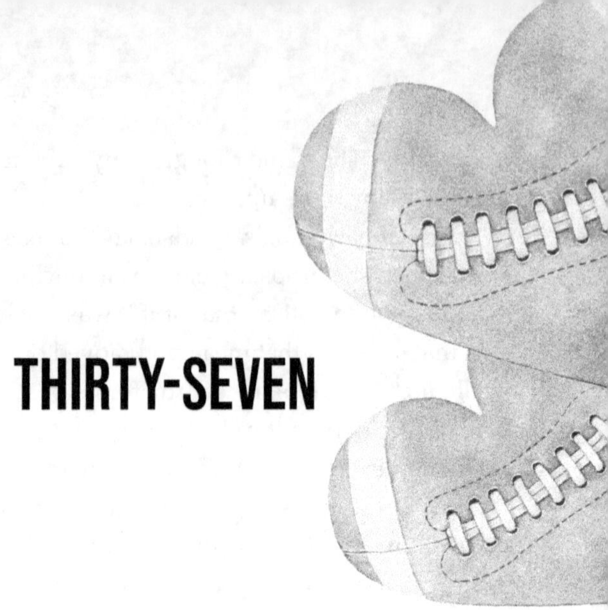

THIRTY-SEVEN

TROY

Charlie is morose after we leave Golden Oaks. I don't need to be a genius to guess meeting my mother put her in that state. Curse the woman and her evil ways. I wish Grandma had told me Mom would be paying a visit today. I'd have canceled ours.

The drive back home is quiet, and not even the radio manages to fill the void.

"Hey, don't let my mother get to you," I tell her once she parks in front of the house. "She's a witch, and she will suck the joy out of you if you let her."

Charlie gives me a pitiful smile. "I'm not upset about what she said exactly. She did remind me about my parents' fight though."

"Do you want to drive to Littleton today? I'll come with you."

She shakes her head, staring straight ahead. "No. Only if Ben needs me. I'm not sure I'm ready to deal with what's coming."

She means if her parents get a divorce. I hate seeing the sadness in her eyes. When my parents split up, I had already been in a dark place, so one more bad thing didn't impact me as much.

"I have an idea. Why don't we invite your friends for another board game party?"

She turns to me, and this time, the smile seems more genuine. She cups my cheek, and because I can't help myself, I take her hand and place a kiss on her open palm.

"Thanks for suggesting it, but everyone is busy today. But I know what can make me feel better."

A sly grin unfurls on my lips as my mind wanders off to Hanky-Panky Town. "What?"

"A Lord of the Rings marathon. It's high time I introduce you to my favorite series ever."

My smile wanes a little as a smidgen of disappointment comes through, but I hide it from Charlie. It's not like we haven't had plenty of sexy times in the past twenty-four hours.

"Sounds good, babe," I reply.

"I promise you'll love it."

"And if I don't and end up falling asleep, I know you have a special way to wake me up." I wiggle my eyebrows up and down.

Her cheeks become bright pink, and suddenly, the air between us is charged with electricity.

"Let's head inside before you get any ideas," she says.

I follow her out of the car, rearranging my cock in a more comfortable position. "Too late; they're already in my head."

When we come to the front door, we find a box waiting for us. It has Charlie's name written on top in block letters.

"What is it?"

She lets out a squeak. "This must be from Fred."

I open the door and let Charlie walk in ahead with box in hand. She sets it on the kitchen counter and peels off the note attached to it.

"What's in the box?" she reads out loud. "Oh my God. No way." She laughs, but I don't get it.

"What's so funny?" I ask.

She widens her eyes. "Come on, Troy. *Seven*? The epic final scene where Brad Pitt loses his mind over the box?"

It finally dawns on me. "Oh shit. Don't tell me Gwyneth Paltrow's head is inside that."

"No, silly. Actually, I have no idea whose head is inside."

Charlie grabs a pair of scissors from the drawer and cuts the tape. The first thing I see when she lifts the flaps is blonde hair and fake blood. Carefully, Charlie pulls the prop from the box. She lets out a yelp and then drops the prop back in the box.

Damn. If she got spooked even knowing what it was, I can only imagine Andreas's reaction.

"Hey, I want to see."

She closes the box again, keeping both hands on top. "Better if you don't."

"Charlie, what the hell? What's in the box?" I know I sound exactly like Brad Pitt now.

She grimaces, keeping her hands in place. "Before I let you see it, you have to understand that Fred has a dark sense of humor, and I'm sure he didn't mean to upset you."

I bristle. "What's that supposed to mean?"

Charlie lets out a heavy sigh. "The head in the box is a fake of your sister."

"What?" I shout, making Charlie wince. "Let me see this."

I pry the package from her and reopen it. Bile pools in my mouth when I remove Jane's fake severed head from the box. It's so lifelike that it feels like I'm holding her actual head.

"This is so fucking wrong," I say. "Why would he pick Jane as his model? Is he a fucking psycho?"

"Oh my God, no. I'm pretty sure it's because he also noticed Andreas's interest in your sister. Like I said, twisted sense of humor."

"We can't use this." I put the head back, wishing now that I had listened to Charlie and not peeked.

"Are you sure? It would be epic."

"Imagine if it were Ben's head."

Charlie's eyebrows furrow, and her eyes become hard, but the moment only lasts a few seconds before she relaxes once more. "Disturbing, but Ben would probably love it."

Now that the shock has passed, I can see the appeal of using the prop. "I guess we could use it if Jane agrees."

"Yeah, and we should totally invite her to come to the party."

"No, absolutely not," I object vehemently. My visceral reaction to the idea surprises even me. I'm protective of Jane, but not to this level. Maybe it's the certainty that Andreas has a thing for her that triggered it.

"Don't get mad at me for saying it, but Jane will start dating soon—guys you don't even know. How terrible would it be if she dated Andreas, your best friend?"

"It's because Andy *is* my best friend that I know he's the last guy on earth I want dating my sister. He's a player, Charlie. The worst kind."

She holds up her hands. "Okay, okay. I'm not going to broach the subject again. What about Fred? Would you *allow* her to date him?" She quirks an eyebrow.

"He just made a fake severed head of her likeness. The answer is a million times no. She's too young to be dating anyone."

Putting her hands on her hips, Charlie stares at me hard. "Troy Wolfgang Alexander, I won't tolerate that kind of Victorian mentality from you. She's eighteen, for crying out loud. I'm sure she's already dated plenty of guys, and you don't even know."

"I seriously doubt it. My mother is stricter than me. And Victorian mentality?" I chuckle. "At least you didn't call me a caveman this time."

"I don't think Neanderthals cared much about who their sisters shacked up with."

"Shouldn't it be *caved* up?"

She throws her hands up in the air. "Ugh! You're impossible.

Just because of that, you're on popcorn duty—and none of that microwave crap. I want the real deal."

I don't move right away, too busy staring at my gorgeous girl. My sexy nerd turns even more irresistible when she's mad and bossy like that. I love it.

I love *her*.

The realization sets in my chest, but instead of becoming terrified, I'm centered, whole. My easygoing smile vanishes when I stride in her direction and slam my lips to hers, claiming her mouth in a possessive way. Her surprise only lasts a moment before she surrenders to the assault.

I'm taken over by a frenzy. I have to connect to Charlie skin to skin right now, or I'll go mad. I yank at her clothes with only one hand since my arm is back in the sling. Mercifully, Charlie is caught in the same urgency as me and shrugs off her jacket and T-shirt on her own. We only break apart when it's necessary to remove a piece of clothing. In less than a minute, I have her bent over on the couch, and I'm fucking her into oblivion.

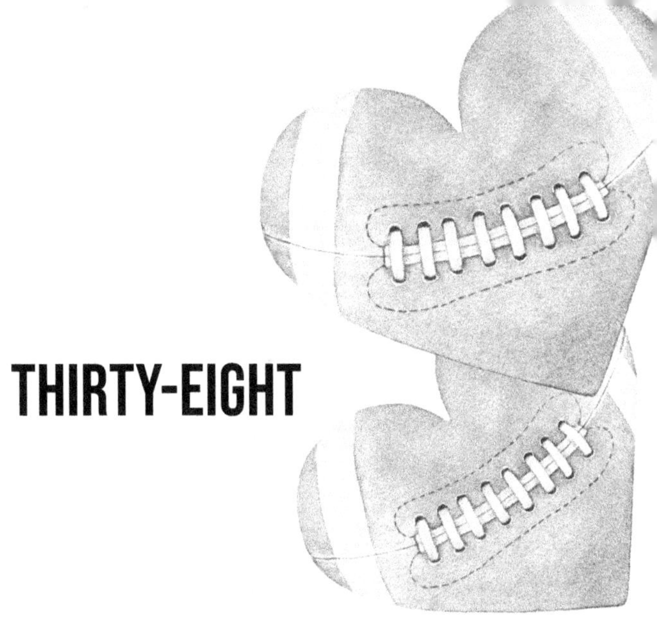

THIRTY-EIGHT

TROY

I'm still trying to come to grips with the realization that I've fallen in love with Charlie fast and hard. I was friends with Brooke first before we went out, and it felt like a natural progression of our relationship. Everything with Charlie is brand-new, and I find myself way out of my depth. I'm only certain of one thing: there's no chance in hell that I'm confessing my feelings to Charlie anytime soon. I don't want to scare her away.

It's no surprise that my protective nature has extended to Ben though. I can imagine pretty well what he must be going through because I also lived through it. Of course, it's worse for him since he's stuck in his parents' house and can't really escape the fights. If his school wasn't in Littleton, I'd suggest he stay with us for a while.

He friended me on social media after we met, so I shoot him a message to ask how he's doing. I was expecting a generic answer, so when he pours his heart out to me, I know I did the right thing by reaching out.

As the week progresses and Charlie doesn't mention any of

the things Ben told me, I suspect he doesn't want to burden her with his problems. I've done that countless times before in order to protect Jane too.

On Thursday, I have a light schedule, but Charlie is stressed about some deadline for the paper. I know I've been keeping her busy, so I decide to make myself scarce and help Ben at the same time. I head to Littleton so we can hang out. The plan is for me to pick him up at school, and then we'll go from there.

I'm a little early, so I park the car and head for the entrance to wait for him. It's easier than trying to tell him where I parked. My head is down, eyes glued to my phone, when the sound of girls giggling catches my attention. I look up and find a cluster of them not too far from me, staring in my direction and whispering to each other. Ah, teenagers making me feel like I'm part of some boy band. I shake my head and return my attention to my phone.

"Hey! Quit staring at my sister's boyfriend like he's a piece of meat," Ben shouts. "Shoo!"

I glance up just in time to see him motion the girls away with a wide gesture of his arms as if they were little birds. The sight is comical. His face is flushed red when he walks over, holding the straps of his backpack.

"I'm sorry about that," he says. "Sometimes I wonder if there's something in the water here that affects the female population of the school. They're more boy crazy than normal."

I chuckle. "It's okay. They weren't bothering me for long. I just got here."

"Good."

We walk back to the car, and I ask, "What do you want to do today?"

"There's something I've been meaning to do for a while, but I've been too afraid to go by myself."

I quirk an eyebrow, curiosity piqued. "What is that?"

"Jane told me you helped her with her fear of heights by taking her bungee jumping. I'd like to try that."

Shit. He's a minor. No operator will allow him to jump without one of his parents present. I'd hate to disappoint him though.

I stop next to my car and wait for Ben to reach the passenger side to break the bad news. "You need parental consent for that since you're under eighteen."

"Got it."

I frown. "You did?"

"Yep. It's all square with the place we're going."

"Okay then. Let's go."

As Ben's turn to jump approaches, I can tell he's getting visibly tenser. It doesn't help that quite a few people had the same idea to jump today. There's a group of guys—probably seniors in high school, judging by their letterman jackets—making a ruckus as they wait in line behind us.

"It's okay, Ben. Try not to think about how high you are. And before you jump, don't look down."

"Okay."

A few minutes later, Ben is all strapped up and ready to go. Right before he steps on the platform, he glances over his shoulder, eyes wide with panic. "I-I don't think I can do this."

"Nonsense. You got this, buddy. Remember, don't look down and let go."

He nods and steps forward. The operator gives him more encouraging words, and after a few more steadying breaths, he jumps with his arms wide open as if he's really letting go of his fear and fully embracing the experience. He shouts in excitement as he drops and doesn't stop hollering when the cord recoils, sending him flying upward again. I take the stairs to wait for him at the bottom. He keeps bouncing up and down for another minute until he eventually loses momentum and swings to a stop.

There's a group of ten kids waiting there as well, and after hearing pieces of their conversation, I realize they're from the same high school as those guys waiting in line with us. This is a senior year dare.

Ben finally comes down, and as the operator helps him out of the harness, I notice a dark stain on the front of his khaki pants.

"Oh my God. Dude! Did you piss yourself?" a guy shouts, pointing at Ben.

Laughter follows and I get ready to step in, but Ben looks down at the mess and, to my surprise, bursts out laughing too.

What the hell?

"I did! I peed in my pants. But it was so awesome!"

A few guys break from the group to high-five Ben, making me relax a fraction. I still eyeball the rest to make sure they aren't talking smack about Ben.

"Hey, Troy. Can you take a picture of me?" he asks.

"Sure."

I snap a few photos, even a few with the guys who high-fived him. We move on when someone else jumps.

"Hey, I have a pair of sweatpants you can borrow," I tell him.

"Okay. Cool. I didn't want to soil your car seat."

"Are you sure you're okay?"

"Yeah. Normally, I would be so embarrassed, but maybe I'm still riding on adrenaline. It's my fault for not going to the restroom beforehand. I usually have to pee when I'm nervous."

"I think everyone does." I laugh.

"Do you ever get nervous before you have to do something?"

I grin. "Heck yeah. I get jitters before every game. But it's also such a rush."

"I get that now."

Back at my car, I open the trunk and pull out the sweatpants from my duffel bag. "Can I be honest with you?"

"Sure," Ben says as he takes the pants from me.

"I'm terrified of going to LARP."

"Really? Why?"

"I had a really embarrassing moment during a school play when I forgot all my lines. I've avoided anything remotely related to theatrical performances ever since."

"That's the beauty of LARP. There aren't any lines to memorize. It's all improv. All you need to know is who your character is, what he can do—such as special powers—and then react to the situation given. It's super fun."

I nod. "All right. If you say so."

Ben heads back inside the building to change. While I wait, I snoop on Charlie's social media profile to check her pictures of past LARP events. It backfires royally when I find way too many images of her with that stuck-up ex-boyfriend. I should put the phone away, but I'm a glutton for punishment and keep scrolling down until I finally come across a few photos of when they were still a couple.

Fuck. Why hasn't she deleted these?

My pulse accelerates as possessiveness takes over. I know it's ridiculous to suffer from retroactive jealousy, but it seems when it comes to Charlie, logic has taken a vacation.

THIRTY-NINE

CHARLIE

Can someone overdose on too much sex? Since I raised the white flag and declared defeat, Troy and I have been doing it whenever we're together. I can't get my fill of him. Even when I manage to carve out time to study or work, thoughts of him invade my brain. It's no surprise that after a week into this sex marathon, I have dark circles under my eyes, and I have to triple my intake of caffeine. I haven't had much sleep.

I'm not complaining. Far from it. Besides all the mind-blowing orgasms I've had, being consumed by Troy keeps my mind from thinking about my parents too much. Dad hasn't returned home, and after a short and painful conversation with my mother, it doesn't sound like he will anytime soon. She mentioned going to couples therapy, but judging by the defeat in her voice, it didn't sound like she believed it would help.

If it weren't for Troy keeping me busy, I would have for sure succumbed to a depressive state. I *am* gutted that my parents might get a divorce, but my main concern in this mess is Ben. I've spoken to him every day. He sounds okay; the upcoming

LARP weekend in a few weeks is keeping his mind occupied. He's helping Tammara with some of the writing too, which is awesome.

It's Friday after lunch, and I'm at the newspaper. I'm behind on an article I have to deliver, and Blake is on my case. He didn't say anything when I came in half an hour ago, but I've been sensing him eyeballing me ever since. Ludwig and Angelica are out, and Blake's constant staring is getting on my nerves. It's already hard enough to concentrate when my eyes want to shut and I can't stop yawning.

Finally, I can't take it anymore and whip my head in his direction. "What?"

"I should be asking you the same question. What's going on with you? I know Halloween is just around the corner, but it's a little early to dress up as a zombie."

"Bite me, Blake."

"See? What's with the attitude?"

"I'm tired, if you haven't noticed, and I have a deadline."

"I'm quite aware of your deadline. I'm the one waiting for it."

I grumble, returning to my laptop. I have to squint my eyes behind my glasses to make the words stop dancing on the screen. It's like I ate magic mushrooms before coming here.

Blake scoffs. "I knew you dating that jock would affect your work ethic."

I jerk my head up to look at him. "Excuse me? How is my work ethic affected?"

"You're late in delivering the article, and Sylvana said you haven't sent your boyfriend's character sheet yet."

"The event is in three weeks. I have time."

"Really? You're just going to deliver that last minute so the other writers have to scramble to fit him in the storyline? Besides, doesn't he want to study the character before he has to play it?"

I rest my head in my hand, letting out a groan. *Crap on toast.* Blake is right. "Shit."

"You forgot you had to do it, didn't you?"

Blake knows me too well.

"I totally did. Troy is going to kill me."

From the corner of my eye, I catch Blake's condescending shake of his head, which turns my irritation into ire. "You don't know what's going on, so keep your judgmental opinions to yourself."

He glowers at me. "No, Charlie, I don't know what's going on with you, and whose fault is that? It's like you've become a different person since you started dating that playboy. You ignore my texts; you don't call back."

"Maybe I'm still annoyed that you stopped by the house to warn him off. That was messed up, Blake."

He sits stiffer in his chair. "It was warranted. Look me straight in the eye and tell me you wouldn't do the same thing for me if the situation were reversed."

I want to keep holding on to my anger, but the truth is, if Blake started dating a girl who had been mean to him beforehand, I'd probably do worse than what he did.

Breaking eye contact, I reply, "You also kept badgering me about this stupid deadline. I wasn't in the mood to deal with Blake the editor."

"I'm sorry if you felt I was only contacting you because of the article." His voice softens. "I've been under a lot of stress too."

Guilt takes away the rest of my annoyance. I've been neglecting my friends since before I started dating Troy. It all began when I moved in with him. "Why are you under a lot of stress?"

He pushes his dark hair back, mussing it a little. "I've applied to a bunch of internships, and so far, I was only called to one interview, and I don't even know if I did well or not."

"I'm sure you aced it."

He shakes his head. "I doubt it. It was last week, and I haven't received a call back asking to come in for a second interview. I'm pretty sure I blew it."

"Where was the internship at?"

"Matrix Media Group."

That's one of the biggest media companies in the country. I'm not surprised Blake managed to snag an interview. He's extremely talented and qualified.

"Wow, that's amazing, Blake."

"It would be amazing if I got the internship. I hate being in this limbo." He dips his chin, threading his fingers through his hair.

"They *will* call you back, and if they don't, fuck them."

"Fuck them?" He chuckles. "It's my dream company."

"So?" I shrug. "If they can't see what an amazing asset you would be to them, then they don't deserve you."

With a smile still on his lips, he glances at his laptop screen. "Only you could make me laugh in my current state."

I lift my cup of coffee in a salute. "Well, at least I'm still good at something. I can't promise I remember how to write though."

Blake's expression becomes serious again. "Writer's block?"

"If only that were the case."

"What's the problem?"

"It's my parents. I think they're going to get a divorce."

Blake glances at me again, his eyes as round as saucers. "Shit, Charlie. I'm so sorry. What happened?"

There's a burning in my eyes and a knot in my throat that I try to swallow. Speaking about my family issues with Blake might not be the best idea. Troy never broaches the subject, and I'm grateful he doesn't. But with Blake, it's a different story. He's almost part of the family, so of course he wants to know what the problem is.

"I don't know. My mother has been complaining he's working too hard, coming home late, and even working on weekends. She accused him of cheating. I think the situation has reached the boiling point." My vision becomes blurry; the threat of a tear spill is very real. But I can't stop now. I have to tell Blake everything. "My father has moved out of the house. I don't know if he'll come back."

A sob escapes my lips just as hot moisture rolls down my cheeks, the first set of tears finally breaking free. I cover my face with my hands, ashamed that I couldn't hold it together in front of Blake. I hate crying in public; it doesn't matter that Blake is my oldest friend and he's seen me at my worst.

I hear the scrape of his chair and then sense his approach. He swivels my seat, then lifts my hands off my face.

"You don't need to hide your sorrow from me, Charlie."

He pulls me up, making me stand so we're almost at the same eye level. I still have to crane my neck a little to stare into his eyes since he's a head taller than me.

"You know I hate crying. I feel so pathetic."

He wipes my cheeks with the pads of his thumbs. "You're not pathetic. This whole situation sucks. It's okay to be sad. I wish you had confided in me sooner. I wouldn't have bothered you about a stupid deadline."

"I was in avoidance mode. If I didn't talk about it, didn't think about it, then I could pretend nothing was going on."

"That's just plain stupid."

I hit his chest playfully. "I'm not stupid."

"I know. But you sure act like it sometimes."

I narrow my eyes. "I thought you were supposed to be consoling me, not making me feel worse."

"You know me. That's how I roll, babe."

He chuckles, and I can't help it, I laugh too.

Then I hug him, pressing the side of my face against his chest. I can't remember the last time Blake and I had a moment like this. I guess since we broke up. That decision was mutual, and there were no lingering romantic feelings on either side. But I think we never wanted to cross the line and give the impression of the contrary. His hand goes to my head, and the soft strokes make me remember the time when we were five and

I fell from my bike and scraped my knee. Blake did the same thing then too.

"Unbelievable." Troy's tight voice sounds in the room, making my blood run cold.

I jump back and turn toward the door. Blake makes an annoyed sound in the back of his throat; I make no sound at all.

Troy is standing there, eyes blazing with fury as he holds a tray with two cups of coffee and a brown bag. He came to surprise me with goodies and found me in an intimate embrace with my ex. No wonder he's glowering, his jaw locked tight.

"Troy, what are you doing here? I thought you had class." I take a step forward, wiping away the remnants of my tears.

He doesn't miss the gesture, which makes his angry expression soften a little. "Class was canceled. The teacher got the flu. I thought I'd surprise you. Funny how things worked out."

His quip feels like a dagger piercing my chest. Even though his expression is no longer murderous, he's still angry.

"Don't get your panties twisted in a bunch, buddy. I was just consoling a friend in need," Blake pipes up.

Troy narrows his eyes. "Right. And I was born yesterday."

Shit. He's not going to let this one go. It's all Blake's fault. If he hadn't shown up at the house to have a talk with Troy, he probably wouldn't be as furious as he is now.

"Oh, what's in the bag?" I ask to change the subject.

He glances at it with a frown, almost as if he forgot he was holding it. "Uh, chocolate-filled croissants."

My favorite. I only mentioned it once in passing, and he remembered. I feel guilty and moved at the same time.

Blake returns to his desk without saying another word to Troy.

Since Troy doesn't seem inclined to move, I walk over and kiss him on the lips. It's like kissing a wooden door. *Damn it.* I feel horrible even though I didn't do anything wrong.

"Thank you," I say.

"Why were you crying?"

"Because her parents are probably getting a divorce," Blake replies bluntly.

"I was updating Blake on the drama, and I kind of lost it. He was just being supportive," I explain.

"Hmm." That's all he says while he glowers at Blake.

What is he thinking?

"Come sit with me." I tug his arm.

"I think I'll go. Don't want to take up more of your time." He heads for the door, and then he's gone. He didn't even kiss me goodbye.

My heavy heart constricts further. In my current weakened state, the tears return to my eyes easily. It's an effort to keep them from falling. I go back to my desk without glancing at Blake.

After a minute, he says, "I knew your boyfriend was an ass."

"Shut up, Blake. Just shut up."

FORTY

Troy doesn't come home for dinner. I begin to worry and call him. It goes to voice mail. I don't trust my voice at the moment, so I text him instead. My stomach is tied in knots as I wait for his reply. I get that he's angry, but why can't he just talk to me instead of giving me the silent treatment? That's fucking mean.

The pasta Bolognese I cooked is now cold and unappealing. If I ate a couple bites, that was a lot. This situation with Troy has taken away my appetite. My heart is too heavy, and my head is too full.

While I wait for Troy to come home, I put on *The Big Bang Theory* in the background and work on his character sheet. He told me he wanted to be a fun troll like Shrek. To me that translates as sarcasm and dark humor. I base the character off Fred, hoping he doesn't notice that Troy will be pretty much acting like him—that is, if Troy still wants to come with me to LARP.

A pang flares in my chest, followed by insecurity. Did I ruin things between Troy and me already? I hate feeling like this, caught in a whirlpool in the middle of the ocean and not knowing which way is up or down.

I have to force the words out, glad it's just a character sheet and not an entire story line. Another five hundred words and I'm done. It's getting late. I check my phone again for the thousandth time. Still no word from him. Maybe he's out with his friends, but he told me he might be playing tomorrow. He wouldn't party the night before a game, would he?

My heart jumps to my throat at the sound of any car that drives by. This is crazy.

I wish Troy had let me explain the scene he walked in on earlier. My fingers hover over his name. I want to ask him when he'll be home, but I don't want to come across as a clingy girlfriend.

Annoyed, I toss the phone aside and stare at the TV screen. It's the scavenger hunt episode, one of my favorites, and yet all the jokes are falling flat.

Tiredness begins to claim me. My eyes are droopy, and several yawns sneak up on me.

I lie down, pulling the blanket over me. My glasses get crooked, so I remove them and set them on the coffee table. Penny just told Raj to run back to India. I want to stay up to catch the final scene of Amy and Howard singing Neil Diamond at The Cheesecake Factory, but I don't.

I wake with a slight shake of my shoulder.

"Charlie, wake up."

I blink my eyes open, and my vision remains blurry for a few more seconds. Finally, Troy's image sharpens. His hair is damp, and I smell fresh soap and toothpaste wafting from him.

Did he just shower?

I sit up, rubbing the sleep from my eyes. "What time is it?"

"It's past eight."

"Past eight? How is that possible? When I lay down, it was already ten."

"It's past eight in the morning."

"What?" I glance at the window, noticing then the light pouring through the blinds. "I slept on the couch? Why didn't you wake me when you got home?"

"It was late, and you looked too peaceful. I didn't want to disturb you."

I get up in a huff, annoyed that Troy let me sleep on the couch even if his explanation makes sense. I would have done the same thing for him. Truth be told, my irritation has a different source. He probably thinks I fell asleep on the couch, waiting for him, which is so not the case.

Liar, liar, pants on fire.

He's already wearing a jacket, and his duffel bag is by the front door. "Are you leaving?"

"Yeah, I have to be at the stadium early." He shoves his hands in his pockets. His sling is gone.

"So you *are* playing today."

"Yeah. Probably not for the entire game though."

The atmosphere surrounding us is thick and uncomfortable with the weight of words unspoken. I can't let him go without talking first.

"Are we okay?" I blurt out, not beating around the bush.

He doesn't speak for several moments, but his hard eyes remain locked on my face. "I want us to be."

I breach the distance between us, even though there's nothing welcoming about his stance. "What you saw yesterday was a friend consoling me. Nothing more."

"And I believe you, Charlie. But there isn't a single guy on this planet who would be okay with their girlfriend being best friends with their ex."

"Are you saying you don't trust me?"

"I don't trust *him*." His eyebrows pinch together.

"Well, then trusting me has to be enough," I retort angrily.

"Please don't ask me to pick between you and Blake, or any of my other guy friends for that matter."

A muscle in Troy's jaw twitches. "I have no issue with you being friends with guys, Charlie. That's not the problem. How would you feel if I started hanging out with Brooke?"

My heart bleeds at the thought. "That's not the same thing. She wants you back!"

Troy takes a step back, pinching the bridge of his nose. "I can't have this conversation with you right now. I'm already running late."

He bends over and grabs the strap of his duffel bag.

"What about tonight? Do you still want me to come to Andreas's Halloween party?"

God, why do I sound so pathetic?

He gives me a quizzical look, and then, forgetting his duffel bag, he steps into my space. He reaches for the back of my head right before he crushes his lips to mine. He kisses me hard and fast, and then, leaning his forehead against mine, he whispers against my lips, "I want you to come. Very much so."

I curl my fingers around his T-shirt, afraid he'll move away. "Good."

I kiss him again, not satisfied with the first one. Troy doesn't end it abruptly like before; he takes his time, savoring my mouth like I'm savoring his. When we finally break apart, we're both a little breathless.

"Was this our first fight as a couple?" I ask.

He chuckles and rubs my cheek with his thumb. "I guess so. Too bad we don't have time for makeup sex."

"I guess we'll have to save that for later." I wink at him, feeling a million times better.

His eyes become hooded and locked on my lips. "Yeah."

I'm not stupid to think this issue is over. I have no plans to cut Blake out of my life, but maybe I need to establish new boundaries. I understand Troy's point of view, and if the situation were reversed, I'd probably be more consumed by jealousy than him.

"By the way, what are you wearing tonight?" I ask.

"Oh, Andy, Danny, Paris, and I are going as the Horsemen of the Apocalypse."

"Who is Paris?"

"A guy on the team. You haven't met him yet."

"And what does your costume entail?"

"An all-black ensemble and skull-painted faces."

"That's cool. I didn't know you knew how to put makeup on." I smirk.

Troy flashes me a toothy grin. "I was hoping you would do it. Of course, if you're busy with your own costume, I'm sure Andy can find another volunteer."

"Hell to the no! I mean, he can get whoever he wants to do his makeup, but no one touches you but me."

Troy's smile grows wider. "That's my girl." He pulls his phone from his pocket and curses. "Shit. I *am* late. Coach will have my balls."

He heads for the door, then stops before walking out to look over his shoulder. "I'd kiss you goodbye, but that would probably make me even later."

"It's okay, babe. My kisses don't expire."

A different emotion crosses his eyes, and I get the impression he wants to tell me something, but all he does is smile before he walks out.

The moment he leaves, my chest becomes heavy again. I rub the spot, trying to soothe the phantom pain away. We parted ways on a positive note, so why the hell do I still feel like the worst of the storm is yet to come?

FORTY-ONE

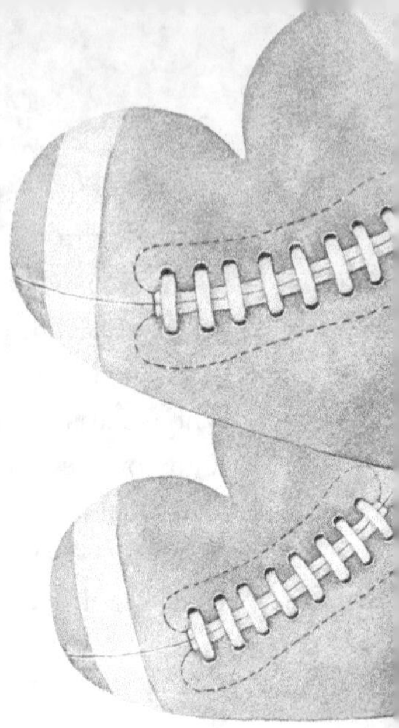

CHARLIE

I watch Troy's game on TV and try not to think about the fact that he didn't ask me to come this time. Was it because he knows I'm not a sports fan, or maybe he secretly regrets me coming the last time? I know my thoughts are irrational and have no merit, but when the camera shows Brooke's face in the crowd, jealousy makes me see red. Her being there might not be because she's still trying to win Troy back. She might enjoy football for real. But that doesn't comfort me. Maybe I should have been a better girlfriend and asked for tickets.

I turn off the TV and stomp to my room. I never asked Troy if Brooke had been invited to Andreas's party, but I'm going to assume she was. I didn't have the chance to put her in her place when I caught her with Troy the last time, but if I see her tonight, all bets are off. What she did was fucked up. Getting drunk and coming on to Troy while I was somewhere in that party. Never mind her cunt of a friend who called Ben names.

This year was the first that I didn't think of a creative Halloween costume. My parents' issue and Troy have kept my mind distracted. It isn't a real problem when half my closet is filled with cosplay outfits, though most of them aren't sexy enough for tonight's party. I only have one that will do. I pull the zipper of the garment bag down and run my hand over the smooth red velvet fabric of Raven the Sorceress's dress. It hugs my curves in all the right places and has a plunging neckline that's made to make men go crazy. She's the master of seduction in our game, a reformed bad girl, per se.

I take my time in getting ready, knowing Troy won't be home for hours. I have a towel wrapped over my head and my body snuggled in my fuzzy robe when I hear the doorbell ring.

Ah crap. Who can it be?

I decide to ignore it, but it rings again.

Shit. I'd better see who it is.

I make sure to tiptoe down the stairs, just in case whoever is outside isn't someone I want to make aware I'm home. I look through the peephole and see Jane standing there.

Doesn't she know Troy has a game?

I open the door a fraction, hiding half my body behind it. "Hi, Jane. What are you doing here?"

"Oh, did I catch you at a bad time?"

"I just got out of the shower. You know Troy is at the game, right?"

"Yeah, but I actually came to see you. Can I come in?"

"Sure." I step away and let her through. This is the first time I've been alone with her, and I'm feeling a little self-conscious to be standing naked under my robe. I pull the lapels closer.

"You must think my visit is super strange, but I have two reasons for being here."

"All right. What are they?"

"I want to see the prop Fred made of me." She sounds eager.

"He didn't make it. His father owns a company that does that for movies."

"Gotcha. So, can I see it?"

"Of course, but let me warn you, it's pretty disturbing." I walk to the closet under the stairs where we stored the box.

"Oh, I'm a horror movie enthusiast. Didn't Troy tell you?"

I wrinkle my nose. "He didn't mention it, but maybe it's because I'm the opposite. I'm slowly going through the first season of *Supernatural*, which, according to him, is the scariest of them all."

Jane laughs. "Oh my God. *Supernatural* is not scary."

"It is to me." I lift the box and then bring it to the kitchen counter. "Here. Have fun."

Jane opens the box like a kid opening a Christmas present. She carefully pulls the head out, then smiles from ear to ear at the sight. "Oh my God. This is awesome."

"Why did Troy think you would have a problem with it?"

She scowls. "Because my brother still thinks I'm a little kid."

"It's because of what happened to your brother, huh?"

"Yeah." Jane's voice grows sadder. My clue to change the subject.

"What was the second thing you wanted from me?"

Her grim expression vanishes, and there's now the hint of a smile on her face. "Oh, I wanted to ask if you could do my makeup for Halloween. Troy mentioned you were doing his."

When did Troy have time to tell her that? I just volunteered for the job this morning. I don't voice my question though. I don't want her to think I don't want to help her.

"Sure. But I warn you, I'm not a professional by any means."

"As long as you're better than me."

"What's your costume?"

"Harley Quinn in the classic black-and-red jumpsuit. I was thinking you could paint my face white and black around the eyes. I want to be unrecognizable."

"That sounds simple enough. Do you have a big party at your high school?"

"Something like that. It's not at my high school. Someone is throwing a party. Don't let my brother know or he might tell my mother."

I don't like that Jane is asking me to keep stuff from Troy, but in this case, I have to agree with her. He's a little too medieval when it comes to her.

"I won't tell. I promise."

"Awesome." She grins. "Oh, one more thing. Can you take a picture of me with the head?"

I laugh. "Sure."

If Fred were here to witness this, he might fall in love with Jane on the spot. But I won't tell him this happened. The last thing I need is one of my friends getting involved with Jane.

Jane is long gone by the time Troy comes home from the game. I'm still wearing my robe, but my makeup and hair are done. He comes straight to my room and sweeps me off my feet while crashing his mouth to mine.

"Troy! You're going to ruin my makeup."

"Fine. I won't kiss you on the mouth, then." He starts to fumble with my robe, pulling the lapels apart while the sash is still in a knot. "Please tell me you're naked under this."

"Yes. Oh my God, what's with you? Is this a postgame shot of libido thing?"

His rough hands cover my breasts, kneading them while he flicks my nipples with his thumbs. "Don't you know sports make men hornier?"

"I never dated a jock before, so the answer is no, I didn't know."

"Well, babe, you're soon going to find out there are more perks to dating a jock than a hot bod." He unties the sash but doesn't bother to remove the robe before he drops to his knees and parts my folds with his hand.

"Troy...." My voice comes out strangled.

Our eyes meet, and I swear I melt under his heated gaze. I run my fingers through his hair, needing some type of anchor. He kisses each side of my thighs, and then he licks my clit, drawing a loud moan from me. With each sweep of his tongue and playful bite, he drives me crazy. My legs can barely support my weight. Troy must have sensed that because he keeps a firm hold on them.

My head is getting dizzy, and suddenly, the room begins to spin. I close my eyes while I try to cling to the sweet moment just before an orgasm, but Troy's caresses are merciless, and when he sucks my clit into his mouth, I lose the battle against my body. I yank his hair and cry out as I attempt to ride the wave of pleasure without collapsing to the floor.

My body is still shaking when Troy unfurls from his kneeling position, picks me up, and almost runs to my bed. A moment later, he's inside me, fucking me so hard that I begin to see stars again in a matter of minutes.

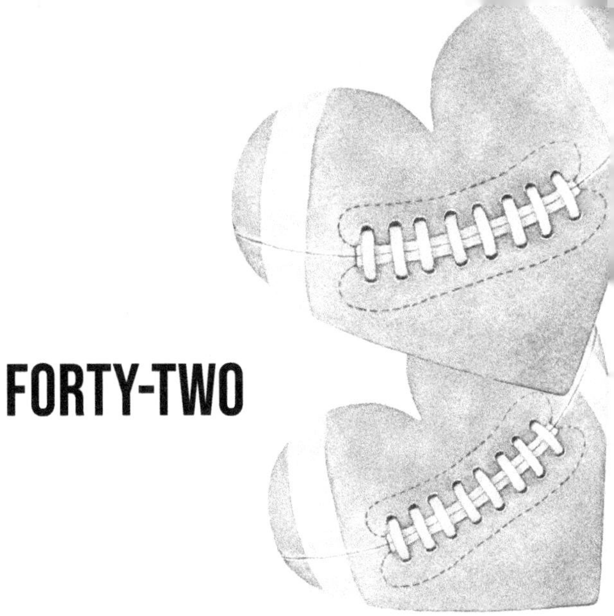

FORTY-TWO

TROY

It was almost impossible to leave the house. When Charlie walked down the stairs, wearing her LARP costume, I couldn't control myself. I dragged her to the couch and begged her to ride me. Now I'm about to park in front of Andreas's building and I'm sporting another boner. All it took was a glimpse of Charlie's golden leg peeking out from the slit in her skirt.

"Ready?" I ask in a gruff voice.

"Yeah." Her eyes drop to my crotch. "Oh, babe. Again? Did you accidentally take Viagra?"

"No, that's all you, darling, and that dress."

She glances outside where a few people wearing costumes are walking in and out of the building. The whole campus is one big Halloween party.

"I could help you out." She reaches for my zipper.

"Oh my God, Charlie. I love you."

Her hand stops, her eyes rounding as she stares at me. Neither of us speaks for a moment. I don't dare to breathe.

What the hell did I just do?

"You love me?" she asks, breaking the silence.

"Hmm." I rub the back of my neck, tongue-tied all of a sudden. How fucking ironic.

"Troy?"

I look away, leaning my head against the car seat. "Fuck. I swore I wouldn't open my big mouth. Please don't get weird on me."

She reaches for my hand. "Why would I do that? I mean, my hands are magical. They get guys to tell me they love me all the time."

There's humor in her tone, but even so, her comment triggers my jealousy. Frowning, I turn to her. "Please don't say that, not even as a joke."

She leans across the gap and kisses me softly on the lips.

"You're going to ruin your makeup," I whisper.

"I don't care." She eases off and stares into my eyes. "Were you scared to confess your feelings to me?"

"Afraid I would freak you out? Yeah." I run a hand through my hair. "This is all new to me. I've never felt this way before. Unsteady, unraveled."

"I feel the same way," she murmurs.

"You do?"

She nods. "I think I've spent the past few weeks equal parts terrified and ecstatic. When I look at you, it almost hurts, like a sweet agony. You rob me of air, Troy."

My heart skips a beat. She might not have said "I love you", but fuck if that doesn't come close enough.

I reach behind her head, tangling my fingers in her hair. Then I lean closer but stop short of kissing her, remembering the reason I can't. "Damn it. Curse my stupid idea to wear skull paint on my face tonight."

A loud knock on Charlie's window makes her jump back and shriek. Paris is outside, grinning like a maniac.

"Holy shit." She places a hand on her chest.

"Come on, Troy. Save sex in the car for the way back home," the idiot shouts.

She rolls her eyes at me. "Let me guess. That's Paris."

"Yep, that's him." I pat her thigh. "Come on. We'd better go before more people start to think we're doing what he said we were."

I get out of the car first, sprinting to circle around it and help Charlie out. Paris and his date are waiting for us by the curb. After introductions are made, we walk together to Andreas and Danny's apartment. Even before we reach the front door, we can hear the loud music echoing in the hallway. This isn't a dorm building, but because it's on campus property, most of the residents are students at Rushmore.

Paris and his date enter the party first, but just as Charlie and I are about to cross the threshold, she grabs my arm. "Oh no. We forgot the head."

"No we didn't, babe. While you were getting ready, I dropped it off. Danny is in the know. He'll place the head in the fridge and signal us."

"I wish Fred were here to see this."

"I'd have invited him if Andy didn't have an issue with your friend," I say.

"I know."

She takes my hand, and we head inside.

Twenty minutes after we arrive at the party, Danny gives us the two-thumbs-up signal. The place is full but not completely packed to the gills. But most importantly, Andreas isn't drunk out of his mind yet. We want him lucid for this.

"Hey, Andy, we're out of Perrier," I say.

"There's more in the fridge," Danny pipes up from the other side of the counter.

Charlie gets her camera ready.

Andreas turns to the fridge. "You and your fucking Perrier, Troy. I swear to Go—" He jumps back, almost falling on his ass. "Motherfucker. Jane!"

I move closer, getting a prime view of Andreas's panicked face. I bet he looks ashen under his makeup.

"What's Andy freaking out about?" Paris pushes him out of the way. "Holy crap. That's freaky." He pulls the prop from the fridge. "Dude, is this your sister?"

I flatten my lips, trying not to laugh. Now that I got used to the sight of Jane's severed head, it doesn't bother me as much anymore.

"It sure is," Charlie replies for me. "Hey, Andreas. Say cheese." She points the camera at him and takes several pictures.

Still stunned, he doesn't lash out at Charlie like I thought he might. Instead, he turns to me, wide-eyed. "What the hell, Troy? That was a sick joke. I'll have nightmares for days. I need a drink." Fumbling through the kitchen, he opens several cabinets until he finds a bottle of Patrón, something he usually hides at parties. He might come from money, but he's stingy as fuck.

Charlie walks over to me, giggling. "Oh my God. That was so epic."

"Did you get everything, babe?"

"Oh yeah. I got the moment on video and then several pictures. Man, Jane is going to love this."

I watch Charlie text my sister, keeping a goofy smile on my face. The crazy feeling in my chest seems to expand. The words Charlie told me in the car make total sense. It's a sweet agony to stare at her and keep my hands to myself when all I want to do is kiss and love her.

Man, I have it bad.

Unable to resist the temptation any longer, I wrap my arms around her waist and bring her back flush to my chest. Leaning close to her ear, I whisper, "I wouldn't mind going home now and having my wicked way with you."

"Troy, we just got here," she replies feebly.

I bite her earlobe. "So? We pranked Andy. That was the highlight of the party."

"When you put it that way," she whispers, leaning against me. "I have to use the restroom first."

Reluctantly, I let her go. While she's away, I step into a conversation with Paris and Puck about today's game. It's easy to lose track of time with those guys. I'm laughing about a joke Paris told us when suddenly, someone yanks my arm, turning me around.

"Charlie?" I frown, noticing her furious expression. "What's going on?"

"What the hell, Troy! I can't believe you would take Ben bungee jumping behind my back!"

"Calm down. Why are you yelling at me? He had a great time."

"Really? You call this a great time?" She shoves her phone in my face. I have to step back and pry the device from her hand to see what she's trying to show me.

It's a video of Ben jumping. Someone caught the whole thing, including when he lost control of his bladder. And then later, there's a shot of him in wet pants. I can't hear what the person who shot the video is saying, but the name of the video makes it clear that it's nothing kind: **Watch this idiot pee in his pants while bungee jumping. HILARIOUS.** If the headline wasn't bad enough, the comments that follow are vile and disgusting. It makes me see red.

Charlie yanks the phone from my hand and strides away.

"Where are you going?" I follow her.

"Leave me alone, Troy."

She bumps into someone coming in and bounces back. Fate would have it that Brooke is the one who collided with Charlie.

"Hey, where's the fire?" she asks with an uncomfortable smile on her face.

Charlie glances at her and, before I can do anything, shoves Brooke so hard that she trips on her high heels and falls down.

"What the hell!"

I'd stop to help her up, but Charlie is already out in the hallway. I can't let her leave in that berserk state.

"Sorry, Brooke," I yell as I run after Charlie.

Charlie took the stairs down and is already one floor below when I catch up with her. I grab her arm, making her stop.

"Babe, please. Don't be like that."

She yanks free from my hold. "Don't be like that? Troy, do you have any idea what this video will do to Ben when he sees it?"

"You don't know if he will."

"Oh my God, Troy. Wake up. Of course he will. Do you know how I came across this disgusting footage? Some guys were watching it and laughing like hyenas." Angry tears roll down her cheeks, making me feel even worse than I already do.

"I'm sorry, okay? Ben was the one who suggested bungee jumping. We couldn't have known that would happen."

"I could have! It's not the first time. Damn it, Troy! And how did you even get the operators to let him jump? He's a minor."

"He said he got your parents' permission."

"That's bullshit. They wouldn't have done that." She throws her hands up in the air. "Ugh! I can't talk to you right now. I have to go home."

"I'll take you."

She raises her hand, halting me. "No. I'm too angry. It's better if you leave me alone."

I get into her personal space. "No, I'm not going to back down, Charlie. You're acting completely irrational. You don't need to talk to me, but I'm taking you home, and that's final."

She shoots daggers from her eyes, and from the way she's clamping her jaw hard and flaring her nostrils, I know she wants to lash out again. But thankfully, she simply whirls around and continues her trajectory down the stairs.

The five-minute drive feels like an eternity. We're seething in silence, and that will only make the resentment fester. I can't believe she lost it like that because of the video. Yeah, it's bad, but she could have talked to me without causing Armageddon.

She's out of the car as soon as it stops. I stay put and let her march up to the front door and disappear inside without following. I'm too fucking angry, and if I go in, God knows what's going to happen. I don't want to make things worse.

I need to cool off, but sitting in the car alone won't do, so I turn the engine on again and take off.

As I drive without direction, I wonder how you can love someone so much and hate the things they do.

FORTY-THREE

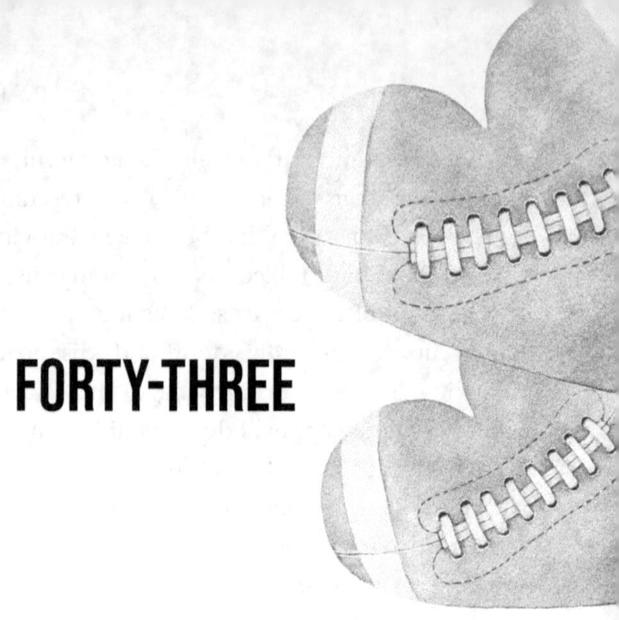

CHARLIE

I'm shaking with fury as I take the steps two at a time. I wanted to punch all those guys who were laughing, watching Ben's video. But when I saw Troy in the footage, all my ire was redirected at him. How could he put Ben in that situation and not tell me about it? I'm so mad, I could scream.

He doesn't follow me in the house. *Smart*. I can't talk to him while I'm so consumed with rage. I hear his car peel away from the curb as soon as I bang the door shut. Once in my room, I pack an overnight bag. I can't stay here. I have to make sure Ben is okay. And when did he and Troy become friends who hang out? Ben never told me about it, and I talk to him every day.

I should change, but I'm afraid Troy will come back, so I just hurry down the stairs and then out the door. Behind the steering wheel, I have to take a couple deep breaths to calm down. I'm glad I didn't have time to drink more than beer at the party, and the anger has burned off all the alcohol from my system.

Traffic is madness. It usually is on Saturday, made worse thanks to Halloween. It takes me forty-five minutes to finally reach the highway to Littleton. My phone rings, and the car dashboard shows it's Troy calling. I guess he's home. Guilt pierces my chest. Now that I'm a bit calmer, I can see that I never gave him a chance to explain. My short-fused temper got the best of me. *Shit*. I even shoved Brooke, unprovoked. *What a mess.*

I let the call go to voice mail. I'm not ready to talk to him yet, and I probably shouldn't while I'm driving. A new song comes on the radio, "Stay the Night" by Zedd and Hayley Williams. It hits me right in the feels. Are Troy and I meant to break?

Tears gather in my eyes, turning my vision blurry. I lean sideways, reaching for the glove compartment. I feel around for the tissue package I have in there somewhere, not daring to take my eyes off the road.

"For fuck's sake, where is it?"

A blaring horn makes me straighten in my seat, and the last thing I see is blinding lights fast approaching.

TROY

Charlie didn't answer the phone. That was hours ago. I've parked my ass on the couch and have been pounding one beer after another. *Where the hell is she?* I would have called Ben if it wasn't so late. Most likely, she went to Littleton.

I still can't believe her reaction. I get she's protective of Ben. I'm protective of Jane too. But she didn't give me the chance to explain. She went total psycho in the blink of an eye. I'd already known she was short-tempered—our beginning is proof of that—but hell, I hadn't expected her to do a one-eighty on me like that.

I'm about to call it a night when my phone rings. My heart skips a beat. Despite the fact that I'm mad at Charlie, the yearning hasn't gone away. I dive for the phone, afraid the call will go to voice mail.

"Charlie, babe, ar—"

"Troy, it's Blake."

My blood runs cold. *What the hell?*

"Where's Charlie?" I jump from the couch, more on edge than before.

"There's been an acci—"

"Where is she?" I'm already veering for the door.

"At Saint James."

"How is she? Is she conscious?"

"She's in surgery. Broke her leg."

"I'll be there as soon as I can. Thanks for calling me."

"Don't thank me. Thank Ben." The line goes silent.

"Asshole."

I slide behind the wheel and gun the engine. The damn beeping sound reminds me to put my seat belt on.

"Yeah, I hear ya, motherfucker."

I click the belt in place right before I take a sharp curve, burning rubber. My heart is pumping like a factory, and my hands are already sweaty from holding the steering wheel too tight. I should be mindful of the speed limit, especially since I've been drinking tonight, but my need to get to Charlie as fast as I can trumps everything.

A traffic jam makes me lose my mind. *No, no, no. I can't get stuck here.* I know if Charlie's in surgery, it'll be hours before she's out, but that doesn't make me less frantic.

Finally, the line of cars begins to move. I decide to take the next exit and get to the hospital via another route. The highway is usually fast, but apparently not tonight.

Another twenty maddening minutes later, I park my car in the first spot I find and then run like a madman through the parking lot. When I burst through the sliding doors of the hospital, I must be quite the sight since I'm still in full skull makeup.

"I'm looking for Charlie Fontaine," I tell the receptionist. "She was brought in earlier an—"

"Troy?" Ben calls out.

I turn toward the sound of his voice.

He walks over and, without hesitation, gives me a hug. "I'm glad you came."

"Thanks for letting me know. Do you know what happened?"

He steps back and wipes the tears from his cheeks. "No. We got the call and rushed here. Mom and Dad talked to the doctors away from me."

We return to the waiting area, and I find Blake, Fred, and a curly haired brunette I haven't met yet. Blake glowers at me but keeps his piehole shut. Fred gives me a sympathetic nod, and the girl simply stares at me blankly. I could be a ghost for all she cares. A middle-aged blonde woman with red-rimmed eyes that are filled with anguish walks over. Charlie's mother, I guess.

"You must be Charlie's boyfriend," she says. "Do you know why she was driving to Littleton so late in the night?"

Her tone is accusatory, and I don't blame her for it. But I can't tell her why without coming across as the biggest asshole in the world. If I had followed her into the house, I wouldn't have let her get behind the wheel.

"She was worried about Ben," I say without elaborating why.

"Why would she be worried about him?"

"Mom, please. It's not Troy's fault Charlie got hurt." Ben jumps to my defense.

Does he already know about the video?

"Is everything okay here?" a male voice asks behind me.

I turn around and lose my ground for the second time tonight. Staring at me is none other than Bill, my mom's boyfriend.

"Dad, this is Charlie's boyfriend," Ben introduces us.

Anger surges within me with the confirmation that Charlie's father has been unfaithful. I can't fucking believe it. There's no trace of recognition in his eyes, and it takes me a second to understand it's because of my makeup.

"Hi, sir. My name is Troy Alexander," I reply coldly, wondering if my answer will trigger his memory. I get nothing.

"Oh. Well, I wish I could say it's nice to meet you, but under these circumstances, I can't. Do you have any idea what Charlie was doing on the road?" His question doesn't have an edge like Charlie's mother's did. Too bad. If it had, I could have given him an answer with a bark.

"She wanted to see Ben," I say.

Guilt shines in the man's eyes, and he doesn't even remember who I am.

Asshole. But I can't think about that now.

"How is Charlie?"

"She has a few bruises on her face thanks to the airbag, but the worst injury is her broken leg. Thank heavens," he replies.

"How long until she's out of surgery?"

"Another hour," her mother replies.

"You look familiar. Have we met before?" Charlie's father asks me, narrowing his eyes.

I know I should lie, but I'm too pissed to do so. In the moment, I want him to know who I am, consequences be damned.

"Yes, we have actually. At a restaurant in Manhattan Beach not too long ago."

He stares at me blankly for a moment, as if he's trying to fish out the memory from his brain. Then his eyes go rounder, his face pale. But instead of confirming it, he schools his expression again. "No, it doesn't ring a bell. If you'll excuse me, I'm going to grab some coffee in the cafeteria."

I glower at his retreating back, but after he disappears around the corner, I feel the full impact of my discovery.

Charlie's father is having an affair with my mother. This will destroy Charlie and Ben.

I'm going to lose her.

FORTY-FOUR

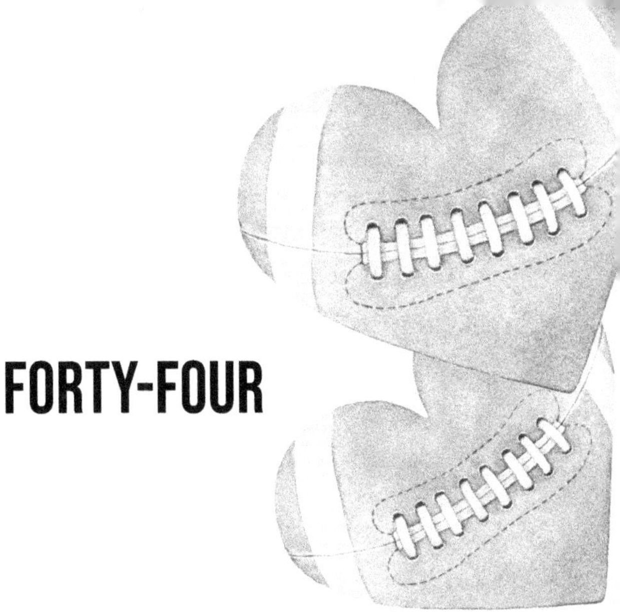

TROY

I ignore Blake to the best of my ability. I don't even know why he's here. Charlie's condition isn't life-threatening, and she's not his girlfriend. As a matter of fact, why was he even called, and who did it?

Charlie is out of surgery now, and her parents and Ben are with her. I wonder if she'll want to see me. I lean my elbows on my knees, resting my head in my hands. If she tells me to go away, I'm going to lose my mind.

A throat clearing catches my attention.

"Charlie is asking for you," her father tells me.

Wordlessly, I get up from my chair and follow him down the hallway. When we turn a corner, he stops in his tracks and turns to me.

"You can't say anything to Charlie."

"Excuse me?"

"Please. I'm begging you. I've decided to end things with Elaine."

I scoff. "A little too late, don't you think? The damage is done."

"No, it isn't done," he grits out. "Tara doesn't know about the affair, and she doesn't need to."

"Oh trust me, she knows."

His face goes even paler than before. He reaches for my arm, gripping it in a tight hold. "Did you already tell her?"

Annoyed, I pull free from his grasp and reply through clenched teeth, "No, I didn't tell her, but she suspects it. Can we go now? I'd like to see Charlie."

He steps back, passing a hand over his face. "She's in room 307."

It's clear that he doesn't intend to walk with me. Whatever. I'd rather not be in his despicable company either.

I continue on alone, and with each step I take, my heart rate accelerates. It's beating at a staccato rhythm by the time I reach her room. The door is open, and from the threshold, I can see her mother sitting in a chair, looking tired as hell as she rests her head on Ben's shoulder.

I knock on the doorframe. "May I come in?"

She stands abruptly, pinching her lips together. I don't know what I did, but she clearly doesn't like me very much. Either that asshole Blake talked trash about me, or she has premonition powers and suspects my mother is responsible for her unhappiness.

"Of course." She glances to the side. "Come on, Ben. Let's give them some privacy."

I step out of the way to let them through, and then I close the door. I don't want anyone eavesdropping on this conversation. Stepping forward, I steel myself for the image of Charlie in a hospital bed, but it does nothing. When I see her bruised face and her leg in a cast, my chest feels like it's caved in.

"Charlie," I murmur.

She smiles weakly. "Hey."

I move to the side of her bed but refrain from touching her. I'm not sure if she'll let me. "Are you in a lot of pain?"

"No. They gave me super-strong sedatives. They're going to

make me sleepy, but I wanted to see you before the drugs dragged me to dreamland."

"I'm here, babe."

"Troy, I'm so sorry for going total psycho bitch at the party. You didn't deserve how I treated you."

A wave of relief washes over me. She's not mad at me anymore. But the sentiment quickly vanishes when I remember the worst of the storm is yet to come. I push those negative thoughts to a corner of my mind, out of the way but easily accessible. A time will come to deal with them, but not right now.

I take Charlie's hand in mine, squeezing lightly before I lean forward and kiss her forehead. "I'm sorry, darling. I should have come after you, not taken off like a coward."

"No, you were right to give me space." She cups my cheek. "I love you that much more for that."

My breath catches, and then a slow grin unfurls on my lips. "You love me?"

"Very much so."

"It's the first time you've told me that, you know?"

Her brows furrow. "No it's not. I told you yesterday."

"Kind of." I run my hand through her hair, unsurprised to see it tremble a little. "When I got the call about you, I got so scared. It was one of the worst days of my life. If anything worse had happened to you, I...." I shake my head as the guilt of Robbie's death becomes a million times heavier. "I couldn't live with myself."

"Troy, what happened wasn't your fault. Just like Robbie's death wasn't."

I recoil as if she'd struck me. "You don't know what you're saying."

"Not the details, but I can read a guilty heart when I see one. Why do you carry such a burden?"

I walk away, giving my back to her. "It was my fault Robbie

died, Charlie. I was supposed to be watching him in the pool. I got distracted, and he drowned."

"You were only eight when it happened. No parent should put that responsibility on a child."

I laugh bitterly. "Oh, my parents were the first ones to put the blame on me."

"That doesn't make it true."

My eyes burn, and the lump in my throat becomes too large. I can barely breathe. "In this case, it does, Charlie."

"Troy, look at me."

Crossing my arms, I look over my shoulder. Charlie's blue eyes are brighter than before, and tears have left streak marks on her cheeks.

I turn fully and stride back to her side. "Babe, don't cry for me. I'm not worth it."

"You're worth these tears and a million more. I'm so sad that your parents let you grow up with that terrible guilt. You're a good person, Troy. Much better than me. Sometimes I think I don't deserve you."

I carefully capture her face between my hands and softly kiss her on the lips. "You've got things twisted around. I'm the one who doesn't deserve you."

The secret that her father asked me to keep comes to the forefront of my mind, making my statement even truer.

She chuckles against my lips. "Fine. Then we're both undeserving rascals who are perfect for each other."

A knock on the door makes me straighten up. Charlie's mother is back and still sporting an unfriendly look.

"Charlie needs to rest. You can come back tomorrow."

"When can she go home?" I ask.

"In a few days."

"I can turn the office room downstairs into a temporary bedroom for you," I tell Charlie.

"Oh, she won't be going back with you. She'll be staying with us for a while."

"Mom, I didn't agree with that," Charlie complains.

"Hush now, honey. You need to rest." Her mother fusses over her, adjusting her pillow and then lowering the bed.

"You should stay with your folks for a while, sweetheart," I tell her softly. "It'll be good for you. I'll come visit every day until you're ready to come back home."

Her mother narrows her eyes, but mercifully, she keeps any retort to herself.

Charlie's eyes are already getting droopy when she replies, "Okay."

FORTY-FIVE

CHARLIE

It's been a week since my accident, and Troy has come by every day to see me. I couldn't fight both my parents when they insisted I recover at their place. Dad patched things up with Mom and moved back. Funny how I don't consider their house as home anymore. The house I share with Troy is home. No, that's not right either. *He* is home. He once confessed I was his endgame. Now I know he's mine too.

Blake, Fred, and Sylvana have come to see me as well, but never at the same time as Troy. I told Blake that he needed to learn to coexist with Troy because he wasn't going anywhere. I don't think he approved of my decision, but he also didn't argue with me. I'm sure me recovering from an accident made him go easy on me.

Yesterday, Troy came over straight after the game, and because it was at the end of the day, he spent the night in Ben's room. Not that he didn't sneak into my room after everyone had gone to bed or anything. It was fun to make out in my old bedroom like two teenagers.

The issue now is, it's morning, and he's still in my room.

"Troy." I shake his arm.

Troy is spooning my side. His arm is wrapped around my stomach, one of his legs is covering mine, and his nose is pressed against the crook of my neck.

"Hmm?" he replies.

"You need to go back to Ben's room. It's morning."

"Five more minutes," he murmurs.

"Psst!" Ben's head pops around the now semi open door. "Mom is up. Just thought you should know."

"Told you." I give Troy a light shove.

He rolls over, miscalculates, and ends up on the floor.

"Ouch," he blurts out.

Ben snorts. "Smooth, very smooth."

"Are you okay?" I crane my neck to get a better view. This whole immobility deal is already driving me crazy.

"Yeah, I'm fine. I'm glad your room is carpeted." He jumps back to his feet with the grace of a cat, and my body responds, remembering Troy's fingers between my legs last night.

Damn it. Now I'm horny again.

At least he's wearing a T-shirt with his sweatpants rather than his usual state of undress, but there's an unmistakable bulge in the front that makes my face unbearably hot.

I glance at the door and let out a relieved breath. Ben is already gone.

"You'd better go before my mother catches you here."

"I'm going. Definitely don't want to lose my visiting rights." He leans over and kisses me on the lips. It's too quick for my liking.

Pouting, I say, "I can't wait to move back home."

"Me too, babe. We'll try to convince your folks again today. If they refuse, I'll just have to break you free like the Weasleys did for Harry in book two."

"Oh my God. I can't believe you know Harry Potter. You're just a nerd in disguise, aren't you?"

"Liking HP is hardly a qualification to be a nerd. Who doesn't like it?"

"Charlie?" Mom's voice echoes in the hallway.

"Crap. She's coming and you're still here."

Troy glances at the door and then back at me. Nonchalantly, he pulls up a chair and sits down.

"What are you doing?" I hiss.

"It's too late for me to sneak out now."

A second later, the door opens, and Mom comes in. "Charlie, wh—oh, Troy. I didn't realize you were here."

"Just came in." He flashes her an innocent smile.

Mom's lips become a thin flat line as she watches Troy through slits for a second. She hasn't warmed up to him yet, and I don't know why. True, she knows about our rough beginning, but he's been the perfect boyfriend from the get-go. I, on the other hand, have messed up royally already.

She turns to me. "I just came to ask what you would like for breakfast."

"I was thinking maybe we could eat out today. I'm tired of being cooped up."

Troy snorts, earning a questioning glance from me.

"What?"

"Sorry, you said, 'cooped up,' and it made me think of chickens."

I don't know if I should laugh or groan and end up doing a mix of both. The source of our amusement flies right over Mom's head, naturally.

"I guess we could go to your favorite diner," Mom replies.

"Really? Awesome."

Troy stands up. "I guess I'd better get into the shower, then."

"What, you're not going to help me with mine?" I joke, loving to see Mom's outraged expression and Troy's are-you-crazy look.

"Ha-ha, Charlie. You're hilarious." Mom comes to help me out of bed, and Troy uses that moment to make his escape.

"I was joking, but it's not like he hasn't seen me naked before."

Mom rolls her eyes. "Trust me on this, save your naked moments for sexy times. You don't want to ruin the magic by making him help you bathe."

I wrinkle my nose. She's right.

Since we're talking about relationships, I ask, "How are things with Dad? Is he going to stay for good?"

"We agreed to go to couples therapy. That's something," she replies in a clipped tone.

"Do you still believe he was cheating on you?"

It makes me sick to my stomach to ask, but I have to think about Ben. I don't want my parents to start fighting all over again. And if Dad was having an affair, that's something I don't think anyone can get past, no matter how hard they try. Once the trust is broken, it's gone forever.

"That's not something I'm comfortable discussing with you, Charlie. Now let's get you cleaned up for that boyfriend of yours." She helps me out of bed.

"How come I have the impression you don't like Troy very much?"

"He took Ben bungee jumping without asking us first, for starters."

"Ben already told you that he lied to Troy and bribed the operator to let him jump without parental consent."

I can't believe he'd do something reckless like that, but considering the shitty situation at home, it's not completely surprising. Ben was only trying to forget about the fighting for a while.

"It doesn't matter. He should have confirmed with us."

Gee, when Mom wants to be stubborn, she's worse than me.

"Well, you'd better get used to him. He's not going anywhere."

Mom locks her eyes with mine. "You love him, don't you?"

"Yes I do."

"I hope he's worth it."

It's impossible to miss the bitterness in my mother's tone. It makes me angry that she can't accept my happiness because her marriage is on the rocks.

"He is, Mom. Troy is worth everything."

<hr>

An hour later, we're finally heading out of the house. My stomach is glued together already, making me regret I ever suggested going out for breakfast. Every little task takes forever with me hopping on one foot. I'm still getting used to my crutches, and Troy doesn't know if he should help or laugh.

"At that pace, we'll get there for lunch," Ben pipes up.

"I don't know, buddy. I think dinner," Troy piles on.

I scowl at them. "Shut up, you two. This is hard."

"Do you want help, honey?" Dad steps closer, but I shrug his outstretched hand off.

"No, I have to practice. I don't plan to sit around the house until the cast is off. I have classes to attend."

"Maybe we should take two cars," Mom says as she joins us outside. "More room for you in the back, Charlie."

I open my mouth to protest, but Troy cuts me off. "I'll take my car."

"Then I'm coming with you," I say, earning a disapproving glance from both my parents.

"Me too," Ben chimes in.

I can see them both gearing up for an argument, but the sound of a car fast approaching draws our attention to the road. This is a residential street; the speed limit is only thirty. Who's driving like this is a Formula One track?

A red sportscar stops in front of our house, burning rubber as it comes to a halt too abruptly.

"Son of a bitch," Troy mutters.

Dad takes a step forward, and a second later, a blonde hurricane exits the vehicle. Troy's mother.

What the hell is she doing here? Looking for him?

"Elaine, what are you doing here?" Dad asks her. He sounds nervous.

She laughs derisively. "Isn't this the picture-perfect image? Jason Fontaine, going out with his precious family." She staggers on her high heels, highly intoxicated, judging by her slurred speech.

"Elaine, you need to leave. Now!" Dad grabs her arm and tries to steer her back to her car.

"No!" She breaks free. "I'm not leaving until I tell everyone what a coward you are."

"I can't believe this," Mom grits out. "Is she the woman you were screwing, Jason?"

My stomach bottoms out. *Troy's mother is my father's mistress?*

I glance at Troy, imagining his shock is the same as mine. But he doesn't look surprised. His gaze is anguished and filled with guilt when our eyes lock.

"I'm sorry, Charlie," he says softly.

"You knew?" I ask, not daring to believe the truth that's right in front of my face.

"Oh yes, Troy's known for a while, right, son?" his odious mother replies. "But instead of standing by me, you betrayed me. You picked his side just so you could keep fucking his daughter."

"Mother! That's enough." Troy grips his mother's arm and drags her to his car. "I'm taking you home."

She doesn't fight him, but even if she did, it wouldn't matter. The damage is done.

I turn around too fast, needing to get away from this scene, and almost fall on my face. Ben reaches for my arm just in time and steadies me. My parents start to argue, but I block them out. I just want to get out of here. With Ben's help, we make it back to the house.

"I think I'm going to be sick," I say.

There's not a chance I can get to a bathroom in time, so I hop on one foot to the kitchen sink and throw up the little bit of food I had in my stomach. My tears come down in rivulets, and even after I quit dry heaving, they don't stop.

"It'll be okay, Charlie," Ben says.

Damn it. I'm supposed to be offering him comfort, not the other way around.

"He lied to me, Ben."

"No, he omitted the truth."

I whip around to face him, incredulous that Ben is defending Troy. "It's the same thing."

Ben drops his chin to the floor. "I like Troy."

His heartfelt admission makes everything ten thousand times worse. I love Troy with all my heart, but how can I stay with him after this betrayal? And even if I could move past it, there's no erasing the fact that his mother broke up my parents' marriage. How can I pick him over my family?

This is hopeless.

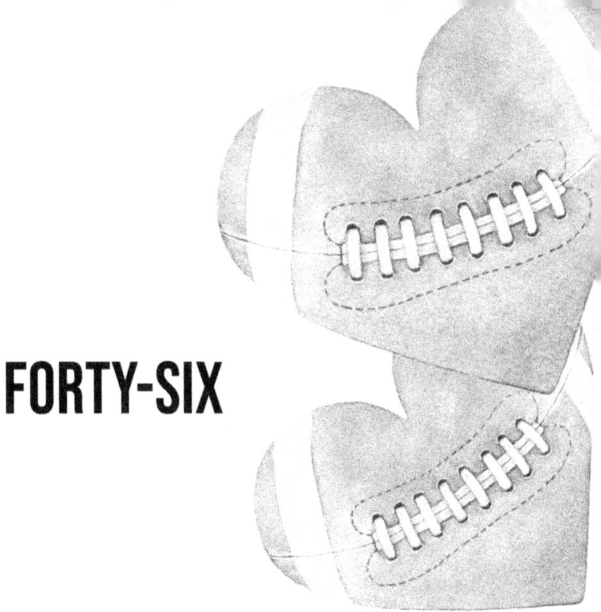

FORTY-SIX

After I drop off my drunk-ass mother at her house, I call Andreas. I know I won't be able to talk to Charlie anytime soon, and I need to vent all my frustrations to someone. I don't disclose anything over the phone, just ask if he's home. He tells me to come over.

I find him slouching on his couch, watching football with a beer bottle in hand and a bag of chips on his lap.

"Where's Danny?" I make a beeline to the fridge. I can't do this without a drink.

"Went to visit his mom." Andreas glances at me and immediately notices something is up. "What's with the frown? Did something happen?"

I chug the beer down, almost emptying the bottle. "Yeah. My mother was screwing Charlie's dad."

"What? Are you serious?"

"I'd never joke about something like that. A few weeks back, Jane and I caught Mom with a mysterious man at a restaurant in Manhattan Beach. It was Charlie's father, only I didn't discover that until I met him at the hospital."

Andreas passes a hand over his face. "That's brutal, man."

"That's not the worst of the story. The asshole asked me to keep it a secret from Charlie. I mean, how fucked up is that?"

"Shit. And you kept your mouth shut and she found out anyway, right?"

I down the rest of the beer. "Yep. In the most spectacular fashion too. My mother showed up at her parents' house, drunk out of her mind, and spilled the beans. I had to drag her ass out of there before things got worse."

"And what about Charlie?"

I stare at the empty beer bottle while I fight to get air into my lungs. I've never felt such agony like this before. "The way she looked at me, man… so broken, and betrayed." I sigh. "I don't know."

"Dude, it's obvious she cares about you. Sure, she'll be mad as hell for a few days, but after you explain you didn't really have a choice, she'll have to understand."

I shake my head, knowing it won't be easy. "You don't understand, Andy. My mother is the person responsible for breaking up her parents' marriage. Even if she could forgive the fact that I kept that information from her, I'll be a constant reminder of the betrayal."

Andreas gets off the couch and heads over to the kitchen. He has his serious expression on, the one he usually saves for game day. "First of all, your mother wasn't responsible for breaking up anyone's marriage. If Charlie's father had an affair with her, it's because he wasn't happy in his marriage."

"Do you think that's going to matter?" I retort angrily, slamming the bottle down on the counter.

"Fine, maybe it won't matter. But if Charlie is really into you like you're into her, she'll forgive you. Grovel, do everything you can to win her back."

"I thought you didn't like Charlie."

He shrugs. "I didn't like her when she was your enemy. I have nothing against her now."

"We haven't broken up."

Yet. I know it's coming. I saw the certainty in her eyes that she believes we're over.

"Then start working on your recover game right away, Troy. You're the fucking Rushmore Rebels' quarterback. You don't know defeat."

I stand straighter. "You're right. I'm not going to give up Charlie without a fight. She's my endgame."

"That's what I'm talk—wait, what? She's your endgame? For real?" His eyes widen.

"Yeah, for real."

"How do you know?"

"I just do. Hopefully, you'll get that someday."

He twists his face into a scowl. "No, thanks. Hard pass. I like my bachelor life too fucking much to give it up. The only chains I'd be down for are the ones that come with whips."

"Why do you have to make everything so dirty?"

He lifts his shoulders in an it-is-what-it-is gesture. "That's how I roll, man. What are you going to do about Charlie?"

"I can't go back to her folks'. It must be war central right now, and my presence would just make everything worse."

"What about your mom's car?"

"Ah hell. I'd forgotten about that."

Andreas grabs his jacket from the back of the highchair. "Come on. We're going back, and now you have an excuse. I'll drive your mom's car, and you talk to Charlie."

"Shit. That means I have to get her car keys first. Great."

"Perfect. That should give everyone time to chill out back at Charlie's."

He heads for the front door like he's about to step onto the field before a game, his shoulders squared and chin high. He said I don't know defeat, but he's the one who doesn't believe in it.

CHARLIE

I've been lying in bed, crying my eyes out since Troy left with his mother. At least my parents are no longer shouting, but only because Mom kicked Dad out of the house. She asked for a divorce—no, shouted for one. Even the neighbors must have heard her.

Troy has called several times and sent a dozen messages. I've ignored them all. I'm not ready to deal with his betrayal face-to-face. I'm so torn about everything. Maybe Ben is right, and Troy was put in a terrible situation. But it changes nothing.

There's a knock on the door, and then Ben pushes it open. "Charlie, are you feeling better?"

"Not yet." I sit up in bed. "How are you?"

"I'm okay. At least now we know."

"You're handling this better than I am."

"I think I accepted it a long time ago." There's a pause, and Ben seems guilty about something. "Troy is here. He wants to talk to you."

"No." My voice comes out in a desperate plea. "I can't talk to him right now, Ben. You know that."

"A-are you going to break up?"

"I'd like to know that too." Troy comes in after Ben, and I feel like my heart stops beating for a second.

"You shouldn't have come."

"No, I had to, Charlie. I couldn't just stay home because it's killing me not knowing where we stand. So, I'll ask you again. Are we breaking up?"

He pierces me with the saddest, most broken gaze I've ever seen on him, and it destroys me. I want to tell him that we can move past this, but I can't form the words.

"I don't think there's any other way," I reply through a choke.

Tears well up in my eyes. My heart squeezes so tight, I can't breathe.

Troy remains stoic, frozen; the only glimpse of emotion I can see are in his anguished eyes. He clenches his jaw and then says tightly, "I'm not going to try to explain myself, or ask for your forgiveness. I know right now, nothing I say will make you feel better or change your mind. I'll walk away and give you the space you need, but I'll wait for you, Charlie. However long it takes, I *will* wait for you."

"Troy—"

"No, don't say anything. You can't ask me to stop loving you. It won't happen. You don't need to move out. I'm going to stay with Andy until you're ready for me to come home."

I'm witnessing the boy I love with all my heart shatter in front of me, and I can't bring myself to end his suffering. I'm frozen, powerless.

Troy turns to Ben and squeezes his shoulder. "Take care of your sister, buddy."

He's gone before I can get a word out.

It turns out, the song was right. We were meant to break.

FORTY-SEVEN

CHARLIE

It's been five days since I broke up with Troy, and I'm a complete wreck. Dad didn't move out like I'd expected him to, but the situation at my folks' is tense as hell. It's gotten so bad that Tammara's parents invited Ben to spend the week with them.

My heart is squeezed tight as I step foot into my house. Good on his word, Troy has moved out, and his absence is like a black hole in what used to be paradise to me.

Fred drove me—I couldn't deal with Blake and his I-told-you-so stare. He sets my bags on the floor and asks, "Do you want me to bring your bed downstairs?"

"What's the point? I still have to go to the second floor to shower and change clothes."

"True."

We don't speak for a while, and the silence begins to smother me.

I sense his eyes burning a hole through my face. Without looking at him, I say, "Out with it already, Fred."

"I know it's not my place to mention it, but are you sure you can't fix things with Troy? You look pitiful."

"Gee, thanks, Captain Obvious."

"I'm serious, Charlie. It's not his fault that your dad is an ass —um, that he cheated."

"I know, but it's his fault for not telling me as soon as he found out."

"Honestly, you can't say you wouldn't have kept your mouth shut as well if the situation had been reversed. You're recovering from an accident."

Fred's words feel like a dagger twisting in my chest. He's not wrong, but I can't even think about Troy without remembering that horrible scene with his drunk mother, telling everyone about the affair.

"Can we please stop talking about Troy?"

"Okay. Well, what do you want to do?"

"I think I just want to be alone for now. Work on some school assignments."

"Okay then. I'm off tomorrow if you want to hang out."

I already know I won't, but it will be easier to decline his offer tomorrow over a text message. If I say no now, he's going to bug me until I agree to do something.

"Sounds good."

As soon as Fred walks out the door, I'm swept under a wave of sorrow. My chest is too tight, and I can't get air into my lungs. I try to watch TV, but quickly, I realize it won't work. The only thing showing is Troy's picture. The sanest thing would be to move out, if I had that option. Everything in this house reminds me of him.

I head to my room. Maybe if I surround myself with my things, it will help. But as soon as I reach the landing, my gaze travels down the corridor to his bedroom door. I move toward it, knowing that opening that door will only make things worse. But I'm a glutton for punishment.

My eyes zero on in his bed, and a choke gets lodged in my

throat. I move toward it and then run my fingers over the mattress. My eyes burn as they fill with tears, and yet I don't turn around to walk away. I lie down and bring his pillow to my nose. I'm drowning in his scent, in his presence, but I don't care.

Can someone die of heartbreak? Because it feels like that's what's happening to me. The tears come through a loud choke, and quickly, they drench Troy's pillow. I hold on to it and don't fight the ugly cry that wrecks me to pieces.

I wake up, bleary-eyed, not knowing where I am for a moment. But Troy's faint aftershave scent reaches my nose, reminding me that I slept on his bed last night. I sit up, rubbing the sleep from my eyes. I feel weak, hollow, but not completely destroyed as I did yesterday. The sharp pain in my chest is still there, though.

Slowly, I get ready for another bleak day. Thanks to the cast, it takes me an hour to get to the kitchen and fix my caffeine deprivation problem. As I wait for it to brew, the tone of a text message draws my attention to my phone. I left it on the kitchen counter yesterday. I'm surprised the battery didn't die.

The name that pops on my screen makes my stomach clench tight. Ophelia hopes I'm going to visit her today. She wants to talk. There's no need to specify the topic. I'm tempted to blow her off, but she's always been kind to me, and in all honesty, I'm in deep need of her advice.

I reply that I'll be there, and then I text Fred. He offered to spend time with me, so that's what we're doing today. His answer comes swiftly. He's a minute from my place. It seems he wasn't going to let me blow him off today and was already en route to kidnap me.

Exactly a minute later, he's knocking on my door. I hop toward it to be faster. I'm getting better with the crutches, but it's still a pain to use them.

"Morning, sunshine," he greets me with a broad smile.

"Why are you so cheerful? Isn't it too early for you?"

"Yep, but I need to bring an extra dose of good vibes to counter your foul mood."

"I haven't had coffee yet." I hop back to the kitchen.

"I brought treats." He follows me.

"Good."

"What are we doing today?" He sets the treats bag on the counter.

"I have to visit Ophelia at Golden Oaks." I grab two mugs from the cupboard, purposely giving my back to him. I'm sure he'll have an opinion about it.

"Do you think visiting his grandmother is a good idea?"

I sigh, turning around. "No. But I owe her an explanation. I broke Troy's heart."

"Hmm. Okay."

Fred doesn't press further, allowing me to have breakfast in peace. I have to force the doughnut down, though because my appetite is gone. The knots in my stomach are taking away all the joy of eating.

We keep the conversation light on the way to Golden Oaks. Fred monopolizes most of it. But by the time he parks in front of the building, I'm a ball of nerves.

"Here we are," he says. "Do you want me to go in with you?"

"No, it's better if I talk to her alone."

He covers my hand with his. "It's going to be okay, Charlie."

I nod, and then get out of the car.

Cheyenne is behind the reception desk this morning, and I wish she weren't here. She hasn't seen me since the accident. Plus, she knows me well and immediately notices I'm a hot mess.

"Honey, is everything okay?" she asks.

"No, not really. But hopefully, it will be better after my visit. Is Ophelia in her apartment?"

"Yes, she's expecting you."

"Okay, thanks."

Ophelia's apartment is an efficient unit with a small kitchen, a living room, a balcony facing the gardens, and a master suite. Once, I asked her if she missed her spacious house, but she said she'd rather live in a small place and have good company than live in a mausoleum alone.

The front door is open, so I call her name as I walk in.

"I'm outside, Charlie," she replies.

I cross the living room, finding her sitting on a chair with a blanket over her lap and a mug of tea between her hands.

"Hi," I say.

She turns to me with a tight smile on her face. "Would you like some tea? The water in the kettle is still hot."

"No, I'm good, thanks." I pull up a chair.

There's a moment of silence when Ophelia just stares at me, making me uncomfortable.

"Where are Jack and Louis?" I ask.

"Probably out, pestering someone. How have you been, dear?"

I shrug. "I've been better."

"Dreadful thing, what happened with your folks." She shakes her head. "Elaine's never had much of a moral compass."

"She didn't sin alone," I reply bitterly.

"No, but that showdown was all her. She's always been like that, creating drama and placing the blame on others instead of owning up to her mistakes."

Ophelia's comment makes me think about what Troy told me. "Did she really blame Troy for Robbie's death?"

Her eyes cloud, and her mouth becomes a flat line. "Yes. She and Jonathan both did. I tried to tell Troy it wasn't true. He wasn't supposed to be looking after Robbie. He was a kid, for crying out loud, and Robbie had his floaties on. Elaine and Jonathan got distracted at the party and didn't notice that he had somehow gotten rid of them. I was the one who found Robbie, drowned in the pool." She closes her eyes and shudders. "It was awful."

"Troy vehemently believes he's guilty."

She shakes her head. "I've lost count of how many times I've told him the truth."

My eyes fill with tears again, and there are too many to keep contained. I wipe off the ones that roll down my cheeks.

"You must think I'm a terrible person to have ended things with him."

Ophelia gives me a pitiful glance. "Oh dear. I don't think that at all. I can read in your eyes how much this separation is costing you."

I drop my gaze to my lap. "I miss him so, so much. But it feels like a betrayal to my mother if I'm together with him. It's stupid."

"No, it's not. You're a good daughter, but remember, you can't keep your happiness on hold because someone close to you is miserable. Life is too short for that kind of nonsense."

Sagging my shoulders forward, I let out a heavy exhale. "I know. I just need more time."

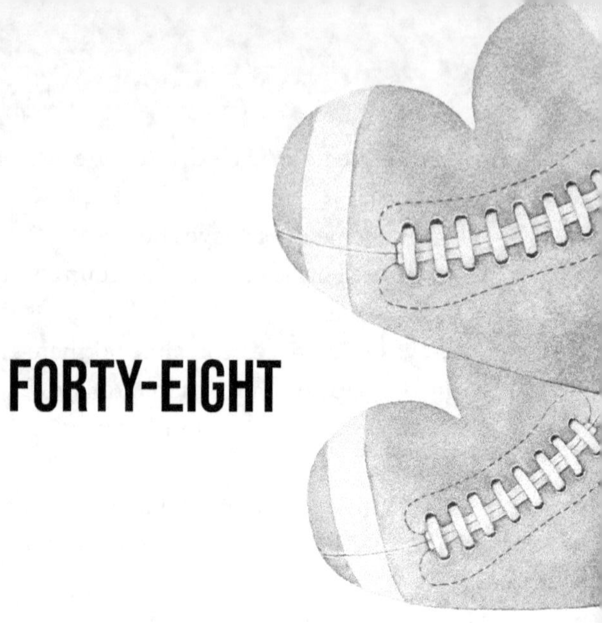

FORTY-EIGHT

CHARLIE

Six weeks have gone by since the breakup. Blake, Fred, and Sylvana all helped me during the first week until I got used to the crutches, and they also alternated in giving me rides to school.

Good on his word, Troy has given me space. He hasn't called or texted. His absence from my life has been glaring, awful. And living in Ophelia's house without him is the hardest thing I've had to do. I thought that with time, the hole in my chest would hurt less, but the pain is as acute as ever.

My parents decided to stay married and give it another try. They've been seeing a therapist, and I hope they can work things out. I don't know how Mom had it in her to forgive him. I know I couldn't forgive my husband if he had an affair, and to be honest, I haven't forgiven Dad yet.

Glutton for punishment as I am, I've been watching all of Troy's games on TV. Whenever I see him on the screen, it feels like a dagger is piercing my chest. God, I miss him so damn much. Is it fair that I'm putting us through this misery when my parents have already decided to put the past behind them?

Ophelia's words come back to haunt me. I said I needed more time, and I think—no, I *know*—I'm ready.

I pick up my phone and pull up Troy's number. I want to text him, but I don't know what to say. Sorry doesn't seem to cut it. He told me he'd wait for me, but I feel like I'm the bitch in this story. He moved out of his own house so I wouldn't have to look for a place to live. He was the perfect boyfriend, and I'm a fucking shrew.

Instead of calling or texting him, I text Jane instead, asking if she can talk. If I'm going to ask Troy to forgive my idiocy, I have to show him how much he means to me. She replies to my message a minute later and tells me she'll come over.

As I wait, I begin to run through ideas of what I could do for Troy. The time speeds by, and before I know it, she's knocking on my door. I've been leaving it unlocked during the day since it's such a pain to move these days.

"Come in," I tell her.

"Hi, Charlie," she greets me, then closes the door. "You know it's not safe to have the door unlocked, right?"

"I know. I'm just too lazy to get up from the couch. Don't tell your brother, okay?"

She makes a face that I can't interpret. "I haven't mentioned you to him at all."

My heart sinks. Why did I think Jane would be sympathetic to me?

"Oh. You must think I'm awful for breaking up with him."

"I get why you did it, but I hate seeing my brother hurting that bad. Are you sure you can't get past what my mother did?"

"I miss Troy terribly, Jane. But I was too caught up in my own pain to be able to stay with him."

"Was?" she asks. "Does that mean you're not sure about your decision anymore?"

"What I did was awful, I know. I hurt him. So saying 'I'm sorry, can I get you back?' won't do."

She widens her eyes in surprise. "Oh my God. You're getting

back together!"

"If he wants me back."

Insecurity takes hold of me. He told me he'd wait, but honestly, I wouldn't blame him if he didn't.

"Charlie, my brother is crazy about you. I've never seen a guy more in love with someone than he's in love with you."

I smile weakly. "I feel the same way about him. You have no idea how agonizing the six weeks have been. Which proves that I'm the stupidest girl alive for ever letting him go."

"I'm not going to say you weren't, but I'm also not going to hold that over your head. I'm guessing you want my help with wooing my brother back?"

"Yes. I want to sweep him off his feet."

Jane laughs. "Sure. It's nice to see a girl making the big, romantic gesture for a change instead of the guy with the boombox outside the girl's window."

"Right? So what should I do?"

She eyes my cast and furrows her brows. "You know Saturday's game is the last one in the season, right?"

"Yeah, I'm aware. I've been following the games on TV."

"I have an idea, but it'll require Andy's assistance and a cheerleader uniform."

My eyes widen. "Oh boy. I'm afraid to ask."

TROY

Six weeks have gone by since I moved out of Grandma's house. I haven't talked to Charlie at all during that time, but I've seen her on campus on a few occasions. Those instances were brutal, and it just made the wound in my chest bleed more. Thank God for football, which has kept me busy. The Rushmore Rebels are kicking ass and taking names. Today's game is the last one of the season, and it feels monumental. It's the end of an era.

The rush of winning games doesn't compare to being with Charlie though. Nothing will ever compare. Ben has been keeping me updated. He's turned into our biggest supporter and believes I've given Charlie enough time to wallow in her guilt. His words, not mine. Their parents aren't getting a divorce after all, and my mother has moved on as well. She's dating a young Hollywood producer. It probably won't last, but at least her new boyfriend isn't married.

A ping from my phone warns me of an incoming text.

> Charlie is going to Golden Oaks this Sunday.
> That's your chance.

I smile at Ben's message. He's the best spy. I text him back saying I'll be there. Despite our breakup, Charlie continues to visit Grandma. I've increased my visits too, but I've purposely avoided going when I knew Charlie would be there. It was an effort to keep my distance from her, but I didn't want to ruin everything by putting the second part of my plan in motion too soon.

On the day we broke up, I had every intention to beg her not to end things. But on the drive to Littleton, I realized groveling wouldn't work. Charlie's protectiveness would kick in big time. So I retreated and bided my time, waiting to strike when her resolve to stay away had weakened. According to Ben, the time is now.

Coach expects us in the locker room in half an hour. Andreas and Danny are already making noise in the kitchen, preparing breakfast. As usual, they're also chatty and loud, but all I can hear from my bedroom are muffled voices as if they're whispering.

When I walk into the room, they stop talking at once and glance at me.

"What are you girls gossiping about?" I grab a box of cereal and fill a bowl.

"Nothing," Danny replies.

"I can't believe this is your last game of the season," Andreas says. "I'm already so fucking sad."

I watch him through slits. "Right. Because you're a big, emotional guy."

"Hey. There's a heart beating underneath all this muscle, bro." He presses a hand against his chest in an exaggerated gesture.

"Yeah, yeah. Just don't cry in your Cheerios, okay?"

Andreas turns to Danny. "Do you see the shit I have to put up with? You'd better treat me better, bro."

Danny shakes his head. "Sure, Andy." He turns to me. "Is Jane coming to the game?"

I stand straighter. Danny's never asked about Jane before. "I think so. Why?"

He shrugs. "No reason. Just curious."

"She asked for six tickets, actually. I wonder who she's bringing with her."

"Maybe your grandma and her two boyfriends," Andreas pipes up.

I groan. "Fuck. You're probably right. I can't deal with them."

"Why? Because they're sharing her?" Danny laughs.

"That's not the problem. The issue is that they love to talk about their sex life."

Andreas wrinkles his nose. "Ew. Why did you have to say that? Now I'm picturing your grandma doing the Eiffel Tower."

"Thanks for putting that image in my head, jackass," I say.

"You started it." He grabs an apple from the fruit bowl. "Come on. Let's go. Talking about geriatric sex is not how I envisioned starting my day."

"Like it was mine," I grumble.

I banish that disturbing visual from my mind and think about Charlie. My heart immediately picks up speed. Tomorrow is the day. If I can't convince her to give me another chance, then that will be it for us. Which means I can't fail.

FORTY-NINE

CHARLIE

I'm staring at my reflection in the mirror, thinking I must be crazy. I'm in the middle of the cheerleaders' locker room, getting ready to perform in front of thousands of Rushmore Rebel fans. This is the grand gesture Jane came up with. With the help of Andreas and his connections, I'm now an honorary cheerleader.

I pull on my skirt, trying to cover more of my ass. Man, their outfit is skimpy.

Vanessa Castro, the soccer player I met at the party I went to with Troy, comes over and stands next to me. "You're looking good, Charlie. The uniform suits you."

"I can't believe I'm doing this." I run my hand over the microskirt.

"Me neither," Heather, Vanessa's twin and cheerleader captain, pipes up. "I don't know how you're going to perform the routine on crutches."

"Please, Heather. All Charlie has to do is stand still and shake the pom-poms while you dance around her. Simple." Vanessa smirks.

"Why are you even here? Don't you have a game or something?"

Vanessa looks at me, then back at her sister. "I couldn't pass up the chance to see this performance. Besides, my game isn't until much later."

"I think it's very sweet that you're doing this for Troy," Jackie, a petite brunette, tells me. "He's such a dreamboat."

"You think every guy on the team is a dreamboat," Heather points out.

"But they are. Why do you think I became a cheerleader?" She shakes her ass and winks at her friend.

Lots of smartass comments pop in my head, but I bite my tongue and keep my opinions to myself. They're helping me, after all. I lock eyes with Vanessa, and she seems to guess exactly where my thoughts went.

"To be fair, most of the girls on campus are boy crazy," she says.

I nod. "I'm slowly beginning to realize that. I've been in my nerd cave for too long."

"And you still managed to snag the most eligible bachelor on campus." She smiles.

"And to lose him." I frown and look around the locker room. "Oh, I'm so nervous. What if I mess up and embarrass not only myself but him as well?"

"You'll be fine." She squeezes my arm.

"Sure, sure. That's why I feel like I'm going to throw up."

"If you need to hurl, you'd better do it now. We're going out in five minutes," Heather tells me.

Shit. Shit. Shit. Why did I let Jane convince me this was a good idea?

TROY

I'm with my teammates, ready to run onto the field. Outside, the crowd clamors, infusing me with the familiar rush of adrenaline. I'm going to miss this. My only regret is that Charlie isn't here to see me play. Hopefully, she'll come to the playoffs. I just have to bring my A-game tomorrow and convince her that we belong together.

With a roar, we storm the field. The crowd goes wild. The band plays our anthem, but not from their usual spot in the bleachers. They're down on the field too. Maybe they've prepared something special for today's game. We head for the bench, and then I notice the cheerleaders are also with the band.

The music changes to a familiar tune. It's only when the actual song spews from the speakers, mingling with the band, that I recognize it. It's "Hey Mickey," but the lyrics aren't the original. Instead of Mickey, the singer is saying Troy.

The band parts, giving space for the cheerleaders to do their routine. Then I see her. Charlie's in a cheerleader uniform, singing along. She can't dance like the other girls thanks to her crutches, but she's shaking her ass to the beat of the song. Her eyes catch mine, and then she winks at me.

"Dude, is that your girl?" Puck, our linebacker, asks me.

"It sure is."

I can't keep my eyes off Charlie. I'm afraid if I do, she'll disappear, and then I'll realize I'm hallucinating the whole thing. I'm grinning from ear to ear as I watch her perform with the cheerleaders. When the song ends, she heads in my direction. I don't wait for her to reach me. I run to her, meeting her halfway, and crush my lips to hers.

The crowd goes even crazier, shouting and whistling.

She drops her crutches and then throws her arms around my neck. God, I missed her mouth, her smell, the sounds she makes when she kisses me. I'm sporting a raging boner in the middle of the football field in front of thousands of spectators, and I don't care one fucking bit.

Charlie breaks the kiss, but her mouth stays close to mine. "I'm so sorry, Troy. I was an idiot for letting my emotions drive you away. Please say you forgive me."

"Babe, I told you I'd wait for you."

"I was afraid you would realize with time that I wasn't worth it."

"You're worth it, Charlie. Get that into your thick head. I love you so damn much. You're not getting rid of me that easily."

I kiss her again, even though I shouldn't. Coach Clarkson is probably about to have an aneurysm because I'm delaying the game.

Someone taps my shoulder. "Okay, lover boy. You'd better save the make-out session for after the game."

I pull back but keep Charlie firmly in my hold.

Andreas bends over, grabs her crutches from the grass, and then hands them over. "Shit, girl, that uniform fits you like a glove. Maybe you should join the squad."

She shakes her head. "I don't think so. I've never felt more self-conscious in my life."

"When do you have to return it?" I ask.

"I don't know. I was planning on bringing it home to wash it first."

My lips curl into a wicked grin. "Good."

We return to the bench, and sure as shit, Coach is fuming.

"Oh no. Did I get you in trouble?" Charlie asks.

I chuckle. "Nah. That's the coach's normal expression."

"I'd better go find my seat. Go break some bones."

"Says the girl with her leg in a cast," Andreas mutters next to me.

I ignore him, way too fucking happy right now to let his comments get to me. I watch Charlie walk toward the bleachers with Vanessa Castro in tow. I didn't even know they were friends. I don't look away until Charlie vanishes from sight.

"All right, everybody, you've had your fun. Now it's time to focus," Coach begins his pep talk.

Knowing Charlie is here to watch me is better than any motivational speech anyone could give me. I've got my girl back, and now it's time to prove that I'm not the unenthusiastic football player she thought I was when we met.

I'm going to play the best game of my life.

CHARLIE

After the game—which the Rushmore Rebels won, by the way—we all head out to celebrate at a pizzeria recommended by Andreas. And when I say we, I mean, Ophelia, her boyfriends, Jane, Ben, and Danny all join us.

I had the best time watching Troy play. It was thrilling, and also sexy as hell to see him in his element. I lost my voice from shouting so much. I couldn't believe how wrong I had been about Troy not giving a fuck about football anymore. He was on fire on that field, and now I understand why his fans treat him like a god. He *is* one.

It's almost eleven by the time we walk through the door. Troy made me keep my cheerleader outfit on, and now he's watching me with that hungry gaze of his that makes my toes curl in my shoes. I thought he was going to pounce as soon as the door closed, but instead, he's just staring at me.

"What?" I glance down. "Something wrong?"

"No, there's nothing wrong. I just want to drink you in first, memorize every inch of your body."

I smirk at him. "I didn't know you had a thing for cheerleaders."

"I don't have a thing for them. I have a thing for *you*. The uniform is just a bonus."

"This cast makes it uber sexy." I lift my leg jokingly.

He walks over, and like they do in the movies, he takes me in his arms and angles our bodies sideways as he kisses me. It's a deep and fast kiss that leaves me breathless. When he straightens us again, I want to jump in his arms. Too bad it's impossible right now. But Troy seems to be having the same train of thought as me. He sweeps me off my feet and heads for his bedroom, taking the stairs two steps at a time.

We don't speak as he carefully sets me on the edge of the mattress. My body is humming with anticipation, and my fingers tingle with the need to touch him. Wordlessly, he kneels in front of me, opening my legs. His warm hands feel like gasoline over my already burning skin.

"You know, I was ready to ambush you at Golden Oaks tomorrow," he confesses.

"Really?"

"I wouldn't have taken no for an answer."

He runs his fingers up my thighs until they disappear underneath my skirt. My clit throbs, ready for Troy's fiery touch, but he stops at the edge of the cheer briefs. Desire spreads through my body like wildfire, but it's my love for the beautiful man in front of me that overflows my heart and takes over everything.

I cup his face, fighting the tears that are quickly gathering in my eyes. "I wouldn't have said no."

His heartfelt smile is like a caress. "You didn't need to make a big gesture to win me over. I would have come running with just a simple text."

"That wouldn't have been enough. I messed up, Troy. I let my fear and anger drive you away. I couldn't accept your love because I was afraid it would hurt my mother and Ben too much. I was a coward." A rogue tear escapes my eye.

Troy reaches for it and wipes it off with his thumb. "No you weren't. It took courage to put your family first."

I capture his face between both hands and bring my face

closer to his. "Never again, Troy. I'll never take you for granted again. You're it for me. Search over."

Looking deep into my eyes, he says, "Search over indeed."

Then he claims my mouth, and we both silently vow to make up for the lost time.

FIFTY

TROY – THREE MONTHS LATER

Today is Robbie's birthday, a date that always leaves me unbearably sad and consumed with guilt. But it's also the first day of a LARP weekend, and after postponing coming to one of those for a month, I couldn't say no to Charlie anymore. I mean, what's a better way to distract myself from the torment of my past than by pretending to be someone else for two days?

The past three months with Charlie have been incredible, but with my looming graduation on the horizon, I have a decision to make. The offer to be an ambassador for a digital media company and travel the world is still on the table. I haven't accepted it yet because I don't want to leave Charlie. I want all my adventures to be with her.

I eye the brochure I picked up from the school administration on my desk. Charlie mentioned once that she considered applying to an exchange program but didn't because of Ben. I could hear the wistful tone in her voice when she told me that story. Ben is thriving now, and their parents are doing okay, so there isn't really a reason for her not to follow her dreams.

My thinking is also self-serving. We could go to Europe together, using our place there as a home base for our travels. I don't know if she's going to see it that way, but fuck it, I won't know the answer if I don't ask.

I grab the brochure and put it in my backpack with my character sheet. Then I glance around my room to make sure I didn't forget to pack anything. When I make it downstairs, Charlie has breakfast ready—coffee, pancakes, and bacon.

"Good morning, babe," she greets me with a big smile.

"Morning. Wow. Is that all for me?" I set the duffel bag down and circle around the kitchen counter to pull her into a hug.

"Yep. You need your energy for this weekend's quest, my dear Gunther."

I chuckle. Gunther Crook is the name we came up with for my character. We must have been drunk when it happened.

I kiss her deeply and would keep it going, but my stomach has other ideas.

"I guess I *am* hungry after that morning workout." I bite her lower lip and then turn around to grab a piece of bacon.

"Don't talk like you were the only one who had to work." She smacks my ass and then saunters out of my reach.

Charlie's phone breaks our silly moment, and I'm glad. I was close to attacking her mouth again, which would have led to more sex. Not a bad thing, of course, but I want to get on the road early to avoid traffic.

She answers, "Hi, Blake."

I try to suppress a groan and fail. Blake and I have agreed on a truce. We'll never become best friends, but we can now be in the same room without arguing... much. It's hard for me to accept their friendship, but he's important to her, and I have to understand that.

Charlie glances pointedly at me, her silent plea for me to be nice. I shove a piece of pancake in my mouth, then smile.

She listens to what he's saying, furrowing her eyebrows a little. "Hold on," she tells Blake.

She covers her phone's mouthpiece and whispers, "Blake's car broke down, and he needs a ride. Fred and Sylvana already left. Do you mind if he comes with us?"

I sigh in resignation. She knows I'd never say no to that, but I appreciate that she asked. "Fine. But you owe me." I point at her.

She rolls her eyes and tells Blake the good news. To be fair, it must pain him just as much to ride with me, so that's something.

It takes just thirty minutes on the road for Blake to complain about something. I've been listening to Iron Maiden, and he has a problem with that.

"Can you please change the music?" he moans from the back seat.

"I guess we can listen to pop for a while." Charlie reaches for the radio control, but I bat her hand away.

"What do you think you're doing?" I ask her.

"Come on, Troy. It's two against one."

I laugh. "Where did you get the impression this was a democracy? I'm driving, and what did we learn from watching your now new favorite show?"

Charlie's shoulders sag forward. Pouting, she replies, "You drive, you pick the music. I shut my cakehole."

I tap her leg. "Exactly."

"Jerk," Blake mutters from the back seat, earning a glower from me via the rearview mirror.

"What was that, bro?"

"Saying what Charlie should have."

Blake is being an asshole, but I choose to let it slide. To be fair, I'm also not playing nice with the music. But to make a point, I listen to Iron Maiden for five more minutes before I switch to a classic rock station. That's my compromise; I'm not going to listen to pop music.

When "Carry On My Wayward Son" by Kansas comes on, I

pump up the volume and sing it at the top of my lungs. Charlie joins me in the singalong, and to my surprise, Blake does too. By the time we arrive at the campgrounds where the event will take place, I'm no longer bothered by Blake's stick-up-his-ass ways.

I'm surprised to see all the cars in the parking lot. I didn't realize it was that big of an event.

"How many people come to these things?" I ask, something I should have done way sooner.

"We usually get ten to fifteen participants, but this is the first spring event, so we probably have double that."

Great, twice as many people to witness my humiliation. I'm glad I'll be almost unrecognizable, wearing my troll costume. It was a good call to not tell the guys I was coming this weekend anyway. Andreas and Danny have been pestering me about it for weeks. If they knew it was today, I wouldn't put it past them to come here to capture my humiliation and post it all over the internet.

I veer for the trunk to grab our stuff, but Blake beats me to it, and not only does he haul out his duffel bag, but also Charlie's.

"I'll take that." I reach for her bag strap.

"Will you relax? I was just being helpful," he says.

"Give it to me. I can carry it," Charlie butts in.

"Nonsense, babe. I'm good." I flash her a smile.

"Fine. Be my guest."

She skips ahead, bouncing her glorious hair. It's longer now, almost to her waist. The movement is hypnotizing, and for a moment, I'm content to just watch her go.

I'm suddenly shoved to the side when someone flings his arm around my shoulders and leans into me. "Troy, my man. I can't believe you actually made it."

Fred, one of Charlie's closest friends, is the one making the fuss. Since he's not a pain in the ass like Blake, and has no past with Charlie, it was easy to warm up to him even after the severed head prank.

"I totally caved. But what can I say? I've seen Charlie's

costume, and it's best if I'm here to fend off any jackass who thinks he has a chance with her." I glance at Blake fleetingly.

"For the thousandth time, I do not want Charlie back," he says before storming off ahead.

Fred pats me on the shoulder. "You really don't have to worry about him. He has zero interest in Charlie as a lover. I think he has a new girlfriend, but you didn't hear it from me. Blake is uber private."

"Like I'd gossip about his love life." I scoff.

Fred grins. "Come on. Let's get you registered, and then it's show time."

CHARLIE

Troy is so nervous, it's adorable. He keeps fidgeting where he stands, watching what everyone does with rapt attention. He told me once that he hated anything theatrical thanks to a bad experience where he forgot his lines in a play, but the beauty of LARP is that it's all improv. You just have to go with the flow and stay in character.

After the dark forces cast a curse across the entire land, my character, Raven the Sorceress, suggests a partnership with Gunther Crook. Blake's character, Philippe Di Biase, is a rogue vampire knight who's against it, but he's also against every idea the group suggests. That's his character.

While Blake is busy with his monologue, listing why trusting a troll is a terrible idea, Troy steps closer to me and whispers, "Why am I not surprised this toad is against me?"

"Shh, you have to stay in character." I elbow him lightly in the stomach.

He pinches my butt in retaliation, daring me with his eyes to say something. I watch him through slits, but then Blake asks Gunther a question.

"Come again?" Troy asks.

"I asked what you have to say for yourself, monster."

"Well, for starters, who are you calling a monster, bloodsucker?"

Blake puffs out his chest. "I'm a valuable member of the king's court. You're nothing but a grotesque creature who lives in a filthy swamp."

Troy crosses his arms and leans casually against a tree. "This 'grotesque creature' is the only one who knows the secret path to the Dark Lord's castle. Don't want my help? Too fucking bad."

Okay, I think he's into it now, but probably because of his feud with Blake. I don't care, he's saying exactly what Gunther Crook would, so everyone is happy.

"Oh, pipe down, Philippe," I intervene. "Gunther is our only hope to save the lands from a much worse threat."

"Besides, if he tries anything, he'll meet my blade," Ben adds, holding his fake sword menacingly.

Troy becomes our guide, and we continue playing until the nonplaying characters make an appearance to put a wrench in our plans. A battle ensues, and when I throw a homemade bag filled with rice at a bad guy and call out a spell, the NP character makes a big show of dying and then drops to the ground. That is apparently too much for Troy, and he immediately loses his shit. He leans his hands on his knees and bursts out laughing. His reaction makes everyone else self-conscious. I grab his arm and drag him away from the scene.

"Hey, where are we going?" he asks.

"You were making everyone uncomfortable when you broke character," I hiss, not wanting to be overheard.

"Ah, babe. I'm so sorry. I didn't mean to ruin the fun."

"I know, but I think that's enough LARP for you for the day. You're still too green."

"I'll show you green." He reaches for my waist and then tosses me over his shoulder.

I smack his back. "Troy, put me down."

He laughs and breaks into a jog, only stopping when we reach our cabin. He kicks the door open, and when he sets me back down, he doesn't give me a chance to talk. His mouth is on mine in an instant, hungry, possessive. His hands explore my body in an urgent way, sliding down my sides until they reach the slits of my skirt. Caught up in his fire, I yank at his costume, fighting with the straps that are keeping his armor in place.

"Ugh, why are there so many of them?" I complain.

"Leave them." He pulls my dress over my head, leaving me standing in nothing but my lingerie.

"Not fair. I'm practically naked."

He answers by getting rid of his pants and boxers. "Not the only one anymore."

His lips claim mine again, and then we're tumbling over the mattress. Troy is between my legs, pressing his erection against my center.

"I'm still wearing my panties," I say against his mouth.

He grabs both sides of them and yanks the fabric, ripping it into two pieces. "Not anymore."

"You owe me a new pair." I grab his face, pulling his mouth back to mine.

"Sure, sure." He enters me fast and hard, drawing a loud moan from my lips.

He doesn't stop or slow down; we're both too horny for making love slowly. The bed creaks dangerously, and I'm afraid we're going to break it. But despite the loud noise the furniture is making, Troy keeps pumping harder and faster until both of us are at the edge of a cliff. He grunts when he comes, and I bite his shoulder when I do seconds later.

This is us. Crazy, impulsive, complete.

Minutes later, I'm resting with my head against his chest. He's still wearing his troll armor, so I make lazy circles with my fingers around his belly button.

"If you're hoping for a second round, I'm going to need a few more minutes," he tells me.

"It's okay. I'm happy just staying like this for a little bit."

We don't speak for another minute, and then I decide to ask something that's been nagging me for a while—what he plans to do after he graduates. We've been avoiding the topic since we got back together, but we can't do that forever.

"Babe, have you decided what you're doing once school is over?"

"I have, actually."

I lean on my elbow so I can see his face, my heart hammering in my chest. "Really?"

"I'm taking that brand ambassador job I told you about."

"The one where you have to travel the world?" I ask through the lump in my throat.

My worst fear is coming to pass. Troy is going to leave me.

"Yeah."

I sit up, putting some distance between us. "It's a great opportunity."

Troy rolls out of bed and then grabs something from his backpack before sitting next to me. "Here."

"What is this?" I grab the brochure from his hand.

"You told me you wanted to study abroad for a semester. There's still time to apply, and the lady at the administration office told me you would be a shoo-in."

"I don't understand."

"I want us to see the world together, Charlie. We'll start with Europe while you're in London. We can travel on weekends. I don't want to go anywhere without you, babe. Those miserable six weeks we were apart were enough."

I'm on the verge of crying, but I keep the tears at bay for the moment. I gave up on the idea because of Ben before, but my brother has proven to me over and over again that he doesn't need me to be his champion. He can fight his own battles.

I want Troy to come to a realization of his own as well. Jane told me what today is, and the haunted glints I caught in his eyes a few times when he thought I wasn't looking killed me. I don't want Troy to keep carrying this immense guilt.

"I will apply under one condition."

"Oh? What is it?"

"I want you to stop blaming yourself for what happened to your brother."

He recoils, closing off his expression in an instant. Facing away from me, he breathes out heavily. "I wish it were that simple, Charlie. My own parents told me it was my fault."

"No offense, babe, but your parents are vile. Ophelia told me what happened. Your parents got distracted, socializing, and didn't see when Robbie removed his water wings. She was the one who raised the alarm when she got near the pool. Do you remember that?"

"No, not really." He presses a closed fist against his chest. "My memories of the pool are blurry at best. My only vivid memory is of my mother shaking me in a rage, screaming it was my fault."

"Oh, Troy." I throw my arm around his shoulders and hug him tight. "I'm so sorry."

He leans into me. "How come Grandma never told me that story?"

"She did, many times over. But I think you just blocked her out."

Troy turns to me. "Thank you for telling me again."

His eyes are so damn sad, but at least the anguish is gone.

"I couldn't let you keep believing that lie. You're a good person, Troy, better than anyone I know. You deserve to be free of that awful guilt."

He cups my cheek. "You're so good to me, Charlie. Sometimes, I think I'm dreaming."

"Not a dream, I promise." I place a featherlight kiss on his lips. "So, do we have a deal?"

"If that means I get to see the world with you by my side, yes, that's a deal."

***** THE END *****

Thank you for reading *Heart Stopper*! Curious to know what's the deal between Andreas and Jane? Keeping reading.

HEART BREAKER

REBELS OR RUSHMORE BOOK TWO

Player. Casanova. Heartbreaker.

I've heard it all. But the truth is, I'm the king of wanting what I can't have.

Jane is a beacon of light I didn't expect to find. Her innocence and joy call to my dark soul.

But she's off-limits, my best friend's kid sister. And I'm a damaged jerk with enough baggage to fill a jet plane.

All it took was one taste for my resolve to stay away to crumble. Now I can't get her out of my head, out of my mangled heart.

If her brother finds out about us, he might kill me. If Jane finds out about my past, she'll never speak to me again.

This love is a disaster waiting to happen, and yet, I can't help going back for more.

ONE

I've lost count of how many times I nearly convinced myself to forget my plan and go home. But I've come this far, and if I chicken out now, I'll spend the rest of my life wondering what could have been.

I'm tired of pining for Andreas from afar. I was fifteen when we met. He was a freshman at Rushmore and my brother's new teammate.

Charming, attentive, and so beautiful it was impossible not to develop a crush on him instantly. I didn't know then about his reputation, but it wouldn't have changed what I did. An impulsive and foolish act that has left me mortified ever since. After that, he simply kept me at arm's length. I was nothing more than his best friend's kid sister.

Everyone says he's a player. It's the reason Troy pretty much forbade me to even glance in his direction. But I need to see it with my own eyes, which brings me to my current situation. I'm standing in front of Andreas's building in the chilly night air dressed as Harley Quinn, an outfit that offers zero protection against the cold, and I can't move.

For fuck's sake, Jane. Seize the moment. It's now or never.

I'm a ball of nerves. There are a lot of people coming and going, all ready to celebrate Halloween. I keep my gaze down, afraid someone will be able to tell I'm a high schooler and don't belong here.

I adjust my Harley Quinn cap to make sure it's hiding my blonde hair. My face is covered by makeup thanks to Charlie, my brother's girlfriend. I'm not even wearing perfume to be safe. I feel bad that I had to lie to her. She thinks I'm going to a party with my high school friends. I hope that with my outfit, she won't recognize her handiwork.

As I get near the party, my heartbeat accelerates, and then it pumps to the rhythm of the loud music coming from Andreas's apartment. No sooner do I step foot inside than someone shoves a red Solo cup in my hand. I hold on to it for a while, trying to blend in, but there's no chance in hell I'm drinking from it.

At first, I search for Troy and Charlie. Wherever they are, I have to keep my distance. Andreas's apartment has four bedrooms and an open living room and kitchen space. For a college pad, it's rather large. With the number of people here, I should be able to fit in and remain incognito.

Andreas has only one roommate, Danny Hudson, who I spot first, and only because of his blond curls. He, like Troy, is dressed as one of the Horsemen of the Apocalypse, and has full skull makeup on. He's chatting with a pretty girl dressed as Gamora from *The Guardians of the Galaxy*. It seems everyone got the painted face memo tonight.

A few other people are familiar, like the guys from the football team. But so far, no sign of my brother, Charlie, or Andreas. I realize then that I might have waited too long to come. A lot of people are already super drunk. If Andreas is nowhere in sight, it's possible he's already hooked up with someone. My heart sinks at the probability.

I berate myself for the idiotic feeling. I don't know what I was expecting. No one gets a reputation for being the biggest manwhore on campus for nothing. Someone bumps into me from behind, sloshing the liquid inside my cup all over the front of my costume. It has a red tinge to it, but for the love of God, I can't figure out what it is. All I know is that I have to clean up before it stains. I whirl on the spot, and fight my way through the throng of people until I reach the hallway leading to the bedrooms.

I've been here once with Troy as soon as Andreas moved in, so I know which one of those closed doors leads to his bedroom. I should use the bathroom in the hallway, but my feet take me to the end of the corridor. My hand reaches for the doorknob, and then I freeze. *What if he's with a girl in there?* My stomach ties into knots. It will probably destroy me, but on the other hand, it would force me to get over him once and for all.

I take a deep breath and brace for the worst, but before I can actually turn on the knob, the door opens inwards, dragging me forward with it. I stumble on my high heels, and crash against Andreas's solid chest. He grabs my arms, stabilizing me.

"Whoa, careful there, girlie." He chuckles.

My heart leaps up to my throat and gets stuck there. I look up, terrified he's going to recognize me. Immediately, I know that's not going to happen. His eyes are a little glazed, and the sexy smile on his lips is not something he ever bestowed upon me. It sends tingles down my spine.

"Were you looking for me?" he asks when I don't say a word.

My tongue feels thick in my mouth. *Come on, Jane, don't fuck it up now. This is your chance.*

"Yes," I croak.

His smile broadens. "You found me, babe. Would you like to come in?"

"I guess."

I guess? Good grief, girl. You're dying to go in.

He opens the door wider and lets me through. I stop in the middle of the room, trying not to show how nervous I am. My heart is pounding furiously inside of my chest, and all I can hear is my pulse drumming in my ears. *Oh my God. I'm in Andreas's bedroom.*

"I dig your outfit," he says, stopping next to me.

I turn to him. His skull makeup is a little smeared and his hair is messier than usual. For a second, I wonder if I'm the second girl to come through his bedroom door, but his bed is immaculate.

"Thanks. I like yours too."

He smiles again, and then reaches for my face, cupping my cheek. "What's your name?"

"Harley," I blurt out.

Andreas chuckles. "For real? Sweet."

He steps closer, invading my personal space. I'm shaking so hard, I don't know how I haven't fallen to the floor yet. He brushes his thumb over my lips, sending shivers of pleasure throughout my body. My breathing catches.

"You're beautiful," he says, leaning down.

He's going to kiss me and I'm seized by overwhelming panic. *What if he remembers?*

"How can you tell?" I ask through a parched throat.

"Trust me, babe. I know."

He closes the final distance between us, pressing his lips against mine, tentatively at first. I thought I'd be ready for it, but I forgot what kissing him was like. It's fireworks in July. It melts my body; it scrambles all the thoughts in my mind.

I reach for his biceps, needing an anchor to remain standing. He pries my lips open with his tongue, deepening the kiss. I taste alcohol, something sweet and potent, but I can't distinguish what. A heady feeling takes over me, like an ice-cold fever. I let go of his arms in order to link my hands behind his neck. A distinctly possessive groan comes from deep his throat, which acts like gasoline poured over my churning fire.

He pulls back suddenly, leaving me lightheaded and unsteady.

"What's wrong?" I ask stupidly.

"Nothing is wrong, babe. I just want to ask if this is okay."

My brain is fuzzy; I'm too lost in him to be able to form a coherent thought.

"I wouldn't be here if I had a problem with it," I say, faking confidence.

He reaches for the back of my head and kisses me again. It's hungry, greedy, and nuclear. It sets me ablaze; it ignites a fire deep in my core that won't be extinguished by anything besides him.

This is completely insane. I came here to finally put to rest my obsession with him. And now all I want is for him to take my clothes off and make me his, even if it's only for one night. There's no getting over him.

He breaks the kiss again to whisper against my lips, "I want to fuck you. Tell me it's what you want too."

I try not to wince at his crude admission. In all the times I fantasized about this moment, in none of them Andreas was drunk and without a clue of who I was. But he's also my weakness, a drug I can't let go of. I want him with every fiber of my body. None of the boys I kissed after him made me feel this way.

"Yes. More than anything," I murmur.

Relief shines in his green eyes right before he pounces. His mouth slams against mine, fiery and intense. His hands make quick work of the invisible zipper on my back. Before I know it, he's peeling off my catsuit, leaving me exposed in only my underwear. Goose bumps spread all over my skin when it meets the cold air. Without breaking the kiss, Andreas continues his eager exploration. He runs his fingers down my arms, and then he moves along to my breasts, squeezing both through my bra.

A moan escapes my lips, followed by his approving chuckle. Dropping his hands to his sides, he steps back to glance at my body.

"Damn, you're more beautiful than I imagined."

I cross my arms over my chest, feeling insecure under his scrutiny.

"What are you doing? Don't cover those lovely tits, babe." He pulls my arms down, and then he steers me to his bed.

I'm shaking so much that it's a relief to sit down. Andreas remains standing as he stares at me with eyebrows slightly furrowed.

Oh God. He finally figured out it's me.

"What?"

He shakes his head. "Nothing."

Grabbing the back of his shirt, he pulls it off and tosses it aside, revealing abs so perfect, they look photoshopped. He's the definition of male perfection. My mouth waters. I've never wanted to lick something as much in my life as I want to lick his taut skin. I'm surprised by my train of thought. I didn't think I had it in me to have such naughty inclinations.

The corners of his lips twitch up, but he doesn't make any comment about my ogling. Instead, he proceeds to get rid of his pants and boxers. My jaw drops to the floor when I take in the sight of his erection. I'm not a prude. I've watched porn before. But this is the first time I'm in front of the real deal. Panic begins to take hold of me. I don't know what to do now. He's going to know this is my first time. *Ugh.*

While I'm freaking out, he steps forward. His cock is right in front of me. Maybe he wants me to suck him. I don't move though, just keep staring at it like a moron. This is a disaster. Maybe I should have drank something before attempting to seduce Andreas. Not that I had any idea this would happen.

"You can touch it if you want, babe," he says in the huskiest voice I've ever heard.

It makes my pussy throb. *Gee, if he can do that with only words, imagine what he could do with his mouth there.*

Before I lose my nerve, I reach for his shaft, curling my fingers around his girth. He hisses, and then reaches for my cap. *Shit.* He can't take it off. He'll figure who I am if he sees my hair.

"I want to stay in character," I tell him.

"That's fine by me." He caresses my cheek and I'm surprised by the tenderness.

My heart overflows with emotion, but I have to remember his gesture doesn't mean anything. To him, I'm nothing more than a hookup.

I return my attention to his cock. The skin is smooth and warm, and when I begin to pump him up and down, he seems to grow larger.

"That's it, babe," he says gruffly.

Encouraged by his words, I bring the head to my mouth, licking it first to get a taste. He grunts loudly, motivating me to continue my exploration. At first, I think I'm doing it all wrong. I don't know if I should keep using my hand while I suck. The silver lining is that if I'm awful at it, he won't know it was me. But soon I find my groove, and my worries take a back seat.

When Andreas makes a guttural sound and pulls back suddenly, it alarms me. I worry that I accidentally bit him.

"What did I do?" I ask, wide-eyed.

"I don't want to come in your mouth. I said I was going to fuck you and I meant it."

He walks over to his nightstand, and takes a condom packet from the drawer. The jitters return stronger than before. This is really happening. *Oh God.*

He turns to me and frowns. "We don't have to continue if you don't want to."

I shake my head. "I haven't changed my mind."

Then why are you staring at him like deer caught in headlights? To prove my point, I reach behind my bra and release the clasp. The fabric drops onto my lap, but Andreas's eyes remain glued to my breasts. My nipples are as hard as pebbles, and I'm not sure if it's because of the temperature in the room or his heated gaze.

"Jesus, are you trying to kill me?" he asks.

"No, not really," I answer, and then realize his question was rhetorical.

Heat creeps up to my cheeks.

He looks into my eyes and smiles, revealing his adorable dimples. Butterflies take flight in my stomach. His dimples were my undoing when we first met three years ago, and they still have the same power over me. Without breaking eye contact, he brings the foil packet to his mouth and tears it open with his teeth.

I swallow the huge lump in my throat when he rolls the condom down his shaft. This is it. No going back now—not that I want to stop what's about to happen. Andreas has awakened something primal in me. He's ignited a rebellion in my heart, in my soul. I'm tired of being the good girl, the obedient daughter. Being with him tonight is not only about sleeping with the man I've pined after for years; it's about me breaking my shackles.

Condom in place, he joins me in bed, sitting next to me. His eyes drop to my lips as he reaches for my face and cups my cheek. The gentle touch is at odds with his callused hand, and yet it sends chills down my spine. Silently, he brings his lips to mine. I expected a gentle kiss, but his tongue is possessive now.

We fall onto the mattress together side by side. While Andreas devours my mouth, his hand plays with my breasts, kneading and teasing them. Then he draws his fingers down my stomach, pebbling my skin in their wake. Right before his hand disappears underneath my panties, I gasp and freeze.

He pulls back, looking into my eyes. "Do you want me to stop?"

My pulse is thundering in my ears, my blood is rushing through my veins. There's only one possible answer.

"No."

I want his lips back on mine, but he maintains eye contact while his fingers slowly continue their travel south. He parts my folds, and then sweeps his index finger back and forth over my clit. I arch my back, closing my eyes as the most amazing sensation quickly spreads through my core. I've played with myself before, but this feels ten thousand times better.

"Damn it, you're so ready for me already, babe."

He keeps playing with my bundle of nerves, but when he teases my entrance, I open my eyes and grab his wrist.

"I don't want your fingers there. I want your cock."

God, did I really say that out loud? My face is burning up. Thank fuck for the makeup.

"As you wish, beautiful."

He takes my panties off and then rolls on top of me. The head of his erection is pressing against me now, slowly nudging in. I kiss Andreas hard to hide the fact I'm shaking like a tree in the path of a hurricane. He matches my enthusiasm with his tongue and with his hips. The first thrust is agony. He's so big that I don't even know how he can fit inside of me. But as he begins to move in and out, the pain morphs into something bearable, and then it becomes really, really good.

"Oh my God. You're so fucking tight," he murmurs against my lips.

On instinct, I raise my knees and hook my ankles behind his ass. He seems to like this new position if I'm to judge by how his grunts become louder and his thrusts faster. A familiar sensation begins to build below. I feel like I'm floating on air. But when the orgasm hits me, I'm unprepared for it. I scream against his mouth, I bite his lower lip, I scratch his back. I've never felt anything remotely similar when I've masturbated.

Andreas's climax follows mine in the next moment. He doesn't scream like I did, but he lets out a string of curses, only stopping when the tremors in his body cease. With his face pressed against the crook of my neck, he collapses on top of me, breathing hard.

My heart is beating so fast, I'm afraid it will burst out of my chest. I did it. I fucked Andreas's brains out like I'd dreamed a thousand times before. I should feel terribly guilty that I concealed my identity from him, but right now, I'm too happy to care.

TWO

ANDREAS – TWO MONTHS LATER

One of my timers is beeping, and I can't find which one. I turn around too fast and end up bumping my elbow against the flour bag, sending it to the floor in a cloud of white dust.

"Motherfucker!"

Danny comes into the kitchen then, rubbing sleep from his eyes. "What happened?" he asks through a yawn.

"I can't find my damn timer."

He raises an eyebrow. "And you decided to get your revenge on the bag of flour?"

"Yeah, that's what I did, smartass."

He circles around the mess and pulls the timer from under a recipe book. "Is this what you're looking for?"

I yank the gadget from his hand. "Yes. Ah, my sponge is done."

Danny eyes the mess over the counter—I'm not a tidy baker—and then reaches for another timer tucked between the sugar and the cart of eggs. "Why do you need more than one?"

"Different things need different times in the oven."

"Makes sense. What are you making today, anyway?"

"Lorenzo's birthday cake."

"Oh, I didn't know it was coming up. What kind of decoration are you doing?" Danny grabs my set of measuring spoons and begins to twirl them around his finger.

With a jerky movement, I retrieve them. He knows I don't like anyone messing with my stuff. "Nothing crazy."

"What? No *Paw Patrol*?" He smirks, earning a droll look from me.

"He's twelve, not five."

Danny shrugs and heads to the living room. "I'd love a *Paw Patrol* cake for my birthday."

"I'll keep that in mind," I grumble.

"The question is: why are you baking a cake? Isn't that your stepmom's department?"

The mention of that snake turns my mood sour. It's bad enough that I have to suffer her presence during special occasions. I don't need my roommate reminding me she exists.

"Probably. But I want Lorenzo to have something from me. Plus, he loves my cakes."

Danny looks at me from the couch. "Dude, do you want me to come with you to his party?"

His question makes me pause. Danny knows why I hate going to my father's. I blabbered my ugly secret to him in a moment of drunken stupidity.

"Don't you have a date or something?"

"I can cancel. It's not like I'm really into this chick." He shrugs.

As tempting as his offer is, I don't want to subject Danny to my personal nightmare. "Nah, it's okay. I'm just going to stay for the cake and then bail. I'm taking Lorenzo out for a proper birthday celebration another day."

"Okay. But do me a favor and quit stressing about baking. It's just cake." He turns the TV on.

"I'm not stressed," I grit out.

"Sure, sure."

"I just don't like to suck at things."

"Dude, you don't suck. Your cakes are better than my mother's. Just don't tell her I said that."

He can't possibly understand where I'm coming from. His mother idolizes him and thinks he can do no wrong. My father, on the other hand, believes I'm always screwing up. No matter how hard I play on the field or how many games I win, he's never satisfied. He's always pushing me to play harder, be better, through any means necessary.

Fuck. My mood is definitely rotten.

If he knew I have a hobby, I'd have to face his wrath. That prospect used to terrify me when I was younger. Not anymore. He wants me to dedicate all my free time to training. He's been pushing me to go pro, even used his connections and got scouts to come see me play. I'm a good player, but not good enough to be drafted to the NFL. That doesn't deter him and his delusional ideas though.

Playing professional football was never my dream. Baking, on the other hand, has always fascinated me. I used to watch my mother in the kitchen when I was younger, and sometimes she let me be her assistant. After she died, I relegated those sweet moments to a far corner in my mind. The memories were too painful. But reality TV, of all things, reminded me of my interest in the craft. I watched *The Great British Baking Show* one day and got hooked.

Now I know what I want to pursue. I'm switching my major from business to hotel management since they don't offer culinary arts as a degree at Rushmore—and my asshole father wouldn't pay for it. I want to own a baking company someday, and a degree in hotel management will offer me more tools than a simple business degree. He's not going to approve, so I'm not asking for his permission.

The man is a NASCAR legend. He was big in the nineties and made a lot of money. Since he was the shit back then, he won't tolerate his offspring being less than what he was. The fact his oldest son won't go pro will be a big hit to his ego.

I push thoughts of him to the back of my mind and focus on finishing Lorenzo's cake. This will be the only good part of my day, and I don't want to spoil it by worrying about my dad and his awful wife.

I arrive at my brother's party late on purpose. I simply couldn't stomach being in my father's house for hours until they cut the cake. My father's mansion is in Malibu. He and Troy's father are almost neighbors.

Not surprisingly, there's valet, but I opt out of it, parking my Bronco on the side of the road. I plan on making a quick exit. Cake in hand, I circle back and enter the house through the staff's entrance. It's the quickest way to the kitchen and the path most likely to be devoid of obnoxious obstacles, such as Crystal's phony friends. They're as bad as she is.

There's a flurry of movement in the kitchen, making it resemble a restaurant and not a home. Immediately, I spot the cake Crystal ordered for Lorenzo. It's weird as shit, more like an abstract sculpture than an actual cake. I bet it cost a pretty penny. I feel like an idiot for bringing my own. Whatever, I'll eat it, and I know Lorenzo will too.

"Who are you?" a man wearing a chef hat asks me in a French accent.

"The birthday boy's big brother." I set my cake in a corner on the counter.

"Oh, you're not supposed to be here. Mrs. Rossi will be most displeased."

"Pardon my French, but I don't give a flying fuck about Mrs. Rossi." My answer drips with venom, and it's a surprise I don't choke on it.

Jesus, Andreas. Get your act together.

"Andy!" Lorenzo's voice pulls me out of my funk immediately. "You made it."

He walks over and aims for a cool handshake, but I'm having none of it. He's my baby brother and he's getting a proper bear hug.

"Happy birthday, squirt." I rub his head for good measure, messing up his hair.

"Dude, cut it out." He tries to break free from my hold, but I have pounds of muscle against him. He'll get there though. He's almost as tall as me already.

I finally let him go, laughing when he tries to fix his hairdo.

"So, what's all this?" I point at the fancy food I know he won't touch.

He shrugs. "All Crystal's idea. This is more a party to show off to her friends than to celebrate my birthday."

"Did you get to invite any of *your* friends?"

"Yeah, a few."

"Any hot babes?" I elbow his arm playfully.

"Hot babes?" He chuckles. "You've been watching *Cobra Kai*, haven't you?"

"You got me there. It's a good show."

"Told ya."

I love my brother. He has the gift to pull me out of my crappiest moods. When our mother died eight years ago, it felt like we had nothing left in the world besides each other. Our father had been absent our entire lives save when he wanted to put the fear of God in me through punches and threats. That didn't change once Mom was gone. It only got worse.

"Don't worry about this party. We'll do something cool this week."

"Okay. You're coming to my race tomorrow, right?"

"Yeah, of course." I fake enthusiasm.

It's not that I don't want to support my brother, but going to his kart race means rubbing shoulders with our father. It's his first time racing in the junior class, so I have to be there.

"Pierre, I'm still waiting for the—Andy, when did you get here?" Crystal sets her soulless eyes on me, and just like that, my cheer is gone.

She walks over in a skintight outfit that's definitely not appropriate for a kid's party. Her fake tits don't even bounce when she moves, not that I'm staring at them. I have too much hatred toward the bitch to ogle her body.

Lorenzo sidesteps quickly, leaving me wide open to be engulfed by her unwanted hug. The scent of her overly sweet perfume mixes with all the vodka she's had already, making me nauseated. I don't return the hug. Instead, I suffer the unwanted proximity stiff as a board.

When she steps back, I'm sporting a glower. She runs a hand over the front of her dress, smoothing invisible lines, and pulling the neckline down to reveal her cleavage. She's trying to use the same tricks as before, only I'm no longer a gullible fourteen-year-old virgin.

"I thought this was supposed to be Lorenzo's party. I don't remember when he acquired a taste for French cuisine," I say.

"It's never too early to learn to appreciate the good things in life," she replies with an air of smug arrogance.

One would think she was born with a silver spoon in her hand by the way she talks. In reality, she's just a generic gold digger.

"Where's my cake?" Lorenzo asks me, interrupting our conversation.

I turn around and point at the white box in the corner. "There. I hope you like it."

"You got him a cake? What for?" Crystal asks in a high-pitched voice. "I spent a fortune ordering from the best bakery in LA."

"Don't care. Have your cake and eat it too," Lorenzo replies with a chuckle.

"Oh, you're a brat. Wait until your father hears about this."

She turns on her heels and walks out of the kitchen, almost

colliding with a server who was coming in. I expect her to lash out at the guy, but she strides forward without a glance in his direction.

Lorenzo makes a face. "Oh, shit. If she tells Dad we were picking on her, he'll probably ground me."

Dad never laid a hand on Lorenzo, at least never in front of me, but my brother's comment makes my blood boil nonetheless. Crystal used to pull that shit every time when I was still living with them, but it was only with me. I was stupid to believe she wouldn't continue her manipulative ways after I moved out.

I don't want her to mess up Lorenzo's party more than she already did, so I follow her, hoping I can convince the viper to forget my brother's quip. He's the only person in the world who could make me seek her of my own accord.

I catch up with her as she's veering toward the main powder room. "Crystal, wait up."

She turns around on her heels, and in her drunken state, almost falls on her ass. She's too shitfaced to appear embarrassed.

"Andy, are you ready to apologize?"

"For what? We did nothing wrong."

Shit. The wrong thing to say. I came to try to smooth things over. But I can't play nice with her.

"Oh?" She raises an eyebrow, and her dark eyes seem to shine with mischief.

She opens the door to the powder room and drags me inside with her. It takes me by surprise, and it's the only reason I don't resist right away. The door is not even closed and she's all over me.

"Oh Andy, I've missed you." She flattens her body against mine, making me sick to my stomach.

I push her off me in disgust, making her stagger back. "What the fuck are you doing?"

"Giving you what you want. What's your problem?" she retorts angrily.

"I didn't come here for this. I want you to leave Lorenzo alone. It's his fucking birthday, for God's sake."

"Oh, Andy. You were always so concerned about your brother. But that didn't stop you from screwing his nanny, did it?"

I'd never punch a woman, but if Crystal were a man, I'd pound her face flat. "Fuck you."

I walk out of the powder room, seething, and make a beeline to the front door. From the corner of my eye, I catch a glimpse of my father, chatting with a guest. I'm sure he wants to grill me about something, probably offer criticism about my last game's performance. *No, thank you.*

I hear him call my name as I walk out the door, but I don't stop. I keep moving, mighty glad that I parked my car outside. Jesus, I was expecting an ambush from my father, not from his deranged wife. I can't believe I ever felt anything for the woman. She's a despicable human being, I can see that clearly now. But to a naïve fourteen-year-old, she was a fucking angel.

THREE

JANE

My head is about to explode. Against my will, my mother dragged me to one of her boring ladies' luncheons and so far, all she and her obnoxious friends have talked about is the upcoming debutante ball they help organize. Mom is the head of the committee, which means this year, I must take part in it.

Debutante balls are not super common in California, but the affair involves planning an uber exclusive and ostentatious party, plus all the pre-event mixers, and those are right up my mother's alley. But if I hear the info sheet of another possible escort candidate, I'm going to hurl.

My stomach twists into knots and the desire to puke the salad I just ate is real. *Shit*. I *am* going to be sick. I excuse myself and make a hasty exit out of the ballroom. The sign for the restroom looms ahead, but when I see a group of girls my age veer toward it, I change course. If they hear me puking my guts out in that bathroom, the gossip will spread like wildfire throughout my mother's circle. The last thing I need is Mom

Dearest thinking I'm knocked up. That's what she would do instead of believing I had an eating disorder.

Hell. What if I am pregnant? Come to think of it, I haven't had my period since my hookup with Andreas. It's been almost two months. *Oh my God.*

I break into a run in the hotel lobby, hoping to find another restroom not currently occupied by anyone I know. A twist in my guts warns me I might not have enough time. On instinct, I follow someone from the reception desk through a door that says "Employees Only". It opens to a narrow corridor with several doors lining each side. One of them says "Restroom". *Thank heavens.*

I make it to a stall a second before my salad comes up my throat. My grotesque noises echo loudly in the tiled room, and I'm glad there's no one here to witness my humiliation. I hug the toilet until I'm dry heaving. There's a film of sweat on my forehead now, and my headache is as acute as ever.

Major disaster was avoided, but my heart is constricted painfully inside my chest. I can't believe I didn't stop to consider the possibility I might be pregnant until now. On the night I slept with Andreas, we used a condom, and I saw him discard it afterward. But what if there was some leakage?

I pass a hand over my face, feeling incredibly lost all of a sudden. I can't tell any of my friends about it because inevitably someone is going to blab to a parent and my mother will find out. I also can't go to Andreas. He doesn't even know it was me at his Halloween party. This is so messed up.

In a daze, I get out of the stall, and wash my face and mouth. My mother must be wondering where I am. I'm still lost in thought when I bump into someone coming into the restroom in a hurry. Her bag slips off her shoulder, falling to the floor and spewing a stack of flyers in the process.

"I'm so sorry," I say, even though the collision wasn't really my fault.

"Don't sweat it. I'm always bumping into people because I'm always running places. Story of my life."

She drops into a crouch to collect the flyers that are spread around her bag. I do the same to help her out. The bright colors and the group of girls wearing tight clothes, helmets, and roller skates catch my attention. I hold on to one and read the text, intrigued.

"Do you like roller derby?" she asks.

"I've never been to one." I keep my eyes glued to the flyer.

"It's so much fun. You should come next Saturday. I'm playing." She taps her index finger over one of the girl's faces. "That's me. I'm a jammer."

I look up, finding her smiling brightly at me.

"Cool. I'll try to make it. What's your team called?" We both unfurl from our lowered positions.

"Second Time Around Divas. I know, it's a mouthful, but it fits us."

"I like the name. I'd better get going before my mother sends a search party for me."

"You're a guest at the hotel?" She raises an eyebrow.

"Not exactly. I'm attending a luncheon."

"Why are you using the staff's restroom? Did you get lost?"

I shake my head. "It's a long story. Thanks for the flyer."

"No problem. I hope to see you at the game so you can tell me your long story." She winks at me.

I nod before slipping out of the bathroom. It's only when I hit the fancy hotel lobby again that I realize I didn't ask her name. I glance at the flyer one more time before I fold the paper neatly into a small square and tuck it inside my bra. *Classy, Jane, so classy.* I can't let Mom see this under any circumstances. She'll criticize my interest. But something about the girls on the picture called to me, and I want to find out what it is.

When I approach the table, I see that the second course has already been served. It's soup, and it's probably cold. It's not likely I can eat anything now. I don't want to risk another bout of nausea.

No sooner do I sit back down than my mother asks, "Where have you been?"

"I had to use the restroom." I give her a meaningful glance, hoping she'll drop the subject. Let her think I was taking a shit. Better than the truth.

"Well, you'd better not eat anything else then."

"Yeah, I probably shouldn't." I slouch against the chair, relieved that I don't have to force any more food down, but worried sick about the possible reason why I can't keep it in my stomach in the first place.

Mom and her friends resume their conversation about the debutante ball, and I tune them out. As soon as we're out of here, I have to slip out of the house and get a home pregnancy test at the pharmacy. I can't have this doubt hanging over my head, but I also know I'm too chicken to face taking the test alone. There's only one person who I trust won't say a thing. Charlie, my brother's girlfriend.

I'm bouncing on the balls of my feet as I wait outside Troy and Charlie's house. They started as roommates, but now they live together as a couple. I've never met two people more perfect for each other than them.

Charlie finally opens the door and lets me through. I called ahead to let her know I was coming, but I made sure to ask if Troy wouldn't be around. If he finds out I might be pregnant, he's going to lose his shit. And if he ever learns Andreas could be the baby daddy, he might actually kill him. Not really, I'm being dramatic, but for sure their friendship will be over.

I greet Charlie with a hug, and then she stares at me with a question in her gaze. "What's up, Jane?"

Knitting my fingers together, I ask, "Troy is not home, right?"

"No, he's running errands for your grandmother. What's going on?"

I take a deep breath. Here goes nothing. "I'm in big trouble. I think I might be pregnant."

Charlie's eyebrows shoot to the heavens. "What? When did that happen?"

I pull my hair back, yanking at the strands. "You're going to be so mad at me."

"Jane, whatever is it, I promise I won't get angry."

I swallow the huge lump in my throat. "It happened on Halloween night."

She stares at me without speaking for several beats, making me even more anxious. "So, the possible father is someone from your high school?"

I shake my head. "No. This is the part you won't like. I lied to you. I didn't go to a party with my friends. I went to Andy's party."

Her jaw slackens. That evening was a disaster for her and Troy, and now I'm adding another sour note to it.

"Troy and I left the party early," she murmurs.

"I don't think you were there when I arrived."

She touches my arm. "Please tell me that whatever happened there was with your consent."

Crap. Why would she think someone assaulted me? Has Troy's insane protectiveness rubbed off on her already?

"Oh yeah. I wanted it to happen. Very much so," I reply with vehemence.

It takes a moment for my words to make sense to her. Her eyes widen a fraction when she connects the dots. She's a smart girl; she must have noticed how hopelessly in love with Andreas I am.

"Oh my God. It was Andy."

"Yep." I stick my hands in my pockets, feeling foolish now that the truth is out in the open.

"Troy is going to flip."

"You can't tell him. Promise me, Charlie," I beg.

I'm putting her in an awful position, but I can't think of a better alternative.

"Does Andy know?"

I scoff. "He doesn't even know he slept with me that night."

She furrows her eyebrows together. "What do you mean?"

"He didn't recognize me. That was my plan all along, remain incognito. I didn't expect to hook up with him—that wasn't my original intent. I just wanted to see firsthand if the rumors about him were true."

Crossing her arms over her chest, she watches me through slits. "Jane, that was wrong on so many levels. You know Andy would never cross that line with you."

"I know, okay?" I snap. "But you don't know what's like to pine for someone for years, knowing it can never happen." Tears gather in my eyes, so I turn around, ashamed of my outburst.

Charlie walks over and pulls me into a hug. "It's going to be okay, hon."

"I'm not sure it will. Like you said, Troy will lose his mind, and my mother…. Oh my God. She's going to flay me alive."

"For what's worth, I think Andy likes you."

I ease off her embrace, shaking my head. "He finds me attractive. That's all. He's a player. I know that now without a shred of doubt."

She lets out a sigh. "Okay, one issue at a time. We need to find out if you're indeed pregnant. Then we'll go from there."

I pull the plastic pharmacy bag from my purse. "I got all the pregnancy tests they had."

"I would have done the same." She smiles. "You can use my bathroom upstairs. Do you want me to come with you? I'll wait outside."

"No, I think it's better if you stay here. I'd be too self-conscious to pee on a stick knowing you're just on the other side of the door."

"All right. I was going to make some tea. Would you like some?"

"Yeah, that's probably all I can handle right now."

ANDREAS

It took me a good couple of hours to get rid of the anger from my system. I can't believe Crystal tried to get with me at Lorenzo's birthday party. That's the lowest of bitch moves. But it's not a surprise coming from her. She's vile and disgusting.

I went straight to the gym from the party. I had to get rid of all my aggression. Usually, I like to work out with a partner, but I wasn't in the right frame of mind to be near any of my friends. When I got home, I baked a batch of cupcakes, and after their sweet smell permeated my apartment, I felt a little better.

Now I'm heading to Troy and Charlie's place to drop off a box of treats. As usual, I made too many and if I don't get rid of them quickly, Danny and I will eat them all. Coach Clarkson will definitely frown if we turn into two round piglets.

It took me a while to warm up to Charlie, mostly because she acted like a total bitch when I first met her. She and Troy were like cats and dogs, and I don't tolerate anyone messing with my friends. In the end, I realized all their hate was nothing more than foreplay. I know now Charlie is crazy about my best friend, so she's cool in my book.

I don't knock before I let myself in. They never lock the house no matter how many times Danny and I tell them it's not safe. My plan is to simply drop off the goods and head out. I know Troy is not home, and since I didn't call in advance, I have no idea what Charlie is up to. She's usually super busy.

The coast is clear downstairs. There's a kettle on the stove, but it's not on. Charlie must be in her room since her car is parked outside. I'm about to set the box on the counter when I hear a toilet flush. A moment later, Charlie emerges from the bathroom near the stairs.

"Andy? What are you doing here?" she asks in a high-pitched voice.

"Uh, sorry to barge in. I came to drop off some baked goods. I'm not staying."

A girlie screech comes from the second floor, followed by the footsteps of someone running. I don't even have time to ask who is upstairs before Jane yells, "I'm not pregnant!"

A second later, she appears at the top of the stairs, holding a home pregnancy test. My blood runs cold. Our eyes lock, and immediately, her ecstasy morphs into horror. She tries to hide the test behind her back, but it's too late. My shock is quickly replaced by fury. Someone touched Jane, almost got her knocked up, which means he's dead meat.

"Andy, wh-what are you doing here?" she stammers.

Flaring my nostrils, I say, "I want a name."

FOUR

ANDREAS

I'm so fucking jealous, I can't see straight. I tried to be a good friend, stayed away from Jane, and now, some douche almost got her pregnant. When she doesn't give me the answer I want, I repeat, "What's his name, Jane?"

"Andy, calm down," Charlie pipes up.

"No, I won't calm down." I turn to her. "Do you know who he is?"

Her round eyes look guilty as hell. She knows.

"It's none of your business, Andy," Jane finally replies.

She comes down the stairs, but the damned pregnancy test is nowhere in sight. She must have tucked it in her back pocket.

"The hell it's not my business. You're my best friend's kid sister. If someone took advantage of you, I have every right to know."

Her face turns beet red. "Oh my God. What makes you think was I taken advantage of?"

"Come on, Jane. You're barely eighteen. Who was it? Is it a guy from your high school?"

She crosses her arms over chest. "You can huff and puff all you want. I'm not telling you jack. You're not my keeper."

I clench my jaw tight to avoid saying something regrettable, and count to ten in my head. "Fine. Don't tell me. I can't wait to let Troy know the wonderful news." I whirl around and veer for the front door.

"Andy, you wouldn't dare." She comes after me.

"Oh, Jane. I would." I walk out of the house, fuming and ready to break things.

She grabs my arm, making me stop. "Please, Andy. I'm begging you. Don't tell Troy. He's going to go ballistic."

Her beautiful green eyes are bright with unshed tears. God, the sight of her desperation breaks my heart. I don't actually want to tell Troy. I just want to protect her at all costs, even if she's not mine to do so.

"Then tell me his name, Jane. Please?"

"I can't tell you."

"Why not? Is he someone I know?" My mind immediately thinks it's a guy on the team, which doesn't help matters.

"Why can't you let it go, Andy? I had sex; it was consensual. End of story."

I notice she doesn't answer my question, which means it *is* someone I know. *Fuck me.* If it's one of my teammates, I'm going to go savage on his ass. Jane is barely legal.

"I can't, Jane. Whoever he is wasn't careful enough and almost got you pregnant."

"You don't know anything," she grits out. "Condoms aren't one hundred percent foolproof."

I wince hearing her talk about condoms so openly. I've always known the day would come when she would start dating, I just didn't expect it to happen so soon or to feel like someone carved my heart out with a saw.

"I'm glad to hear you weren't completely stupid and used one," I retort angrily, regretting my outburst immediately.

Her lower lip quivers. She's fighting to not cry, making me

feel ten times worse than I already do. One rogue tear rolls down her cheek, which she wipes away hastily.

"You're such a jerk," she says in a broken voice. "Fine. Go ahead and tell my brother. I don't fucking care."

She walks away with her chin raised high. I should stop her, say I'm sorry, but I don't move from the spot. I'm too caught up in my turbulent emotions. Plus, there's a high chance that if I stop her from leaving, I might do something even more stupid, such as kiss her senseless like I did three years ago.

THREE YEARS BEFORE

I can't thank Troy enough for inviting me to spend Thanksgiving with his family. I couldn't bear the thought of being in the same room with my father and Crystal and pretending I am grateful. I feel guilty for abandoning my brother, but he never experienced our stepmom's toxic ways like I did. Or our father's fists. I've only been free of them for a few months. I need more time before I can face that vipers' nest again.

Troy's mother's house is in the Hills. It's not as big as my father's mansion in Malibu, but she and my father share the same taste for modern and cold things. I hate the minimalist shit. It makes me feel like I'm in a spaceship waiting to be probed by aliens.

He warned me that his mother might be a bit prickly. She doesn't like last-minute changes. I told him not to worry about it. She can't be worse than Crystal.

True to his word, the woman is cold to me when Troy introduces us. She warms up a bit when I give her a bottle of expensive champagne. It cost five hundred dollars, a small price to pay for some peace of mind.

I meet the rest of the guests—two of his mother's friends, and his grandmother, Ophelia Holland. I quickly understand why he won't stop praising the old lady. She's a hoot and a half, completely different from her stuck-up daughter.

"Troy, can you find your sister and tell her dinner is almost ready?" his mother asks in a testy tone.

"I'm here, Mom," a pretty blonde answers from the other side of the room.

My eyes widen in surprise, and my heart skips a beat. I knew Troy had a younger sister. I didn't know she was a knockout. Tall and curvy in all the right places, she's exactly the type of girl I gravitate to. Her hair is blonde like Troy's, but that's the only similarity they share. Her eyes are big and almond-shaped in the most beautiful green shade I've ever seen. High cheekbones and bee-stung cherry lips complete the look that seems to have been designed to bring me to my knees.

"Jane, come meet my friend Andy." Troy's voice wakes me from my daze.

Shame immediately takes hold of me. His sister is only fifteen, for crying out loud. I'm such a perv for ogling her like that. I try to hide my reaction as I watch her come over.

"Hi, Andy. Nice to meet you." She extends her hand, and it takes me a second to snap out of my paralysis and shake it.

"Same," I reply, dropping her hand quickly, as if the contact burned me.

I'm acting like a complete idiot. It's not like I don't meet beautiful girls all the time. *So what's my problem?*

"Jane, what in the world are you wearing?" her mother says, making her wince.

"Elaine, leave the poor girl alone," Ophelia intervenes, but the damage is already done. I can see how deflated Jane is now.

"For what's worth, I like your clothes," I say.

She glances down at the flannel shirt-style dress she's wearing, and then she looks at me again from under her eyelashes. My chest takes another hit. *Fuck me. Why am I having such visceral reactions to her?*

"You do?" she asks.

"I like it, too. Don't let Mom get into your head." Troy throws his arm around her shoulders. "Let's head outside. It's getting too stuffy in here."

I follow behind them, purposely keeping my eyes glued to the back of Troy's head. I barely noticed what Jane was wearing. I was too stunned by her pretty face. But I refuse to check her out. I have to remain in control here. My body betrayed me once, and it led to nothing good. I can't go down that path again, especially with Troy's sister.

We hang out on the terrace for as long as we can, but eventually we have to go back inside to eat. The dinner runs smoothly, and I dare to believe Troy's mother's obnoxious behavior was only a fluke.

I'm stuffed like a pig, ready for a nap or some serious caffeine intake, when my phone vibrates in my pocket. A quick check tells me it's Lorenzo calling. Guilt once again pierces my chest. I excuse myself from the table and take his call on the terrace.

I'm relieved he's not calling to complain I didn't come. On the contrary. He's ecstatic about the gift Dad got him. A kart. Lorenzo, unlike me, is obsessed with racing, which obviously pleases our father to no end. We talk for about five minutes before I tell him I'm being rude to my hosts. On my way back, I make a pit stop at the restroom.

I wonder when Troy wants to leave. As Thanksgiving dinners go, this wasn't bad. But I'm tired of keeping my inappropriate reaction to his sister concealed. My eyes kept wandering in her direction throughout the meal. I hope no one noticed. I need some strong liquor and maybe a hookup to set my head straight.

It's just my luck that when I step out in the hallway, I bump into the girl.

"I'm sorry," she blurts out and then dashes down the corridor.

Troy's loud voice warns me something changed while I was taking a piss. He's arguing with his mother about something she said to Jane. I remain in my spot, not knowing what to do. In the end, I go after Jane, justifying to myself that someone needs to check on her.

I expect to find her in her room, but I didn't hear a door banging shut. To my surprise, she's in the laundry room, sorting out clothes.

"Hey, are you okay?" I ask.

"Yeah, I'm fine," she replies in a choked voice.

"What are you doing?" I walk over even though my senses are warning me I should leave her alone.

"Folding laundry."

"Why?"

"Because it's menial work and it helps me calm down."

I look closely at her face and notice the tear streaks. *Ah, man.* Whatever her mother said made her cry.

"It's not worth it, you know."

"What isn't?"

"Trying to please a parent no matter what."

"It sounds like you speak from experience. Is your mother a bitch too?"

A sharp pang in my chest robs me of words for a second. "My mother is dead."

Jane stops her maniacal folding and glances at me with round eyes. "I'm so sorry. I had no idea."

"It's okay. She passed away a long time ago."

"But you still miss her very much, don't you?"

"Every day. Missing her is a constant ache. It will never go away."

"At least she was a good mother to you, even if briefly."

The pain I see shining in Jane's eyes echoes with my own. My mother died, leaving Lorenzo and me alone with an egomaniac. Unable to restrain myself, I reach for Jane's face and wipe off the moisture from her cheek. She gasps out loud, making me drop my hand in an instant.

"I'm sorry. I shouldn't have done that," I say.

She doesn't say a word as she stares at me with those

beguiling eyes. I expect her initial shock will give way to revulsion in the next moment. Instead, she grabs me by the shirt and seals her lips to mine. I'm frozen, completely astonished by what's happening. But soon my body wakes up and seizes control. I grab her by the hips and deepen the kiss. Her lips taste like cherry, her tongue is sweet and demanding, and it's wreaking havoc on my mind.

I devour her mouth like I'm a starved man and she's the only sustenance I need. But when she steps closer, pressing her belly against my erection, it serves as a wake-up call. I break the kiss suddenly, pushing her back. *She's fifteen, damn it! What am I doing?*

"We can't do this," I say.

A blush spreads through her cheeks. She steps away from me, covering her mouth. "I'm so sorry."

"Andy?" Troy's voice echoes in the hallway.

Jane walks around me and runs away, going in the opposite direction of where Troy's voice is coming from. I'm still stunned by what happened when he finds me.

"I was looking for you. How did you wind up in the laundry room?"

I pass a hand over my face. "I got lost."

He chuckles. "Only you, man. I'm ready to bail. Have you seen Jane?"

"Why would I have seen her?" I ask defensively.

Shit. Get your act together, Andreas. You're acting hella guilty.

"She must be hiding from Mom. Oh well. I'll call her later. Come on, let's get out of here before more shit hits the fan."

I follow him silently, hating myself already for lusting after his sister, and for kissing her back. I'm a fucking scumbag. There's no denying it.

FIVE

ANDREAS

I'm not proud to say I'm stalking Jane online. We've been friends for a while, but I've never paid much attention to what she posts—or to what anyone posts, for that matter. Social media is a waste of time. There are a few photos of her with friends from school, and also of her in several different kinds of volunteering work. There's only one picture where she's standing next to a guy in Disney character scrubs. He's much older than her—around thirty would be my guess. Immediately, my perverted brain marks him as a suspect even though I know the guy is probably a doctor at the children's hospital where she volunteers.

I shut my laptop and then go make myself some coffee. I'm tired as fuck thanks to a sleepless night. My mind was partially obsessing about Jane and also agonizing about what I must endure today. I blew off Dad yesterday, which means he's going to make me pay today, and at the tracks, there aren't a lot of places to hide.

What I need is a buffer. I veer toward Danny's room. The door is partially open.

"Danny?" I call out as I stick my head in.

There's no answer, and his bed is made. It takes me a moment to remember he went to visit his mother today. *Damn it.*

I pass a hand over my face. Troy would come with me in a heartbeat. That is, if he doesn't already have plans with Charlie. I'm not keen on seeing him face-to-face, knowing about Jane's secret, but I can't hide from my best friend forever.

"Ah, screw it."

It's only ten past nine, he may not be up already. I call him before I change my mind. It rings a few times before he answers with a groggy voice.

"Hello?"

"Yo, dude. Don't tell me you're still in bed."

"What time is it?"

"Not as early as you think."

In the background, I hear sheets rubbing together and then Charlie's faint voice asking who is on the phone. Sometimes I forget they're still in the honeymoon phase, so they're probably not getting much sleep either. A strange tightness forms in my chest and I can't make sense of it. *I'm not jealous of Troy's relationship bliss, am I?*

"It's Andy," Troy tells her.

"Oh, what does he want?" she asks in a tense tone.

Shit, she must think I'm calling to tell Troy about what happened yesterday.

"Lorenzo has a kart race today," I say. "Do you guys want to come?"

My original idea was to invite only Troy, but there's no reason to not extend the invite to Charlie as well. The more the merrier. Fewer chances for Dad to corner me. Plus, it might also give me an opportunity to grill Charlie about Jane's secret hookup.

Troy asks Charlie, and a moment later, he replies that they're game.

"Do you want me to pick you up?" I ask.

"It's easier if we meet you there."

"Sounds good. See you in an hour."

Troy and Charlie are ten minutes late, but one glance at their faces tells me why. With a smirk, I say, "I'm surprised you two can still walk."

Charlie's cheeks turn a shade pinker while Troy widens his eyes innocently. "I have no idea what you're talking about, bro."

He hits me on the shoulder playfully while trying to hide his own grin.

"Have you been waiting long?" Charlie asks.

"Not long. Don't worry about it."

"I've never been to a kart race before. Thanks for inviting me."

I smile to hide my guilt. She doesn't know I had ulterior motives when I invited her here and that makes me feel bad. I don't know why the sentiment persists every time I do something shady. It shouldn't affect me anymore, considering my asshole ways.

"No problem, dudette."

"Dudette?" Charlie and Troy ask at the same time, making me laugh.

I shove my hands in my pockets. "It's what I call all my friends' girlfriends."

"Since when?" Troy arches both eyebrows.

"Well, since now. You're the first of my buddies who got serious about a girl."

"Don't Paris and Puck have girlfriends? Do you call them dudettes too?" Charlie asks.

"Uh... Puck would kill me if I even said hello to his girl, and I don't think I was ever officially introduced to Paris's jailer."

Charlie looks at Troy with an eyebrow raised. "Jailer? I hope that's not a word used to describe all your teammates' significant others."

Troy sighs heavily. "No, only Geneva has claimed that title. I'll tell you about it later."

"Yeah, let's not sour the mood with tales of Geneva, the Ball Buster," I pipe up.

"There'd better be a pretty good reason for calling her all those names." Charlie crosses her arms over her chest, sobering me up.

"There is, babe. You'll see." Troy tosses his arm over her shoulders.

I shouldn't have said anything about Geneva. Charlie would eventually pick up on the weirdness of Paris's relationship with his girlfriend. But now she clearly thinks I'm the jackass calling an innocent chick names. She's still not sure about me, all thanks to my horrible behavior last year.

"Let's get inside. The race will start soon."

We head to the pit where conversation will be difficult once the race starts. I immediately spot my father speaking with one of the crew members. Lorenzo is standing apart from everyone else, staring at the tracks. He's shifting his body weight from foot to foot while chewing on his thumbnail. He's nervous.

I sense my father's stare when I walk past him, but I don't stop until I'm standing next to my brother.

"Jitters getting to you, little brother?"

He turns to me, dropping his hand from his mouth. "No."

The furrow on his eyebrows worries me. I know how my father gets when the Rossi name is on the line.

"You're going to kill out there."

"I can't mess up," he says, then switches his attention to Troy and Charlie before I can get another word in.

While Troy introduces his girl to Lorenzo, I search for my father. He's still talking to the crew member, but maybe sensing my stare, he lifts his eyes to mine. I catch the slight narrowing of his gaze, which tells me a storm is coming my way. I lift my chin in response. *Bring it on.*

"I can't believe you're already competing at junior level. Time flies," Troy tells my brother.

I turn around in time to see the simple nod Lorenzo gives in response. *Shit.* I've never seen him act like this before a race. Something is definitely eating at him. I lock gazes with Troy. He seems to have caught on the how weird Lorenzo is acting. Wordlessly, he steers Charlie away so I can have a private moment with my brother.

"What's going on, buddy?" I ask.

"Nothing. I'm trying to get in the zone."

"It's our old man, isn't it?"

He glances at me with wide eyes, and then looks over my shoulder. Like someone flipped a switch, his green eyes turn darker, and the muscles around his mouth tense. He's too fucking young to be sporting such a somber expression.

"It's nothing, Andy. Drop it, okay?" He walks off before I can get another word in.

Seething, I stride toward my father. The asshole must have said something to Lorenzo to make him act like that. He used me as his punching bag for years. I won't let him do the same to my brother. I didn't have anyone to protect me from his evil ways, but my brother has me.

"What did you do to Lorenzo?" I ask loudly, not caring about who hears it.

"Watch your tone, Andreas. You're not talking to one of your friends."

I step into his personal space. "You'd better not pull the same crap with him as you did with me."

A shrill horn announces the race is about to start. My father glances at the track for a second, and then back at me. "I don't have time for your bullshit right now."

He walks away, leaving me choking on my anger. My

breathing is coming out in bursts when Troy and Charlie join me again.

"Are you okay?" he asks.

"I'll be fine in a moment," I grit out.

"Let's find a good spot to watch the race. It's the reason we came, right?" Charlie links her arm with mine, and without hesitation, steers me closer to the tracks but far away from my father.

To say I'm shocked by her initiative is an understatement. I'm pretty sure she only puts up with me because Troy is my best friend. And after my caveman display at their house yesterday, she has even more reason to be leery of me.

Troy is sporting a satisfied grin when I glance at him. His reaction serves to dissipate my fury a little. I force my mind to stay in the present so I can cheer my brother on properly. But the worry won't stop gnawing at my insides. If I discover Dad is hurting Lorenzo in any way, there'll be hell to pay.

SIX

JANE

I spend the entire week pretending nothing happened last Saturday, but I kept waiting for Troy to come over and demand the name of the guy who took my virginity. But he never did, which means Andreas kept his mouth shut. It's so fucking ironic that he went crazy over it when he's the culprit. One more reason to take this secret to my grave. He's never going to forgive me if he finds out I tricked him. I hope Charlie doesn't cave and tell Troy.

With the fiasco of Mom's love life a couple of months ago, she spent too much of her spare time focused on me. She has eased off a little now that's she dating again, but still, the entire week was all about the stupid debutante ball. She has narrowed down my potential escorts to three candidates, and they all sound like complete toads. I'm supposed to meet them at another luncheon where the girls get to meet and pick their dates. It's like *The Bachelor* on steroids since there are only a few candidates who are considered top prizes. *Gag me.*

This weekend I manage to keep my calendar free so I can check out the roller derby game. Getting out of the house without Mom grilling me to the umpteenth degree will require deception. My go-to person would have been Troy, but I was afraid he'd offer to tag along. I don't need a chaperone.

Without options, I have to involve Sheila, my closest friend at school. She's a nice girl, but she stresses way too easily, especially when she needs to lie. It takes a lot of cajoling to convince her to cover for me tonight. I tell her I'm going to the movies on a date. She asks the name of the guy, which forces me to make one up. He can't be someone she knows.

The game doesn't start late, so I'm hoping it's over at a decent hour. Mom has a date, which means she might come home super late, but I can't be too careful. I definitely don't want to get grounded.

The game is being held at a gymnasium thirty minutes from my house. The parking lot is full, which surprises me. I didn't know there were so many roller derby fans. It feels weird to be going in alone when everyone around me is in groups. I shove my hands in my jacket pockets and try to become smaller. Years of public reprimands by my mother made me dislike crowds.

I take a seat on the row farthest from the banked track and wait. Slowly, the place begins to fill up, but everyone is trying to find a spot closest to where the action is, so my row remains empty. To keep busy, I pull out my phone and read more about the rules. I did some research before, but I haven't memorized all of them yet.

"Jane?" Someone taps me on the shoulder.

I turn toward the voice, completely surprised when I find Fred Johnson, Charlie's friend, standing there with the biggest smile on his face. I haven't seen him in over a month. His hair is back to blond. When we met, it was bright green.

I jump to my feet. "Oh my God, Fred. What are you doing here?"

"I could ask you the same thing. I didn't peg you for a roller derby fan."

A short brunette with curly brown hair walks up to him holding a large popcorn bucket. "Hey, I found us seats closer."

"Hold on, Sylv. Do you know who this is?" Fred asks.

She glances at me. "Haven't the faintest clue."

"I'm Jane, Troy's sister."

"Ah, you're the famous Jane." She smirks, then looks meaningfully at Fred.

Did I miss something here?

He rubs the back of his neck, looking sheepish. "Yeah, this is Jane."

"I'm Sylvana, Fred's cousin. Are you waiting for someone?"

"Oh, no. I'm solo tonight."

"Oh, then you must sit with us. Come, there are better seats down a few rows."

Not wanting to be rude, I follow them. To be honest, I feel better now that I'm not alone anymore. Sylvana enters the row first, and then Fred tells me to follow her. Now I'm sandwiched between them.

When I first met Fred, he was a bit of a flirt, but I didn't think much of it. It was actually nice to be on the receiving end of his attention. He's funny, cute, and smart. But then Andreas showed up and ruined the evening with his antics. He acted like a jealous boyfriend, annoying me, and also giving me hope something had changed between us. It was all just in my head.

"Never in a million years would I have pictured you as someone who enjoys roller derby," Fred comments.

"Why?"

He shrugs. "I don't know. You seemed like the type of girl who does ballet or plays the piano."

"Dude, stereotyping much?" Sylvana butts in before I can reply. "Don't listen to him, Jane."

"That's okay. I've done both things actually, at my mother's insistence. I didn't care for either."

"What do you like to do?" Fred asks.

"I'm a horror movie fanatic, but I think you already know

that." I smirk, remembering the severed head he got made in my likeness.

"Oh yeah." He chuckles. "Man, that prank was epic. Did you see the video?"

My heart squeezes in my chest. The night of the prank was when I seduced Andreas and kicked off my current problem.

"Yeah, Charlie sent it to me. So, what brings you here tonight?" I ask to change the subject.

"My girlfriend is a jammer on one of the teams," Sylvana replies.

"Oh really? Which one?"

"Second Time Around Divas."

"Shut up!" I say enthusiastically. "I've met her. That's why I'm here."

Sylvana frowns. "You've met Katja? When?"

"I bumped into her in a restroom at the Magnolia Hotel last weekend. More like collided with her, actually, and sent her roller derby flyers flying."

She chuckles. "Ah, that makes sense. She's always running somewhere."

I turn to Fred. "What about you?"

"Sylvana didn't want to come alone."

She snorts. "Like it's a hardship for you to be here."

"I never said it was. What's not to like about a bunch of badass chicks wearing skimpy outfits and playing for dominance on skates?"

"This is my first time watching a live game. I've seen *Whip It* though. It looked fun."

"Well, it's not as dramatic as in fiction, but it's pretty entertaining to watch. I'd join the team if I didn't have the coordination of a giraffe on stilts." Sylvana laughs.

"Can you skate, Jane?" Fred asks.

"Yeah. I used to do it all the time when I was younger."

There's a sudden rush in the crowd, and a moment later, the

game starts. Sylvana yells when her girlfriend enters the track with her teammates, almost making me deaf.

Fred leans closer. "Do you want to trade seats with me? Sylv will be obnoxiously loud the entire time."

"It's okay." I force a smile.

He's so nice and adorable. I should be flattered that he seems to be into me. But I can't even entertain the idea of dating anyone when my heart is still bleeding over Andreas. There's not a day that I don't relive my evening with him. I'm constantly craving the taste of his lips, and the feel of his arms around me.

I shove the memory to a dark corner of my mind. One of the reasons I came here tonight was to take my mind off Andreas, my mother, and the clusterfuck that is my life right now. And don't get me started on my father pushing me to attend Stanford, his alma matter.

It doesn't take long for the game to capture my full attention. I'm enthralled by the rules, the ferocity of all the girls on the track. It's clear both teams have a tight bond among their members, and I find myself wanting that too.

I never had strong female friendships growing up. Most of the girls in my private school are phony bitches. Half of them only wanted to be my friends so they could get closer to Troy. Sheila is the exception, but it's because she's pathologically shy, and her parents are even more controlling than mine.

The game goes by in a blur. Katja's team wins, which sends Sylvana into a fit of cheers and shouts. We wait until the crowd begins to walk out, and then I follow her down to the track. After Sylvana congratulates her girlfriend for the win, she steers the redhead to where Fred and I are.

Katja recognizes me immediately. "Hey, you made it."

"Yeah. Awesome game."

"Thanks."

Fred steps forward and hugs the girl before returning to my side.

"How do you know Syl and Fred?" she asks.

"Jane's brother is Charlie's boyfriend," Fred answers.

"And we just met," Sylvana adds.

"Wow. Small world. What did you think, Jane?"

"It was incredible. I wish I knew about roller derby when I was younger. I'd totally beg my parents to let me join a team."

Katja's blue eyes light up. "Are you a good skater?"

"I think so."

"You should come to our Fresh Meat tryouts next Saturday."

"What's that?"

"It's tryouts for our league's bootcamp program. If you're good, you might make it to our team. We're losing a teammate to the East Coast."

"I haven't used my skates in ages."

"You have a week to shake off the dust," Fred pipes up. "You have to try. It will be epic."

The insecure little girl inside of me wants to say no, but I'm tired of feeling small and unworthy. Maybe I've been obsessing about Andreas because he's the only person besides Troy and Grandma who actually saw something in me.

"Okay. Tell me where and what time, and I'll be there."

SEVEN

ANDREAS

I'm half asleep, rubbing the tiredness from my eyes as I make my way to the kitchen when I find my father sitting on the sofa as if he owns the place. Technically, he does, but that doesn't give him the right to barge in whenever he feels like it. Oh, wait. It does. He's such an asshole.

"What are you doing here?" I grumble, aiming for the state-of-the-art espresso machine.

I can't deal with the man without caffeine in my system. I haven't forgotten about our little interaction at Lorenzo's race. My brother ended in third place. Considering it was his first time racing in that class, it was a pretty good result, even for Giancarlo Rossi.

"You've been avoiding my calls."

"Yeah. On purpose. Take the hint."

My back is to him, but the rise of the small hairs on the back of my neck warn me he's walking over. My spine becomes tense, an involuntary reaction thanks to the many years of abuse. I turn around, bracing for what's to come. He hasn't laid a hand on me since I got strong enough to fight back, but that doesn't mean I can let my guard down around him.

"You changed your major without my consent."

"I fail to see how my degree choice is any of your damn business."

He narrows his eyes while a muscle in his jaw twitches. Faster than a cobra, he grabs me by the T-shirt and pulls me close to his furious face. "You seem to be forgetting who pays for your tuition and all this luxury. I can take it all away with a snap of my fingers."

"Do it then. I don't care."

He shoves me away, and I hit my lower back on the edge of the granite counter. Pain shoots up my spine, but I ride it in silence. I won't give him the satisfaction of knowing he hurt me again.

"Yo, Andy, what's up with the no—Mr. Rossi, I didn't know you were here." Danny walks into the kitchen wearing nothing but his boxer shorts.

My father's murderous expression vanishes. When he glances at my roommate, he has his friendly and approachable persona on—the one he uses on a daily basis to fool strangers into believing he's a nice guy.

"Hi, Danny. I had an urgent matter to discuss with Andy. I never got the chance to congratulate you on your game performances this past season."

"Thanks." He shrugs. "I couldn't have done it without the rest of the team."

"Nonsense. Let me tell you something, son. This whole team mentality is bullshit. If you're a star, you should flaunt it. I expect great things from you next year."

Fuck him. He's only praising Danny like that to rub in that I'm not good enough. Not that Danny doesn't deserve praise, but I know how my father operates.

Danny glances at me as if he's looking for a clue for how he should behave. He knows I don't get along with my father, but he doesn't know the man used me for his punching bag while I was growing up. Thankfully, the only dirty secret Danny knows about me is the Crystal deal.

"Thanks, sir," Danny replies.

Dad knocks once on the island counter with his knuckles, looking pointedly at me. "This conversation isn't over. You *will* reverse your idiotic decision."

I cross my arms over my chest. "My decision is final. Don't force me to involve Coach Clarkson in this matter. You don't want to tarnish your reputation, do you?"

I'm bluffing. My father could very well stop his financial support and I'd have no choice but to drop out. It's too late to apply for a scholarship, and I wouldn't qualify anyway. I come from money.

If looks could kill, I'd be dead on the spot. But I no longer tremble under my father's cruel gaze. I lift my chin in defiance. Wordlessly, he turns around and walks out of the apartment.

"Whoa, that was intense," Danny pipes up as soon as the front door shuts.

"You don't know the half of it." I focus on making another espresso. The first one has gone cold already.

"What happened?" He pulls up a stool and rests his forearms on the counter.

"He found out I switched majors. He wasn't happy about it."

Danny whistles. "Yeah, I definitely noticed that. I don't see what's the big deal. Hotel management is almost the same as business, but focused more on what you want to do. Why is he angry?"

"He thinks it's beneath the Rossi name," I reply bitterly.

"I'm sorry, man. I don't envy you, and this is coming from a guy who has always wanted to have a dad around."

Danny was raised by a single mom. I don't know what the situation is with his biological father, but he's never been in the picture. Like me, Danny is private about his life, only telling Troy and me the bare minimum. We all have skeletons in the closet. Maybe that's why we bonded as friends.

"Yeah, you definitely have nothing to be envious about my fucked-up family. The only saving grace is Lorenzo."

"He's a cool kid." Danny smiles. "Hey, want to make me a cappuccino?"

I chug the hot espresso, not caring that I burn my tongue and throat in the process.

"What's wrong with your hands?" I ask after I set the cup down.

"You know yours is better than mine."

I roll my eyes. He always gives me the same excuse. I'm not fooled, but Danny is the perfect roommate. He never makes any messes, he doesn't complain about all the parties I throw here, or the noise I make when I have company. Sure, I charge him ridiculously cheap rent, but he could be a jackass.

"Fine, but this is the last time," I tell him.

He grins from ear to ear. "Thank you. Are we hitting the gym before class?"

"Yeah. Today more than ever I need a good workout."

It's not a surprise I couldn't get into a better mood even after pumping iron at the gym. I barely paid any attention during my morning classes. After lunch, I have to escape campus. There's only one place I can think of going that will probably ease some of the heaviness in my chest. I head to Jane's high school. I've done that more times than I can count in the past. It's something utterly absurd. I come at the most bizarre hours and never get to see her leave the building. Just the fact that I know she's somewhere inside is enough for me.

But today of all days, she leaves early. I'm instantly suspicious. Why is she leaving school before everyone else? Jealousy erupts in my chest like a churning volcano. She must be skipping class to meet with the asshole who almost got her pregnant.

I sink in my seat, hiding from view, and wait until she gets into her car. Then I follow her. I have to know who she's seeing in secret. *Fuck.* If it's someone I know, I'm going nuclear on his ass.

She heads to the mall, and I think that makes perfect sense. What better place to have a clandestine meetup than in a busy location where you can easily blend in with the crowd?

I keep my distance. My Bronco is too recognizable. Lucky for me, an upscale store in the mall offers valet. I don't have to waste time finding a parking spot. If I lose sight of her, it's game over. I shove a fifty-dollar bill in the valet's hand along with my car key and then run across the parking lot. I didn't want him to give me shit for not entering the mall through the fancy store.

I pull my hoodie over my head as I follow Jane. She speed-walks ahead, as if she's in a hurry. Maybe she's late for her date. My anger increases at the thought, making me grind my teeth hard until my jaw hurts. When she stops suddenly, I'm forced to duck behind a column, afraid she sensed someone was following her. I wait a couple of seconds to peer around my hiding spot. Her head is down; she's looking at her phone. A moment later, she veers inside a small boutique that has colorful and racy outfits on display. *What the hell is she doing there?*

Like a stalker, I linger nearby. Maybe she's meeting her guy there. I wait ten minutes and not a single dude goes inside the store. *Fuck it.* I'm going in. Patience is not a virtue I possess.

As soon as I step foot inside, two salesgirls smile at me, and the closest asks in a flirtatious tone if she can assist me. I shake my head, and wordlessly head toward Jane. She's far in the back, distracted as she peruses a rack of clothes.

"Hey," I say when I'm standing next to her.

I shouldn't have done that. Her sweet perfume reaches my nose, bringing back forbidden memories.

She whips her face to mine, widening her eyes. "Andy, what are you doing here?"

"I was in the mall when I saw you come in here." My eyes drop to the clothes draped over her arm. "What are those?"

Cagey, she steps back, attempting to hide them from view. "Workout clothes."

I reach over and pull one pair of flimsy spandex shorts from the stack. It's small enough to pass for underwear.

"You're joking, right? You can't work out in these."

She pulls the scrap of fabric from my hand with a jerky movement. "My God. When did you become Troy's second-in-command? I told you, I don't need another overprotective brother."

Her remark makes me wince. I don't want to be her brother. Not now, not ever.

"These clothes aren't you, Jane. Please tell me you're not buying them to please your fuckboy."

Her face turns beet red, right before she shoves all the clothes in her hands at me. "You're unbelievable. Stay out of my life!"

She walks around me and strides to the door. When did she develop a temper like that? My astonishment lasts a couple seconds before I snap out of it. The stupid clothes she tossed at me meet the floor, and then I run after her.

"Jane, wait."

"Leave me alone, Andy. Don't make me call mall security on you."

I grab her arm, forcing her to halt. "Will you just stop for a second?"

She whirls around still trapped by my steely hold. "Why? So you can keep pestering me with your misplaced protective attitude?"

"I care about you. I don't want you to get hurt."

Her green eyes become brighter. "Well, it's too late for that."

Her admission feels like a punch to my stomach. Some asshole did hurt her, like I suspected, and now he has to pay.

"Jane, babe. Just tell me his name, please."

"*Babe?*" Her eyebrows arch.

Shit. I can't believe I called her that.

"Sorry, slip of the tongue."

My answer seems to add fuel to the fire. Incensed, she pulls her arm free from my grasp, and then pokes me in the chest.

"I'm not your *babe,* asshole. Don't insult me by putting me in the same league as the girls you fuck."

I'm taken aback by her remark. Jane has always been shy and soft-spoken. This new side of her is terrifying and exciting at the same time.

"I'd never do that. You're high above them, Jane. They're nothing, barely a hazy memory."

She recoils, almost if I physically hurt her.

"Whatever. Just stop harassing me about my love life."

She turns around and speaks over her shoulder. "If you follow me again, I *will* scream for help. Don't try me."

EIGHT

JANE

I'm still fuming when I cross through the gates of my mother's house. I can't believe Andreas cornered me in that store and started pestering me. I'm pretty sure that encounter wasn't a coincidence, which means he followed me there. What was he trying to achieve? I do not need a bloodhound on my case, especially him.

I decided to skip art class to get to the mall and buy clothes for the roller derby tryout. I was totally going to buy regular gym clothes until Katja told me to check out the store with the inappropriate attire—according to Andreas.

Jackass. Even when he's annoying me, he makes my pulse skyrocket with yearning. I don't know what I have to do to eradicate him from my heart once and for all. *You shouldn't have lost your virginity to him, Jane. Now there's no forgetting him.* Ugh! Am I doomed to be forever in love with Andreas?

All I want is to hide in my room and not come back until dinner. That is, if Mom is around. I'm hoping she has a date. But that idea flies right out of the window when I find her and two other guests in the living room, and a plethora of evening gowns on hangers and draped over her furniture.

"What in the world?" I mumble.

Mom lifts her gaze to mine. "Jane, I'm glad you're home early. Come see all these beauties."

Leery, I walk closer. "What's all this?"

"Dresses for your debutante ball!" she replies in a high-pitched squeal.

Lorena Meester, one of her closest friends, walks over holding a flute of champagne. "When Elaine told me you hadn't picked your dress yet, I knew I had to intervene."

Mom rolls her eyes, a reaction I rarely see on her. "Please. You just wanted an excuse to hit up all your favorite designers."

"Why do you need an excuse?" I ask.

Lorena is married to one of the wealthiest men in the country. He's also ancient, but she doesn't seem to mind that as long as he keeps showering her with jewelry and fancy trips.

"Pete claims I don't need more gowns." She pouts, glancing at my mother.

"He clearly doesn't know his wife." Mom laughs, reaching for her own glass of champagne.

My jaw drops. I can't remember the last time I've seen her in such a good mood.

A tall man with bleached white hair and pale complexion to match comes over holding an ethereally beautiful gown in his hand. "I think this will look phenomenal on you, darling."

"Oh, Jane. This is Caz, the best stylist in Hollywood," Lorena pipes up.

The man smiles a little. "You're making me blush, dear."

There's literally no change in his skin color, so I guess he's being fake modest.

"I guess I can try that," I say.

"Oh for heaven's sake, Jane. Can you stop being such a Debbie Downer for a moment? How about showing some excitement?" Mom retorts.

Ah, there's the criticism. I was beginning to suspect I had walked into *The Twilight Zone.*

I clap my hands together and force a phony smile on my face. "Oh my God. I can't wait to try that on!" My squeaky tone is fake as hell too, which only makes Mom glower more.

"Don't be a brat."

I shake my head and then take the dress from Caz's hand. "I'll be right back."

He twists his brows into a frown. "Uh, I have to help you with that. It's a piece of art, very delicate. We can't risk getting it ruined."

Wait. Does he want me to undress in front of him? Not a chance.

"I'll be careful. Besides, if I snag the fabric, Mom has to buy the dress. So it's a win for everyone." I smirk at her.

"Ha ha. You're hilarious today, Jane. No one is asking you to get naked in the middle of the living room. Go behind the partition Caz brought and get the dress on already. He'll help you zip up."

Grumbling, I do as she says. The quicker I pick a gown, the quicker I can disappear for a while. Behind the partition, I undress fast, grimacing when I look at the underwear I'm wearing today. It's hot pink with black skulls all over it. It will totally show through the thin fabric of the dress. *Oh well.*

Caz was right though. The dress is so fine that I fear any tiny movement will cause the fabric to rip. As beautiful as it is, I'd be terrified to wear it, but I'd like to see how I look in it. I step into it and then pull the bodice up until it covers my breasts. It's a corset draped with the most beautiful lace I've ever seen. It even has tiny crystals woven through it.

Holding the top part in place, I step from behind the partition, and immediately Lorena and Caz gasp.

"Oh my. Look at you, Jane. You're a vision." Lorena presses her hand over her chest.

"That dress was made for you. That's it, no need to try anything else." Caz waves his hand.

I turn to Mom, waiting for her to tear me down. "Hmm, I don't know. Maybe if Jane ever learns to stand straight without slouching. A dress can only do so much."

My spine goes rigid, and I hate how she can manipulate me like a puppet. I don't have bad posture. In fact, my ballet teacher couldn't praise me enough for my stance.

"I don't like this dress anyway. It's too flimsy."

"Pity. You look like an angel in it," Lorena declares.

"Who is your escort?" Caz asks out of the blue.

"Undecided," I say.

"You haven't secured an escort yet?" Lorena screeches, and then turns to Mom. "How come, Elaine?"

"Jane has been most uncooperative. If she had followed my guidance, she would have already made headway with Hanson van Buuren."

The name doesn't ring a bell. But again, I only pretended to listen when Mom prattled on about escorts. He must be one of the top three candidates she'd already pre-selected.

"Who? It's the first time I've heard of him," I ask out of spite, knowing very well she must have said his name a hundred times.

Mom narrows her eyes to slits. "That goes to show how little effort you're putting in all this. It's *your* debutante ball, Jane. Not mine."

"Are sure? I never said I wanted to take part in this archaic ritual."

Lorena widens her eyes. "Jane, dear. Don't say that. It's a rite of passage and so much fun. Many girls even find their future husbands at the ball."

"How is that not an ancient mentality?"

"Don't waste your breath on her, Lorena. Jane is determined to make me suffer. She's going through a rebellious phase."

"Oh, you think I'm rebellious? Watch this."

I drop the gown to the floor, not caring that I'm standing now in the middle of the living room in my underwear. Lorena and

Caz stare at me with mouths agape, but Mom maintains her bitchy face.

"How mature, Jane. Keep acting like that and you'll have to attend the ball with some idiot with bad skin."

"Why can't I find my own date?"

Mom snorts. "Oh, that's rich."

"Your escort can't be just anyone," Lorena chimes in. "Hanson's mother owes me a favor. I'll set up a date for you two to meet."

Shit. I don't want to go on a blind date set up by anyone. It's bad enough that I have to attend the stupid ball with a guy who's probably a snob.

"I thought that's what the bachelorette luncheon was for."

Lorena furrows her brows. "I don't follow. What bachelorette luncheon?"

"Jane is being a smart-mouth. She's referring to the luncheon at the marina."

"Oh, no. That's just a formality. You can't wait to snag an escort there. All the good ones will have made commitments by then."

"You'll need a dress for your meet-cute," Caz chimes in. He turns to the rack of cocktail attire. "What are you thinking, Lorena? Will it be a lunch date or dinner?"

"Definitely lunch," Mom replies. "Dinner implies other things. Saturday will be best."

Oh my God. Is she for real? Not that I want to have dinner with a complete stranger. But I don't want to have lunch either. Besides, the Fresh Meat tryouts is this Saturday. I can't miss that.

"I already have plans for Saturday," I reply.

"Cancel them. Nothing you have on your schedule can be more important than a date with Hanson van Buuren."

I curl my hands into fists. "I have a meeting to work on a school project," I grit out.

"I'm sure you can reschedule that," she replies dismissively.

"Lorena is right, I've slacked off. You do need to secure the best bachelor available to make up for your lack of polish."

Heat spreads through my cheeks. Why does she have to bring me down all the time? Now I regret dropping the gown to the floor. Exposed like this, her insults seem to hurt more.

"And Hanson goes to Stanford. I'm sure he can answer all your questions about your future school," Lorena pipes up.

"I'm not going to Stanford," I declare.

Up until this moment, I have pretended to follow along with my parents' plan to send me to my Dad's alma matter. I never said out loud I have no intention of going there.

Mom's eyes narrow. "We'll see about that. I'm sure once you meet Hanson, you'll change your mind. He's quite the looker."

"Like that ever mattered to me."

Yeah, right. I never cared about all the pretty boys in my school because I was already head-over-heels in love with Andreas.

"I've had enough of this nonsense. You're going on this date, Jane, even if I have to drag you by your hair."

Her comment makes me see red. I'm done being her punching bag. She wants me to meet this Hanson guy? Fine. I will. But I can't promise I'll behave or that I will stay past starters.

I glance at the rack and spot a rich sapphire blue dress. "How about that one?"

Caz pulls the dress from the rack and holds it up for my inspection. "The Versace?"

"Too over the top for a lunch date." Mom wrinkles her nose.

Ignoring her remark, I say. "Sold."

Good girl Jane is gone.

NINE

ANDREAS

I watch Jane walk away from me in a daze. I can't fucking believe the sweet girl I used to know turned into a hurricane. And the worst of all is that I'm so onboard with this new version it's not even funny. My heart is pumping like a machine, and it feels like it's going to pierce through my chest. Not to mention what's going on in my pants. I'm sporting wood in the middle of the mall, lusting after my best friend's little sister. I'm despicable.

It's no use. I have to accept that this obsession with Jane is no longer only a matter of wanting what I can't have. Something has changed, and now I'm so screwed. Even if by some miracle Jane gave me the time of day now, there's no chance in hell Troy would ever accept me dating his sister. He knows too much about my heathen ways. He'll never believe I could give up all the women and partying for Jane. To be honest, I don't know if that's something I can do either. I'm broken and there's no fixing it.

I pass a hand over my face, at loss about to what to do. I can't keep going on this path, following Jane everywhere like a fucking psycho with murder intent in my mind. If I see her with the motherfucker who almost got her pregnant, I won't be able to restrain myself. I'm going to teach him a lesson he'll never forget.

My phone vibrates in my pocket, pulling my mind from turbulent thoughts. It's a message from Troy asking if I want to hang out later. *Fuck.* Now I feel even worse than before. I don't reply, needing time to think of an excuse. I can't hang out with him now after my epiphany.

I call Danny, the only friend I can trust with this shit. He answers on the second ring.

"Hey, you home?" I ask.

"I'm just about to walk through the door. Why?"

"Wanna meet me at Goldsboro Mall?"

"What the hell are you doing there?"

"It's a long story. They have an Irish pub somewhere here. I think it's called O'Shea's."

"Yeah, sure. I'll be there in twenty minutes.

Danny takes at least half an hour before he walks into the pub. I'm already on my third pint and trying my best to ignore the big-titted server who keeps giving me come-hither glances. The old Andreas would be all over her like a hobo on a hot dog. Now her obvious interest makes me uncomfortable. It's like I've traded places with someone else.

"About time," I grumble.

"Sorry, I had a delay." He sits across from me and flags the waitress.

She stops next to our table, all smiles. Now she has two of us to try her luck. She'd probably be down for a threesome. The idea is depressing. Another side effect of the new me.

"What can I get you, hon?" she asks Danny.

"Same as him." He turns to me. "Need another round?"

I chug the rest of my beer, and then reply, "Sure."

When she's gone, Danny levels me with a serious gaze. "What's going on, Andy? Is this about your dad's visit earlier?"

"No. And don't remind me of that. I'm fucked, bro."

"How so?"

I lean back and run a hand through my hair. "It's Jane."

His eyebrows arch, but his surprise only lasts a split second. "So, you're finally ready to admit you have feelings for her."

"What the hell are you talking about?" I'm on edge in an instant.

"Dude, only a blind man couldn't see that you have a major crush on little Jane."

"Don't call her that," I snap.

"Sorry. But I'm right, aren't I?"

"Fuck. I don't know. Truth be told, I've been obsessing about her since we kissed."

"Wait. You kissed?" His eyebrows shoot up. He leans forward and asks, "When did that happen?"

I sigh, forgetting that I never told anyone about my lapse in judgment. "The first time Troy brought me over to his mother's house, three years ago."

"Jesus, she was only fifteen then." Danny stares at me like I'm the biggest perv on the planet.

He's not wrong.

The waitress returns with our drinks, interrupting the conversation for a moment. As soon as she leaves, I continue. "I didn't plan to kiss her, all right? She was upset about something her mother had said. I was just consoling her when she attacked me."

"She kissed you?" His tone is incredulous.

I don't blame him. I wouldn't believe it either if I were in his shoes.

"Yeah. It caught me completely by surprise. But I'm not guiltless. I didn't end the kiss right away as I should have. I kissed her back and enjoyed every second of it." I pinch the bridge of my nose and close my eyes for a second. "I'm fucking scum."

"Just because you were weak once doesn't make you scum. Please don't rip my nut sack off for saying this, but Jane is hot."

I glower at him. "Watch it."

He leans back, raising his hands. "I'm just making an observation. You haven't done anything else with her since then, have you?"

I take a large sip of my drink, needing to dull my guilt somehow, before I answer. "No. I haven't crossed that line yet, but I want to."

"Man, Troy's going to flip."

"I know. That's the problem. He's one of my best friends. I don't want to ruin our friendship."

"There's only one solution. You have to tell him."

I rest my elbows on the table and then yank my hair back. "I can't. He's never going to forgive me for even thinking about Jane in that way."

"Bro, you don't think he already suspects? Like I said, it's pretty fucking obvious."

I shake my head. "No. There has to be another way."

"If you're thinking about sleeping around, that won't work. You do that plenty." He chuckles, earning a glare from me.

"Thanks, jackass."

His amusement vanishes as he sits straighter. "Do you think Jane is into you as well?"

Danny's question makes me pause. She did kiss me first, but that could have been just a teenage impulse, a way to get back at her mother.

"I don't know. We've always been friendly, but never flirtatious or anything. She's pretty mad at me at the moment."

"Why? What did you do?"

The answer is on the tip of my tongue, but I stop just in time. I can't betray Jane's secret, not even to Danny, who I know won't tell a soul.

"I bumped into her earlier. She was in the mall buying provocative workout clothes. I gave her a piece of my mind."

Danny rolls his eyes. "Translation: you acted like a caveman."

"Kind of. I was jealous as fuck. The last time I felt this way was… you know when."

Bitterness pools in my mouth. I can't even speak about the past without feeling the need to puke. After what happened to me in my teen years, I swore to never let myself be vulnerable like that again, and here I am, desiring the impossible.

"You can't compare the two situations. That piece of shit used you to get to your father. Whatever you thought you felt for her wasn't love. With Jane, you might actually experience the feeling."

He takes a large sip of his beer while I stare at him with mouth agape. "Are you sure you're only eighteen?"

"Shh. Do you want to get me kicked out?"

I give him a droll stare. "Like that waitress will ever do that to you."

"One can't be too cautious. But seriously, man. I think you should tell Jane how you feel. If she reciprocates, then you tell Troy."

A humorless laugh escapes my lips. "You clearly don't know Troy very well. Or me."

Danny's brows furrow. "What do you mean?"

"Even if I fall head-over-heels in love with Jane, I *will* hurt her. It's unavoidable, and Troy knows that."

"Bullshit, Andy. I don't believe it."

I snort. "I appreciate the trust, but it's misplaced. I'll never be able to fully commit to anyone. That's who I am. A broken, heartless asshole."

My phone rings on the table. Troy's name is boldly displayed. "Shit."

"Aren't you going to get that?" Danny asks.

"He wants to hang out, but I've been avoiding him."

Danny reaches for my phone and answers before I can stop him. "Yo, Troy. What's up?"

"Why are you answering Andy's phone?" he asks.

The jackass gives me a pointed look. "Andy is in the restroom. Wanna meet us at—"

I yank the phone from his hand. I don't want Troy to come here. "Hey, Troy."

"Where have you been? I haven't talked to you since Lorenzo's race."

"Busy with school and family stuff."

"And pussy," he adds, making me grimace.

I haven't been with anyone since I found out about Jane's secret. She's all I can think about—her and the asshole she's been seeing.

"Actually, no girls."

Danny seems surprised for a second, but then understanding shines in his eyes. I feel like punching his knowing face.

"Jesus, are you sick or something?" Troy asks.

"I guess something," I grumble. "So, do you wanna hang out?"

I might as well face the music. I can't avoid Troy forever.

"Can't now. I've made plans with Charlie. The reason I'm calling is to ask for your help with something."

"All right. I'm listening."

"Jane has this silly ass debutante ball next month and Mom is pestering her to find an escort."

For a split second, I fear Troy is going to ask me, but then I remember he'd never steer Jane in my direction.

"She's going on a blind date with someone called Hanson van Buuren. Wanna help me dig up intel on the guy?"

Immediately, my pulse skyrockets and my vision becomes tinged in red. I don't want Jane going out with anyone, especially a douchecanoe with that name.

"When is the date?"

"Saturday, I think."

I hear Charlie's voice in the background, but it's muffled so I can't make out what she's saying.

A moment later, Troy continues in a lower tone. "Charlie is unhappy with my attitude right now. I had to promise her I won't do anything. But it doesn't mean you can't. I'm counting on you, buddy."

"Don't worry. I'll get all the dirt on this schmuck."

When I end the call, Danny is watching me through slits. He must have heard every word Troy said.

"What if that guy doesn't have any skeletons in the closet?" he asks.

"No one is perfect. And if I can't find anything before Saturday, then I guess I'll have to crash Jane's date."

TEN

ANDREAS

I'm hunched over my laptop, distracted, when Danny comes into the kitchen. He covers his mouth, trying to suppress a yawn, and then says, "You're up early."

"I haven't been to bed." I reach for the cup of coffee next to me.

It's empty. I don't even remember drinking from it. I'm definitely going to need ten more if I'm to survive the day.

"Why? Please don't tell me you spent the night looking up the dude Jane is supposed to meet Saturday."

I groan. "No, I didn't. I couldn't find anything on the guy yet. As far as his social media profiles are concerned, he's clean. But that doesn't mean anything."

"Then why didn't you sleep?" He opens the fridge and grabs a jug of orange juice from it.

"Today is my first class in my new major track, Introduction to Food Service Management. I spent the night studying the syllabus."

"Was that necessary?" He raises an eyebrow.

"I don't want to be unprepared. I'm already behind thanks to switching majors this late in the game."

"But falling asleep in class because you're too fucking tired is okay?" He chuckles.

I peel my eyes from the laptop to glower at him. "Don't you have some place to be?"

"I'm going soon. What are you going to do about that Hanson guy? You're not really going to crash Jane's date if you can't find anything compromising, are you?"

As tempting as the idea is, I can't cross that line. Jane is already furious with me. If I show up at her date, she might not ever talk to me again.

"No, but maybe I can convince her not to go on the stupid date, period."

Danny leans against the fridge, crossing his arms over his chest. "Oh, and how do you plan to do that?"

"I don't know. I'll think of something."

"I have an idea. Why don't you just offer to be her escort? And maybe, I don't know, tell her how you feel?" His grin becomes wider.

"Quit trying to turn me into a Nicholas Sparks hero."

"The fact you know who the guy is, is telling."

I close my laptop and glare at him. "Are you trying to get your ass kicked, buddy? Because I *will* if you keep pestering me about confessions of love."

"Yeah, yeah." He chugs his orange juice, and then says, "Just don't do something crazy like lock her in the house."

"That's the stupidest shit you've said today. I'd never do that to Jane or anyone else for that matter."

"I was joking. Jesus, I'd better get out of here before you do kick my ass."

"Yeah, you do that," I say. Then I look at the time and let out a string of curses. I stand in a rush. "Shit! I'm going to be late."

Curse Danny for distracting me with his ideas on romance. I had to race to get to class in time. I can't make a bad first impression today. I was so damn lucky to snag a last-minute spot, and I want the teacher to know it wasn't wasted.

Out of all of the classes that are now available to me thanks to switching majors, Food Management is key in order to run a successful business in my chosen area. I plan to take specialized cooking classes too, now that football season is over.

I'm not the first to arrive like I had planned, but I'm not late either, which is a miracle. I take a seat in the middle row next to a wiry guy who looks as nervous as I feel. I notice his legs are bouncing up and down. Freshman jitters, I guess.

"Hi, I'm Andy," I greet him.

"Taiyo. Nice to meet you."

"Are you from LA?"

"Yeah. And you?"

"Same."

Could this conversation be any stiffer? Gee, it's like I've forgotten how to socialize.

The classroom begins to fill, and I pay attention to the newcomers. I don't recognize any of their faces, but it's no surprise. This is an introduction class, after all. A minute later, the professor comes in. He's sporting a serious countenance that immediately reminds me of Coach Clarkson.

The rattling coming from Taiyo's desk increases. I cut him a look. "Are you that nervous?"

"Yeah. I heard Professor Norman is pretty tough. He rarely gives his students an A, but I can't let my average go down. My parents would kill me."

"I'm sure you'll be fine."

"You don't know them. They're strict as hell."

I bet they don't punish you with punches and kicks when you don't meet their expectations.

"My father is strict too, but I've learned that the only person I have to please is myself."

Taiyo stares at me with his jaw slack. I sense he wants to comment, but Professor Norman begins his lecture. I face forward and ignore my neighbor for the time being.

In the first ten minutes, he explains what he expects from us, and then goes over the required work assignment at the Rushmore Hotel we all must complete for the class. My father will love that. A Rossi doing manual labor is going to severely abuse his ego. Too fucking bad.

After Professor Norman finishes his introduction, he asks each of us to introduce ourselves and explain in a short sentence why we choose hotel management as a major. When it's my turn, I try not to squirm when all eyes turn in my direction. I should be used to attention, but this is different than when I'm on the field, dressed in my uniform and surrounded by my teammates.

"Hi, I'm Andy Rossi. I want to own a bakery business someday, so I figured a degree in hotel management would be the smart course of action for me."

"You're on the football team," someone pipes up.

"Yep," I reply curtly.

I don't know why it matters that I play sports.

"You switched majors late in the game, something that doesn't happen often," Professor Norman says. "I hope you didn't make that decision on a whim."

"No, sir."

"I'm sure you're used to receiving special treatment from my colleagues, but let me warn you, it won't happen in my class. I won't tolerate diva-like behavior here."

My entire body becomes rigid in an instant. I never acted like an ass in class because of my status as a football player or expected to be treated differently by my professors. I'm royally pissed now for Professor Norman to assume so.

"Don't worry, Professor. I won't pull a Kanye West move on you," I reply through a fake smile.

He narrows his eyes for a brief moment, and then turns his attention to Taiyo who stutters through his answer. I get lost in my head throughout the rest of the student introductions, still riding the anger. But eventually, my thoughts wander to Jane and what I'm going to do about the stupid feelings swirling in my chest. I vowed I'd never let them take control of me again, but it seems I'm losing the battle.

When the class actually starts, I have to force myself to pay attention. Professor Norman has already taken my measure and found me lacking. I wanted to do well in this class before—I'm already too far behind—but now I have the extra motivation of proving him wrong.

ELEVEN

JANE

I had to look for an hour until I found my old roller skates. The Hello Kitty print is faded—thankfully—and they're a bit snug, but they'll have to do until I can get to the store and buy a new pair. I was planning on doing that the last time I went to the mall, but Andreas's sudden appearance derailed my plans.

A spike of anger surges within me. I can't believe he followed me there. He'd better not pull that crap again. The worst of this situation is that a part of me—the idiotic, in-love part—is gleeful that Andreas was watching me.

The house is silent. Either Mom is still sleeping, or she didn't come home last night. I tiptoe in the dark anyway until I'm outside. Then I put my skates on and try a few laps on the driveway first. I'm not wearing knee or elbow pads, so I'd better not fall. It takes me a minute to get used to being on wheels again, but once I get my groove, happy memories trickle back. The rush of excitement makes me giddy and for a moment, I forget my problems.

Okay, Jane. Now that you know you still remember how to skate, it's time for the real test.

I press the code to open the gate, and then venture out on the street. The issue is that my mother lives in the Hills. I have to be extra careful not to break my neck going down. My bravado vanishes when I begin to pick up speed and see my death flashing in front of my eyes. I swerve to the side, reaching for the neighbor's gate. My heart is hammering loudly inside of my chest while I try to get air into my lungs.

"Holy shit. That was dumb."

I sit on my ass and remove the skates before I trudge back to the house. I'm so glad the sun isn't up yet, and no one saw my humiliating moment. I have to practice skating on a flat surface. I hurry inside the house to grab my purse and shoes, and then I'm off to the beach. There's no better place to practice than the boardwalk.

Traffic is still relatively light at this time and thus, I arrive at my final destination in no time. School starts in a couple of hours, which means I have at least an hour to practice. Surprisingly, there are quite a few people out already either jogging or exercising on the beach.

I get on with it, and it's like I've been doing this for years. But soon my breathing becomes labored and sweat dots my forehead. I might feel like I'm a pro, but I'm clearly out of shape.

I stop next to a popular cafe to catch my breath and berate myself for not bringing a bottle of water with me. My throat is parched. I don't think they'll mind if I go in with my skates on. I turn to the entrance and then spot a familiar face approaching the cafe from the opposite direction.

"Fred?" I call out since his gaze is down, glued to his phone.

He looks up and a second later, a wide smile blossoms on his face. "Jane. What in the world are you doing here?"

"I could ask you the same question."

He drops his eyes to my skates and slowly looks up. "I see you're practicing for tryouts. Nice."

"Yeah. I have to. I've been skating for less than ten minutes and I'm already winded."

"You'll be fine." He pockets his phone, but the easygoing smile stays in place.

He's an attractive guy. More so now that his hair is no longer an unnatural color. And he's so nice. Why can't I get butterflies when I'm in his presence? Why did I have to meet Andreas first?

"Have you ever been to a tryout?" I ask to keep my thoughts from wandering where they shouldn't.

"A couple of times. They're fun. I could probably give you some pointers."

"Really? That would be awesome."

"Do you have time now? I was going to grab a quick breakfast before heading to work."

"Yeah, I could use a break."

"All right then."

We head to the cafe side by side, but then I remember I don't have any money. "Shit. I forgot my wallet in the car."

"Don't stress about it. It's my treat." He points at a table outside and waits for me to go first, but I'm too self-conscious already.

"No, go ahead. I feel like a giraffe on stilts wearing my skates here."

He laughs. "Trust me, you look nothing like that."

I know he's being flirtatious and it's a nice stroke to my ego, but I feel guilty for enjoying it when my heart is pining for someone who doesn't care.

As soon as we sit down, an energetic waiter comes to take our order. I select the first thing I see on the menu, plus water.

Once he leaves, Fred asks, "Aren't you a little far from home?"

"I felt like coming to the beach to train."

"Hermosa Beach is a good spot. I love living here."

"It's definitely a different vibe than the Hills."

"Don't you have school today?"

"Yeah, but I still have time before first period. Plus, it's not a big deal if I'm late. I'm always on time. Getting a tardy won't kill me."

"Oh, I like this rebellious side of yours. But then again, I always knew you had sass in you."

My cheeks become warmer and I end up lowering my gaze. As much as I want to pretend that I'm a bad girl, I feel like an impostor.

"Thanks? I guess." I shrug.

"So, what do you want to know about the tryouts?"

"How good is the competition? I mean, do I even have a chance?"

"No one expects you to know the rules. If you're a good skater, then you have a strong chance. How fast are you?"

"I don't know. I've never timed myself."

"If you're fast, you'll increase your chances even more. Teams are always looking for potential jammers. And since you're on the slim side, I think that's probably what they'd want you to be."

"What? Are you saying I'm not tough enough to be a blocker?" I fake being offended.

"No, not all. I mean, I don't know. I suppose you're tough since you have an older brother."

"I don't know what having an older brother has anything to do with being tough."

"You remember my cousin Sylvana, right? She has two older brothers, and they were pests to her growing up. She had to toughen up or she wouldn't survive their antics. Even I had to get some brawl in me to deal with them." He chuckles.

"They sound like a fun bunch," I joke. "Troy never picked on me. On the contrary, he was super protective—still is."

"Yeah, I got that vibe from him. What else you want to know about the tryouts?"

"What are they going to ask me to do?"

"Run a few laps on the banked track, see how you do when there are obstacles, etc. Nothing crazy."

The waiter returns with our food and drinks, interrupting our conversation. I dig in, surprised how hungry I am. I'm too busy shoveling food in my mouth to speak. When I'm done, I find Fred looking at me with glee.

"What?" I ask.

"If you skate with the same ferocity you eat your food, then I think you have nothing to worry about."

My cheeks turn as hot as lava. "Oh my God. I wasn't eating like a wild animal, was I?"

He shoves a piece of muffin in his mouth and grins in answer.

I watch him through slits. "Shut up. I wasn't."

"Did I say you were?"

"You implied. But whatever. I don't care. Mother Dearest is not here to chastise me."

His amusement seems to vanish. "Does she give you a hard time often?"

I shouldn't have mentioned her. It's not like me to complain about my mother to anyone. Suffer in silence is my motto. "She has expectations for my future that I don't agree with."

"Let me guess, roller derby isn't something she'd approve of."

"Nope. Hence the appeal."

"See? You're a rebel girl. I can't wait to see you rock on that track."

I cover my face with my hands. "Oh, the pressure. I hope I don't screw up."

TWELVE

JANE

I practiced for the tryouts in any free time I had during the week. I was lucky that Mom was super busy with her business and didn't check on me often. But I still don't think I'm prepared enough for today. I couldn't sleep last night because I was worried about the tryouts.

Restless, I go to the boardwalk again at the crack of dawn for one final practice. I don't return home until eleven, and when I walk through the door, my mother is home and in a tizzy.

"Where the hell have you been?"

"I went to the beach for some exercise."

She looks me up and down, furrowing her brows in a disapproving manner. "You look dreadful. Get in the shower immediately. Your date with Hanson is in less than two hours."

I turn around, and head to my room. She misses my eye roll, not that she'd care. I lost track of time at the beach. I do actually want to look my best today, but not because I want to snag the most eligible bachelor. I don't plan to pick him as my date for the debutante ball anyway, no matter how the lunch goes. This is a test for me to see if I can actually shed the good girl persona. Fred said I was a rebel, and I'm ready to see if it's true.

You've been bad once already, Jane.

My inner voice can be such a bitch sometimes. Yeah, I tricked Andreas into sleeping with me, and look where that led me. Now I have another pain in the ass on my case, as if Troy wasn't bad enough.

I rush through the shower so I can have enough time to blow dry my hair and put my makeup on. I wish Charlie lived closer. She did such a good job with my Harley Quinn makeup. But alas, that's not the case, and anyway, she's probably busy today.

An hour later, I'm satisfied with the way I look. The royal blue dress is stunning and brings out the color in my eyes. It is a bit much for a lunch date, but fuck it, no regrets now. To finish up, I choose strappy sandals that make my legs seem longer. It's a pity that my ensemble is wasted on a date I don't want to go on. But at least I won't be staying long. The tryouts start at two, which gives me just enough time for an appetizer before I have to bail.

Looking in the mirror, I practice my confident posture. If I can get past the dragon—aka Mom—without crumbling under her criticism, then I'll be fine. I need to find my inner strength more than ever today.

She screams my name, telling me I'm going to be late. I glance at my phone and wince. For once, she's not wrong. I'd better hurry or I won't make it on time. I had the foresight to leave my duffle bag and roller skates in the trunk of my car, so I just grab a light jacket and blast past Mom in the living room, going straight for the front door.

"Jane!" she calls me, but I don't stop.

"I'm late," I yell over my shoulder and keep striding toward the front of the house where I parked my car.

My heart is already hammering inside of my chest, but when I see who is waiting for me outside, it stops beating for a second. My steps falter.

"Andy, what are you doing here?"

ANDREAS

It didn't take much to find out the time of Jane's date. I just casually asked Troy when the deadline was to find intel on the guy, and he told me everything I needed to know. On the drive to his mother's house, I agonized over what I was going to tell Jane. Danny wants me to confess, but how can I when I don't even know what the hell is going on inside my heart?

To be sure I wouldn't miss Jane, I arrived early. I've been waiting fifteen minutes when I finally spot her coming down the driveway. I get out of my car, and as she comes near, it seems like a burning fever takes over me. My throat is suddenly dry, and my tongue is stuck in my mouth. There's a crazy commotion in the pit of my stomach, which unfortunately reminds me of what I used to feel for the viper when I was a teen.

Jane stops in her tracks when she notices me. "Andy, what are you doing here?"

I step forward as my mind races at the speed of light. Trying to remain calm is impossible when Jane is wearing a dress that's meant to give men wet dreams. It's a miracle—and a blessing—I'm not sporting a boner right now.

"I heard you were being forced to go on a date with some preppy boy from Stanford."

She snorts. "Let me guess. Troy told you that. Did he send you here to be my chaperone?"

"Actually, he doesn't know that I'm here."

Her eyebrows shoot to the heavens. "Why did you come?"

Here it is, the opening I need to tell her something meaningful, something true. But I can't get the words out. I'm unable to tell her that I don't want her going on any dates or to balls with another guy because I'm jealous as fuck even thinking about it.

"Listen, you don't have to attend that debutante ball with a stranger. I'll gladly be your escort."

Her mouth makes a perfect O, drawing my eyes to her deliciously plump lips. I feel a stirring in my pants and curse my cock for not behaving. She doesn't answer for a moment, but when she does, it's not the answer I was hoping for.

She shakes her head, laughing without humor. "My God, Andy. You are one conceited prick. I'd rather go to the stupid ball with some random guy than suffer your presence for another minute."

Her barb feels like I've been hit by a cannonball. Words shouldn't hurt me so much, but the fact hers did means I've let my guard down again. I should be mad at myself for being weak, for breaking the promise I made years ago. But I don't care that Jane managed to pierce through my barriers.

"Come on, Jane. You can't still be mad about the incident at the mall."

She walks around the front of her car and opens the door. "I'm not. I'm just done with overprotective men in my life. Tell Troy to mind his own business."

"I told you he didn't send me here."

"Whatever. I don't have time for this crap. Bye, Andreas."

She disappears inside the vehicle and takes off in the blink of an eye. I don't move from my spot, processing what just happened.

"Fuck!"

What did I expect? I gave her nothing, not even an apology. Of course she wouldn't accept my offer. Clearly, she's still pissed at me.

I get behind the wheel, but don't drive off right away. There's a good chance that if I catch up with Jane's car, I might end up following her. What I need to do is get Jane alone for more than five minutes so I can plead my case. Maybe I won't choke next time.

THIRTEEN

JANE

I'm still fuming when my phone pings, warning me of an incoming message. I glance briefly at the screen, expecting to see Andreas's name on it, but the text is from Hanson. At a traffic light, I read the message.

> Sorry, Jane. Something came up and I won't be able to meet you today. Let's reschedule. I AM looking forward to meeting you.

I can't believe it. *This fucker is canceling on me?* Ugh, all the time I wasted getting ready I could have spent practicing for the tryouts.

Fuming, I make a U-turn and head to the gymnasium. I'll be early, but it's better if no one sees me wearing a cocktail dress. I don't want them thinking I'm a pampered girl from the Hills. My annoyance quickly vanishes when I encounter more traffic than I expected. What I thought would be a thirty-minute drive ends up taking an hour. When I arrive, I'm not the first one there. Great.

I put on my jacket, but it's short and you can still see the bottom half of my dress. My windows are tinted, so I could change in the car. *Ah, fuck it. I'm doing it.* I fumble with the zipper at the back, but eventually I managed to get the dress off. No one comes near the car, but I'm still uber self-aware that I'm half naked. *You're a rebel girl, Jane. Stop worrying.*

I never went back to the funky store at the mall after Andreas ruined my shopping trip that day. I did go back to buy a new pair of roller skates, but I opted for getting regular workout clothes.

There's a mix of everything today. Girls who are clearly into the culture and went all out with fishnet tights, tiny, colorful shorts, and rock-and-roll makeup. Others, like me, chose the blend-in style. Fred said being a good skater is what's important, not theatrics. I hope he's right.

I follow the herd toward the registration desk. I'm happily surprised to see Katja there, even though the knot in my stomach is tighter than ever.

"Jane! I'm so glad you came. I've heard you've been practicing." She hands me a form to fill out.

"Yeah. Not sure if it will be enough though."

"Don't stress about it. Just try to have fun."

"Oh, stressing is my middle name."

"I'm the same," a girl to my right says.

She's a head shorter than me, and stocky. Her hair is curly and short, dyed hot pink at the tips. But it's her crazy T-shirt that draws my attention the most. It's a pattern print of her face sporting different expressions.

"Nice shirt," I say.

She stretches the fabric down proudly. "I know! I'm Alicia Jackson, by the way."

"Jane Alexander. Nice to meet you."

We get out of line and find a place to sit in the crowded room. It's crazy how popular the sport is. I had no idea. We manage to snag two chairs and for a minute, neither of us speaks, busy filling out the registration form. When I have to list a contact person in case of an emergency, I freeze. *Shit. Who am I going to list?* No one knows I'm doing this.

I nibble on my lower lip and then finally decide to write down Troy's information. I'll tell him if I join a team. I don't want to live a secret life.

"Are you all done?" Alicia asks me.

"Yeah."

"Come on then. Let's pay the registration fee and then check out the competition."

I follow her back to the front of the registration desk. After we pay, Katja hands over blank name tags. Alicia quickly scribbles "Thunder Rose" on hers and places the tag over her chest. *Ah crap, I don't have a moniker.*

"I didn't realize I was supposed to have thought of a nickname," I say.

Katja laughs. "You don't need to pick a name now."

"Thunder Rose is what my grandma used to call me when I was little because I was such menace and my middle name is Rose," Alicia explains.

I follow her to where a cluster of girls are facing the banked track. Alicia butts in the conversation, introducing herself as if she owns the room. Some of them give her a haughty look, others offer names but quickly ignore us. Alicia gives me a what-can-you-do shrug and continues on her recon mission.

"This is so wild. I can't believe I'm here." She leans over the railing, smiling from ear to ear.

"When did you become interested in the sport?" I ask.

"Oh, since I was maybe five. My mother introduced me to it. She was a jammer."

"Oh, how cool. She must have taught you everything."

The happiness vanishes from her face. "Not really. She died when I was young. Breast cancer. I went to live with my aunt after that and she has zero interest in roller derby, or anything extreme for that matter."

"I'm so sorry."

She shrugs. "Don't be. Everyone always gets a look when they learn about my mother. Playing roller derby is a way to keep her memory alive, that's why I'm stoked to finally have turned eighteen so I can participate."

I notice she doesn't mention a father, so I don't ask.

"I just recently learned about roller derby."

She gives me a surprised look. "Shut up. You didn't know about this awesome sport?"

"Well, I knew about it, but I never gave it a second thought. It wasn't until a couple weeks ago that I came to a game and became fascinated by it."

"How do you know Katja? She's a badass jammer. I hope to join her team."

"I collided with her in a hotel restroom. She had flyers for a game and invited me to come."

"There you are," a male voice says from nearby.

Alicia and I turn. Fred is walking in our direction holding a big cup of soda in his hand.

"Hi, Fred. You weren't kidding when you said you'd be there."

"I never joke about roller derby." He turns to Alicia. "Who is your friend?"

"This Alicia Jackson. She's a roller derby legacy."

"Nice." Fred raises his hand up for a high five, which Alicia immediately reciprocates.

"Are you Jane's boyfriend?" she asks.

A blush creeps up my cheeks. "Noooo, Fred is just a friend."

"Damn, girl. Way to put emphasis on that no." He laughs.

"Oh God. I didn't mean it like that. I'm sorry."

"Don't stress." He looks over the gymnasium and whistles. "Wow, there are more girls here today than the last time I came."

"Fantastic," I mumble.

A guy wearing a tracksuit and holding a clipboard begins to steer all the hopefuls to the center of the banked track.

"We'd better get ready," Alicia pipes up.

My pulse accelerates as anticipation shoots up through my veins. I try to remain calm, or project a serene expression, but my hands are shaking as I put my skates on.

"Good luck, girls." Fred waves from his spot near the railing.

I'm too nervous now to respond, so I just follow Alicia and then sit on the floor among the other girls.

The guy with the clipboard proceeds to separate us in groups of five. He does it by alphabetical order, which separates Alicia and me. I'm in the first group, which doesn't help with the nerves.

We run laps on the banked track first, which is harder than it looks. I fall behind on the first loop and when I'm finally getting the hang of it, a girl collides with me and we both fall down in the most ungraceful manner. Laughter echoes in the room. Mortified, I don't make eye contact with anyone as I get up. The girl who bumped into me got back on her feet faster and is already speeding ahead.

It takes another full loop for me to regain my confidence and then it's time for the next group on the track. My face is still in flames when I skate back to where Alicia is sitting.

"That wasn't so bad," she says as sit down.

"It was horrible. God, I fucked up already."

"No, you didn't."

"Didn't you see? I fell."

"So what? Falling is part of the game. Getting up is what matters."

Despite her words of encouragement, I sulk throughout the rest of the first trial. Alicia does extremely well when it's her turn, which doesn't surprise me. She must have been practicing her entire life.

My group is called back on the tracks, and this time, there are cones on it. We must skate in a zigzag while they time us. I put my game face on and try to forget everyone else. My goal is to remain standing and not finish last. Pumping my legs and swinging my arms, I take off, glad that Fred told me about the obstacles so I could practice. I'm so focused on the course that when I approach another girl from behind, I wonder when I fell behind her. I zoom past her, and another. It's not until I pass the fourth girl that I hear Fred shout, "Go, Jane, go!"

I don't slow down until the whistle sounds, and even then, I need another moment to skate off the track. When I return to my spot, Alicia is smiling from ear to ear.

"Jane, that was amazing! I have to step up my game."

"Well, I didn't fall this time." I remove my helmet to cool off my head.

"Not only that. You skated so fast; you were a blur."

"Really? I didn't notice. I was too focused on not falling."

"If you don't make it on a team, I'll be shocked."

I don't want to jinx things by getting my hopes up. After everyone goes through the obstacle course, we practice playing the actual game with some of the team members. I'm first positioned as a blocker. Katja is a jammer for the opposing team. Trying to block her is impossible. She speeds past me before I can move into her path. After a while, it's clear that I'm not cut out to be a blocker. Fred was correct in his earlier assessment. That means I have to do my best as a jammer.

My chance comes up after an hour. The teams switch again, and this time I'm a jammer and Alicia is a blocker on my team. A mean-looking chick with long jet-black hair is my opposing jammer.

"Are you ready to eat dirt?" she asks me with a sneer.

I can't think of a comeback, so I don't say anything.

"That's what I thought," she adds.

The whistles blare and off we go. She takes the lead easily, but I can't let that discourage me. I have to give my all. Adrenaline and motivation fill me with energy. I pump my legs, keeping my gaze sharp to find openings to breach through. And when I can't find them, I make them. Alicia sees me coming hot on her heels, and without a second thought, body slams against the blocker in my path. I blast through and finally score a point for our team.

In the end, we lose, but not by much. I run a lap over the track to catch my breath, and finally search for Fred. He's clapping enthusiastically with a proud smile on his face. I feel a slight tug in my chest. I don't know if it's the high of the game or if I'm actually beginning to see Fred as something other than a friend.

Maybe I'm ready to let go of Andreas once and for all.

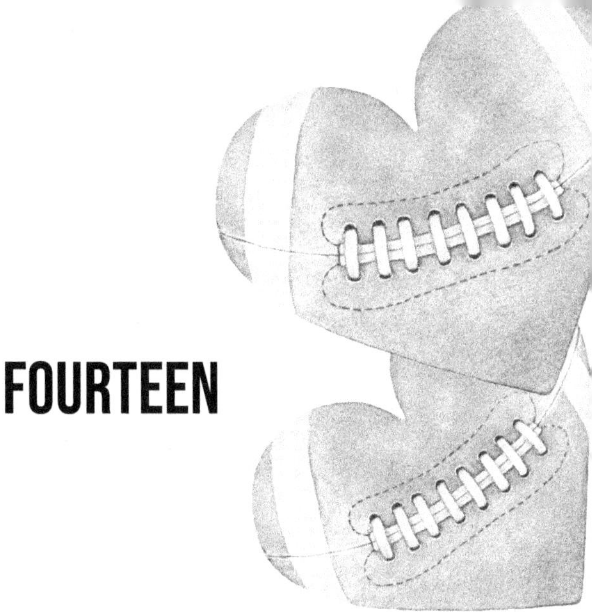

FOURTEEN

"How did it go?" Danny asks the minute I walk into the apartment.

I throw him a glower in response.

"That bad, huh?" His eyes drop to my crotch. "Well, you still have your nuts attached. That's a good sign."

"Ha ha. You're such a comedian." I fall on the couch like a sack of defeated potatoes.

"What happened?" He joins me in the living room, still holding a can of Pringles, but sits as far away from me as possible.

"I offered to be Jane's escort, and she shot me down."

"Did you apologize first?"

"No. And before you say I told you so, I know I messed up, okay?"

He pops a couple of chips in his mouth, chewing loudly as he observes me. I reach for the remote control and pretend to watch whatever game is on TV.

"What's your next move?" he finally asks.

"I don't fucking know. I have to get Jane alone for more than a minute to figure shit out."

"I have an idea."

As annoyed as I am with this whole situation and with the fact that Danny knows too much about my inner turmoil, I still turn to him, showing clear interest in whatever he has to say.

"I'm all ears."

"Two words: barbecue party. The weather is supposed to be nice tomorrow, so let's have a barbecue at Troy's and invite some guys on the team, plus Jane, naturally."

I give him a droll look. "I said I need time alone with Jane. How do you think I'm going to get that in a full house and with Troy watching her every move?"

He grins, his eyes gleaming with mischief. "Simple. It's all a matter of giving Jane the wrong time and creating a reason to get Troy and Charlie out of the house."

I shake my head. "Jesus, where do you get those convoluted ideas? This is real life, not a soap opera."

He shrugs, popping another chip in his mouth. "Make fun of me all you want. My plan will work. Do you want to get Jane alone or not?"

There's no point denying the obvious. I'm desperate. "Fuck yeah."

"Okay then. Don't worry. I'll take care of everything. All you have to do is not muck things up on your end."

I grumble, sinking further into the couch as I cross my arms. "That, my friend, is the biggest challenge."

JANE

I'm on pins and needles as the organizer reads from this clipboard, announcing the names of those who have been selected for the league's bootcamp and what teams they will join after the four weeks of intensive training. When he says Alicia's name, she lets out a squeal and squeezes my arm so hard, I know it will leave a mark. I don't mind the pain. I'm sore in so many places already, what difference does one more spot make?

My heart is racing; there are only two spots left. The second-to-last name he calls is not mine. My heart sinks. That's it. I didn't make it. Alicia laces her fingers with mine and holds my hand in a death grip. *Gee, she's strong.*

"And last, but not least, Jane Alexander, for Second Time Around Divas," the organizer calls.

"Yes!" Alicia throws her arm over my shoulders. "I knew you would make it!"

"Oh my God. I can't believe it," I murmur, still stunned.

She helps me to my feet, and in a daze, I let her steer me toward the railings where Fred is waiting for us. No sooner am I within reach than he hugs me enthusiastically, almost sending us both to the floor.

"Easy there. I can't fall now in front of the organizers. They might realize they made a mistake."

He pulls away. "No way, Jose. You were the fastest skater today. They'd be crazy if they didn't snatch you."

Katja approaches us, grinning from ear to ear. "Congrats, Jane. I'm so stoked we got you on our team. And Alicia, wow. Your mother would have been so proud."

"Thanks," she beams.

"What happened to your voice, Katja?" Fred asks, noticing how rough it sounds.

"Oh my God. You have no idea how hard it was to snatch Alicia and Jane for Second Time Around Divas. It ended in a screaming match."

"More than one team wanted us?" I ask, unable to hide the surprise from my tone.

"Oh yeah. The Bay Hurricane team wanted you badly. But in the end, Scary Samantha made our case for us."

"Scary Samantha? Who is that?" I ask.

"The jammer who gave you a hard time," Alicia replies.

"Oh. The brunette?"

"Yup." Katja nods.

"How did she make the case for you?"

"She didn't want you on her team. She doesn't like competition. So in the end, her refusal to accept the obvious worked in our favor."

"Accept the obvious? I don't follow."

"You're way faster than she is. She's afraid you'll dethrone her," Alicia pipes up.

"Aren't you worried that will happen to you?" I ask Katja, even though I really don't think that's possible. She was so good in the game I watched.

"Of course not. I don't care who is the lead jammer on our team. I care about winning, and with you two on board, damn, there's no stopping us next season."

"When do we start bootcamp?" Alicia asks eagerly.

"Next weekend, bitches. We train Saturday and Sunday from eight to four, so you'd better clear all your weekend plans for the next four weeks."

Ah, crap. I have the stupid luncheon at the marina and the debutante ball is in six weeks, which means more long and boring social events until then. How am I going to get out of them?

"That sounds great," I say through a fake smile.

Fred lingers while I remove my skates, and then walks out with Alicia and me. She asks for my phone number and we make plans to meet up next week to practice. Once she leaves, Fred turns to me.

"You did really well out there. I even recorded some of it if you would like to see."

I twist my face into a grimace. "Ugh, better not. I probably look awful."

"Not at all. Anyway, I feel like such an achievement needs to be celebrated. Do you want to go somewhere grab a bite to eat?"

Now that I'm coming down from the high, my body remembers that I've been running on fumes. I never ate lunch, thanks to Hanson canceling our date. But looking at Fred's open and expectant face makes me hesitant to accept his invitation. I know he likes me, but I'm not sure yet if I'm ready to see where this will lead. He's not a rebound guy, that's for sure. I need more time.

"Gosh, I wish I could, but my mother is expecting me, and I don't want to push my luck."

Disappointment washes over his face, but he quickly buries it under a smile. "That's okay. Raincheck?"

"Yeah, sure. Thanks for coming today to cheer me on."

"You're welcome. I can't wait to watch your debut."

"Four weeks. Boy, that's going to fly by." I hug my middle when a sudden tension forms in the pit of my stomach again.

I thought surviving the tryouts would be the hardest part and that once it was over, I wouldn't have this ball of dread in my belly. I was obviously wrong. First, I have to find a way to come to bootcamp without my mother finding out. And then I actually have to get out there, and be part of a team of badass chicks.

Did I bite off more than I can chew?

I say goodbye to Fred and once inside my car, I check my messages. Mom texted me a few times to ask how the date went. I ignore her for now. There's also a missed call from Troy. Did he call to apologize for sending Andreas over to do his dirty work? I still don't buy that he came of his own accord.

Curious, I call my brother back. He answers on the second ring.

"Hey, Jane. How's it going?"

"What's up, Troy?" I reply coldly.

"Do you have any plans tomorrow? I'm throwing a last-minute barbecue party at my place since the weather will be nice. Wanna come?"

I consider his invitation for a second. My body is too sore

after today, so there's no practicing tomorrow. And if I come, Mom won't have much opportunity to pester me about the debutante ball or how I still don't have an escort. The only issue is that Andreas will probably be there.

"Who's coming?"

"Danny, Andy, Puck, I think Paris too, and a few other people you don't know. It's not a big party or anything. It will be chill. That's what I told Danny, anyway, when he made the suggestion."

"Oh, so this barbecue was Danny's idea, not yours?"

"Yeah. Does it matter?"

Considering Danny is Andreas's roommate, I have reason to be suspicious. On the other hand, Andy wouldn't be crazy enough to pull a stunt in front of Troy.

"No, not really," I say. "What time?"

"Eleven."

"Okay, I'll be there."

FIFTEEN

ANDREAS

Danny and I arrive at Troy's a little before ten to have enough time to setup for the barbecue. I still don't know how he plans to get them out of the house for at least an hour so I can a have chance to speak to Jane alone. He told me not to worry about it, so we'll see what he comes up with.

I'm in the backyard getting everything ready when Troy sticks his head out and shouts. "Yo, Andy. We have to run to the store. Charlie needs something and I forgot to buy the veggie burgers for Paris's fancy ass."

I'm about to ask why Paris can't buy his own damn burgers when my brain catches up with my mouth. That's the excuse to get Troy out of the house. How he fell for it will remain a mystery until I can grill Danny later.

"Okay. I'll keep working here."

I wait a couple of minutes before I head back in to make sure the coast is truly clear. I also don't want to miss when Jane arrives. My stomach is tied in knots, a sensation I never thought a girl would make me feel again. I pass a hand over my face, fighting the urge to grab a cold beer from the fridge to take the edge off. But alcohol won't help me now. I have to be stone-cold sober for this. The likelihood I'll say something wrong is already high enough as it is.

Whenever I'm nervous, keeping my hands busy helps. I search Troy's pantry, hoping he has the basic ingredients for something simple. Surprisingly, I find everything I need—thank you, Charlie—and that alone already calms me down. I spot a few bananas that are turning brown and decide to make a banana cake. As I measure the ingredients, I keep an eye on my phone. Jane was told to get here at eleven, and it's already ten to.

A minute later, I hear a car door slam outside. My heartbeat kicks up a notch. Another moment passes before Jane walks in, carrying two grocery bags. We both freeze as our stares connect.

"Hi Jane," I croak.

"Where is everyone?" she walks over slowly, her eyes shining with apprehension. Any wrong word will send her into flight mode. I have to be careful here.

"They had to make a quick run to the store."

She sets her groceries bags on the counter and glances at the mixture bowl in front of me. "What are you making?"

"Banana cake. I was bored."

"I never knew you baked."

"There are many things you don't know about me."

She doesn't reply, but she also doesn't break eye contact. There's something different about her today. She seems more confident and I wonder if it has anything to do with her date yesterday. I become blind with jealousy, but fight to appear unaffected.

"How was your date?" I ask, making an effort to keep my tone normal.

Her eyes narrow. "Don't start."

I widen my eyes innocently. "What? It was just a question. Can't a friend ask?"

"We were never friends." She crosses her arms over her chest. "You're my brother's annoying sidekick."

Ouch. Jane one, Andy zero. I walk over the counter, needing to get closer to her. She seems leery of my approach, but at least she doesn't step back.

"My mistake. I thought we were more than that." My voice drops to a low timbre, giving my words a double meaning.

Satisfaction rushes through me when I catch Jane swallow hard. She noticed it too and is not unaffected.

"That's because you think the world revolves around you," she retorts.

I stop in front of her, an inch away from invading her personal space. My heart is beating savagely inside of my chest, almost as if it wants to burst out. *Jesus fucking Christ. What's happening to me?*

"You didn't answer my question," I press.

"God, you can't drop anything, can you? You're like a dog with a bone."

"You have no idea how much that statement is true."

"Fine, if you must know, the douchecanoe canceled the date."

Yes! I shout in my head, punching the air.

"Try not to look so smug about it," she continues.

"I'm not." I grin.

"Ugh. You're insufferable." She slams her open palm over my chest as she tries to sidestep me, but I grab her arm, stopping her.

She whimpers, causing me alarm. I let go of her at once. "I'm sorry. Did I hurt you?"

Without making eye contact, she steps back, massaging the place I held her. "No, don't be silly."

I watch her carefully. She's hiding something. "Let me see your arm, Jane."

"What for? I told you I'm fine." Her voice rises an octave.

She's definitely lying. *Why?*

"Let me see your arm, Jane." I stalk her, not caring if I invade her personal space now.

"No," she replies stubbornly.

I reach for her again, grabbing her arm and squeezing a bit tighter this time.

"Ouch! Let go of me, you brute."

"I'm not pressing that hard. You're hurt."

Done with her bullshit, I yank her hoodie's sleeve off her shoulder, and see then the massive bruise on her arm. She pulls away from my grasp, face red with fury, and adjusts the sleeve.

"What the hell, Andy!"

"I could say the same thing, Jane. What the hell? Who did this to you?"

Her eyebrows shoot to the heavens. "No one."

"Don't lie to me. You're protecting that fuckboy who almost got you pregnant, aren't you?"

Her mouth opens, but no sound comes from it.

"That's it, isn't it?" I whirl around, pressing my knuckle against my forehead. I'm so furious that I could break something. "Fuck! I'm going to kill him."

"For fuck's sake, Andreas! No one hurt me," she shouts, frustrated.

I look at her again. "Then what happened?"

She takes a deep breath, dropping her gaze to the floor for a second before meeting my eyes again. "I got hurt during roller derby tryouts yesterday."

"What?"

"You heard me." She lifts her chin higher.

"Roller derby? For real?"

Her green eyes darken. "Yeah, for real. What's with the surprised tone? You don't think I can handle roller derby?"

I shake my head. "It's not that. I just didn't know you were into extreme sports."

"It's a new interest."

I'm relieved her injury wasn't caused by an asshole. But now I have so many questions.

"Fair enough, but why are you keeping it a secret?"

She runs her hand through her hair. "Well, my mother will never approve, for starters. And I don't know yet what Troy will say. I'm tired of having people dictate what I can and cannot do. It's my life, damn it."

Shit. I'm one of the assholes who was trying to keep Jane in a cage. I feel wretched, worse than the lowest scum.

"I'm sorry."

"For which part? Acting like a deranged caveman, or calling me a liar?"

"For everything. I lost my mind when I learned you were no longer...." *Ah, fuck, I can't go there.*

"I was no longer what? A virgin?" She raises an eyebrow in challenge.

I shake my head, not meeting her eyes. "Forget I said anything."

"Oh my God. That's what you were going to say. Why do you care? I'm nothing to you, just your best friend's little sister who stole a kiss from you a million years ago."

Her reminder of that day forces me to look at her. Her cheeks are red from anger, but it's her eyes that are my undoing. They're so open and vulnerable. This is it. It's now or never.

"You have no idea how wrong you are. There hasn't been a day that I haven't thought about that kiss. It might be a distant memory to you, but to me, it's like it happened yesterday."

She snorts. "That's rich. Do you want me to believe that the kiss of a clumsy fifteen-year-old is imprinted in your mind? Maybe as a horrifying memory."

"Horrifying? Are you insane? It's one of the best memories I have."

"What are you trying to say, Andy? Do you have a thing for me now? Is that it?"

I yank my hair at the strands. "I have no other explanation."

Disappointment washes over her face and it's clear I said the wrong thing.

"No other explanation, huh? I have one for you. How about you're a player, and I'm just something new that caught your eye?"

"No, you're not just another plaything. I care about you." I step closer. "More than I should."

She laughs with derision. "You know, if you had told me that a few months ago, I might have believed you. But I've seen you in action. I know you don't mean a word you say."

"You've seen me action? What's that supposed to mean?"

Her face turns ashen as guilt shines in her eyes. "Never mind."

"Don't 'never mind me'. Tell me, Jane. Where and when did you see me in action?"

"I don't have to answer anything." She turns around and veers for the door.

"Oh no. You're not going to run away from me without answering the question." I run past her and block the exit.

"Get out of my way, Andy. I'm serious."

"I will if you tell me when you got proof that I'm too much of a player to possibly develop feelings for you."

This is going all wrong. I'm confessing, but not exactly how I planned in my head.

"You don't have feelings for me. Stop saying that!" she snaps.

"You want proof that what I'm saying is true?" I step closer, but this time, Jane steps back.

I don't stop though; I keep going until she has nowhere to go. I back her against the wall, caging her in.

"How about I've been going crazy out of my mind imagining you with someone else? It kills me that you slept with another guy. And do you want to know why? Because I don't want you with anyone else but me. I tried to fight it, Jane. By God, I did. You've always been off-limits for more reasons than one."

Tears gather in her eyes, confusing the hell out of me. I reach for her face to wipe the first tear that rolls down her smooth cheek. "Why are you crying?"

A storm of dark emotions forms in her eyes. She bats my hand away. "Because you're saying everything I've always wanted to hear, but it doesn't matter now. It's too late."

The truth hits me like a steely punch. Jane might have had feelings for me before, but I waited too long and now she's in love with someone else.

I step back, not wanting to prolong this awkward moment any further. My whole life, I've always fought for what I wanted, but with Jane, I can't force my will. She should run far away from me.

"You're not going to ask me why it's too late?" she asks in a tight voice.

"No need. I get it now. I lost my chance. Don't worry. I won't bother you anymore. I'll try to rein in my jealousy. I hope this dude is worthy of you."

Speaking those words out loud is like stabbing myself in the chest. It seems now that I've confessed my feelings for her, everything hurts ten thousand times more. I've lowered my shields. There's no protection from the blows.

She watches me with round, bright eyes, and when more tears streak her face, she doesn't bother to dry them off. She should be relieved that I'm backing off without a fight. So why is she staring at me like I broke her heart?

"It was you," she blurts out.

"It was me what?"

"You were my first and you don't even remember."

The floor seems to vanish beneath my feet. My pulse skyrockets, blowing my head off its orbit, making my ears ring. How could I have done something so careless and not remember? Fear grips my insides. I'm terrified to find out the truth, but I have to know how low I managed to go.

"Jane, what did I do?"

SIXTEEN

hat have I done? I swore to take my dirty secret to the grave, and I just go and blurt out the truth to Andreas?

"Jane, what did I do?" he asks in a pitiful voice.

Hell, he must think he did something horrible to me, when in reality, I'm the one who did the despicable act. I can't backtrack now. I have to tell him everything and risk him hating me forever.

"I went to your Halloween party."

He furrows his eyebrows together, probably trying to fish out his drunken memory from a forgotten corner of his brain. Suddenly, his eyes widen.

"You were Harley Quinn?"

I close my eyes for a second, fighting a new wave of tears. "Yes."

"I was drunk out of my mind that night, Jane. You knew I hadn't recognized you. How could you?"

"I'm sorry."

"You're sorry? You're sorry!" he yells, making me wince.

"You tricked me into crossing the line with you, something I tried so hard not to do."

"I know! And that's why I did it. It was wrong, no denying that. You weren't ever supposed to know."

"Oh, that makes it so much better." He throws his hands up in the air. "Why would you want your first time to be with someone so wasted he wouldn't recognize the girl he had been pining after for years?"

I hastily wipe the tears from my eyes. "Because it was *you*! I've been in love with you since I stole that kiss."

There's no point keeping that part a secret anymore. I'm already in a pit of despair, might as well get all the truth out.

His face contorts as if he's in pain. "You lied to me. I've been going crazy, hating the asshole who almost got you pregnant. Little did I know that jerk was me."

Dropping my chin, I glance at the floor. "You weren't supposed to know," I repeat weakly.

"I can't be here. I have to go."

I look up and watch Andreas stride out of the house. As soon as he closes the door with a loud bang, I cover my face with my hands and let the ugly tears fall. The torrential stream gets worse when I hear the loud rumble of his Bronco. He's never going to forgive me. If only I had known that he had feelings for me. *God, what a mess.*

A moment later, the door bursts open again. My breath catches. Andreas is back and he's coming for me.

"Andy, I—"

He captures my face in his large hands and crashes his lips against mine. His possessive tongue invades my mouth with fury and passion. I can taste the anger in his savage kiss, but also all the suppressed feelings he hid from everyone, even me.

When I don't think I can remain standing any longer, he pulls away, leaving me confused and lightheaded.

"You're coming with me." He takes my hand and steers me out of the house.

I'm too dazed to question him, so I just let him take me wherever he wants.

"Where's your car?" he asks.

"I had to park it a block away."

"Good."

He opens the door of his Bronco for me, waits until I slide inside, and then shuts it again. I don't take my eyes off him, trying to decipher what's going on in his head. The intensity in his eyes is still there, but I can't read the emotion.

Silently, he takes his seat behind the steering wheel. He left the engine running when he went back into the house to get me. But he doesn't drive off immediately.

He turns to me. "Buckle up."

With shaking hands, I do as he says. It's only then that he puts the car in Drive.

"Where are we going?"

"Back to my place."

"Why?"

"Because I need to make things right."

I have no idea what that means, but there are excited butterflies and a knot of dread in my stomach competing for space.

"What about Troy? The barbecue?"

"Don't worry about that."

Andreas's jaw is locked tight, and I can't see his eyes anymore since he's wearing sunglasses now. He kissed me, but now he's acting like he didn't set my body ablaze a minute ago.

I face the road ahead, but I couldn't recall the color of the car in front of us if asked. My mind is racing, going at hundred miles an hour. My heartbeat is not far behind. The thumping inside my chest is as loud as the car's engine.

The drive is shorter than I remember, maybe because Andreas broke the speed limit to get us here faster. I force my body to move and get out of the car before he can circle around to open the door for me. I feel like I'm inside a vortex and I need to regain some control.

The corners of his lips twitch upward as he steps in front of me, then he takes my hand again and together we enter the building. We bump into two sorority girls in the lobby. They both greet Andreas in a sugary tone, completely ignoring me. But he doesn't acknowledge them, and despite my nervousness, I smirk, pleased beyond measure.

We ignore the elevator and head for the stairs. Andreas's apartment is on the top floor, but it's only four flights up. Whatever is on his mind, he's in a hurry to get to it. We race up the stairs, taking two steps at a time. My leg muscles protest; I'm still sore from yesterday. I suck it up though. I'm eager to reach his place too, because the suspense is killing me.

Andreas doesn't let go of my hand, not even to fish his key out of his pocket or open the door. When I step foot in his apartment, all the memories come rushing back. I haven't been here since the Halloween party.

The sound of the door slamming shut again makes me jolt, but I don't have time to recover from it before Andreas spins me around and kisses me again. He drops my hand to capture my face once more, almost as if he's afraid I'm going to run away. He obviously doesn't know how intoxicating his kiss is. I wouldn't be able to move from this spot even if his apartment were on fire.

He moves one hand to the back of my head, tangling his fingers with my hair, while his other hand runs down my side, grazing the underside of my breast before resting on my hip. He digs his fingers in my skin, pulling me closer, and I moan in response, not sure if this is really happening or if I'm dreaming.

The sound of a phone ringing bursts through the rose-colored haze surrounding us. With a groan, Andreas pulls back, biting my lower lip before letting go.

"To be continued. Don't go anywhere."

Like I'd be able to move even if I wanted to.

"Hey, Danny. What's up?"

"Where are you?" Danny asks.

I'm close enough to Andreas I can hear him clearly.

"Something came up." He looks at me, smiling cheekily.

"Troy is bitching that you left a mess in the kitchen."

"Ah, crap. I totally forgot about the banana cake."

"What do I tell him?"

"Shit." He threads his fingers through his hair, pushing his long bangs back. "Tell him Lorenzo needed me."

"Okay, but you know you'll have to elaborate on your excuse. Does your disappearing act have anything to do with you-know-who?"

"Yeah, it does."

The heated gaze he gives me makes my entire body go haywire. I'm craving his touch, but at the same time, I have to know what's going on here. This little break worked to get some of my sanity back.

"I have to go." Andreas presses the End button and shoves his phone back in his jacket pocket.

"Wait," I tell him when he steps closer to me. "Why did you bring me here, Andy? I thought you were furious with me."

"I was mad for a hot second, but I was the idiot who didn't realize who you were." He tucks a loose strand of hair behind my ear. "Right now, I'm angry at myself for not remembering much of that evening. You didn't deserve for your first time to be a rough tumble in the sheets with a drunk bastard like me."

"You might not remember much, but it wasn't a bad experience."

"Did I hurt you?"

My cheeks become hot. It's silly to get embarrassed when we've already done more than fool around.

"It hurt just a little."

He kisses me again sweet and fast, and then presses his forehead against mine. "I'm sorry."

"I'm the one who needs to be apologizing here. For tricking you, for lying."

"You've been a naughty girl, sweet Jane." He chuckles. "Now what you said makes sense. I acted like a jackass that night. I've been bad for the longest time. My reputation is not a lie."

"What does that mean for us?" I ease off. "If you don't think you can com—"

He presses a finger against my lips. "I wouldn't have started anything with you if I wasn't serious. But I am a broken asshole, Jane. There's a good chance I'll fuck up. I always do."

I search his eyes and read nothing but the truth. He believes wholeheartedly in his statement and that breaks my heart.

I hold his face between my hands. "I won't let you."

"Well, I already did."

"Let's agree that we both messed up. Which means we get a clean slate."

He kisses my nose, and then the corners of my lips. Goose bumps break out on my arms and a shot of desire travels down to my core.

"I'd like that. I want to make it up to you if you'll let me." He kisses me again, long and hard this time.

I reach for his arms, digging my fingers into the fabric of his jacket. At once, the fire he ignited when he kissed me at Troy's returns. I match the tempo of his tongue beat for beat while I step closer to his inferno. The man is incendiary and I'm burning hot for him.

He breaks the kiss suddenly to whisper against my lips, "Is that a yes?"

"It's a hell yeah." I try to capture his lips again, but he stops me.

"Wait. We're not rushing through this. Since I don't remember our first time, this is a do-over. We're taking things slowly."

"How slowly?"

He smiles wickedly. "I'll show you."

His fingers lace with mine and we head to his bedroom. Everything is as I remember, but this time, he knows who I am. I look at the bed, letting those memories assault me. My clit throbs, recalling the feel of his length inside of me.

Andreas kisses my neck while he pulls my hoodie off. I close my eyes, letting out a whimper. He runs his fingertips over my bruise and whispers, "Does it hurt a lot?"

"Not right now."

He bends over and kisses the spot. "Do you have any other places in need of attention?"

"Yeah, right here." I touch the side of my thigh.

"I'm afraid I'll have to inspect that closer."

He drops into a crouch in front of me and tugs my leggings down. I reach for his shoulders, needing the support to remain upright. When he sees the huge purple mess, he freezes.

"What the hell. How did you get this?"

"Someone collided with me on the banked track and we both fell."

He glances up. "I don't like to see you injured like this."

I furrow. "Do you really want to start this relationship by giving me grief over roller derby?"

"I'm not giving you grief. I'm just saying I don't like to see you covered in bruises."

"You'll have to get used to it."

He narrows his eyes. "Only if I get to see you kick ass on the track."

A bubble of laughter goes up my throat. "I still have to go through bootcamp."

"Yes, you do. Right here in my bedroom." He runs his tongue over my bruised leg, erasing my amusement in an instant. All that's left is yearning for this beautiful man.

He curls his fingers around the sides of my panties and looks up. "May I?"

I nod, unable to form words. My throat is dry now. Anything I say will probably sound like a croak.

Keeping eye contact, Andreas rolls down my underwear, exposing my sex. He keeps going until they're off.

"Did I taste you here, Jane?" he asks in a husky voice.

"No."

"Tsk. That needs to be remedied."

His face disappears between my thighs, and when his tongue finds my clit, I cry out, unprepared for the sensation. He laughs, blowing hot air against my core, and then continues his delicious torture.

"Oh my God, Andy. Take me to bed."

"Why? I'm perfectly fine here."

"My legs are about to give out."

"All right."

He grabs me by the hips, applying pressure to the bruise. I bite my tongue to keep the whimper bottled in. I don't want to get him distracted by my injuries again. He doesn't notice because as soon as I'm sitting at the edge of his mattress, he reaches for my breast with one hand, and pushes me down while he opens my legs with his other. Then he resumes eating my pussy as if it were candy.

The room begins to spin. I'm back inside the vortex, only there's no regaining any kind of control anymore. I let go of all restraint and soon, the orgasm hits me, more intense than the first time. I moan, and call his name, shaking from head to toe. Andreas only stops when I can't take the assault against my sensitive spot any longer and beg for mercy.

I don't move while I catch my breath. The room is no longer spinning, but I am still floating on air.

The mattress dips to my right when Andreas lays by my side, propping his head against his fist.

"How did I do?" he asks.

"Do you want me to give you a score?"

"Not exactly. I want to pretend this is our first time together."

His eyes soften, and if it's possible, I fall in love with him even more. "Technically, it is. On Halloween, you fucked Harley Quinn."

He glowers. "Don't talk like that. I hate that you experienced my asshole self."

I roll on top of him, holding his arms above his head as I straddle him. "Fine. I won't talk about the past anymore, but only if you stop calling yourself names."

"Why? It's the truth."

He can be a jerk, controlling, a veritable pain in the butt. But when he belittles himself, it causes a pang in my chest. I curl my fingers tighter around his wrists, putting more weight on them.

"Promise me."

"Fine, I promise. Can I have my hands back now? I have plans for them."

"Hmm, I don't know. I kind of like you in this submissive position."

He narrows his eyes to slits. "You know you weigh nothing, and I can easily break free."

"I wouldn't be so sure about th—"

In a swift move, he dislodges me, rolling over to cover me like a blanket. "You were saying?"

"Not fair. You caught me by surprise."

"Do you want to see unfair moves?" He rotates his hips, pressing his rock-hard erection against my clit.

I whimper, drawing a smirk from him. *Oh yeah? Two can play at this game.* I lift my knees, hooking my ankles together behind his ass, and then pull him to me.

"How about my moves?" I capture his lower lip between my teeth and tug slightly.

"One hundred percent unfair. I think it's time to be reintroduced to your sweet pussy."

SEVENTEEN

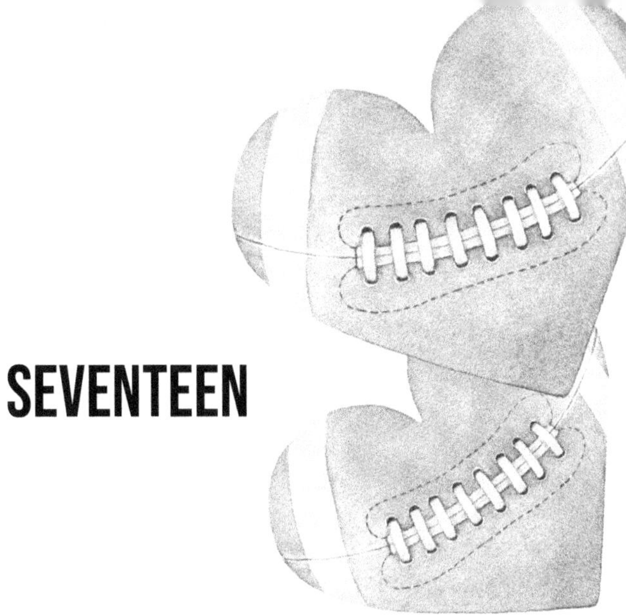

ANDREAS

I roll off Jane for a second to search for a condom in my nightstand drawer. The box is almost empty, a sign I haven't been myself for a while. I always make sure I've got plenty on hand. Maybe there's hope for me after all. Maybe my father and Crystal are wrong, and I'm not a fuck-up.

I can't think about those two hateful people now. Not when I have the most beautiful girl—inside and out—next to me.

I turn to her. "Where were w—"

My words get stuck in my mouth. Jane has gotten rid of the rest of her clothes, and is now lying naked on her side, watching me with a Cheshire cat smile. My gaze drops to her glorious breasts, causing me acute pain, especially in my crotch. My dick seems to grow larger at the sight.

"You were saying?" she asks.

"My God, you're beautiful."

A blush spreads over her cheeks, but she holds my gaze. "It's your turn now. You're wearing far too many clothes for my liking."

I jump from the bed and get rid of my jeans and shirt faster than I've ever done anything in my life. Jane's eyes drop to my cock, and I swear they widen a fraction.

"You can touch it if you want to."

She lifts her gaze to mine again. "You said the same thing to me on…. Never mind."

We agreed to leave the past behind, but I'm too curious to let that one go. It's fucking sad that I don't remember the details of that night.

"Oh? And what did you do?"

Groaning, she rolls on her back and pulls a pillow to cover her face. "I don't want to talk about it. I shouldn't have even mentioned it."

Damn it. Now I really have to know. I take the pillow away from her. "Come on, sweetheart. Tell me. This is a safe space." I smile.

She snorts. "Safe space? You're having too much fun at my expense."

"I'm not making fun of you. But like you said, I can't let things go. I'm a dog with a bone."

Her gaze narrows. "Fine. But this is the last time we're going to discuss that night."

"Cross my heart and hope to die." I make the sign across my chest.

She sighs, resigned. "I tried giving you a blow job, but I'm pretty sure I sucked at it. You didn't even let me finish."

A burst of laughter escapes my mouth. "That's what you're embarrassed about?"

"Don't laugh!"

"I'm sorry, sweetheart, but it's pretty funny."

"No, it isn't. Shit. Now I'm mortified all over again."

I cover her with my body, pressing my cock against her belly. "I probably didn't want to come in your mouth."

"That's what you said, but I wasn't sure if it was true. I've never sucked a guy before."

Her confession makes me feel crazy good. "Don't worry,

babe. I'll teach you, but now, I want to fuck you until you see fireworks."

She opens her legs wider and arches her back. "Hmm, I'm fine with that."

I pepper her neck with open-mouthed kisses, loving the goose bumps that form on her skin. "Tell me, Jane," I whisper in her ear. "Did I make you come the first time?"

"Yeah."

I draw my tongue across her collarbone. "Good. It wasn't a total bust then."

"No, you were amazing and considerate, despite not knowing who I was."

I lean on my elbows to peer at her face. "I'll never forgive myself for that."

She cups my cheek. "You have to, because I already did."

My chest overflows with emotion and I can't breathe for a moment. I thought I knew what I felt for her. I mistakenly confused it with the same feelings I had when I was a naïve teenager. But this is different. It's so much more and I can't quite describe it.

I bring my lips to hers again, kissing Jane deeply and slowly. I want to savor her mouth, be consumed by her taste. Jane's hands find my back, her nails scratching my skin softly. She begins to gyrate her hips underneath me, and immediately, I mimic the movements of what's to come.

My cock is now pressed against her heat. She's so slick between her legs that it won't take much to slide in. I can't let that happen. One pregnancy scare is way too many.

"Hold on, sweetheart. I have to put protection on before I lose my mind."

I reach for the condom, and then sit on the balls of my feet. I keep my eyes locked with Jane's as I tear the wrapper and fish the condom out.

"Can I put it on?" she asks.

"Yeah," I say in a voice I barely recognize.

Her fingers are nimble and gentle, but her hands on my cock is absolutely torture. My balls tighten. This could very well end up with me pulling a quick draw move on her. I squeeze my butt cheeks and focus on not coming yet.

As soon as the condom is in place, I fumble forward, locking my lips with hers as I sheathe myself inside her tight pussy. I said I was going to take things slow, but my body seems to have other ideas. I'm fighting against three years of lusting after the impossible, three years of wanting to the most beautiful girl I've ever laid my eyes upon.

Jane's hands find my back again, but this time she digs her nails deep. It will leave a mark and I don't care. She can brand me all she wants because I'm as much hers as she is mine.

The bed begins to rattle. The headboard is banging against the wall loudly and in sync with the pumping of my hips. I'm glad this isn't Jane's first time. I'm fucking her so hard, it'll be a miracle if we can walk straight afterward.

Her knees are up, her legs crossed behind me. She's kissing with tongue and teeth. This isn't as a sweet moment as I thought it would be. This is raw need. This is letting go and being consumed by a passion that's been brewing for the longest time.

"Jane, babe, please tell me you're close," I whisper against her mouth.

"Oh my God," she breathes out, capturing my face between her hands.

Her body convulses, her walls tighten around my dick, and I lose it. I'd scream if I wasn't busy kissing the hell out of her. Now my body is shaking too as I empty myself inside of her. I don't stop moving. I piston in and out even faster, trying to prolong the best orgasm of my life.

Eventually, all good things must come to an end. I shudder with one final thrust, and then collapse next to her.

"Fuck," I say out of breath.

When Jane doesn't reply, I roll on my side toward her. Her eyes are closed, but her breathing is as erratic as mine.

"Jane, babe. Are you okay?"

"Give me a second. I'm trying to reassemble my body after it burst into a million pieces across the galaxy."

"Are you saying I gave you an out-of-this-world orgasm?" I ask, amused.

She pries one eye open. "Yes, you turned me into stardust."

Unable to resist her beautiful, sexed-up face, I kiss her. It was meant to be a quick one, but now that I've tasted her, I'm greedy for more. She brings her body flush with mine, as eager to keep going as I am.

"Hold on, babe. I have to get rid of the condom first."

"Oh, sorry."

It takes me only a few seconds to discard the condom in the bathroom bin, but when I return to my room, Jane is already half dressed.

"What do you think you're doing? I thought you wanted round two."

"I heard my phone ring in the living room. I bet it's Troy asking me where I am."

I push my hair back. "Oh shit. I totally forgot about the barbecue."

She pulls her leggings up, and I know I won't be taking them off again today. The magnitude of what we did hits me at once. Troy will kill me when he finds out about us.

Hastily, I put a pair of sweatpants on and follow Jane to the living room. My eyes drop to her sweet ass, and I don't feel an ounce of guilt. I can finally ogle her freely now—at least when we're alone.

"It was Troy. I'd better call him back."

"What are you going to tell him?"

She turns around. "I don't know. Definitely not the truth. I don't want his reaction to spoil things for us yet. I hope he hasn't spotted my car."

"We can't keep our relationship a secret from him forever."

She bites her lower lip, causing a stirring in my pants. *Jesus, settle down, Andreas.*

"I know we can't, and I don't want to. But this is so new, I don't even know yet where we stand."

I walk over, and then pull her closer to me. "I want you, Jane. I've wanted you for a long time. I'm not going to let you slip through my fingers. I'm yours."

"Exclusively?"

"What kind of question is that? Of course, exclusively. Unless you want to date other people."

She twists her face into a scowl. "Now you're being thick on purpose. It has always been you, Andy."

"Good. That means I'm taking you to the debutante ball."

Her eyebrows arch. "It's in six weeks. That means we have to come out to Troy way sooner than that."

"Why?"

"You don't know your best friend? He's going to flip, and it will probably take him ages to get over his overprotective brother issues and accept that you're my boyfriend."

I smile from ear to ear, letting the happiness flow freely through me. "I love that you called me your boyfriend."

"You do?" Her eyes twinkle.

"I do, sweet Jane." I kiss her on the cheek—it's safer—and then step back. "Now call your annoying brother back so we can resume our activities."

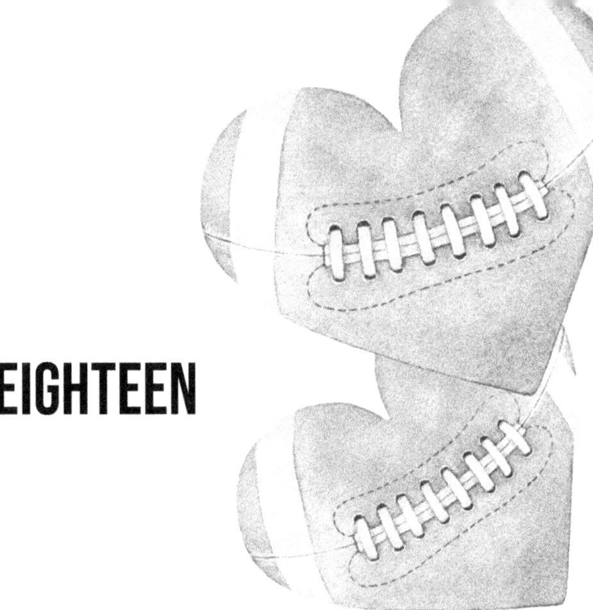

EIGHTEEN

JANE

I wish I could have spent the entire day with Andy, but if I didn't come home, my mother would probably call Troy and my ruse would be up. Andreas had to drive me back to my car. For the first time since Troy moved to Grandma's house, I was glad finding a parking space on this street during the weekend is a nightmare.

I was hoping Mom wouldn't be around when I got home, but unfortunately, she is, and she has company. Her friend Lorena, the one who arranged my date with Hanson van Buuren, and another woman who I believe is also on the ball committee. They're all around the dining room table, which is now overrun by packages and samples of merchandise.

Mom lifts her gaze in my direction. "Where have you been?"

Crap, can she tell that I've spent the entire afternoon having mind-blowing orgasms?

"At Troy's. He had a barbecue."

"You spent the whole day at your brother's?"

"Yeah. Why?"

"A text letting me know would have been nice."

"Oh, Elaine, leave the poor girl alone," Lorena pipes up. "So, how was your date?"

"I wouldn't know. Your boy Hanson van Buuren canceled last minute. What a gentleman, huh?" I reply sarcastically.

The pitiful look on Lorena's face is comical. "Oh no. I'm sure he must have had a good reason to cancel."

"I wouldn't know. He didn't say."

Mom shakes her head, making a disapproving sound. Of course she's going to blame Hanson's assholery on me.

"It's back to the drawing board then. Who else is still free?"

"Enough already with trying to pawn me off on some random guy. I can find my own escort."

"Jane Marie, we've already discussed this. Your escort must be from a reputable family."

"No, it doesn't. I looked into it," I lie. "There's no rule that says the escort of a debutante has to belong to an elite family."

"It's not a rule, my dear, but it's tradition," the other friend says.

"Screw tradition."

"Jane! That's unacceptable behavior."

"Oh really? Like you having an affair with a married man was?"

I never thought I'd use Mom's affair with Charlie's dad as a weapon, but I'm sick and tired of being her punching bag. She's not perfect by any stretch of the imagination. Why does she want me to be?

"How dare you?" She rises from her chair. "Go to your room and don't come out until you're ready for school tomorrow."

"Gladly." I turn on my heels and stomp away.

Maybe now that I fought back, she'll stop pestering me about the ball. If I'm lucky, she won't make me attend it at all. *Yeah, that's wishful thinking.* She'll do it out of spite. I could refuse to go, but unfortunately, while I'm still living under her roof, I can't declare open war against her. Besides, I can't risk her getting suspicious and searching through my things. If she finds out about roller derby, she might ship me off to a boarding school in the middle of nowhere.

Once in the safety of my room, I pull my cell phone out to text Alicia and ask when she wants to meet to practice. But a message from Andy is waiting for me, which I read first.

Hey, babe. Missing you already.

Missing you too. The dragon was home and she went ballistic when I told her I'd find my own date to the ball.

The dragon? LOL. She needs to suck it up. Besides, I'm a pretty good catch.

Yes, you are. Did you talk to Troy yet?

No. I need to speak to Lorenzo first since he's my alibi.

Are you telling him about us?

Yeah. He's cool. He won't tell anyone.

I'm not worried about that.

Hold on. He's calling me back now. I'll call you later to wish you goodnight.

Okay.

I keep my gaze glued to the phone, smiling like an idiot for a minute. I also re-read Andy's texts several times. I still can't believe this is all real. Andreas Rossi is my boyfriend.

My phone pings, announcing an incoming text. It's from Fred. *Ah shit. What am I going to do about him?* I don't click on it yet. I'm afraid he's texting to ask me on a date and I'm not ready to deal with that. I hate disappointing people, especially kind ones like him.

I text Alicia instead, remembering the reason I grabbed my phone in the first place.

> Hey, when do you think you can practice this week?

> Hey, girlie. Yikes. It's going to be pretty tough. My schedule is hell. One of my coworkers is sick and management is forcing me to work a double shift.

> Oh no. Can they do that?

> Technically, no. But they know I need that job. It's cool. I can use the extra cash.

> No worries then. I'll see you next Saturday at bootcamp.

> You betcha!

I flop on my bed, suddenly bone-tired. I showered at Andy's, but I should change. My clothes smell like I've been in a sex dungeon. But they also smell of him. I hug one of my pillows, and pretend I'm hugging him instead. There's a delicious ache between my legs that reminds me of the most amazing day I've ever had. I'm pretty sure if I could spend the night at Andy's, he'd fuck me all night long.

I become hot and bothered again, and now, another shower is in order. A yawn catches me by surprise. I look at the time. It's only a little bit past eight. Not late at all. But I'd better get ready for bed. I need to get enough rest. This week promises to be hella busy. Between school, practicing, and sneaking around to see Andy, I don't know when I'll have time to slow down. And that's not taking into account whatever social function Mom will try to shove in my schedule. She insisted I not take any volunteering work this month, which means she plans to keep me occupied.

I take my time in the shower. I'm sore in several places, and the sex marathon didn't help. Not that I mind that at all. The bruise on my arm and thigh is more purple than before. I have to be extra careful to hide them from Mom. That means no trying on clothes in front of her. Thinking about it reminds me that I still have to pick a dress for the ball. I only got the blue one for the stupid date with Hanson.

Silver lining: I'm sure Andy will love that dress. I'm still smiling when I walk out of the bathroom, but it vanishes immediately when I find my mother there, waiting for me. Panicking, I look for my phone. I left it on my bed, but the screen is face down.

"What are you doing here?" I ask.

"This is my house. I can go wherever I please."

"So privacy doesn't mean anything to you anymore?"

"You'd better watch your tone. If you think behaving like that in front of my friends will get you kicked out of the debutante ball, you're mistaken. And since you don't have a date yet for the ball, don't even think of skipping the marina luncheon next Saturday."

The blood drains from my face. The fucking luncheon. I completely forgot about it. *How am I going to get out of that?*

"I said I'll find my own escort," I grit out.

She laughs. "Who? Some loser from your school?"

"Any loser from school would be better than that prick Hanson van Buuren."

"Well, Lorena was overreaching with him."

My phone rings. It must be Andy calling. *Crap.* I ignore it, hoping Mom will too.

She doesn't even glance at the device. She's busy staring me down. "I already put a dress on hold for you at Nordstrom. Go try it on tomorrow after school."

"Really? No personal stylist anymore?"

"It's pointless to get you in an exclusive gown. Off the rack will do just fine."

She walks out, leaving me fuming. I can't wait to get out of this house. If I didn't like my life here in LA, I'd attend a school across the country just to stay away from the woman.

Before I check who called me, I lock my bedroom door. I know Mom has a spare key, but it makes me feel a little better to do so anyway.

The missed call was from Andy. Seeing his name on my screen makes me crazy happy, even if I'm still angry at my overbearing mother. I press the Call button. He answers on the first ring.

"Hey, babe. Where were you?"

"My mother was in the room, giving me a hard time."

"Ah hell. Was it because I kept you hostage the entire day?"

"No. I told her I'd find my own date to the ball and she flipped."

I decide to keep the nasty details to myself. He knows how bad my mother can get. I don't need to elaborate.

"Do you want me to come over and officially request to be your escort?"

I laugh. "How gallant of you. But that won't be necessary. I do, however, have to find a way to miss the bachelorette luncheon next Saturday. I have roller derby bootcamp all weekend."

"Ah man. When am I going to see you?"

"After bootcamp. But can you please focus for a second? How am I going to evade the dragon? She'll be at the luncheon, watching me like a hawk."

"What time is it at?"

"It probably starts at noon."

"And bootcamp starts at eight, right? I suppose you have an hour of lunch break?"

"Yeah, I think so."

"You could show your face at the luncheon, and then head back to bootcamp."

"I'll never be able to pull that off with LA traffic."

"Don't worry about the logistics. I'll get you where you need to be."

It's so sweet that he's determined to help me, but unless he can rent a helicopter, I don't see how his plan will work. Maybe I can fake food poisoning.

"Let's not talk about my problems anymore. What are you doing now?"

"Baking the banana cake I started at Troy's. Well, not that one. I had to start from scratch."

"When did you get into baking?"

"My mother introduced me to it. After she died, I forgot about it for a while, but now it's back in my life."

"Oh, I'm going to get so fat. You know I love treats."

"I don't care if you get fat. You'll still be the most beautiful woman I've ever seen."

"Yeah, yeah. You say that now. Wait until I look like the Pillsbury Doughboy."

"You're silly. What's your favorite cake?"

"Hmm. That's a tough one. Probably chocolate lava cake."

"Okay, I'm making a note of that. Anything else?"

"Wait. Do you want a list?"

"Yeah, I want a list."

"Who is being silly now?"

"Why is it silly to want to spoil my girl with delicious treats?"

Giddiness overtakes me at hearing him call me his girl. I'm so happy, I could burst into song, Disney style.

"I have to stop by the mall after class to try on a dress my mother has on hold for me. Do you want to come?"

"Is this the dress for the luncheon?"

"Yeah."

"I'm definitely coming then."

"Don't be a pest like you were at the other store."

"To be fair, those clothes *were* provocative. Were they for roller derby?"

"Yep. And full disclosure, I still want to go back there. I liked those clothes."

He groans. "God, it's going to drive me insane to see baboons drool over you."

"That's what you get for dating a hot piece of ass," I laugh.

"Shit, babe, don't remind me of your booty. I have a hard-on already only imagining you in those skintight clothes."

"Really? And what are you going to do about it?"

"I guess I'll have to make do with my hand. Keep talking. I'll pretend you're here."

Heat rushes over me. I've never imagined I'd be having phone sex with Andreas, not even in my wildest dreams. But in this case, the reality is so much better than the fantasy.

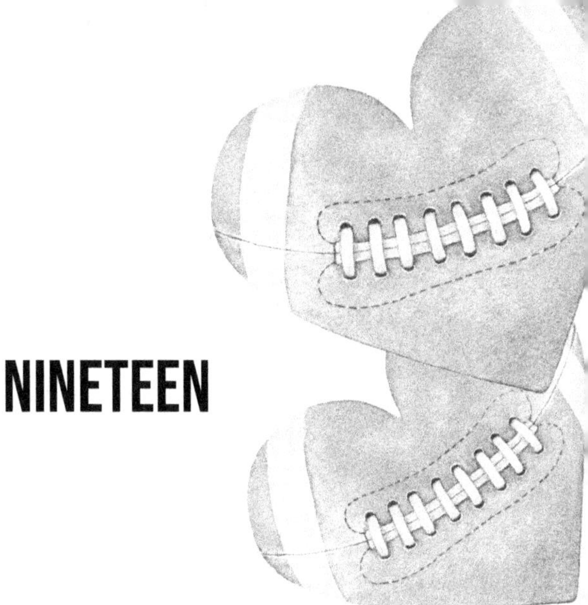

NINETEEN

ANDREAS

I'm still on cloud nine when I enter the classroom. It's Norman's class—the douche professor who wants to see me fail—and I'm smiling from ear to ear. No surprise, Taiyo is already here, face buried in a book. *Damn, the dude is serious about his academics.*

I drop on the chair next to him as loudly as possible. "Morning."

He jumps on his seat, startled. "Jesus, where did you come from?"

"Don't you know? I'm a wizard. I can apparate."

He stares at me blankly. Not a Harry Potter fan then.

"Anyway, what are you studying so hard there?"

"I have a Finance quiz after this class. I feel wholly unprepared."

"Ugh. I barely passed that class. Can't help you there."

A guy with wild curly hair takes the seat in front of us. He dyed the tips of his hair blond, which immediately makes me think of Justin Timberlake circa the nineties. Yikes.

He turns around and asks, "Hey, what you guys think of Professor Norman?"

I snort. "You don't want to know."

"Yeah, he didn't seem to like you very much. Total jackass move, in my opinion."

I nod, not wanting to agree and risk getting caught dissing the guy by a teacher's pet or the man himself.

"Anyway, my name is Ricky Montana. Big fan."

Taiyo looks at me. "I didn't realize you were famous."

"You don't like sports very much, do you?" I ask.

"No time for that."

"Dude, this guy is a legend," Ricky replies enthusiastically. "It's wild that you're taking the same class as me," he tells me.

"I'm not a legend. Calm down," I joke.

"Sorry. I tend to get overexcited easily. Hey, do you know of any cool parties happening this week?"

"Not really."

"Well, if you hear about any, please, let me know." He scribbles something on a piece of paper and hands it over. "Here are my digits."

"Sure." I tuck Ricky's note inside my book, knowing very well I'll forget about it by the time this class is over.

Professor Asshole walks in, silencing all the chatter in the room. He has a reputation, and no one seems to be willing to get on his bad side. He gets settled behind his desk, and not a minute later, begins his lecture. This time, he doesn't put me on the spot, and I start to hope he's forgotten about his dislike of me.

I get into the zone, not daring to look away from the white board, and taking notes as furiously as Taiyo. Ten minutes before the class is over, he announces he has the schedule for the hands-on portion of this course. We're expected to work at the Rushmore Hotel in different functions to get real life experience.

I log in to the class's portal to see what my first assignment will be. I'll be serving at the hotel's restaurant during my first week. I curse when I see my schedule. I'm supposed to work this Saturday during the lunch shift. *Fuck.* I promised Jane I'd help her sneak out of the luncheon. I can't let her down.

I raise my hand. "Sir, what if the schedule conflicts with prior plans?"

He glowers at me. "Then I suggest you change your prior plans. Like I said before, I'm not going to give any student special treatment. If you can't take this class seriously, I suggest you quit wasting my time."

Asshole.

"Am I allowed to switch with another student?"

He sighs, intensifying his death glare in my direction. "If you can find someone willing to trade with you, then be my guest. However, if they don't show up to cover your shift, you are the one who will get an F."

Ricky raises his hand. "Sir? Does that mean if we get sick and miss a shift, we get an F too?"

"For Christ's sake. Of course not, Mr. Montana. This is America, not China." He glances at Taiyo meaningfully.

What a racist prick. I can't keep my mouth shut.

"Taiyo is from Japan."

"Actually, I'm second genera—never mind," he whispers.

I don't glance at him. I'm too busy in my staring contest with Norman. I'm not going to look away first.

"Oh, okay," Ricky mumbles.

Norman caves first, giving the classroom a glance. It's a small victory, but I know I just made my life ten times more difficult.

"Anyone else have an asinine question to ask? No? Good. Class dismissed."

People can't get out of their chairs fast enough. I refuse to rush out. Ricky turns in his seat.

"I can trade shifts with you," he says in a low voice, probably afraid to be overheard by Norman.

"Oh yeah? What do you have?"

"I've got serving on Friday, dinner shift. Does that work?"

I'm not keen on wasting my Friday evening. I'd much rather spend the time with Jane. But I don't have a lot of options. I doubt anyone else will want to trade with me now that I'm on Norman's shit list. They're probably afraid to attract his wrath too if they help me.

"I'll take that. I'm on Saturday lunch shift. Are you sure you can cover for me? I can't get an F."

"Yeah, man. I got your back. But… I need a favor in return."

I knew there was a catch.

"Spill it already."

"Can you get me a date with a cheerleader?"

From the corner of my eye, I notice Taiyo sitting straighter in his chair. Finally something catches his interest, but I'm too annoyed right now to care.

"Do I look like a pimp to you?" I ask.

Ricky's eyebrows shoot up. "I heard you got Leo Stine a date with Heather Castro."

Shit, I did do that. But Leo is the Pike's president. It wasn't that difficult to convince Heather to go out with him.

"Those were rumors. But I can introduce you to a bunch of chicks the next time there's a Greek Row party."

"For real? Man, that would be awesome."

"Can I come too?" Taiyo asks.

I turn to him. "I thought you didn't go to parties."

"Right, I don't. Never mind."

"You can come if you find the balls to do so." I switch to Ricky. "You have a deal. You'd better not screw me over, Montana."

"Are you crazy? I'd never do that to you." He stands, hoisting his backpack over his shoulder. "When is the next party?"

"Don't have a clue. I've been out of the loop. I'll text you, but it won't happen this weekend. I have plans."

"Right. No worries." He glances at his phone. "Oh fuck. I'm late for my next class."

"Shit, me too," Taiyo says in a panic.

Both hurry out of room in an ungainly fashion. I shake my head, wondering when the hell I turned into the king of nerds.

—————

"**I**s the situation with Lorenzo resolved?" Troy asks me.

I forgot I made plans to meet the guys for lunch today. Danny, who was about to take a big chunk out of his burger, pauses to look at us. *Damn, could he seem any more suspicious?* Luckily, Troy and Paris aren't paying attention to him.

"Yeah, I called a repair company. They came over and fixed the glass on our father's trophy case in a jiffy. He'll never know it was broken in the first place."

The lie feels bitter in my mouth. I hate that I have to lie to my best friend like this, but I can't tell him why I bailed yesterday before Jane is ready to deal with Troy's reaction.

"Damn. Your father must really love those trophies to send Lorenzo into panic mode," Paris pipes up.

"You have no idea," I say.

I'd never have come up with an alibi involving my asshole father. That was my brother's plan. The story worked because everyone knows my old man is a self-absorbed jerk.

"Barbecue was fun, but man, when are we going to go on a guys-only trip?" Paris asks. "Now that football season is over, I need a healthy dose of adrenaline."

"Are you sure you're allowed to go on a trip without your girlfriend?" I tease.

"Bite me, Andy. Geneva is not my keeper. I can do things without her."

"Could have fooled me." I shove a piece of fry in my mouth.

"I'm game for a trip. We could go rock climbing at the Arches. I haven't done that in a while," Troy says.

"You want to go all the way to Utah?" Danny frowns. "I don't think I can swing buying a plane ticket."

"We could go somewhere closer," I suggest. "Like Yosemite Park. But when are you thinking? I started my practical portion of Intro to Food Service Management and I have to check my schedule. Some are weekend shifts."

Plus, I don't want to leave town for a whole weekend and miss spending time with Jane. *Jesus, I sound as whipped as Paris and Troy.*

"I don't know. I have to check with Charlie," Troy replies.

"Oh, look who is actually in jail," Paris laughs.

"Shut up, jerkface. I don't have to ask for Charlie's permission, but maybe she already has things planned for us."

"Like LARPing." Danny chuckles.

Paris perks up on his seat. "We have to come see Troy run around in a full troll outfit. How come we haven't done that yet?"

"LARPing is not a performance. You can only come if you participate," he replies.

Paris makes a face of disgust. "No, thank you."

"Don't dismiss it until you try it." Troy throws a fry in Paris's direction.

"Not happening, bro." He shoves the food missile in his mouth and smirks.

I thought hanging out with Troy today would be weird as fuck. The guilt for keeping shit from him is still in the background, but it's easy to ignore that while this banter is going around.

"Did you read the email Coach sent us about that benefit gala?" Danny asks.

"Ugh, don't remind me of that." Paris sighs in an exaggerated manner. "Geneva read the email and now she can't stop talking about ball gowns."

"First of all, why is she reading your emails?" I ask.

"She was sitting next to me when I clicked on it."

"Why are you asking about the gala, Danny?" Troy asks.

"I don't want to rent a tux. Any of you have one to spare?"

"Wait? That's a blacktie event?" I glance at him.

"Galas usually are," Paris pipes up.

"I barely glanced at the email," I confess. "When is it again?"

When my phone vibrates in my pocket, my remorse heightens. I bet it's Jane calling. She said she would let me know when she planned to go to the mall. I reach for it and press the Ignore button. A moment later, my phone pings again with an incoming text. I shouldn't check now that all eyes are on me, but I don't want her thinking I'm blowing her off.

I glance at it quickly, making sure no one sees the screen. She wants to go the mall now. My heartbeat picks up its pace as excitement takes hold of me. I can't wait to see her again and it hasn't even been twenty-four hours since I saw her last.

"Who is that?" Troy asks.

I try to school my face into the perfect mask of innocence, but I'm not sure if I'm pulling it off. Remorse returns with a vengeance.

"No one. I actually have to go." I stand, taking my food tray with me.

"No one, huh?" Troy leans back, smiling knowingly. "I bet that was a booty call."

Shit. I'm so transparent. He wouldn't be smiling like that if he knew I was about to nail his sister.

"Yeah, yeah. You got me. Later, fools."

I walk out of the cafeteria as fast as I can, hating myself for being such a douche. I don't disagree with Jane. Troy is a fucking pain in the ass when it comes to her. But I also know that if the situation were reversed, I wouldn't want a guy like me messing around with my sister either. If I were a better man, I would have never let things get this far. But I'm too weak and Jane is everything I've ever wanted.

TWENTY

JANE

I'm giddy with excitement, restless as I pace back and forth in front of Nordstrom. I told Andy I'd meet him here. It's better if we go in together instead of sending the poor guy on a wild goose chase inside the store.

It's risky meeting him in a public space when no one is supposed to know about us, but as long as we don't do any PDA, it will be okay.

I let out a yelp when strong arms wrap around me, and Andreas's lips find my neck. There goes the no PDA idea down the drain.

"Hey, babe. Miss me?" He spins me around so now I'm facing him.

"Andy! People can see us."

"So?" He ends any further protest I might have with a long and sensual kiss that makes me melt on the spot.

I find myself leaning into his body while my own bursts into flames. Oh my God. This man is going to be the end of my sanity. I could kiss him forever, and proof of that is that he's the one who eases off, breaking the moment too soon in my opinion.

"You were saying?" He chuckles against my lips.

"We shouldn't be kissing in public," I whisper without making any motion to move away.

"I know, I know. But I couldn't resist. You're breathtaking today." He steps back and gives me a once-over. "I love school uniforms. Does that make me a perv?"

"It totally does. You're lucky that I'm into the forbidden stuff."

"Is that why you want to keep our relationship a secret?"

His question erases my amusement in an instant. *He doesn't really think that, does he?*

"Of course not."

"Hey, I was joking. I get why. Troy is my best friend. I know him better than anyone."

"Sorry. This situation is giving me a lot of anxiety. I feel like I'm keeping too many secrets and eventually they're going to come crashing down on me."

He caresses my cheek. "I'm sorry, sweetheart. I'm ready to let the world know about us. Just say the word and I'll message Troy right now."

Panic grips me. "No. That's not what I meant. We *will* tell Troy, but I can't afford to have him angry at me. I need an ally in case Mom finds out about roller derby."

"It's okay, babe. I'm not pressuring you to do anything. But it's so fucking hard to be in your presence and keep my hands to myself."

"If it makes you feel any better, I feel the same way."

He scrunches his eyebrows together. "No, it doesn't make me feel better."

I sigh, defeated. "Let's go. I can't wait to see what kind of atrocity Mommy Dearest thinks is suitable for me."

Andy reaches for my hand, but I pull away with regret. *This sucks.*

"Oops. Sorry. Told you it was hard," he says.

"I know."

We walk side by side, leaving a gap between our bodies. For all intents and purposes, we're just friends.

"Who picked that blue dress you were wearing the other day?"

"I did. Mom was against that choice."

"Hmm."

"What?" I glance at him.

"Just wondering why you chose that dress to go on a date with a random guy."

Andy is jealous, something that used to irritate me, but it warms me like a soft blanket now that we're together.

"I wasn't planning to stay. I just wanted Hanson to see I wasn't a charity case. I had roller derby tryouts that afternoon."

Andreas touches the back of my wrist with the tips of his fingers. It's an innocent caress, but it sends a zing of pleasure to my core.

"No one in their right mind would think you're a charity case, Jane. You're perfection."

I don't know if I should laugh or jump in his arms. "I'm perfection?"

"Too corny?" He gives me a crooked smile.

"A little."

My cheeks are warm, and I'm a second away from breaking my own rules and kissing him in the middle of the store. A cheerful sales associate saves me from myself when she welcomes us to Nordstrom.

"This store has so many departments. Do you know where you're going?"

"Yeah. Follow me."

I find the department that has my dress on hold. While I speak with the sales associate, Andreas hangs back and pretends to be interested in the accessories displayed on the mannequin. He's completely out of his element, but seems to be enjoying himself. Many guys seem to get an allergic reaction when they have to go on a shopping trip with their girlfriends, and here's Andy, the most macho guy I know, taking everything in stride.

While the associate goes to the back to find my dress, I join him in his exploration.

"I bet I'm not going to like what my mother picked. Help me find alternatives?"

"Really? You want my help?"

"Of course. You're the one who has to see the dress on me."

"Okay." He turns to the rack behind him and quickly browses through the options.

I look at the dress on the mannequin. It's cute and I wonder if they have it in my size.

"Hi." The associate returns. "This is the dress your mother put on hold." She shows me an off-white dress that's as boring as they come. It's also too long to be cute.

Andreas steps closer. "What's this? A grandma's nightgown?"

The woman laughs politely. "It's a little on the conservative side. I have other options that are a bit more fun."

"I like fun," he pipes up, and then looks at the dress on the mannequin, the one I had been eyeing before. "What about that one?"

"We just got it in. It's my favorite dress in the collection."

"I'd like to try that on, please," I say.

"Of course."

She finds my size on the rack without having to ask—she can probably judge by looking at me—and asks us to follow her to the fitting room, which is bigger and more private than the ones I'm used to. When Andy slips in with me, she doesn't bat an eyelash.

He takes a seat on the velvet bench, getting comfortable while I stand in the middle of the room in my school uniform, feeling awkward all of a sudden. *Nonsense, Jane. He's seen you in your birthday suit already.*

"I'm ready for my show." He leans back, lacing his fingers behind his neck.

"Ha ha. I didn't ask you to come for your entertainment."

I begin to unbutton my shirt, remembering at the last minute I'm wearing a boring cotton bra. I should have worn sexier underwear today. Andreas doesn't seem to care though. His eyes are hooded, swimming with desire. His heated gaze feels like a sensual stroke against my skin. My breathing turns shallow. My panties soak through. He got me hot and bothered with a single glance.

"Oh? And why did you ask me to come, sweetheart?" He leans forward, resting his elbows on his knees now.

"To help me pick a dress." I lob my shirt in his direction, and he catches it with perfect dexterity.

"I can't help you if you don't try it on. You'd better hurry up, or that sales chick will think we're up to no good in here."

He had to go and remind me that the woman is only a few feet away from us. *Ugh!*

Quickly, I take off my skirt, and then put on the strapless dress. The zipper is in the back, and I can't quite close it all the way up.

Andreas jumps from his seat. "Allow me."

With him close behind me, it's impossible to ignore how much I crave him. My pulse skyrockets.

He zips me up slowly, sending ripples of pleasure down my spine. Then he captures my gaze in the mirror's reflection and tugs the bra straps with his index fingers.

"You don't need this," he whispers seductively.

"No," I croak. "I didn't want to tempt you too much."

He kisses the corner of my neck, making me shiver. "That's an impossible task. I'd burn for you even if you were wearing a shapeless potato sack."

He continues his torture, drawing his tongue up my neck until he captures my earlobe between his teeth. His left arm snakes around my waist, pulling me flush against his muscled body—and obvious erection—while his right hand disappears underneath the skirt of the dress.

"Andy." I melt against his embrace, reaching behind me to keep his head where it is.

He touches the edge of my panties, and there go my legs, turning into jelly. He tugs at the fabric, sliding it to the side so his fingers can play with my sensitive flesh without barriers.

"Oh my God." I close my eyes and arch my back.

"Do you like that, sweetheart?"

"Yes," I hiss.

He makes small circles over my clit, quickly building a delicious tension between my legs. A moan escapes my lips.

"I'm obsessed with the sounds you make," he whispers, blowing hot air against my skin.

And I'm obsessed with you. I don't say that out loud, instead, I whisper, "I love your hands on me."

In response, he inserts two fingers inside of me.

"How about now, babe? Do you love that too?"

"Ye—oh my God. Don't stop," I beg as the first wave of the orgasm hits me.

"Open your eyes, babe. I want you to see how beautiful you look when you come."

I do as he says, and watching Andy finger fuck me as I climax is the hottest thing I've ever seen. The image seems to double my pleasure, and I have to bite my lower lip to keep from moaning out loud again.

Andreas works his magic until my body goes slack against him and the tremors subside. My heart is pumping like a factory and sweat dots my forehead now.

With a smile, he fixes my underwear back in place, and does something utterly shocking. He licks his fingers.

"Fucking delicious," he says.

"How did the dress work for you?" the sales associate asks outside our door.

My face bursts into flames. I jump out of Andy's embrace,

mortified now. What if she heard us? He chuckles at my reaction, earning an exasperated glance from me.

"I love it. It fits like a glove," I reply.

"Great," she says.

Andreas still has a stupid grin on his face after she leaves. I slap his arm. "Quit laughing. This isn't funny."

"Sorry, babe, but it kinda is." He sits on the bench again, and I notice the bulge in his jeans is still there.

"I don't know what you find so amusing when you have to deal with your lack of release."

He drops his eyes to his crotch for a second. "This is nothing. Besides, I know you're going to take care of me soon."

Smirking, I reply, "Maybe."

"You're a mean one."

I stick my tongue out at him. Then I take the dress off and place it back on the hanger while still in my underwear. I know I'm making the situation for him worse, but that's what he gets for laughing at me.

"I'm not mean," I laugh.

"I don't know about that. And if you don't want me to fuck you against the wall in the next second, you'd better put your clothes on. This is cruel punishment."

Crap. Now I want him to follow through on his threat. But if I stay another minute alone with Andy in this room, I won't be able to face the associate outside.

"Okay, okay." I hastily button my shirt and put on my skirt.

I said I wanted to be a bad girl, but one orgasm in a public place is all I can handle today. When we finally walk out of the fitting room, there are more customers browsing through the department. I feel like they all know what Andreas and I were doing. I can't look the sales associate in the eye when I pay for the dress, and I practically drag Andy with me as I stride away.

"Babe, what's the hurry?" he asks with humor.

"I just want to get out of here."

"Are we going to the other store now?"

Ah shit. I forgot about that. But I can't take Andy to that store and try on a bunch of sexy outfits in front of him. He *is* going to want to bang me in the fitting room and I won't be able—or want—to stop him.

"No, I think we should go home."

"Oh? I thought you were coming to my place."

I stop in my tracks when I realize I meant his place when I said the word home. It's probably too soon to be thinking that way. We literally just start dating.

"I didn't want to assume you didn't already have plans," I reply to save face.

"You'd better start getting used to the idea that any plans I have involve you, babe."

The butterflies in my stomach become radioactive. I beam, smiling like the crazy-in-love girl that I am.

"Is that so?"

Still holding hands, he tugs me closer to him. I know we shouldn't be doing this out in the open, but right now, I don't care about being discreet.

"You'd better believe it."

He kisses me softly, a quick peck on the lips. I obviously want more, but Andreas has more restraint than me.

He steps back and says, "Let's get out of here before I drag you back to that fitting room and make good on my promise."

TWENTY-ONE

ANDREAS

I've never had a hard-on last this long. I'm usually able to take care of the problem or it goes away naturally—and painfully. But after a thirty-minute drive back to my place, my cock is still as hard as a rock. Maybe if I hadn't kept talking to Jane on the phone during the ride, this wouldn't have happened.

We agreed that I would go up to my apartment first, and she'd wait five minutes and follow me. It's one thing to steal kisses in the middle of a packed shopping mall, but quite another to walk into my apartment building with Jane in my arms. There are too many people coming and going, and everyone knows Troy and me.

I'm grinning like a fool when I open the front door, but a sickly sweet perfume reaches my nose the moment I walk in. Immediately, my muscles tense. I know that fucking smell too well. Crystal is sitting on my chair, holding a glass of whiskey in her hand as if this is her house.

"What the fuck are you doing here? How did you get in?"

She takes a sip of her drink before replying. "My, my. Is that how you greet your stepmother?"

"Answer the fucking question, Crystal."

"I might have borrowed your father's spare key. What's the matter, Andy? Aren't you happy to see me?" She smiles wickedly, knowing very well her presence here is unwelcome.

"Quit with the bullshit. Why are you here?"

She stands up, revealing another skintight outfit. "I thought we should continue our conversation from the other day."

"Are you out of your goddamned mind? We have nothing to talk about."

She sashays in my direction, once again trying to pull her old tricks on me. "I know you don't mean that."

"Oh my God. This was the most inten—" Jane walks in but stops abruptly when she sees Crystal there. "Oh, hi. I didn't know Andy had company."

"She was just leaving," I grit out.

Crystal turns to me, smirking. "Of course. I don't want to ruin your afternoon delight." She chugs the rest of her drink before heading for the door. "We'll catch up another time, sweetie."

I'm fuming. Any happiness I had in me Crystal sucked out with her vile presence.

"That was your stepmother, right? Is everything okay?" Jane asks as soon as the bitch walks out of the door.

I glance at Jane, all innocent and pure, and I hate myself for allowing her to come into my corrupted world. Crystal's presence here reminded me that I'm tainted, unworthy of someone like Jane.

Shit. I need a drink.

Without answering, I make a beeline for the booze cabinet in my kitchen. I need something stronger than beer. The bottle of expensive tequila I keep hidden from Danny needs to make an appearance. I twist the cap off and drink from it, not bothering with a glass.

"Andy?" Jane walks over. "What happened?"

I close my eyes, letting the warmth of the tequila wash away my guilt. "Nothing happened, babe."

She stops in front of me and pulls the tequila bottle from my hand. "Bullshit. Don't lie to me."

"Sorry. I don't mean to push you away. My home life growing up wasn't exactly all sunshine. Crystal's presence here was… triggering."

"Did she let herself in?"

"Yeah. She knows I wouldn't have let her come in otherwise."

Jane steps into my space, wrapping her arms around me. I hug her back, kissing the top of her head. She doesn't comment on my confession, and my affection for her grows. Just the feel of her body against mine is enough to dissipate the darkness swirling in my chest.

"Are you hungry?" I ask. "I can cook you something."

She lifts her gaze to mine. "The only thing I'm hungry for is you."

And just like that, my body is on fire again. I take her face in my hands and crush my lips to hers. My mouth takes possession starvingly, as if I want to drown in her taste, in her essence. The world ceases to exist. It's only Jane and I lost in each other.

I let go of her face to lift her off the floor. My hands find her sweet ass while her legs wrap around my hips. Without breaking the kiss, I stride to my bedroom. I'd take her right there on the kitchen counter, but Danny could come in at any time.

Hands busy squeezing her tight ass, I shut the door with a backward kick. Then we're falling on the bed together, already tugging at each other's clothes, fighting to get them off as fast as possible. I don't know if I should rip her uniform shirt off or kiss the bit of skin already exposed.

Roughly, I push her bra up and suck her nipple into my mouth. I guess it's tasting her with clothes on for now. She arches her back as she threads her fingers through my hair.

"Ouch," she blurts out when I get too eager and bite her a little too hard.

I lift my eyes to hers. "Sorry, babe. You're too delicious."

"I want to taste you too."

God, the idea of her mouth on my body almost makes me climax on the spot. I've never felt such insatiable hunger for anyone before.

"That can be arranged." I lean back and impatiently get rid of my shirt.

Jane's hands find my chest and then my abs. I don't move, letting her explore me with soft fingers and hungry eyes.

"I love your body. It's almost not fair how perfect you are. I could look at you all day."

"I wouldn't mind that at all as long as I can touch you as you do so," I reply.

Her hands travel south. She unbuttons my jeans and pulls the zipper down. "I want your cock in my mouth."

"Babe, I'm hanging by a thread here. This could end fast."

She curls her lips into a grin. "If it does, we'll just start it all over again."

With that sassy smile across her face, she sits up, pushing me down as she does. I'm now lying on my back and Jane is straddling my thighs.

"You know, I wish you were a Scottish lad wearing a kilt. That would make things so much easier." She pulls my pants low enough to grant her easier access to the goods.

"I don't have an ounce of Scottish blood in me, but I can role-play."

"Don't tease me, or I'll be ordering you a kilt as soon as I get home."

I chuckle. "That's okay."

She holds my gaze for a couple of beats before her eyes drop to my crotch. I notice her slight hesitation when she tugs my boxers down and frees my dick.

"Do you want me to tell you what I like?" I ask softly.

She meets my eyes again, and I see as clear as day the vulnerability and insecurity shining in her gaze.

"Am I lame if I say yes?"

I run my fingers over her exposed thighs. "No, on the contrary, sweetheart. Although I'm sure you know exactly what to do to drive me wild."

She rubs her thumb over the sensitive skin, spreading precum over my cock's head. My balls tighten, making me hiss.

"Do you like that?" she asks.

"God, yes."

A little smile appears on her lovely face. She leans forward, bringing her plump lips closer to my shaft. I inhale deeply, bracing for the sensation. I don't want to come too soon. I never had this problem before until Jane came along. This must be pent-up desire thanks to all the long nights I spent fantasizing about her.

Her fingers curl around the base, then she licks my length from bottom to top. My hips buckle, and I dig my fingers into her legs.

"How about this?"

I nod, closing my eyes, fighting to maintain control, but it's pretty fucking hard. I thought she was going to keep taking things slowly, but she surprises me when she swallows my cock all the way to the hilt.

"Fuck!" I blurt out.

Jane is not playing around anymore. I know she wasn't lying when said she never sucked a guy before me, which means she's just talented. With expert hands and tongue, she quickly takes me closer and closer to the edge.

"Oh my God, babe. You're a magician," I whisper.

I give everything I have to keep my shit together, to fight the tidal wave that's fast approaching. But this is a fight I can't win. My release crashes against the shore like a tsunami, obliterating everything in its path. My body seems to disintegrate and become whole again in the span of a second.

I realize I kept my eyes shut in the final moment like an idiot. Maybe it was instinctual to try to maintain some kind of control because looking at Jane as she sucked me into oblivion would be my demise.

When I open my eyes, I catch her wiping off the corner of her mouth. There's not a drop of my release in sight. She took it all.

I reach for her open shirt and tug her forward. "Come here."

She leans closer, and I use the opportunity to roll over her and switch positions. Now she's trapped under me, my reawakened cock lodged between her legs. She laughs, but I cut the sound short by kissing her long and hard.

I'm already ready to go for round two, but I decide to take my time now and make out in bed like teenagers, something I never did, all thanks to Crystal. I can't change the past, but maybe I can have something good for once.

TWENTY-TWO

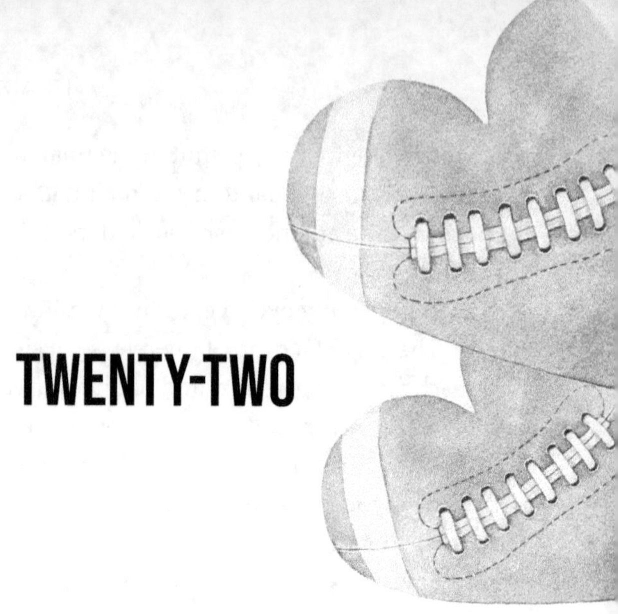

"Wow. I didn't think guys could recover that fast," I say against Andy's chest.

After I gave him the best blow job of his life—his words, not mine—we did nothing but kiss for an hour. I thought he needed that time to recover—not that I minded in the least. But I was so wrong.

"Most don't, but they don't have a Jane in their bed."

I lift my chin to look at him. "Are you saying I have magical powers that can recharge your dick with a mere touch?"

He chuckles. "Yeah, you do."

I rest my face against his chest again. "I wish I could spend the night and put that theory to the test."

The sun has set already. I have to leave soon or my mother will start hunting me down. I completely blew off my plan to get some skating practice. I don't want to be one of those girls who drop everything to spend time with their boyfriends, but considering our illicit affair, finding the time to spend together might be more complicated.

"I wish you could stay here too, babe." He kisses the top of my head.

His phone vibrates on his nightstand, an invasion of our peace. The world has come knocking. I try to sit up, but Andy's arms around me become tighter.

"Stay for just another minute."

"You don't want to see who's calling?"

"Whoever it is can wait."

I relax in his arms, loving the feel of them around me. Exhaustion is slowly creeping into my bones. I've done a lot of physical activity in the past few days. Between roller derby and screwing Andreas's brains out, it's no surprise I'm beat. I'm sore now in a lot of places, some I don't mind one bit. My bruises from roller derby are still tender to the touch, but they're already beginning to yellow out. I'll probably gain new ones next weekend, though. I'm glad it's not bikini season yet.

I should get up, especially when my eyelids grow heavy and my eyes begin to shut. I'm beginning to doze off when loud male voices in the apartment makes me tense on the spot. Danny is home, and he brought company. *Shit.* I hope whoever it is it doesn't have a big mouth.

"Hell. Our solitude is over," Andy murmurs.

We both get out of bed and start to get dressed. All he does is put some sweatpants on that don't hide much. I get now why some girls from school love sweatpants season. You can see everything, especially when guys don't wear underwear like Andy isn't now.

He snaps his fingers in front of my face. "Hey, my eyes are up here."

"If you don't want me to objectify you, don't wear provocative clothes. You're asking for it." I smirk.

"Well played, babe. Well played."

I'd love to shower first before doing the walk of shame, but it's really getting late. Andy leans against his desk with arms crossed and watches me get dressed. He's ogling my body on purpose now, payback for my earlier comment. A tent forms in the front of his pants, and I can't help my laughter.

"Oh my God. Again? Did you take Viagra or something?"

He twists his face into a scowl. "Please. I don't need help in that department. But man, I do love that uniform on you."

I finish fastening the last button, and then I try to smooth the wrinkles on the skirt. It's pointless. I make a quick run to the bathroom to check the state of my hair. *Crap.* It's as bad as I feared. There's no way in hell I'll be able to comb through this tangled mess, so I just make a quick bun, securing it with a strand of my own hair since I don't have a hairband, and if I find one in Andy's bathroom, I'm going to go blind with jealousy. I'd better not open that Pandora's box.

"Okay, I'm ready to go," I say as I walk out of the bathroom.

Andy has his cell phone in hand. He turns to me, his face completely ashen.

"We have a problem. Troy is here."

"What?" My voice rises to a pitch.

Then I berate myself. What if Troy heard me?

"Danny was the one who called to warn me. Then he texted."

"Why is my brother here?" I shout-whisper, panicked.

"We were hanging out before I went to meet you at the mall. I have no fucking no clue why Danny came home with Troy and Paris. I'm so sorry, babe. I'll go out and try to get rid of them as quickly as possible."

I can tell that Andy feels guilty as hell over the situation, but this is not his fault. I'm the one who's afraid to tell Troy I'm in love with his best friend.

"No, this happened for a reason. It's ridiculous to keep our relationship a secret from him when Danny and Charlie know. Lying about it is only going to mess things up more."

"Wait. Charlie knows about us? You told her?"

"She doesn't know that we're together. She knows we hooked up at the Halloween party."

He passes a hand over his face. "Man, now I get why she looked so guilty when I asked her about it."

"Yeah, I put her in a super-tight spot with my brother and it's not fair. I'm doing the same to you. The longer we keep this a secret, the more betrayed Troy will feel."

"I'm ready to face the music if you are." He offers me his hand.

We lace our fingers together, but before we step out of his bedroom, Andy leans in and kisses me on the lips. "It will be fine."

Yeah, right. We both know that's a lie. My heart is thundering inside of my chest as we step into the living room. Troy is on the couch, playing a video game with Paris, and doesn't see us right way. Danny, on the other hand, is in the kitchen and balks at the sight of us.

"Shit," he says.

Troy begins to turn around. "What is it?"

He freezes the moment his eyes land on Andreas and me holding hands, my uniform looking like a cat chewed it and spat it out, and Andy wearing nothing but sweatpants.

"What is this?" Troy stands, body coiled tight with fury.

"Bro, calm down," Andy says.

"Calm down?" He walks around the couch, eyes bulging out of his skull. "Jane was your afternoon hookup?"

"I'm not his hookup," I retort angrily, but Troy doesn't even spare me a glance. His murderous gaze is on Andreas.

"I can't believe this. You could have any girl on campus, but you had to go after my sister, didn't you? Nothing is off-limits to you."

"I don't want any girl. I want Jane," he replies calmly.

"Yeah, for how long? A day, a week?"

I step in between them. "Back off, Troy. You don't have a say about who I date and don't. If I want to date Andy, I will."

"Date Andy?" he scoffs. "Don't be naive, Jane. Andreas doesn't date. He's a player, he always has been."

"People can change," Andy replies. "I care about your sister. I've cared about her since the day I met her."

Troy's eyes widen. *Fuck.* That's not good.

"Are you telling me you've had a thing for my sister for three years?" he shouts. "Three fucking years? She was fifteen, you perv."

He advances, hands curled into fists. If I weren't standing in between them, he would have punched Andreas by now. Danny and Paris, who had been trying to stay out of the situation, must have noticed that Troy is about to blow. Paris pulls Troy back while Danny stands next to Andy, worried.

"Let go of me!" Troy pulls his arm free from Paris's grasp.

"Calm down, bro," he says. "You're not thinking straight."

"Andy didn't do anything, you jackass!" I yell. "He stayed away from me this whole time. I was the one who started this."

Troy snorts. "Are you saying you seduced the biggest manwhore on campus?"

"Yes. That's what I'm saying." I throw my hands up in the air. "Get a grip, Troy. I'm no longer a kid. I'm eighteen. I'm capable of making my own decisions."

He looks at me with contempt. "So, you want to hook up with him until he gets tired of you and breaks your heart? Is that the plan?"

My eyes burn. I'm about to cry, but not out of sadness. I'm so fucking angry I could punch Troy in the throat. I knew he would get ugly, but I didn't imagine it would be like this.

Andreas walks around me. "I'm not going to break your sister's heart. I wouldn't have let things get this far, wouldn't have risked our friendship, if all I wanted was to bang her."

Troy laughs without humor. "Oh, you're worried about our friendship now? That's rich. You should have thought about that before you screwed my sister behind my back."

I wince, mortified that we're airing dirty laundry in front of Danny and Paris. The tears finally spill, making me even angrier that I let them fall in the first place.

"You're such a jerk!" Propelled by fury, I pull my arm back and punch Troy in his gut, something I haven't done since we were kids.

Back then, all I accomplished was to tickle him. Now, he doubles over, and grunts, "Jane, what the hell!"

Andy throws his arm around my shoulders and pulls me closer. "That's my girl."

Pride surges within me. Not because Andy validated what I did, but because Troy is finally seeing me, instead of arguing with Andreas as if I wasn't in the room or like my opinion doesn't matter. I don't know why he's like that with me. I know he doesn't treat his girlfriend with that backward attitude. She wouldn't date him if he did.

"She's not your girl." Troy straightens to his full height.

"Yes, I am. Get used to it."

ANDREAS

Seeing Jane stand up for herself and put Troy in his place is hot as hell. For three years, I had this image of a shy and sweet girl. I had no idea there was a lioness inside of her, ready to fight for what she wanted. And the fact that she's fighting for me, someone who doesn't deserve that fierce loyalty, is humbling.

"Are you seriously going to date *him*?"

The venom in Troy's voice cuts like a knife. I knew he wouldn't be happy about this situation, but the way he's staring at me with such loathing rips me apart.

"Yes, and you either support my decision, or you stay out of my life," Jane replies.

His face falls. "I'm just trying to protect you. I don't want you to get hurt."

I open my mouth to rebuff his words, but he looks at me and

cuts me off. "Don't even try to deny it. You know you're going to break her heart, even if you don't mean to."

The words to defend myself won't come. Troy knows me better than anyone. He might not know all the sordid details of my past, but he can see I'm rotten inside. I've told him time and time again I'd never settle with anyone. Why would he believe me now?

But he's upsetting Jane with his behavior. Despite her bravery, she's shaking next to me. And no one is going to make her feel that way, especially not in front of me.

"You'd better leave before you say something that can't be unsaid," I grit out.

"I'm not going anywhere without Jane."

My spine goes taut as I prepare to forcibly remove him from my apartment. But Jane surprises me once again.

"Fine. I'll go with you, only because I don't want Andy to kick your ass for being such an idiot."

He snorts. "Like he could."

I narrow my eyes to slits. "Don't push your luck, pal. I can whoop your ass with one arm tied behind my back."

"Okay. No one is going to whoop anyone's ass today," Paris pipes up. "Unless it's in video games."

I glance at Jane. "You don't need to go if you don't want to. Don't let Troy bully you into anything."

"I'm not bullying her!" he yells.

"Just wait outside, Troy," Danny chimes in. "You're not helping anyone with that attitude."

"Fine! But if Jane doesn't come out in five minutes, I'm coming back in."

"Bite me, Troy," she retorts. "You're not my keeper."

He spares me another murderous glower before he strides out of the apartment and shuts the door with a loud bang.

With him finally gone, I turn to Danny. "Why the hell did you bring him here?"

"Hey, I called to warn you."

"Five minutes before you got here. Fantastic timing."

"It was my fault. I wanted to play your new game," Paris chimes in.

"Guys, please don't beat yourself up for this. I'm the one to blame. It's my mess." Jane looks at me. "I'm sorry, Andy. I'll talk to Troy. He'll come around."

"Don't worry about me, babe." I caress her cheek. "Call me when you get home, okay?"

"Okay."

I plant a soft kiss on her lips, dying for more, but refraining from devouring her mouth in front of my friends.

My heart feels like lead as I watch her leave. She's putting on a brave face, but she must be torn inside over her fight with her brother. I wish I could do something to ease her pain, but I've caused enough damage as it is.

TWENTY-THREE

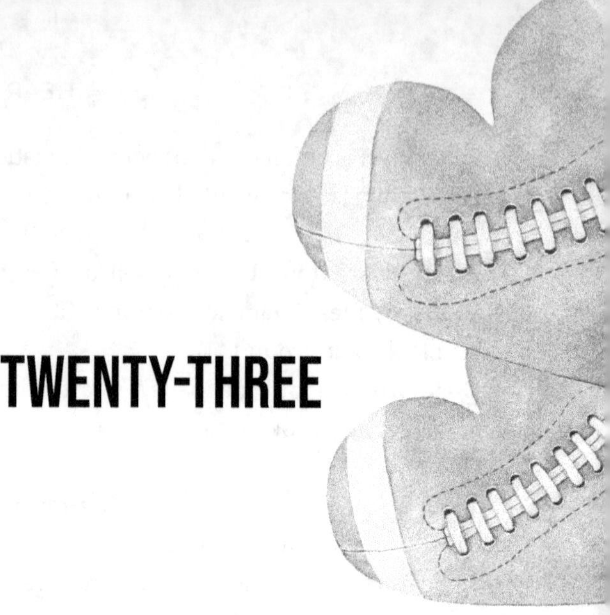

JANE

Troy is leaning against the wall opposite Andreas's apartment with his arms crossed and an expression capable of leveling an army. I match his furious glare and then walk away from him without a word.

"Jane, wait."

"What for? So you can yell at me some more? Humiliate me in public?"

"That's not my intention. But you have to understand where I'm coming from. I just found out that my best friend is sleeping with my sister behind my back. That's fucked up, Jane."

"Yeah? And whose fault is that? If you weren't so pigheaded when it comes to me, maybe we would have told you we were together from the start."

"That's a lame excuse. He should have manned up and told me."

I stop and whirl around, stepping into his personal space to poke him in the chest. "He wanted to tell you from the start. The only reason he didn't was because I asked him to wait. So if you need someone to aim your misplaced anger at, I'm your target."

I resume my escape, getting angrier by the second. Troy follows me, but at least he refrains from saying another word until we reach my car.

Before I can get in, he touches my arm. "I'm never going to blame you for what happened. You're only eighteen. Even if you think you started all this, he should have put a stop to it."

"You're so full of shit, it's not even funny. Do you know how Andy and I got together the first time? He didn't know it was me. That's right. I tricked him into sleeping with me."

Troy's eyebrows shoot to the heavens. "Why would you do that?"

"Because I've been in love with Andy for three years, but I knew he would never cross that line with me. I'm not denying it was a terrible thing to do. Andy was furious when he found out. He felt horrible he didn't recognize me."

"And that doesn't tell you to run for the hills? Come on, Jane. I thought you were smarter than that."

"Don't patronize me!" I snap.

"I'm not. I'm just trying to open your eyes. I get being so infatuated with someone that you ignore the red flags."

"I don't need your help. I know about the risks. But Andy is worth all of them."

Troy clenches his jaw hard, narrowing his eyes. "I hope he feels the same way about you."

There's a myriad of things I want to tell him, the top one on the list being a big "fuck you," but I don't voice any of them. Troy walks away, and I lose my chance to have the last word. My pulse is pounding in my ears when I slide behind the steering wheel. My eyesight is blurry thanks to all the unshed tears, and my chest is heavy. I don't know what makes me sadder—the fact this is the biggest fight I've ever had with Troy or that he spoke out loud all my fears in relation to Andreas.

Mom's ringtone breaks the silence inside the car. I let out a string of curses. It's already past eight. She must have just gotten home, and now she's wondering where I am. I'm too wretched to deal with her, so I let the call go to voicemail, and then put the radio on as loud as I can. I have at least half an hour to come up with an excuse for why I'm out.

About five minutes into the drive, I see the sign for an In-N-Out restaurant. My stomach grumbles, reminding me I haven't eaten anything in hours. That's my alibi right there. Delicious junk food. Mom doesn't need to know I haven't been home since the trip to the mall.

I order all my favorite items from their menu, including their six-hundred-calorie strawberry shake. After the day I've had, I've earned it. I start drinking it as soon as I get a chance, but the treat is not making me feel any better. I hate that I fought with Troy. He's a pain in the ass, but I love him.

I've never felt more alone than I do now. I don't have any close girlfriends who I can trust with my problems. The only person who could actually give me some advice is Grandma, but even so, I'm afraid to tell her about Andreas. What if she agrees with Troy that I'm risking too much, that I will get my heart broken? I can't handle another person I trust and love telling me I'm making a mistake.

I should be on cloud nine. I'm dating the boy of my dreams, but I've never been more depressed. And when I walk through the front door, knowing I'm about to be on the receiving end of criticism and reproach, my stomach bottoms out.

Mom is sitting at the dining room table busy working. A glass of Chardonnay is next to her laptop, but no sign of food. She subscribes to the idea that wine is an excellent meal replacement. If I were a better person, I would have bought her at least a burger. She's eternally on a diet, but she eats junk food like everyone else.

She lifts her face from the computer. "Where have you been?"

"I went to grab dinner." I lift the In-N-Out bag.

"Junk food on a Monday, Jane? Really?"

"Alcohol on a Monday, Mom? Really?" I mock.

She watches me through slits. "Don't start with me. Did you pick up your dress?"

"Yep," I reply.

She doesn't need to know I didn't pick the dress she selected. It's better if she finds out at the luncheon Saturday. My stomach ties into knots. I still don't know how I'm going to manage bootcamp and that event.

"I've made a list of all the candidates that are still available. They aren't at the same level as Hanson van Buuren, but beggars can't be choosers."

I grind my teeth, fighting hard to not fall for her trap. I know she's goading me to talk back so she can either ground me or say more hurtful things.

"Sounds good, Mom. Just shoot me an email." I veer for my bedroom.

"Where do you think you're going with that greasy bag? You know you're not allowed to eat in your bedroom."

I count to ten in my head. I'm not going to engage. With a fake smile on my lips, I say, "Right. I forgot. I'll eat my dinner in the kitchen."

She keeps watching me with her resting bitch face. I'm sure she's raving mad that she doesn't have a solid excuse to grill me further. I'm almost out of earshot when she adds, "Oh, your father called. He wants to have dinner together to discuss your application to Stanford."

"I'm not going to Stanford," I blurt out, and just like that, I give her the opening she needs.

"If you botch your application to Stanford on purpose, we aren't paying for any other school. So I suggest you reconsider your attitude."

I give her the mother of all death glares while saying in my head, *Fuck you, Mom.*

TWENTY-FOUR

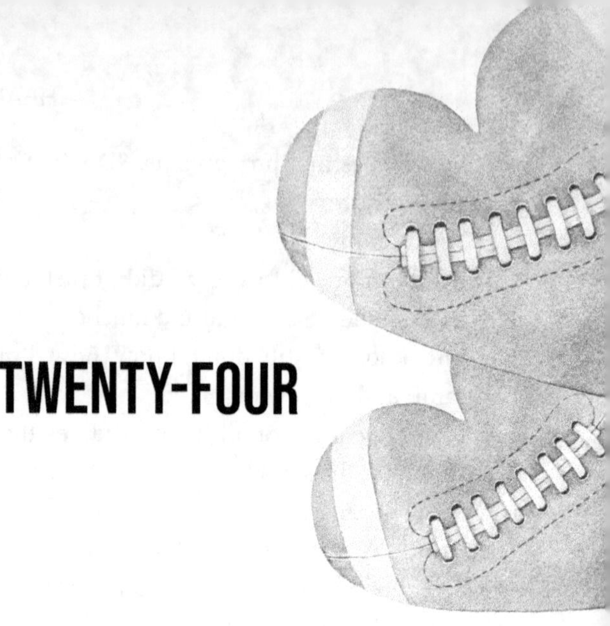

ANDREAS

Going against Danny and Paris's advice, I decide to pay Troy a visit after class the very next day after our fight. They said I should give him more time to cool off, but I can't stand to see Jane suffering. I have to patch things up with him because I'm not giving her up.

I call Charlie to make sure he's home. It rings for a long time and I fear it will go to voicemail. She finally answers it, but judging by the tone in her voice, I might have called at a bad time.

"Hey, I want to check if your boyfriend is home."

"He is, but if you're planning to swing by, I'd suggest you don't."

"Why is that?"

She sighs. "I told him I knew you had hooked up with Jane at the Halloween party. Now he's mad at me too."

"Ah hell. I'm sorry. Troy can be such a stubborn jerk sometimes. I'm coming over anyway. I'll see you in a few."

Maybe Charlie is right and going right now while Troy is

already pissed is not such a great idea, but I can't leave things alone. I can be as pigheaded as he is.

I snag a prime spot in front of his house, but I stay in my car for a minute, running over in my head what I'm going to tell him. Saying that I care about Jane is not going to be enough for him. But I won't lie and tell him that I love her, because I don't even know if that's true. To be honest, I don't know what the hell I feel for her. That's how fucked up I am. I crave her body like nothing else, and she makes me crazy happy. But is that love?

"Shit! I'm a bastard."

"You got that right," Troy says, looming only a few feet away from my car.

I was so immersed in my thoughts that I didn't even hear him walk out of the house. I get out of the car. It's time to do what I came here for.

"I'm glad we're in agreement about something then," I reply.

"What do you want, Andreas?"

"I want a chance to explain things."

"Nothing you can say will change the fact you pursued my sister after you told me countless times that you'd never commit to anyone. Do you want me to be happy that Jane is now another notch in your bedpost?"

"That's not what she is to me. I ca—"

"Care about her, yeah, I heard you the first time. And the second. Even Charlie tried to feed me that bullshit. But I've seen you in action too many times. I have watched you leave a parade of girls brokenhearted after you fucked and ditched them. Do you think I want Jane to be one of them?"

"That won't happen. I'm giving you my word."

"You can't promise me that."

"Why not? Because I have a reputation? Maybe I slept around because I didn't know what I was missing until I found Jane."

Troy presses a closed fist against his forehead. "As angry as I am right now, I do want to believe you, man, but I just can't." He glances at me, his eyes shining with conflict. "Jane might have finally found the confidence to speak her mind, but that doesn't mean she isn't vulnerable. Don't you fucking know how hard she has it now at the hands of my narcissistic mother?"

"I do know. And that's why I'm here, risking getting punched in the face. She's miserable about your fight. Don't let your anger with me drive you away from her."

"If you're that worried, there's a simple solution. Walk away now before it's too late."

"It's already too late!" I lose my patience. "I can't walk away from Jane. She's all I think about."

"Are saying you love her?"

Damn it. He had to ask me the only question I'm not able to answer truthfully.

He laughs without humor. "Never mind. Your face says it all. Don't worry about Jane. I'm not going to shut her out of my life because you're now in hers. Someone will have to be around to pick up the pieces when you obliterate her heart."

He walks away, leaving me feeling worse than I did before I came here. I didn't expect him to forgive me. I don't think he ever will, even if end up marrying Jane and we have a bunch of kids. Warmth spreads through my chest at the thought of one day starting a family with her. Right now, it seems like a dream and I don't dare let my thoughts go there.

I knew patching things up with Troy would be impossible. My main goal was to make sure he wouldn't stop talking to Jane on my account.

I text her once I'm in the car. I probably should give her some space, but I wasn't lying to Troy. I can't stop thinking about her.

Hey, what are you doing today, babe?

She doesn't text me right away, and I begin to worry, which is fucking stupid. She might be busy. *Hell.* I went from Casanova to clingy boyfriend in the span of days. I'd better find a distraction fast before I head to her house uninvited. Wouldn't it be the cherry on the top of the cake if I got Jane in trouble with her mother too?

You already agreed to help her escape the luncheon, dumbass. What do you think is going to happen?

I did agree and I can't back down now. Her mother will be furious, but at least Jane will get what she wants, which is to play roller derby instead of being paraded around like she's a fucking prize horse.

Anger surges within me, making me tighten my hold on the steering wheel. Her mother is almost as bad as my father. Mine punished me with his fists, hers does so with words and actions. Maybe that's why I'm so drawn to Jane. We both have fucked-up parents.

My phone chimes, announcing a new text message, and my heart skips a beat. I glance at the screen, smiling from ear to ear when I see it's her reply. At a traffic light, I read the whole message.

> I have a ton of homework to do, and I have to get my skates on later.

I'm disappointed that, most likely, I won't have a chance to see her today. The feelings I keep having are a surprise to me.

Another text pops up.

> I'm going to Hermosa Beach to practice. Do you want to come?

And just like that, my spirits are lifted. I feel giddy like a kid on Christmas Eve. I say "Yes" before thinking things through. I never learned how to skate properly. *Shit.*

> Do you have roller skates? I should have asked that first, huh?

No, but I'll figure it out. I'll pick you up. Just tell me when.

I half expect her to say it's better if I don't or her mother might create issues, but when she texts back with an "Ok," a stupid grin appears on my face. Now I have to find some skates.

JANE

I can't focus on my homework to save my life. And once Andreas's text comes through, impossible. But I can't let my grades slide off. I need to maintain my GPA, or forget getting accepted at Rushmore. They might not be as prestigious as Stanford, but they have a tough selection process as well.

I'm still reeling from Mom's latest threat. I bet it was her idea to withdraw financial support if I refuse Stanford. One more reason to graduate top of my class. I might have to apply for a scholarship if that's the case. The only issue is that I'm not a star in any sport, and since my parents are wealthy, it will be tough getting financial assistance any other way.

I wish Troy were speaking to me. He'd have a word of advice. But knowing him, he'll stew on his anger for a while.

I force my mind back to the book in front of me. I have to memorize all these historical facts by the end of the day. I have a quiz tomorrow, and I want to head to Hermosa Beach to practice later. I'm jonesing to go skating.

But my phone with Andy's message keeps taunting me. I glance at the screen every thirty seconds. *God, forget it.*

He asked what I'm doing today. I guess he wants to hang out. So tempting. With the way we left things off last night, I'd like nothing more than to see him in person to make sure he hasn't changed his mind about me. Any other guy would say the hell with it if they had to deal with a brother like mine.

With regret, I tell him that I have homework to do, and I'm going to practice after. He doesn't reply immediately, so I shoot another message, asking if he wants to come.

The "Yes" comes swiftly, and like a fool in love, I let out a shriek. I didn't stop to think if he has skates or not. I've never seen him rollerblading before. He says he doesn't own a pair, but he'll figure it out. The worry in my chest eases a little. If he wasn't sure about us anymore, he wouldn't go through the trouble.

When he tells me that he's going to pick me up, a sliver of worry pierces my chest. The last thing I need is Mom finding out about Andreas and forbidding me to see him. She would do it out of spite—or jealousy. Then I remember she won't be home until much later. She texted earlier to let me know she has a dinner with a client.

That thought and the prospect of seeing Andy today is all the motivation I need to get done with schoolwork as fast as I can.

TWENTY-FIVE

ANDREAS

It took me a while to find someone who had a pair of skates I could borrow. Buying was also an option, but I didn't feel like going all the way to the mall. In the end, I got a pair of rollerblades from a dude on the hockey team. In hindsight, in the amount of time it took me to find these damn things, I could have gone to the mall and back in less time.

I'll be late to pick up Jane, and I feel horrible, knowing she probably wants to get as much practice as possible. I tell her she can go ahead of me and I'll meet her there. She doesn't sound upset over the phone, but I could be completely wrong. My lack of experience having a girlfriend is coming back to bite me in the ass, big time.

After suffering the brutal LA traffic during rush hour, I finally arrive in Hermosa Beach, but I can't find a parking space near the pier to save my life. I end up parking closer to Redondo Beach, which is the next neighborhood south of Hermosa. I call Jane as soon as I'm out of the car, but it rings and rings until it goes to voicemail. *Hell. What now?*

I text her instead, and walk toward the beach, carrying my

borrowed rollerblades. I won't put them on until it's absolutely necessary. The sun is about to set, and the boardwalk is busy. Too many people to witness my poor skating skills. I look at my phone again, and nada.

"Come on, baby. Where are you?" I mutter to myself.

I hope she didn't forget her phone in the car. It seems I won't have a choice but put the skates on and look for her on wheels. I hope I don't break something in the process.

JANE

When Andreas said he would be late and told me he'd meet me here, I was disappointed. I was looking forward to the ride with him. I even dressed like a cute eighties roller skater girl especially for him. But now that I'm at the beach, I'm glad he gave me the option to practice longer.

The boardwalk is as busy as I expected it to be. The weather is lovely and the sunset promises to be phenomenal. I put my roller skates on, and then I make sure my phone is off vibration mode. I don't want to miss when Andy calls. I brought a mini crossbody bag that fits the device, my wallet, and my car keys. It's small enough that it won't get in the way.

I skate from my car to the boardwalk, and it feels like I'm in a video game where the objective is trying to reach the beach without running over any of the pedestrians. This is good practice for me. I'm sure there will be obstacles on the banked track this Saturday.

I finally reach the boardwalk without killing anyone, and then skate toward Manhattan Beach. Andy said he was probably running thirty minutes late, so that should give me enough time to get there and back. Then I'll wait for him near the pier.

My legs are still a bit sore from the tryouts. It was good that I wasn't able to practice yesterday—in more ways than one.

Remembering what kept me busy brings a blush to my cheeks and a wonderful feeling in my belly. I couldn't have imagined, not even in my wildest dreams, how wonderful it would be to be with Andy.

My brother thinks it's crazy to be so in love with someone I don't really know well. But the heart wants what the heart wants. Besides, he only knows one side of Andreas. Even when he was drunk out of his mind, he was kind and gentle. A true asshole wouldn't have cared if I was comfortable or not.

I reach the edge of Manhattan Beach in ten minutes. I could keep going farther, but I decide to head back in case Andy manages to get here earlier. Sweat is pouring down my back and covering my face. I'm no longer as cute as I wanted to be, but there's nothing I can do about it. I'm blazing past a busy restaurant with an outside area when I hear someone call my name. I look over my shoulder and find Fred waving at me. Sylvana and Katja are sitting at the table with him.

I whirl around and head back to them. Fred jumps over the restaurant's pony wall, grinning from ear to ear.

"Jane, we have to stop meeting like this," he says.

"I know, right? What are the odds?" I glance past his shoulder and wave at the girls. "Hi."

"Are your ears burning, Jane? We were just talking about you," Katja pipes up.

"Really?" My smile wilts a bit.

I hope it wasn't Fred talking about me. With everything that happened recently, I forgot all about him and the date I postponed. A raincheck is not a refusal, and judging by the way he's looking at me, he believes he has a chance.

"Yeah, Fred was spewing poetic shit about you," Sylvana laughs.

My face becomes as hot as lava while my chest tightens. *Crap.* I really wish she hadn't said that.

"I was not!" Fred retorts. "Don't listen to my cousin, Jane.

She's crazy. I was just saying how awesome you were during tryouts."

"Thanks. I'm still pinching myself that I made it through."

"You did really well," Katja says. "I'm glad to see you're training. Bootcamp is intense."

"I have a question about the schedule. Do we have a lunch break or something?"

"Yeah, of course. You'll get an hour, but I advise you to eat something light. Puking on the track is never fun."

An hour. I still don't know if I'll be able to make an appearance at the luncheon and then get back in time. Andreas said he could make it happen. I have to trust him because with the way things are between Mom and me, if I miss the luncheon, I don't know what she'll do to me.

"Right," I reply.

"What's with the furrow?" Fred asks.

I shake my head, forcing a smile on my face. "Nothing."

"You look like you need a break. Do you want to join us?"

"Uhh...."

"Yeah, Jane. Join us." Sylvana smirks.

"Jane!" I hear Andreas yell my name from somewhere nearby.

I turn toward the boardwalk, squinting to try to find him in the crowd. Suddenly, he appears, coming fast on rollerblades. He doesn't slow down, even when people walk in his path.

"What is he doing?" Fred asks.

"Oh my God. I don't think he knows how to brake," I reply.

And I'm right. Andy manages to miss a couple in his way, but only because he swerved to the right at the last second. He's going to crash into us if I don't help him. I skate in his direction, but instead of meeting him straight on, I loop my arm around his waist, using his momentum to spin us. It would have worked if he didn't freak out and flail around. I can't maintain my balance and compensate for his lack of it at the same time. We're going to fall and it's going to hurt.

My back meet someone's chest and hands reach my arms, stopping my descent.

"Gotcha," Fred says near my ear.

I'm still holding Andreas in my arms, so this must look like the most awkward scene ever. But since we stopped moving, he finally finds his balance and eases off me.

"Are you okay?" I ask.

"Mortified, but yeah." He looks over my shoulder at Fred. "You can let go of her now, pal."

There's no mistaking the hint of threat in his tone. Fred steps back, but he leaves a hand on my lower back. *Crap on toast.* I'd increase the distance myself if Andy wasn't blocking my way.

"Maybe you should be the one to give her some space after you almost killed her with your poor skating skills."

"I didn't—"

"You're both smothering me. Back off, please," I say.

Andreas glances at me, surprised, but then gives me some room. Fred also drops his hand and stands next to me.

"I'm sorry I almost made you fall, babe."

"*Babe?*" Fred's tone rises to a pitch. "Are you two dating?"

I turn to him. "Yeah."

"Since when?"

I feel Andy's stare burn a hole through my face. *Oh boy, that's going to be a bitch to explain.* I hope he doesn't have another fit of jealousy in front of everyone.

"Why do you care?" he asks.

Fred doesn't try to hide his disappointment. He ignores Andy and glances at me. "You could have told me."

"I'm sorry."

He cuts a quick look in Andy's direction, and then back at me. "I'd better go before your boyfriend punches me in the face."

Damn it. I feel awful now. Fred heads back to the restaurant with his shoulders slumped forward. I was a total ass for not being straight with him from the beginning.

"What was that all about?" Andy asks.

His posture is tense, but it's the hardness in his gaze that worries me. Now he's upset with me too.

"It's not what it looks like."

"Whenever someone says that, it is *exactly* what it looks like. Were you going out with him before we got together?"

"What? No! Can we go somewhere else and talk, please?"

He turns toward the beach, skating away without answering. I follow him until he sits on the pony wall separating the beach from the boardwalk. He removes his rollerblades, still not saying a word or meeting my gaze.

"Are you mad at me?" I ask in a small voice.

He lifts his face to mine. His green eyes are softer now. *Thank God.*

"I'm not angry at you. I'm just trying to come to grips that my girlfriend is a knockout, and it's my own damn fault for taking too long to stake my claim."

Sweet baby aliens. I've just melted on the spot. I move into his personal space, then I run my fingers through his hair. "There's no need to be jealous. It's always been you, Andy."

His eyes focus on my lips, and in the blink of an eye, I'm blazing from inside out.

"Did you get enough practice already?" he asks.

"Yeah, why?"

"I want to do something, but unfortunately, what I have in mind is NSFP."

"What's that?"

He curls his lips into a crooked smile, and then he whispers in a husky tone, "Not safe for public, meaning it involves my cock buried deep inside your pussy."

TWENTY-SIX

ndreas walks me to my car. Since I left my shoes in the vehicle, I have to skate slow so I can match his leisurely pace.

"You didn't answer your phone," he says.

"I didn't hear it. I'm sorry. But you found me anyway." I squeeze his hand.

"Don't remind me of that scene."

"Why didn't you tell me you didn't know how to skate?"

"I know how to skate," he grumbles.

Through laughter, I say, "Fine. Why didn't you tell me you didn't know how to skate well?"

He reaches over and pinches my waist. "Ouch!" I drop his hand and move away from his naughty fingers.

"I wanted to see you today. If that meant making a fool out of myself, so be it."

"That's the sweetest thing someone has ever done for me. Who said romance is dead?"

"Some schmuck who never had anyone loveable in their life."

When we reach the sidewalk, I ask, "Where are you parked?"

"All the way at Redondo Beach."

"Wow, really? Well, my car is right there." I point to my right. "I can drive you to yours."

"Hmm, sure, but later."

"Later? Where are we going?" I unlock the doors, waiting for an answer.

Andy doesn't say a word. He gets into the car, leaving me hanging. I quickly follow suit, dying to know where he wants to go first. While I remove my skates, the suspense gets to me. "Are you going to tell me or is it a secret?"

"It's not a secret."

"So where?" I press.

"Not far."

"You're acting very mysterious." I toss my skates to the backseat and then turn the engine on. "But if I'm driving there, I need a location."

"Just drive, babe. I'll give you directions on the way."

I watch him through slits. "You'd better not be taking me to fleabag motel."

He throws his hands up in the air. "Ah hell. There goes my plan."

"You were seriously going to take me to one?"

He looks at me, trying to maintain a serious expression, but the twitch of his upper lip gives him away. "Nah, I'm just yanking your chain."

I smack his chest. "You're awful."

He grabs my hand, keeping it trapped under his, and tugs me to him. His lips find mine, possessive and hungry, like always. I soon forget that what we were talking about a minute ago, and get lost in the feel of his stubbled chin against my face, in the taste of his tongue as it dances with mine.

A familiar throbbing between my legs makes me wish we were anywhere but inside my car. Even a fleabag motel would do. I want to straddle him and take care of the ache so badly, I could cry. But there are too many people walking around.

I pull away before my brain short-circuits and I do something foolish. "What was that for?"

"I realized I didn't say hello to you before."

"Hmm, I like the way you greet me."

"And let me add that I fucking love what you're wearing." He runs his fingers over my exposed legs.

"I'm glad you approve. This is all for you."

He smiles broadly, revealing the dimples I adore. "Good. Now, what was the deal with Fred? Why did he sound so butthurt to find out about us?"

Way to kill the mood, Andy.

"Uh…." I look forward, putting distance between us. "I was trying to get over you and might have encouraged him a little."

"Only a little? You didn't go out on a date with him, did you?"

I glance at him, trying to guess how jealous he is right now. I can't tell.

"No. He wanted to go somewhere to celebrate me surviving the tryouts and making the team."

"Wait? You told him about that?"

Ah hell. He's probably not going to like this. But I can't lie to him. "Fred was there."

"I see." Andy faces forward, clenching his jaw hard.

I touch his arm. "Hey, the only reason he knew about it in the first place is because his cousin's girlfriend is a player on the team."

"Hmm."

"Are you mad?"

"Nope." He crosses his arms over his chest. "Not mad at all."

"You could have fooled me."

He watches me sideways. "Fine. I'm jealous as hell, okay? But I'm trying my hardest to get over it."

"There's no need to be jealous, but I get it. I'd be jealous too if the situation were reversed. Let's not talk about Fred anymore, okay? Where do you want to go?"

He's still pouting when he answers, "I wanted to take you to a boutique hotel a block away, but maybe that's not much better than a motel. It's okay if you just want to go home."

Heavens above. Guys can be such babies sometimes.

"I was joking about the motel. I don't care where I am as long as you're with me."

I can tell he's trying not to smile, but the grin wins. "Okay, babe. Then drive."

No sooner do I pull out of my parking spot than Andreas's hand finds my pussy. He presses his fingers against my clit through the fabric of my shorts, making me gasp.

"Andy, you're distracting me."

"You can't multitask, babe?"

With regret, I bat his hand away. "Not when one of the tasks has the power to send me into oblivion."

He chuckles. "Okay, okay. I'll try to keep my hands to myself. Turn right at the next traffic light."

The boutique hotel appears as soon as I turn on the next street. It's so close to where I was parked that we could have walked. There's a tiny parking lot in front of the building, full save for one spot.

"We got lucky," he says.

"No, you got lucky. Imagine if there was no free space. You would have made me lose my parking spot for nothing."

"You sound way too grumpy for someone who's about to have some awesome sex." He gets out before I can offer a retort.

I grab my bag and follow him. He didn't go far. He's waiting just in front of my car with his hands shoved in his pockets. The pose makes his jeans hang lower on his hips, showing a peek of tanned skin. It's impossible to stay annoyed when the man looks like Adonis. He offers me his hand once I'm near, sending a zing of pleasure everywhere in my body.

I hate to admit it, but he's right. Grumpiness has no place

with him next to me. I ignore how strange this situation is, getting a hotel room just for sex. I feel all grown-up and a little dirty too.

Andy got us a suite with a separate living area from the bedroom. There's also a huge balcony with an ocean view.

"This is incredible, but we're not spending the night. Why waste the money?"

"Because I can."

He grabs me by the waist and spins me around. Then he leans in and rubs his lips over mine, teasing me with the promise of another mind-blowing kiss. He doesn't follow through though. Instead, he presses his forehead against mine and takes a deep breath. His fingers run up and down my arms, leaving a trail of goose bumps in their wake.

"I thought you said something about awesome sex," I murmur.

"In good time. Let me just breathe you in."

"Is this going to be our thing? Fancy hotel rooms?"

He pulls back, frowning. "No, I just knew I couldn't make the drive back to my apartment in my condition."

"Your condition?"

He takes my hand and guides it to his crotch.

"Ah, this condition." I smile.

"Be straight with me, Jane. Does it bother you that I brought you here? I don't want you to feel uncomfortable."

"It doesn't bother me. I just wish I had my own place to make things easier for us."

"You're always welcome in my apartment. And your mom works, right? I can come over when she isn't around."

"I think I'd rather go to your place. My mother's schedule is unpredictable."

"That's fine." He tucks a loose strand of hair behind my ear. "I went to see Troy today, by the way."

His confession takes me by surprise. I step back so I can look at his face properly. "What happened?"

"He's still mad as hell at me. I don't expect him to forgive me any time soon. But I wanted to make sure he didn't make you pay for my sins. I don't want to be the reason you don't speak with your brother."

"You're not the reason. Troy's stubbornness is."

"Even so, I had to explain to him I'm not simply fooling around with you. I'm serious about us, Jane. I haven't been this happy in a long time and I'm not going to give you up."

My heart takes off, skipping gleefully toward the sunset. If I wasn't already in love with Andreas, I'd fall in love now. I throw my arms around his neck and crush my mouth to his. He matches my enthusiasm, encircling my waist with his arms and pulling me closer to his body. Together we create an inferno. His heat fuels my own, and suddenly, I no longer know where I end and he begins. Clothes get snatched off urgently, and then we're tumbling down on the white leather couch.

Andreas abandons my mouth to place open kisses on my neck and then he moves south, sucking my nipple into his mouth while he plays with my other breast with his hand. I arch my back, begging for more.

"Andy, shouldn't we head to the bedroom?"

"What for, babe? I got you right where I want."

He lets go of my nipple to continue kissing my stomach until he's in between my legs. He lifts one of them over his shoulder, exposing me even more to him. When his warm tongue finds my clit, I cry out. He licks my bundle of nerves with gusto while he continues to play with my breast.

I'm quickly losing control. I'm floating on air. I want to hold on to sanity for as long as I can, but Andreas is too good at sex. He inserts two fingers inside of me, torturing me in every possible way.

"Oh my God," I moan just a second before he makes me come.

His fingers fuck me harder; his tongue works my clit faster while my body shakes from head to toe. I don't realize I was screaming until I stop and find my throat hoarse. My eyes are closed when Andreas finally shows me mercy. I'm boneless.

I hear a condom wrapper rip, and a moment later, Andy's body is covering mine, and his length slides into me. *Holy fucking shit.* I didn't think I was ready for round two. But I guess I am.

TWENTY-SEVEN

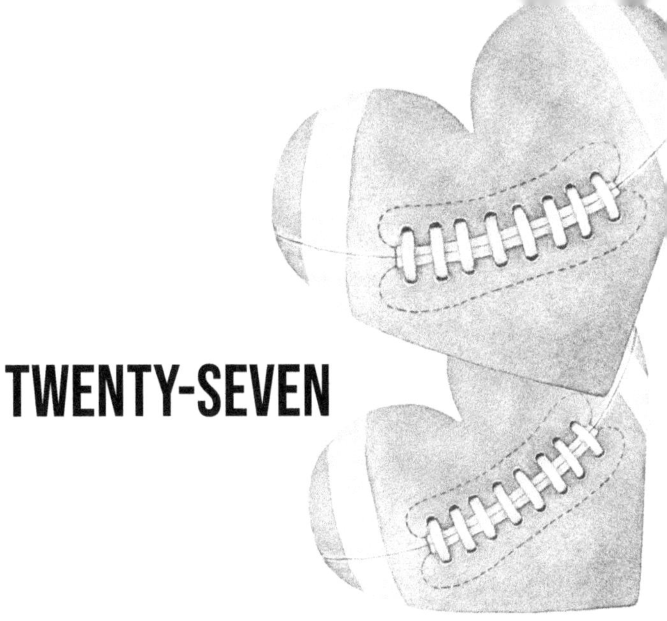

ANDREAS

Eventually we made it to the bedroom. It would have been a waste to not take advantage of the king-sized mattress. I'm now resting my head against Jane's stomach and she's running her fingers through my hair. I could seriously fall asleep like this. It's heaven.

"How was your day today?" I ask.

"School was a bore. I'm so ready to graduate."

"Only a few more months and then you'll be a Rushmore Rebel."

"That's what I want. But my parents want me to go to Stanford, no matter what."

I lift my head to look at her. "They can't force you to go to a school you don't want to."

"As long as they control the financial strings, they can. My mother told me the other day that if I botch my Stanford application on purpose, they won't pay for my tuition anywhere else."

"That's seriously fucked up, babe."

"I know. But even if I did try to sabotage my chances, I'd still be a shoo-in with my father being a famous alumnus and all."

"I don't want you to move to San Fran," I say. "But I'd respect that if it were your choice."

"It's not my choice and I won't go. I love my life here in LA. Now I have you and roller derby. If that means attending community college and working my way through, so be it. Lots of kids in America do it. I can too."

"Of course you can, babe. Have you talked to Troy about it?"

"The last time we spoke, he wasn't completely against Stanford."

"Maybe he was trying to keep you away from me. I think, deep down, he suspected I had a thing for you."

"Why do you say that?"

"He never wanted me to tag along when he had plans with you."

"You say you had a thing for me, but tell me the truth. When exactly did that start? It can't possibly have begun after I stole that kiss from you."

I frown. "Why not? You were a damn good kisser for a first-timer."

She yanks a fistful of my hair. "Hey. How do you know it was my first kiss?"

"Are you saying it wasn't?"

Her cheeks turn a beautiful pink color. "No, Mr. Know-It-All. For your information, my first kiss happened when I was in seventh grade. His name was Enrique Garcia, and he wore braces."

"Fine, I accept that I wasn't your first everything. But I'm sure my kiss was the first one that made you go weak in your knees."

"Aren't you cocky?"

I roll on my belly, resting my chin in between her lovely tits. "Are you saying that it isn't true?"

She narrows her eyes. "Fine. It's true."

I chuckle. "There's no need to feel embarrassed about it."

"Who says I'm embarrassed?"

I poke her cheek. "Your lovely red face."

She bats my hand away, and then leans on her elbows, dislodging me from my comfortable position. "All right. Enough of making fun of me."

"I'm not making fun of you."

I'm about to blurt out that she's the first girl who ever made me feel alive, but the truth gets stuck in my throat. Her phone interrupts the moment.

"Crap. That's Troy's ringtone."

I roll off her and reach for the device on the nightstand. "Here, you should answer it."

She bites her lower lip, staring at the phone without making any motion to take it from me. "I'm not sure I'm ready to talk to him."

"Babe, he's probably calling to apologize for being an ass. Give him the chance. And he if doesn't, then I'll head back to his house and kick his ass for making you suffer."

Her beautiful eyes turn as round as saucers. "Please don't. I don't want you two fighting because of me again. I feel bad enough as it is."

"Please, Jane. Answer the phone."

She finally takes the device from my hand and clicks the Accept button, putting it on speaker.

"Hi, Troy."

"Hey, Jane. Are you busy?"

"No. But with I'm Andy."

"I figured as much. Anyway, I want to apologize for the way I reacted Sunday. To be honest, I'm still reeling from it."

I roll my eyes, making the same gesture Jane does. Troy can be so dramatic sometimes.

"You make it sound like I'm dating the devil."

"Not the devil, but close enough."

I twist my face into a scowl. As apologies go, this is one of the worst.

"I thought you were calling to say you're sorry. All you've done so far is criticize Andy."

"Right. Well, I *am* sorry for the way I treated you. But I'm not sorry for the things I told hi—ouch! Charlie, come on."

I laugh, guessing that Charlie must have pinched him or something. If she's comfortable doing that, then it means they've made up. No surprise there. Troy is crazy about her.

Just like you're crazy about Jane.

The random thought takes me by surprise. Up until now, I couldn't make sense of my feelings. Sadly, my only experience with love is too fucked up. Danny said what I had with Crystal wasn't real. She manipulated me. He's right, but that doesn't mean she didn't leave scars deep enough to confuse the hell out of me.

I shouldn't be listening to this conversation, so I slide out of bed and return to the living room. Jane must have taken the call off speaker because I can still hear her talking although Troy's voice vanishes. It's better this way. He's clearly too angry, and all the things coming out of his mouth were beginning to get to me.

I put my boxers back on and head to the balcony. Fresh air will do me good. It's much colder now that the sun has set. A T-shirt would make me more comfortable, but the cool air against my skin isn't too awful.

The boardwalk is much quieter now, and I can hear the waves crashing against the shore. I take a deep breath, enjoying the peaceful moment. A few seconds later, Jane hugs me from behind, resting her cheek against my back. I feel a pang in my chest like a broken piece clicked back into place. I can't breathe for a moment, caught between being scared and elated.

I cover her arms with mine and ask, "All good?"

"Yeah. After you left the room, Troy was much more reasonable. I think he was saying all those hurtful things because he knew you were listening."

"I figured as much. Did you tell him about Stanford?"

"Not yet. We made plans to visit Grandma this Friday. I'll tell them both at the same time."

"Are you also telling Ophelia about us?"

Jane releases me from her hold and steps to my side. "Yeah. I don't want to hide from anyone that you're my boyfriend."

I throw my arm over her shoulders, pulling her closer. "Only your parents," I chuckle.

"Not even them." She turns in my arms, looking up. "I'm telling Mom at the luncheon that you'll be my escort to the ball because that's what boyfriends do."

My face splits into a grin. "That's right. And I'm going to prove to you that I'm the fucking best boyfriend in the world."

"Better than Troy?" She arches an eyebrow.

"Hell yeah. No offense, but your brother's got nothing on me."

"All right. But now that you've raised the bar, you'd better deliver."

I kiss her long and hard, loving how she immediately melts into me. When I pull away, her face is ethereal.

"Oh, I'll deliver, sweetheart. You'd better believe it."

TWENTY-EIGHT

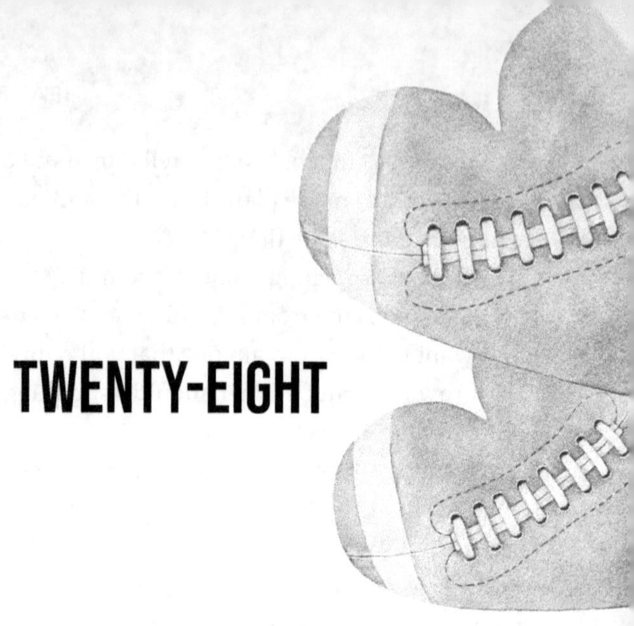

JANE

I've been avoiding Mom since we clashed over Stanford. But I couldn't keep that up forever. This morning she reminded me that we were meeting my father for dinner tonight, which totally blew the plans I'd made with Andreas and left me in a bad mood all morning.

I didn't text him right away because I knew I had to vent, and messaging wouldn't do. As soon as I come home from school, I call him, knowing he should be home already.

"Hey, babe. How's your day so far?" he asks.

I flop on my bed and stare at the ceiling. "Pretty crappy. I have to cancel our plans. I'm having dinner with the parentals tonight."

"Oh, no worries. Is Troy going to be there?"

"I don't think so. This is a dinner to talk about my future at Stanford. Gag me."

"I've been thinking about that. Maybe it's better if you just pretend to follow along with their plan until you have a solid counterattack strategy."

"Yeah. It's good advice. The problem is, now that I've found my voice, it's hard to keep quiet. Meek Jane is gone."

He chuckles, infusing my body with warmth.

"You were never meek."

"I beg to differ."

"A meek girl wouldn't have attacked me in the laundry room."

"Oh my God. You're never going to drop that, are you?"

"No. I'll be telling that story to our grandkids."

I stop breathing for a second. *Is he only joking or is he serious about that statement?* Andy has told me I make him happy and he's not giving me up, but he's never mentioned a distant future like that. He knows I'm in love with him, and yet, he has never said it back.

"Hello? Jane? Are you still there?"

"Yeah, I'm here."

"Anyway, just think about what I said."

I want to ask which part, but I know he's referring to dinner with my folks. "You're right. The smart thing to do is to bite my tongue. Dinner is going to be brutal though."

"Why don't you ask Troy to tag along?"

"I thought about it, but he's been protecting me from Mom my entire life. Maybe that's why he feels entitled to an opinion about us. I need to do this on my own."

"And you will, babe. I wish I could come over right now, but I have to write a paper."

"It's okay. I also have schoolwork to do."

"Call me when you get home from dinner, okay?"

"I will. Love you," I say automatically and immediately freeze.

Fuck me. I can't believe I blurted that out. Maybe it was his talk of grandkids that made me daft for a moment. The line goes silent, but I can hear his breathing. *Oh my God.* If he says thank you, I'm going to die.

"I know," he finally replies. "Talk later."

He ends the call, leaving me reeling. My heart feels tight, and my stomach is now twisted in knots. The urge to cry comes swiftly like a tidal wave. He didn't say it back, and it hurts so damn much. I know I'm being melodramatic. We have been dating for less than a week. The fact I've been in love with him for three years doesn't change that.

But what if he thinks I'm a pathetic, needy girl?

"I'm such a moron." I hit my mattress with a closed fist.

My phone vibrates, sending me into a flutter. But it's not Andreas texting me back. It's a message from Hanson van fucking Buuren. *What the hell does he want?*

I should delete it after the douche move he pulled, but I'm too curious for that.

> Hi, Jane. I'm sorry it took so long to get back to you. I feel awful for canceling our lunch the other day, but I want to let you know I'll be at the luncheon this Saturday. I hope we have a chance to talk then. Looking forward to meeting you in person.

Oh joy. I'm sure Lorena has something to do with Hanson's resurrection. Mom might have given up pairing me with a top candidate, but her friend clearly didn't.

ANDREAS

"I'm a fucking idiot." I stare at my phone, fighting the impulse to throw it against the wall.

"What did you do?" Danny asks.

He has an uncanny ability to show up at the exact time I'm doing or saying something stupid.

"Jane said she loved me, and I replied with 'I know.'"

"So you pulled a Han Solo on her. That's not too bad."

"No, it's bad. I hesitated. Besides, I've never said those words to her before. The Han Solo line only works after the fact in real life. I haven't risked my life for Jane time and time again like Han did in the movies."

Danny's eyebrows arches. "Wow. And I thought I was the romantic sap in this household."

"Just because I know my pop culture doesn't make me a romantic. Han wore his feelings on his sleeve, unlike me."

"You haven't been dating long. I'm sure she didn't expect you to say it."

I push my long bangs back. "I'm not sure, man. She's sensitive. The last thing I want is to hurt her."

"You're feeling awfully guilty about this. Is it possible that you're already on the same page as she is, but you're just too afraid to admit it?"

I throw him a glower. "Stop psychoanalyzing me, Dr. Phil."

He lifts both hands up. "Hey, I'm just trying to help. I'm going to hit the gym. Wanna come?"

"I can't. I have to finish a paper for Professor Douchebag's class."

My phone pings with an incoming message. My heart skips a beat, thinking it's from Jane, but when I glance at it, it's from a random chick, wanting a hookup. This one included a picture of her rack. *Jesus.* What if Jane saw it by accident? I can't give her any reason to believe I'm still a player.

The problem is so many girls have my phone number. Most of the time, I don't know who they are or how they got my digits in the first place. That detail never bothered me before. Now it's a fucking problem. This is the fifth text I've received since I started dating Jane. And like the others, I delete the message and block the number.

"Why are you glaring at your phone now?"

"Just another random message from a stranger."

"Ah, booty call. Maybe you should make an announcement

on the school paper that you're officially retired as the campus Casanova. I'm sure Charlie can hook you up."

Danny's eyes are swimming with glee as he drinks his pre-workout shake.

"You're such a comedian, Danny. I thought you were leaving."

He sets the glass down on the counter. "Don't be a hater. I'm just trying to help."

"Sure."

I get comfortable on the couch and fire up my laptop. This damn paper won't write itself. Danny doesn't say another word, and five minutes later, he walks out the door. I should be able to get into the zone now that the house is quiet, but my mind keeps going back to my phone conversation with Jane. I didn't want to tell Danny, but the reason I was cursing to myself is that I almost said the L-word back but choked in the end.

The only time I've said those words before was to Crystal, and now, I'm terrified to open myself up for more heartbreak. Crystal was a fucking bitch who only used me to get to the top prize, my father. Even knowing I was played when I was too naïve to know better doesn't make the memory of that pain less acute.

I'm hardwired now to walk away from any chance of getting hurt again. Admitting that I've fallen for Jane could be the hardest thing I have to do.

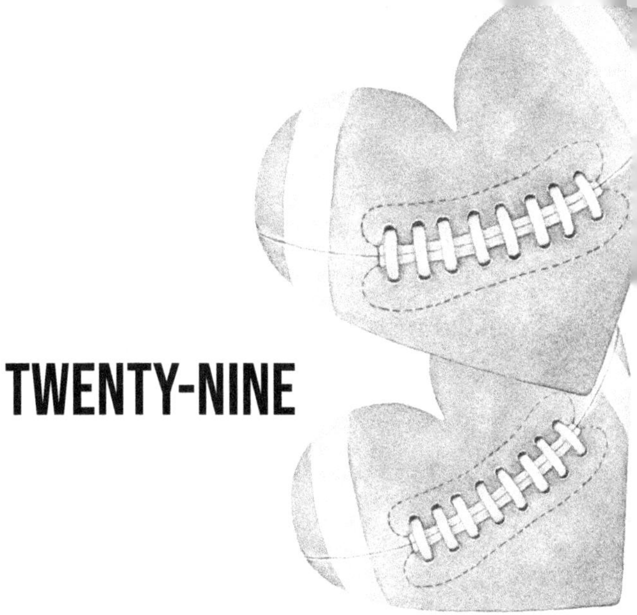

TWENTY-NINE

JANE

When we arrive at the restaurant, my father—punctual man that he is—is already there waiting for us.

"You're late," he says as soon as we take our seats.

"I had an important call with a client," Mom replies without looking in his direction.

They've been divorced for ages, and still, they can barely tolerate each other's presence. I can't remember the last time they exchanged more than a few words at social events. The fact they've agreed to this dinner means it will be an uphill battle to convince them I don't belong in Stanford.

He glowers at my mother for another second before switching his attention to me. "How have you been, Jane? It seems like I haven't seen you in months."

"That's because you haven't. The last time was last year at your employees' barbecue party."

"Ah, that's right."

"Your father is too busy for family, Jane. You should know that by now," Mom retorts.

I let out a heavy sigh. *Here we go.* I wonder how long they'll keep tossing barbs at each before they remember the reason for this dinner from hell. I look around until I catch the waiter's attention. He walks over to our table and takes our drink orders. His interruption serves to reset my parents. They stop bickering for a moment to pay attention to the menu. I'm not hungry, but if I don't order anything, it's just going to cause me more grief with them.

"So, how's school?" Dad asks, resuming his phony interest in me.

"School is fine. Same old, same old."

"I hope this silly debutante ball business is not distracting you from your studies." He gives Mom a meaningful glare.

"This 'silly debutante ball' will help Jane's chances of getting into your precious Stanford. Her extracurricular activities were lacking."

"That's bullshit." I set the menu down, fuming.

My parents look at me as if I had suddenly sprouted a second head. I promised Andy I wouldn't antagonize them, but I can't keep my mouth shut and let Mom walk all over me.

"Jane, what in the world?" Dad says.

"See what I have to deal with? Jane has suddenly developed a rebellious side. Back talking, staying out late, and God knows what else she's doing."

"I've finally found my backbone, and I'm not going to apologize for that. I've been busting my ass, picking up any volunteer work I can, and you know it."

"You're not doing any volunteering work now."

"Because you told me not to!" I snap.

People are now staring, which is probably what's bothering Mom the most. Like she's one to talk after the spectacle she pulled last year in front of Charlie's family.

"She didn't want me to sign up so I'd have free time for debutante events," I continue in a lower tone.

Dad continues to stare at me calmly without saying a word.

Mom, on the other hand, looks like she's about to blow a fuse. The waiter returns then with our drinks, and no sooner does he set her martini on the table than she chugs half of it. Dad glances at her in disgust before thanking the man.

"I'd be more than okay if you didn't participate in such a ridiculous affair, Jane," he finally tells me.

I want to shout, demanding why didn't he say something before, but then I remember he's not that type of parent. The only thing he cares about is making sure I attend his alma mater.

"You'd have to be involved in her upbringing to have decision power."

"Mom already put a lot of work into it. I think it will be fun," I say.

She looks at me, surprised, and I don't blame her. She knows I'm not keen in the least. However, now that Andy is coming with me, the prospect of a dull gala is not daunting anymore. I can't wait to show him off to all those snobby bitches I know talk trash about me behind my back.

"I'm glad that some sense has finally returned to you." She takes another large sip of her drink.

"Anyway, I didn't ask for this dinner to discuss frivolous social affairs." Dad folds his napkin on his lap, keeping his shrewd eyes on me. "Your mother told me you don't want to attend Stanford, and I want to know why."

"I don't have anything against it. I just don't think it's the right school for me."

"I don't see why you would think that. You loved the campus when I took you on a tour."

"I was eight. I didn't care about the school's campus. I enjoyed spending time with you."

He seems taken aback by my honest remark. Maybe he's just too focused on his career and is truly unaware of his shortcomings as a father.

"Besides, how come you've never pressured Troy to attend

Stanford?" I continue, taking advantage of a weakness in his demeanor.

"Because John Rushmore has a better sports program, and that's where your brother excels. Your talents would be wasted there."

"Rushmore is a good school."

"Stanford is better. Jane, I'm sorry, but I'm not going to back down on this. You're going to Stanford. You *will* thank me later."

Tears gather in my eyes and I hate myself for showing weakness. "No, I won't. I happen to like my life in LA."

"Oh, please. San Francisco is only a few hours away. You're being dramatic, as usual," Mom pipes up.

She flags the waiter again since she's already finished with her drink.

It's clear that there isn't a way to win this argument. Nothing I say will convince my father to let go of his Stanford dream. I have to swallow this bitter pill for now and, like Andy suggested, come back with a strategy in place.

I check out during the rest of the dinner, only replying with short answers whenever I'm asked a question. I lose count of the number of martinis Mom drinks, and when the dinner is finally over, she's positively drunk. I have to drive us back home.

She stumbles out of the car when I park in the garage. It's a miracle she doesn't fall on her stiletto heels. I guess she's had a lot of practice. She disappears into her room and I know she will be dead to the world until late morning tomorrow. It's a blessing and a curse. I'm free of her annoying presence tonight, but I'll have to deal with her bitchy hangover mood tomorrow.

I get ready to call it a night, feeling immeasurably drained from the whole affair. I pick up my phone and pull up Andy's contact info. I promised to call him, but I'm not sure I want to after I blurted out that stupid love declaration. I set my phone on my nightstand, deciding it's better to just go to sleep and hope he forgot what I said.

Twenty minutes later, he calls. If I don't pick up, he's going to think there's something wrong.

"Hey," I say.

"Hi, babe. Did you just get home?"

"Yeah," I lie.

"You sound upset. How bad was it?"

I didn't think I sounded upset. I don't know how he could tell. But hearing the worry in his tone does something to me. Sadness and a sense of impotence overwhelms me. My eyes burn as the tears form once again.

"Jane?"

I let out shuddering breath, which I'm sure he heard.

"It was exactly like I thought it would be," I say through the choking in my throat. "My mother got stinking drunk and nasty, whereas all my father cared about was my future at Stanford. He's determined to send me there. He thinks he's doing what's best for me."

The hot tears finally roll down my cheeks. I'm glad Andreas is not here to see me bawl my eyes out, but I can't keep talking and hide the crying. I feel so weak and pathetic; I don't want him to know.

"Jane, bab—"

"I'm actually super tired. Can we talk tomorrow?"

There's a poignant pause before he replies, "Yeah. Sleep tight, babe."

I end the call without replying, burying my face in my pillow. I know I'll feel better tomorrow, but tonight, I'm going to let misery win.

ANDREAS

Something is wrong. Jane was crying, I'm sure of that, and trying to hide it from me. There's no way in hell I'm going to wait until tomorrow to check on her. I jump off the couch, grab my keys from the entryway table, and head out. I'm glad Danny is not home to try to stop me. It's not that late yet, and Jane said her mom got drunk, which means she's probably passed out already.

I drive as fast as I can, propelled by a gripping sense of dread. I wish Jane lived closer to campus, but the twenty-minute drive is nothing compared to the six hours from here to San Francisco. I told Jane we would find a way for her to stay here, but there's a small part of me that fears that might not be possible. I still have another year of school to go, which means not seeing her every day until I graduate.

The thought fills me with anguish, spurring me to press the gas pedal harder. I'm lucky I don't get a speeding ticket. When I park outside of Jane's house, all the lights are off. I could jump the gate, but there's a security camera mounted on top. Plus, there's the issue that I don't have the house keys and I can't pick a lock. Besides, I don't want to surprise Jane. I just want to make sure she's okay with my own eyes.

I call her, hoping she hasn't fallen asleep yet. It rings and rings, until finally, her croaky voice comes through.

"Hey."

"Babe, I'm outside, can you open the gate for me?"

"What? You're here?" Her voice gets more agitated, and then I hear the sound of sheets being tossed aside.

"Yeah. I couldn't sleep without checking on you."

"Okay, I'm coming."

The call goes silent. She must not want to be overheard on the phone. A moment later, the gate opens, and I slip through. Jane is waiting by the front door wearing loose flannel pajamas. There's barely any light save for the crescent moon. It's enough to see the streak marks of tears on her cheeks though.

"You didn't need to come. I'm fine."

"Well, I'm here now. Are you going to let me in?"

"Yeah, but you have to be super quiet. The dragon sleeps for now."

She closes the door softly after me, and we tiptoe to her bedroom. We're lucky that it's at the opposite side of the house from her mother's suite.

As soon as Jane closes her door, I pull her into a bear hug, hiding my face in the crook of her neck. She hugs me back, and we don't move for a minute or so. I'm in not in a hurry to let her go.

"You didn't need to come, Andy. As you can see, I've survived."

I pull back to look at her face. "You don't need to lie to me, sweetheart. It's okay not to be all right."

She drops her eyes to my chest. "I don't want to be the girl with all the emotional baggage. First my brother goes berserk, and now my insane parents are dead set on making my life a living hell."

"You don't think I have enough baggage to fill a jet plane?" I pinch her chin between my index finger and thumb and lift her face back to mine.

"You seem to be handling it better than me."

"Babe, I wish that were true. I think I just learned to hide it better."

"You know you can tell me anything, right?"

"Yeah," I say, even knowing it's unlikely I'll ever confess my dirty secret to her. "You know that applies to you too. So tell me. You're feeling down only because of your parents, or did I contribute to it as well?"

Her eyes widen a fraction. "What do you mean?"

"You were hurt that I didn't say I love you back."

She steps back, putting an unwanted distance between us. "No, I wasn't. I didn't expect you to say it."

"I want you to know that I want to say it, but... I can't."

"Why?" she asks in a small voice, breaking me.

I'm such a fucking mess. I'm hurting the girl of my dreams

and I can't help it. "Because I'm broken, babe. It's not you. It's me. I'll never be able to say those words out loud. It's beyond what I can give."

She wipes away the tear that rolls down her cheek. "Why is that? What happened to you, Andy?"

I swallow the huge lump in my throat. "I can't tell you that either."

"You don't trust me?"

I bridge the distance between us and capture her face between my hands. "I do, babe. I do. I'm just not ready yet. I need time."

It's a cop-out. I'll never be ready.

"I can give you time. This is not a race."

I kiss her lips softly. "You're too good to me, sweet Jane."

She steps away from me again, leaving me adrift. But when I look into her eyes, I don't see sadness anymore. I see passion and love. She undoes the buttons on her shirt slowly, not stopping until the swell of her breasts peek through the open fabric.

"You said you can't say you love me. But can you make love to me, Andy? Even if it's only tonight?"

I inhale sharply. My pulse accelerates, and other parts of my body react accordingly at the sight. Not only my cock, but also my stomach that now seems to house a thousand butterflies.

I step into her space again and rest my hands on her hips. "I can make love to you tonight, and every other night. I'm damaged goods, but I'm yours, babe. For as long as you want."

THIRTY

JANE

My alarm blares, ending a pretty good dream prematurely. With my eyes still closed, I reach for my phone on my nightstand, trying to shut it off. A male grumble makes me open them in a flash. *Oh my God.* In my semi-asleep state, I forgot that Andreas spent the night. He tosses his arm over my stomach, trapping me against his solid chest as he spoons me.

"Andy, you have to go," I whisper.

"Five more minutes, babe."

"I have to get ready for school. And don't you have class too?"

"What time is it?"

"Quarter to seven."

He pulls my hair off my shoulder and kisses my neck. "Plenty of time for a morning quickie."

I want to say no, but his hand finds its way between my legs, effectively shutting off the cautious side of my brain.

"You really know how to make your case."

"Is that a yes?" he whispers in my ear.

I moan in response, and he bites my earlobe before releasing me to search for his jeans on the floor.

Wanting to get a better view of his ripped backside, I lean on my elbows. Andy straightens when he finds the condom he was looking for and then turns to me with lopsided grin on his face.

"The last one. I need to keep you stocked."

"Why? Are you planning more midnight visits?"

"First of all, I didn't come at midnight. And secondly, why not?" He rips the wrapper and quickly rolls the condom down his length.

My eyes remain focused on his erection when Andreas returns to bed.

"My eyes are up here, babe," he smirks.

"Is that s—"

A knock on the door cuts off my sassy reply. My heart jumps to my throat at the same time that Andreas jumps off the bed, grabbing a pillow to cover his crotch area.

"Jane, are you up?" Troy asks outside the door.

He glances at me, panicked. If Troy finds him naked in my room, God only knows what's going to happen.

"Barely. What are you doing here?" I ask.

"I thought we could have breakfast together."

"Is Mom up yet?"

"I walked by her room. Heard her snoring pretty loudly."

"I have to shower. I'll be out in a minute."

"You do that, but tell Andy to come out first."

"Shit," he curses under his breath.

"I saw your car parked outside, moron," Troy replies.

Andreas gives me a look that's equal measures guilt and exasperation. It would have been comical if I knew what's going to happen once he walks out of my room alone. Maybe I should forget the shower.

He removes the condom and gets dressed in a flash. My lady parts are crying now that the morning quickie got canceled.

Stupid Troy. Why did he have to show up unannounced like that? It's almost like he knew Andy would be here. I wonder if it's a big brother radar thing.

I get going as well, putting my underwear back on before finding my school uniform.

"You're not showering first?" Andreas asks.

"I don't want to leave you alone with Troy."

He walks over with a smile. "Babe, I can face Troy by myself. I don't need you to be my lady in shining armor."

"I don't need to shower," I pout.

He leans closer and takes a whiff of my neck. "You smell like you've been thoroughly fucked all night. I think that will set your brother off more than me having a conversation with him alone."

"Okay, fine. But please, try to not to argue. We don't want to wake the dragon."

"I hear ya. Don't worry, babe. I'll behave."

He leans down and kisses me softly on the lips. I'd enjoy it more if my stomach didn't feel like it was filled with pinballs.

ANDREAS

I can't believe Jane bought into my reasoning. If she smells like sex, so do I. However, I'm sure it would bother Troy more to smell my scent all over her then the other way around.

I find him in the kitchen making way too much noise for my liking as he prepares breakfast.

"What are you trying to accomplish here, buddy? Wake your mom up so she can bust Jane too?"

He stops in his tracks and glances at me, sporting a glower. "No. I'd never unleash my mother on Jane on purpose. I can't believe you'd think that."

"You sure are making a ruckus." I pull up a chair and rest my elbows on the counter.

"I got a text from my father last night. I know Mom got trashed. She won't be waking up before noon."

"You need to help Jane out with this Stanford deal," I say, even though Jane told me she'd tell Troy and their grandmother later today.

He crosses his arms over his chest. "Why? Would you be upset if she moved to San Fran?"

"Of course I would." I pull my hair back, yanking it at the strands. "I can't bear the thought of her going to live almost four hundred miles away from me."

Troy doesn't say a word, but his eyes…. They feel like a drill trying to make a hole in my brain.

"I don't know what else I can say to you to prove I'm not messing around with Jane," I continue.

"I guess only time will tell. But if you're that worried about not getting her in trouble, you shouldn't be sneaking in and spending the night."

"I was worried about her. She sounded off when I called her after dinner."

Troy's hard stare softens. "I wish she'd told me she was having dinner with our folks last night. I'd have come."

"She wants to fight her own battles."

Jane walks into the kitchen, looking like a ray of sunshine as usual. Her hair is damp, and her cheeks are still flushed from the hot shower. She's not wearing any makeup, but she doesn't need it. I feel a stirring in my pants, and immediately curse my body for betraying me.

"Are you talking about dinner last night?" She looks from me to Troy.

"He wanted to know why I risked being caught by your mother. I was explaining I had a valid reason."

"Dad won't change his mind about Stanford. He's a stubborn son of a bitch," Troy tells her.

"Like father, like son," I mutter under my breath.

He throws me a warning glare. "Watch it, pal."

"Please don't start," she says. "I really wish you wouldn't be at odds because of me."

"I'm not the one being difficult here," I reply.

"I'm trying, Jane. But seeing you two together is going to take time getting used to."

"Well, that's better than nothing. Are you going to help me get Dad off my case about Stanford?"

"I don't know what I can do to help. Like I said, he's committed to sending you there."

"Shit. I don't know what to do." She pulls her hair back, frustrated.

I wish I could do something to help, but if Mr. Alexander won't listen to his own son, he won't listen to me either.

"Would it be so terrible to move to San Fran?" Troy asks, earning the mother of all glares from me.

I just told him how I'd feel if she moved. *What a jerk.*

"Really, Troy? You're that petty?" Jane retorts.

"I'm not being petty. And before you say it, I'm not playing devil's advocate because I want to separate you two. I just don't want you to make this decision because of a guy."

"This has nothing to do with Andy, and you know it," she grits out. "Besides, he's not the only thing that I'd be giving up if I moved."

"I'd visit you."

"She's not talking about you, jackass," I butt in, annoyed as hell. "And you're not going to be around anyway. Aren't you going to Europe with Charlie?"

He narrows his eyes at me, probably dying to say something, but in the end, he simply turns to Jane and asks, "What are you talking about then?"

"What in the world is all this yapping in my house?" Jane's mother whines as she walks into the kitchen.

My spine becomes tense in an instant. Jane and I lock gazes, and I read fear in her eyes. *Fuck*. I'm about to make her home life a thousand times more difficult.

"Troy, what are you doing here?" his mother asks.

She hasn't acknowledged my presence yet, and I suspect it's because she's still drunk. I can smell the alcohol she drank last night from where I sit.

"Having breakfast with my sister. Why? Do you have a problem with that?"

"I fucking do have a problem when I have a migraine and you're talking so loudly." She whirls around and finally sees me. "And why are you here?"

"He came with me," Troy answers. "But don't worry, we're leaving. Come on, Jane. Let's have breakfast out."

"Let me get my bag." She runs back to her room, and away from a very uncomfortable situation.

Staggering to the fridge, their mother mutters, "I can't wait for Jane to start college and get out of my hair."

My hands curl into fists as I scowl at the back of her head. Troy shakes his head, a sign for me to keep my mouth shut. It's with effort that I stay silent. Jane deserves so much more than the awful parents she has. At least I had a mother who love me unconditionally.

Jane also deserves a man who can offer that same kind of love, not someone who is too fucked up to even say the words out loud.

My conscience is my fucking worst enemy. *Jesus.*

She returns with backpack hanging from her shoulder, and an expression that says let's get out of here. I get up and follow her and Troy to the front door. I don't bother saying goodbye to their mother. She's too hateful to warrant proper manners.

Outside the house, Jane seems unsure of what to do.

"Well, I guess I'd better head home. You kids have fun," I say.

"Will I see you tonight?" she asks me.

"Sorry, I can't tonight. I forgot to tell you. I have to work at the Rushmore Hotel as part of the practical portion of my Intro to Food Service Management class. But don't worry, I haven't forgotten about my promise." I move to kiss her on the lips, but Troy is watching us like a hawk, so I kiss her on the forehead instead.

There's no need to poke the beast with a short stick.

THIRTY-ONE

ANDREAS

Before I drive to the hotel for my shift, I make a pit stop at one my father's dealerships. There's something I need to arrange. I figured out a way to get Jane to the luncheon and back to the tryouts in time.

I hate my father's guts, and I wouldn't use his resources under normal circumstances. But for Jane, I'll make a deal with the devil if necessary. For this to work, I need to talk with the right person. Being the heir of my father's empire doesn't mean I can do whatever I want. The asshole has loyal employees who would immediately call him to inform him of my visit.

But I have my own contacts, people who would gladly help on the down-low in exchange for the right amount of cash. The entire transaction doesn't take more than ten minutes.

I'm in good spirits when I leave the place, but as I approach my final destination, apprehension takes hold of me. I've never served in my life. In hindsight, I should have practiced carrying a tray at least. One of the syllabi had the basic rules, but nothing beats the real deal.

The instructions said to use the employees' entrance at the

back, and wear black slacks, a white button-down shirt, and tie. I took a selfie before I left the house and sent to Jane, asking what she thought of my new look. She replied with a thirsty emoticon and told me to save the tie.

She is the fucking best.

I'm grinning like a fool when I finally join tonight's crew. But sadly, Professor Douche is also present, killing my good humor in an instant. He gives me a loathing glance before introducing us to Paul Leggett, the restaurant's manager, who will be our instructor tonight. The restaurant opens in an hour, which means Paul only has time to explain things once.

A petite brunette wearing glasses bigger than her face moves closer to me and whispers, "Do you think this is going to be like Ramsay's *Hell's Kitchen?*"

"I hope not. I might punch someone in the face."

She chuckles, earning a glare from Paul and Norman. She doesn't say another word throughout the rest of the lecture.

Paul assigns our sections and then all we have to do is wait for the crowd to come. I'm in my designated section, ready to engage, when suddenly Norman appears next to me.

"I'm surprised that you actually found someone to trade places with you. Must be that star power."

"Must be," I reply through clenched teeth, fighting the urge to ask what his problem with me is.

But I can't start an argument with the man here of all places. He'll take great pleasure in flunking me. He departs soon after, and all I can do is stare daggers at this back.

"What did you do to piss off Professor Norman like that?" glasses girl asks.

"Nothing. I think he hates jocks."

"I'm Amelia, by the way." She offers me her hand for a handshake.

This is probably the first time a girl in school introduced herself to me in such a businesslike manner. Her expression is neutral too; I see no signs of flirtation.

"Andy," I say.

"Nice to officially meet you, Andy." Her gaze travels past me. "Oh, the first customers are coming in. Shit, I have butterflies in my stomach."

"It will be fine."

"I hope so."

Soon, a party of three sits at a table in my section. I'm a little nervous when I greet them and take their orders. As the time goes by, I get more comfortable with the job, and the first hour passes by in a flash.

I'm feeling pretty good about myself, but the feeling goes up in smoke when I catch sight of my father and his fucking wife being escorted to a table in my section. This can't be a coincidence. The question is, how did he know I'd be working here tonight?

I need to take a couple of calming breaths before I veer for their table. I have every intention to treat him like he's just a regular customer, but my tongue has a mind of its own.

"What are you doing here? This is not your regular spot."

"I had to see for myself this despicable display," he replies with disdain, looking me up and down.

"How did you know I'd be here?"

"Norman is an old buddy of mine." He smiles wickedly.

Mystery solved. Now I know why Norman had it out for me since the beginning.

"Did you pay him to make my life a living hell in his class?"

He ignores my question and picks up the menu. "I have to say, the service is appalling. Do I have to call the manager to get my order taken?"

"I'd like to start with a cocktail. What do you suggest, Andy?" Crystal asks in overly saccharine tone.

"How about a Redheaded Slut?" I blurt out without thinking.

Dad whips his face up, glaring, but Crystal simply laughs.

"Nah, I think I'll have a Cosmo. I'm feeling *Sex and the City* tonight."

The way she watches me as if I'm a piece of meat twists my stomach. And to think I used to crave her heated glances once upon a time. The recollection makes me feel dirty, unworthy of my sweet Jane.

My father opens his mouth to order, but I cut him off. "Yeah, I know what you'll have, Dad. I haven't forgotten."

How could I when the smell of his expensive whiskey was always on his breath whenever he pounded me with his fists?

I put their drink orders in the computer, fighting the sudden nausea that has gripped me. Amelia joins me, and makes a comment about something, but I don't know what. My mind is reeling, stuck in the past.

She touches my arm. "Andy, is everything okay? You look ill."

"I'm fine. I just want this evening to be over already." I stare at my father's table, and the loathing and sickness grows.

She follows my line of vision. "Do you know them?"

"Unfortunately, yes."

"Do you want me to cover their table for you?"

"No, but thanks."

Accepting Amelia's offer would be cowardice. No, I'll serve Daddy Dearest and his Stepford wife with a smile on my face even if it kills me.

The evening that was going by in a blur suddenly begins to move at a snail's pace. Every time I have to attend to their table, my skin crawls. When the asshole finally asks for the check, I can't help the sigh of relief that whooshes out of me.

He signs the bill without looking or speaking to me. I expect him to not give me any tip, so when I see the amount he wrote down, I can't hide the surprise.

"I think you've made a mistake here. There's one zero too many."

"No mistake." He stands. "Consider this my parting gift. I've warned you I'd cut you off if you insisted on dragging the Rossi name through the mud. Surviving on tips will be your life now."

"What the hell are you saying?"

"I'm done with you, Andreas. You can finish the semester since it's already paid for, but if you want to remain a student at Rushmore, I'd suggest you find a way to pay your tuition fees from now on. Oh, and I'll be collecting rent too."

I remain rooted to the floor, fighting to get air into my lungs. I can't believe he's actually following through with his threat.

"Don't look so sad, darling," Crystal purrs. "I can try to convince your father to give you a second chance, for old time's sake."

She takes advantage of my paralysis and kisses me on the cheek before sashaying away.

Her unwanted touch works like an electric shock. I can move again, and I use my recovered ability to run to the restroom to empty the contains of my stomach.

I'm not even that upset about the loss of financial security or the fact I'll have to drop out. I'm distraught because now I have nothing to offer Jane. Absolutely nothing.

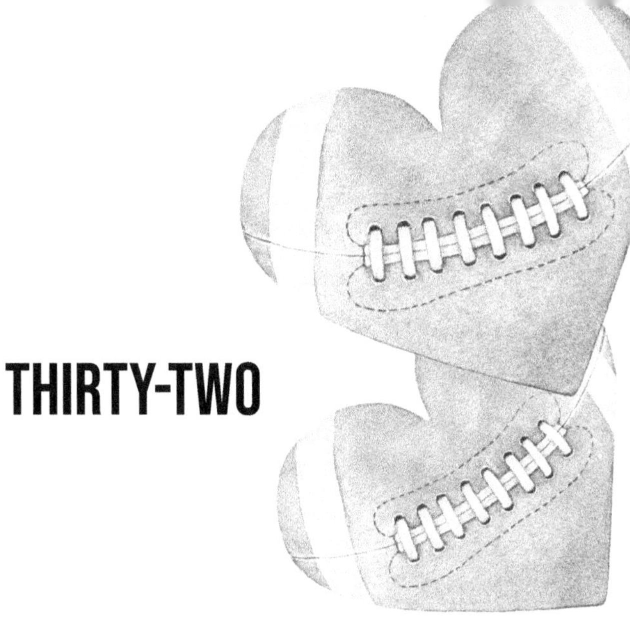

THIRTY-TWO

JANE

Andreas said he'd call me after his shift. I ended up falling asleep early last night, but this morning there wasn't a missed call or single text. His radio silence worries me, so I call him right away.

"Hey babe," he answers on the second ring.

I exhale in relief. "Hi. You didn't call last night."

Great. Way to sound needy, Jane.

"I know. I'm sorry. It was late, and I was pretty tired."

"Oh. How was it?"

"It was… okay, I guess. I didn't drop spaghetti on anyone."

His attempt at a joke falls flat in my ear. He sounds miserable. *What is he not telling me?*

"Are you ready for tryouts?" he asks.

"Yeah, I'm just about to get ready. I have to sneak out before my mother wakes up."

"I can't wait to see you in that dress you picked. It's giving me happy memories."

Even though I know he's distracting me from whatever is bothering him, I can't help the smile that spreads across my lips.

"I know there will be hell to pay afterwards, but I can't wait to see the look on my mother's face when I tell her you'll be my escort to the ball."

"You know, we don't need to tell her today. Maybe I'll just wait outside and let you do the rounds."

Disappointment floods through me. "You've changed your mind about being my date?"

"No, babe. Not at all. I'm just thinking logistics. We don't have a lot of time before I have to take you back."

"Right. I still don't know how you're going to work that magic."

"Don't worry. I'll make it happen. Do you trust me?"

"Yeah, I trust you."

I wish you would trust me too.

"Lunch break is from noon to one," I continue.

"I'll be there at a quarter to twelve. Now go get ready. I don't want you to be late."

"Okay. I'll see you later."

I keep staring at my phone for at least a minute after I ended the call. Even though Andreas said all the right things, I still sensed something off about him. If there's one thing I wish he would do, it's to let me in. I actually crave that more than hearing him say he loves me.

I managed to slip out of the house without Mom being any the wiser. My dress for the luncheon is safe in the backseat of my car, and I'm already wearing makeup. It's probably going to be ruined by lunchtime, but it's easier to retouch than apply everything from scratch.

As much as I hate that Mom is forcing me to attend this stupid luncheon at the marina, I want to make an impression. I want Hanson van Buuren to know what he missed out on. I'm no longer upset that Andy doesn't want to come in with me. I don't need to have a gorgeous man on my arm to prove to everyone I'm worth it.

My head is still filled with thoughts of him, my mother, and the debutante ball when I step foot in the gymnasium. The sound of skates on the banked track and the excited chatter of the other new recruits push all my personal problems to a corner in my mind. A rush of excitement goes through me. This is where I belong.

I head to the locker room and find Alicia sitting on a bench, lacing up her skates.

"Ready for this?" I ask, setting my duffle bag next to her.

"Jane. How are you, girlie?" she replies with a smile.

"I'm good. Excited."

"Same. It's too bad we didn't have a chance to meet this week to practice. Work was brutal."

"It's okay. We have the weekend to catch up. Did you manage to get any skating in at all?"

"Here and there."

She waits for me to put my skates on and together, we head to the track. The same guy who was judging us during tryouts is in the center of the track with a clipboard in his hand. Katja is standing next to Scary Samantha, the mean brunette who ended up helping me get picked for the Second Time Around Divas.

"Good morning," I greet them cheerfully.

Scary Samantha sneers in my direction. "Great. Kindergarten has arrived."

She skates off before I have a chance to reply.

"She's upset that Jane broke her record, huh?" Alicia pipes up.

"Right. She never forgets shit. You'd better keep an eye out for her. She's one of the most savage players in the league," Katja tells us.

"I'm not afraid of her," I say.

"Good." She smirks. "So, who was that hottie at the beach the other day?"

"Oh, that's Andy. My boyfriend."

"I didn't know you had a boyfriend," Alicia chimes in. "I thought you had a thing for Fred."

"Oh no. Fred is just a friend. And I just started going out with Andy."

"I think you broke poor Fred's heart," Katja says. "I've never seen him so quiet as I did after that encounter."

Guilt enters my chest and squeezes my heart tight.

"I didn't mean to hurt his feelings."

"The face of an angel, the attitude of the devil." Alicia laughs. "I knew I liked you for a reason, girlie."

"I'm not the devil," I reply, faking indignation.

I like that for once, I was not described as meek or shy. I'm a fucking badass rebel.

"I do hope you have a devilish streak in you. There's no room in roller derby for nice girls." Katja smirks.

"Nice girls can be bad." I follow her to where the rest of the girls have gathered.

It seems we're about to start training.

"I like that," Alicia says. "We should make T-shirts with that quote. So, do you already have a game name?"

I had been thinking about several options, but it wasn't until Scary Samantha sneered at me that I settled on the winner.

"Yeah, Blaze Jane."

"Blaze Jane," Alicia repeats. "I love it."

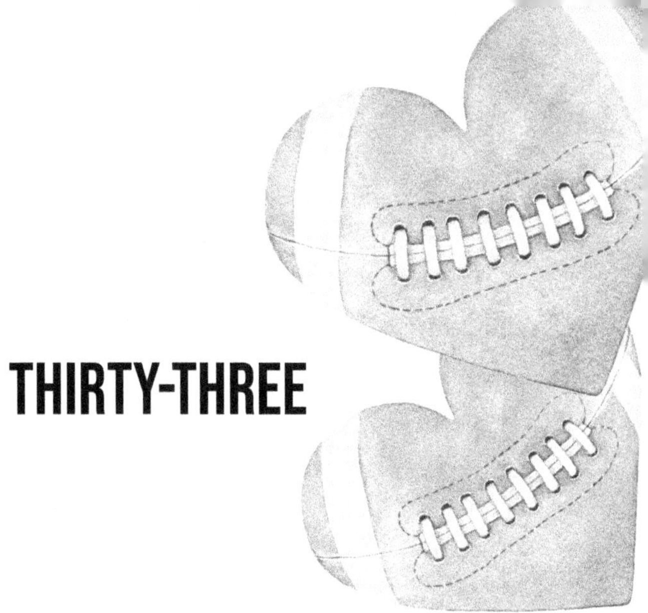

THIRTY-THREE

JANE

My lungs are about to burst when the whistle finally echoes in the gym. Our trainer, Roger, is in fact, a torturer. Sweat covers my skin, and I know there's no chance that my makeup survived the intense workout. I need a shower. I glance at the giant clock on the wall. It's a quarter to noon, which means Andy should be already waiting for me outside.

Alicia skates to me slowly with her hands on her hips. Her breathing is coming out in bursts like mine.

"Fuck. That was intense. My legs are liquified. I don't think I'll survive the afternoon."

"Do you think we can start break before noon?"

She glances at the group being tortured now by Roger. "I don't think we'll be going back on the track until after lunch. Do you want to go somewhere to grab a bite to eat?"

"I can't. I have to be somewhere."

"Oh?" She raises an eyebrow.

"My mother is forcing me to attend a luncheon at the marina. I have to make an appearance."

"Why?"

"Because she doesn't know about roller derby. If I don't show up, she'll probably wonder where I am."

"Not to sound negative, but how are you going to make it to the marina and back before our break is over?"

"I don't know. Andy said he could make it happen."

"Oh, is Andy Superman then?" She laughs.

"Maybe he is. Anyway. Can you cover for me? I have to shower first."

"Yeah. You're good. If anyone asks me where you are, I'll tell them you have the shits."

I wrinkle my nose. "Gee. Thanks."

I look around, making sure no one is paying attention to me. Not that this is a jail or anything. I'm allowed to use the restroom. In the locker room, I practically yank my clothes off and jump into the shower. My hair, unfortunately, I can't wash. Showing up with damp hair will surely be seen by mother as an affront. But I had the foresight to pack dry shampoo. It should do the trick. I'll have to do my makeup in the car.

Five minutes later, I'm running to the gym's front door, hoping no one will see me sneaking out in my fancy dress. But it's my luck that Scary Samantha is standing there, talking on the phone.

She gives me a once over and smirks. "Where's the ball, Cinderella?"

"Shut up," I say as I run past her.

My reply will probably come back to bite me in the ass, but I can't worry about that now. Outside, I search for Andreas's Bronco in the parking lot. My heart sinks when I can't find it. *Shit. Is he late?* In my hurry to get ready, I didn't even check my phone. I dig for it in my bag, but the sound of a motorcycle's engine approaching catches my attention. The rider stops right in front of me and then removes his helmet.

"Andy! Oh my God. Whose bike is that?"

"I borrowed it for the day." He pulls an extra helmet from his backpack, and a leather jacket. "Here, put them on."

I hesitate and the smile on his face wilts. "What's the matter?"

"I've never ridden a motorcycle before."

"You can add that to our list of firsts."

His dimples make an appearance, turning me into goo. I put the jacket on first, and then helmet—there goes my idea of putting on my makeup on the way to the marina—and hop behind him. The smell of leather and Andy's cologne reaches my nose, infusing me with heat. I wrap my arms around his waist, getting as close to him as I can.

"Are you comfortable?" he asks over his shoulder.

"As comfortable as I can be."

"All right. Hold on tight, babe."

He revs the engine, making me acutely aware of its power. Then he takes off and my entire body tenses. I curl my fingers around his jacket, pressing my helmet against his back.

"Relax, babe."

"I'm trying."

"I'm not even going fast yet."

"I know."

Stop being pathetic, Jane.

In another minute, we enter the freeway, and my heart lodges in my throat. I'd scream if I could, but I'm too busy closing my eyes and pressing my face against Andreas's back. It can't be comfortable for him with my helmet jamming into him like that, but he didn't complain when he had the chance.

Okay, I'm not pathetic. This is awful, and I'm going to die.

I keep my eyes shut during the entire trip, but I'm keenly aware that Andreas is zigzagging through traffic. The ride that would normally take thirty minutes, we make in ten. When he finally slows down and I open my eyes, my heart is beating so fast, I'm afraid it's going to burst through my chest. I lean back and remove the helmet, but I make no move to dismount.

"Are you okay back there?" he asks.

"I need a minute."

I glance around and take in my bearings. We're in the parking lot of the fancy marina restaurant, which is almost full, save for the few motorcycle spots. I guess there aren't a lot of guests riding bikes today. The luncheon started a half an hour ago, so we're the last ones to arrive. My legs are still shaking, but the whole point of this hellish ride was to save time. I'm not going to waste it now by sitting outside.

I jump off and try to smooth the wrinkles from my dress's skirt. Andreas hops off and then removes his jacket. Underneath, he's wearing a jacket, shirt, and tie.

"I thought you wanted to wait outside," I say.

"I'm sorry I said that. I was having a rough morning, and I thought that by suggesting that I was being helpful. I was an idiot. If you still want me to be your date today, I'm here."

"I do, but for different reasons now. Before, I wanted to show you off. Now, I just want you by my side because you're my boyfriend, and that's where you should be."

He pulls me to him and kisses me deeply. I'm glad that I'm not wearing makeup because this is a lipstick-smearing kiss. When he pulls back, I'm a little breathless.

"Okay, then," he replies with a lazy smile.

I step back from his embrace and take off the leather jacket. "How do I look?"

"Hot as sin."

I frown, looking down. "My dress is a disaster."

"Who cares if your skirt has a few wrinkles?"

"I do, and not because I'm afraid what my mother is going to say. I really dislike wrinkled clothes."

"Really?" His eyebrows shoot up.

"Yeah."

He chuckles. "Okay. Well, there's nothing we can do about it now." He offers me his arm. "Shall we? I'm kind of hungry."

ANDREAS

Hungry for you, I want to add, but getting Jane hot and bothered now is not going to do me any favors. I'm already sporting a semi all thanks to that kiss. I swear I must have reverted to a horny teen because my dick is out of control whenever I'm in her presence.

I know she wishes she looked more polished, but she's stunning no matter what.

The restaurant's maître d' greets us and lets us know where to go. The affair seems to be pretty casual. There are high tables spread around an open room, a buffet with food, and an open bar. The presence of that surprises me.

"Aren't all the debutantes under twenty-one?" I whisper to Jane's ear.

"Yeah, but not all escort candidates are. Plus, the organizing committee depends on alcohol to survive."

I chuckle. "What's the plan?"

"Find my mother, eat something, and bail."

"Jane Marie Alexander," a woman shrieks behind us.

"Ah, I believe she found us," I say.

We turn around, coming face-to-face with a veritable dragon. The woman is spiting fire from her nostrils.

"Where have been? I woke up to find you gone. You don't answer your phone, and you show up late and wearing…" She gives her a glance over, twisting her face in disgust. "That."

"Sorry, Mother. I had things to do in the morning. But I'm here, aren't I? Now, what's for lunch? I'm starving."

She makes a motion to grab Jane's arm, but my protective instinct takes over. I block her without stopping to think about it.

"I wouldn't touch her if I were you. Besides, everyone is looking."

If looks could kill, I'd be dead on the spot. She takes a step back, yanking her fancy suit down as if it's she trying to smooth invisible lines.

"I'd like to know what you're doing with my daughter."

"Andy is here because I asked him to be. He's going to be my escort to the ball."

She snorts. "*Him?*"

I try not to wince when she stares at me with profound disdain. *Who the fuck does she think she is to judge me?* But I keep my mouth shut because I don't want to embarrass Jane in front of all these people.

"Why not? He's Troy's best friend, and his father is a legend and filthy rich. Isn't that all you care about? Money and connections?"

Shit. I wish Jane wouldn't have mentioned my asshole father. At least that wasn't the first qualification she mentioned. I know she doesn't care about status, but how would she feel if she knew my father disowned me?

"Sorry to interrupt, but are you Andreas Rossi? Son of Giancarlo Rossi?" a preppy-looking dude with pushed back straw-colored hair and a fucking chin dimple asks me.

"Yes, that's me."

"I'm Hanson van Buuren. Huge fan of your old man." He extends his hand, and I stare at it without taking it.

After an awkward moment, he drops the offending appendage, and continues. "You must be Jane. I'm so pleased to finally meet you."

"I bet you're regretting canceling that date now, huh?" I ask, not hiding the aggression in my tone.

He looks at me, surprised. "Of course. I wouldn't have done it if I hadn't had an emergency."

"Sure, pal. Or maybe you didn't know how smoking hot she was."

Jane tugs on my arm. "Let's get something to eat, Andy."

"We're not done yet, young lady. I demand an explanation for all this," her mother tells her.

"With all due respect, Mom, I've done what you asked me to. I'm here, and hey, I have a date to the ball who isn't a teenager covered in pimples."

Her mother opens and shuts her mouth without making a sound. The fish-out-of-water look is great on her. Pride fills my chest. Jane keeps surprising me every day.

We hit the buffet, but in reality, I'm not hungry at all. Jane doesn't seem to have much of an appetite either. To be fair, the food looks too pretentious to be enjoyable.

I take the plate of uneaten appetizers from her hand, setting it down on the high table. "Let's get out of here. Like you said, you've done your part."

"I still have to eat something. I won't survive the rest of bootcamp running on fumes."

"Don't worry, babe. I got you covered."

With her hand firmly in mine, I rush out of the restaurant. I'm sure our attitude will be the talk during the rest of the event, which will mortify her mother to no end.

Jane and I put our leather jackets and helmets on, and then I take her to a place that can make any day better, an In-N-Out restaurant. When Jane hops off the bike and takes her helmet off, I see her grin.

"The gym building is just around the corner. We have fifteen minutes. I hope you're okay with my choice."

"Are you kidding me?" She jumps into my arms and kisses me soundly.

I could taste her mouth forever, but she does need to be somewhere.

"As much as I enjoy your lips on mine, I do need to get you fed, babe."

"I know. Thank you so much for taking the time to help me today. If there's anything I can do to repay you, just say the word." She watches me from under her eyelashes.

Jesus fucking Christ. There she goes again, making me wish we were somewhere private with one single glance. *God, I'm crazy about this girl.*

Stepping away before I attack her mouth again, I reply, "I can think of something."

THIRTY-FOUR

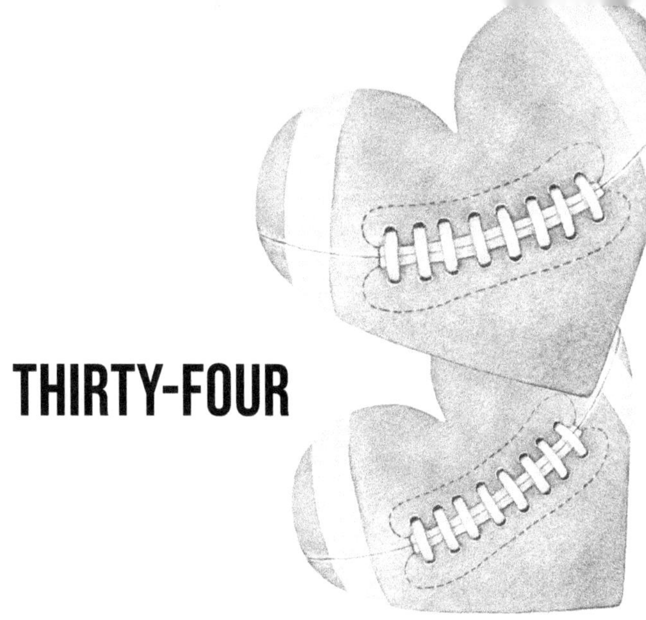

ANDREAS

After I drop Jane off at the gymnasium, I return to the dealership to get my car. I drive the motorcycle to the service lot and leave the key with the service area receptionist, per my agreement with Juan, the guy who I paid to loan me the bike.

I left my car in the clients' area, however, when I walk to the spot I parked, I find another vehicle in its place.

"What the hell."

Did I park at a different spot and forgot? I run around the lot, covering the area in less than a minute. My Bronco is most definitely not here. There's no way some asshole came in and stole my car out of the lot in broad daylight. There's got to be an explanation for this. I head inside and look for the dealership's manager. I've met him once, and he's a total jerk.

He's in his office on the phone. I don't fucking care.

"What the hell have you done with my car?"

He gives me an impatient glance and tells whoever is on the line that he'll call them back. Then he leans back on his chair, crossing his hands over his protruding belly. "You mean what I've done with your father's car?"

"Don't play games with me. Where is my car?" I grit out.

"Back where it belongs. In Mr. Rossi's garage. I had it towed there per his instructions."

Son of a bitch.

I can't believe he did that. How the hell did he know my Bronco was parked here in the first place? Juan must have sold me out. *Asshole.*

"Now if you'll excuse me, I have work to do." The manager reaches for his phone, dismissing me.

My hands curl into fists, and my body is shaking in anger, but there's nothing I can do. The car was never in my name. At the time, I didn't care. But now I see it was another way for my father to control me.

I stride out of the manager's office, shoving his Nespresso machine to the floor.

"You punk! You're going to pay for that," he yells.

"Send the bill to my father."

I keep walking until I'm off the dealership's property. I wouldn't put it past the manager to call the cops on me. Once I'm out, I call Danny. It rings until the call goes to voicemail. *Damn it.* I can either call Paris or Troy. Paris is most likely with his obnoxious girlfriend. *Pass.* I guess Troy it is.

I'm surprised when he actually answers the phone.

"What do you want?"

"I need a favor."

"Is that so? Why don't you call Danny?"

"I tried. Dude, this a fucking emergency, okay? I wouldn't have bothered you otherwise."

"Does your emergency have anything do with Jane and the stunt you pulled at the luncheon?"

"You know about that?"

"Yeah, I know. I just spent the last twenty minutes listening to my mother yell in my ear that I let you corrupt Jane."

I pinch the bridge of my nose. "This has nothing to do with Jane. She's back at…." *Hell, he doesn't know that she's at roller derby bootcamp.*

"She's back where? Home?"

"Yeah," I lie.

Shit. This is fucked up. I can't keep lying to Troy and expect him to forgive me.

"What's the emergency then?"

"My father cut me off. He took my Bronco away and now I'm stranded in front of one of his dealerships."

"Damn. Is that because you switched majors?"

"Yup. Can you give me a ride home or what? I could call an Uber, but I'm afraid my credit cards probably aren't working right now."

"Yeah, man. I'll be there as soon as I can."

"Thanks again for picking me up," I say to Troy.

"As much as I don't like you right now, I'd never leave you stranded like that."

I look out the window, thinking about what I'm going to do with my life now. I can't even take Jane out on a proper date without having to ask to borrow one of my friend's cars. I can't afford to take her anywhere either. No more impromptu afternoons at fancy hotels.

Some might call me a hypocrite for spending my father's money without a care when I hate him so much, but I've earned every dime of the money I spent. I paid in blood.

"I can't believe your father cut you off. You need to speak to Coach Clarkson about that. The team needs you."

"I will, although I don't know what he can do besides try to convince my father to reconsider."

"You could apply for a sports scholarship."

"I'd never qualify. They'd look at my father's bank account

and laugh."

"You know athletic scholarships aren't need-based. You can't just give up and quit school."

"I'm not going to give up. I just don't know yet what I'm going to do."

"I'll talk to Grandma and ask if you and Danny can move in with me."

Troy knows I charge Danny almost nothing for rent, which means we'll both be homeless soon.

"What about Charlie?"

"She supports the idea one hundred percent."

"You already told her? You just found out."

"Bro, as soon as you told me your father cut you off, I knew that meant you'd have to give up your place."

I let out a heavy sigh. "You're a good friend, Troy. I'm sorry I fucked up things royally between us."

He clenches his jaw. "I know you're sorry. I can also see now that you'd never go after Jane if you didn't care about her. What you did today was awesome. Thank you for that."

"So you're cool with me dating her now?"

"Let's say I'm resigned to the idea. But you hurt one single strand of her hair and I'm coming for you."

"I don't plan to ever hurt her, but if I do, you have my permission to pound my ass to the ground."

He snorts. "Like I need your permission."

When I glance at him, he's smirking.

"How did your visit with Ophelia go? Does she have a solution to keep Jane in LA?"

"Jane didn't tell you?"

"No, there hasn't been time. She had to rush to…." Damn, there I went, almost blurting out Jane's secret.

"To roller derby bootcamp."

"Wait, she told you already?"

"Yeah, yesterday."

"So you knew I was lying and you didn't call me out?"

He turns to me. "I was testing you. Don't get me wrong, I'm not happy that you lied to me, but the fact you did shows me you really have Jane's back."

I shake my head. "Boy, you have a twisted way of seeing things."

"I don't know why she felt like she had to keep that a secret from me."

"Hmm, maybe because it's a savage sport and you think she's made out of porcelain?"

"I don't think she's breakable."

I laugh. "Yes, you do."

"Fine. I guess I *am* overprotective. I'm working on it. But anyway, Grandma said that if Jane is truly set on attending Rushmore, she'd pay for her tuition."

"That's great news. I wonder why Jane didn't tell me."

"I'm sure she was stressing about bootcamp and the luncheon, and she wanted to tell you in person."

No, she didn't tell me because I didn't call her last night like I said I would, and today, she probably forgot. I keep my thoughts to myself though.

"What are your plans for the rest of the day?" Troy asks.

"For starters, I have to look for a job."

"What are you thinking?"

"I have no clue. I could do serving."

"You could probably make some serious money depending on where you work."

"Yeah."

"Doesn't Paris's girlfriend's family own a chain of upscale restaurants?"

"I don't know. I usually check out when he talks about her. She hates my guts, though. I doubt she'd help."

"She doesn't hate your guts."

"Dude, she does. She said that to my face. I'm a bad influence on Paris, apparently." I laugh, even though this situation is far from humorous.

It's better than crying, right?

"It doesn't hurt to ask. Paris is a good guy. He'll help."

"Sure." I look out the window again, hating my situation.

"You don't sound convinced. What's the matter?"

"I don't like this. I'm a fucking charity case now."

"You're not a charity case. You're in a tight spot, that's all. There's no shame in asking for help, Andy."

Maybe for someone like Troy, there's no shame. But I've been told time and time again I'm a failure. At a certain point, you start to believe it.

THIRTY-FIVE

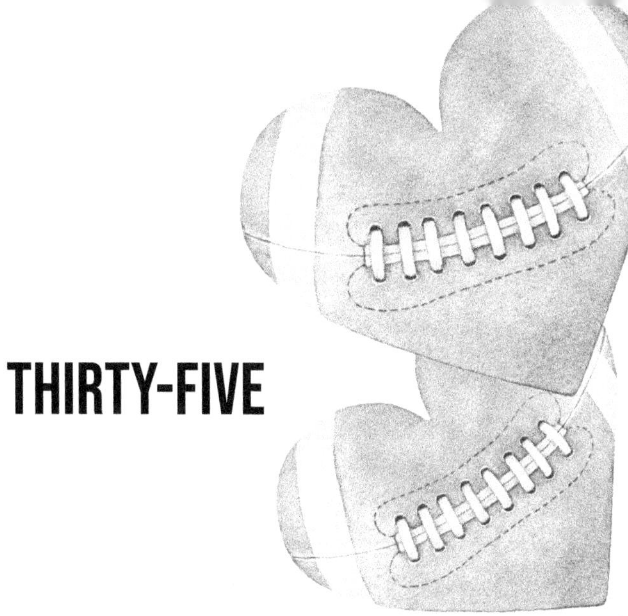

JANE

I don't really want to face my mother after an entire day of practice, but if I don't come home, it will only make things worse. I'm physically and mentally exhausted. I can't say that altercation at the luncheon didn't affect me, even if it felt fucking amazing to stand my ground against her.

No surprise, my mother is waiting for me in the living room, nursing a glass of white wine. Her expression tells me I'm about to receive a major tongue-lashing.

"Where have you been?"

"I was out with friends."

"Bullshit. I know you were hanging out with Troy's buddy."

"Troy's buddy has a name. And I wasn't hanging out with Andy. I don't care if you believe me or not. I'm done trying to please you. I'll never measure up anyway."

"That's right. You never will. I should be used to your mediocrity by now."

My blood is pumping in my veins. I'm about to blow a fuse, and I don't care.

"You know what? Fuck you, Mom. I'm sorry that your life

didn't turn out the way you wanted, but I'm done being your punching bag." I whirl around and stride to my room.

"Jane Marie, come back here this instant!" she yells.

I'm beyond listening to her threats. I go straight to my closet and I take my duffle bag out. She finds me shoving random clothes in it.

"What do you think you're doing?"

"Isn't it obvious?"

"Oh, where do you think you're going to live?"

"I don't care. Under a bridge is better than here."

"You can't leave. I won't allow it."

I laugh like a crazy woman. "I'm eighteen. You can't force me to stay. Besides, I'm sure Dad will be more than happy if I go to live with him."

Now she's the one laughing in derision. "I wouldn't be so sure. You might hate me, but at least I take an interest in your life. He wouldn't care if you were dead or alive."

I wince because she's right about that, but I won't allow her to weaken my resolve. "That might be true, but he will take me in to spite you."

I don't even know what I packed, but I zip the duffle bag shut and walk around her. She grabs my arm, digging her long nails in.

"You walk out that door, you're not coming back."

I yank my arm free from her grasp. "Fine by me. I don't plan on ever returning."

Hot tears are streaming down my cheeks by the time I step outside. I'm glad my roller derby gear is in the trunk of my car and everything else I didn't pack I can either replace or ask Troy to come get for me when the monster is not home.

I drive off, needing to put as much distance between me and my mother's house as I can. But when the anger subsides, I feel hollow and alone. I can't see shit in front of me thanks to my blurry vision. I turn into the first parking lot that I come across because driving in my condition is dangerous.

The silence in my car is broken by the sound of my phone ringing. With shaking hands, I fish the phone out of my bag. My heart does a backflip when I see Andy's name flashing on my screen.

"Hi," I say in a trembling voice.

"Babe, what's the matter?"

"I had a huge fight with my mother and I... I left home."

"Where are you now?"

I look outside my window and notice for the first time where I am.

"I'm in front of a McDonald's five minutes from my mother's house."

"Do you want me to call Troy to get you?"

His question takes me by surprise. "Why would you do that?"

"I don't have my car right now or I would be already on my way."

I should ask what happened to his Bronco, but I don't have it in me for small talk. "It's okay. I just needed a minute to calm down. I can drive."

He curses softly under his breath. "I don't like this, babe. Let me call Troy."

"No. I'm fine."

"Why are you so stubborn? I'm beginning to think it's a family trait."

"Would it be okay if I came over and spent the night? I was planning to bunk with my dad, but I can't handle another parent right now."

"Of course it's okay, sweetheart. Do you want to keep talking as you drive here?"

"Better not. I'll see you soon."

"All right. Please drive safely."

"I will."

ANDREAS

I'm on pins and needles, burning a hole in my living room floor as I pace left and right.

"Relax, Andy. Jane will be fine," Danny says from the couch.

He got home five minutes ago. If he had been home earlier, I'd have borrowed his car and left to get Jane myself. For her to make the decision to move out means the fight with her mother must have been ugly.

"You didn't hear her on the phone. She was broken, man." I pull my hair back. "I hate that I wasn't there to protect her from that viper."

"I know you do. That shows how much she means to you."

I turn to him. "She's my entire world."

He levels me with an intense stare. "Have you told her that yet?"

His question feels like a punch to my chest. I can't answer him, so I do the cowardly thing: I look away. A knock on the door prevents him from pestering me further. I stride toward it, and open it without bothering to look through the peephole. Jane is standing there, carrying a duffle bag too big for her. Her beautiful green eyes are red and tear streaks mar her cheeks.

I pull her to me, engulfing her into a bear hug as I drag her inside my apartment. She hides her face against my chest, curling her fingers into my T-shirt.

"It's going to be okay, babe."

She eases off and glances up. "I know it will be. I feel a million times better already just being here with you."

"Do you want anything to eat? I can make you a sandwich."

"No, I'm not hungry."

"A drink then?"

"Maybe some water."

"Okay, coming right up."

I take the duffle bag from her and set it down next to the couch. Danny already made himself scarce, giving us privacy. I couldn't have asked for a better roommate, even when he's acting like a pain in my ass about my inability to voice my feelings.

"Where's Danny?" Jane asks.

"In his room."

She pulls up a barstool and sits at the counter, resting her head in her hands. "I've made a mess of things."

"I doubt it. Whatever you told your mother, she had it coming."

"Maybe. But shouldn't I be feeling relieved then? How come I now have this immeasurable guilt swirling in my chest?"

I set the glass of water on the counter and then I turn her around to face me. "Because you're too good. She doesn't deserve your guilt, sweetheart. Trust me. I know what it's like to be raised by a narcissistic parent."

Jane stares into my eyes intensely, as if she's trying to peer into my soul. She'd only find a black smear there.

"Did your father hurt you, Andy?" she asks softly, probably afraid I'm going to take flight at any moment.

My automatic reaction is to tense and step away. She holds me by my forearms, keeping me in place. "You can tell me anything. I love you and nothing will change that."

I look away, unable to withstand her gaze. My heart is bleeding in agony. I want to surrender to her, lay myself bare at her feet, but my primal survival instinct won't let me. I can't handle the pain of being betrayed again.

"It doesn't matter, babe."

"It *does* matter. Keeping things bottled inside is never good."

I glance at her again. "Why are you asking me if my father hurt me? Did your moth—"

"No. She never laid a hand on me. But not only fists cause pain. She's an expert at verbal torture."

I cup her cheek, needing to offer comfort as much as I need the contact.

"Yes, he used to hit me," I confess. "After my mother died, he became uglier than he already was."

"Did he hit Lorenzo too?"

The possibility that he might be doing to Lorenzo what he did to me robs me of air. The times I spoke to my brother after his races, he was the same cheerful kid as always, but what if he's gotten good at hiding like I did? I shake my head, more to convince myself than anything else.

"No. He never laid a hand on him. Thank God."

"I'm so sorry, Andy."

I close my eyes, hating the pity I see shining in hers. "Don't."

"Don't what?"

"Don't feel sorry for me."

"Andy, look at me."

I do as she commands because there's nothing I wouldn't do for her. *Besides tell her you love her,* my perverse mind reminds me.

She holds my face between her hands. "I don't pity you. I pity your father for being so consumed by darkness that he failed to see what an amazing son he has."

"I'm not that great, babe. Trust me."

"Shut up. I don't want to hear you demean yourself like that. You're great. No, you're amazing. A loyal friend, smart, funny, a beast in bed," she smiles, and that sight fills me with happiness.

I chuckle. "A beast, huh?"

"Yes. My world is better because you're in it. Never forget that."

"For what it's worth, my world is better because of you too."

Her face splits into the most radiant smile, and it's my undoing. I shorten the distance between us and slam my lips to hers. I should be gentle, but I can't restrain myself. If I can't find the courage to tell her how I feel, then I have to show her.

She jumps into my arms, hooking her legs behind me. My hands find her lovely ass, and with our mouths still fused together, I make a beeline for my bedroom. We could tumble down on my bed, but as much as I'm ready to fuck her into oblivion, I want to worship her body first. I set her back on her feet, and reluctantly pull away.

"Where are you going?" she asks, keeping her hooded eyes glued to my lips.

"Maintaining my vow to make love to you always."

"What if I want, no, what if I *need* to be fucked hard?"

Jesus, how can I remain in control when naughty things keep coming out of her angelic mouth?

"Is that what you need, babe? My cock plunged deep in your tight pussy?"

"Yes," she hisses.

I take my T-shirt off. "What else do you need?"

"I need you to pound into me until my body leaves a permanent imprint on your mattress."

Shit. I'm so hard, it's painful. Quickly, I remove my jeans and boxers. But freedom doesn't alleviate the ache. Only doing exactly what Jane wants will give me any kind of relief.

"Take off your clothes."

She follows my request in the same order that I did, first the T-shirt, and then her jeans. She's standing in front of me now wearing no-fuss black underwear with pink roller blades printed on them.

I smile. "I love those."

"I figured I should wear something thematic today."

Unable to keep my distance any longer, I step into her space, kissing her again so hard that she can't tell whose air she's breathing. She runs her fingers down my abs, leaving a trail of goose bumps. I smirk against her lips, knowing exactly where she's going. When she wraps her hand around my shaft and gives it a little tug, I bite her lower lip softly.

"Do you want to do something new, babe?" I whisper against her lips.

"Another first?"

"Yeah."

"Is it a sixty-nine?"

I chuckle, nodding my head. "How did you guess?"

"Hmm, maybe I'm a psychic."

"Oh, yeah? Can you guess what my next move is, then?"

"That's easy. I don't need special powers. You're going to toss me on the bed and eat my pussy."

"Damn straight I am."

"Not if I toss you first." She yanks me by the arm and lobs me toward the bed. I could have put up resistance, but I'm having too much fun.

I bounce on the mattress, laughing like I haven't in a long time. Jane joins me, taking advantage of my lowered guard to straddle me. She's still wearing her underwear though, and that's way too much of a barrier in my book.

My cock is nudged nicely between her folds, and when she gyrates her hips, the friction makes us both moan loudly. She doesn't stop, driving me wild with need. If she keeps at it, I'm going to come. I flip us over, caging her in now with my arms on each side of her head.

"Are you trying to make me want to skip foreplay and fuck you right this second?"

"No, I want to do the new thing first."

I invade her mouth with my tongue again, while hooking my fingers on each side of her underwear.

"Okay, then we need to get rid of a certain piece of clothing."

Peppering kisses on her chin and continuing my trip south, I roll her panties down her legs. I run a lazy tongue around her belly button, loving how Jane arches her back and whimpers like a kitten. But now her pink secrets are exposed to me, and I can't resist the temptation of having a quick taste. I sweep my tongue over her clit, once, twice. *Shit, I can't stop.*

Jane threads her fingers through my hair and pulls hard.

"Ouch!" I complain.

"This is not a sixty-nine."

"Okay, okay." I flip on my back. "Come on, it's easier if you hover over me."

She moves slowly, and a little awkwardly. Her cheeks are bright pink, and I want to tell her there's no need for embarrassment, but then her pussy once again comes within reach of my tongue, and what can I say, I'm easily distracted.

I grab her by the hips and bring her closer to me. Jane cries out when I resume my merciless assault. Like me, she's at the edge of pure ecstasy. I groan when she takes my entire length into her mouth while holding the base with her hand.

Fuck me. I'm not going to last. But hell if I'm going to let that happen before I take care of her. I suck her clit into my mouth, and that does the trick. Her body convulses, and her ministrations turn a little clumsy with the distraction, but I was already on the verge. I dig my fingers deeper into her hips and suck her clit harder as I climax. I'd keep eating her up if she'd let me, but she moves away from me and collapses sideways on the mattress.

For a moment, neither of us move. We're both trying to catch our breath. I run my fingers up and down her thigh—the only thing I'm capable of doing. I never thought I'd say this, but I'm boneless. Jane has taken me to a state of pure bliss and I never want to leave it.

THIRTY-SIX

JANE

I t's almost midnight, but neither Andy nor I are ready for bed. We're in the kitchen eating ice cream. I feel a bit better, but I'm still worried about the future. What if Dad takes my mother's side? There's no way in hell I'm going back to live with her. I might just have to move in with Troy.

"Penny for your thoughts," Andy pipes up.

"I'm just thinking about practical things."

"Like what?" He licks his spoon slowly, distracting me for a moment. "Jane?"

I blink out of my lustful daze. "Whether my father will let me live with him or not."

"Isn't his house far from your school?"

I shrug. "I don't mind the commute. It beats living with my mother for sure."

"I might have to move out too."

"Why?"

He takes a deep breath, avoiding my gaze. "My father cut me off. It's the reason I couldn't come pick you up. He took my Bronco, and said I have to pay for tuition next year."

"Why would he do that?"

"Because he's an asshole." He shoves his bowl of ice cream to the side. "I recently switched my major from business to hospitality against his wishes."

"Are you serious? Because of that he decided to cut you off?"

"Hey, who's winning the awful parents award now?" He smiles, but it's a sad one.

I reach over, covering his hand with mine. "It's going to be okay. I'll help you."

"I need to find a job ASAP. I'm sure my credit cards have been canceled by now."

"I have money in my savings. It's yours."

"Jane, I couldn't possibly take money from you."

I sit straighter in my chair. "Why? Because of a macho thing?"

He slides his hand from under mine, and then pushes his long bangs back. "It's not a macho thing. It's a… *pride* thing."

"Andy…."

He stands and walks away from the kitchen counter. His back is to me now, but there's a new tension there that tells me how much this subject bothers him.

"I've spent my entire life trying to please my father. It's fucking stupid, I know." He rests his hands on his hips, and glances at the floor. "The guy used to beat me to a pulp whenever he had a few drinks. But besides the physical aggression, he also loved to bring me down with words. Nothing I did was ever good enough. No matter how many games the Rushmore Rebels won, or how great my performance was, he'd find a way to criticize me."

I walk over and hug him from behind. "I know how it feels. You hear so much that you're not good enough that you start to believe it."

He turns in my arms, revealing his tear-filled eyes. "You're good enough, babe. Don't let that hag get into your head."

"Fine. As long as you don't let your asshole father get into yours."

Andreas's gaze darkens. "I'm trying not to, but it's so damn hard. Do you understand now where I'm coming from? I need to prove to myself I'm not the failure my father believes I am."

My heart is breaking for him. I don't know what to do or say that will make him see the truth. He's not perfect—no one is—but he's perfect to me.

"You're not a failure, but I understand wanting to do it all alone. You don't have to, though. You have me, and your friends."

His lips curl into a crooked grin. "Troy gave me the same spiel."

"Wait? When did you talk to my brother?"

"He helped me out today. We talked. If there's a silver lining in all this it's that we're on the way to patching things up."

A sigh of relief whooshes out of me. The whole feud between Andy and Troy was stressing me out.

"That's great, babe," I say.

"Babe?" He raises an eyebrow. "I think that's the first time you've called me that."

"You don't like it? I can always call you Beast."

He throws his head back and laughs, a sound so infectious that it affects me too.

"What's all the racket?" Danny comes into the kitchen, rubbing his eyes.

He's only wearing pajama pants, and holy moly, the freshman can give Andreas a run for his money.

Andy pinches my arm. "Hey, stop ogling my roommate."

My face becomes hot. "I wasn't ogling."

Danny doesn't seem to register the exchange between us. He opens the fridge and takes a jug of filtered water from it.

"How was your first day at bootcamp, Jane?" he asks.

"Oh, it was intense, but so much fun."

"I can wait to see you in action," Andreas tells me.

"Well, I have another three weeks to go. Grandma already said she wants to come to my first game too."

"With her two boyfriends?" Danny smirks.

"Yeah, of course."

Danny turns his attention to Andreas. "What are you doing tomorrow, bro?"

"I thought I'd hit all the restaurants in the area, see if they're hiring."

"Have you thought about trying a bakery instead? That would you give you a ton of experience that you won't get anywhere else."

"Oh, that's a great idea," I say. "Actually, I might be able to help."

"How so?"

"Grandma. She knows the founder of Sugar Loaf Cupcakes."

"The biggest bakery chain in LA?" Andreas's eyes bug out.

I nod, grinning. "Yep. Do you want me to ask her? I'm sure she can score you an interview."

"An interview would be amazing, but I think I should be the one asking her."

Of course he would say that, but at least he didn't flat out say no to the idea. That doesn't mean I can't give Grandma a heads-up though.

"It'll probably count toward school credit too," Danny pipes up. "It can be an internship."

"As long as it's paid, it can be anything."

I clap my hands together. "This is great. Who wants to celebrate with more ice cream?"

"I can't say no to ice cream," Danny replies.

Andy eyes the one-gallon container greedily. "I don't know if there's enough for three."

Danny opens the lid and widens his eyes. "It's half full. How much were you planning on eating?"

Andreas turns to me, watching me with a smoldering gaze. "All of it."

My face bursts into flames. He's not only talking about dessert. I don't know what part the ice cream plays in his dirty mind, but I can't wait to find out.

THIRTY-SEVEN

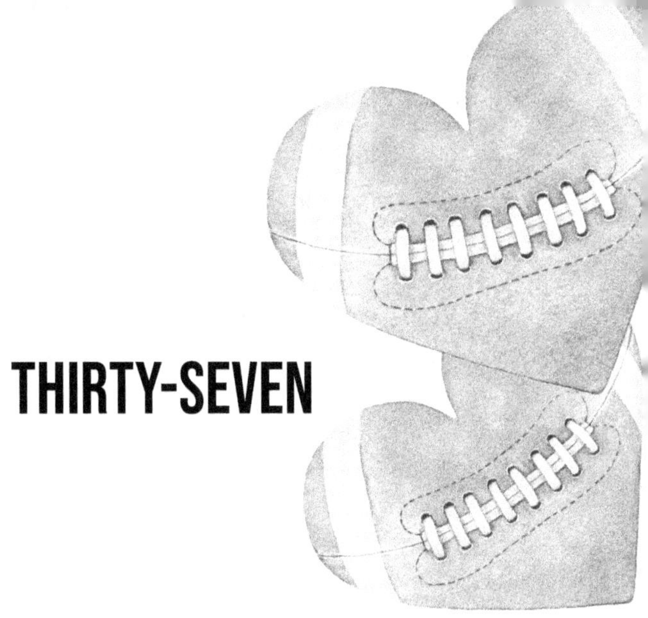

ANDREAS

While Jane is at bootcamp, I spend the day working on school assignments, sending out resumes, and when the restaurants nearby open for lunch, I visit them.

It was a bad call to look for a job while the restaurants are dealing with the Sunday crowd. No one has time for me. I'm told to try during the week when it's less busy. Either way, I'm not very hopeful anything will come out of it.

I stop by the bank to withdraw the money I have left in my account. There's not much in there, but it will cover my living expenses for a few weeks if I'm frugal. No more eating out for sure until I find another source of income. I'm surprised my father didn't zero out my account. It's a joint one. Maybe he forgot. There's no way in hell he'd make things easy for me.

On the way home, I stop by the grocery store. We're getting low on food. I've never shopped before with a budget in mind, and it blows my mind how expensive everything is when you're low on funds. I buy generic shit, and the only splurge I make is buying Jane's favorite brand of ice cream. A smile crosses my lips when last night's memories come to the forefront of my mind. We did finish that half-gallon of ice cream in the exact manner I wanted. Licking every drop of it off Jane's body.

I become aroused in an instant. Thank fuck there's a grocery cart in front of me to hide the bulge in my jeans.

I'm whistling happily while the cashier rings up my stuff. My amusement wanes a fraction when I see the bill. Over two hundred dollars, and I only bought the basics. *Jesus.* The money I got might not last me as long as I expected.

My phone vibrates in my pocket when I'm on my way to Jane's car. Since she'd be in the gymnasium the whole day, it made sense for me to drive her there so I could run errands.

I don't look first before I answer the call. Bad mistake.

"Hi, Andy," Crystal's sugary voice greets me.

Every cell in my body rebels against the sound, and the small hairs on the back of my neck stand on end. She shouldn't be able to reach me. I blocked her number a long time ago.

"What do you want?" I ask.

"Is this the way you greet the only one who can help you out of this mess?"

"I don't know what you're talking about. Being cut off from that dick you call a husband is the best thing that could ever happen to me."

"Oh, Andy. There's no need to play tough around me. You've been a spoiled brat your entire life. No one raised with a silver spoon does well when they lose everything."

"You clearly don't know me at all."

"Oh, we both know that's a lie."

"Fuck off, Crystal. And stop calling me."

I end the call before she can get another word in. I'm ready to block this new number too, but the bitch used Lorenzo's phone to call me. Rage courses through me. If she got her hands on Lorenzo's phone, then she must have read all the messages exchanged between us. I told him about Jane and other personal stuff. I feel violated, which brings back awful memories of growing up with her as my stepmom.

I'm in a funky mood when I come home, a fact that Danny immediately picks up on. "Dude, what happened?"

"Nothing." I dump the grocery bags on the kitchen counter.

The TV is on, displaying a war video game. Paris and Troy have taken over my couch, and barely acknowledge my presence.

"Since when has my place turned into gamers' central?" I ask no one in particular.

"Charlie has a school deadline and kicked me out of the house. She said I distract her too much," Troy replies.

"Geneva is out of town visiting family," Paris adds.

"Basically, their girlfriends let them off their leashes," Danny jokes.

"At least we have girlfriends," Paris retorts.

"Been there, done that. I don't need to enter another serious relationship any time soon. I'm enjoying my freedom," he replies while peering inside one of the bags. "Did you get soap for the dishwasher?"

"That's not in the budget."

"Okay. Did you get detergent then?"

"Ah fuck. I forgot."

"I guess we can use shampoo for the time being."

"Hell no. Do you know how much shampoo costs?"

"I don't know about yours, but I get mine at the Dollar General." He shrugs.

Damn it. Why didn't I think of going there? I bet I could have found half of what I bought for much cheaper.

"So, your dad cut you off for good?" Paris asks.

"He sure did. It's better this way though. He can't control me anymore."

"I can ask Geneva to try to find you a job in one of her family's restaurants."

I grimace, ready to say thanks, but no thanks. One look at

Danny's frown and meaningful stare reminds me I can't be picky.

"Thanks, man. I appreciate it."

Paris nods. "No problem."

Troy puts the game on pause. "Listen, I spoke to Grandma. She's okay with you and Danny moving in. Her only condition is that you don't throw rave parties when Charlie and I are in Europe."

"When did I ever throw a rave party?" I ask, offended.

"Sorry, man. You have a reputation."

Shit. That's not good. "Do you think it would be all right if I went to visit her?"

He frowns. "Why do you want to do that?"

"She might be able to help me find a job. Plus, I need someone in your family to not think I'm an irresponsible jerk."

Troy grimaces, and guilt shines in his eyes. "I don't think that about you... *anymore.*"

I should feel offended by his remark, but what's the point? I was reckless and stupid before.

"Fair enough. So, what do you think?"

"I think that'd be okay. You can probably go today. Do you want me to call her?"

"Yeah. Sure."

I shouldn't feel nervous about visiting Ophelia Holland. This is not my first time meeting the lady, but I'm jittery when I walk through Golden Oaks' entrance. A youngish receptionist is behind the desk and greets me with an overly cheerful tone.

"Welcome to Golden Oaks. How can I help you?"

"Hi, I'm here to visit Ophelia Holland. I'm Andreas Rossi. She's expecting me."

The receptionist's eyes become wider, and her smile has now the hint of a secret. "Oh, you must be Jane's boyfriend."

I watch her through slitted eyes. "Yes. I don't mean to sound rude, but how do you know?"

An embarrassed flush spreads over her cheeks. "I'm so sorry. I shouldn't have said anything. Ophelia is waiting in the gardens. Just follow the signs and you won't miss it."

"Awesome. Thanks."

After the receptionist's comment, I'm now more nervous than before. I wouldn't put it past the sassy lady to be plotting a trap of some kind. God, what if she's going to tell me I'm not good enough for her granddaughter? She didn't want me living with Troy when she let him stay in her house. I never thought much about it, but now I wonder if there were serious reasons behind her rule against me.

I have no problem finding her today. She has a preference for Easter egg coloring in her hair, and the turquoise blue is hard to miss. She's wearing huge sunglasses and colorful clothes that are either too high fashion for me to appreciate or they're just plain awful. She's sitting at a table with her two boyfriends, Jack Morris and Louis Romano. I'm surprised to see them there. I thought I'd get a private meeting with her.

"Good afternoon, Mrs. Holland, Mr. Morris, Mr. Romano," I say.

She smiles broadly. "Stop with the formality. You can call me Ophelia, like always."

"All right."

I glance at her boyfriends, who, unlike her, are not all smiles. On the contrary, they're glowering at me. *Fuck. What did I do to them?*

"It's so nice of you to visit. Have a seat." She points at the chair opposite them.

It's only when I'm seated that I notice the peculiarity of the seating arrangement. It's a round table, and the trio is facing me as if they're a judging panel. Hell, I bet they are.

"So, Andreas Rossi," Jack starts. "We heard you're now Jane's boyfriend."

"Yes, sir." I squirm uncomfortably in my chair.

Ophelia brings her cocktail to her lips, partially hiding a smirk.

"We're not going to beat around the bush here," Louis chimes in. "What are your intentions with her?"

I blink several times. "Excuse me?"

"We know about your reputation. The manwhore of campus, they say," Jack pipes up.

"That's in the past," I grit out, fighting not to lose my cool.

"So you say," Louis snorts.

I glance at Ophelia, trying to judge if she shares her boyfriends' opinion of me. I can't make sense of her expression. She seems amused. *What the hell!*

"If you came here to ask for her hand, you'd better have prepared a list of reasons for why that should be granted," Jack says.

"What? She's only eighteen!"

Are they for real? I turn to Ophelia, who's trying to hide her amusement, but failing miserably at it.

I narrow my eyes. "You guys are yanking my chain, aren't you?"

The boyfriends look at one another and then burst out laughing.

Son of a bitch. They totally had me for a moment.

"I was wondering when you would figure it out. When Jack and Louis suggested we prank you, I was sure you'd catch on right away," Ophelia replies.

"I hope you're not cross with us," Louis adds, wiping off tears off laughter from the corners of his eyes.

Jackass.

"I'm not mad. You had surprise on your side," I say. "Besides, it was my fear that you would judge me by my bad rep."

"I'm much more inclined to judge you based on your recent

actions. What you did for Jane was unbelievable. It showed me you truly care about her," Ophelia says.

Even behind the sunglasses, I can sense her intense stare.

"I do. Very much so."

She nods in approval. "Now, Troy was tightlipped about the reason for your visit."

"Yeah, I asked him to not say anything so you wouldn't have the chance to think it over too much and dismiss me right away."

She raises an eyebrow. "And who is sneaky now?"

I chuckle. "I need all the advantages I can get. He told you that my father has cut me off because I switched majors, right?"

She nods. "Yeah, we know."

"Your father is grade-A asshole," Louis pipes up, sporting a frown now.

"He truly is. But in all honesty, it's better this way. Now I have nothing tethering me to him save for my brother."

"Did Troy tell you I've lifted the ban on male roommates? You and Danny are more than welcome to stay at my house."

"Yes, he did tell me that and I appreciate it. But I'm here to ask you for another favor."

"Anything that I can help."

"I was hoping you could put in a good word for me with the owner of Sugar Loaf Cupcakes."

"Ah, yes, you like to bake, I hear."

"It's my calling. I know that now without a shred of doubt."

Ophelia doesn't speak for several beats, pinning me to the chair with her stare. I don't dare to breathe while she ponders my request.

She takes a sip of her cocktail, and finally replies, "Consider it done."

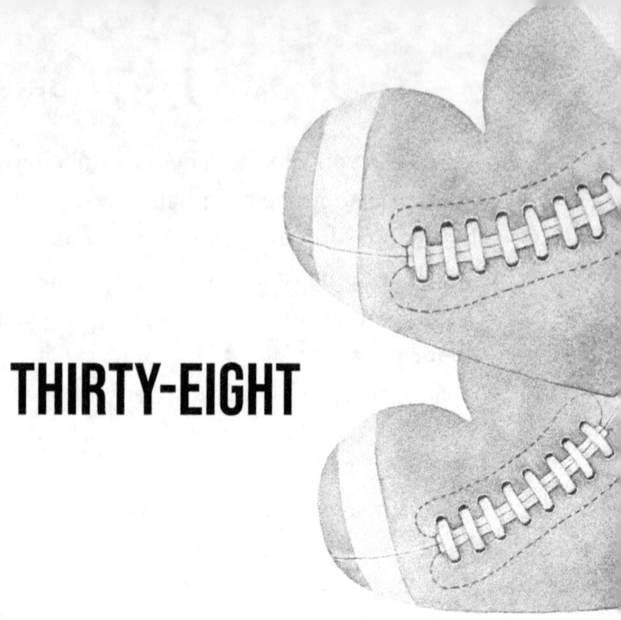

THIRTY-EIGHT

ANDREAS

I come straight to the gymnasium to pick up Jane after my visit to Golden Oaks. Ophelia told me she'd contact me as soon as she spoke to Howard Honeywell, the owner of Sugar Loaf Cupcakes.

There was some traffic, and by the time I arrive, Jane is already waiting for me in front of the building. She's chatting with a short brunette who by Jane's description must be Alicia.

They glance in my direction when I bring the car to a stop in front of them. Alicia's attention switches to the interior of the car. She's squinting, probably trying to see what I look like. I put the car in park and get out.

"Hey babe. How was practice?"

Jane walks over and kisses me softly on the lips. I'd pull her closer to me and devour her mouth properly if we didn't have an audience. Not everyone is a fan of PDA.

"Practice was good." She turns to her friend. "This Alicia, roller derby legend."

Keeping my arm firmly looped around Jane's waist, I offer my right hand to the girl. "Hi Alicia, nice to meet you."

"Nice to finally meet you too, Andy. And I'm not a legend. Not yet, anyway."

"I like that way of thinking," I reply sincerely.

Jane needs positive role models in her life after all the toxicity her mother gave her throughout the years.

"Anyway. I'd better get my ass home before my big sister freaks out," she continues.

"Okay," Jane replies. "And let's try to meet this week."

"For sure, girlie. See ya."

No sooner than Alicia gives her back to us, I turn Jane around and greet her properly. My mouth covers hers hungrily. My tongue opens the seam of her lips with impatience while my fingers dig into her hips, pulling her closer. Jane clutches my arms, melting into me. She fits perfectly into my embrace, into my world. I never want to let her go. If this ain't love, I don't know what is. Why can't I tell her that?

She pulls away, and breathlessly asks, "How was the meeting with Grandma?"

"It was good." I lean forward, my eyes dropping to her lips.

Jane presses two fingers against my lips, preventing me from claiming her mouth again. "We should go. You're making it almost impossible to behave in public."

I chuckle, stepping back. "I thought you were a rebel."

"I *am* a rebel, but I'd rather save my bender of rules side for the bedroom."

Jesus fucking Christ. How can she know exactly what to say to drive me crazy?

"Woman, you're playing with fire. Let's go before I break into that gymnasium building and have my way with you pressed against the wall."

A wicked smile unfurls on her lips. "I like that idea."

My body automatically moves closer to her. She flattens her palms against my chest, halting me. "In your apartment," she continues.

I reply through a groan, "Fine. Get your sweet ass in the car."

"Yo, Danny. Are you home?" I ask as soon as I open the front door.

Jane is supposed to be moving in with her Dad, but he's out of town, which means she can stay with me for a while longer.

Silence greets us, but to be sure my roomie is really not home, I check his room.

"Are we alone?" Jane asks from behind me.

I pivot around, smiling already from ear to ear. "Yeah. I remember something about a wall."

Jane widens her eyes when I pull my T-shirt off and move closer to her.

"Your bedroom has walls."

"The one behind you is just fine."

We're in the hallway, and it would take nothing but a couple of steps to disappear inside my room, but I like the idea of fucking Jane out here where we could get caught at any moment. I cage her in, resting my hands against the wall on either side of her head. Her ragged breathing fans across my jaw, making it hard to maintain my distance and think straight.

Without breaking eye contact, she runs her fingers across my abs, and then she licks her lower lip. "What are you waiting for then?"

"In good time, babe." I lean closer and rub my lips against hers. A distraction while my hands disappear underneath her skirt. She's wearing the simple cotton panties she prefers.

"I love that you're wearing a skirt, but these are in the way."

"Is that so?" She reaches for my jeans, slowly undoes my button, and pulls the zipper down.

Her nimble fingers so close to my cock snap the little bit of restraint I have left. I pull her panties down with the patience of a starving man and crush my mouth to hers. As motivated as me, she pulls my dick free from the confines of my boxers, drawing a feral groan from deep in my throat.

There's no turning back now. I lift her off the ground and she opens herself to me, hooking her legs behind my ass. Her pussy is so wet and ready that one little nudge is enough to drive my cock home. I hesitate though, and curse in my head for forgetting a crucial detail.

"We need protection," I murmur against her lips.

"I'm on the pill." She digs her heels against my ass, pulling me closer

I lose the battle against caution and thrust forward, sheathing myself in her. I don't move for a second, getting used to the feeling. I haven't had sex without a condom in a very long time, and I forgot how fucking amazing it feels.

"Andy?" Jane captures my face between her hands and makes me look at her. "Are you okay?"

"I'm more than okay, babe."

I slam my mouth against hers, kissing her with teeth, branding her with my tongue while I piston in and out of her heat. With each thrust, my grunts become louder. Jane digs her nails in my back, leaving her own mark on me. Our exposed skin becomes slick, and my sweaty hands have a harder time maintaining Jane at the right height. But I keep going, chasing the promised land.

"Oh my God, Andy. I'm going to co—" I cut her off with my mouth because I need to be fused with her in every way possible.

She tightens around me, and her moans of ecstasy are muffled by my tongue. Her body shakes as she clings harder to me. I'm about to lose my mind too. I thrust harder, and when my release finally comes, it's an explosion of bliss. I don't stop moving until I milk every single drop of pleasure.

After a minute, I become still save for my chest, which is keeping my heart from bursting out. My breathing is ragged, just like Jane's.

I press my forehead against hers and whisper, "Jesus. That was...."

"Amazing," she completes.

A chuckle escapes my lips. "Yeah."

"Ah hell." Danny's disgruntled voice reaches us from the beginning of the hallway. "Are you guys kidding me?"

Shit. Roomie is home. I angle my body forward to hide Jane, and glance in his direction. I catch him heading back to the living room.

"Oh my God. I want to die," Jane whispers in my ear.

"Relax, sweetheart. I don't think he saw anything."

"I saw enough," he yells from the couch.

A bubble of laughter goes up my throat and I can't stop. Jane disentangles herself from me, and before running to my room, she hits my arm. "This is not funny."

"Sorry, babe. I don't know what's taken over me."

I have the giggles, and I can honestly say that's never happened to me before. Jane has already disappeared into my bathroom by the time I close the door. I don't follow her, choosing to let her recover from the embarrassing moment alone. I clean myself with my discarded T-shirt and then I go check on Danny to find out how much he's seen.

He's playing a video game while sporting a serious frown.

"Hey." I jump on the couch.

"You're an ass," he says without looking at me.

"Why?"

"You have a room. Why did you have to screw your girlfriend in the hallway, man?"

"Living recklessly, I guess." I shrug. "What's the big deal?"

"The big deal is that I see Jane as the sister I never had, and now I have that racy image in my mind. It's doing my head in. I feel like I need to wash my brain with Purell."

"Nobody forced you to watch."

"I didn't watch, asshole! But the quick glimpse was enough."

I roll my eyes. "You're so dramatic."

My phone rings from somewhere nearby. I don't remember where I left it before Jane consumed my thoughts. I get up and search, finding it on the kitchen counter.

"Great," I mumble.

"Who is it?"

"It's Ricky Montana, the guy who traded shifts with me on Friday." I press the Answer button, knowing he won't stop annoying me until I fulfill the end of my bargain. "Hello?"

"Hey, Andy. My man. What's up?"

"Not much."

"Do you have any plans for tonight?"

"Yeah, chilling with my girl. Why?"

"Rumor has it that the infamous Glitter Club party is happening tonight at Pike's headquarters. Dude, you have to get me in."

I pinch the bridge of my nose. The Glitter Club party is a seventies-inspired event that's always announced last minute and is super exclusive; mainly jocks and Greeks are invited. I probably got an email about it.

"How did you get wind of it?"

"A guy in my dorm did the sound system hookup. Are you seriously not going to this?"

"No, wasn't planning on it. And we have Professor Asshole's class first thing tomorrow morning."

"I know, I know. Dude, you don't need to stay long. Just get me through the door and introduce me to some hotties, and I'll consider us square."

I can tell Ricky won't leave me alone until I help him out. Might as well get this shit over with. There's no chance I'm going to a party without Jane though.

"Fine. I'll meet you in front of library in two hours and we'll walk from there."

"Cool, man. I'll see you there."

I drop my phone back on the counter and then push my long bangs back.

"What was that all about?" Danny asks.

"Fulfilling an oath. Get dressed. If I have to suffer a Glitter Club party, so do you."

"What the hell is that?" He looks over his shoulder.

"Ah, right. You're still a noob. I'll tell you all about it on the way to Troy's."

"Wait. Why do we need to head to Troy's first?"

"Because we need supplies and the only girl I know who has a Halloween costume store in her house is Charlie."

"What about Charlie?" Jane asks as she walks over, freshly showered and wearing clothes that show zero skin. *Overcompensation, maybe?*

"We're going to a dress-up party."

"On a Sunday?" Her eyebrows arch.

"Hey, we're rebels, remember?"

Her cheeks turn bright pink. She glances briefly at Danny. "I'm not so sure about that anymore."

"Don't worry, he saw nothing."

"True. I didn't see a thing," he pipes up.

Still sporting a frown, she looks in my eyes. "What kind of dress-up party?"

"The glitter kind." I smile, loving how her eyes slowly widen in surprise.

"Okay. You should have started with that. I can't wait to see what that entails."

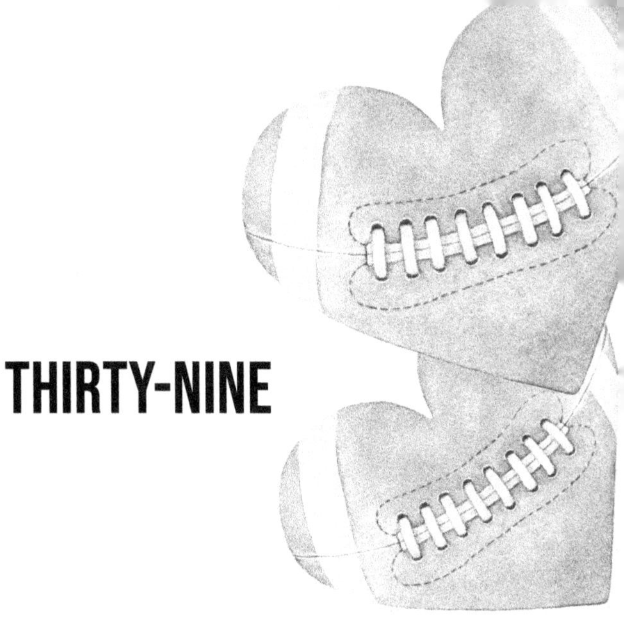

THIRTY-NINE

JANE

I'm still in awe at how quickly our Sunday evening turned into a Club 54 outing. Charlie had everything we needed to glamorize any outfit. The glitter usage went unchecked and now Andy, Troy, Danny, and Paris look like they all came out of a unicorn's ass.

I have on the same eighties outfit I wore to the beach minus the roller skates. My long hair is in pigtails and I'm wearing more makeup than a drag queen.

On the way out of the house, I hear Troy ask Andy, "Are you going to let Jane go out like that?"

I turn around with my hands on my hips, ready to tell Troy to fuck off, but Andy beats me to the punch.

"I see nothing wrong with her outfit. Besides, if any punk even thinks about harassing Jane"—he raises his fists—"he's going to meet Chuck and Norris."

He catches me staring and rewards me with a panty-melting smile. As excited as I am to finally be going to a college party with Andy, I'd trade that for a quiet evening with him in a heartbeat. But he does have to return a favor.

"Did you tell Geneva you were going to a party?" Danny asks Paris.

He rubs the back of his neck, looking sheepish. "Er, not exactly. I said I was hanging out with you guys."

Troy shakes his head and Andy coughs, "Whipped."

"You're both in the same boat as me, so shut up," Paris retorts, walking ahead of us.

"Why do you guys keeping pestering him about his girlfriend?" I ask.

"You'll understand when you meet her." Andreas throws his arm over my shoulders and leans closer to my ear. "You're not cold, babe?"

"I'm fine. But if you want to keep me super toasty, don't let go."

"Sweetheart, I'll be glued to your side like chewing gum on the bottom of a shoe."

"What if I have to pee?" I ask through a laugh.

"I'll come with you."

"Ew. No, you won't."

"Ugh. Can you please cut it out?" Troy opens the door to his car. "Watching you two play the lovebirds game is nauseating."

"That's nothing compared to what I had to witness," Danny says under his breath.

Andy and I cut him a warning glance. He pulls his upper lip in, grimacing. Then he mouths "Sorry."

Troy looks pointedly at us. "Fuck, I definitely don't want to know that."

Charlie giggles, following my brother inside his car. I veer for mine, but Andreas already claimed the driver's seat on the way here, so I take shotgun. Danny is riding with us, and Paris with Troy and Charlie.

"Tell me more about this guy Ricky Montana," I say.

"What's to tell? I barely know him."

"He's not in any of my classes, but he's notorious in the freshman circle," Danny chimes in.

I turn on my seat to glance at him. "How so?"

He shakes his head and laughs. "He's obsessed with meeting girls and keeps talking about his homies from back home."

"Pretty much the real-life version of 'Pretty Fly for a White Guy' then," Andreas laughs.

Danny shrugs. "I guess. It should be interesting going to a party with him."

Ten minutes later, Andy finds a parking spot near Rushmore's main library building. The wind has picked up, and the air is a little chilly. I shiver inside my short jacket, and now my tush is freezing.

"Are you okay, babe?" Andy pulls me to his side, and I feel better immediately. The man is like a human furnace.

"Yes. I'll be fine once we go inside."

"Yo, Andy, my man." A guy ahead of us waves in our direction.

"That's Ricky," Andreas tells me.

He's tall and wiry, reminding me immediately of Shaggy from *Scooby-Doo* even though his hair is curly, not straight. He's not alone. A shorter dark-haired guy is with him.

"I'll be damned. Taiyo?" Andreas asks, amused.

"Hey, Andy. I hope you don't mind that I tagged along."

"Not at all. I'm glad that you found the time to live a little." He turns to me. "This is Jane, my girlfriend."

I should be used to Andy calling me his girlfriend by now, but I still get butterflies in my stomach when I hear it.

"Hi, nice to meet you."

"Wait, you're Troy's sister, right?" Ricky chimes in.

"Yep, so?" Troy answers as he walks over, holding hands with Charlie.

Paris is right behind him.

Ricky looks at them and his eyes bug out. "Holy crap. Troy Alexander and Paris Mackenzie. I didn't know you were coming too."

Danny shoves his hands in his pocket. "What's his deal? I'm on the football team too."

"I'm sure you'll have a legion of fans next year," I tell him.

He smiles. "Thanks. I was kidding though. I don't care about having a legion of fans. I just want to play football."

"All right. Let's get going." Andreas steers me toward the beginning of Greek Row, taking the lead.

It doesn't take long to hear the sound of loud music coming from one of the biggest houses in the street. Andy told me this is a semisecret party, but much like Poppy's party in the forest in the *Trolls* movie, anyone in the vicinity can hear the music or see the purple and blue lights coming from the building.

The front lawn is peppered with people wearing skimpy and outrageous outfits. Two huge guys in Greek togas and golden glitter spray all over their exposed skin greet us at the front door.

Andy fits bumps the one closest to him. "Nice outfit, Keevan. Who are you supposed to be? Apollo?"

The guy's lips curl into a grin. "That's right." He glances at Ricky and Taiyo behind us and lifts his chin. "Who are those two?"

"Friends. They're cool."

"All right, then."

And just like that Ricky and Taiyo gain access to their dream party.

Inside, it's crowded and dark. The lights keep changing from purple to blue, but they don't provide much illumination. Music is coming from a small stage set up in the living room where a live band is playing catchy seventies tunes to a crowd of enthusiastic dancers. The disco ball reflects against their glittering costumes and colorful wigs. At one point, I spot a unicorn floatie being passed around until it reaches the stage. As parties go, this is pretty wild.

Andreas still has his arm wrapped around my waist, but it becomes more and more difficult to walk like that. I free myself from his hold and link our hands instead.

"It's easier this way," I shout through the loud music.

"Okay. Stay right behind me."

He carves a path through the throng of people, using his elbows when necessary. No one seems to mind. They're either already too drunk to care, or they idolize Andy too much to complain. We finally reach a spot where there's more breathing room. It's a games space. There are two large leather couches, a pool table, foosball, and a dartboard on the wall.

Once my eyesight adjusts to the difference in lighting—no purple glow here—I notice that this seems to be the make-out room. There are mostly couples here, or people in serious flirtation mode.

Andreas turns to Ricky and Taiyo. "All right. This is it, boys. I'm going to introduce you to some girls, but then it's up to you."

Charlie steps next to me. "Give Andy some room and see what happens."

Curious about her statement and amused tone, I do as she says. Andreas glances at me with eyebrows furrowed and a question in his eyes.

"Go on, help your friends out," I tell him.

Not even a minute goes by before the first flock of pretty girls moves closer to the boys. A stab of jealousy pierces my chest when one overenthusiastic redheaded gets up close and personal with Andy and runs her hand over his arm.

"Is that what you meant?" I cross my arms over my chest, not in the slightest bit happy about the sight.

"Yep. That happens all the time with Troy. It's like I'm invisible to them."

"Pretty sad, isn't it? The boys are like chum in shark-infested water," another girl says next to me.

I turn to find a gorgeous brunette standing there. She looks familiar.

"Vanessa, oh my God. I was wondering if I would see you here," Charlie says.

"You almost didn't. These types of parties are not my jam anymore. Ever since my sister started dating Leo Stine, I avoid Greek events like the plague." She glances at me. "You're Troy's little sister, right?"

"Yeah. Jane. Have we met before?"

"I've seen you on TV during the boys' games. I'm Vanessa Castro. I'm on the soccer team." Her attention switches to the guys, and a moment later, she frowns. "Isn't that Paris Mackenzie?"

"Yeah. Do you know him?" Charlies asks.

"No, I know his girlfriend. She was my neighbor growing up. I fucking hate her. Stupid snobby little bitch."

With wide eyes, I glance at Charlie and we share a similar expression. Maybe the guys were right about Paris's girlfriend after all.

"I'm sorry. I shouldn't have said anything. I'm just surprised she's not attached to his hip."

"It's okay. No one seems to like the girl," Charlie pipes up. "They came to a barbeque at our place, but I can't say I got to know her. She was pretty antisocial."

The guys are still surrounded by the bimbo sharks. Even though Andy has stepped away from the redhead, she's still too close to him for my liking.

"You know what? I've had enough of watching those girls fawn over my boyfriend," I say.

"Yeah, me too," Charlie chimes in.

Vanessa laughs. "And I'm so glad I'm a free agent. No boyfriend for me, especially the pretty ones."

Someone's slimy hand covers my butt, sending a chill down my spine. I jump forward with a yelp, looking over my shoulder.

"Relax, girlie." A drunk jackass smiles leerily at me, stepping into my personal space.

"Back off, asshole." Vanessa shoves him back hard. The idiot staggers back but somehow remains upright.

"I wasn't talking to you, bi—"

A blur appears in front of him, and his face gets knocked back by a punch. He does fall down this time. Andreas looms over him with closed fists by his sides, and then turns to me, eyes gleaming with fury.

"Did he touch you?"

I swallow the huge lump in my throat. If I tell him the truth, he'll go ballistic.

"Oh yeah, he grabbed her ass," a guy standing not too far from us replies before I can.

Thanks, pal.

Andy grabs the drunk from the floor by his T-shirt with one hand, and his right arm is pulled back, ready to deliver another blow.

"You touched my girlfriend, motherfucker?" he yells in his face.

"I-I didn't know she was your girlfriend," he stammers.

"No excuse. You shouldn't be touching anyone without consent."

The jab comes quickly, followed by another. Danny and Troy jump to get Andreas off the fallen drunk before he can get another punch in and drag him far away from the guy.

"That's enough, man," Troy says to Andy.

He's breathing hard, almost as if he's coming down from a frenzy. I hug my middle, not knowing what to do make this situation better.

After a moment, Andreas shakes himself free. "I'm fine."

Troy and Danny step aside and I move closer. "Are you okay?"

Andy pulls me into his arms and kisses the top of my head. "I'm the one who should be asking you."

"I'm fine."

"Damn," Ricky says as he steps closer to the douche on the floor. "Do you know who this is?"

"Don't fucking care," Andreas grits out.

"That's Professor Norman's nephew," Taiyo chimes in. "Shit, man. If he didn't like you before, now he's really going to hate you."

FORTY

ANDREAS

I shouldn't have let my anger take control like that, but the moment I saw that asshole get near Jane, my vision turned crimson. Leaving her alone for a minute was a mistake. Guys at those frat parties can't see a pretty girl alone without thinking she's there for their entertainment.

The ride back to my apartment was quiet. Jane looked out the window the entire time. Even Danny, who usually tries to defuse tension, was tightlipped in the backseat.

Troy asked Jane to stay over his place, but she denied him. I should take that as a sign that she's not mad at me, but the doubt has entered my chest and it's now festering. I'm not even concerned about the fact that the jerk I knocked out is Professor Norman's nephew. I guess the apple doesn't fall far from the tree.

Maybe I went too far and spooked her. I am a hothead; I've never hidden that. With me it's punch first, ask questions later. It might earn me an F in Norman's class, which is a small price to pay to protect Jane. What I hope I didn't achieve is making her afraid of me.

No sooner are we alone in my room with the door closed than I pull her to me and look into her eyes.

"Are you okay, babe?"

"I'm fine. Why do you keep asking me that?"

"Because you haven't said a word since we left the party."

"I'm just sad that it ended on such a sour note. I was having fun up until that moment."

"I'm sorry you had to see me like that."

Her delicate eyebrows furrow. "That guy deserved what he got. I'm not sorry you punched him. I'd have done the same thing after I recovered from the initial shock."

"I'm still raving mad he laid his hands on you. I would have kept punching him if Troy and Danny hadn't stopped me. That's who I am, Jane. Impulsive, reckless."

She cups my cheek tenderly. "And I love you just like that."

I kiss her sweet lips, knowing deep down she's too good for me.

"I don't deserve you," I whisper against her lips.

"I already told you to stop saying stuff like that. You *do* deserve me, Andy. You're worthy of love."

A shiver runs down my spine. I close my eyes, fighting the sudden tightness in my throat and the burning in my eyes. Why can't I be like her, someone who is not afraid to say time and time again she loves me even though I offer nothing in return? *Why am I such a coward?*

"I never thought I'd feel this way about anyone, Jane. But you're my entire world. Even if I'm too fucked up to say the words, I want you to know you're here." I press a fist against my chest. "Forever."

Her beautiful green eyes fill with tears. "That's all I ever wanted. I don't care about words. Your actions say it all."

She rises on her tiptoes and presses her lips against mine. As always, the moment we touch, sparks ignite, and I'm filled with the urge to devour her where she stands. But tonight, I kiss her slowly, savoring her taste as if time stands still. Tingles run down my spine at the same time that my chest overflows with emotion.

I pick her up in my arms and take her to bed. Desire is running rampant through my veins, but I'm in no hurry to cross the finish line. Reluctantly, I detangle myself from her and sit on the balls of my feet. Jane is on her back, watching me with hooded eyes. I take my shirt off first, knowing she loves to run her fingers over my abs, and I love her hands on me.

We don't speak. There's no need for words. I help her out of her top, leaving her pink bra in place. The clasp is on the front, which makes me smile. I flick it open, freeing her lovely breasts. The sight of them almost makes me weep. With greedy hands, I cover them both, kneading them softly. She arches her back, letting out a kitten moan.

Unable to resist such an offering, I lean down and suck one of her nipples into my mouth. It turns as hard as a little pebble against my tongue. I take my time playing with it, alternating between flicking and sucking it.

Jane's fingers find my hair, tangling with the strands. She begins to move her hips in a restless manner, and I know where my attention should divert now. Still latched on her tits, I move my left hand south until I'm cupping her pussy. I should have removed her tiny shorts first, but I got too distracted. I can still find her clit through the layers of fabric though, and judging by how Jane's breathing is coming out in bursts now, she's enjoying what I'm doing.

Even so, I'm surprised when she shouts, "Yes, oh God, yes!"

With a chuckle, I let go of her nipple with soft pop and kiss her hard while she rides the orgasm. Only when her body relaxes against the mattress, I stop moving my fingers.

"Wow, that was so damn good," she breathes out.

"I'm here to please." I kiss her cheek.

"Now it's my turn, which means pants off."

"I love that bossy side of you," I say without thought.

Jane's eyebrows shoot up to the heavens, and then grins. "You do, huh?"

I realize then that I said the *L* word and it was the most natural thing in the world. The fear I'll get hurt again is still there, but refusing to say the word out loud is no protection. The truth is, I love this girl whether I confess it or not.

I roll on top of her, resting my elbows on the mattress. "I love every part of you, Jane, with all my heart."

Her eyes widen. "I thought you couldn't say the words."

"I didn't think I could. I guess you fixed me."

She throws her arms around my neck, trapping me as much as I trapped her. "We fixed each other. I was broken too. You made me whole again."

I lean down and rub my nose against hers. "How about we become one now?"

It's a cheesy line, but Jane doesn't call me out on it. Instead, she answers me with one of her scorching kisses and the promise of a sleepless night. Rest is overrated anyway.

My head is pounding when a blaring sound wakes me from too little sleep. I swear I just closed my eyes. Blindly, I search for the source of the noise—my damn phone. I press the side button, cutting off the annoyance. It starts up the nonsense again a couple of seconds later.

"What the hell." I grab the device and look at the screen with one eye open.

It's not the alarm, it's Coach Clarkson calling. I sit up at once as adrenaline jolts me awake. Coach wouldn't be calling at six in the morning if it wasn't something serious.

"Who is it?" Jane asks softly.

"My coach. Something is wrong."

I press the Answer button. "Hello?"

"Andy Rossi, you'll be the reason I choose to retire early," he grumbles.

"What happened?"

"Did you knock out a student last night?"

I pinch the bridge of my nose. "Yes. He got handsy with my girlfriend."

Jane is now sitting up as well, and looking at me like deer caught in headlights.

"So I heard. It doesn't matter. The dean called me late last night. An official complaint has been made. It seems the guy you punched is related to one of your professors."

"Yeah, I learned that after the fact. What now? Am I in trouble?"

"Yes, son. I'm afraid so. He's being pressured to make an example out of you. You know the school has a zero-tolerance policy for violence, and the fact you're an athlete doesn't bode well."

"How about the school's stance on sexual predators?" Jane asks loudly next to me.

I guess she heard every word Coach said.

"Is that your girlfriend?" he asks.

"Yes."

"Put the call on speaker, please."

I do as he asks. "You're on it."

"Did Derek Norman do anything to you, dear?"

She glances at me briefly and I want to tell her she doesn't need to say anything she's not comfortable with.

But she replies with chin raised high, "Yes, sir. He grabbed my butt. I didn't even see him coming. I'll testify if I need to."

"That's brave of you, Jane, but I don't think it will come to that."

"What's going to happen now?" I ask.

"Professor Norman has asked that you be expelled."

"That son of a bitch. He's as dirty as they come. My father is paying him to make my life hell."

"I'm afraid that without proof, we can't use that argument. I'm calling to let you know we're having a meeting at eight this morning with the dean to discuss this matter. Your presence is required."

"Should I come too?" Jane asks.

"No, dear. You're not a student at Rushmore, so I'm afraid your presence there won't help Andy's case."

I'd rather her not go either.

"I'll be there, sir," I say.

"Good, I'll see you soon. And don't worry, son. I'm not letting an asshat kick one of my best players out of school."

When I end the call, Jane is looking at me with guilt-ridden eyes. "This is all my fault."

"No, it isn't. It's Derek's fault. He shouldn't have touched you."

She drops her eyes to her lap. "I know, but I still feel responsible for the mess you're in now.

I pinch her chin between my thumb and forefinger and bring her face back up. "Hey, stop this nonsense. I'm the one who chose to pound his ass to the ground. It's going to be fine. You heard Coach Clarkson."

"Okay. We'd better get going. I don't want you to be late." She throws her legs over the side of the bed and gets up.

I follow her example, keeping my face a mask of serenity and confidence. In reality, I don't know if Coach Clarkson will be able to save my ass this time. And if he does, I still have no means to pay for my tuition fee next year. Whatever happens today, my future is still looking grim as hell.

FORTY-ONE

ANDREAS

My heart thumps loudly inside of my chest as I stride down the hallway toward the dean's office. I don't regret punching the scumbag who touched Jane. But the possibility that I may get expelled because of it has strengthened the constant anger that simmers in my guts whenever I think about Professor Norman.

I have to keep calm though. Taiyo texted me to say Norman's class was canceled this morning, which means he must be in attendance at this meeting too. I wonder if his nephew will be there as well. Hell, thinking about that bastard brings my blood to the boiling point.

The dean's office looms closer. I have to stop for a moment to take deep breaths. I can't let my emotions take control. My future and Jane's depend on it. She deserves more than a college dropout can give her. I know she's the one. Maybe I've known that for a while, but I was too cowardly to admit it.

With her at the forefront of my mind, I enter the reception area of the dean's office. His assistant lifts her gaze from her computer screen.

"Good morning, Mr. Rossi. They're already waiting for you."

I frown, and glance at the time on my phone. I'm not late. In fact, I'm ten minutes early.

"What time did the meeting start?"

"Oh, about half an hour ago."

"What? Coach Clarkson told me to be here at eight."

The door to the dean's office opens and Coach fills the frame. "Andy, I thought it was you."

"Did the time of the meeting change?"

"No. We wanted to discuss matters before you arrived."

My hands curl into fists. Quickly, the anger swirls up my guts. "Why?"

"Don't worry, son." He steps aside and points inward. "We're ready for you."

My nostrils flare, but I clench my jaw tight and swallow the angry retort in my throat. I have to trust Coach Clarkson.

Keeping my rage in check becomes even harder when I find Norman in the room and his piece-of-shit nephew. A great sense of satisfaction enters my chest when I notice the shiner he's sporting. I know it doesn't make me look good, but I don't fucking care.

"Good morning, sir," I say to the dean, purposely ignoring the douche family.

"Good morning, Mr. Rossi. Please, have a seat." He points at the chair farthest from my accusers.

Coach Clarkson takes the chair next to mine. He's now in between me and the others, probably a safety measure on his part. He knows I have a temper.

"What's going on?" I ask. "Why is that weasel here?"

"Andy...," Coach warns me.

"What? I want to know why he was allowed to come in earlier to this meeting."

"You assaulted my nephew. He doesn't feel safe in your presence. That's why," Norman replies.

"Spare me the victim speech. Your nephew is a perv who thinks it's okay to touch girls without their permission."

"I didn't touch anybody," the rat complains. "You jumped me for no reason."

"That's not the account we have from the event, I'm afraid," the dean interjects.

"Oh, please, sir. You can't take the word of his girlfriend. She's clearly lying," Norman retorts.

I make a motion to stand, but Coach grabs my arm and forces me to stay in place. The dean glances at me briefly, and then turns his attention to Norman and his nephew.

"Miss Alexander's account of the altercation is not the only testimony we have. Miss Vanessa Castro also testified Mr. Derek Norman verbally assaulted her."

"She pushed me!" Derek replies angrily.

The dean twists his face into a scowl. "And we have several eyewitnesses who saw the moment you, Mr. Norman, approached Miss Alexander from behind and touched her inappropriately."

Professor Norman throws his hands up in the air. "They were probably bribed to lie by Andreas and his friends."

"You'd better watch your tongue, Norman. I won't let you smear my players' reputations," Coach grits out.

Norman stands abruptly. "This meeting is absurd. It's clear this school's administration doesn't have any intention of punishing their beloved football players. We're taking this matter elsewhere."

"I suggest you sit back down, Professor Norman," the dean replies sternly.

His eyes flash with cold fury and I doubt his reaction is caused solely by my issue with his nephew.

"We're pressing charges," Norman continues.

His declaration makes Derek's face turn pale. "Uh, I'm not sure if that's nec—"

"Sure, go ahead," the dean interrupts, leaning against his

chair in a relaxed manner. "I'm sure the authorities would love to see what our internal investigation uncovered."

Now it's Norman's turn to look like he's seen a ghost. I sit straighter in my chair. This just got interesting.

"What are you talking about?" he asks.

"You know exactly what I'm talking about. I suggest you rethink your strategy here."

Norman swallows hard, and then turns his hateful gaze in my direction. If looks could kill, I'd be dead. He forgets about his nephew and walks out of the office.

"Uncle?" the idiot finally stands, but he seems unsure if he should follow Norman or not.

"I'm not done with you yet, Mr. Norman," the dean says.

The idiot sits back down and grips the sides of his chair in a vise grip. "Wh-what do you mean, sir?" he asks.

"Mr. Norman, your conduct at a social gathering on campus grounds was appalling, to say the least. Even though Mr. Rossi shouldn't have reacted in the way he did, we must take into account the circumstances. We can't punish him for protecting the victim. You, however, not only violated our code of student conduct, but you tried to cover up your misbehavior with lies."

"It wasn't my idea to press charges against Andreas. My uncle made me do it."

I knew it. That son of a bitch.

"That doesn't excuse your behavior. We're placing you on academic probation."

"What? No! Sir, you can't do that. My parents will kill me."

"Consider yourself lucky that you're only getting probation. I was more than ready to expel you. You can go now, Mr. Norman."

"Yes, sir." He jumps out of his chair as if he were electrocuted, and pretty much runs out of the office.

As soon as he's gone, I ask, "What's going to happen with Norman? You heard his nephew. He's been gunning for me ever since I switched my major. My father put him up to it."

"Coach Clarkson already filled me in on your situation."

I glance at Coach. I haven't told him yet about my change in financial status.

Guessing my train of thought, he says, "Troy told me about what happened between you and your father."

"When?"

"When he called me about last night's incident."

"I don't want you to worry about your tuition fee next year, Mr. Rossi. We'll sort it out. All I want you to worry about for now are your grades," the dean says.

"And football," Coach Clarkson adds.

"Wow, I don't know what to say."

"Let's start with thank you and a promise to stay out of fights from now on," the dean replies.

"Yes, sir. You have my word."

"Good."

"What's going to happen to Professor Norman? He's probably going to fail me in his class out of spite."

"That's an administration issue now. I'm afraid I can't discuss it with you. But rest assured, we know what he's been up to and we'll take the appropriate measures."

Coach Clarkson stands, giving me the cue to the same. The dean has just dismissed us.

I follow Coach out of the office, and when we're in the hallway, I remark, "That went better than I expected."

"It did. We got lucky so many witnesses came forward to support your story."

"I was surprised about that."

"I think you have your teammates to thank for that too. Troy, Danny, and Paris tracked down everyone who was in the room when the incident happened."

The news stuns me. I'm tight with them, but I still didn't expect that.

Coach laughs. "Don't look so shocked, Andy. No one on the team wants to see you gone. We actually like your sorry ass."

"Thanks." I chuckle.

He claps me on the shoulder. "Now, try to stay out of trouble. Got it?"

"Yes, Coach."

"You'd better hit the gym soon. You're looking a little small."

I flex my arm. "What are you talking about? I'm in my best shape."

"Yeah, yeah. We'll see about that during pre-season training."

He walks away, whistling. *Shit.* I don't think I've ever seen Coach in such a great mood. It can't be because he saved my ass from expulsion. Something is up with him. I laugh, shaking my head, and then pull my cell phone out. I need to tell Jane the good news.

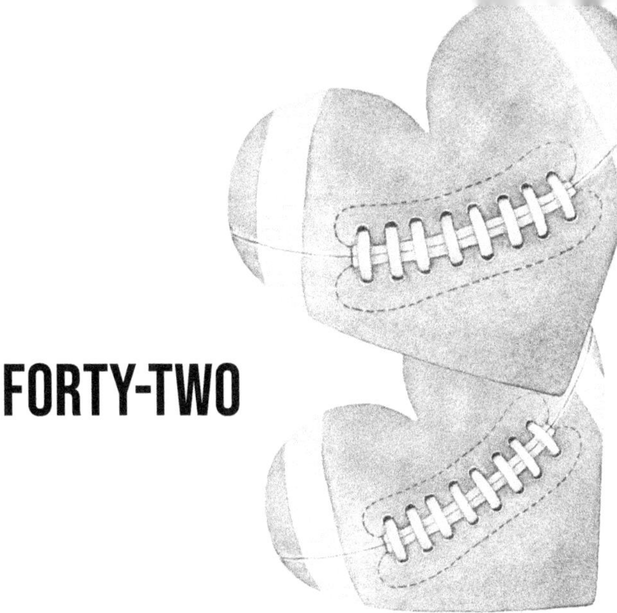

FORTY-TWO

Danny let me borrow his car today. It's a pain that I have to depend on my friends to go places, but until I find a job, I have to suck it up. Jane moved in with her father a couple of days ago, and I miss her more than anything. I loved playing house with her, even with Danny around. I'd ask her to move in with me for good, but since I won't be staying in my apartment for much longer, I can't do that yet.

From not being able to say I love you to wanting to shack up. My life sure as hell has done a one-eighty on me.

I'm on my way to the interview at Sugar Loaf Cupcakes. Ophelia finally came through and scored me an interview with the hiring manager. It's for a paid internship, which is perfect for me.

My mood couldn't be better today. We learned this morning that Norman resigned. Taiyo suspects he was forced to leave, but either way, the fact he's gone is good enough for me. I'm curious, of course, to know what transgressions the dean hinted at, but I will probably never know.

I'm singing along with the radio as loud as I can when Lorenzo calls me. It's midmorning; he should be in school.

"Hey, buddy? What's up?"

"Andy, I don't feel well," he croaks.

My relaxed posture becomes rigid in a flash. "What's going on?"

"I think I have a fever."

"Where's Crystal?"

No point asking where our father is. He wouldn't be home at this hour.

"She's at a spa in Santa Monica. She won't be back until Sunday. Dad is away for business."

Son of a bitch.

"How about the housekeeper?"

"I don't know. I haven't heard her at all today. I think Crystal gave her a few days off."

"Are you saying that viper left you alone in the house?"

"Yeah, it's not the first time. I'm used to it."

I press a closed fist against my forehead. "I don't fucking believe this. Don't worry, buddy. I'm on my way."

"Okay."

Shit. Lorenzo sounded awful. I make a U-turn, and then I call my contact at Sugar Loaf to try to reschedule my interview. Unfortunately, I get his voicemail. *Hell.* I leave him a voice message, hoping he won't be completely put off by me and cancel the interview altogether.

The sign for a drugstore looms in the horizon. I signal to turn. I'm betting there isn't a single dose of cold medicine in my father's house.

I shoot Jane a text before I head into the store. She's in the middle of class, so she probably won't see it until later.

Not knowing what's wrong with Lorenzo, I buy every imaginable medicine I can find. The cashier gives me a funny look during check out, but doesn't offer a comment.

It's a forty-five-minute drive to Malibu, and I'm lucky that traffic is not heavy at the moment, or it could take much longer. I call Lorenzo again to keep tabs on him. He should probably drink water if he has a fever. He doesn't answer the phone this time and that fills me worry. My foot becomes lead on the gas pedal. Danny's car is an old Subaru, but it has juice.

I never thought I'd feel relief to be pulling up in front of my father's mansion. My heart is stuck in my throat when I burst through the front door. I kept the spare key even though I'm cut off from anything he owns. But Lorenzo lives here, and that asshole can't ever take my brother away from me.

"Hello?" I call out, just in case Lorenzo was mistaken and the housekeeper is working today.

My greeting is met by silence. *Goddamn it.* How can my father be so fucking careless as to leave Lorenzo in the care of such a selfish bitch? Who am I kidding? The man cares about nothing but himself.

I make a beeline for my brother's bedroom. He's in bed, passed out. I run to his side, and one touch is enough to tell me he's burning up.

"Lorenzo, wake up."

Whimpering, he blinks his eyes open. "Andy?"

"It's me, buddy. Let's get you out of these clothes. You need a cold shower."

"Why?"

I fish the thermometer from the shopping bag and take his temperature. One hundred three degrees. *Jesus.* He needs medication STAT.

"Because you have a high fever." I rummage inside the shopping again, until I find the Tylenol. "But first, you need to swallow these. Open your mouth."

He does as I say without a fight. Things weren't this easy when he was younger. Crystal always disappeared whenever Lorenzo got sick. Most of the time, the housekeeper would tend to him while I was in school. But at night, I was the one on duty.

"I feel like roadkill," he complains.

"I know. You'll get better soon. I promise."

I help him out of bed, and then I drag him to the bathroom.

"Shower or bath?" I ask him.

"If it's going to be cold, shower."

I turn on the water for him. When I face him again, he's struggling to get his shirt off. It's stuck to his back, thanks to the sweating. I help him out of it.

"There you go. Can you manage your pants now?"

"Yeah, I think so. But you might need to hold my arm."

I steady him and wait. Distracted, I glance at the mirror, and stop breathing. Lorenzo's back is a patchwork of bruises. Some deep purple and fresh. Others are older and already yellowing out.

"What happened to you?" I ask in a tight voice.

Lorenzo tenses in my arm. "Nothing. I fell."

Bullshit. I force him to stand straighter and look into my eyes. "Did Father do this to you?"

Lorenzo's eyes swell with tears. He nods, keeping his jaw locked tight.

My own eyes prickle. I'm overwhelmed with too many emotions to even know which one is the strongest. I'm enraged that the son of a bitch hurt my brother. Furious at myself that I didn't follow up on my suspicion and get the truth sooner. But most of all, the guilt that pierces my chest leaves me weak.

I pull him into a bear hug. "I'm so sorry. I should have known."

"It's not your fault."

"How long has this been going on?"

"Not long. A month maybe."

Long enough. Bile pools in my mouth. His answer breaks me. I failed my brother. I should have spent more time with him. I naively believed that just because our father never laid a hand on him when I was around, Lorenzo was safe. I should have known that monster would turn on my brother. It can't be a coincidence that it started when I switched majors. God. I'm such a fucking idiot.

"Let's get you cleaned up and under the covers. You need to rest." I try to keep my voice steady for his benefit, but I'm screaming inside.

"What are you going to do, Andy?"

"I don't know yet. But one thing I promise you: you won't live under this asshole's roof any longer."

"But he cut you off. No judge will let you become my guardian."

"Don't worry about any of that. What we need now is to get you better."

The shower and the meds work to get Lorenzo's temperature down. I also found him chicken soup in a can that I'm sure was not meant for my father or Crystal. He's sleeping now, which means I'm all alone with my remorse. I can't look at him without seeing those awful marks on his back. I feel like crying, screaming, breaking things.

I walk out of his room and make a beeline for the bar in the living room. My father keeps it well stocked with the most expensive shit. The first bottle I find is of his preferred whiskey. It's brand new. I open the sucker and pour it all down the drain. Then I find a bottle of tequila. He doesn't drink it, but he likes to have top-shelf spirits for his guests.

Without bothering to look for a glass, I remove the cap and take large gulps straight from the bottle. The premium brand goes down my throat smoothly. I keep drinking until it numbs the pain swirling in my chest.

I stagger to the couch nearby and drop like a potato sack. I'm not drunk yet; it's the sense of failure that's dragging me down. I take another large sip, not caring that the tequila is hitting my hollow stomach. My head is getting fuzzy. I'd better take it easy. I can't pass out in a drunken stupor. Lorenzo's fever might return.

I sense a vibration in my pocket, but my clumsy fingers can't fish my phone out fast enough and I miss Jane's call. It's better that way. I don't want her to hear my pitiful voice. I text her saying that I'm going to spend the night here since Lorenzo is alone.

Instead of replying to my text, she calls again.

Hell, I can't ignore her call twice in a row. *Suck it up, man.*

"Hey, babe."

"Hi. How's Lorenzo?"

"Sleeping now. His fever has gone down." I hiccup.

"Andy, are you drunk?"

"Me? Nah. I just had a shot to get rid of the edge."

The lie rolls off my tongue easily, but it still leaves a bitter taste behind.

"It's hard being at your father's house after everything he's done to you, isn't it?"

Hell, she has no idea. If I tell her what I found out, she's going to reach the same conclusion I did. How could I possibly have not known my father was abusing Lorenzo?

"Yeah," I say.

"Do you want me to come over? I can spend the night."

"There's no need, babe. Besides, you have bootcamp tomorrow."

"Are you sure?"

"I'm sure. I want you rested. If you get injured because you're tired, I'll feel responsible."

"That's stupid thinking."

I wince. She has no idea how true that is. I was fucking stupid. I saw the signs something was off at Lorenzo's kart race and I didn't do anything besides ask him about it. He'd never tell me the truth. That's what victims of abuse do. We hide it at all costs.

"Truly. I'm fine," I insist.

"Okay then. But if Lorenzo gets worse, please call me."

"Sure, babe. I will."

I hiss in pleasure. Jane's mouth is wrapped around my cock, sucking me into oblivion. I curl my hands into fists and start to help her out, fucking her mouth.

She laughs. "That's it, Andy darling. Come for me."

My body tenses immediately. That's not Jane's voice. It's Crystal's. This is not a dream, it's a nightmare. My head is fuzzy as hell when I open my eyes. My vision is blurry, but I see her white-blonde head bobbing up and down, my cock in her mouth. My heart is hammering inside of my chest as I watch frozen what's she doing to me. Again.

"Andy?" Jane's strangled voice calls me from near the front door.

She's staring at the scene with big round eyes and jaw slack.

The sight of her is like a jolt of electricity running through my body. I push Crystal off me and jump from the couch. But I drank more than I should have, and the room begins to spin.

"I can't believe this," Jane says before she turns around and runs out of the house.

"Jane. Wait!" I follow her but end up tripping on my two feet and falling to my knees.

Behind me, Crystal cackles. "Oh, how fickle young love is. She didn't even stay to hear your explanation. But then again, actions speak louder than words."

I look at her, ready to commit murder. "What the hell did you do, bitch?"

She flicks her hair over her shoulder. "I didn't do anything. You were the one who texted Jane and invited her to come over. It's too bad your cock missed my tongue so very much. All it took was one lick and you were mine again."

I get back on my feet slowly, breathing hard. "You set me up?"

She raises an eyebrow. "What if I did? You need to

understand, darling. I was your first, and I'll be your last. Everyone knows no one forgets their first and true love."

"You're not my true love!" I take a step forward with fists ready to punch.

"Hmm, all that rage. Go ahead, babe. Hit me. You know I like it hard." She runs her hands over her breasts, as if that sight did anything for me.

It does actually. A bout of nausea hits me, and I end puking all over my father's Persian rug.

"Oh, babe. That's probably going to stain. Don't worry. I'll tell your father the housekeeper did it."

"No, you won't," Lorenzo says. "I like Fatima."

Hell, when did he get out of bed? And how much has he heard of this disgusting exchange?

Crystal gets up from the couch, not bothering to adjust her skintight skirt.

"Whatever. I'm exhausted. The spa was a bust. I'm going to bed."

I watch her leave, bracing my hands on my knees. Lorenzo walks over, looking worried.

"Did you catch a cold too?"

"No, buddy. How are you feeling?"

"A bit better."

"Good. We're getting out of here."

FORTY-THREE

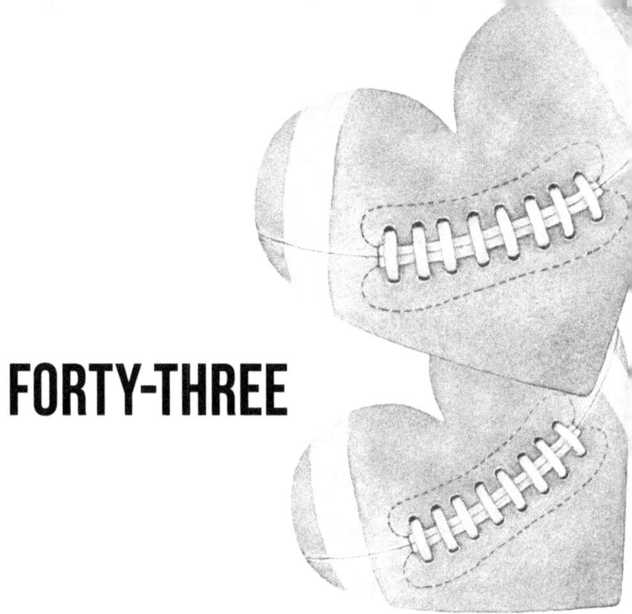

JANE

My eyes are blurry, and I can't see shit in front of me. But even if my vision hadn't been compromised, all I can see is Andy's stepmom giving him a blowjob. My stomach is twisted in knots and I want to throw up, but that means stopping the car and I won't do that. I have to put as much distance as possible between that house and me.

I feel like a fool. Now her presence in Andy's apartment makes sense. How long has he been fucking his stepmom?

Bile rises up my throat and I know I won't be able to keep my food down. I swerve to the side of the road and stop the car. I almost don't open the door in time. My throat and eyes burn as I expel the contents of my stomach. When the dry heaves stop, ugly sobs replace them. I close the door again, but I don't drive off right away. I'm too brokenhearted to do anything but cry my eyes out.

My phone rings, and the car's dashboard shows it's Andy calling. I reject the call and turn my phone off for good measure. Fear that he might have followed me spurs me into action. I have to get out of here. I put the car in Drive and return to the freeway.

The tears are still rolling down my cheeks as I blow past my father's house. I don't know where I'm going until I find myself suddenly in Troy's neighborhood. By some miracle, I manage to get a prime parking spot in front of his house. I stumble out of my car at the same time that the front door opens and Troy walks out.

"Jane, what are you doing here?" he asks.

I break into a run and collide into his arms. He engulfs me in a tight hug, and I hide my face against his chest.

"You're scaring me, Jane. What happened?"

"Oh God, Troy. It's Andy. It was awful."

His body tenses against mine. "What did he do?" he asks in a tight voice.

The sound of tires screeching make me tense. Immediately, I know that Andreas has followed me here.

"Jane!" he yells.

I untangle myself from Troy's arm and face him. "Go away! I don't want to hear it. I've seen enough."

"What have you seen, Jane?" Troy glances at me, fury sparkling in his eyes.

"Jane, please, it's not what you think." Andy is closer now.

Troy steps forward and stands in front of me like a human shield. "You gave me your word you wouldn't hurt Jane. And now she's in pieces. You'd better get the hell out of here before I break your face."

"I'm not leaving until I can explain."

"What's to explain?" I say as step from behind Troy. As destroyed as I am, I'm not going to let him fight my battles for me. "I found your stepmother sucking your dick. That's pretty fucking clear to me."

"You did what?" Troy asks in shock. Then he turns to Andreas. "You son of a bitch."

He pulls his arm back and punches Andy square in the face.

He never stood a chance. He staggers back, fighting to keep his balance. It's in vain. He falls flat on his ass, and almost immediately, blood begins to drip from his busted nose.

"Andy!" Lorenzo screams from the curb.

I didn't see him until now. Why would Andreas bring his brother here to witness this?

He leans on his elbows and touches his bleeding nose before looking at me with such a pitiful stare, it almost makes me cry again. But I bite the inside of my cheek and fight the tears.

From the corner of my eye, I see someone running toward the house. When the porch light catches his frame, I see Danny's blond curls. He stops short when he sees Andy on the ground and Troy's aggressive stance.

"Fuck. What happened?"

"What do you think? Troy sucker punched me," Andreas gets back on his feet.

"What are you doing here, Danny?" Troy asks in an aggressive tone.

"I called him." Andreas pulls his T-shirt up and wipes off the blood from his face.

With wide eyes, Danny glances from him to us. Then he says, "Everybody needs to calm down."

"There's no calming down as long as this asshole is here," Troy spits with venom.

"It was a setup!" Andreas shouts.

"What?" I ask in a high-pitched tone.

"What you saw. Crystal set me up. I got drunk and she found me passed out on the couch. She's the one who texted you and waited until the she heard your car outside to do what you saw her doing."

"Come on. Do you seriously believe Jane will buy that half-baked excuse? Why would Crystal do that?" Troy asks.

"Because she's a fucking psycho!" Andreas pulls his hair back and starts to pace.

"You need to tell them the whole thing, Andy," Danny chimes in.

He gives him such a tortured look that it twists my heart even more. I hug my middle, afraid to know truth. Whatever it is, I know it will be ugly. Andy said he was damaged, unworthy of me. Maybe his feelings are not only related to the abuse he suffered at his father's hand.

"I need to speak to Jane privately first."

"Over my de—" Troy starts, but I cut him off.

"It's okay. I'll hear him out."

"Jane, are you sure?"

"Yeah. I'm sure. Is Charlie home?"

"No, she's visiting Ben."

"Do you mind waiting outside then?"

Troy glances at Andreas and clenches his jaw. "You have five minutes."

Andy glances at his roommate. "Danny, could you please take Lorenzo back to the car? He shouldn't be up and about."

"Yeah, sure." He steps closer to Andy's brother and steers him away from the house. "Come on, buddy."

Lorenzo throws Andreas a confused glance before going with Danny. He's not himself or he would have already pieced things together.

I head inside, and sense Andreas close behind me. He closes the door, but I keep walking until there's a good distance between us. I can barely look at him after what I saw. That scene will be imprinted on my mind forever.

"You heard Troy. You have five minutes," I tell him.

"Crystal was the first woman I slept with. I was fourteen, she was twenty-eight and Lorenzo's nanny."

Andy's admission that he slept with his stepmother is like a punch to my stomach. Everyone has a past, but that one is too cruel.

"I was naïve and thought I was in love with her. I didn't know she was only using me to get to the top prize, my father.

When I caught her in bed with him, it destroyed me. I never felt more betrayed in my life. Then she married the asshole."

"Did you continue to sleep with her after she married him?"

"No. She wanted to, but I couldn't do it. I wouldn't share her with a man I hated so much."

"Are you still in love with her?" I ask in a small voice.

"No, God no. Jane, babe. I have no feelings toward that viper besides loathing. I didn't know what true love was until I fell for you. I'm in love with you."

I let out a ragged breath, my shoulders sagging. "Why did she do that to you?"

"Because she's a jealous bitch. She couldn't accept someone else had taken her place. Little did she know, you didn't take her place. She never had my heart. It has only belonged to one person. You."

He moves closer slowly as if he's afraid I'm going to run away. I won't though, because as crazy as the story sounds, I believe him. I replay all the tender moments we've had, and everything Andy has done for me, and I know in my heart that this man loves me.

I take a step forward. "I wish you had told me that story sooner."

"I couldn't. I never planned for you to know because I'm so ashamed of what I did."

"What you did? Andy, you were fourteen. She was the perv who seduced you. You did nothing wrong, she did. She should be in jail."

"It doesn't matter. I'll carry this stain in my soul forever."

I stop in front of him and punch his arm.

"Hey. What was that for?"

"That's for being such a dumbass. You're not tainted."

His eyes widen, followed by the lopsided curl of his lips. "What's up with you and your brother physically harming me?"

Ah hell. He has blood all over his face, and here I am, giving him a hard time. "I'm sorry. Do you think it's broken?"

"No, it's not broken. But you know what could make it better?"

He snakes his arms around my waist and pulls me flush against his body.

"What?"

"A kiss from you."

I lean forward, but stop short of pressing my lips to his. "She didn't kiss you on the mouth, did she?

He grimaces. "To be honest, I don't know. I was passed out."

"I swear to God that I will kick that skank's ass the next time I see her."

"Hopefully we won't have to suffer her presence ever again. But how about my kiss? I'm still in pain here."

I rise on my tiptoes, but only have the chance to brush my lips against his before Troy comes barging through the door.

"My five minutes aren't up yet, Troy," Andy says without looking in his direction.

"Something happened, Andy," he replies in a sad voice.

Andy turns around, noticing the change in my brother's demeanor. "What now?"

Lorenzo comes in with Danny by his side. He looks like he's in shock, his eyes bugged out and his skin definitely paler.

"It's your father," Danny replies. "He's dead."

FORTY-FOUR

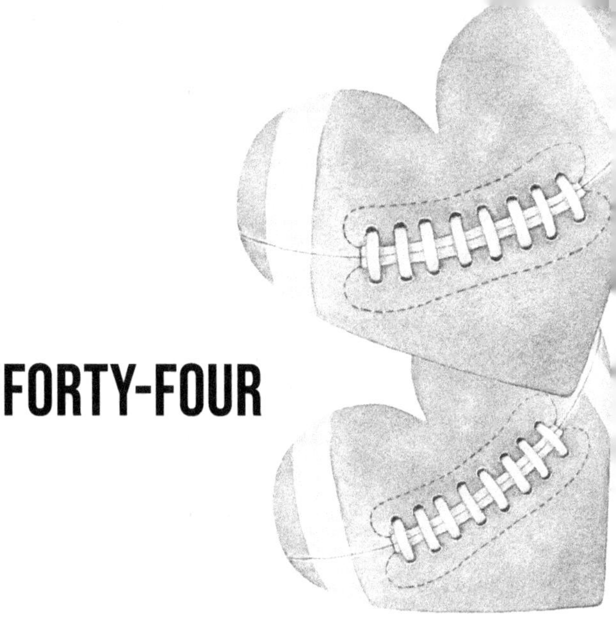

My father is dead, and my biggest regret is that I didn't get to punish him with my bare hands for what he did to Lorenzo. The asshole died of a heart attack while in bed with a hooker and the tabloids had a field day. Crystal played the victim role, milking it to the max. Several gossip magazines booked interviews with the "grieving, wronged widow."

The funeral was yesterday. I would have gone for Lorenzo's sake, but he was the first to announce he didn't wish to attend. It saved me from seeing Crystal face-to-face after the stunt she pulled in front of the cameras, but avoiding her is impossible. She was married to my father, and until all the red tape regarding his estate is over, I'm forced to deal with her.

Today, it's the reading of my father's will. I told Jane she didn't need to come, but she insisted on being by my side. She can't come into the meeting, though. The reading is only for the beneficiaries and their lawyers.

Troy and Danny came as well, plus Jack Morris, Ophelia's boyfriend who is a retired attorney and offered to help. I don't know what's in store for me, or if my father had a chance to cut me out of his will like he said. I don't care about the money though. My biggest concern is Lorenzo. I'll fight tooth and nail to become his guardian. It's a blessing that Crystal never wanted to adopt him, but I wouldn't put it past the bitch to want him if there's financial gain for her.

We arrived at the lawyer's office before the viper, but I know the exact moment she steps into the lavish reception area even though my back is to the door. Jane stiffens next to me and her gaze hardens. I follow her line of sight and see Crystal standing on the other side of the room wearing, for once, a dress that doesn't scream gold digger. She's still playing the demure widow for the cameras. I bet she's hired a paparazzo to follow her around and sell her images to the tabloids.

She doesn't remove her sunglasses, but I can feel her gaze on me. Her red lips curl into a smirk as she steps forward, veering in our direction. My skin crawls, remembering her unwanted touch. I brace for what's going to come out of her mouth. I can't be a hothead here. Jane jumps from her seat and strides ahead before I can stop her.

"Jane," Troy calls.

Fuck. I can't let her cause a scene here, even though she has every right to bitch-slap Crystal. I stand as well and follow her, ready jump in between them. The tension in the air becomes a live entity. This could turn ugly at a moment's notice. But Jane stops before she reaches Crystal, and I realize she wanted to block the snake's path to us. The shy girl I met three years ago has turned into a fierce lioness. Pride and love fill my chest, pushing back the anxiety that has riddled me ever since I found out about my father's death.

I stay a step behind, knowing that whatever Jane wants to do or say, she doesn't need me.

"You'd better think twice before you get any closer to Andy and Lorenzo," she warns Crystal in a defiant tone.

"Really? What are you going to do if I don't?"

Jane snorts. "It would be so easy to let your reporter friends know about your sex predator past. Statutory rape applies to both genders, in case you didn't know."

Crystal's lawyer widens his eyes as he glances at his client. I bet she didn't tell him about her dirty secret.

I told Jane I would only press charges against Crystal if it meant getting Lorenzo's guardianship. Does she deserve to be punished? Yes. But I don't want to subject our family to further scrutiny. I don't begrudge Jane for putting a little fear into that bitch's heart though. I used to be so ashamed of my past with Crystal. I feared people would look differently at me if they knew. But the secret lost its stigma and hold on me once Jane knew the truth. She didn't look at me in repugnance like I feared. On the contrary, I've never felt more loved by her, more connected.

The muscles around Crystal's mouth tense. She doesn't know Jane is bluffing. She harrumphs—the only sound she makes—and turns around to take the farthest seat away from us.

I'm fighting a grin when Jane spins around. It dies completely as I meet Jane's steely gaze. Yeah, she's still furious about the disgraceful trap Crystal set up for us. I can't blame her. I'd be enraged too if the situation had been reversed. I might have actually committed murder.

Both Troy and Danny are glowering in Crystal's direction when we return to our chairs. Lorenzo doesn't know about what went down that night, and I prefer that he never finds out. He has no lost love for the woman though. She embraced the wicked stepmom stereotype to a T.

She doesn't glance in our direction until we're called into the lawyer's office. I lean closer to Jane and kiss her on the lips.

"Thanks for having my back, babe."

"Always."

I get encouraging nods from Troy and Danny. Their support means a lot. They have no idea how much I need the encouragement. I honestly couldn't have survived the past week without them. I'm faking confidence here for Lorenzo's sake, but I'm way out of my depth.

I squeeze my brother's shoulder. "Ready?"

"Yeah. Let's get this over with."

Our father's lawyer is an ancient-looking man, frail in appearance, but his eyes are sharp behind his thick glasses. He's one of the top lawyers in the country, and smart as hell. It's hard not to feel intimidated by him. I keep my confident mask on because I can't show weakness in front of him or Crystal.

Once everyone is seated, he breaks the seal of the envelope to my father's will and begins to read from the document.

It's all filler to me until it comes down to listing the division of assets. Crystal leans forward, clutching her designer bag with a death grip. I can't help the sneer that crosses my face.

When the lawyer announces that Daddy Dearest left his entire fortune to Lorenzo and me, I'm stunned into silence.

Crystal shrieks. "What? That can't be right. I deserve half of it."

"Actually, according to your prenuptial agreement, you were only entitled to five hundred thousand dollars per year of marriage provided that you remained faithful. We have proof that wasn't the case, therefore your prenuptial agreement is void."

She turns to her lawyer and continues yapping like a banshee, but I tune her out, keeping my attention on the man behind the massive mahogany desk.

"What about Lorenzo? Does the will mention anything about him?"

"Your lawyer already made me aware that you wish to request guardianship of your brother. Since you have no close kin, and the will doesn't provide guidance regarding this issue, it's all a matter of following protocol now."

Jack pats me on the shoulder. "I'll take care of everything, son."

Crystal rises from her chair in a huff and turns her ire on me.

"If you think I'm going to let that bullshit will stand, you're sorely mistaken. I'm coming for every fucking penny."

She marches out of the office, blowing smoke through her nose. Her lawyer trails after her in a much calmer fashion. He's probably loving this setback. It means more billable hours. Scumbag.

"Can she get in the way of my guardianship request?" I ask both Jack and my father's lawyer.

"I'm sure her lawyer will try every venue to guarantee she gets some of your dad's money," Jack replies.

"He can try, but he won't succeed. I drafted that contract. It's solid, just like the evidence she had several lovers throughout their marriage."

"So Dad knew she was cheating on him?" Lorenzo asks.

"Yes, he's known from the beginning."

"I don't get it. Why didn't he just divorce her? She was awful."

The older man shakes his head. "I can't answer that, kid."

I'm still dazed from the surprising developments when I walk out of his office. Troy, Danny, and Jane are deep in conversation. I don't need to guess the topic. They abruptly stop talking and glance at me just as I loosen the tie around my neck.

Jane gets up and walks over. "How was it? That awful woman left the office spitting fire from her mouth."

"She got nothing."

Jane's eyebrows shoot up to the heavens. "Really?"

"She cheated," Lorenzo pipes up. "That voided her prenup."

"Does that mean you got everything?" Danny asks my brother.

Lorenzo shakes his head. "No. Andy and I did."

"What? For real?" Troy looks at me, surprised. "I thought your father cut you off."

"So did I. Maybe he didn't have time to change the will. But it doesn't matter. All I care about now is making sure I become Lorenzo's guardian."

"Still. That's huge. Now you don't have to worry anymore about how to pay for your tuition next year," Danny chimes in.

"Honestly, if I had the luxury of not touching his money, I would." I pull the tie off my neck and shove it in my jacket pocket. Everything I'm wearing feels so damn constricting.

Jane steps into me, looping her arms around my waist. "I know you won't need his money soon. You'll make your own way."

Her embrace disperses some of the darkness swirling in my chest. Despite the outcome of today's meeting, I know the war is far from over. Crystal will be back to torment us.

But a lazy smile blossoms on my lips, and a peaceful warmth spreads through my chest. I don't know what I did to deserve this beautiful woman, but I'm so fucking glad that she chose me. I capture her face between my hands and bring her lips close to mine.

"I love you," I say before I kiss her deeply in front of everyone.

In the background, I hear Troy complain. But he'd better get used to it. If I have my way, Jane and I will be one of those annoying couples who can't keep their hands off each other. I've wasted too much time stuck in the void. Jane is my sun, and I'm never letting her go.

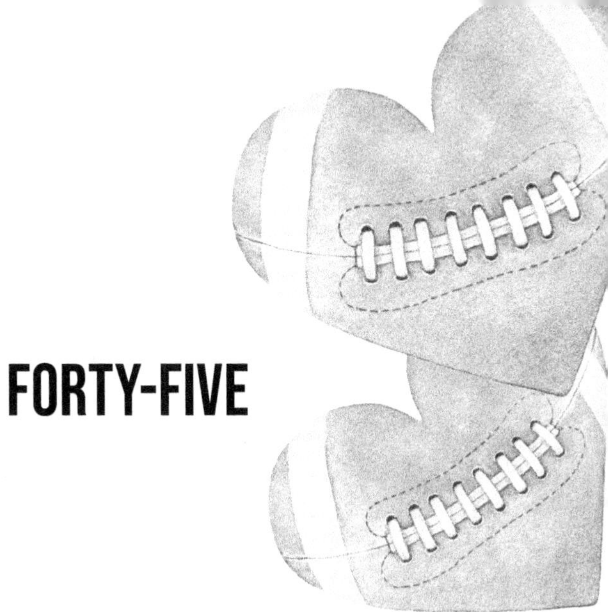

FORTY-FIVE

JANE

The entire week after the death of Andy's father was a whirlwind. I spent every single moment I could with him and was barely home. My father was too busy with work to notice my absence.

I had to skip school in order to attend the meeting with Andy this morning, but unfortunately, I have a test next week that I must prepare for. So I come home, intent on putting a few hours of studying under my belt. I also made plans to meet with Alicia later to practice. I need to take my mind off of upsetting things.

My father's car is parked in front of the house, which surprises me. The sight doesn't fill me with anxiety like it used to whenever I came home and noticed Mom's car in the garage.

I've been meaning to talk to him alone, and this might be my best chance. The door to his office is open, and from the entryway, I hear his voice. He's on the phone. If I try to wait until he's done, he'll probably get into another call. I step toward his office, but a pile of thick envelopes on the dining room table catches my attention. The top one has Stanford's logo on the corner.

Shit. It's thick, which means it must be my acceptance letter. I wonder if that Dad was the one who left those for me or if it was his housekeeper.

There's a sudden lump in my throat as I change course and veer for the table. I don't care about Stanford—I knew I'd be accepted. The other envelopes in the pile are what interest me. I push Stanford's to the side. My breath catches when I see John Rushmore's logo on the next one. It's also a thick envelope.

Impatiently, I rip the paper and pull everything out. The letter on top is what I care about. I scan through the document in a flash, looking for one word: Congratulations.

My heart jolts forward. I read the same line a few times to make sure I'm not seeing things. But it's there. I've been accepted.

"Yes!" I shout, my outburst echoing in the room.

I read the entire letter more slowly now, but not calmer. My hands are shaking, and the thumping inside of my chest seems to intensify.

I'm in. I'm in.

My father finds me while I'm sporting the biggest grin on my face.

"Is that Stanford's letter?" he asks.

His question erases my smile. Grimacing, I lift my face from the letter.

"No. It's Rushmore's." I show him the paper with the school's logo.

He stares at me in silence for several beats. My mind is spinning like a top, working on all the arguments I have collected in the past month to convince him I don't belong at Stanford.

"Are you sure that's where you want to be?" he asks finally.

"Yes, Dad. I'm sure."

He sighs, glancing away. "If that's what you want, I'm not going to stand in your way."

His statement stuns me. I can't believe he's simply giving up after two years of relentless pressure.

"Wait? Really?"

"Your brother came to my office last week. We had a serious conversation about not only you, but our family. I'm not a good parent, I know that. My number one priority has always been my business." He passes a hand over his face and looks at me. "I had no idea what your mother was doing to you, Jane. And I'm so sorry for that."

I drop my eyes to the floor as an old feeling of failure sweeps over me. I've tried my hardest to not think about Mom since I moved out. She's selfish and cruel, and yet a small part of me still wants to make her love me. It's fucking stupid.

"Okay," I say.

Dad comes closer. "Jane, look at me."

I lift my face, fighting to remain calm and not crumble into a mess of tears. I've been doing so well for the past weeks. *Why do I feel like a weak little girl now?*

"I can't go back in time and fix my mistakes, but I promise to make up for them if you let me."

"Is that why you're not going to force me to attend Stanford?"

"In part. But I also realized I was projecting my dreams onto you and that wasn't fair. I was doing the same thing Elaine was doing to you."

"Okay, but what does that mean? Are you going to spend more time in LA from now on?"

"Yes, to start. I also want to get to know you. I have no idea what your likes and dislikes are. You also need to bring Andreas here for an official meet the parent dinner."

"Dad, you know Andy."

"I know him as Troy's friend. I don't know him as your boyfriend." He gives me a meaningful glance.

My cheeks become warmer. He must know I've been spending a lot of time in Andy's apartment.

"All right. I'm not sure when we can make it happen though.

He's still dealing with the aftermath of his father's death."

"My assistant is keeping me updated on that. If he needs any support with anything, you can always ask me."

"Thanks, Dad. You have no idea how much this means to me."

He nods once and seems to run out of things to say. An awkward silence follows. We have a long way to go before we can create some kind of rapport. He took the first step, and now it's my turn to the take the second. I give him a hug, which feels weird. I don't remember ever hugging him, not even as a child. He stiffens at first, but then he throws his arms around my back.

I ease off after a brief moment, and then decide now is the time to tell him about roller derby.

"You said you wanted to know more about me. Are you free three weeks from now?"

"I'll have to check my schedule. Why?"

"I'd like you to come to an event. A sports event."

He raises his eyebrows. "Are you into sports too?"

"Not any sport. Are you familiar with roller derby?"

I expect many reactions from my father, not the goofy grin that splits his face. "Yeah, I'm familiar."

I watch him through narrowed eyes and point at his face. "What's that?"

He shakes his head. "What's what?"

"That dreamy smile."

His face becomes his usual impartial mask. "Nothing. I don't know what you're talking about. Make sure to let my assistant know the date and put a ticket aside for me. I'll be there."

He spins around, sticking his hands into his pockets, and walks back to his office with a new lightness to his steps.

It occurs me that I also don't know much about my father, and I might have unveiled a side of him I had no idea he possessed. Roller derby seems to have been the trigger. Now I have more reasons to look forward to the first game of the season.

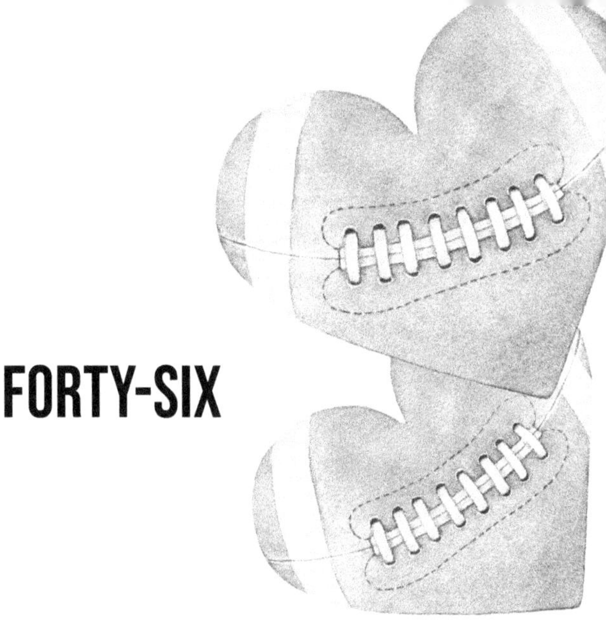

FORTY-SIX

ANDREAS – THREE WEEKS LATER

I'm on pins and needles today, waiting for my damn phone to ring with good news. Lorenzo is sitting on the couch facing the TV, playing a video game with Danny. Jack managed to get temporary permission for Lorenzo to stay with me while we wait on the finalization of my guardianship request. He's supposed to call me today about that, hence why I keep maniacally checking my phone.

I wish Jane were here to keep me calm, but today is her debut roller derby game and she's at the gym with her teammates. She's been my rock during the past few weeks, the only one who managed to keep my head from spiraling into a dark abyss of pessimism.

Crystal and her lawyer haven't gone away. As we predicted, she's fighting the will, and as a last resort, requested to be Lorenzo's guardian as well. Jack guaranteed me she doesn't have a leg to stand on, but there's always the possibility that things could go her way.

I told Jack to use our trump card if necessary. I will disclose how she seduced me when I was a teen if it comes down to it.

I'm not playing around. There's no chance in hell I'll let that snake take Lorenzo away from me.

When the phone finally rings, I jolt in my seat. That's how wound tight I am. It's Jack. I reach for the device in a hurry, almost dropping it to the floor.

"Jack, please tell me you have good news."

"You can pop that champagne, son. The judge has just signed the papers. You're officially Lorenzo's guardian."

I punch the air. "Yes!"

Danny and my brother pause the game and look at me.

"Did you get it?" Lorenzo asks, eyes filled with hope.

"Yes, bro. You're not going anywhere."

He smiles from ear to ear. "Awesome."

"Now we need to find a new place to live."

His grin wilts a fraction. "Why? I love living here. I can't wait to meet some hot college babes."

Danny snorts. "You have a little growing up to do, buddy."

"No way. Girls love a tragic story. They won't be able to resist consoling poor little orphan me." He bats his eyelashes in an exaggerated way as he presses his palm to his chest.

I twist my face into a scowl. "Yeah, yeah. That story will still work when you're out of diapers. You'd better stick to the hot babes in your age group."

Lorenzo rolls his eyes. "Fine. I won't go after any girls from Rushmore, but that doesn't mean I have to stick to the annoying girls in my class."

"Why don't you just concentrate on your studies for now?" I tell him sternly, not sure if I'm pulling it off.

His entire life I was the fun older brother who didn't hesitate to break the rules. Now, I have an entirely different role. I can't let him get away with shit anymore.

"What about karting?" He turns serious. "Am I not allowed to compete anymore?"

"Do you want to?"

I'm surprised by his question. I thought he'd want nothing to do with the sport that reminds him of our father.

He nods decisively. "Yeah. My interest might have started because of Dad, but I actually love to race."

"Well, if that's the case, of course you can compete."

"Great. I can't wait to go back to the tracks." He switches his attention back to the TV and unpauses the game.

I watch him play for a bit, noticing that he's definitely more relaxed now, even though I didn't think he was nervous before. He's better at hiding things than me.

My phone pings, announcing an incoming message from Jane.

Hey, any news?

Yeah. I got it. I'm officially Lorenzo's guardian.

That's amazing, babe. I'm so happy for you.

I'm so relieved. I can't wait to celebrate it later with you.

Me too. If I survive the game. I have to go. I'll see you later. Love you.

I chuckle as I type my reply.

I know.

You're an ass, but I still love you.

"What's so funny?" Danny asks.

"Nothing, man. I just happen to have the fucking best girlfriend in the world."

JANE - A FEW HOURS LATER

Tonight, it's my first game in the roller derby league. From inside the locker room, we can hear the wild clamor from the crowd. It's a full house and the knowledge is wreaking havoc with my nerves. Adrenaline is pumping in my veins as I absorb the rush of excitement that's floating in the air.

I'm still pinching myself to prove that this is real. After four gruesome weeks of intense training, the moment has finally arrived. I'm equal measures excited and terrified. Alicia waits next to me, sporting her game face. This is a special moment, more significant for her than for me. She's keeping the memory of her mother alive. Unlike me, who is trying to forget mine.

I won't think about her tonight. I'm not the daughter she wanted, and hence, she's not the mother I deserve. I haven't heard from her since I moved out, but Grandma told me she's traveling with her new boytoy.

At least Dad is trying to make up for his years of neglect. He promised he'd be here tonight. I got him a ticket and judging by how excited he was this morning when I left the house, I know he's out there.

I told Andy to look for him in the crowd and maybe they could sit together. The expression of sheer horror he gave me was priceless. I wish I had caught it on camera. We still haven't had the official boyfriend dinner, and Andy seems petrified of the idea.

"All right, ladies. Are you ready to kick some ass?" Katja shouts enthusiastically.

"Hell yeah!" we all reply in unison.

"Put it in." She shoots her arm forward, and we all stack our hands, ending our team huddle with a war cry.

Then we're putting our mouthguards on, checking the straps on our helmets, and for me, trying not to puke. I'm so nervous, I'm not sure if I know how to skate anymore. I let everyone go ahead of me, but Alicia notices I'm stalling and throws her arm over my shoulders.

"Come on, girlie. This is going to be awesome."

She drags me with her, and when we emerge from the locker room and I see the crowd filling the entire gym, I balk.

"Oh my God. I think I'm going to pass out."

"No, you're not. Come on, they're going to announce us."

We skate faster to join our teammates. I purposely don't glance at the stands, fearing that if I see a familiar face, it will make me even more nervous.

Stop freaking out, Jane. You got this.

The announcer says our team's name, and then I really have to get over my pre-game jitters. I hop onto the banked track for the greet-the-crowd round. I can't avoid looking at the stands now, and the first thing I spot is a homemade sign with hearts, roller skates, and Jane Blaze in big glittery letters. My heart somersaults to my throat when I see who is holding the sign. Andy.

The butterflies in my stomach fly away as sudden calm washes over me. Seeing the love of my life there supporting me has that effect.

I barely notice my other supporters next to him. My eyes remain glued to Andy as I blow past him. I'm in the middle of the pack, so I can't skate closer to the railing, but I blow him a kiss.

We finish our lap and then wait for our adversaries to do the same. We're playing against Bay Hurricane, Scary Samantha's team, which is the strongest in the league. We might lose tonight. I'll probably get a lot of bruises. But I wouldn't trade this moment for anything in the world. This is where I belong.

ANDREAS

I have lost my voice. I never screamed so much in my entire life. Or yanked my hair back so often. I probably lost a good chunk of it. Lorenzo and Danny had to restrain Troy and me on several occasions when Jane got roughed up on the track. It'll take time to get used seeing her get hurt. It never occurred to me she probably felt the same way when Troy got sacked on the field, or I collided with an opponent.

Second Time Around Divas lost the game, but it was close. After they run their final lap, Jane veers straight to where we're standing, sporting the biggest smile on her face.

I reach over the railing and pull her to me for a scorching kiss. I don't care that Troy and her grandma are standing right next to me. The crowd near us goes crazy, wolf-whistling and shouting.

When I pull back, Jane's face is redder than before.

"What was that for?" she asks out of breath.

"Can't I congratulate my girlfriend?"

"We lost." She laughs.

"Not in my book." I grin from ear to ear.

I won't tell her my second reason for kissing her like that. I want all those baboons ogling her to know she's taken.

"It was an amazing game, dear. I'm so proud of you," Ophelia pipes up.

"Thanks, Grandma." She turns to Troy. "Have you seen Dad?"

"No. I'm sure he will find you outside."

"Jane, come on!" Alicia waves her over.

"I'm coming." She looks at me. "I have to go. Meet you out front in fifteen minutes?"

"I'll be there."

I watch her skate away and join her teammates Alicia and Katja, who hug her from both sides. Someone elbows me hard on my arm.

"Get your shit together, man. You're drooling," Troy says.

"I wasn't, jackass."

Charlie shakes her head. "Don't mind him, Andy. He still can't handle seeing you all chummy with Jane."

Troy crosses his arms. "I'll never get used to that."

The crowd begins to shift toward the exit, and we do the same. It takes at least ten minutes to get out of the stands since we were closest to the railing. The majority of people are hanging outside the building where a few food trucks are serving morsels that make my stomach growl.

"I'm hungry," Lorenzo pipes up. "Can we see what they have?"

"Uh...."

I want to linger close to the exit, so I don't miss when Jane walks out.

Sensing my hesitation, Danny offers, "I'll go. I'm starving too."

"Hey, look. It's Fred and Sylvana," Charlie says.

I follow her line of sight, and sure as shit, the tall blond dude who had the hots for Jane is standing not too far from us, talking to his cousin.

Charlie waves and calls his name. I scowl. *Fucking great.*

"Try not to murder the guy," Troy tells me under his breath.

"As long as he stays away from Jane, I won't."

The duo walks over and take turns hugging Charlie. Troy— the traitor—shakes hand with him. I shove my hands in my pockets and try not glower... *too much.*

Fred briefly glances at me, but does nothing to acknowledge my presence, not even a nod. Whatever. Not like I'll ever be buddies with him.

Someone sneaks up from behind me and covers my eyes. It only takes me a second to recognize Jane's perfume.

"Guess who?" she asks in a different voice.

"Harley Quinn," I joke, and she pinches my arm.

I spin her around and trap her in my embrace, blocking her view of Fred on purpose.

"Were you testing me, babe?" I ask.

Her eyes dance with mischief. "Maybe."

"Hi Jane. Great game," a girl says.

She breaks free from my arms and looks over my shoulder. "Hey, Sylvana. I didn't see you there. Hi, Fred."

I step aside and let Jane talk to them for a moment. I'm jealous, but letting it show would give the blond too much power. It'd let him know I'm afraid to lose Jane to him, which is not true, at least not exactly.

I *am* afraid to lose her, but not to another guy. If that happens it'll be because I fucked up, which means I have to bring my A game to this relationship. Jane doesn't need another watchdog. She already has Troy. She needs a man who will support her decisions and let her grow as an individual. I will spend the rest of my days being that person for her.

She keeps her conversation with Fred and Sylvana brief, and then we go after Danny and Lorenzo. Before we locate them, another person finds us. Jane's father.

Hell and damn. I was hoping to avoid the man tonight. Wishful thinking.

"Dad, you came." Jane drops my hand to hug him.

He kisses the top of her head, the most affectionate gesture I've seen him do around people. I always had the impression he was a robot without a soul. I guess he's getting better, which makes me happy for Jane and Troy. They deserve a parent who cares. Like I had Mom.

"Why are you surprised? I said I would."

"Nice to see you, Jonathan," Ophelia greets him.

"Likewise." He nods, and then he switches his attention to me.

I try not to squirm under his scrutinizing gaze.

"Andreas Rossi, finally we meet again."

He offers me his hand, which I shake in an automatic reaction. I don't know why I'm freaking out, but I am.

"Sir."

"Sir? You can keep calling me Jonathan."

"Oh, okay. Sure."

"How about we pencil in that dinner we've been meaning to have?"

I swallow hard, but when Troy chuckles next to me, I forget my nervousness for a second to give him a death glare.

"What's so funny?"

He shakes his head, grinning. "Oh, nothing."

"How about tomorrow? Does that work for everyone?"

"It depends who you're including in your invitation," Ophelia chimes in.

Embarrassment seems to wash over the man's face. I suspect he forgot the feisty lady was nearby.

"Er… all of you, naturally," he replies.

She nods. "Good. Jack and Louis are dying to visit your house."

Troy groans and now it's my turn to laugh.

"Shut up," he says.

"I didn't say anything."

Glowering, he replies, "I know what you were thinking."

I snort. "Sure, you're a Vulcan now."

"I can't believe you know what a Vulcan is," Charlie pipes up.

Jane steps next to me and loops her arms around my waist. "Andy is secretly a nerd."

I wrinkle my nose. "Not quite. I just know my pop culture references."

"Well, I'll let you know the time tomorrow," Jonathan continues.

"We were planning on going somewhere to celebrate my game and the fact Andy got guardianship of his brother. You're more than welcome to come."

The man glances into the distance briefly, almost as if he's searching for someone in the crowd, and then back at Jane. He seems torn.

"I'd love to come, honey, but I have a prior commitment."

"Oh, okay. We'll see you tomorrow then."

"Perfect."

He kisses her forehead, says goodbye to the rest of us, and then strides away. He's definitely in a hurry.

"If we're heading somewhere, we'd better go now. These old bones can't handle too much excitement," Ophelia says.

"I need to find Lorenzo and Danny. Do you know where we're going?" I ask.

"Yeah, I'll text you the address. Go find them and meet me there. I have to get Grandma in the car," Troy replies.

"All right."

Jane drops her arms from around me, making me miss her warmth in an instant. I lace our fingers together and bring our joined hands to my lips to kiss her knuckles.

"Where do you think they went?" she asks.

I look over the sea of people to check out the assortment of food offerings. "Hmm, if I were to guess, I'd say they went for hotdogs."

"Really?"

"Oh yeah. Lorenzo doesn't care for experimental cuisine, and Danny loves all-American junk food."

"Oh yeah. Pringles Boy."

"You know about that nickname?"

"Charlie told me."

I find the diner food truck and make a beeline for it, while I gather the courage to broach a subject that's been nagging me since Jack told me I was Lorenzo's guardian. I never asked Jane how she felt about it. It's a lot of responsibility, and maybe she wants no part in it.

"Andy, you're squeezing my hand."

"Oops, sorry."

She stops, forcing me to do the same. "What's up? You got tense suddenly."

Damn. My girl is too observant. I can't really hide anything from her.

"You know that now that I'm Lorenzo's guardian, my life will be very different."

"Yeah, so?"

"So? I'm pretty much a parent now. And you're with me, which means…. Hell, I don't know. I never asked you if you wanted that kind of responsibility."

Jane's lips make a perfect *O*.

"Andy, I'm with you for better or for worse. Lorenzo is your brother. There's no doubt if I want to be part of his life or not. It's a hell yeah. He's my family now too."

I can't help the tears that well up in my eyes, or how my chest feels that much lighter. I pull her to me and kiss her soundly for as long as she lets me. When we finally break apart, we're both short of breath.

"Do you feel better now?" she asks.

"Yeah, babe. Much."

"Good. To be honest, I thought you were going to say something about Fred."

I frown. "Why? I was on my best behavior."

"I know. And that surprised me."

"I won't deny it, jealousy reared its ugly head for a moment. I'm not perfect, babe, but I'm trying to be the man you deserve."

She cups my cheek tenderly. "You *are* the man I deserve."

"If you say so, but I think one can always become better."

Narrowing her eyes to slits, she asks, "What are you saying, Andy? Is that a hint that I need to improve?"

I chuckle, reaching for her face to rub my fingers over her lips. "No, my sweet Jane. You are perfect."

She wrinkles her tiny nose. "No one is perfect."

"You are to me."

I lean closer to kiss her again, but an oversized ice cream cone appears between our faces.

"Andy, look what Danny bought me."

I step back, wiping the bit of whipped cream from the tip of my nose. The white stuff is all over Lorenzo's face.

"What the hell did you get him?" I ask. "That thing is bigger than his face."

He shrugs. "He wanted it. What was I supposed to say? No?"

"Yeah. We're going out to dinner and that much sugar is going to put him in a coma."

Jane chuckles next to me. "He's twelve, Andy, not five."

"You laugh now, but you'll wait and see."

She rises on her tiptoes and kisses me on the cheek. "You'll be a wonderful father. I can't wait to see it."

"Skipping the early years and going straight to pre-teen. Piece of cake." I laugh.

"And you love cake." She smiles.

"Not as much as I love you."

"I know."

***** THE END *****

Thank you for reading *Heart Breaker*! The next story in the series is about Danny! Read his story in *Heart Starter*.

HEART STARTER

REBELS OF RUSHMORE BOOK THREE

My plans were simple. Graduate from college, get a job, and not worry anymore if I can make next month's rent.

It turns out I might have a shot of getting drafted to play in the NFL, and nothing will distract me from that goal.

I didn't count on Sadie Clarkson wrecking my plans. Our first meeting was explosive, to say the least. Now I can't stop thinking about her sassy attitude or sexy mouth.

On top of being a distraction I don't need, she's also the coach's daughter and off-limits.

But forbidden fruit always tastes better. She might cost me everything I've worked for, and yet I'm willing to risk it all.

My sanity.
My heart.
My world.

ONE

SADIE

I blink my eyes open and don't know where I am at first. Then I hear a faint and constant beeping sound, which draws my attention to the machine to my right. It's monitoring my heartbeat. Fragments of memory rush through my brain, and then I remember being at the pub with my teammates after we won the championship game.

There were some wankers at the pub, drunk out of their minds. They followed Anika and me when we left, and then… *fuck*. The flash of a steely blade, the white-hot pain in my side.

"Sadie, darling. You're awake." My mother moves into my line of vision, face scrunched in worry, making the lines on her forehead deepen.

"Apparently. I could be dreaming though," I croak.

"Even heavily sedated, her sarcasm is intact. She'll live, Mum," my brother Dominic pipes up from somewhere in the room.

"Piss off, Dom," I grit out and try to sit up. A sharp sting flares in my side. "Bloody hell."

"Sadie, you can't move. You'll open your stitches."

Mum fiddles with the bed's control panel, raising the back until I'm in a comfortable sitting position.

"How is Anika?" I ask.

Her gaze narrows, getting darker with anger. Mum is usually a mellow person; she rarely gets aggravated, but when she does, you'd better pray you're not the one in her path of wrath.

"Distraught, naturally. She came to visit you yesterday. Brought you those flowers." Mum points at the vase with white lilies, my favorite.

"And the motherfuckers who attacked us?"

"In custody."

A wave of relief washes over me. "Good."

"Yes. But what were you thinking, Sadie? Jumping in front of someone carrying a knife? You could have been killed."

Anger bubbles up my throat. "What was I supposed to do? Stand aside and let them stab my best friend instead?"

Something like remorse flashes in my mother's eyes. She steps back, and then Dominic walks over to take her place next to the bed.

"Come on, Mum. Let Sadie rest before you lay on the guilt-trip," he says with an easygoing smile, but his eyes are serious.

I must have scared them to death. The knowledge makes me feel guilty, but I don't regret my actions.

"I called your father," she tells me, and in a flash, I'm as rigid as a board.

"Why?"

"Sadie." Her tone is reproachable. "He loves you. You really ought to let go of your resentment."

I clench my teeth so hard it hurts my molars.

"What did he say?"

"He wanted to come see you."

"What? No way." The heart monitor starts beeping faster, picking up on my distress.

"I told him there's no need," Mum adds quickly.

I sag against my pillow, feeling the tension whoosh out of my body. I can't handle seeing Dad on top of everything else.

"And he just accepted that, right?" I can't help the bitterness that seeps into my voice.

Mum and Dominic trade a look, and immediately the small hairs on the back of my neck stand on end. Bad news is coming my way.

"He did on the condition that you attend college in the US, like we agreed when your father and I…." She looks away.

"You can say divorce, Mum. It's been twelve years. And I told you I didn't care about your agreement. I don't want to study in the States. Dominic didn't."

He puffs his chest out. "That's because I'm a genius and got into Oxford. Don't be a hater. Besides, I know what you're saying is pure rubbish. I've seen you staring at Rushmore's brochure for ages. Their football program is legendary. You'd be a fool to pass up that opportunity."

I try to cross my arms, but it hurts when I move. I settle for pouting like a five-year-old. "They call it soccer over there. I can't take them seriously when they don't use the correct name for the sport."

He rolls his eyes. "Yeah, sure. Let's go with that horse-shite excuse."

Mum hits him on the chest with the back of her hand. "Dom, language."

He scowls. "What? Sadie can drop f-bombs and I get told off when I use 'shite'?"

I smirk. "You didn't almost die."

He sticks his tongue out at me like he's a little boy, not a twenty-year-old man.

He's not lying though. John Rushmore does have a wicked football program. It's why—despite my protests—I applied. As much as I want to stay mad at my father and piss him off, I can't do so at the expense of my future.

"I can't make that decision right now," I say, just to be

difficult. "I'm still recovering from getting shanked, for crying out loud."

Dominic's lips curl into a knowing grin. "California, here we come, babe."

I shake my head, struggling to keep my scowl. "You're delusional."

He knows me too well. There was never a doubt that I'd go to Rushmore, but protesting until the end is how I roll. I'm too stubborn to acknowledge defeat.

DANNY– A MONTH LATER

My heart is about to burst from my chest when I skid to a halt in front of Coach Clarkson's office. He called me in even though we don't start preseason training for another week. I had a shift at Three Dudes Smoothies and ended up staying past my shift due to the crowd, so I had to race here.

I knock on the door, still breathing hard.

Shit. He's going to think I'm out of shape.

"Come in," he says.

"Hey, Coach. Sorry I'm late."

He turns his gaze away from his computer screen and frowns. "What in God's name happened to you?"

I remove my uniform hat and wipe the sweat off my forehead. "We were busy at work today, and then I had to ride my bike. My car is in the shop."

He swivels around in his chair and bends over to retrieve a bottle of water from his mini fridge. "Here. I can't have you passing out on me due to dehydration."

"Thanks, Coach."

I twist off the cap as I take a seat. Then I pretty much inhale the whole water bottle in the blink of an eye. I was parched.

"Do you need another one?" Coach asks with the hint of a smirk.

"I'm okay. Thanks."

"All right, I won't keep you waiting. You must be wondering why I asked you to see me before preseason training starts."

"Yeah. I'm not in trouble, am I?"

Worry has been consuming me since I got his call. I'm on a sports scholarship, which is the only reason I can afford to attend Rushmore. If that went away, I don't know what I'd do.

"No, of course not."

"Nothing wrong with my grades?"

"Your grades are fine. You're probably the best student on the team. Really, Danny, relax."

I sink against the back of the chair as relief sweeps over me.

I had been obsessing about this meeting, much to Andy's amusement. He says I stress too much. I do, but only about things that matter. My status on the team is one of the things I worry about. It's my ticket to a better life. He experienced what it was like to be in my shoes for a hot minute, and he almost lost his mind. But I've lived in constant survival mode my whole life.

"Okay, so why am I here? Do you need something from me?"

"I want to talk about the NFL. Have you ever considered going pro?"

My heart suddenly speeds up, and my tongue gets stuck to the roof of my mouth. After a moment, I reply, "Yeah, of course. Isn't every kid's dream to play in the NFL?"

He chuckles. "True. But in your case, it could become a reality."

"How so?"

He furrows his eyebrows again. "Danny, come on. Surely you know you're one of the best quarterbacks we've ever had on the team."

"Troy was pretty good too. Honestly, I'm only trying to fill his shoes and not mess up, sir."

I'm not only saying that because Troy is one of my best

friends. He legit kicked ass during his time as the Rushmore Rebels' quarterback.

"Troy was good, but he lacked focus and ambition. I suspect his heart wasn't one hundred percent in the game. You, on the other hand, have a fire I haven't seen in all my years of coaching. When Troy got injured, you hit the ground running. If it hadn't been his senior year, I'd have benched him in favor of you."

I'm at a loss for words.

"Wow."

Coach laughs. "Another great quality you have. Humbleness. You're not cocky, and you always put the team above your own interests. I appreciate that. But, son, this year, I want to see you shine."

"Yes, sir."

"A buddy of mine is a scout for the NFL. He saw your tape, and he was impressed. He's interested, which means other recruiters will soon be as well. However, if you want to give the NFL a shot, you have to train harder than before, be focused solely on the game and your academics. No excessive partying, no distractions."

"I want to make the NFL happen, sir. I'll do anything. No parties, no distractions. You tell me what I need to do, and I'll do it."

He nods. "That job of yours. I assume it's only during the summer?"

It wasn't, but I can't tell Coach I was planning on keeping my job at Three Dudes Smoothies for as long as I could. I want him to know I'm committed to the goal. So what if I have to live on a tighter budget? I've made do with less before.

"Yes, sir."

"Good. Well, that's it for now. Enjoy the rest of your summer break."

"Will do, sir. And thanks for the opportunity."

He shakes his head. "Don't thank me, Danny. You've earned it."

TWO

SADIE

I'm bleary-eyed when I push my trolley through the arrival gate of LAX and search the crowd. In the end, Dominic didn't come with me. He got the internship he'd been vying for, and I couldn't ask him to drop that to accompany me on this trip, only to be a buffer between Dad and me.

It's easy to spot my father in the sea of people. He's taller than most, and he always wears a baseball hat with his school's logo on it. I haven't seen him face to face in three years, and our online calls have been sparse. I simply never had much to say to him. Now I'm back to my home country—a place I never wanted to leave to begin with—and it feels surreal. I'm not sure if I belong here anymore.

He has a tentative smile on his scruffy face as he walks over. "Hi, Sadie."

"Hey, Dad."

He circles around the trolley with the clear intention to pull me into a side hug, but he stops abruptly and asks, "Is this okay, or are you still healing?"

It's hard to school my face into neutral. I don't like to talk about my battle wound. I thought I was fine when I was in the hospital, but when I returned home, my brain decided having PTSD was the way to go.

"It's been six weeks. I'm fine."

He hugs me awkwardly, and I can't help the stiffness of my body. Mercifully, he steps back fast.

"Let me help you with that."

He takes the trolley from me, which was acting like a shield. With that gone, I can increase the distance between us. I can't stray too far, though, or he'll notice. I clutch the straps of my backpack tighter while I pretend to people watch.

"How was your flight?" he asks.

"It was good. The seat next to me was empty."

"I love when that happens. Did you manage to sleep?"

"Couldn't. I was too wired."

"Nervous?"

I glance at him, frowning. "About what?"

"New school, new teammates."

I shrug. "It's not like this is my first rodeo moving across the ocean and starting from scratch."

He falls silent after that, which is what I wanted. The jab was intentional. Before my parents' divorce, Dad and I were close. I was your typical daddy's girl. Mum decided to move back to England after the split, and Dad agreed with giving her full custody of me and my brother. I begged to stay and live with him. I didn't want to move to a country I knew nothing about, save that it rained a lot. And according to my six-year-old mind, Mum was to blame for breaking up our family. She was the one who wanted to move back to her country. Naturally, things were way more complicated than that, but still, I resented my father for not fighting for me.

The sun has yet to set in California, but back in London, it's way past my bedtime. I can't wait to crash into a bed, any bed.

"I bought In-N-Out Burgers if you're hungry." Dad offers me a paper bag once we're in the car.

I was determined to keep up with the grumpiness, but a grin unfurls on my lips. "I haven't had one in years."

Eagerly, I take the bag from him and dive in.

"I remember you and Dominic ate so much the first time, you both had a tummy ache."

I wish Dad would stop reminiscing. Those were the happy days before the implosion of our happy family, and there's no point in dwelling there.

"I want to ask if you changed your mind about staying over for a couple of days, and give us a chance to catch up."

My stomach twists into knots, forcing me to stop chewing for a moment. "Nope. I haven't changed my mind. I'd like to get settled in my dorm room as soon as possible. Preseason training starts in two days. Besides, I think it's best if we keep our relationship on the down low at campus. I don't want to be treated differently because my father coaches the American football team."

"It's just called football, honey."

"No, *I* play football." I shove a fry into my mouth.

I'm only saying that to annoy him. I obviously know the difference in terminology.

"I like your accent. It's cute."

"I hope it'll help me get laid as much as it helps Dominic whenever he comes to visit you."

"Sadie!"

"What? Americans love a British accent."

It's hard to keep a straight face when Dad is redder than a tomato.

"I thought you had a good head on your shoulders," he grumbles.

"Will you relax? I was just taking the piss. I have no intention on dating. Football will be my only focus."

"And your classes too."

I roll my eyes. "Sure, and classes."

"We need to go shopping for cars. Any model you have in mind?"

Tension sweeps over my body. I forgot that owning a car is a must in America. I hate to drive mainly because I suck at it.

"Nope. Anything will do."

"Okay. I'll start looking online and then send you links."

"Brilliant."

"Are you sure you want to go to the dorms now?"

I nod. "Yeah, I might as well get settled. I've already emailed my roommate and told her I'd be moving in today. It's all arranged."

"Okay, Sadie. If that's what you want," he says, resigned.

I look out the window, not feeling an ounce of satisfaction in getting my way.

Since I only brought two suitcases and a backpack, getting settled in my minuscule dorm room took less than five minutes. I didn't unpack, just shoved my suitcases under the bed. Dad didn't linger, for which I had to thank my roommate, Katrina Montana, an extremely enthusiastic girl from my original hometown of Austin, Texas.

As soon as my father left, she started talking a mile a minute. "I'm so excited to finally meet you, Sadie. I had no idea your father was the football team's coach. You know what that means, right?"

"No idea." I flop on my bed, trying to give her a clue that I'm bone-tired and in no mood to chat right now.

"You'll get access to all the cute boys on the team." Her voice rises to a shriek.

"I guess. I don't really care, to be honest. I'm here to play football, not chase jerseys."

"Well, you'll be chasing jerseys anyway. I mean, when you play soccer, you're technically chasing jerseys."

Oh God. She's one of those Miss Smarty-pants girls. I pull a pillow over my head and groan.

"Are you okay?" she asks.

"Please don't take this the wrong way, but I'm super tired. It's been a long day."

"I'm so sorry. Of course you are. You probably want to take a nap before the party."

I pull the pillow away from my face and lean on my elbows. "What party?"

"The preseason party at the Red Barn. It's a jock thing. You don't know? The girls' soccer team is always there."

Ugh. I've received a few emails from Vanessa Castro, the team's captain, which I ignored. I was not in a good place emotionally. I was afraid she'd mention the attack in them. Now I know it was stupid to be so cowardly. I hope my radio silence didn't shine a bad light on me; I don't want to be perceived as a liability to the team.

"I've been traveling all day. I'm sure I was invited and just missed the email."

"Yeah, I'm sure. What time do you want me to wake you?"

All I want is to sleep until tomorrow, but now I have to do damage control. If this is a preseason kickoff party, my presence is a must.

"Whenever you're ready to go. I need a ride anyway, as I haven't gotten around to getting a car yet."

"Sure. Will do."

Katrina leaves the room, and not a second later, I pass out.

THREE

"Earth to Danny. Hello!" Andy snaps his fingers in front of my face.

"What?" I glare at him.

"Please don't tell me you're still worried about your car."

I had to park in a heavy pedestrian traffic area, and knowing how drunk everyone gets at parties on campus, I wasn't happy. The last time I drove, a few idiots used the hood as a make-out spot and left a big dent behind. So the truth is, I *am* still stressing, but if I confess, Andy won't stop bugging me.

"No," I lie.

"Where was your head, then? I've been talking to myself for the past five minutes."

"So the usual for you, then?" Paris pipes up with a smile on his face, joining us in the small space we carved out in the jam-packed area.

"Bite me, Paris," Andy retorts. "Flying solo tonight?"

Andy's question erases Paris's amusement in a flash. "No, Lydia stopped to chat with some old friend from her high school."

"I'm shocked she has friends," Andy mutters before he takes a large sip of his beer.

Paris doesn't reply. Either he didn't hear it or he's choosing to ignore Andy's comment. He knows his longtime girlfriend is no one's favorite. He's a pretty chill guy, friendly and outgoing. The little I've seen of his girlfriend suggests she's the opposite, but I won't join the hate bandwagon based solely on first impressions.

I take a sip of my beer—the only one I'm drinking tonight— as I scan the crowd. The Red Barn preseason party is one of the most popular events on campus, and it's bursting at the seams with people. Most in attendance are part of an athletic program or a Greek. Last year, I got totally trashed. It was my first college party, after all. But after my convo with Coach Clarkson, I'm one hundred percent dedicated to not letting Rushmore's social life deviate me from my goals.

"Where's Jane tonight?" Paris asks Andy.

"She has a game out of town. She'll be back tomorrow."

Paris drops his jaw, widening his eyes in an exaggerated surprised expression. "And you let her go?"

I snicker when Andy's spine goes taut and he clenches his jaw in displeasure. "What are you insinuating, buddy? I trust my girlfriend completely."

"Gee, relax. I'm just busting your balls. It doesn't feel great, does it?"

Andy grumbles before chugging his beer. Since getting together with Jane, this is his first big college party without her, and I can already tell he's in the mood to get wasted, which sucks for me. Drunk Andy is a fucking pain in the ass.

Despite there not being enough space to walk from one side to the other in the open room without using elbows to make way, I can still see distinct division lines among the crowd. Everyone is hanging out with their own teammates, groups, or cliques. However, that will change as the evening progresses and alcohol consumption increases.

Not far from us, I spot the girls from the soccer team. They're cool chicks, drama-free, and focused as hell on their game. It's no surprise they're at the top of their league. The same can't be said about their counterparts. Rushmore's men's soccer team not only sucks but also their players are mostly dicks, especially their captain, Nick Fowler.

I catch sight of him making his way to Vanessa Castro, the captain of the women's soccer team. He gets into her personal space and whispers something in her ear. It's obvious by her body language that she's not happy about the proximity or whatever Nick has to say.

"Shit. The douche king has arrived," Andy sneers.

Paris follows his line of sight. "What the hell is that weasel doing?"

He stands to his full height, body tense all of a sudden. Paris is a beast, the tallest player on our team and as strong as a bulldozer. He seems ready to run interference, but Vanessa doesn't seem to need his help after all. She says something to Nick that sends him away scowling. Unfortunately, he's coming in our direction now.

When he's within earshot, Andy speaks up. "Need some aloe vera for that burn, Nick?"

His expression turns murderous, but he quickly covers it up with an arrogant smirk. "Don't know what you're talking about, Rossi. Vanessa and I were chatting about the upcoming season."

"Not what it looked like from here," Paris replies, his tone harsh and cold.

Nick's eyebrows arch. "Sounds like you're jealous, Andino. Does Lydia know about your other interests?"

It's Murphy's Law that Lydia would show up just in time to hear Nick's comment.

"What other interests?" She loops a possessive arm around Paris's waist.

"Nothing, babe. Come on, let's get a drink. The air here has gotten rotten."

He steers her toward the nearest bar before Nick can get another malicious comment in.

"You're such a dick, Fowler." Andy glowers at the douche.

Like the idiot he is, Nick steps into Andy's space. "Oh, I'm a dick, huh? Do you think I'm afraid of you, Rossi?"

Andy has already curled his hand into a fist, and I can see things are about to turn bad in the blink of an eye. Nick's buddies from the soccer team are already striding our way. *For fuck's sake.* I toss my cup to the floor and get between Andy and Nick, pushing the jerk back.

"Get lost, Fowler," I tell him.

"Make me, Hudson," he grits out, bringing his ugly mug inches from my face.

Knowing full well that if I get into a fight, Coach will have my head, all I can do is swallow my anger and not fall for Nick's goading.

Suddenly, Puck and Paris are there, pulling Nick off me. His buddies lose their bravado and hang back. It was stupid of them to think they could take on Andy and me, and suicidal to face off against Puck and Paris, the Rushmore Rebels' linebackers.

"Get lost, Fowler. You're stinking up the place." Puck shoves the jackass toward his friends.

Shaking with anger, he points a finger in our direction. "This isn't over."

I rub my face, annoyed as fuck that the asshole managed to get under my skin. I wish I could have made a pancake out of his face.

"I can't believe you got into a fight, Paris," Lydia complains loudly.

"I didn't get into a fight. I helped avoid one," he retorts, sounding annoyed, which is a surprise. He always treats his girlfriend as if she's breakable.

"Why did you have to meddle?" she continues.

"Are you serious right now?"

I hear the frustration in his tone, which reminds me of how I used to sound by the end of the only serious relationship I've ever had.

Not wanting to witness Paris and Lydia argue, I turn to Andy and Puck. "Let's get another drink."

"Fuck. Let's." Andy leads the way.

It's impossible to walk side by side, so I end up following Andy and Puck. But a hand on my arm stops me in my tracks. I put my game face on despite the fact that I don't feel like socializing with strangers now. Only, the person staring at me is not unfamiliar. Gwen, my ex-girlfriend, is standing there with a big smile on her face. I have to blink twice to make sure I'm not seeing things.

"Gwen?"

"Hi, Danny."

My heart is pounding fast, and not in a good way. The end of our relationship wasn't amicable. It was ugly, and it made me swear off serious relationships for the next decade or longer.

"What are you doing here?" I ask, on edge.

Her smile wilts to nothing. "I didn't come here to follow you, if that's what you're worried about."

I'm still in shock from seeing her here, so it takes me a moment to process her words.

"What do you mean, come here?"

"I transferred to John Rushmore."

I feel the blood drain from my face. *She didn't follow me, my ass.*

"You transferred to the school I go to and you expect me to believe it's a coincidence?"

She drops her hand from my arm. "I don't care what you believe, Danny. I've always wanted to come here, but I didn't in our freshman year because of you. But why shouldn't I attend the school of my dreams to spare your feelings?"

I scoff. "Trust me. My feelings are fine. The question is, are yours?"

She watches me through slitted eyes. "Yes, Danny. I've finally moved on. You don't have to worry about me anymore."

She seems hurt by my question, and despite the shit she made me go through in our senior year in high school, I feel guilty.

I sigh. "Listen, I'm sorry, okay? It's been a shitty night, and the last person I expected to see here was you. I'm glad you're at your first-choice school."

"Thanks. Well, I'd better get back to my sorority sisters."

I watch her disappear into the crowd, but the foreboding feeling still lingers in my chest. *Damn it.* I sure hope Gwen is telling the truth about why she transferred here. I glance around, trying to find the guys, but the crowd has swallowed them up. *Whatever.* I need fresh air more than I need a beer.

When I finally manage to get outside, I keep walking until I'm back in the parking lot. Hell, it's clear that what I really want is to go home. I pull my cell phone out and text Andy. He can ride back with Puck or Paris. No sooner do I get near my car than I notice one of the taillights is busted and my bumper is crooked and bent.

Fucking hell. Someone rear-ended my car, and now there will be hell to pay.

FOUR

SADIE

"Sadie, wake up." Someone shakes my shoulder, but instead of doing what they want, I roll on my side and pull the pillow over my head.

"Sadie! You said you wanted to go to the party."

Finally, my dead-tired brain recognizes Katrina's voice. I'm tempted to tell her I've changed my mind, but I suffer from major FOMO. If I don't go, regret is going to make me her bitch tomorrow.

"I want to go," I mumble as I try to open my eyes, but it seems Mr. Sandman poured superglue over my eyelids. They feel heavy and stuck together.

"It doesn't look like you want to."

"I do. It's just my body that has other ideas. I can't even open my eyes."

"Should I do something to help?" she asks.

"Like what?"

"I don't know. Throw cold water at your face?"

"If you do that, I'll punch you in the throat."

Katrina gasps, and because I don't have a visual of her, I can't tell if her indignation is fake or genuine. I push the pillow aside and manage to open one eyelid. "I'm kidding. I'm not a psycho, you know?"

She laughs nervously and waves her hand. "Oh, I knew that."

Sure, sure. I'd better watch what I say to Katrina. She seems to be the oversensitive type. I've been told on multiple occasions that I have an abrasive personality, which is true. I've made people cry without even trying.

I push my covers out of the way and throw my legs to the side of the bed. A yawn sneaks up on me, and it takes me several seconds to be able to close my mouth again.

"How long do you need to get ready?" Katrina asks, bouncing from side to side.

Gee, I wish I could steal some of that nervous energy. It's better than this damn lethargy.

"It depends. How do I look?"

"Do you want an honest opinion or the polite answer?"

"Honesty always. The quickest way to get on my shit list is to be fake with me."

"Okay. Well, you look like a cat chewed on you for days and spat you out."

I jump off the bed, rubbing my eyes. "A shower is in order, then. I'll need twenty minutes."

"Twenty minutes?" Her eyebrows shoot to the heavens. "It takes me at least an hour to get ready to go to school. Just doing my hair for tonight took me half an hour." She points at her perfectly arranged curls.

I smile. "I'm not fussy about my looks. Not aiming to impress anyone." Blush spreads through Katrina's cheeks, and I sense I said the wrong thing. "I just want to focus on my career for now," I amend.

"So that's what you want to do? Play soccer professionally?"

"Yes. It's been my dream since I started playing in the wee league."

"Wee league? Isn't wee a Scottish word?"

I chuckle. "Yeah. My neighbors growing up were from Scotland. I picked up a few things from them."

She tilts her head to the side and narrows her eyes. "If you were given the chance, which national team would you pick? England or USA?"

I thought I knew the answer to that. Back in London, I never considered another alternative besides playing for England. But I'm back in the States now, and their national team is the best in the world. What athlete wouldn't want that?

"I never stopped to think about it," I lie. "Well, I should get going or we'll never leave this room."

Okay, it didn't take me twenty minutes to get ready. It took double that, but only because I wasted precious time looking for bathroom shit in my suitcase and my favorite pair of jeans.

Katrina was shocked that I planned on leaving the apartment without drying my hair first. I did put makeup on because I'm not anti-beautification. I might not be interested in dating anyone, but this is my first social event at this school, and I don't want anyone thinking I'm a troll.

I guess I *do* want to impress people.

As we walk out of the dorm building, I can feel excitement in the air. Classes haven't officially started, so right now, only people in the summer program or athletes here for preseason training are in residence. I follow Katrina to her car in silence, distracted by my surroundings. I was so knackered when I arrived and keen on getting rid of Dad that I didn't really pay attention to anything.

The buildings are a little disappointing. They're bricks without anything appealing to them design-wise. I should be glad the interior is clean though. I've heard horror stories of student dorms back in England.

Katrina stops abruptly and points at a silver Honda Accord. "That's my car."

"Okay?"

She offers me the key. "Here, you need to drive."

"Why?" I stare at her hand as if she plans on killing me with that key.

"I had a few pre-party drinks while you took your nap. I shouldn't get behind the wheel."

"But the party is on campus. What's that, a five-minute drive?"

I'm freaking out that she wants me to drive. I barely passed my driving test back in London, and also, we drive on the other side of the road. I'm bound to run over someone or collide with another car.

"It's not five minutes, and it'd be irresponsible to drive. I'm drunk, in case you couldn't tell."

I want to say, *"How was I supposed to tell? I've just met you, and I was barely conscious for most of the time."*

"Ugh. Fine. I'll drive, but only if you promise not to judge me if I drive like an arse."

"Arse." She giggles. "I love your accent."

"Yeah, it's brilliant. I'm still waiting for your answer."

She arches her eyebrows as if she already forgot what I said earlier. "Oh, don't worry. I won't make fun of you. I promise."

Like an idiot, I automatically open the wrong door. Yeah, that bodes well. Katrina doesn't make a comment though. Either she's keeping her promise, or she's too drunk to notice.

The positive side is that her car is automatic, so I don't have to worry about shifting gears with my left hand.

The first minute of the drive is the worst. I'm nervous and queasy. It gets better after a while, and there isn't a lot of traffic at this hour. I begin to relax, only to regress to a panic state when we get near our destination. Way too many drunk pedestrians walking in the middle of the road and not a parking spot in sight.

"Keep your eyes peeled for a place to park," I tell Katrina.

"Ah, man. I had no idea it would be this busy already. We might have to park farther back."

I choose a random lane, because at this point, it'd be sheer luck to find anything. It turns out it was the wrong choice, and this one is a dead end. Bloody fantastic. I have to make a T-maneuver to get us out of here, which wouldn't be a big deal if the space wasn't tight as hell and I didn't have an audience.

"Why don't you get us out in reverse?" Katrina asks.

"I guess I could."

I had already started to get the car turned around, but going in reverse would be easier. I switch gears again—at least I think I do—and press the gas pedal, but instead of going backward, the car lurches forward, and I bump into the vehicle parked in front of me before I can stomp on the brake.

"Shit!"

"Oh no," Katrina mutters.

I back up a little and then get out of the car to inspect the damage, trying my best to ignore the group of jackasses lingering nearby and now laughing at my expense.

"Who had the bright idea to let women drive?" I hear one of them say.

My face is burning, but I refuse to acknowledge those arseholes. I'm also more preoccupied with the damage I caused. The taillight is busted and the bumper bent. Bloody hell. Whoever owns this car will be pissed.

"Do you know whose car this is?" I ask Katrina.

"No idea."

"Oh well. We can't just stand here and wait for the owner to show up. Got a piece of paper and pen?"

"Yeah. One sec."

She hands me a Post-it notepad and a Sharpie. I jot down my

name and email address, then shove the note under one of the windshield wipers.

"Shouldn't you also put down your cell phone number?" Katrina suggests.

I glance quickly at the idiots who are still watching us with interest. I wouldn't put it past them to read the note. I definitely don't want those dumbasses to have my phone number.

"Better not. Email will be fine."

"What are we going to do now?"

I give Katrina a droll look. "What do you think? After this ordeal, I need a bloody distraction. We'll find a parking spot, and then it's party time, babe."

FIVE

DANNY

My blood is boiling as I stare at my car. I even checked underneath the windshield to make sure the person responsible didn't leave a note. Nope. The asshole just took off, hoping I'd never find out their identity.

"Danny, my man. What's up?"

I look over my shoulder and find a freckled kid holding a red Solo cup.

"Someone hit my car and bailed."

He whistles as he assesses the damage. "Dude, that sucks."

"Do you have any idea who could have done it?" I ask with zero hope that there were any eyewitnesses.

"No, man. I just came out for some fresh air."

And pot, if the stench wafting from him is any indication.

"I know who did it," someone else pipes up.

I turn toward the guy's voice. "I'm listening."

"It was a blonde chick. She had a British accent. Hot as sin but as blind as a bat. I still can't believe she managed to bump into your car."

There are a ton of pretty blondes at the party, but I doubt

many have a British accent. However, I can't talk to every single girl who matches the description in order to find the culprit.

"Do you happen to know her name or the car she was driving?"

"Uh, I think she was driving a silver sedan, maybe an Accord? Don't know her name though. Never seen her before."

Great.

"Hey, I've heard the soccer team got a new player from England," the freckled guy chimes in. "I actually saw her talking with Vanessa Castro not too long ago."

"No shit. Thanks, man. That helps."

I head back to the party, ready to confront this new girl who thought it was okay to damage my car and get away with it. Who does she think she is? I thought English people were supposed to be the epitome of good manners. Apparently not.

I'm so worked up by the time I get back to the party that I ignore anyone who attempts to say hello. I spot Andy and Puck first, but I'm in no mood to talk to them either. They'd probably try to calm me down, which is the last thing I want. I'm pissed, and I need to yell at someone.

I push my way through the crowd, going in the direction I last saw Vanessa, hoping she didn't head someplace else. She's still there and, what do you know, speaking with a pretty blonde who is gesturing exaggeratedly with her hands. Vanessa says something that makes the blonde laugh like she doesn't have a care in the world. I clench my jaw hard and march in her direction.

Vanessa notices my approach first. She turns to me and smiles, giving me an opening to address her new teammate. I've been mulling over what I was going to say to her on the way here, but when she looks at me, I forget my spiel. The guy describing her wasn't wrong. She's hot all right. But that's not what's making me tongue-tied. I honestly don't know what it is about her that has rendered me speechless.

"Hey, Danny. I thought you left," Vanessa chimes in.

"I was going to, but someone rear-ended my car." I turn to the blonde. "You don't happen to know anything about it, do you?"

Her pretty blue eyes widen. "That was *your* car?"

"Yes," I grit out. "Does it matter? You damaged it and left."

"Uh, what's going on here?" Vanessa butts in.

"Oh God. I messed up. I had an issue with the car's gear and crashed into a vehicle that was parked nearby. But I left a note. You didn't get my note?" Her voice rises to a pitch. She sounds sincere, but I don't really know her. She could be lying to save face.

"There was no note," I reply.

"I tucked it under the windshield wiper."

"That's the first place I looked."

She shakes her head. "I'm not lying. I swear."

"Are you saying someone simply got rid of your note? To what end?"

"I don't know. There were some drunk wankers nearby."

"Danny, come on. If Sadie is saying she left you a note, she left you a note," Vanessa intervenes.

Damn it. I'm letting my emotions get the better of me. I'd usually give the other person the benefit of the doubt. This evening has just been a clusterfuck of bad surprises.

"Fine. Don't believe me if that's what you want to do," Sadie retorts. "I'll give you my information again. Get your phone out."

I was ready to apologize, but her bossy tone rubs me the wrong way. *Why am I suddenly the bad guy here? There was no note!*

"Really? No 'please' or anything?"

She narrows her eyes. "What exactly do you want from me?"

"Maybe a fucking apology, for starters?"

"I said I was sorry."

I scoff. "Uh, no you didn't."

"I said it in the note."

"And we've already established I never got your note."

"Jesus Christ." Vanessa throws her hands up in the air. "Can we please move on from the note that wasn't there? I swear to God, if you two become a thing, this is the worst meet cute ever."

Sadie and I wince at the same time and turn our attention to Vanessa.

"Are you mental? We're not going to become a thing," Sadie retorts, then turns to me. "No offense."

"Ditto," I reply curtly, not understanding why her comment annoyed me.

Even if I hadn't sworn off romantic relationships, she'd be the last person I'd date. Yes, she's gorgeous, and don't get me started on her accent and raspy, sexy voice. But her attitude spells trouble. I've dated one crazy chick already; don't need to repeat that same mistake twice in a row.

I need to get the hell out of here as quickly as possible. Phone out, I glance at her. "Number?"

"I haven't gotten around to getting an American number yet." She takes my phone from my hand even though I didn't offer it to her. "But I'll give it to you anyway. You can WhatsApp me."

Not wanting to sound like an ass, I bite my tongue and don't complain about her rudeness.

"Here." She returns my phone.

I glance quickly at the information she wrote before pocketing it again.

"And for the record, I *am* truly sorry I busted your car," she continues.

She's remorseful, that much I can tell—or she's an amazing actress. I'd try to make her feel less guilty about the whole deal, but I swallow my words of reassurance. I guess tonight, I'm not a nice guy.

"I'll let you know how much you owe me."

SADIE

My heart is still beating like a mad drum a minute after Mr. Too Hot to Handle stormed off.

"That was intense," Vanessa says. "I've never seen Danny so angry like that before."

"He's never met me before. I have a reputation. I can aggravate the most patient people in the world."

She cocks her head to the side and watches me closely. "Are you saying you're like the bee that stung Ferdinand?"

"You can't possibly be implying that the huge football player is a peaceful flower-sniffing bull."

"How did you know Danny was a football player? I thought you just landed and didn't have a chance to learn anything about our school."

Shame makes my cheeks warm. I'm glad it's dim here. I wasn't completely honest with Vanessa about why I didn't check her emails. She knows I got hurt, but she doesn't know how, and I'd like to keep it that way.

"Just a hunch. He has the physique." I shrug.

"Danny is one of the good guys. Super chill and humble. Actually, most of the guys on the football team are nice, even the cockiest ones like Andy Rossi."

No surprise there. Dad wouldn't tolerate rubbish from his players. I don't make a comment though. Vanessa knows who my father is, but I don't want to remind her.

"If you'd arrived earlier, you'd have had the displeasure of meeting Nick Fowler, the captain of the men's soccer team. He's a dick with a capital D. Obnoxious and a perv."

"So basically a total creep."

"Yep. I don't hate a lot of people, but he's one of them. Fucking asshole." She takes a large sip of her drink and then continues. "I'm sorry. I shouldn't have been so candid about my opinion of him."

I shake my head. "Don't apologize about that. If you have a list of wankers I should avoid, send it my way."

"You betcha. I'm glad you could make it tonight despite the drama."

"Me too. I shouldn't have driven my roommate's car. I'm not a good driver, and I'm not ashamed to admit it."

She snorts. "I'm glad we don't need your talents behind a steering wheel. We want you for your skills on the field. You're good to play again, right?"

I grimace. "Yeah. I've been cleared to practice. It wasn't a big deal, just a superficial wound," I lie.

My new coach is the only one who knows the extent of my knife injury and how I got it. I don't want anyone else on the team to know I was attacked.

"That's good to hear. You probably need to work extra hard to compensate for the time you were recovering. I'm sure Coach Lauda already talked to you about that, but as the captain, it's my job to reinforce the message. We worked fucking hard to get where we are."

Whoa. Straight to business. I'm not mad though, just surprised.

"Sorry if I'm being too blunt," she continues.

"No, don't apologize. I appreciate your honesty. I abhor people who beat around the bush. Your directness is refreshing. And don't worry, I have no intention of being a deadweight to the team. I don't do anything half-arsed. No time for losers and all that."

She smirks. "Nice Queen reference."

"Queen songs make the soundtrack of my life."

Vanessa laughs and then asks, "Where's your roommate, anyway?"

I glance around me, and sure as shit, Katrina is not in the vicinity.

"I'd better go look for her. She said she'd been drinking since God knows when."

"Good luck."

The moment I'm alone in a sea of strangers, I rehash the argument I had with Danny. I came across like a jerk, even though I didn't mean to. And I was in the wrong to begin with. I did smash his car. But he put me on the spot and accused me of being a liar. It triggered my self-defense mechanism, and the bitch came out.

Of course, the altercation had to happen in front of Vanessa. I can't have the captain of the team thinking I'm a liability. I'm an acquired taste—I have enough self-awareness to know that. So I have to be extra careful, let them get to know me slowly. Unleashing the full Sadie Clarkson hurricane on them too soon will only blow up in my face.

SIX

SADIE

I spent the entire weekend agonizing about my first day of preseason training. Besides Vanessa, I only met a couple of the girls last Friday before I had to haul Katrina back home. If I couldn't tell she was drunk on the way to the Red Barn, there was no mistaking her drunken state when I finally found her at the party. She couldn't even stand up straight; I had to practically drag her to the car.

I made sure to set my alarm clock an hour earlier than my usual wake-up time. I simply couldn't arrive late on my first day. Anxiety kept me up all night, so the alarm wasn't needed in the end. I was wide awake.

I still don't have a car. Dad was busy all weekend prepping for work today and only sent me a few links. The options all looked fine to me. I'm not fussy about what car I drive.

The training field isn't far from my dorm building, so I simply jog there. It's a good warm-up. I'm surprised when I find Vanessa in the locker room, already in practice gear.

"Wow, I can't believe you beat me here," I say in greeting.

"Coach Lauda wanted to talk to me about the season before the rest of the team arrived."

"Oh."

I turn around and look for the locker with my name on it. One of the topics of the conversation was probably me. I'm the new recruit recovering from an injury, after all. I've spoken with Coach Lauda a few times online before I flew over, but I haven't met her in person yet.

"She told me you're aware we have two strikers already. Melody McCoy and Joanne Barnes."

"Yeah, I'm aware. But she said she'd let me play during a portion of the second half depending on my performance during training."

I'm not conceited when I say I was the star of my former team. But I *am* worried my performance won't be the same. Six weeks without playing is way too long. I don't voice my doubts out loud though. I sure hope Coach keeps her promise, because that's all I need, a chance to prove I should be starting the game. I've seen a few tapes. McCoy and Barnes are good, but I'm better—or *was* better.

No, Sadie. You can't think like that.

"Don't worry though. This is Melody's senior year. You'll have plenty of time to show off your skills. Just be patient."

"I'm a team player. I'll do whatever is best for the team."

"I'm glad to hear that," Coach Lauda pipes up from outside her office.

Wearing a tracksuit in dark green with our team's logo embroidered on the chest and a determined glint in her eyes, she's the epitome of a badass coach. Her short blonde hair and businesslike stare remind me a bit of Coach Sue Silvester from *Glee*.

"Good morning, Coach," I say.

"Good morning, Sadie. I'm happy to see you're here bright and early. You're sweaty. Have you been running already?"

"Yeah, I jogged here. No car yet."

"Nothing wrong with a good cardio to begin the day. There are three new girls starting today besides you. Two are freshmen like you, and the third is a sophomore transfer from Florida. You might have met them at the mixer last Friday."

I almost giggle at her use of "mixer," but I manage to swallow my amusement down. Glancing at Vanessa, I catch her trying to hide a smirk.

"No, I didn't stay long at the party," I reply.

"You'll meet them today. Vanessa will show you around before we start." She returns to her office and shuts the door.

Despite the circumstances surrounding my admission to John Rushmore, Coach Lauda was clear that she wanted me on her team. I'm not a favor Dad had to call in. From the get-go, I knew she had a no-bullshit attitude and didn't play favoritism. All she cares about is having the best players on the field and winning games.

Once I change clothes, Vanessa shows me where everything is in the locker room plus the showers, and by the time she finishes her tour, some of my other teammates have arrived. The three newbies—Charlotte, Phoebe, and Steff—are standing close together and looking a little uncertain about themselves. Super easy to tell they're fresh meat. I made sure to learn who they were before coming here, because as the newest people on the team, we have to stick together. I'm sure there will be some kind of hazing to welcome us to the Rushmore Ravens.

Tessa and Gabi—who I met at the party on Friday—are also already here, way less chatty this morning. They barely look awake. I say hello to them, and they grunt and nod in reply.

"Hi, I'm Sadie." I wave at Charlotte, Phoebe, and Steff.

"Nice to meet you, Sadie. I'm Charlotte," the shortest of the group replies.

What she lacks for in height, she makes up for in solid muscle. Her kicks can turn a ball into a missile. She's a midfielder. In high school, she alternated between center midfielder and attacking midfielder. Vanessa usually plays the latter, and she's damn good at her job.

Phoebe and Steff proceed to introduce themselves, and then the conversation veers toward the Red Barn party. Since I didn't have a jolly good time like everyone else, I choose to simply listen.

Steff is the transfer from Florida. I couldn't find out in my research why she transferred, but I'm sure I'll learn that soon enough. She's a keeper, but despite being new to the team, there's a good chance she'll be starting. Her nickname at her previous school was The Wall because getting through her was almost impossible. I'm glad she's on my team.

And finally there's Phoebe, the girl with the multicolored hair. She plays defense. While Steff and Charlotte chat away, Phoebe remains quiet like me. It's hard to get a read on her.

A minute later, Melody walks into the locker room, acting like she's a bloody rock star. She even has sunglasses on. She says hello to everyone in a cheerful tone, and then she spots our little group.

"Oh, you're the new blood. Welcome to the team." She pushes her shades up and stares at me.

"Thanks," I say.

"I heard you're a striker. I can't wait to see what you got."

"Melody holds the record for most goals scored in the championship two years in a row," Gabi pipes up from across the room.

"That's awesome. I'm looking forward to beating that record." I smile from ear to ear.

Melody's grin fades, and her eyes flash with annoyance.

Oooh, the claws are already coming out. If there was a record for bringing the worst out in people, I'd win it.

"You'll have to actually play in a game to score," she replies sweetly and then walks to her locker.

Vanessa comes over and whispers, "Why did you have to poke the bear with a short stick?"

"I didn't realize we had wild animals among us," I joke, earning chuckles from my companions.

She rolls her eyes. "Antagonizing Melody the first time you meet her was not smart, Sadie. She's fiercely competitive and has a mean streak."

"Oops?"

"Yeah, joke now. Don't come crying to me later." She walks away.

"Vanessa is right. I should know," a cute brunette with short hair says. "I'm Joanne Barnes." She shakes my hand in a businesslike manner. "Welcome to the team."

"Thanks."

I'm not sure if Joanne was joking or not, but it's unlikely their advice will scare me off. If Melody is mean, then I'm her 2.0 version. Maybe I should have played nicer until I get the lay of the land, but what's the fun in that? And a little competition among teammates is healthy. It keeps us on our toes. It's not like I'm showing off my scary side yet. This is just letting them get to know me slowly.

After Joanne heads over to her locker, Charlotte asks, "So, any guesses as to what our welcoming prank will be?"

"No bloody clue," I reply.

The Three Musketeers and I—that's what I started calling Charlotte, Phoebe, and Steff—couldn't guess what our welcome to the team hazing was, and our imagination had been wild. After practice, we were more than ready to hit the showers and go home, but it wasn't meant to be.

Our wonderful teammates let us shower in peace, but when we were all fresh and wearing clean clothes, they turned us into oversized chicken tenders ready for the fryer. First came the egging, and I tell you, being hit by dozens of eggs at once hurts. And I'm certain Melody aimed most of her attack at me.

After the first coating was done, it was time for the flour part. And for the grand finale, we have to go back to our dorm rooms in a walk of shame from hell. The mix of egg and flour formed a disgusting coating over our bodies, which is turning hard as we trudge under the hot California sun.

"I thought I was prepared for the prank, but this is a nightmare," Charlotte moans.

"I have egg and flour everywhere, even in my ears," Steff joins the cryfest.

"And it itches like crazy," Phoebe adds.

"Well, it could have been worse," I say.

"Worse than this?" Steff's voice rises an octave.

"We're not bleeding."

A heavy silence descends on our group. I glance at the trio and find them looking at me with their jaws hanging loose.

"What?" I ask.

"What exactly did you think they'd do to us?" Charlotte asks.

I shrug. "Well, they could have whooped our arses, for starters."

"Jesus, is that what they do in England?" Phoebe asks.

I open my mouth to reply, but the sound of a car approaching distracts me. I glance over my shoulder and grimace when I notice the vehicle is slowing down. It's one of those open Jeeps that fuckboys like to drive, and that seems to be exactly who is behind the steering wheel.

"Good afternoon, ladies." The driver smiles at us, exulting cocky attitude and amusement. "Need any help?"

For a second, I suspect he's from the soccer team until I notice the guy riding shotgun.

Bloody hell. It's Danny, looking like a damn Greek god with his blond curls shining under the sun. And here I am covered in junk.

"If by help you mean a hose down, sure," I say, trying my best to avoid making eye contact with Danny.

"Sorry, don't have enough water here to get all that gunk off you. But even if I did, I wouldn't meddle in the Ravens' affairs. Vanessa would have my balls."

"You could give us a ride," Charlotte pipes up.

The driver twists his face into a scowl. "Are you crazy? And let you guys mess up my car? Hell no."

"So did you just stop to laugh at us?" I ask, annoyed.

"I stopped because Danny-boy here asked me to." He points at his friend, and like an idiot, I shift my attention to him.

I can't guess what he's thinking since he's wearing sunglasses and has a poker face on, but I feel oddly exposed.

"Is that so? Did you want to make sure I hadn't skipped town?"

Danny scoffs. "I wanted to make sure you were all right. Clearly you are."

"Yep, we're all fine and dandy here. Run along now." I wave my hand impatiently.

I expect him to scowl, but he laughs instead, shaking his head. "I'll call you later, Sadie. Come on, Andy. We've been dismissed."

"See you later, alligator." Andy waves at us and then accelerates away.

I keep staring at their car while I wrestle with my emotions. *Why didn't Danny bite my head off? Or better yet, why did I want him to?*

"What was that all about?" Charlotte asks.

I blink fast, peeling my eyes off the road. "Nothing."

"It didn't sound like nothing," Steff chimes in. "When did you meet Danny Hudson?"

"It's a long story." I resume walking.

"It's a long trek back to the dorms." Charlotte nudges my elbow.

Bollocks. I guess there's no escaping rehashing the stellar beginning of my new life.

SEVEN

"**Y**ou've been holding out on me, Danny-boy," Andy says as soon as we leave Sadie and her teammates on the side of the road.

"I don't know what you're talking about."

"You never said the girl who crashed into your car was one of the Ravens."

"How is that important?"

He shrugs. "I guess it isn't important. But that accent of hers? That's hot."

"Dude, you have a girlfriend."

"I just said her accent is hot. That doesn't mean I want to bone her. Jeez."

I snort. "Yeah, that'd fly well with Jane."

"Jane knows I'm one hundred percent devoted to her. Besides, I'm not telling her, I'm telling *you*, in case you want to do something about it."

"Do what exactly?" I turn to him, glowering now.

He shrugs. "The tension between you and that girl was obvious. I couldn't really tell if she was pretty thanks to all that crap covering her, but I'm going out on a limb here that she has a face to match that voice."

I clench my jaw tight and look at the road ahead. I'm annoyed now for a myriad of reasons. The main one is that Andy was able to guess what was going on with me during only a few minutes of conversation. The second reason is that I *do* find Sadie attractive to the point that I haven't been able to stop thinking about her. As soon as I take care of my car repair, I have to avoid her at all costs. She's a distraction I don't need.

"Really? You're not going to say anything?" Andy continues.

God, he won't leave me alone now.

"The only thing I want from Sadie is money to repair the damage she did to my car. That's all."

"So when you said you'd be completely focused on football this season, did you mean you would turn into a eunuch? That's not healthy, man."

"I didn't say that."

"Okay… then why are you so bent out of shape because of my comment? I didn't say you should date the girl."

"Why are you interested in my love life all of a sudden?" I ask.

"Dunno. Maybe payback for all the times you butted in mine."

"You should thank me that I did."

"Yeah, yeah. You did me a solid, and I'm never going to forget that. But anyway, when are you planning on taking your car to the garage?"

"Whenever you're free. The sooner the better."

Andy shakes his head. "No can do today. I've got to see Jane."

"I'll ask one of the guys, then."

"Why don't you ask Sadie to give you a ride? She's the one responsible for the damage, right?"

I roll my eyes. "Will you quit trying to matchmake me with that girl?"

"That's not what I'm doing, but whatever."

If I tell him the reason why I want to spend as little time as possible with Sadie, Andy will never drop the subject. So I pull up my phone and text Paris to check if he's available. His reply comes a minute later. He's busy today, but he can do it tomorrow. Waiting another day wouldn't be too bad if I hadn't promised Mom to run some errands for her. I can't drive around LA with a busted taillight. Getting a fine is not in the budget. The sooner I get my car fixed, the better.

Hell, if I can't get a ride with anyone today, I can always take the bus back to campus.

Immediately, I feel better that I have a plan that doesn't involve Sadie in any way.

SADIE

I've been back in the dorms for an hour, and it took me that long to wash the egg and flour paste off my body and hair. I'm ready to veg out in bed and watch TV when Dad calls me.

"Hello?"

"Hi, kiddo. How was your first day at training?"

"Good. We got pranked."

"You did? How bad was it?" he asks.

"Mild compared to what I was expecting. I'm glad it's out of the way."

"Do you have plans for dinner? I thought I'd take you out. Any place you want."

I could eat, but I'm not ready to spend a couple hours alone with Dad yet. I don't know what I'd say to him. Maybe if there was someone else there to be a buffer, it'd be better.

"I'm knackered, to be honest. I was planning to go to bed early."

"Oh, of course. And you're still not over your jet lag, I bet."

"Yeah, right. Not over it yet."

"Right. Well, I got something for you."

"Oh, what is it?"

"A car."

"You got me a car?" My voice rises to a shrill.

"It's nothing fancy. It's a Toyota, a good car. It has low mileage, and I got a deal."

He's rambling, which is not something I remember him doing before. He must be nervous. I'd been so caught up in my awkwardness around him that I never stopped to consider that this situation must be strange for him too.

"That's cool, Dad. When are you dropping it off?"

"As a matter of fact, I haven't picked it up yet. But I can take you there now, and you can drive back to campus."

Instant sweat dots my forehead. "How far is the dealership?"

"Not far at all. Fifteen minutes or so."

I swallow the huge lump in my throat. "Do I have to take the highway?"

"Yeah. What's the matter, honey? You have your driver's license, right?"

God, I'm acting like a ninny.

"Yep. But…. Never mind. When can you come over?"

"I'm two minutes from your building."

"Okay, I'll see you soon."

I was so nervous about the prospect of driving on my own on the highway that I barely cared about the awkwardness of being alone with Dad again in a moving vehicle. I'm glad he kept the chitchat to a minimum.

Now with key in hand and standing next to my new car, my heart is beating so fast and hard, it feels like it might burst out of my chest at any second. I'm queasy too, but I try my best to hide my nervousness from Dad.

"What do you think, Sadie?" he asks me, not hiding his satisfied grin.

"It's lovely." I clutch the key tighter in my hand.

"We're all set here. You can follow me back to campus."

"Yeah, that's a good idea. Getting lost in LA is not my idea of fun times."

He nods and then walks toward his car. I slide behind the steering wheel, trying my best to keep my body from shaking. While I wait for Dad, I glance over the dashboard to learn where everything is. Then I fix the side mirrors and adjust the seat.

A minute later, Dad pulls up next to me and nods.

All right, then. Here we go.

My hands are sweaty from holding the steering wheel too hard, and when we enter the highway, my stomach is twisted so tightly it hurts. I thought following Dad would be the best idea, but I quickly realize that making sure I don't lose him in the heavy traffic while trying to avoid a car wreck is stressing me the fuck out.

I freak out for a second when I lose visual of Dad's car, and I almost end up colliding with the dickhead who cut me up. I should have honked, but pressing on the brakes seemed more important. When I finally manage to switch to a faster-moving lane, I can't find Dad's car anywhere.

Shit. Did he take an exit?

I should have kept my phone handy so I could call him. There's nothing for it now. I have to get off the highway, grab my phone, and use Google maps to find my way back to campus. The international roaming fee is going to be murder, but this is an emergency.

My phone rings. It must be him wondering where I am.

The next exit leads me to an industrial area where most of the buildings are warehouses. There's less traffic here, which helps with my nerves. I turn toward the commercial building that has a parking lot and stop in front of an old car repair shop.

I'm just about to fish out my phone from my purse when the

last person I expect to see here walks out of the building: Danny Hudson. He must have brought his car to get fixed.

"You have got to be kidding me," I mumble to myself.

He doesn't see me as he walks right next to my car. Instead, he veers toward the street.

Wait. How is he getting back to campus?

Before I can overthink it, I get out of the car and call his name.

He stops and looks over his shoulder, eyes going wider as he sees me there. "What are you doing here?"

"I got lost," I reply as I walk over.

Don't know why I feel the need to move closer to him. It's like he's the sun or something and I'm a cold planet in need of his warmth.

For fuck's sake, Sadie. What kind of rubbish are you thinking?

"You got lost," he repeats as if he doesn't believe me. "So, are you saying Andy didn't tell you I'd be here?"

I squint. "Who's Andy?"

He shakes his head. "Never mind."

"Anyway, I assume you dropped off your car to get it fixed?"

"Yep."

He shoves his hands in his jeans pockets, pushing the waistband lower and revealing a strip of golden skin. I want to be able to say my eyes didn't linger there for a second too long, but I'd be lying.

"How are you getting back to campus?" I ask after I force my eyes to look up again.

"The bus."

"God. Aren't they bloody awful here?"

"They aren't that bad."

"Well, I can take you back. I pulled over to pull up Google maps, but having you to give me directions would be easier."

He seems unsure for a hot second.

Damn, did I make such a terrible first impression that he doesn't even want to accept a lift from me?

"I suppose you owe me a ride back home." He cracks a tiny smile.

I'll take that.

As we walk back to my car, I ask, "Why were you taking the bus anyway? Couldn't find a friend to give you a lift?"

"I need my car fixed ASAP, and everyone was busy today."

God, way to make me feel even guiltier. Though to be fair, I don't think he's doing it on purpose.

Distracted by his presence, I once again veer for the wrong side of the car

"Oh, do you want me to drive?" he asks.

I pull my hand from the door handle with a jerky movement. "Bollocks. I keep doing this."

Pure amusement dances in his blue eyes now. "*Should* I drive? I mean, you don't have the best track record."

A part of me wants to take him up on his offer, but hell, I'm too proud to let a dude drive my car because I'm afraid.

"Ha ha. Very funny."

I circle around the car and pretend I'm not a bundle of nerves inside. It's much harder than I thought though. I didn't count on Danny taking so much space inside the vehicle. It's not because of his size—the car is roomy. It's his presence that seems to take over everything. He doesn't make it any easier when I can sense his eyes on me.

"What?" I whip my face to his.

"I was wondering if you know how to start the car." The upturn of his lips tells me he's teasing me.

"I'm beginning to regret offering you a lift," I mutter as I turn on the ignition.

"I'm not." He laughs.

My phone rings again, and I finally remember Dad. *Shit.* Where's my purse now?

Danny leans forward and then lifts the accessory from the floor. "Are you looking for this?"

"Yeah. Thanks."

The ringing stops. It was indeed Dad calling. Not willing to disclose my father is Danny's coach, I text him instead of calling back. Then I shove my phone back in my purse and toss it to the back seat.

"Is everything okay?" he asks.

"Of course. Why wouldn't it be?"

He snickers. "You seem awfully tense."

I clench my jaw and swallow the retort on the tip of my tongue. His mocking comments are better than the angry ones I received when we met. I was never one to care much about what strangers thought about me, and yet I don't want Danny Hudson to think I'm a bitch.

Ignoring him is hard, but if I can keep my cool during a penalty kick that will decide a championship game, I can drive with him by my side.

Mercifully, he doesn't tease me any more after and only opens his mouth to give me directions. When he's not being a pain in the arse on purpose, he has a calming effect. A few minutes into the drive is all it takes for my anxiety to melt away.

"Did the mechanic give you a quote for the repairs?" I ask.

"Yeah. Five hundred should cover it."

Not too bad. I thought it would cost more.

"Hey, I can give you cash right now."

"You carry that much money on you?"

"Well, I don't have it with me. It's in my dorm room, you know, left over from my trip."

"No, I don't know."

He sounds prickly all of a sudden, so I chance a quick glance at him. He's looking out the window with his jaw locked tight.

Did I say something wrong?

"Anyway, if you have time, we can make a pit stop at my place and I'll pay you."

"Sounds good."

Does it though? How come I have the impression he's angry at me again?

EIGHT

DANNY

I shouldn't have let Sadie's comment about money get to me. I know five hundred bucks is not a lot for most of the students here at Rushmore. And she's a foreign student, which means she must not be lacking in the finance department.

It's so damn stupid. I never had a problem with my friends being richer than me. Why am I feeling so small that Sadie didn't even bat an eye when I told her how much she owed me for the car repair?

Like a total grump, I follow her in silence to her dorm room. She must have picked up on my mood change because she doesn't try to make conversation. This is for the best. I was trying to avoid the girl anyway, and now that we're about to settle the car issue, there won't be any reason for us to hang out.

Then why the hell do I feel so gloomy about it? I have this stupid feeling that I'm going to regret the way I'm acting the moment she drops me off.

She stops suddenly in front of a door and says, "This is me. Hmm, there's a sock on the doorknob though."

"We probably shouldn't go in."

She turns to me, piercing me with her beautiful blue eyes. My heart seems to lurch forward.

Fuck me. I can't be having visceral reactions for her—or any other girl, for that matter. I promised Coach no distractions, and Sadie would be one with a capital D.

"Wait. So the sock thing is for real? She's in there with someone?"

I shrug. "I don't know what kind of rules you guys have, but in most cases, that's what it means."

"Blimey, we didn't talk rules."

Sadie presses her ear against the door and furrows her eyebrows. "I don't hear anyth—" She jumps back suddenly. "Scratch that. Katrina is definitely busy."

Her face is bright red now, and she won't meet my eyes. I can't help the laugh that bubbles up my throat.

"What's so funny?"

I shake my head. "Nothing."

She glares at the door. "This sucks. What am I supposed to do? Wait out here in the hallway until she's done?"

"You could hang out at my place."

Shit. I can't believe I just said that. Didn't I just acknowledge that Sadie would be a distraction I don't need?

"Are you sure? I don't want to impose."

"Yeah, it'll be fine. I'm sure Lorenzo will appreciate the extra company."

"Who is that?"

"My roommate's brother. He's twelve."

Sadie's mouth makes a perfect O, drawing my attention to her full lips.

Stop staring, you idiot.

"And he lives with you on campus?"

"Yeah. It's a long story."

She glances at her door once again and sighs. "All right. Let's go."

"Gee, could you at least pretend going to my place isn't a

burden?" I half joke. I'm a little annoyed, if I'm being honest with myself.

"Oh, you got it all wrong. I'm not upset that I have to hang out with you. It's just… well, I was looking forward to taking a nap. I haven't adjusted to the time difference yet, and today at practice was brutal."

I remember Sadie's walk of shame, and that brings a broad smile to my face. "Ah, yeah. I can imagine."

She narrows her eyes. "You're picturing me covered in all that gunk, aren't you?"

I try to convey an air of innocence by widening my eyes. "Me? Of course not."

"You're lucky you don't have any aspirations of becoming an actor."

Grinning, I reply, "Nope. Not at all."

"I'd never take you gambling either."

"I'm not a gambler, so I'm totally unfazed by your remark."

She cocks an eyebrow. "Really? You've never gambled in your life?"

I narrow my eyes. "Why do I have the impression that's a loaded question?"

With a shrug, she walks away from her dorm room. "It wasn't. I'm just making conversation."

"Okay."

Our gazes lock, and for a moment, neither of us moves. The air between us becomes heavy, almost as if there's a magnetic field trying to push us closer.

The spell is broken by the loud voices of strangers approaching. I look away first, glancing in the direction of the noise. Two girls are walking over, and when they notice me, giggles follow.

Sadie snorts next to me before she strides down the hallway toward the exit. I follow her, matching her stride. I chance a look at her face. She seems annoyed. Did she get jealous? The notion should raise a red flag in my head. I barely know her, after all, and she has no reason to act territorial. But instead, I'm feeling idiotically pleased about it.

"Are you hungry?" I ask to fill the silence.

"I could eat."

"There's an awesome diner not too far from here."

She peeks at me, smirking. "I hope that's not a roundabout way to ask me out on a date."

I scoff. "Please. If I were asking you out, you'd know."

I expect her to be offended by my remark, but instead, her grin broadens. "Brilliant. I don't have time for dating. But oddly, I don't mind your company."

Surprisingly, I chuckle. "Ditto on both counts."

We hop back in Sadie's car, and I give her directions to the diner. She grabs her phone and texts someone before driving though.

She catches me staring and says, "I asked Katrina to let me know when her visitor is gone."

"Smart."

I consider texting Andy to ask if he wants to join us, but I scratch that idea fast. He'll give me too much grief over Sadie, and I don't want him trying to play matchmaker.

It's getting close to dinnertime, and the parking lot is beginning to fill up. Odette, the waitress who always waits on Andy and me, smiles when she sees me walk in. Her shrewd eyes notice Sadie right away, which only makes her grin wider.

Great. I bet she thinks I'm on a date.

"Hi, Danny. I haven't seen you in a while."

"I've been super busy," I lie.

That's not the main reason. Eating out is simply not in the budget, which really doesn't explain why I suggested bringing Sadie here. Date or no date, I don't expect her to pay since it was my idea. I have manners.

Odette grabs a couple of menus and leads us to my usual booth in the far corner. I try to ignore the stares that seem to follow Sadie and me. In my head, I'm cursing. It won't take long for the rumor mill to churn and for Andy to find out I brought Sadie here.

Once we're seated across from each other, Odette hands over the menus and takes our drink orders. We both ask for water.

Sadie opens the menu and asks, "What's good here?"

"Everything is good. It depends on what you're in the mood for."

She looks up. "Would you think I'm weird if I order something from the breakfast options?"

I smirk. "Sorry, sugar. That boat has sailed. I already think you're weird."

Twisting her face into an exaggerated scowl, she leans back and says in a thick British accent, "I beg your pardon?"

Laughter shakes my entire frame. "I'm just yanking your chain."

"So you don't think I'm weird."

"I don't know you well enough to have come to that conclusion. All I know is you're a terrible driver."

Her jaw drops. "Rude!"

"Not a lie though."

I watch her closely. I'm joking to mask the fact that I'm attracted to her. But this all could blow up in my face.

Sadie's expression remains serious for a couple of beats until the corners of her lips twitch up.

"Bloody hell. It's definitely not a lie. I'm dreadful behind a steering wheel. Didn't have many chances to practice back home."

"Where is back home, anyway?"

"London." She drops her eyes to the menu again. "I think I'll have pancakes with eggs and bacon."

I don't miss the quick change of subject. If she doesn't want to talk about her life before coming here, I shouldn't pry. But I'm damn curious.

I scan the offerings in front of me and decide on the half sandwich and small soup combo.

"What are you having?" she asks.

"Something light. I can't pig out or Coach will have my balls."

A shadow crosses Sadie's eyes, and her lips pinch together. I can see the difference this time. She's not pretending. What did I say that caused that reaction? She might not be weird, but she's certainly a mystery.

"How do you like Rushmore so far?" I ask.

She shrugs. "It's all right, I guess. I haven't been here that long. I flew in on the day of the Red Barn party, actually. I can probably blame the jet lag for that unfortunate event with your car."

I smirk. "Sure, let's go with that."

"Do you know when your car will be ready?"

"By the end of the week. They're busy at the garage."

"That's shite." She pauses and nibbles on her lower lip for a second. "I can give you rides while your car is being fixed. I mean, if you dare, considering how appalling my driving skills are."

I don't answer right away. Instead, I take a large sip of my water to buy time. I don't want Sadie to drive me anywhere, though not because she sucks at driving. I simply can't afford to spend more time with her. She beguiles me like no one ever has before. I can honestly say no girl has made me more curious, more interested from the get-go, and I'm not simply talking about her looks. Something about her speaks to me on a deeper level.

I should say, *"Thanks but no thanks."*

"Are you sure you're up for it?" I ask instead.

Clearly my mouth is a rogue agent now and is disregarding all my logical arguments.

"I wouldn't have offered if I didn't mean it. It's self-serving too."

"Oh?"

"I feel bloody guilty about it. So if I add driving you around as my penance, it will probably help with my heavy conscience."

"Maybe, or it could double your guilt when you kill me in a car wreck."

"Oh my God." Her voice rises an octave. "What a terrible thing to say."

I reach over and cover her hand with mine. "I'm just kidding. You're so easy to tease."

Sadie tenses a little as she drops her gaze to our joined hands. I realize my mistake then and quickly pull back.

Note to self: no touching, even if it's innocent.

Odette stops by our table just in time to diffuse the awkward moment. She takes our orders in a businesslike manner, but before she walks away, she gives me a meaningful glance and then winks.

Fucking hell. So it starts.

I'll have to do some serious damage control before we leave. I can't have Odette believing Sadie is my date. She means well, but she loves to gossip.

"I'm not easy to tease," Sadie replies to my earlier comment. "I'm just... I don't know, trying not to assume people are like me."

"I don't follow."

"Your comment that I could kill you in a car wreck. That's something I'd totally say because I'm savage like that."

I lean against the back of the booth seat. "Are you saying I'm a savage?"

Her eyebrows arch. "Oh no. That's not what I'm saying at all." She shakes her head and then rests it in her hand. "You see what I'm saying though? I just offended you without meaning to."

"You didn't offend me. That was also a joke. Told ya you're too easy to tease."

She looks up, narrowing her eyes to slits. "All right, Danny Hudson. It seems I've been holding back with you for nothing. You can obviously take whatever I have to dish out."

"I never said I couldn't."

She presses her index finger over her lips. "Hmm. I wasn't sure. I mean, you were pretty mental at the party."

"Only because someone had wrecked my car and not left a note."

"I left a note."

I give her a droll stare. "Really? Are we going to start the note debacle again?"

She smirks. "Better not, huh?"

Odette returns with our orders, and I'm thankful the service here is fast. Keeping myself busy with food will give me time to reset the thoughts in my head. I'm feeling out of my depth with Sadie, and I don't like it one bit.

My eyes are on my soup when a moan escapes her lips. The sound seems to shoot straight to my cock, making it twitch. *Damn everything to hell.* I shove a spoonful of hot soup into my mouth, burning my tongue in the process. Anything to stop the sudden awakening happening in my pants.

"This is real good nosh," she says. "Do you want a bite?"

I glance up, finding her offering a piece of maple syrup–drenched pancake to me.

Why is the idea of Sadie feeding me so damn erotic? Am I missing pussy that much? No, that's not it. I wouldn't be reacting like this with anyone else, that much I know.

"I'm good, thanks."

"Your loss." She shoves the piece of pancake in her mouth, not caring that it is obviously too large.

"You eat like a dude," I say, and I don't know why.

She swallows before replying, "No, I eat like a person who didn't realize they were starving. This is not a date anyway, so I don't have to pretend to be all prissy. Although, I've never done that before."

"You've never gone out on a date or pretended to have manners?"

"Both. And for the record, I *do* have manners. But I also have an older brother."

"Ah, mystery solved." I swallow another spoonful of soup. "How come you've never dated before?"

"Seriously? Teenage boys are gross. Besides, I was too busy with football. I'm not saying I've never snogged or shagged anyone. I'm not a blushing virgin, for crying out loud. I have needs."

Fuck, how did I wind up talking about Sadie's sex life? I'm trying to ignore how attractive she is, and the mental pictures popping in my head are not helping.

"Hi, Danny." An annoyingly sweet voice that makes my skin crawl draws my attention away from Sadie.

I glance up and find Gwen standing near our booth. Two other girls wearing sorority hoodies are flanking her.

"Hey," I reply, cold enough that she won't miss the hint.

Her eyes turn to Sadie, who has not slowed down inhaling her food on Gwen's account.

Shit, I think I already love this girl.

What the hell am I thinking?

"We have to stop meeting like this," Gwen continues.

"Yeah, for real."

Sadie raises a questioning eyebrow at me. Hell, I hope she doesn't decide to play the ten-thousand-questions game once Gwen leaves.

"Are you going to introduce me to your friend?" Gwen asks through clenched teeth.

For fuck's sake. She's acting like she did at the end of our relationship.

"The name is Sadie. And if all you wanted was an introduction, you should have said so. I will sign a napkin if you want, but I draw the line at selfies."

"Why would we want your autograph?" one of Gwen's friends asks. "Are you famous or something?"

"Oh, you don't know who I am? How refreshing." Sadie smiles. "I knew coming to America was the right decision for me. Grammy didn't really think so. It was hard to convince her, especially after the whole scandal with Harry and Meghan. The poor thing was brokenhearted."

"Wait. Are you implying the Queen of England is your grandmother?" The girl's voice turns high-pitched.

I'll be damned. She's actually buying Sadie's bullshit.

"Of course she's not related to the queen, Carol. Come on," Gwen retorts, but I detect a hint of uncertainty.

Sadie shrugs. "Believe me or not, I don't bloody care. Now, if you don't mind, bugger off and let us get back to our dinner."

"That was rude," Gwen replies.

"No ruder than you stopping here and acting like Danny owes you anything."

Wow. When Sadie said she was holding back with me, she wasn't kidding.

"Are you going to let her talk to me like that?" Gwen turns her ire on me.

"Did she say anything that wasn't true?"

Gwen's friends trade a glance that looks a lot like third-degree embarrassment. Her face is bright red when she storms off and walks out of the diner.

I should be relieved she's gone, but I'm rattled. My hands are shaking when I break my sandwich into pieces. I can't believe I let her get to me like that.

"Dear Lord. That was pleasant." Sadie sticks a piece of crispy bacon into her mouth.

I don't offer a comment; instead, I shove a piece of bread into my mouth and chew on it with excessive force.

"You don't need to tell me who that was, even though I can guess," Sadie continues, clearly unfazed. "We all have a past that we wish stayed in the past."

"What's yours?"

She doesn't answer until she chews and swallows her food, all the while keeping her eyes locked on mine.

"Maybe I'll tell you one day."

NINE

SADIE

By the time Danny and I finished having dinner, Katrina had already texted me back, so instead of hanging out at his place, I simply dropped him off. I didn't think spending more time with him after we bumped into his crazy ex would be enjoyable anyway. The encounter messed him up, which obviously made me uber-curious to know what their deal was.

I'm completely beat when I finally walk into my dorm room. Katrina is watching a movie on her laptop with her headphones on. I inspect my bed to make sure she didn't use it as an extension of hers. She's burning a scented candle by the window —probably to mask the scent of sex.

Ew. Fucking gross, now that I think about it.

She glances up and pulls her headphones off. "Hey, you're finally home."

"I was here sooner, but the room was at full capacity."

I take off my jeans and then jump under the covers. I don't want Katrina to see my scar, so I keep my T-shirt and bra on. I used the restroom before I got here, and there's no chance in hell

I'm going back out to brush my teeth. I'm too exhausted for that.

"I'm sorry about that. It wasn't a planned hookup."

This is where I should ask who the lucky guy was, but I honestly don't care to hear the story right this second. My eyelids are heavy, and all I want is the sweet oblivion only my pillow can provide.

"Fine. But I think we should establish a schedule of when we're allowed to bring guests. I had a full day, and I was planning on going to bed early."

"Totally. But I heard your evening wasn't a total bust."

"What do you mean?"

"You were spotted having dinner with Danny Hudson," she says way too chipperly.

"He was with me when we found the sock on the doorknob."

"What?" she shrieks. "Were you hoping to score a hookup yourself?"

"Will you tone down the excited poodle behavior? He came by to grab the money I owe him for his car repair. We decided to kill time at the diner. That's all."

"Really? So it wasn't a date?"

"No, it wasn't a date. You can stop planning our wedding now." I roll onto my side, giving my back to her, hoping she'll cease with the inquisition.

I can't believe she already knew I was with Danny tonight. Blimey, gossip travels fast here.

"Too bad. I heard you bumped into his ex," she continues, ignoring my blatant sign that I want to go to sleep.

Shite. She had to go mention something that'd pique my attention. I roll onto my other side so I can see her face.

"We did. She was a nightmare."

"I'm not surprised. I heard from a girl who is rushing her sorority that she forbade any of her sisters to even look in Danny's direction."

"She sounds like a psycho. Poor bloke."

"For real. But anyway, nothing for you to worry about, right? I mean, you said you weren't interested in boys."

"Nope. Still haven't changed my mind." I yawn heavily. "I'm going to sleep now. I'm destroyed."

"Okay, sweet dreams." She puts her headphones back on.

I try to get comfortable again, but even returning to my favorite sleeping position doesn't help me. My body is tired, but my mind is now whirring nonstop.

I wasn't lying when I said I wasn't interested in boys. They can be such a nuisance.

So why is Danny living rent free in my head?

It took me a while to fall asleep last night, and it was equally hard to get out of bed this morning. My internal clock is still wonky. I skip breakfast and, bleary-eyed, trudge toward the school. I didn't bother brushing my hair, just simply pulled it back into a messy ponytail. I couldn't tell someone what clothes I'm wearing if they asked me. It's only when I'm a block away from my building that I remember I actually own a car now and don't need to walk.

Bollocks. I can't believe I forgot. I'm having way too many Bridget Jones moments for my liking.

I turn around, and on the way to my car, I debate if I should stop to grab coffee somewhere. I could use some caffeine.

My phone rings when I slide behind the wheel. I don't recognize the number showing on my WhatsApp, and for that reason, I almost reject the call. Then I realize telemarketers wouldn't be calling me on the app.

"Hello?" I say, suppressing a yawn that sneaked in.

"Hey, good morning, Sadie."

"Who is this?" I grumble.

"It's Danny."

My pulse quickens, and in an instant, I'm wide awake. It seems Danny Hudson is better than coffee.

"Hey. Hi, I'm sorry, I didn't recognize your voice."

Shite. I sound like an idiot.

"It's okay. I hate to do this last minute, but I was wondering if your offer to give me a ride still stands."

"Of course. Do you need one now? I'm about to drive out of my parking lot."

"No, I'm going to practice with Andy. I need a ride later today. What time are you done?"

"Around three. Where do you need to go?"

"I gotta run an errand for my mother. I wouldn't ask you if it wasn't important."

Taking Danny on an errand run means spending more than just a few minutes with him. I'm not sure I should be doing that. He's already taking up too much space in my mind.

I could offer to lend him my car. I wouldn't have to play chauffeur, but then he might think I'm avoiding him.

Blimey. Why am I having such a hard time with this?

"Sadie? Are you still there?"

"Yeah, sorry. I spaced out for a moment. I didn't have coffee yet. Where am I picking you up? At your place?"

"Uh, probably easier to swing by the field. I'll be done with practice around the same time as you."

"Okay. Sounds good. I'll see you later, then."

"Thanks a lot, Sadie. I appreciate it."

"No worries."

It's not until I end the call that I see the problem with the logistics. What if my father sees me when I come by to pick up Danny? Would he think I'm messing with one of his players just to get to him?

Hell, it's too late to change plans now without sounding like a dimwitted fool.

Shoving all my concerns related to Danny to a dark corner in my mind, I drive to practice. I managed to avoid boy drama throughout school back in London; I won't fuck it up now when being the best on the field matters the most. I have to make up for lost time while I was recovering and prove to Coach Lauda that I shouldn't be benched.

Despite getting out of bed later than I planned, I'm one of the first ones in the locker room. None of the Three Musketeers are there, only Joanne and Vanessa, who are already in training gear. Both are covered in a sheen of sweat.

"Hey," I greet them.

"Morning, Sadie," Joanne replies.

Vanessa simply stares at me with a grin. *What does she find so amusing?* I choose to ignore it for now.

"When did you get here?" I ask.

"An hour ago," Vanessa answers. "We wanted to get a cardio session in before today's training."

"I should have done the same, but getting out of bed this morning was almost impossible."

"Someone keeping you up at night?" Vanessa raises an eyebrow.

I roll my eyes. "Ugh. For fuck's sake. Not you too."

Joanne glances between Vanessa and me. "What did I miss?"

"Sadie went out on a date with Danny Hudson last night." She laughs. "I knew I saw sparks when you guys were at each other's throats."

Joanne's eyes widen. "Sadie got into an argument with Danny? How is that possible? He's the most mellow football player I've ever met."

I point at Vanessa. "First of all, that wasn't a date." Then I turn to Joanne. "And you're wrong if you think Danny doesn't have a temper. You should have seen his reaction when his ex showed up."

Both Joanne and Vanessa watch me with renewed interest, making me regret my big mouth.

"Oh, don't stop there. Tell us more, tell us more," Vanessa sings to the tune of the *Grease* song.

"Now you're just taking the piss."

I give my back to them to shove my duffel bag in my locker.

"We're not making fun of you," Joanne pipes up. "Well, at least *I'm* not."

"There's nothing to tell. She acted like Danny still belonged to her, all jealous. He wasn't amused."

More of our teammates join us, effectively killing the conversation. I hope the subject dies for real. This is only the first week of preseason training and I'm already headlining gossip. I don't want to be known as Danny Hudson's date, hookup, whatever. I'm here to make a name for myself, not be arm candy to a football player.

TEN

DANNY

I'm drying my hair with a towel when Andy bumps his shoulder with mine.

"You were on fire today, bro."

"Thanks. It was a good day."

"Keep it up and nothing will stop us this season."

"That's the plan." I grin.

"Did you find someone to take you shopping today?"

I grimace, not keen on telling Andy who is giving me a ride.

"Ah, man. You didn't?" he asks. "You know I'd lend you my car if I didn't have to take Lorenzo to the dentist."

I shake my head. "I know. Don't worry though. I found someone."

"Oh yeah? Who?"

"Sadie," I mumble, purposely avoiding making eye contact.

"Come again?"

"Why are you surprised, Andy?" Puck butts in. "Danny was spotted having a romantic dinner with her last night."

I glower at him. "I hardly consider eating at a diner having a romantic dinner."

"You went out on a date with the hot English chick and didn't tell me?" Andy's voice rises.

"For fuck's sake, it wasn't a date," I growl. "A guy and a girl can hang out together without leading to anything sexual."

"Sure, if they're related. Even so, sometimes not even blood relation stops that." He shrugs.

"Ew. Can you please spare us your impure thoughts, infidel?" Puck retorts.

"Bite me, altar boy."

Puck jumps forward, ready to wrestle Andy into silence, but Andy was prepared and danced out of Puck's reach. Now that they're occupied with their stupid antics, I finish getting dressed without interruption and slip out of the locker room before they remember me.

On my way out of the gym building, I text Sadie to let her know I'm ready. She replies saying she'll be here in a minute, but she's obviously just around the corner, because I barely have time to slide my phone back in my pocket before I see her car approach.

She stops right in front of me. When I open the car door, loud music pours out, a pop beat I don't recognize.

"What are you listening to?" I ask by way of greeting.

"Oh, Boyzone."

"Boyzone? What is it, some new boy band?"

She laughs. "No. They're old school. Like popular in the '90s and early 2000s. My friend Anika put together a playlist on Spotify that includes only the top British songs from the last decades. She demanded I listen to it regularly so I don't forget home."

"I don't know if that's nice of her or if she's trying to torture you a bit."

She laughs. "Probably both."

"What's this jewel of the UK charts called, anyway?"

"'Picture of You.' Come on. It's not that bad."

"It'd probably be more tolerable if it was a smidge less deafening."

"Okay, okay."

She lowers the volume until we can actually carry on a conversation without having to resort to shouting.

"Thank you."

"Where are we going?" She puts the car in drive again.

"Ikea. I'll give you directions."

"Seriously? You're making me suffer through an Ikea shopping experience?"

"Come on. I thought girls loved buying shit for their dorms."

She shakes her head. "Not this girl. But it could have been worse."

"Oh yeah? What would you consider worse?"

"Going to a home improvement shop."

I chuckle. "You're lucky. Not today."

The cheesy song ends, and it's followed by another oldie. This one, at least, I've heard before, but I can't name the band or song.

After a while, I ask, "How was practice?"

"It could have gone better. I woke later than I planned and didn't have a chance to go for a run beforehand."

"You're hard-core dedicated to soccer, aren't you?"

"Yeah. I want to go pro."

"Me too."

She pulls her eyes from the road for a second. "You're that good?"

"Why do you sound so surprised?"

"I'm not surprised you're a good player, although I haven't seen you play yet. I just thought getting drafted to play in the NFL was as hard as winning the lottery."

She's not saying anything I don't know, but the reminder makes me less confident that it's an achievable goal.

"Coach Clarkson seems to believe I have a chance," I reply meekly.

"If he said that, then it must be true." Gone is the levity from a second ago, her voice suddenly cold and tight.

"He could be wrong though. But I'll give my all to make it happen."

"He's never wrong, at least not when it comes to football."

I frown. "How do you know that about my coach? Do you know him?"

"Bloody hell," she mutters and then falls silent.

"Sadie?"

She lets out an audible sigh, her shoulders sagging forward. "Okay, I didn't want anyone to know this, but, uh, your coach is my dad."

I stare at her without blinking, frozen as I process her words. "Coach Clarkson is your father?"

"Yep."

"I knew he was divorced, but that's about it."

She lets out a humorless laugh. "I'm not surprised. Why would he talk about the children he so easily gave up?"

I open and shut my mouth, but no word comes forth. I've always seen Coach Clarkson as a father figure. I can't reconcile that with the image of a man who walked out on his family.

"Are you saying he abandoned you and your mom?"

"No. My parents got a divorce, and then he let my mother take us to England."

"I'm sure it wasn't an easy decision to make. He was probably trying to avoid a custody battle."

Sadie's nostrils flare, and she's holding the steering wheel so tight now that her knuckles are white.

"And that's the reason I didn't want to tell anyone Coach Clarkson is my dad. I know his players idolize him."

"I'm sorry, Sadie. I clearly know a different man than you do."

"Yeah, clearly. Can we please not talk about him?"

"Of course." I look out the window, feeling conflicted about this revelation for more reasons than one.

It was already bad enough that I was letting Sadie reel me in. Now that I know she's Coach Clarkson's daughter, she's not only a terrible idea, but she's completely off-limits. I can't even dream about getting involved with the coach's daughter, especially knowing their relationship is rocky. I won't jeopardize my rapport with him, or my future, because of a girl, no matter how alluring I find her.

"What exactly do you need to buy at Ikea?" she asks after a few minutes of uncomfortable silence.

"Bookshelves."

"That's it?"

"Yeah. Mom is a bookworm, and she has a bad habit of hoarding novels she's already read. She had an old bookshelf that finally collapsed, and now all her books are scattered around her small apartment. She's been nagging me to buy her a new one for weeks."

"Couldn't she have waited a few more days until you got your car back?"

"Probably, but I know training will only get harder as the preseason progresses. I might as well go now before Coach trains us within an inch of our lives."

She falls silent again, and I realize I shouldn't have brought up her dad.

"And that's the last time I'll mention him. Promise."

She laughs. "God, you can mention him to me. He's your coach, after all, and a big part of your life. If we're going to be friends, I don't expect you to edit him out of conversation."

My stupid heart latches onto the "friends" bit of her speech and rejoices. Damn stupid muscle.

"So that's where this is going? Friendship?"

"Am I not driving you to bloody Ikea?" She glances at me, sporting a smirk.

"Sure, but I thought you were doing this to ease your guilty conscience."

"Nah. I'm only doing it because I like you."

"You like me?" I try not to sound too eager and fail.

"Down, boy. I like you as a friend. Don't get any ideas."

I scoff to hide my humiliation and disappointment. Friend zoned. I can't say it doesn't hurt.

"You think too much of yourself. I have zero interest in dating you. It's nothing personal. I just can't get distracted."

"We're on the same page, then. Besides, you're not my type."

"Ouch. Tell me how you really feel, why don't you?"

She winces. "Sorry. I did warn you I was savage. My tongue is a lethal weapon."

Hell. She had to go and mention her tongue. Now I'm thinking what kissing her would feel like. I bet she tastes sweet and dangerous. It's almost as if after I learned she's forbidden fruit and she doesn't want me, she became even more irresistible.

I have to stop this stupid shit. If I were any smarter, I'd say forget being friends. But I'm not, and if all I can get is Sadie's friendship, it's better than nothing.

ELEVEN

SADIE

I'm glad the cat is out of the bag, but at the same time, I'm peeved that Danny was so quick to defend my father. He acted exactly how I expected one of my dad's players would, and it pissed me off. I can't blame him though. He didn't know what it was like for me when my entire life fell apart.

I can't believe I told him we should be friends. This has disaster written all over it. Despite what I told him, he *is* my type —or at least I think he is. I'm not sure. I've never been so at ease with a guy before, and maybe that's doing my head in. The good thing is, he isn't interested in dating me—or anyone—either. We have that in common, so maybe this experiment of being friends with a bloke won't blow up in my face.

After another fifteen minutes driving on the highway, which went better than I expected, the blue and yellow Ikea building finally looms on the horizon. The car park is half full, which makes me wonder if people don't have any jobs. It's the middle of the afternoon on a weekday, after all.

"You'd better pray it's not a zoo inside," I tell Danny once I park the car.

"Ah, where's your sense of adventure?"

"Never had one."

"Somehow, I don't believe you."

He gets out before I can offer him a retort.

For the sake of keeping the peace and also not revealing too much about myself, I let his remark go.

We take the escalator up to the showroom, but since we know exactly what we're here for, I look for the sign pointing to the store area. Danny veers in the opposite direction.

"Where are you going?" I ask him.

"I don't know what kind of bookshelf I need yet."

I groan. "Great."

To my surprise, he throws his beefy arm over my shoulders and pulls me against his side. "Come on, Sadie. It'll be fun."

Alarm bells sound in my head when a ripple of desire travels down my spine and butterflies I never felt in my tummy before spring awake. Being this close to him is wreaking havoc in my body, but I'm too stunned to do anything besides bask in his warmth.

"We'll see," I reply weakly.

He steps aside in the next moment, releasing me from his embrace. I let out a breath of relief, but at the same time, I miss his proximity.

Note to self: no more getting close and personal with Danny Hudson if I want to keep my sanity.

The problem is that now I'm too aware of his presence, and the damn insects in my belly are still throwing a rave.

To distract myself from my problematic reaction to Danny, I focus on the knickknacks on display. Maybe I should buy something for my dorm room after all. My bed could use some colorful pillows, and a pinboard would be nice.

I stray from Danny when I find something that catches my eye in the home office section. It's a print of a picture of London in black and white with only the two-decker bus in color. I stare at it for a moment while I decide if it will work on my wall.

"Do you like that?" Danny stops next to me.

"Yeah. I know it's cheesy, but it's also cool."

"You should buy it, then."

"It might be too big."

"If it doesn't work, you can return it."

Wrinkling my nose, I say, "That means coming back here. No thanks."

I pivot around Danny and walk away from him and the picture. I should just stick to my original three items: a couple of pillows and a pinboard. I find one that will fit above my desk and promptly grab it. A second later, Danny pries the board from me.

"I'll carry this."

"There's no need to be chivalrous. You're not trying to get into my knickers, remember?"

He raises an eyebrow. "Do you think that's the only reason a guy would do something nice for a girl?"

I shrug. "Basically."

He laughs, shaking his head. "I don't know if I should be offended or sad for you."

"Hey! Don't you dare feel sorry for me."

"Fine, I'll stick with feeling deeply hurt, then."

I nod. "That's better. I always prefer when I'm inflicting pain on blokes."

"Even your friends?"

"Truth be told, I've never had a guy friend before. But if you ask any of my girlfriends back home, they'd tell you I'm not one to spare their feelings either. I'm too blunt for that."

"I don't mind brutal honesty as long as you can take as much as you can dish out."

"I've got thick skin. Don't worry."

We spend the next ten minutes looking at various bookshelves in the showroom until we get to where they're all displayed together. Mercifully, Danny doesn't take long to decide which one he wants. He takes a note of their model number and where they're located in the pickup area. We head downstairs, and on the way to the big warehouse, I wind up grabbing more items for myself than I intended.

"I thought you weren't one of those girls." Danny chuckles.

"Shut up. These are all basic necessities."

"Pillows are a basic necessity?"

"When they brighten my sleeping space, yes."

"Maybe you should grab some succulents too." Danny points at the miniature plants in cute vases.

"Oh God, no. They'd be dead in a week."

He stops offering comments as we continue to the warehouse. Then I try not to ogle him too much as he loads the large boxes in our trolley. It's pretty hard not to notice the muscles straining against his T-shirt though. The boy is damn gorgeous.

Curse football players and their top-shape physique.

"I think that's it," he declares as he turns and catches me staring. A broad smile splits his face. "Are you okay there, Sadie?"

I blink fast, trying to clear my mind of its lust-induced fog. "I'm hunky-dory."

"Hunky-dory." He chortles. "I don't think I've ever heard anyone our age say that before."

"I like to be different."

His eyes seem to shine with appreciation, making my face feel hot. "Okay, then."

He pushes the trolley forward, but I lag behind, still pissed that I let him see me drooling over him and also confused about that loaded glance.

"What are you doing back there? Checking out my fine ass?" he teases.

I snort. "Your arse is not that fine."

"So you *were* checking it, then?" He laughs.

I walk faster to catch up and, in retaliation, pinch his waist.

"Hey! What was that for?"

"Punishment for being a bellend."

"A what?"

I sigh. "A dickhead."

"How does stating the obvious make me a dickhead?"

"When it's nothing but a bold lie."

"Fine, Sadie. From now on, I'll pretend you don't find my tush appealing."

"Good," I say, then immediately realize my error.

Danny smirks but refrains from commenting.

When it's time to pay, I try to cover the cost of everything since I owe him money, but he doesn't let me pay for the bookshelves.

"What difference does it make how the money is spent?" I ask.

"Huge difference," he replies, and that's the end of it.

He then veers for the line where you can arrange for transportation.

"I think those will fit in my car, Danny."

He eyes them with a frown. "I'm not so sure."

"We should try anyway. If they don't fit, we'll come back."

"Okay."

We return to the garage, and after some maneuvering and a few cursed words, the boxes are in and the boot is closed.

"Told ya," I say.

"You don't need to gloat. I'm not a macho man who doesn't believe women can be right. I know better."

I snicker. "Your mother obviously trained you well."

He grins while his eyes fill with pride. "She did."

I'm not sure what it is about his look, but my chest feels warm and fuzzy all of a sudden.

TWELVE

DANNY

I wasn't expecting the bookshelves to fit in Sadie's car, so when I approach my mother's humble apartment building, a sense of shame takes hold of me. I don't know why I don't want her to know that I don't have a lot of money. Maybe it's stupid male pride.

Sadie doesn't bat an eyelash at the faded paint on the building or the yellowed grass and sad-looking garden at the front. When she gets out of the car, she does glare at the stairs leading to the second floor with her hands on her hips though.

"Please tell me your mother's apartment isn't on the top floor."

I circle to the back of the car and open the trunk. "I can't say that."

She looks over her shoulder, glowering. "You suck."

"Come on. It'll be great exercise. You were upset you missed your morning run. This ought to compensate for it."

"Breaking my back is not how I envision leading the Ravens to victory."

"Leading the Ravens? Does Vanessa know you're vying for her position as the team captain?"

She waves her hand dismissively as she walks over. "I don't want to be captain, but I do want a starting position. Melody McCoy thinks she's Megan Rapinoe, and someone needs to knock her off that pedestal."

"Ah, naturally. Because there can't be two queens on the field." I smirk.

Instead of backtracking, Sadie smiles wickedly. "Of course not. There can be only one."

My eyebrows arch. "Please tell me that was an actual *Highlander* reference and not a coincidence."

"You can't drown, you fool, you're immortal!" she replies, trying her best to sound like Sean Connery as Ramirez.

I throw my head back and laugh from the belly up.

"Blimey, I didn't know my Sean impression was that bad."

I wipe tears from my eyes. "It's actually spot on. I'm laughing because… well, I don't even know."

Deep down, I do know the reason. I've never met a girl who was into classic '80s movies, especially that particular one. My laughter wasn't from amusement but a rather pleasant surprise.

She shakes her head. "You're such a confusing boy. Come on. These boxes won't get themselves up those steps."

She nudges me out of the way and slides the top box off the trunk.

"It'll be easier if we carry the boxes together," I suggest.

"Are you implying I can't lift one by myself?"

"Not at all, but go on, try."

She narrows her eyes at me, and I sense she's taking my comment as a dare. Bending her knees, she lifts the box using her core strength and legs. But getting the box off the ground was the easy part; balancing the long board is what I predicted would be hard. Sadie staggers back as she tries to find her equilibrium, bumping into me.

"Watch it," I say through a suppressed laugh.

"If you laugh, I swear I'll do more than just pinch you."

I grab the end of the box. "Stop being stubborn and let me help you. I know you're strong, but there's no reason to make your life harder just to prove a point."

She moves forward to hold the other end of the box. "Fine, Hudson. You win."

We trudge toward the building and then up the stairs, carrying all the boxes up first before I open the front door and bring them into the apartment. As usual, the scent of baked cookies hits my nose. Mom always has them around when she knows I'm coming by. What she doesn't know is that I never eat everything she makes. If I did, I'd be a round little pig. Instead, I bring her treats to school and share them with my classmates or teammates.

"This is cozy," Sadie remarks. "Is your mum not home?"

"No. She's at work."

After all the boxes are inside the apartment and propped against the wall, Sadie glances around the room. "Where do you want the bookshelves to go?"

"Oh, we don't need to put them together now."

She gives me a droll stare. "I bet you were planning on assembling them right away. Two can get the job done faster than one."

"Are you sure you're up for it? I think I've already abused your friendship too much."

"Abuse away. I always prefer to have people indebted to me instead of the other way around."

"Is that so?"

"Yep. So they can't say no when I call asking them to help me bury a body."

"Jesus, Sadie. You have a twisted mind."

She sticks her tongue out at me, and all the blood in my body seems to whoosh south. This cannot happen. It's the second time in less than an hour that the urge to push Sadie against the wall and claim her mouth hits me. I need to reset my brain somehow.

"So, where are they going?"

I point at the wall where several book towers are lined up. "There. I need to make room first so we can set up the working area."

With Sadie's help, I move the furniture around. It's a small living room, so there isn't much space to work with. In the end, I have to carry the coffee table to the kitchen so we can spread out on the floor. It takes an hour to get all the bookshelves up, and we manage to do it without cursing at the furniture, or worse, bleeding all over Mom's rug.

"Done. Finally." I wipe the sweat off my forehead with the back of my hand.

"Not quite. What about all those books?"

"It's probably better if we let my mother organize them as she prefers. I'm sure she has a system."

"Fair enough."

"I'm parched. Do you want something to drink?" I head for the kitchen.

"Yeah. Water, please."

I fill a tall glass with cold water from the fridge and hand it over to Sadie, brushing the tips of her fingers with mine during the transfer. I've never believed in romantic nonsense such as sparks, but as we both drain our glasses of water, it does seem that the air around us is crackling with electricity. Maybe I shouldn't have locked gazes with her while I was drinking, and I most definitely should have looked away after I set the glass back on the counter.

"So, what now?" she asks.

I'm so caught up in the fight between reason and desire going on in my head that I totally misunderstand her question.

"What now what?" I ask in a high-pitched tone. Shit. My heart is racing.

"Do you have any other chores you'd like my help with while I'm here?"

Fuck. It seems only *my* mind was in the gutter. I'm glad I didn't do something stupid.

"No. We're all done. We should be heading back to campus."

No sooner do I say that than the sound of a key turning announces Mom's arrival.

Hell and damn. I wasn't planning on making introductions today. Probably never, if I'm being honest. Mom has always been able to tell what I'm feeling at any given time. If I don't control my emotions around Sadie, Mom will know I have the hots for the coach's daughter. She was never a fan of Gwen and was secretly hoping I'd find a new girlfriend soon. I don't need another matchmaker. Andy is bad enough.

"Danny, I didn't think you'd be here today. Isn't your car in the shop?" She walks over and then stops when she spots Sadie. "Oh, hello. I didn't know Danny had company."

Sadie steps forward, extending her hand. "Nice to meet you, Ms. Hudson. I'm Sadie, Danny's friend from school. I gave him a ride today."

"Oh, how nice of you. You can call me Martha." She smiles as she shakes Sadie's hand, then turns to me. I can see the glint of curiosity shining in her eyes.

"I owed him the favor considering I'm the reason he doesn't have a car."

Mom's brow furrows. "I don't follow."

"Sadie was the one who wrecked my car," I explain.

"Oh." Mom's eyes grow larger. "Well, it's still nice of you to offer."

"She also helped put the bookshelves together," I add.

"She did?" Mom's eyebrows arch slightly. "Well, thank you, dear."

"You're home early," I say, trying to divert her interest on Sadie.

"Slow day at the office today, and Dr. Francis is out of town."

I turn to Sadie. "Mom works at a plastic surgeon's office."

"Cool. You must be busy all the time, huh?"

"Oh yeah. Everyone in this town wants to look younger, better, or different. So, what brings you to LA?"

"Sadie's Coach Clarkson's daughter," I blurt out thanks to nervous agitation.

I look at Sadie, trying to convey that I'm sorry about my outburst. She shakes her head as if to say I'm the worst.

"Really?" Mom asks. "I didn't realize Coach Clarkson had kids. But you have an accent."

"Yeah, I've lived in London since I was six, after my parents split. I would have gone to uni there, but my parents had a deal that I'd come back to attend college in the US."

That's way more information than she volunteered to me in the car. Maybe she's telling Mom all that to avoid questions she isn't keen to answer.

"Well, we have to go now to try to beat traffic," I butt in.

"It's already too late for that, hon. Why don't you stay and have dinner?"

"Eh…." I can't think of an excuse to refuse, but I know I don't want to subject Sadie to my mother's inquisition.

"Oh, I can't stay," Sadie replies. "I promised I'd take my roommate out tonight. Maybe another time."

Mom's face falls. "Oh, that's too bad. Thanks for driving my son around and for helping him with the bookshelves."

"It was my pleasure," Sadie replies through a beaming smile.

Before we rush out, Mom shoves a bag of cookies into my hand and also Sadie's. By the time we make it back to her car, she's already on her second cookie.

"I thought you had dinner plans. You're going to spoil your appetite eating all that."

"I don't have dinner plans. I only said that because you looked so pained. I figured you didn't want me to hang out with your mum."

Shit. That's what she thought?

"Sadie, you got it all wrong. I was just trying to protect you from her billion questions. I'm sorry I told her who you were."

"I didn't mind that. It's the truth, after all."

She stops in front of her car and offers me the keys. "Do you mind driving back? I'm knackered."

"Not at all."

Our fingers connect again, and I try not to react to it. I should have learned my lesson when I pulled her into a side hug back at Ikea. She felt too damn good in my arms, which means I have to keep my distance and avoid all contact, even innocent ones like this.

"Since I'm driving, maybe I should pick the music this time?" I ask once we're both inside.

"Sure. Go ahead. I'm curious about what your musical tastes sound like."

"I like a lot of different styles."

"I'm the same. Don't judge me through my friend's choices."

"Oh, it's already too late for that."

She rolls her eyes but refrains from replying.

I pick a random radio station and drive away from my mother's building. We don't speak for several minutes, but this time around, the silence isn't uncomfortable. When traffic slows to a stop, I glance at Sadie. Her head is propped against the window. She's sound asleep. Glutton for punishment that I am, I stare like a creep until some asshole honks behind me.

I see then that the line of cars has moved and I had been holding traffic.

Mom was right; it was too late to avoid rush hour, and it takes me an hour to get back to campus. Instead of driving to my place, I head to Sadie's building instead.

"Sadie." I shake her arm lightly. "We're home."

She blinks her eyes open, looking a little confused. Her gaze is unfocused as she stares at me, but when she looks out the window, her body seems to tense.

"You drove to my place, not yours."

"You were passed out. I didn't want you to have to drive back alone when you're that exhausted."

"How are you getting home?"

"I'll figure it out. Don't worry about me."

"Take my car."

My eyes widen. "What? No. How are you getting to practice tomorrow?"

"I can jog there. Seriously, it's no big deal."

I shake my head. "No, I'll pick you up. What time do you have to be there?"

"Six. Is that too early for you?"

Yes, but I don't tell her I don't need to be at practice until eight.

"Not at all. I'll see you tomorrow, then. And thanks for the ride and everything."

She leans across the gap between our seats and kisses me on the cheek. My breath catches.

What the hell is she doing?

"What's that for?" I ask when she returns to her side.

"That's my thank-you for today. I had fun. See you later, alligator."

She's out of the car before I can recover. In fact, it takes me a full minute to finally snap out of my paralysis and drive away.

I'm so fucked.

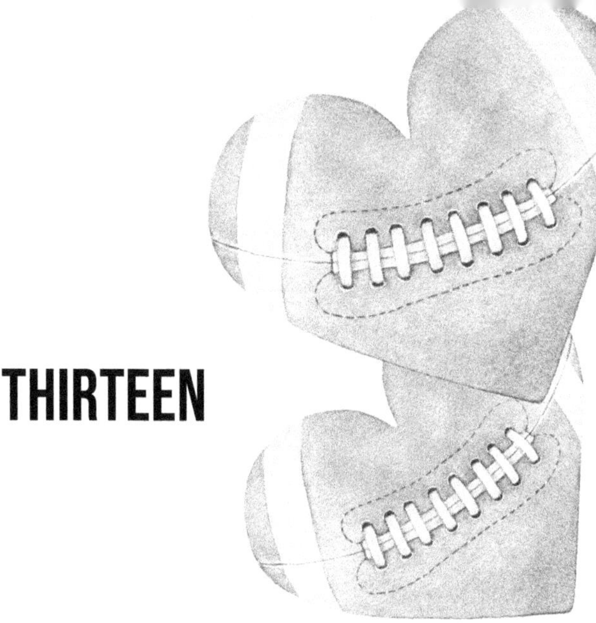

THIRTEEN

SADIE

I was tired until I decided to play dead from the neck up and kiss Danny on his cheek. My lips were still tingling by the time I slipped into my dorm room. Lucky for me, Katrina wasn't around, and I didn't have to make small talk while freaking out that I fancy Danny way too much and I really, really want a snogging session with him.

I can't allow myself to fall for a boy, especially one of my dad's players. That'd be more stupid than getting into the path of a knife.

I prop my new pinboard against the wall and then toss my new pillows on the bed before changing into my pj's. Once under my covers, I try to get comfortable, but now I'm too wired and can't relax.

You're just horny, Sadie.

Ugh. How did I let Danny sex me up like that? He wasn't even trying. God, I'm such a twat.

Well, there's nothing for it now. I have to get rid of this pent-up sex drive or I'll jump Danny the next time I see him. I send Katrina a WhatsApp message to ask when she thinks she'll be home. I don't want her to burst in when I'm playing with my toys.

She replies that she'll be back in a few hours and to not wait up.

Wasn't planning on it, sugar.

I get out of bed again and pull my suitcase from under the bed. *I really need to finish unpacking.* After a minute rummaging through the mess of clothes, shoes, and other junk, I finally locate my stash of toys, which I had the foresight to put in a small pouch just in case some nosy airport employee decided to check the contents of my luggage.

I want fast relief because I do need to sleep, so I choose my favorite toy, a bullet that can make me come in less than a minute.

But tonight it seems my body refuses to cooperate, and my faithful device is not doing the trick. *Goddamn it, Danny. You'd better not have ruined me for my toys.* I close my eyes and remember how he made me feel when he hugged me briefly, how his cheek felt against my lips. Then my imagination runs wild, placing him in my room. In my head, he kisses my neck and touches my body with his big hands. I pinch my nipple through the fabric of my shirt and arch my back when I finally feel the tendrils of pleasure build between my legs.

When I climax, I pretend it's Danny between my legs, pumping into me and fucking me into oblivion. I may have said his name out loud.

Blimey, I didn't realize I had it that bad for him.

I do need to find a way to get him out of my head. In hindsight, getting off while thinking of him is not the best way to do it, but at least I'm relaxed now. I'll figure out how to stop wanting him tomorrow.

The sound of someone knocking on my door disturbs my peaceful dream. I groan, hiding my head under the pillow and hoping whoever is bothering me will go away.

"Sadie? Are you there?"

Fuck. That's Danny.

I jump out of bed as if I've been electrocuted. *What's Danny doing at my door at this hour?* Katrina's bed is empty, so she must not have made it back home yet.

I hurry to open the door, tripping over my duffel bag's strap and colliding with the door.

"Ouch!"

"Jesus, what was that?" he asks.

I open the door with a jerky movement, not caring about how I look. If he's here, there must have been an emergency. It takes me a second to notice he's fresh out of the shower. His curls are still damp, and he smells soapy.

"What happened?" I ask.

His eyes widen when he sees me there, standing in all my just-out-of-bed glory. I must be quite the sight.

"Uh, you told me you had to be at practice at six. It's a quarter till," he says, smirking.

"What?" I shriek. "It's morning already?"

"Yeah."

"Bloody hell." I pivot around and try to find my phone in the dark.

"Uh, should I wait in the car?"

"No, you can come in. It's fine. I'll change in the bathroom. Would you mind hitting the light switch? I can't see a damn thing."

The sudden brightness makes my eyes burn, but when I get used to it, I regret not sending Danny to wait in the car after all. My room is a fucking war zone.

"Better?" he asks.

"Uh, probably not."

He steps around my stuff, looking at everything with curiosity. "What happened here?"

"I was too tired last night to tidy up my room." I yank the cover off my bed so I can at least straighten it and accidentally send my bullet flying right into Danny's hand.

"What do we have here?" He looks at the pink device, fighting to keep a straight face.

My cheeks are burning as I reach for it. "Give me that."

I step back fast, clutching my bullet tightly, while Danny is watching with mirth shining in his eyes.

"Quit looking at me like that."

"Like what?" he asks innocently.

"Like this is amusing to you."

"I can't help that it is."

"Shut up. This is the most embarrassing moment of my life." I bend over to grab the little pouch from the floor, but I forgot to zip it closed last night and, in my haste, end up spilling all my toys onto the floor. "Shite!"

"Whoa. That's quite a stash. You weren't kidding when you said you had needs."

"I take it back. *This* is the most embarrassing moment of my life."

I keep my gaze down, hiding my face behind my hair as I quickly shove everything into the container and out of sight. Then I drop the pouch in my luggage, close it, and slide it back under the bed. When I finally rise from my crouch and dare to look at Danny again, he still has a shit-eating grin on his face.

"What?" I cross my arms over my chest.

"Nothing. Maybe I should wait in the car and give you time to recover."

"Recover from what?" I snap, even though I know exactly what he's saying. I just told him I was embarrassed.

"Uh...." He rubs the back of his neck while his cheeks turn pinker.

Ha! I managed to turn the tables on him and I wasn't even trying. It doesn't make me less mortified, but at least I'm not the only one feeling uncomfortable as hell.

"Just sit down and wait for me. I'll be back in a few minutes."

I grab the first pieces of clothing I can find in my dresser drawer plus my toiletry bag and then rush out of my room. I usually take a shower in the morning, but since I'm already late, I just brush my teeth and wash my face. I try not to cringe too much at the state of my hair. It's good that Danny saw me at my worst. I need him to remain in the friend zone at all costs. It'll be easier if he perceives me as one of the guys and not at all attractive.

I return to my room in less than five minutes and find Danny browsing on his phone. He looks up when I enter, no longer red-faced.

"Ready?" he asks.

"Yeah."

He stands up, and the room becomes much smaller suddenly. He's a tall guy, over six feet, with wide shoulders. But it's not the size of his frame that makes it feel like the place has shrunk. It's his presence that gives the illusion. He's everywhere.

His eyes shift focus to something over my shoulder, so I turn to see what caught his attention.

"Do you need help putting that up?"

"Oh, the pinboard? Nah, I just need a nail and a hammer."

"Do you have those tools?"

"No."

He chuckles. "Okay. I'll bring them next time."

"Next time?" I arch my eyebrows.

He shrugs in a cute, boyish way, and my insides turn into gummy bears.

Danny Hudson must have a horrible flaw, and I need to find out what that is before my attraction to him gets out of hand.

"We're friends, aren't we?"

"Yep. Let's go already before my roommate decides to show up and get the wrong idea about us."

"She didn't spend the night?"

"It doesn't look like it."

My intention of avoiding gossip becomes moot when we encounter several people in the hallway, either heading out or going to the bathrooms. Danny and I earn curious glances, which only sets my teeth on edge.

In the car park, he veers straight to the driver's side but stops suddenly when he realizes his mistake. "Eh, you probably should be driving since it's your car."

"It's fine. I'm not fully awake yet."

I slide into the passenger side before more people see us together, pulling the hoodie over my head.

"Cold?" he asks me.

"Yeah."

"If you weren't late already, we could stop to grab coffee."

My stomach growls at the prospect of the warm and delicious caffeine treat, but I can't indulge.

"Maybe next time. I'm sorry I wasn't ready. I forgot to set my alarm."

"No worries. I didn't mind coming up to your room."

"I bet you didn't," I grumble.

He laughs. "You know, girls have it much easier. You have all those cool toys. I have to make do with my hand."

I sink farther into the seat. I just pictured Danny wanking off, and that makes my core throb. My memories of last night come to the forefront of my mind, making my face feel hot again. I'm glad the hoodie is hiding it. But instead of changing the subject, I make it worse.

"That's not true. What about blow-up dolls?"

"Have you seen the size of those? It's not like I can hide them under my pillow."

"There's also this device made out of silicone or something

that's supposed to replicate a woman's vagina. Dudes say it feels almost like the real deal."

Danny groans. "Sadie, stop talking about sex toys."

"You started it."

"Well, now I want to stop," he grits out, almost as if he's in pain.

"Why?" On a hunch, I drop my gaze to his crotch and see the huge bulge his sweatpants can't hide. *God have mercy.* "Oh. Sorry."

He tries to fix his pants in a way that it's not obvious he's sporting wood. Of course I have to open my big mouth again.

"It's fine. I get that guys can't always control what their wieners do."

"It would help if you'd stop staring at it," he grumbles.

I look out the window, covering my mouth and trying to suppress the laughter that bubbled up my throat. I fail.

"Stop laughing, Sadie. This isn't funny."

The giggles take over, and I can't stop.

"I'm sorry, but you have to see the humor in this situation." I wipe the tears from the corners of my eyes. That's how hard I'm laughing.

He grins. "Fine. It was funny. I'm glad we're friends. I'd be double mortified if you were a girl I was trying to score with."

My heart constricts in my chest at his reminder that he isn't interested in me. But I can't complain. I was the one who set the rules, after all.

FOURTEEN

DANNY

Getting Sadie out of my head after the sex toy convo was hard. I kept imagining her playing with them, which left me in a state of semi-arousal in the most inappropriate moments. I couldn't even look Coach Clarkson in the eye. What would he think about me if he knew I was lusting after his daughter?

Mercifully, Andy didn't give me a hard time about Sadie, even after I revealed she was Coach Clarkson's daughter. I have to thank Jane for that reprieve; whenever she's around, Andy only has eyes for her.

In an exercise of self-restraint, I manage to keep my contact with Sadie to a few messages here and there throughout the rest of the week. I felt tempted to invite her to hang out, but that wouldn't help me at all. In just a few days, she managed to get under my skin. It's crazy how much I miss her already, and I barely know her.

Friday morning, I get a call from the garage to let me know the car is ready. The damage was more extensive than their first assessment, so the repair cost was more than five hundred dollars. The knowledge made me consumed with guilt, which is nonsense. Sadie wrecked my car, after all. But I still avoided telling her until the last minute, right before Andy was getting ready to give me a lift.

I send her a message on WhatsApp. She doesn't answer, and a moment later, I get a call from a number I don't recognize.

"Hello?"

"Hey, Danny. It's me. Sadie."

"Whose phone is this?"

"Oh, I finally got a US number. You'd better save it in your contacts. Anyway, I'm calling to ask if you need me to drive you to the garage. Then I can pay the bill."

I glance at Andy, who's eating a snack in the kitchen. I should tell Sadie I don't need a ride, but I would still need to swing by her place to get the money. It'd be easier to just let her drive me there instead of bothering Andy.

"Yeah. Sounds good. What time do you think you can be here?"

Andy snaps his head in my direction, frowning.

"Ten minutes tops. Does that work?"

"Yeah."

"Okay, see you soon."

"Who was that?" Andy asks after I put the phone away.

"Sadie. She's taking me to the garage."

His lips curl into a knowing grin. "Is she now? You sure enjoy spending time with the coach's daughter."

"Shut up, man." I flop on the couch and turn the TV on.

Not satisfied, Andy walks over and sits next to me. "I get the appeal. Forbidden fruit always tastes better."

"Oh yeah? Was that why you went after Jane?"

My comment erases the mirth off his face in an instant. "You know it wasn't like that with Jane."

"Fair. Just like it isn't like that with Sadie. We're just friends."

"Uh-huh. Sure. I'll pretend I believe you."

"I'm not kidding, Andy. So stop with the cupid shit, all right?"

"Are you saying if the opportunity presents itself, you're going to hook up with someone else at the Pike party tonight?"

I scoff. "Shit. Is it tonight? I forgot about it."

"Yeah, it's tonight, and you're going."

"*I'm* going? What about you and Jane?"

"Nah, we're staying home tonight. Gotta make up for the time she was away."

"What about Lorenzo?" I ask.

"He has a sleepover. Everything is arranged. All I need is to get rid of you for a few hours."

"Gee, way to make me feel good about being your roommate."

"Come on. It's not like I'm asking you to find a place to crash tonight. Just do me a favor and don't come home before midnight."

Before I can reply, I receive a text from Sadie saying she's downstairs.

"Fine. I'll go to the stupid party." I get up and head for the door.

"Maybe Sadie wants to go," Andy chimes in before I walk out.

"Right. Whatever. See you later."

Like I'd ask her to come to the party with me. Maybe I *should* hook up with someone just to stop obsessing about her.

As soon as the idea enters my head, I reject it. I don't want to sleep with a random girl.

Outside, I search for Sadie's car. She must not have parked near the building's entrance.

"Hey, Danny," a female voice says from behind me.

I turn but haven't the faintest clue who the girl is smiling at me.

"Hi."

"Are you going to the Pike party tonight?"

I'll never get used to people acting like I owe them information about my life. Popularity was never my goal. I just want to play football.

"I'm not sure yet."

She steps closer and places her hand on my arm. "I hope you do."

A loud honk makes her jump back. We both turn to the street. Sadie just stopped in the middle of the road. Her passenger window is down, and she's leaning closer to it.

"Hey, lover boy. Get in here," she says.

My face splits into a broad smile. My reaction is not for this random chick's benefit. I'm genuinely happy to see Sadie. Too happy, actually.

Settle down, stupid heart.

"Is that your girlfriend?" the girl asks.

"Sure," I reply absentmindedly and rush to Sadie's car.

She takes off before I have the chance to put my seat belt on.

"Whoa. What's the hurry?"

"I was blocking traffic."

"There was no one behind us." I click the seat belt in place.

"Well, I don't want to get stuck in traffic. Katrina invited me to a party, and she wants to doll me up. I have no idea what that entails or how long it will take."

"Are you talking about the Pike party?"

"I don't know. Some Greek party. I wasn't paying attention. Why? Are you going?"

"I was thinking about it." I look out the window to hide my lying face.

I don't know why I felt the need to lie to her about it when I know I'll be there. It's just a party. I'm an idiot.

"Cool. Then maybe I'll see you there. Although, considering Katrina has roped me into being her guinea pig, maybe it'd be better if you didn't go. There's a fifty-fifty chance that I'll look like a lost pageant contestant."

I laugh. "Damn. Now I have to go."

"Shite. I should have kept my mouth shut, huh?"

"Probably."

She yawns. "God, I'm so tired. The last thing I want is to go to a stupid party. But I promised."

"I hear ya. If you hadn't promised, I'd offer to hang out with you."

"What? In my tiny dorm room? Why couldn't we hang out at your place?"

"We can any other night, but my roommate has planned a romantic evening with his girlfriend, and he wants me out of there for a few hours."

"Ah, I see. So you *are* actually going to the party." She smirks.

"Well, I'm not sure yet. I was thinking of catching a movie."

"Ugh. That's sounds like a better idea, but like I said, I promised."

"I'll go to the party if that will make you feel better."

Not because I want to spend more time with you.

I can hear Will Ferrell saying I sit on a throne of lies. Shit.

"Hmm. Would I get to witness you fend off all those jersey chasers?"

I fidget in my seat, not liking where she's going with this.

"Uh...."

She laughs. "For fuck's sake. Relax. I'm just taking the piss. I don't care if you have a bazillion arse lickers all over you."

"You don't?"

She glances at me for a second. "Why should I?"

I grind my teeth, annoyed.

"No reason."

Fuck. I'm doing a hell of a job pretending Sadie and I are just friends.

FIFTEEN

"What do you think?" Katrina turns my chair around and finally allows me to see her masterpiece.

My jaw drops. I don't look like me.

"What did you do?" I ask. "I look so pretty."

"You *are* pretty. I just enhanced your natural looks with makeup."

"My hair feels so luscious." I run my fingers through it. The blonde seems even lighter.

"That's the effect of brushing it." She laughs.

"Hey! I do brush my hair… on occasion."

"I know. But it's always in a ponytail."

"Of course. I'm always training. It'd get in the way otherwise."

"What are you planning on wearing?" she asks as she collects all her beauty products and puts them away.

I glance down at my favorite pair of jeans and flouncy top. "This."

She glances at me with an eyebrow raised. "Really? You don't want to wear a dress?"

"I only own one dress, and it's boring as hell. I prefer jeans anyway." I stand and go in search of my shoes.

"How about a skirt? You've got those soccer player legs. You shouldn't hide them."

I do have nice legs, but I never bothered flaunting them before. I want to look my best tonight though, and it has nothing to do with a certain someone who's going to be at the party. My pulse accelerates just by thinking about Danny. Crap.

"I suppose I could wear a skirt." I look in my drawers, remembering I already unpacked my micro jean skirt.

Anika made me buy it on a dare, but I never felt like wearing it, to be honest. It still has the tag on it. I change out of my jeans and into the skirt, then grab my Doc Martens from the closet.

Katrina scrunches her nose. "Are you seriously wearing those ugly boots?"

I press a hand over my chest. "How dare you offend my Doc Martens? They're classic."

She shrugs. "If you say so. It doesn't really matter. No one will be looking at your feet."

I roll my eyes. "I'm not going to this party in the hopes of scoring. I just want to have fun with my friends."

"And is one of your friends a tall and handsome football player?" She smiles slyly.

I watch her through slitted eyes. "Yes, Danny is one of my friends. And that's all we are. Don't get any ideas."

"So you wouldn't care if I went after him?"

A sliver of jealousy spears my chest. I can't help but glare at Katrina, even though I should be keeping my expression neutral.

"I don't care," I say through clenched teeth.

"Holy shiiit. That was the most intense death glare I've ever received in my life."

I sit on my bed to put my boots on and effectively avoid making eye contact with Katrina. "Whatever."

Boots laced up, I jump up with sudden jittery energy and reach for my small purse on my desk. I can only fit my phone, keys, and some cash, but Katrina is driving tonight, so I don't need to worry about bringing my license.

"I'm ready. Let's go."

"Eager, aren't we?" she teases.

"Yes, I'm eager to mingle with people who are not getting on my nerves."

"Gee, you're so touchy. I won't say another word about Danny. Promise."

Good on her word, Katrina doesn't mention Danny on the drive to the party. It seems we arrive just when the place is filling up. We follow the flow of partygoers going into the house, but soon Katrina is swarmed by her sorority sisters. Not wanting to be engulfed by that sea of high shrieks and phony smiles, I step aside and lose sight of her. My teammates said they'd come, so I pull my phone out and send a message to our WhatsApp group.

SADIE: I'm at the party. Where is everyone?

VANESSA: We're all the way in the back.
Beware of the dicks in the kitchen.

SADIE: You have to be more specific than that.

JOANNE: Nick Fowler and his buddies.

SADIE: Don't worry. I can handle a few tossers.

I'm tempted to text Danny too, but think better of it. There are a lot of people here and we might end up missing each other, but I won't seek him out, no matter how much I want to see him.

I push my way through the throng of people until I finally reach the kitchen. There is a group of guys huddled together, filling red Solo cups and laughing about something. They look positively pissed already. I ignore them and continue toward the door to the back. One of them sees me and steps in front of it, blocking my way.

"Hello, gorgeous. Where do you think you're going?"

"Taking into account that you're not my father or anyone who matters, I don't bloody need to tell you anything. Now move."

"Burn, Fowler!" One of his friends laughs, and the others join in.

So this is the wanker Vanessa warned me about. His eyes flash with annoyance as he takes a step into my personal space. "Such a bitchy attitude for a pretty face. Don't worry, I can fix your bad manners in no time."

"Listen up, creep, because this is the only warning you're getting. Move any closer and you can forget procreation. Although, thinking about it, I'd be doing humanity a favor by ripping your nut sack off."

I can see Nick is not taking my threat seriously by the way his lips curl up in amusement. Sometimes, words aren't enough; people need to be shown you mean business. I really wasn't looking forward to getting into a brawl with anyone tonight, but hell, I'm not going to be coerced by an asshole who thinks a penis gives him the power to say and do whatever he pleases.

"Hello, party people!" a male voice shouts from behind me. "Welcome to La Casa Pike."

Nick looks over my head and twists his face into a scowl. I half turn to see who came in. There's a guy wearing a paper crown on his head with a pretty blonde who doesn't look too happy to be standing next to him.

"Hey, Leo," one of Nick's friends says. "You're out of booze, man."

"Only because you drank it all, jackass."

He staggers forward in my general direction. His eyes are glazed over, and to avoid getting pushed right into Nick, I jump aside. Leo's drunken antics distract Nick enough to allow me to shove him out of my way.

"Hey, where do you think you're going?" he asks, grabbing my arm.

In a knee-jerk reaction, I kick back, hitting his shin hard. He releases my arm and curses.

"Fucking bitch!"

"I warned you, arsehole."

I'm out the door before he can say anything else. My heart is racing as I stride through the backyard. I didn't expect such a high-intensity situation tonight. It wasn't the same, but it put me back in the evening in London when Anika and I were accosted. I hate that someone like Nick Fowler made me relive my darkest nightmare. Fucking hell.

There's a bonfire going, but I don't see any of my teammates near it. I do see Danny though, talking to some girl I don't know. I get jealous all over again, and that just adds insult to injury. This evening is turning out to be a total bust, and I'm a second from going home.

I pivot, changing my course of direction, and end up bumping into someone else I didn't care to see tonight.

Danny's ex.

"Watch where you're go—oh, it's you." Her lips twist into a malicious grin. She looks over my shoulder, probably in Danny's direction, then back at me. "Ah, it seems you've been replaced already. Too bad."

"Piss off, psycho." I push her out of my way, seeing nothing in front of me. My temper isn't rising—it's already reached boiling point. If I bump into another annoying person, I might punch them in the throat.

"Sadie! Over here." Vanessa waves at me.

I walk toward her and see she's hanging out with Melody and Joanne. No sign of the Three Musketeers.

"Jeez, what happened to you?" Joanne asks.

"I've met the dick, the witch, and now I need a drink."

"Oh my God. She's spewing bad poetry. Give her a beer already," Melody tells Vanessa.

"I'd prefer something stronger."

Melody raises an eyebrow. "Sorry, sugar. This isn't a bar. We only have beer."

"I didn't mean it like that."

Vanessa shoves a bottle of Corona in my hand. "Don't listen to Melody. Here, drink this. It'll take the edge off."

"Thanks."

I twist the cap off and take a couple big chugs, emptying half the bottle. Then I wipe off my lips with the back of my hand. Classy I'm not.

"Better?" Vanessa smirks.

"Not yet, but I'll get there. You weren't kidding. Nick Fowler is a major arsehole. I had to kick him to get rid of the wanker."

"You kicked Nick?" Joanne asks. "Where?"

"Please tell me in his junk," Vanessa pipes up.

"I got his shin. Sorry to disappoint."

I drink some more, then ask, "So this is it? We just hang out here and drink beers?"

"For now. Why? Too boring for you?" Melody retorts.

"No, I'm just wondering. There's music inside. I don't mind dancing."

Vanessa opens her mouth to reply, but then something behind me catches her attention. "Ah shit."

"What?" I turn and see the blonde girl who came with Leo into the kitchen marching in our direction.

"It's my twin sister, Heather."

"Oh."

A moment later, Heather joins us, and Vanessa asks, "What's up, sis? Got tired of your boyfriend already?"

"Leo is a jackass. Can I have a beer?" She reaches for the cooler next to Melody without waiting for an answer.

"Hold on a second, honey. This is for Ravens only. Why don't you go back to your flock?"

"Mel, come on. Let Heather have a beer," Vanessa chimes in.

"Fine."

"Thanks." Heather takes a bottle from the cooler and, just like me, drains half of it in large gulps.

"Whoa. Slow down, Heather," Vanessa says.

I'm distracted when I feel a tap on my shoulder. I turn around and stare right into Danny's eyes. The breath whooshes out of my lungs. I wasn't expecting him and therefore didn't put up my shield.

"Hey," he says.

"Hi," I squeak.

"Did you just get here?"

"Uh, no."

"Hello, Danny, how are you?" Melody says in a mocking tone that indicates she caught on to his rudeness. He didn't acknowledge any of them.

"Oh, hi, girls," he replies sheepishly, then turns his attention back to me. "You look nice. Nothing at all like a lost pageant contestant."

"Yeah, Katrina did a good job."

"I don't think I've ever seen your hair down." He reaches over to take a strand between his fingers.

Fuck a duck. What the hell is he doing?

I clear my throat. "It's not like we hang out all the time."

He drops his hand as his expression becomes more serious. "True. Well, I'd better go look for Puck and Paris."

"What? Andy and Jane aren't coming?" Vanessa asks.

"Ah, not tonight. They're still in the honeymoon phase." He shrugs. "Well, I guess I'll see you guys later."

"Sure," I try to reply, like I don't care, but I think I end up sounding a bit snobbish. *Shite.*

Once Danny is out of earshot, Joanne says, "Was that weird or what?"

"I don't know if it was weird, or he simply felt that Sadie's cold behavior was too much like Siberia," Vanessa replies.

"What are you talking about?" I look at her, genuinely surprised.

"You acted like you couldn't wait to get rid of the guy," Heather replies, then takes a sip of her beer.

"I did not!"

"Uh, you kinda did." Joanne nods.

Stumped, I glance in the direction Danny went. *Fuck. Did I mess up already?* I didn't mean to act like a cow.

"Ah, who cares? He's just another dude who thinks he's the king of the world because he has a sausage between his legs," Melody butts in.

"Danny is not like that," I retort. "Shite. I have to talk to him."

"You do that," Vanessa says, smiling from ear to ear.

I don't have time to dissect that expression. I finish the rest of my beer and head after Danny. He went back into the house already, and I can't find him that easily. It's too busy. *Come on, now. He's tall. It shouldn't be that hard.* I wind up in the main room where the DJ is set up. People are dancing to an upbeat tune that, at any other time, I might appreciate. But I'm too concerned about Danny to care.

Bloody hell. A dude is making me act like a deranged twat. What the actual fuck? I'm doing exactly what I said I wouldn't do.

I stop in my tracks, but the crowd's motion pushes me forward until I'm right in the middle of the dance floor. I don't know how, but someone managed to ride the wave of writhing bodies while carrying a tray of shots. He stops in front of me and hands me one.

"What is it?" I take the small plastic cup.

"Tequila."

All right. I can use that. I toss the shot back, then take another cup from the tray. Why the hell not?

It doesn't take long for me to feel the effects of the drink. My body relaxes, and I forget Danny for a while. I dance and dance, losing track of time. And when "Blinding Lights" by The Weeknd starts to play, I close my eyes and let the music take control. All my problems evaporate into thin air and nothing matters besides the beat of the song. I'm definitely buzzin'.

I feel hands touching me, pulling and pushing in different directions. Even with my eyes open, I can't make out the faces of the people around. The room is spinning, and everything is blurry. Maybe I drank too much, but hell, I've never gotten that drunk after a couple shots of tequila and a beer. I decide that maybe I need fresh air and some water.

Moving through the crowd isn't as easy as before, and my legs don't seem to want to cooperate. Vertigo hits me, and I end up staggering forward and bumping into a body. Arms circle around my waist, and I'm pulled closer to a bloke who is smiling too broadly and smells of beer and sweat. I try to push him off me, but he only keeps his hold on me tighter.

"Not so fast, sugar. We have a score to settle."

"Let me go," I say feebly.

I push against his frame, but it's like my arms are made out of cotton candy. With me firmly in his grasp, he steers me farther away from the dance floor. I have no idea where he's taking me. I just know I have to get away.

"Sadie," I hear someone call out, but I can't pinpoint the direction the voice came from. Everything is so damn loud.

A second later, I'm pulled from whoever was holding me into the arms of another person. At this point, dark dots are clouding my eyesight, and I feel like I might pass out at any moment. There are shouting and angry words exchanged, but I'm too far gone to distinguish the words.

Then my legs seem to vanish from under me, and everything is pitch black.

SIXTEEN

DANNY

When I saw Sadie being dragged by Nick Fowler, I knew something was wrong. She'd never associate with that jackass. The moment I got close and saw her condition, anger like I'd never known surged through me, making me see red. I wanted to punch the asshole's face into a pulp. Sadie was barely conscious.

But I couldn't get into a fight with him while he had Sadie trapped under his arm.

Good thing I wasn't alone.

While I pried her from his grasp, Paris got into his face. If some of the frat boys hadn't come in to intervene, I'm sure he'd have done what I wanted to do myself. They dragged Nick away, preventing a fight that would cost us big-time.

Now Sadie is passed out in my arms, and I don't know what to do.

Paris turns his attention to her, still breathing hard from the altercation.

"She's out cold," I tell him. "I don't know what happened. She was fine when I talked to her earlier."

"Was she drinking?"

"She had a beer in her hand."

Paris peels her eyelid back. Being premed, he's more qualified to figure out what's wrong with her than I am.

"Her pupils are dilated. You said she was fine. How long ago was that?"

"I don't know. Maybe an hour."

He rubs his face. "I don't want to make you even more worried, but I think she was drugged."

"What? Are you sure?"

"I'm almost positive."

"I should take her to the emergency room, right?"

"Danny?" Sadie asks in a small voice.

"Sadie, honey. Are you okay?"

Her eyes are only half open and unfocused.

"I can't feel my body. Where am I?"

"We're still at the party."

"What party?" Her eyelids begin to close again.

"Maybe you should take her to the hospital," Paris tells me.

"What? Why?" she asks in a high-pitched voice.

I don't like how people are staring at us, so I move toward the front door and don't answer her until we're outside. Paris is right behind me.

"What did you take, Sadie?" I ask.

"Two shots of tequila, I think."

"Do you remember who gave you those shots?" Paris asks.

"No."

"Shit. There could be more people affected," he says as he stares at the house.

"Go back and tell Puck and the others to keep an eye out for possible victims," I tell him. "I'll take Sadie to the emergency room."

"I don't need to go to the hospital," Sadie insists. "I just need to sleep this off."

"Sadie, I think you've been drugged."

"Roofied?"

"We don't know."

"I can't go back to the hospital, Danny. Please don't take me back. Please," she begs, twisting my insides.

"Don't take me back," she said. What does that mean?

"If she was given a roofie, the effects should wear off between sixteen and thirty-five hours," Paris explains. "If you keep an eye on her, she should be fine."

I glance at her, and agony rips through me. Her eyes are shut again, but I can see the streak marks the tears left on her cheeks.

If I find out who gave her those shots, I'm going to kill him.

Paris returns to the party, and I head to my car. People stare at us, and I know tomorrow the gossip mill will be running wild with crazy stories. Not important right now. My only concern is to make sure Sadie is okay.

Afraid she'll throw up if I lay her down in the back seat, I place her in in the front and buckle her seat belt. Her head lolls forward, heavy and almost lifeless, making my heart twist painfully with worry.

During the drive, I make the decision to go back to my place. I don't know her roommate, but I can't rule out the possibility that she might bring back company.

I hope Andy and Jane are done with their evening activities. Both will have a myriad of questions if they see me carrying an unconscious girl into the apartment, but I can deal with them later.

There's no sign of the lovebirds in the living room, and the apartment is quiet. Hopefully they're asleep already.

Walking softly, I make a beeline to my room. I'm glad I tidied up earlier and got rid of the mountain of dirty clothes scattered everywhere. Carefully, I lay Sadie on my bed. Her short skirt has hiked up to her hips, giving me a view of her black underwear. Damn. I feel like a pervert for accidentally looking. I have to cover her.

I head out to grab a blanket from the living room, and when I get back, I find Sadie leaning over the side of the bed, making retching sounds.

"Shit." I rush to her, skidding to a halt before I step over the mess she left on the floor.

"I'm so sorry, Danny. I couldn't run to the bathroom."

I push her hair out of the way. "It's okay, Sadie. Do you think you're still going to throw up?"

"I don't know. I got vomit all over me and your bed."

"Don't worry about it. Let's get you cleaned up." I lift her from the bed and prop her up against me.

She can barely walk on her own, which makes me furious all over again. What would have happened if Nick Fowler had managed to leave the party with her?

In the bathroom, I feel torn about how to proceed. Sadie can't stand on her own, and unfortunately, there's no bathtub here.

"Do you think you can sit on the toilet for a second?"

"Yeah."

She drops like a sack of potatoes and clutches the side of the counter to keep upright while I turn on the shower.

"You got vomit all over your shirt," she says.

"It's fine."

I take it off because it seems I need to get into the shower with her anyway.

Then it hits me. I can't take off her clothes.

"Uh, Andy's girlfriend is here. Should I ask her to help you?"

"Are you mental? I don't want a stranger seeing me like this."

"You need assistance. You can't even stand up."

"Why can't you do it?"

"I don't want to make you uncomfortable."

She waves her hand awkwardly. "I puked all over your room. We passed uncomfortable five exits back."

Sadie lets go of the counter and tries to pull her soiled top up, but she topples forward instead. I catch her just before she plunges headfirst into the tiled floor.

"Careful there."

"I think you need to help me out of my clothes."

"Okay."

"I don't care if you peek. Although, I don't think I look that attractive right now."

"You're always attractive, Sadie, no matter what."

She lifts her gaze to mine. "Really?"

I shouldn't have said anything. I don't even know how the words left my mouth.

"Come on. Let's get you out of these filthy clothes."

She attempts to sit straighter, but it's clear the drug has reached its peak. I can't believe she hasn't passed out yet.

"Lean back a little. I won't let you fall."

She does as I told her and braces her hand against the counter. I pull her top up, glad it doesn't have a zipper on the back. I didn't think to check first. I was expecting to find a bra underneath, but she isn't wearing one, and I get a full view of her breasts. My face and ears burn because despite what she said, it doesn't feel right to see her topless. I have every intention of looking away, but something else catches my attention—a red scar on her side. It looks recent judging by the color.

Her words come back to me. She didn't want to go back to the hospital. Does this scar have anything to do with it?

"Are you looking at my battle wound?" she asks.

I force my eyes to return to her face, embarrassed she caught me staring. "Sorry. I didn't mean to."

"It's okay. I don't mind that you see it. I don't mind a lot of things when it comes to you. Why is that, Danny?"

I swallow hard, not knowing how to answer the question. She's pretty loopy, and I'm sure she won't remember this conversation tomorrow, but somehow, she's never been more honest. Maybe that's the drug at play too.

"I don't know, Sadie. It's the same for me too. Probably why we're friends."

Her eyebrows furrow. "Bollocks to friendship. This is way bigger than that."

I couldn't agree more, but now is not the time to discuss what's going on between us.

"We can talk about that tomorrow. Let's get you cleaned up."

I can't bring myself to remove her skirt as well, not when her comments have made me even more aware of my conflicted feelings about our relationship. I hoist Sadie up, throwing her arm over my shoulder, and then head into the shower stall. It's big enough that both of us fit in it. The water is already warm, but she still jolts when the jets hit her head.

"Ugh. Why am I getting all wet? Is it raining inside?"

"It's just the shower. You had vomit all over you, remember?"

"No."

She doesn't complain further; instead, she lets out a soft moan and rests her head against my chest, making it really hard to wash her, or ignore how her breasts are now pressed against me. I'm keenly aware how the water turned her nipples into pebbles too.

Fuck me.

I decide that just rinsing her off will have to do. There's no way I'm lathering her with soap. I shut off the water and then dry her off with a towel. Sadie finally passes out on me then. I lift her up, cradling her like a baby with the towel covering her upper body, and return to my room. It stinks of vomit, reminding me of the mess I still have to clean up. She did get some on my bed, so I set her in my chair, then quickly change the sheets and wipe off the floor.

Sadie is snoring by the time I finally put her into bed. Even with her makeup all smeared, she's so beautiful that I can't help but stare at her for a moment. My chest feels tight suddenly, like I can't breathe.

A soft knock on the door draws my attention away from her. I'm not surprised to find Andy and Jane standing outside my room. I did make more noise than I intended when I took my dirty sheets to the laundry and started the machine.

"Hey, guys," I say.

"Is everything okay?" Jane asks.

"Yeah. Sorry if I woke you."

"We weren't sleeping." Andy tries to peer over my shoulder into my room. "Got company there, Danny-boy?"

"Yes. But it's not what you think."

"Oh?" His eyebrows arch.

"Since you're going to find out tomorrow morning anyway, I may as well tell you now. I've got Sadie here. She took something she shouldn't have, and I thought it was best to bring her here to keep an eye on her."

"What do you mean, she took something she shouldn't have?" Jane asks, her eyes growing rounder.

"Paris believes she was roofied."

"What?" Andy's voice rises in anger. "Please tell me we know by whom."

His fury rekindles my own, but I put a damper on it. Getting bent out of shape now won't help me. My focus tonight is taking care of Sadie.

"No. But I left Paris and the rest of the guys to investigate when I left the party."

"I can't believe that happened. It's horrible. What if other girls were drugged too?" Jane says.

"The guys were keeping an eye out for other possible victims," I reply.

Jane hugs her middle, looking distressed. Andy pulls her into a side hug and kisses her temple. "Don't worry, babe. The Rebels won't let anyone get taken advantage of."

She nods and then asks me, "Where are you going to sleep? In the living room?"

"I want to stay nearby in case she pukes again, so I'll just sleep on the floor."

"Dude, we have sleeping bags. Hold on."

Andy disappears down the hall.

"I'll grab some extra blankets and pillows," Jane adds.

A minute later, they return with their items. Jane also grabbed a couple bottles of water, which hadn't occurred to me. They head back to Andy's room, but not before they make me promise to call them if I need anything. I close the door but keep it unlocked, then set everything down by the end of the bed and go check on Sadie. She seems fine, and her breathing is steady.

I sit next to her for a moment and brush her damp hair off her forehead. I probably shouldn't have dunked her under the shower. What if she catches a cold because I made her sleep with wet hair?

Shit, I'm an idiot. Maybe I can dry it off a bit more with a towel.

I begin to slide off the mattress when Sadie murmurs my name.

Her eyes are still closed though. She's probably dreaming.

"Don't go, Danny. Don't leave me alone."

"I'm not going anywhere, sweetheart," I reply, even though I don't think she's really talking to me.

I forget about the towel and lie next to her for a moment. I had every intention of moving to the floor in the next minute, but when my eyes begin to shut, I tell myself I'll relocate in a second.

Should have known it wouldn't happen.

SEVENTEEN

My mouth is as dry as a desert and tastes like a dead animal has been rotting inside for weeks. Every muscle in my body hurts, and the pounding in my head makes me wish for a swift death.

What the hell happened last night?

When I finally manage to open my eyes, I don't recognize the room I'm in. I'm also naked from the waist up, and there's a towel bunched around my waist. But what makes my pulse skyrocket is the muscled arm across my stomach.

Fuck. What did I do?

I turn my head and only see a mop of blond curls at first. *No. No. No.* Did I sleep with Danny last night? I don't remember anything. The last bit of memory I have is dancing by myself at the party.

I try to push Danny's arm off me slowly without waking him, but my movements are lethargic, and I feel weak as hell. I only manage to move him an inch when he stirs and pulls me closer to him. My heart wrestles with the meaning of this gesture. On one hand, if I did sleep with Danny, it's because I finally accepted that we're more than friends. But on the other hand, the reason why I wanted to keep things platonic between us has not simply disappeared.

I'm totally freaking out and don't know what to do.

There's nothing for it. It seems I can't escape without waking him, and I probably should find out what exactly happened last night. Running away won't make my problems vanish.

I shake him. "Danny, wake up."

He groans and then turns his face to mine. His eyes only open halfway, still clouded by sleepy fog. A couple of beats later, they fly open, and faster than lightning, he pulls not only his arm off me but his entire body in a movement so sudden, he ends up rolling off the bed in the process.

Shite. That doesn't bode well.

Pulling the towel up to cover my tits, I lean on my elbow and ask, "Danny, are you okay?"

He sits up and looks at me, startled. "Sadie, I'm so sorry. I didn't mean to fall asleep next to you."

Relief washes over me. He wouldn't be saying that if we had shagged last night. At least I don't think he would.

"What the bloody hell happened? Why am I in your room and half naked?"

His expression contorts into a grimace. "You don't remember anything?"

Fear makes my heart feel tight in my chest. "The last thing I remember is dancing for a bit."

He begins to get up but stops mid-motion, drops his gaze to his crotch—I'm guessing—and then returns to his sitting position on the floor.

"Do you mind throwing me a pillow? I'm only wearing boxer shorts."

"And I'm only wearing my skirt."

"Only because you puked all over your shirt last night."

Shame makes my face erupt in flames. I lean back, sinking

against the pillow and closing my eyes. "Shite. I got too drunk, didn't I?"

"That's not what happened."

Danny's voice comes from a different place in the room, so I open my eyes. He decided to get up in the end, and I get a perfect view of his fine ass. His boxer shorts leave nothing to the imagination. I know this is the worst possible moment for it, but the sight turns me on.

Why am I getting horny during one of the most embarrassing situations of my life, and when I'm feeling like crap to boot?

"What happened then?" I ask, wincing when I notice the yearning in my voice.

I hope he didn't.

He grabs a pair of sweatpants from his drawer and puts them on too fast. This situation must not be easy for him either.

With a grim expression on his face, he walks over, holding a T-shirt. "Put this on. I'll turn around."

"You probably already saw them anyway."

And something else too. My scar.

"Well, it couldn't be helped last night." His cheeks become pinker.

Damn. Embarrassment is too cute on him, and it's turning my insides into mush. Also, how unfair is it that Danny looks like a fucking god with bed hair, while I probably look like a witch? I'm afraid to look at my reflection in the mirror.

Brat that I am, I drop the towel before he can turn around just to see his reaction.

"Sadie!" He pivots, crossing his arms. "Can you please not make this harder?"

"Why is it harder, Danny?" I tease, but I do want to know.

"You were drugged last night," he blurts out.

I'm not sure what I was expecting him to say, but it definitely wasn't that. The blood seems to freeze in my veins, and I'm unable to string a sentence together.

I. Was. Drugged.

The words seem to ring in my ears, drowning all other sounds. I feel sick all of a sudden, and not wanting Danny to see me throw up again, I jump off the bed, still topless, and rush to the bathroom. Kneeling in front of the toilet, I pull my hair back and puke whatever is left in my stomach. It turns out there isn't much, but I keep retching as if my body wants to expel not only the drug from my system but also the fact that it happened.

My eyes are teary when I finally fall on my arse. I'm too tired to even pull my legs up and hug them.

"Sadie, do you need anything?" Danny asks from outside the bathroom.

"No. I just want to be alone for a moment."

"Okay. I'll be outside if you need anything."

I don't move from my spot for I don't know how long. During the time, I'm bulldozed by a myriad of different emotions. At first I'm mortified that I was drugged and needed to be rescued like a damsel in distress. Then I'm ashamed for feeling guilty that I got drugged, followed by angry at myself for allowing it to happen in the first place. Any shrink would say that's displaced anger. The only person at fault here is the motherfucker who drugged me.

I feel like crying, but the tears won't come. It's no surprise, since I don't usually cry when I'm feeling sad or angry, and rarely when I'm in pain. All I know is I can't hide in Danny's bathroom forever, so I push myself off the floor, hating how my legs shake in the process. Some arsehole turned me into a puny victim, and that makes me want to yell and break things.

A new sense of urgency takes hold of me. I have to find out everything Danny knows.

I glance at the mirror and wince. As I suspected, I look like I've been dragged through hell. My hair is a bloody mess, half of it twisted into knots and the other half hanging limp like a forgotten dirty rag. I also still stink of vomit. And Danny slept next to me. If there was ever any chance for a possible romance between us, what happened last night effectively killed it with acid.

I need a shower, pronto.

I jump into the stall, not bothering to wait for the water to warm up. I wash my hair twice, getting lost a bit in the scent that my brain has already associated to Danny. An ice-cold fever sweeps over my body when goose bumps form on my arms, despite the fact that the water has already heated up. I'm on edge, wired, and I don't know if that's a side effect of the drug or if it's my stupid body wanting Danny's cock between my legs.

I brace my hands against the wall, letting my head drop between my shoulders. *Football. That's the only thing that matters. That's what I need to focus on from now on. Not stupid parties, not friendships with impossibly good-looking guys. Just football.*

I repeat the mantra in my head as I finish washing up. The bathroom is foggy when I finally step out of the shower. In my rush, I didn't look for a towel first. There's one hanging on the peg—probably Danny's, and I'm not about to borrow it. Luckily, I find clean ones in the cupboard under the sink. As I dry off, I stare with disgust at my skirt and knickers. I can't bring myself to wear them. They also have a faint smell of puke. Great.

Wrapped in the towel, I grab my clothes and return to Danny's bedroom. He's not here, but getting closer to the now made bed, I see he left me more than a T-shirt to wear. There's a pair of girl sweatpants and a brand-new pair of undies with the tag still on.

Blind jealousy rushes through me. Did these belong to Danny's ex? I think I'd rather parade naked than wear them.

The door opens, and Danny comes in carrying a tray of food. He stops in his tracks. "Oh, I didn't know you were out of the shower already."

"Where did these clothes come from?" I ask brusquely.

"They're Jane's. Andy's girlfriend."

"Oh."

Now I feel foolish for getting all worked up about it.

He nods. "I'll just set this on the desk and let you get ready."

"Okay."

When he's on his way out, I say, "Thank you, Danny. For real."

He smiles, and my heart beats faster. *Stop betraying me, traitorous muscle!*

"You're welcome. For real."

DANNY

"How is she?" Jane asks when I return to the living room.

"I think she'll be okay."

"We probably shouldn't be here when she comes out." Jane reaches for her purse and gives Andy a meaningful glance. "Come on, Andy."

"Guys, you don't need to leave. I can talk to Sadie in my bedroom."

Andy stands from the couch despite my protest. "We have to pick up Lorenzo anyway. It's all good, bro. Go take care of your girl."

"She's not my girl," I grit out.

He smiles wickedly. "Whatever you say."

I wait until they're gone to check on Sadie. I knock first this time; I do not need to see her naked again. As much as I want to forget what I saw last night, it's hard to erase the image of her perfect breasts from my mind.

And now I'm officially in perv territory.

"Come on in," she says.

She's dressed in the clothes I left her, and I won't deny that seeing her wearing my T-shirt stirs feelings in me I shouldn't look too closely at.

"How are you feeling?"

"Really awful." She glances at the food I brought her and twists her nose.

"What's wrong?"

"I want to eat, but I'm afraid my stomach will expel anything I put inside."

"Try the Saltines. They should be okay to handle."

She nibbles on one, then immediately puts the cracker down. "What happened at the party, Danny?"

I swallow the lump in my throat, hating what I have to tell her.

"I don't know who gave you the drug, Sadie. You said someone gave you a couple tequila shots. When I found you, you were with Nick Fowler."

"What?" I shriek. "I'd never go near that guy of my own free will."

"I know that. I was so angry, I wanted to punch that motherfucker in the face. But whisking you out of the party was my number one priority. He's getting what's coming to him though. Don't worry."

Her eyes blaze with fury. "Do you think he's the one who spiked my drink?"

"I don't know. Paris went back into the party to investigate and also to see if anyone else had been drugged. I haven't talked to him yet."

She pulls her hair back. "I can't believe I was that stupid. I know not to accept drinks from strangers."

"Don't you dare blame yourself for what happened, Sadie," I say angrily.

Her eyes widen at my outburst. "Trust me, I've already given myself that spiel. I ran through the entire gamut of feelings when I was in your bathroom."

I rub my face. "I'm sorry I didn't find you sooner."

"Hey, don't you go blaming yourself for it, either. You're not my bodyguard. And why would I need one at a party anyway? Everyone should feel safe."

"You're right."

We stare at each other for a moment, and I fight the urge to walk over and pull her into my arms. She breaks the connection first by looking at her feet.

"Was I a terrible burden to you after the party?"

"Nothing I couldn't handle. Don't worry."

"Nice evasion, Danny." She looks up, her lips curled into a grin. "That means I was a nightmare."

I smirk. "Fine. If you want to know all the gritty details of what a pain in the ass you were, I'll tell you."

"Go on. Spare me nothing."

"After you puked all over yourself, my bed, and the floor, I had to stick you under the shower, hence why you weren't wearing your shirt."

"Why didn't you take off my skirt too?"

"Uh…." I rub my neck. "Honestly, I already felt guilty enough that I'd seen your breasts."

She laughs. "So what? They're just tits, Danny. Cows have them."

"Nothing like yours," I reply, exasperated.

The satisfied smile Sadie rewards me with tells me I fell for her trap. Devious woman.

"You let me sleep with a wet skirt on. And if you felt so bad about seeing me topless, you should have given me a shirt to wear."

"I covered you with the towel." I cross my arms. "Stop making me feel worse."

She shakes her head. "God, you're so easy to tease."

"You must be feeling better if you can think of ways to torture me."

She raises an eyebrow. "Talking about my boobs is torturing you? Good to know. As for feeling better, I'm not so sure. I'm not quite myself yet. There's the nausea, and I'm feeling weak as hell."

"I can take you to the hospital. They can run some tests and find out what drug is in your system."

The playfulness leaves Sadie's face in an instant.

"No hospitals. I can't deal with them."

"Does your scar have anything to do with it?"

She looks away, bracing her hands on the back of the chair. "Yes. Maybe one day I'll tell you about it, but not today."

"I'll be here to listen whenever you're ready."

"You're a good friend, Danny." She gives me a half smile that doesn't reach her eyes.

"Ditto."

"Even after I reenacted a scene from *The Exorcist* in your room?"

"Yeah, even after that."

Friends. That's all Sadie and I can ever be. I want to make peace with that, but I can't.

It seems this is going to be the lying season.

EIGHTEEN

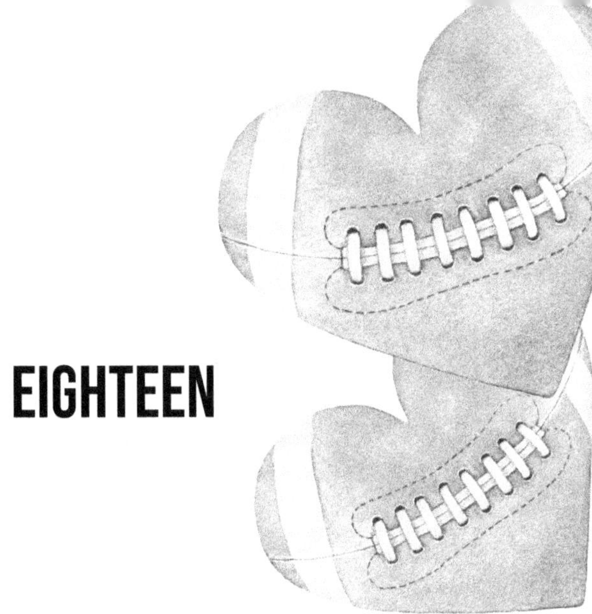

SADIE

Upon Danny's insistence, after I ate a bit, I took a nap and didn't wake up until midafternoon. Danny left my phone on the nightstand in case I needed to ask for something. The boy is too sweet for his own good, and if I'm not careful, I might fall head over heels for him. I can already feel the butterflies waking up in my belly. Hell, I'm giddy just thinking about him.

When I glance at my phone, I see a bunch of notifications stacked on top of one another on the screen. I open WhatsApp and find out that my teammates blew up our group chat. Vanessa is the one sending most of them.

Before they decide to march into Danny's apartment to check if I'm alive, I reply to all.

SADIE: I'm fine, still a little groggy from whatever I was given.

VANESSA: Thank heavens. Can you talk? I wanna call you.

SADIE: Sure.

A second later, the phone rings.

"Hey," I say.

"Sadie, I'm so sorry. Are you really okay?"

"I am. Don't worry. Danny is taking good care of me."

"Is he now?"

Bollocks. I shouldn't have let that slip out.

"Yeah. He's an angel."

She laughs. "What kind of angel? I hope Lucifer."

I rub my legs together as my mind takes a nosedive into the gutter once again. Maybe the drug made me horny too.

"Stop it. I don't want to picture Danny doing wicked things to me. We're just friends, and that's all we'll ever be."

"Why? If you like him and you're attracted to him, I don't see the problem. He's clearly into you."

I don't want to rejoice at her statement, not when he made it clear that he only wants to concentrate on football.

"We're both trying to focus on our careers. No time for relationships."

"Are you saying you're going to turn into a nun and not hook up with anyone?"

"I have toys. They'll do. Besides, apart from Danny, the quality of blokes I've been subjected to so far at this school is appalling."

"Slim pickings, I know. I'm livid that Nick Fowler tried to take advantage of you when you weren't yourself. He's an asshole through and through. I wouldn't be surprised if he was the one who spiked your drinks."

I share the same thought, but without proof, I can't accuse the tosser of anything.

"You didn't hear anything about who did it, then?"

"No. I know the guys on the football team were looking and asking questions, but that party was a fucking zoo. No one saw or remembers anything. At least we don't think anyone else drank what you did. Small blessings, I guess."

"Yeah."

"Anyway, I'm glad you're okay, and that you have a sinfully good-looking guardian angel looking out for you." I can hear the grin in her voice.

"Thanks for checking on me."

"Of course. We're Ravens. That means family in my book."

"I don't think Melody considers me family." I snort.

"Nah, she does, but she's jealous as fuck that you're as talented as she is."

"*As* talented? What the hell? I'm better than she is."

She snorts. "God, I forgot humbleness is not your forte."

"No, it isn't."

"When are you going home? Tomorrow?" she asks.

"Why tomorrow? I was planning to head back to the dorms today."

"Paris told me the drug is likely to stay in your body for thirty-six hours. I'd stay at Danny's if I were you, just in case you require his *assistance*."

I sigh. "For fuck's sake, Vanessa. Nothing is going on here."

"Yeah, yeah. Remember, I called it first. I demand to be in the wedding party."

"I'm hanging up now. Bye."

I end the call and lean back against the pillow. It's hard enough to lie to myself when I'm around Danny. It doesn't help when my friends keep reminding me that I'm the biggest pretender there ever was.

I scroll through my other messages. There are a few from Katrina. The first she sent soon after I left her with her sorority friends, asking where I was. The second one was drunken nonsense, and the last one was from this morning, again asking where I was. She didn't sound worried that I didn't go back to our shared room last night. I'm sure she assumed I hooked up with someone.

I send her a quick text so she knows I'm not missing, but there's not a chance in hell I'm telling her where I am.

There's a missed call from Dad, and I fear he somehow heard about what happened to me. My stomach coils tightly. I should call him back, but what if he knows? Is he going to get mad? Probably.

Ugh. What if he doesn't care? I don't know which is the worst scenario.

I'm freaking out while I stare at my phone.

A knock on the door jolts me out of the stupid panic mode.

"Sadie?" Danny calls.

"You can come in. I'm up."

I run my fingers through my hair, remembering belatedly that I just woke from a nap and must look like shite.

He sticks his head in first and catches me in the act of preening. I drop my hands quickly, making it even more obvious that I was trying to hide that I want to be pretty for him.

Kill me now. I want to go back to when I barely noticed boys. None of the blokes I knew in London looked like Danny though.

"How are you feeling?" He walks in and shuts the door.

My pulse accelerates. Why am I all of a sudden so aware that I'm alone with Danny in his room? It didn't affect me when I woke up in the morning as much as it is now. Maybe because I was too busy puking my guts out.

"Much better. Hey, quick question. Did you tell my father about what happened to me?"

His eyes widen. "No. Of course not."

I exhale loudly in relief. "Thank God. I can't handle any more drama about this. I just want to forget the whole deal."

My statement doesn't seem to sit well with Danny. He's scowling a little.

"What? You don't think I should move on?"

"That's not it. I understand your reasoning. I'm just pissed that someone did that to you and they're going to walk away unpunished."

I shrug. "That's life, Danny. Most of the time, the bad guys don't get what they deserve. Hoping otherwise just leads to disappointment."

"Was that what happened to the person who gave you that scar?"

All my barriers fly up in the blink of an eye. "What makes you think that scar was from an attack?" I snap.

Remorse seems to shine in his eyes. "I'm sorry. I didn't mean to assume or pry. You don't need to tell me."

"I know I don't."

Irritated, I throw my legs to the side of the bed and stand up too fast. The room begins to spin, and I find myself tumbling forward. In two long strides, Danny reaches me and prevents the fall.

"Careful there. You're not completely recovered yet."

"I feel fine. As a matter of fact, I want to go home."

"Sadie, is this because of my stupid question about your past? I'm sorry, okay? But I want you to stay."

I should insist about going home, but I can't think straight when I'm this close to Danny, when I can feel his accelerated heartbeat under my flattened hand over his chest. Actually, those are the very reasons I should go. But I'm weak, and I can't say no to him.

I step back, even though Danny keeps holding my arms. "Fine. But I need a change of clothes. I feel funny wearing borrowed pants."

"Okay, if you give me your keys, I can bring your stuff."

"I'll come with you."

"Sadie, you should rest. If your roommate is home, I'll ask her to pack your things."

I scrunch my nose. "Honestly, it wouldn't make a difference who packs my stuff. It's still two strangers going through my knickers."

His eyebrows furrow. "I thought we had moved past the

strangers phase after you puked all over my room and I saw your tits."

My jaw drops. "I can't believe you're throwing that in my face. You're such a bellend."

"Sorry if the truth hurts, sugar." He smirks.

I watch him through slits. "Are you trying to get on my bad side, Danny Hudson? I'm only weak for another ten hours or so, but after that, you don't really want to mess with me."

He flicks my nose. "You're cute when you're angry."

I'd kick his shin if I thought I could do it and not lose my balance. "Stop saying stuff guys say when they're trying to get laid."

Danny twists his face into an exaggerated scowl. "That may have been true before I saw the insides of your stomach. You ruined it for me, Sadie."

It's hard not to wince, but I think I manage not to give away how his joke upset me. I'm such a basket case. I want us to remain in the friend zone, yet I want him to secretly want me.

"Listen, it doesn't matter. If I'm to stay another night, I have to pack my own overnight bag. Besides, I don't want any more rumors spreading about me. If you show up at my dorm alone and leave with a duffel bag, people will think we're shacking up."

"Would that be so terrible?" My heart skips a beat, thinking he means the question, but then he continues. "Do you find me *that* abhorrent?"

"Absolutely. Now let's go. If we're lucky, Katrina won't be around."

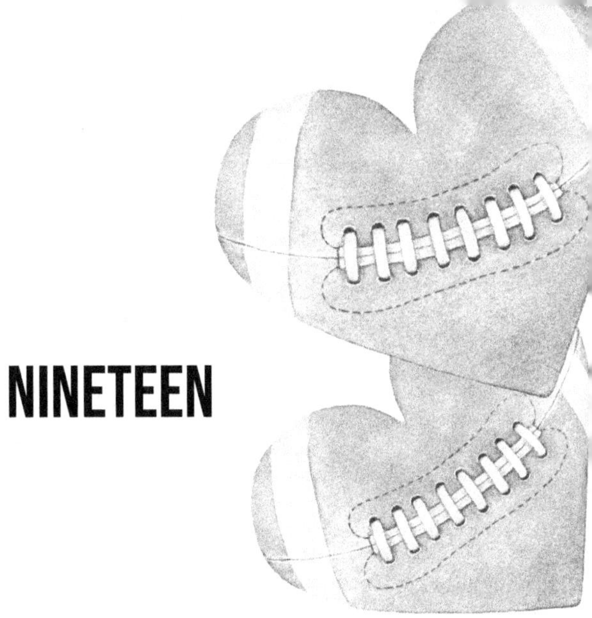

NINETEEN

I didn't feel like an A-lister being chased by the paparazzi in the streets of London when I went back to the dorms to grab my stuff. I didn't run into that many people, and I made Danny wait in the car. Spending another night at his place wasn't as hard as I thought it would be either. He slept on the couch in the living room, and I was so tired that I fell asleep as soon as my head hit the pillow.

I was back in my dorm room on Sunday morning, and mercifully, I didn't have to fight Danny on that. He was probably sick of me already.

I called Dad back since I'd forgotten to do so on Saturday. It turned out he was just checking on me, then invited me over to his place whenever I had the time. I said I would get back to him on that, which was code for "I will avoid you as much as I can." Is it horrible that I keep blowing him off? Sure. But it'll take more than moving closer to him to erase all the years he wasn't there for me.

Monday morning at practice, I feel the weight of all the stares of my teammates when I enter the locker room. It was foolish of me to think they would have already forgotten Friday's incident. The thing is, I had already moved past that, and their scrutiny just got under my nerves.

"Can you guys piss off with the concerned looks? Like I said, I'm fine." I veer for my locker.

"The bitch is back. She's clearly fine," Melody pipes up.

"You haven't seen the bitch yet," I murmur.

Vanessa stops next to me. "I guess your sleepover was a bust, huh?"

"If you're inferring it was a bust because nothing happened, then you're correct and wrong at the same time."

"You lost me."

I give her a droll look. "Nothing happened, like I said it wouldn't, and it wasn't a bust."

"Then what's up with the foul mood?"

I close the metal door with a bang. "I don't know. I'm just on edge, like I have all this pent-up energy that needs to be released. I'm keen on a good practice game."

"Or pent-up sexual tension." She laughs, stepping away from me.

"Dude, you'd better pray you're playing on my team today."

"What were you guys talking about?" Joanne asks.

"Vanessa was being nosy." I sit on the bench to switch my shoes.

"Sadie, I want to apologize for Friday night. I feel awful that I didn't go check on you after you disappeared."

I look up. "What's with everyone feeling bad about Friday? It wasn't anyone's fault that some wanker gave me a spiked drink."

Joanne shoves her hands in her hoodie's pockets. "We still should have come after you sooner, especially with the likes of Nick Fowler at the party."

The anger that was simmering in my gut returns with a

vengeance. Nick may not have put the drug in my drink—that's something we'll never know for sure—but he didn't hesitate to take advantage of the situation, and I won't forget that.

"He'd better stay away from me if he has any sense of self-preservation."

"I heard Paris almost smashed his face," Steff says. "Pity the Pikes dragged Nick away and saved his sorry ass."

"Paris would probably get benched if he got into a fight. It's best that it didn't happen, even as much as I'd like to see Nick get an ass whooping," Vanessa replies.

A loud rumble shakes the building, interrupting our lovely convo.

"Whoa. Was that thunder?" Joanne asks.

A moment later, heavy rain pelts the windows, and the world outside looks like nightfall has come earlier. That type of storm is the kind that hurts when it hits you and makes playing football not fun at all.

Couch Lauda joins us in the common area a minute later.

"Well, it looks like this rain won't stop until the afternoon. I'm switching the schedule. You're going to do some weight lifting now."

Almost everyone groans, including me. Weight lifting is boring as hell and not what I was looking forward to. I retrieve my duffel bag from the locker and change shoes again.

"Crap. We'll get drenched walking from here to the car," Phoebe moans.

"We used to get heavy showers like this all the time in Florida. It's not a big deal." Steff shrugs.

"Sadie must be used to it too since all it does is rain in London." Joanne smiles.

"One never gets used to bad weather," I reply. "Or the cold."

No one was expecting rain, so naturally, no one had an umbrella. To be fair, I didn't carry one with me in London either because they're such a hassle. I'd rather use a raincoat.

In clusters, we run to our cars. The distance is short, but puddles have already formed on the pavement, and I manage to step in every single one of them.

The gym building is only a minute from the field, but all the parking spots near the entrance are taken. Before I head out in the rain again, I check my duffel bag, hoping I packed an extra pair of sneakers. Working out in wet shoes won't do. I sigh in relief when I see my old gym shoes in the bag. I meant to toss them out and forgot. Sometimes, having a shite memory is a good thing.

When we enter the building, I wrinkle my nose, getting a whiff of something awful.

"What's up with the wet dog smell?" I ask no one in particular.

Vanessa's eyes sweep the open room, where half the machines are currently in use. "It must be Nick."

I follow her line of vision and spot the tosser far back, standing next to a bench press while his friend goes through his reps.

"For fuck's sake. What is he doing here?" I glower in his direction.

"His coach probably had the same idea as ours." Vanessa tugs on my duffel bag's strap. "Come on. Ignore him. We're here to work out. Don't let him distract you."

Grumbling, I follow Vanessa and the rest of my teammates to the gym's locker room. It's hard to let go of my anger though. Maybe instead of weight lifting, I should take out my aggression on a punching bag.

That's exactly what I do. While my friends spread out through the gym to work on the machines, I head to one of the workout rooms where I spied a punching bag the other day I was here. There's no one here, so for a good fifteen minutes, I have the punching bag all to myself. But then a couple of girls come in, chatting too loudly, and end my solitude.

Not in the mood to listen to idle gossip, I head out and search for a familiar face. I should probably work out my legs now. I spot Vanessa and Joanne sharing a leg press machine and make a beeline in their direction. My pulse is still pumping loudly in my ears thanks to the cardio, and for that reason, I don't pay attention to what's going on in my periphery.

That's when bloody Nick decides to show up, sporting a sneer. The wanker once again blocks my path.

"I was wondering where you were, darling."

"Get the fuck out of my way," I say, loud enough to draw attention.

He grabs my arm tightly, as if he has the right to touch me. "You have to learn some manners."

"How about this for manners?" I bring my knee up, slamming it against Nick's balls.

He howls, stepping back and leaning forward as he cups his junk with both hands. "You bitch."

"What the hell is going on here?" Coach Lauda asks, looking none too happy.

"She kicked me in the balls," he moans.

"Sadie?" She looks at me, frowning but not yet glowering.

"He got handsy. Men need to understand they can't go pawing whoever they like without asking."

"You wish I touched you," he lies.

I glance around, searching for a witness that will step forward and confirm my accusation. No one meets my eye, not even the girls.

Wankers. The whole lot.

"All right, Sadie. Come with me." Couch Lauda turns around and walks away without bothering to wait.

That wasn't a request, it was an order, so I follow her quietly. My face is burning, which means it must be as red as a tomato. It's not embarrassment as some of the people staring might think. I'm red from anger.

Coach Lauda leads me to a back room in the gym, which must be used as administration slash storage. There's a small desk and two chairs. She motions for me to go in first and then closes the door. She doesn't make a motion to take one of the chairs, so I remain standing as well.

"Explain to me what that was back there."

"Nick Fowler is a dick," I say angrily.

Coach pinches the bridge of her nose. "I'm aware that Fowler is problematic, but his behavior is not my problem. Yours is."

"How is that fair? The bellend grabs my arm and I'm supposed to just ask politely for him to let go?"

"That would have been better than kicking him in the nuts. Everyone saw you do that. No one stepped forward to say he touched you first."

"Because they're all a bunch of cowards."

"Probably. But you need to understand, Sadie. Whatever you do reflects on the entire team. I can't have one of my players assaulting another student. You're a promising star. I'd hate to bench you because of a weasel like Nick Fowler."

My blood is boiling, and it's taking every bit of self-control to keep my angry retort bottled inside.

"What's going to happen now?"

"Hopefully I can smooth things over with Coach Phillips. We go way back. But you have to promise me there won't be a repeat. If you must defend yourself, make sure there are willing witnesses to confirm your story. Is that clear?"

"Crystal."

"Oh, and one more thing. Skip parties throughout the rest of preseason training."

My chest feels tight suddenly. Does Couch Lauda know about last Friday?

"Why?"

"Drinking to the point of passing out is not something I want to hear about my players."

Shame washes over me, even though that's not what

happened. But I can't confess to Coach Lauda what actually did. She might want to tell my father, and that's something I want to avoid at all costs.

So I swallow my pride and let her believe the lie.

"Understood. It won't happen again."

TWENTY

DANNY

Coach Clarkson trained us harder than ever, despite the rain. By the time practice was over, I could barely walk. I welcomed the exertion though. Focusing on not slacking off, I barely had time to think about Sadie. And in the locker room, my teammates kept me occupied with their banter.

It's not until I'm riding home with Andy that thoughts of Sadie invade my mind and I can't think of anything else.

"You're awfully quiet," Andy points out.

"I'm just tired."

"A certain soccer player definitely kept you busy last weekend."

"Dude, come on. You know Sadie is only a friend."

"Get your mind out of the gutter, will you? I wasn't insinuating anything, just making an observation. Taking care of someone who is sick is draining."

"Sorry, I can't tell with you. Ninety-nine percent of the time, your comments have double meaning."

"That's true." He grins. "I guess I'm improving my ways."

"What are your plans for the evening?" I ask to change the subject.

"Jane has derby training. She also has a game next weekend if you want to come. Lorenzo is psyched about it."

I grin. "I'm sure he is. Does he still have a crush on that dark-haired player? What's her name again?"

"Oh, Scary Samantha? I don't know. He hasn't mentioned her again since Jane told him we weren't allowed to speak her name in the house."

That makes me laugh. "She's still bitter about that black eye, huh?"

"Totally. I mean, I was livid when it happened, but then I reminded her that's the nature of the game, and she can't cry when things get tough."

"You probably didn't get any sex that evening, did you?"

"Nope."

"Sadie would probably love going to a roller derby game," I say without thinking.

Andy groans. "Bro, it's really hard not to make a comment about the girl if you keep mentioning her as if she were your girlfriend."

I clench my jaw hard and look out the window. I have no one but myself to blame for that. "Hell, can't I invite a girl to a game without it being a date?"

"Yeah, but we both know you're into Sadie. If you want to insist on not dating anyone because of whatever, then it's a smart idea to stop hanging out with her."

"I know."

We fall silent for a minute or two before Andy continues. "If you want to bring Sadie to the game, I guess it'd be all right. You'll have me, Lorenzo, and I believe Jane's grandma is coming with her two boyfriends. That's plenty of buffer."

Despite my gloomy mood, that makes me laugh. "Damn it, now I have to bring her. I can't wait to see Sadie's reaction when she meets Ophelia Holland."

"Yeah, that will be epic, I bet."

No sooner are we home and I'm back in my room than I pull my cell phone out to text Sadie. I begin to ask how her day was but decide to go with something less clingy in the end.

Hey, what's up?

Not much. Veg'ing out in my room and listening to Katrina talk about her Greek life.

That sounds fun, LOL.

Barf. But it's distracting me from the shitty day I had.

What? Did your coach make you train in the rain?

I wish she had. Something else.

Come on, Sadie. You can't leave it at that.

A moment later, she calls me.

"Hey. Got tired of typing?" I ask.

"Yeah, the story is too long, and my fingers were cramping up already. Anyway, if you must know why I had a crappy day, here it is. Coach Lauda made us do weight lifting because of the rain, which I hate on most days. But then we bumped into the king of arseholes at the gym, and he acted like his usual obnoxious self."

My entire body becomes tense. The memory of him dragging a barely conscious Sadie out of the party on Friday pops in my mind, making me relive the anger all over again.

"What did he do?" I grit out.

"The usual BS. But because I exchanged barbs with the wanker, I received a reprimand from Coach. To cut a long story short, I have to train harder and stay out of trouble if I want to play in our first game."

Sadie's evasion makes me suspect it was more than the usual BS. But I can probably get the details from someone else.

"That's harsh," I say. "You can do it though. If you want, I can help you on both counts."

"What do you mean?"

"I also need to train harder. Maybe we can run in the mornings or hit the gym together."

"Hmm, that's not a bad idea. But how is that going to help me stay out of trouble?"

"I'll help you make better decisions because I'm older and wiser?"

"You did not just quote Rolf from *The Sound of Music*." She laughs.

"Guilty. I couldn't help it. My mom got me hooked on it when I was little. I think I know most of the lines and the song lyrics by heart."

Sadie laughs harder at this, and the sound is infectious.

"You're going to make me piss my pants."

"That wasn't the intention."

"Did you burst into song at the most inappropriate moments too?"

"Yeah."

"Blimey, your dad must have loved that."

I grow quiet suddenly, not knowing how to reply to that. It's normal for people to assume I grew up with a dad, but coming from Sadie, it's a surprise. She didn't have her father around either, after all.

"No dad," I reply.

"Bollocks. I'm such a moron. I don't know why I made that comment. It was word vomit, really. I'm not that thick, I swear."

I don't know what to make of that comment. Did she guess my father was never in my life? Probably. I bet most guys she knows talk about their fathers all the time.

"It's okay, Sadie. It happens."

I could tell her I've never met my father. In fact, I do want to share that with her, but now is not the time.

"If it makes you feel better, I accept your offer to tag along when I train, despite the blatant sexist comment about helping me make better decisions."

Her joke does pull me out of my sudden funk. Very few people are able to do that when I enter my dark moods.

"Tag along, huh? We'll see about that when I leave you behind, eating dust."

She scoffs. "You don't seriously believe you can run faster than me. I play soccer, in case you forgot."

"I sense a bet coming on. Should we put a wager on it?"

"That sounds brilliant. I love entering bets when the winning is guaranteed."

"That's what the hare thought."

"The hare was a dumbass and fell asleep."

"Okay, then. Let's meet for a run in front of the library tomorrow. We'll see who's the fastest. How about five?"

She groans. "I'm already not liking this, but hell, I'm game."

I smile from ear to ear, even though I know spending more time with Sadie is exactly what I don't need.

"All right, see you tomorrow, Sadie."

I'm still sporting the goofiest grin minutes after the call ends.

I see the warning signs flashing in front of me, and I'm choosing to ignore all of them.

When I crash and burn, I'll have no one to blame but me.

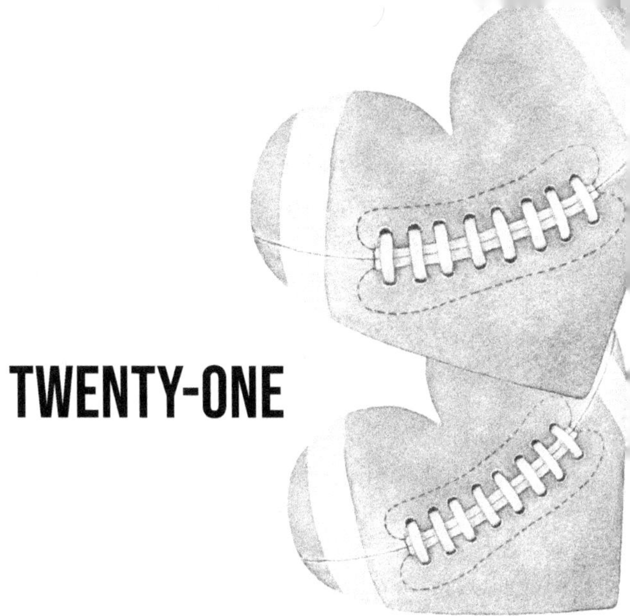

TWENTY-ONE

No matter how long I've been waking at the crack of dawn, I'll never get used to it. Some people don't even require an alarm clock after a while. I'm the one snoozing mine until I'm late. But this morning, I was up before the shrill sound disturbed my peace.

I move around on my tiptoes, careful not to wake Katrina, who is snoring softly. My phone tells me it's four thirty, which gives me plenty of time to shower and get ready. Ten times out of ten, I wouldn't bother showering before a morning run—I'm getting sweaty within minutes. But after an entire weekend of Danny seeing me at my worst, I want to look good.

Yep, I'm preening for a guy who I don't want to date.

I'm such a liar.

I want Danny so badly that it hurts, which also proves I'm a glutton for punishment. But every time I make a promise to myself to cut down on the time I interact with him, I break that vow. He's my weakness, and I don't even know how I let that happen. Sneaky little bastard must have slipped through a crack in my barrier when I wasn't paying attention—or was too distracted by the way he looks.

The bathroom is empty at this ungodly hour. I'd appreciate the lack of people and take my time if I wasn't so anxious to finish quickly and head to the library. I don't wash my hair, but I do make a point of brushing it until it shines. I'm about to put it in a ponytail, but in the end, I slip the hair band around my wrist instead. I'll put it up later.

I have dark circles under my eyes, and I wish I could put some makeup on, but that would be pushing it and beyond ridiculous. I'm already wearing my sexiest workout outfit; I don't want him to notice I tried hard to look my best.

No matter how many times I repeat in my head that Danny is just a friend, my stomach is twisted in knots the entire drive to our meeting point. The clock on my dashboard is flashing that it's five minutes to five, but when I walk over to the building a minute later, I find Danny already standing there, wearing shorts and a snug, long-sleeve shirt.

"Good morning." He smiles broadly, making his eyes twinkle under the streetlights.

My butterflies decide to wreak havoc in my belly because apparently the knots weren't enough. Or maybe the damn bugs were the ones that tied my insides in the first place.

"Morning. I can't believe you beat me here. It's not even five yet."

"I was up early."

"Same," I reply.

"You didn't put your hair in a ponytail though."

He noticed, and that makes me feel all warm and fuzzy inside. *Dumb girl.*

"Eh… I forgot."

"I like your hair down like that."

His confession renders me speechless, and a new tension develops between us. We don't speak for a while, just stare at each other as if we forgot how to string sentences together.

Quickly, I comb my hair back with my fingers and use the hairband around my wrist to tie it together in a messy ponytail.

Danny clears his throat, breaking the awkward silence. "So, what are the rules of our bet?"

"Are you sure you want to do this?" I smirk.

He raises an eyebrow. "What's the matter, Sadie? Are you scared to lose?"

"No, I'm just trying to save you from the humiliation."

"Aren't you sweet? So, first and foremost, we need to establish the track."

"Right. It's a pretty straight path from here to the practice fields. How about whoever gets there first wins?"

"Sounds good. And what's the prize for the winner?"

I know Danny is a scholarship student and isn't swimming in riches, so I'm not going to be a cow and suggest we bet cash.

"How about a favor?"

His lips twist upward. "What kind?"

"It can be anything, but it has to be major, like—"

"Burying a body?" he finishes for me.

"Something like that."

"Sounds good."

We stretch first, and I try to ignore the radioactive insects in my tummy. A couple of minutes later, we're both ready to start.

"On the count of three?" he asks.

I nod, getting into position.

"One, two, three!" he shouts.

We sprint forward, going neck and neck in the beginning. Danny's legs are longer, but I compensate by being faster. However, I know not to use all my gas at the start. Instead, I save some of my energy for the final stretch. That allows Danny to take the lead. I'm banking that he'll tire out and slow down, but it's possible that strategy will backfire. The guy is a top athlete, trained by my dad.

I can't allow the distance between us to increase too much or I'll never catch up. I push my legs, loving how my muscles protest at first. It's a sweet pain that will soon fade into the background.

My guess is the distance between the library and fields is around two miles.

I'm far from winded by the time we near it. When I get a visual of the finish line, I push myself to the limit, propelled by the need to win this race at all costs. Nothing motivates me more than being at the top. I hear Danny grunt as I blow past him. I'm tempted to wave, but that type of distraction could cost me. I don't want to be like the hare from the story.

I'm a few feet from reaching the wire fence when I sense Danny close behind me. Then, in the final steps, he takes the lead.

No fucking way.

In an act of desperation, I leap, reaching the fence a second before he does. Well, not reaching, more like colliding with it. Danny was too close to me when I jumped in front of him, which results in him crashing against my back and sandwiching me between him and the fence.

My left cheek and my chest take the blunt of the impact. It hurts to the point that I cry out.

"Sadie, what the hell!" Danny steps back and turns me around. "Are you hurt?"

His breathing is coming out in bursts as his frantic eyes search my face.

"Of course I am. You smashed into me."

He touches my face with the tips of his fingers, making me hold my breath. A shiver runs down my spine from the contact.

"Wh-What are you doing?" I breathe out.

"You're bleeding."

He shows me his smeared fingers.

"Blimey." I touch my cheek, feeling the moisture too. "How bad is it? Do you think I'll need stitches?"

"Nah. It looks superficial. But we should definitely clean it up properly."

"Yeah."

My heart is still racing, but I'm not sure if it's because of the run or the close proximity to Danny.

"I'm sorry, Sadie."

"You should be. I won."

His eyebrows furrow. "That's not why I'm sorry. And you only won because you cheated."

"I didn't cheat," I retort angrily. "I won the race fair and square."

"I don't think jumping in front of your opponent counts as fair and square."

"You're just a sore loser," I grumble, pushing him to the side so I can put some distance between us.

"Oh, I think you've got me confused with yourself." He throws his arm over my shoulders, effectively ruining my plan to get some much-needed space. "Come on. Let's get that boo-boo taken care of."

"Don't tell me you have a first aid kit in your car."

"Yeah. You don't?"

"Uh, no."

"Unwise considering what a klutz you are."

"I'm not a klutz!" I elbow him in the ribs, hoping to dislodge him from my side. No such luck.

Instead, he laughs and laughs.

"Are you done?" I ask after a while.

"Sure. I concede victory to you. What favor do you want from me?"

I almost say that I want him to stop making fun of me, but that'd be a waste of my winnings. Besides, the deal was for the favor to be something big.

"Don't know yet."

"Hmm, we probably should have agreed on an expiration date. I can so picture you knocking on my door fifty years from now, all wrinkled and shit, asking me to help bury the body of someone you killed."

I try to pretend I'm offended, but I snicker instead. "That could happen. Guess you'll just have to wait with bated breath until I call to cash in my favor."

"The anticipation will probably send me to an early grave. Please don't wait fifty years."

"I can't make such a promise."

He sighs. "You have a mean streak, woman. I thought I was your friend."

"You're my friend."

"I feel sorry for your enemies."

I shrug. "Unfortunately, I can't deal with all my enemies like I want to. Society really frowns upon maiming and castrating."

"Are you referring to Nick Fowler? What did he do yesterday at the gym?"

I tense, not wanting to tell Danny for fear he'll try to play the knight in shining armor. I don't want him getting into trouble because of me.

"Nothing worth repeating, Danny. Don't worry, I can fight my own battles."

He tenses next to me and then drops his arm from my shoulder. I wanted some space, but now I feel like the distance is more than physical.

"We didn't think this through," I say.

"What?"

"We should have left one car parked near the fields."

"I assumed we'd be running back. I didn't count on you getting your face slashed by a fence."

I can tell there's no real humor in his attempted joke.

"I can still run."

Danny stops and looks at me. "Shit. You look like an extra from a horror movie."

I touch my face again, noticing it's way wetter than before. "Danny! You said the cut was superficial."

"And it is. But even those bleed a lot."

"Great." I stop moving so I can take off my tank top.

"What are you doing?"

"What do you think?" I ask mid-motion. "Don't worry, Danny. I won't flash you my tits this time. I'm wearing a sports bra."

I manage to find a piece of fabric that's not completely drenched in sweat, then use it to dry off my cheek. We resume our trek back to our cars, but the absence of the easy banter feels like a heavy cloud hanging over our heads.

Thirty minutes later, my tank top has soaked up all the blood from the shallow cut, but even so, Danny insists I get it cleaned in his car. I would have protested and insist he do it outside, but rain decides to make an appearance.

Danny is half into his car while I glare at the sky.

"What are you waiting for, Sadie? Get in. You'll get soaked."

Grumbling, I circle around the front of the vehicle and slide inside.

"What were you hoping to do? Break into song and start tap dancing over puddles?" he asks.

"Sure, let's go with that." I cross my arms over my chest.

Danny leans toward me, making me tense.

He's just reaching for the glove compartment, dumbass.

"Okay, let's start with cleaning the wound. This might sting a little."

He sprays an antiseptic solution on a piece of gauze and taps it to my cheek. This moment is too intimate, and it's making me feel all kinds of things. Like an idiot, I stare right at his face. His attention is solely on the task, but my heart is racing just the same. When he pulls back, his eyes meet mine, making breathing much harder than it already was.

"There. All better," he says in a voice that's thicker, almost if he's having trouble drawing air into his lungs as well.

Then his eyes drop to my lips, which part automatically, almost an invitation for a kiss. And God, I do want Danny to kiss me now. I inch closer, allowing myself to get pulled into his orbit. He seems to lean forward too.

This is going to happen, even though it's so stupid. We're friends. Friends don't make out in cars.

At the last second, Danny's attention moves from my lips to my cheek.

"Oh, crap. You're bleeding again. We'd better put a Band-Aid over it."

He grabs a clean strip of gauze and reaches over, but I take it from him. We were a second away from making a huge mistake. I won't let that happen again.

"I'll do it."

I tap my cheek way harsher than Danny did, and then I grab a Band-Aid from his first aid kit myself. Using the passenger mirror, I apply the bandage over the cut, trying my best to ignore the weight of Danny's stare.

"All right. I'm all patched up. I'd better get going." I open the door, avoiding making eye contact with him.

"Okay. Sadie?"

"Yeah?" Like an idiot, I look.

Yep. Still want to kiss him.

"Same time tomorrow?"

"Sure."

Bloody hell. What. Am. I. Doing?

He smiles. "All right. See you later."

I slip out, ignoring the fact that it's still raining. In a daze, I walk to my car, and it's not until I'm behind the steering wheel that I feel the significance of what just happened.

Danny and I almost kissed.

How long until we finally cross the line and everything changes?

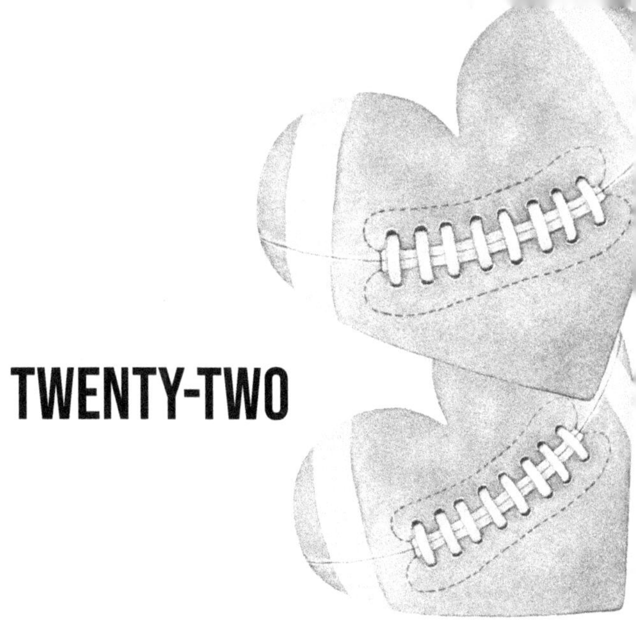

TWENTY-TWO

Danny and I ran every morning during the week, but we didn't place any bets, and we most definitely kept our distance. It seems both of us realized how dangerously close we were to making a big mistake the first time, and we weren't willing to take the risk again.

Without too much proximity and definitely not touching, it was easy to push it to the back of my mind that I fancy him. By the time Friday rolled around, I was confident that I had my crush under control and, therefore, totally let my guard down. So when he asked me if I wanted to come to Jane's roller derby game Saturday, I said yes.

Now here I am, standing in front of Danny's building, waiting for him to come down. I didn't want him to pick me up because it felt too much like a date. I also didn't want to drive alone to the game. My compromise was to meet him here.

He walks out of the building accompanied by a young kid with brown hair and green eyes. He looks like a carbon copy of Andy, so it's easy to guess it's Lorenzo, Andy's younger brother.

"Hey." I wave at them both.

"Hi, Sadie. This is Lorenzo."

"Nice to meet you."

He doesn't answer right away, just stares with his jaw hanging loose until Danny pipes up, "Dude, quit staring at her like that."

A sheepish expression falls on his face, and he drops his gaze. "Sorry. You didn't tell me she was so pretty."

"Aw, thanks. You're sweet." I smile.

Danny throws me a glower. "Don't encourage him. The Casanova gene is strong in the Rossi family."

"Is that so?" I raise an eyebrow at Lorenzo.

"He's just jealous that the girls like me best."

"Quit being such a pest." Danny ruffles Lorenzo's hair in an affectionate way.

It reminds me of Dominic and how he used to do that to me all the time. It drove me bonkers. Like me, Lorenzo complains and steps away.

"We'd better go, or we'll get stuck in traffic," he says.

"Is Andy not coming with us?"

"He's already there. He drove Jane."

"Ah, gotcha."

I fall into step with Danny but choose to walk next to Lorenzo. I shouldn't even be here, because seeing Danny dressed in jeans and a casual T-shirt is worse than his running gear. And his aftershave is making it hard to ignore how my body reacts when I'm near him.

When we come close to Danny's car, Lorenzo calls shotgun.

"Come on, kid. Let Sadie sit up front."

"Oh, it's fine. I don't mind sitting in the back seat," I say.

He looks at me. "Are you sure?"

"Positive."

DANNY

The gymnasium where the roller derby game takes place isn't busy yet, and that allows us to find Ophelia and her boyfriends with ease. I'm also surprised to see Jane's dad in the audience, sitting next to Andy. As we approach their row, Ophelia spots us and waves. Her hair is bright orange today, clashing—or complementing, however you see fashion—big-time with her colorful print outfit.

"Is that Jane's grandmother?" Sadie asks.

"Yep. And her two boyfriends, Jack and Louis."

"Wait? Boyfriends as in plural?" Sadie glances at me with eyebrows arched and eyes wide.

I chuckle. "Oh yeah. You're in for a treat."

Lorenzo enters their row first, followed by Sadie, then me. This is the first time since the almost kiss incident that we're going to be in close proximity again. We saw each other every day of the week, but there's an effort from both of us to keep things planted firmly in the friend zone. I considered not inviting her to come tonight, but I have to believe I can be strong and not succumb to my urges. Mind over matter and all that.

She had to go and wear something sexy though. Those jeans of hers fit her tight ass perfectly, and the crazy asymmetric top shows peeks of skin here and there that are seriously impairing my ability to not think about kissing her.

"Hello, darlings. Long time no see," Ophelia greets us.

"Hi, Grandma." Lorenzo kisses her on the cheek.

Since Andy got custody of Lorenzo after his dad died, Lorenzo got the habit of calling Ophelia "grandma," much to her delight. It makes sense, considering everyone knows it's only a matter of time until Andy proposes to Jane.

Lorenzo says hello to Louis and Jack before taking his seat next to Ophelia. Her sharp gaze travels past him and focuses on Sadie and me.

"Danny, you brought a date."

My cheeks become warmer. "Not a date," I say quickly.

Ophelia's smile wilts a fraction. "That's too bad."

"Not really. Danny and I can never be more than friends. We're way too competitive for that. I'm Sadie, by the way. Nice to meet you."

"Nice to meet you, darling. These are my beaux, Jack and Louis. And the grouchy man with his eyes glued to his phone is my former son-in-law, Jonathan."

The man in question raises his head upon hearing his name. "What?"

"Jane's friends arrived. I was making introductions," Ophelia explains.

He says a halfhearted "Nice to meet you" and returns to his device. The man is a workaholic, and no one really cares anymore that he's only partially present whenever he's around. At least he comes to Jane's games, unlike her estranged mother.

Introductions are made, and then we take our seats. Immediately, I feel the tension build between Sadie and me. It's like whenever we get in close proximity, our bodies create an electric spark. Or maybe it's just in my head. I chance a look at her and notice her jaw is tense. Hell, I don't want things to get awkward between us because of pesky physical attraction. I like to hang out with her. If I just could stop wanting to kiss her, it would be great.

"Have you ever been to a roller derby game before?" I ask.

"Dude, you asked me that question already when you invited me, remember?"

"Right." I rub the back of my neck, dropping my chin slightly so my long hair can hide my embarrassment.

"So, have you?" Lorenzo asks.

"No. All I know about the game I learned from Elliot Page's movie."

"Ah yeah. *Whip it*. I like that movie. It's fun."

"The soundtrack is also brilliant."

"What's your favorite song from it?"

"Let me guess," I butt in. 'Bad Reputation.'"

She smirks. "You know me too well already, Hudson."

"Don't call me Hudson. Only my teammates call me that."

Her eyebrows shoot to the heavens. "Oh, sorry. I didn't mean to offend you."

I shake my head, not knowing why I made that comment. "I'm not offended. It's just... weird when you call me that."

"Why? Because I'm a girl?"

No. Because you're a girl I want to kiss so badly, it hurts.

"You're not a guy on my team. That's why." I face forward, resting my elbows on my knees.

"It's getting busy. How long until the game starts?" she asks.

"It'll be another ten minutes, I think," I reply.

"Oh good. I have time to pee." She stands and stares at me. "May I?"

Since the row is too narrow, the only way she can walk through is if I stand too. Even so, there's literally no space between our bodies when she walks past me. Chills run down my spine with the contact, which prompts me to make a hasty decision.

"Hey, Lorenzo, wanna trade seats with me? I haven't seen Ophelia in a while."

The kid shrugs and then switches places with me.

"Hi, Danny. How is everything with you?" she asks me, smiling kindly.

"Great. Preseason is kicking my butt, but Coach Clarkson thinks I have a shot at going pro."

"Oh, that's wonderful news."

We chat a little about football and then about how Troy and Charlie are doing in Europe before Ophelia brings up the topic of Sadie.

"So, tell me why you haven't staked your claim on that lovely girl you brought tonight."

I shift uncomfortably in my seat. "I'm not interested in dating anyone. I want to focus on football."

"Danny, you're only a sophomore. You can't simply put your life on hold like that. Besides, why does having a girlfriend mean you can't also succeed on the field?"

"Ophelia is right, son," Jack pipes up. "This whole idea that no sex helps athletes stay focused is BS."

My face and ears are in flames. I so don't want to talk about my sex life—or lack of one—with Troy's grandma and her boyfriends.

"Well, there's also a complication. Sadie is Coach Clarkson's daughter."

"Oh really? How marvelous. That just made this story so much more interesting." Ophelia claps her hands.

"Shh," Jack says. "The girl is coming back."

I turn and see that Sadie is, indeed, on her way back to her seat. She pauses when she notices the change in seating arrangement but doesn't make a comment about it before she sits next to Lorenzo and proceeds to ignore me for the rest of the game.

Lorenzo is more than happy to fill the void and talks nonstop. He explains how the game works, who the players are, even tells Sadie about his crush on Scary Samantha, to which Sadie comments that she can see the appeal.

Before I know it, the game is over and we're out of our seats, shuffling toward the aisle. Sadie continues to ignore me as she walks ahead with Lorenzo by her side. The kid is beaming with the attention. As for me, I just trudge along, feeling like a dirty dog who was kicked to the curb.

Andy catches up with me and throws his arm over my shoulders. "What's up, Danny-boy? Feeling blue because Sadie traded you for someone younger?"

I push him off me. "Shut up, Rossi."

He just laughs. "If she's giving you the cold shoulder, it's your fault. Why did you have to switch seats with my brother?"

"I wanted to chat with Ophelia."

"Right. Well, I have a solution to your problems."

"I don't have problems."

He taps my shoulder. "Don't worry, buddy. I got you."

"Andy, for fuck's sake. I already asked you not to play cupid."

He widens his eyes innocently. "I'm not."

Like I believe the asshole.

My suspicions are confirmed when Andy shows his hand outside the building.

"All right everyone. I think Jane's epic win deserves a celebration. We're all going back to La Casa Rossi for pizza."

"I should probably go home," Sadie says.

"Nope. I'm not taking no for an answer," Andy replies and then turns to wink at me.

Jackass.

"Come on, Sadie. You have to come. We can play *Mario Kart*," Lorenzo pleads.

While Lorenzo is busy giving Sadie the puppy eyes, I'm glaring at his brother.

"You're going to pay for this," I mouth silently.

The idiot just laughs.

"Fine, I guess I can hang out for a little bit," Sadie tells Lorenzo.

Even though she's not coming because of me, my stupid heart beats a little faster just the same.

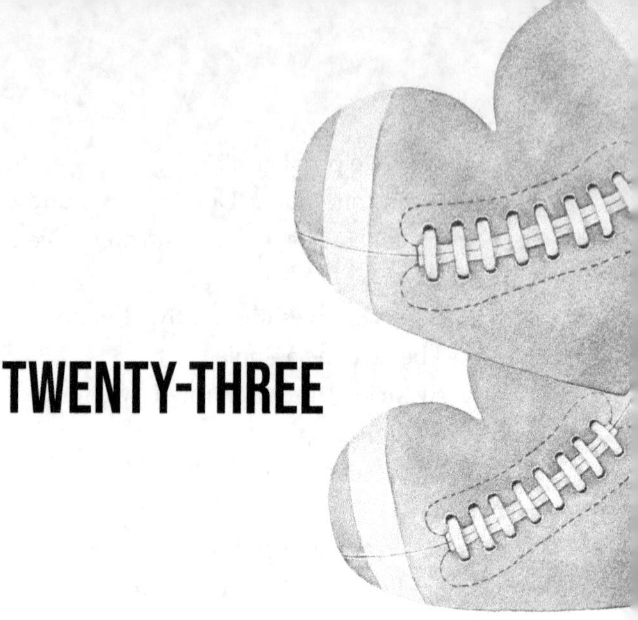

TWENTY-THREE

SADIE

I t was obvious that Danny switched seats with Lorenzo at the game because of something I said or did, so I ignored him while we were there. But I couldn't keep doing that while hanging out at his place. I'm not a total bitch.

Danny leans forward and reaches for the last slice of pizza, but then he stops and looks at me. "Do you wanna share?"

"God, no." I lean back on the couch and stuff my belly out. "I look like I'm six months pregnant."

He drops his eyes to my stomach and shakes his head. "You look nothing like a six months pregnant woman. Four tops."

He takes a bite of the pizza, and gooey cheese drips down the sides. That sight should have been gross, but hell if Danny doesn't make it look sexy. His tongue darts out to capture the string of melted cheese, and I can't look away.

He turns, catching me staring. "What?" he asks with his mouth full.

I sit straighter. "Nothing. I should get going. It's late."

"What? No way," Lorenzo complains. "You promised another round of *Mario Kart*. I have to reclaim my title."

From the other side of the couch, Andy says, "Yeah, Sadie. Stay. Besides, how many beers did you drink? You probably shouldn't be driving."

I'd take him seriously if he hadn't said that with a smirk.

"I'm fine to drive," I grumble.

"Says the girl who crashed into my parked car when she was sober," Danny chimes in.

Narrowing my eyes, I whip my face to his. "Really? How long are you going to hold that over my head?"

"For as long as it annoys you." He takes another bite of his pizza.

"Teasing aside, I also think you should stay," Jane says. "Danny can sleep on the couch again, right, Danny?"

"Yep. I like the couch."

I have hundreds of reasons why staying over is a bad idea, but I did drink one too many beers. Maybe I did it deliberately, so I'd have an excuse to stay. My mind is weak when it comes to Danny.

"Fine. I'll stay. But I've got nothing on me. I have to borrow one of your shirts," I tell him.

"That can be arranged."

"Maybe you should leave some stuff here since you and Danny are such close friends." Andy smiles like a cat that ate the canary.

I want to say "Hell to the no," but it would probably offend Danny. I choose to glare at his roommate instead.

"So, *Mario Kart*?" Lorenzo asks.

"Sure, but since I'm staying, I guess I can have another beer." I make a motion to stand, but Danny puts his hand on my arm.

"I'll grab it."

He heads to the kitchen, taking the empty pizza box with him. My eyes begin to follow him, but I catch myself in time and snap my gaze to the TV.

Lorenzo and I get busy picking our avatars and then customizing our race cars.

"Sadie, we're out of regular beer," Danny calls from the kitchen.

"What's not regular beer?"

"Cherry."

"Oh, I like those."

"How in the world did we end up with cherry beer in our fridge?" Andy asks.

"I don't know. I think Charlie brought them the last time she and Troy were here."

"I miss them," Jane says in a morose tone.

"Me too, babe." Andy kisses her on the cheek.

"Who are they?" I ask when Danny returns with the bottle of cherry beer.

"Troy is my brother, and Charlie is his girlfriend," Jane explains. "They're living in London now."

"Really? If they need suggestions on the best places to go, I'd be happy to give them some tips."

"Oh, that'd be great. I'm sure they'd love it."

"Are you ready, Sadie?" Lorenzo draws my attention back to the game.

"Oh, yeah. I'm so going to smoke your arse again."

"No chance."

We play until my fingers are numb and Lorenzo finally beats me. Andy and Jane have gone to bed already, and after a silly victory dance, Lorenzo trudges to his room. I stand and stretch my arms, eyeing the three bottles of cherry beer I drank between rounds of *Mario Kart*.

It's then that I notice Danny is also not in the living room anymore. Gee, I guess being in any type of competitive game takes all my focus.

I bring the empty bottles to the kitchen, setting them on the counter. They probably have a recycling bin somewhere, but I'm too tired now to go look for it.

On my way to Danny's bedroom, I realize I *am* tipsy. His door is open only a sliver. I have no idea what I'll find inside.

Maybe I should have knocked first, but the thought only occurs to me after I've already opened the door all the way. To my regret, I don't catch Danny in the middle of changing clothes.

He's asleep with a thick book lying across his stomach. I tiptoe toward him, and upon closer inspection, I see he was reading *Harry Potter and the Goblet of Fire*. My favorite book in the series. A smile tugs on my lips.

Since there are no witnesses, I give myself permission to stare at Danny unabashedly. Giddiness takes over, and who can blame me? The boy is swoonworthy. I don't know what I love more about his face: the kissable lips, his chin dimple, or his blond curls. I sit next to him and lightly run my fingers over his hairline.

Danny wakes with a start and a second later squints. "Did I fall asleep?"

"Yeah."

"Sorry. I'll go set up my bed in the living room." He begins to sit, but I push him back.

"I'm not going to make you sleep on the couch. I'll do it."

Undeterred, he rises despite my hand pressing in the opposite direction. If he wants to sit up, I'm not going to manhandle him into bed. Although I'd love to manhandle him in other areas.

Bollocks, my train of thought is already derailing into smutty territory. Next stop, O-town.

"You're not sleeping on the couch. Don't be ridiculous."

"I'm not going to let you sleep there either. So I guess we're sharing the bed."

Oh my God. What am I saying? I can only blame my behavior on alcohol.

"Fine. If that's what you want, we'll share the bed. But if you start to hog the covers, I will push you over the edge."

Since my hand is still on Danny's shoulder, I pinch his arm.

"Ouch!" he complains.

"If you push me off the bed, I'll do to you what I did to Nick Fowler at the gym."

Danny's back turns rigid as his face twists into a scowl. His hand ends up on my leg. "That's the day you said nothing important happened."

Ah hell. Stupid drunk tongue revealing all my secrets.

"Nick grabbed my arm at the gym when I told him to get out of the way, so I did the only thing I could. I brought my knee up to his nuts. Crushed 'em."

His eyebrows shoot up, and his lips curl in a grin. "You did that? For real?"

"Yep. It's not like I hadn't warned him before." I shrug.

To my surprise, Danny pulls me into a hug, and damn it if I don't melt into his arms.

"You're the best."

"I know." I laugh.

Too soon, he releases me and gets out of bed. I watch him go with lovesick puppy eyes. He pulls a long T-shirt from his drawer and tosses it in my direction.

"You can wear this. It should look like a dress on you."

I eye the piece of clothing, loving how it smells of him. I might have to steal it. "Only because you're a giant."

"I'm not a giant, at least not compared to Paris or Puck. Those two are Hagrid wannabes."

I smile. "I love that you're an HP fanboy."

He gives me a crooked smile. "Oh yeah. I got my membership card and everything."

"What house are you? No, let me guess. You're a Hufflepuff."

He glares. "Woman, I'm offended. I'm a Gryffindor."

"Oh yeah. I get that now. Soooo proud."

He narrows his eyes. "I bet you're a Slytherin."

I jump from the bed and shorten the distance between us. "How dare you? I'm also a Gryffindor."

He pinches his lips together, trying to suppress a chuckle.

"Laugh again and you get another pinch," I say.

"Stop being so bossy, *Hermione*. If you want to brush your teeth, there's a new toothbrush in the bathroom cabinet."

Immediately, I fear I have bad breath. I step away from Danny before I say anything else.

"Cool. Thanks."

I disappear into the bathroom and look for the aforementioned toothbrush. It's not in the cabinet above the sink, so I search the drawer. I do find it, but also a box of condoms. Great, like I need another reminder that I want to jump Danny's bones.

I close the drawer with a shove, then take my time brushing my teeth. I even brush my tongue—something I never do. Staring at my reflection in the mirror, I list in my head all the reasons why I should keep it in my pants. But my tipsy brain is keen on ignoring every single item.

Bloody hell.

In a hurry to change clothes before Danny decides to check on me, I almost end up falling on my butt, trying to remove my tight jeans. I bang my elbow against the wall, which sends white-hot pain up my arm.

"Fuck," I grit out.

"Sadie? Are you okay in there?"

"I'm fine."

I change into Danny's shirt next, and like he said, it covers every bit that counts. It's still short though, so he'll get a good visual of my legs.

Why is that important?

You know why, Sadie.

God, the little voice inside my head is annoying.

When I return to the bedroom, Danny is already under the covers sans a T-shirt.

"You'd better not be naked under there."

He rolls his eyes. "Come on. I'm not a perv. If my bare chest bothers you, I can put a T-shirt on. But I usually get hot at night."

Hell and damn. I won't survive sleeping next to him.

"Just stay on your side of the bed and we'll be fine."

I slide under the sheet, trying my best to act like this is natural. I can't get comfortable to save my life though. I turn around and hit the pillow to see if it helps, all the while ignoring Danny's stare.

"Are you done abusing my stuff?"

"Yeah. Keep talking and I'll abuse you next."

"Okay."

Ah, hell. That sounded bad.

"Sorry. I didn't mean to imply I'd… well…. Ugh. Forget it." I turn on my side, giving my back to him.

"I got what you meant. Can I shut off the light?"

"Yeah."

The room turns pitch black for a moment, but my eyes remain wide open. After a while, they get used to the darkness and I can see the outline of the furniture. Danny fidgets next to me, switching positions several times.

Is he as uncomfortable as I am?

"What are you doing?" I ask after a minute of his restlessness.

"Nothing."

He grows quiet after that, yet I can't relax enough to fall asleep. He sighs after a while, and like an idiot, I turn so I'm facing him.

"What is it?" I ask.

"Nothing."

"Is 'nothing' the only word you know now?"

"Apparently."

"You sound mad. Was it the abuse comment?"

"What? No. And I'm not mad."

"I can see your furrow even in the dark." I touch the spot between his brows.

"Don't do that," he says in a voice that's suddenly thick.

"Why not?" He doesn't answer right away, and I begin to really freak out. "You're angry with me."

"I'm not angry." He turns his face to mine. "You seriously don't know, Sadie?"

I lean on my elbow and boldly trace his collarbone with my fingers. "Are you saying you like when I touch you too much?"

"Yes," he hisses and then reaches for my hand, stopping what I'm doing.

"I like touching you. As a matter of fact, I think about touching you constantly."

"Don't say that."

"Why not? It's the truth."

"Because it's taking every bit of self-restraint I have to remain on my side of the bed."

"Well, I have none left."

I roll on top of him, bringing my face inches from his. I can feel his accelerated heartbeat, I can hear his sharp intake of breath, and, most importantly, I can feel his erection pressing against my belly.

"We're supposed to stay friends."

"Why can't we be friends with benefits?" I ask softly. "You have needs, I have needs."

"You have your toys."

"You can't honestly believe my toys are anything like the real deal."

"Sadie, you know this is a bad idea. You're only saying all that because you're drunk."

I seriously didn't expect him to put up so much of a fight, especially considering his body is more than on board with the idea. But there's only so much begging I can do.

"I'm not drunk." I slide off him. "But okay, I won't ask again. Good night, Danny."

I begin to turn, but he stops me, looping his arm around my waist and bringing me flush against his body once more.

"Forget good night," he says right before he slants his lips over mine.

Oh my God. All nerves in my body short-circuit. This is not a tentative kiss. It's demanding, rough, intense, pure fire. His tongue invades my mouth, claiming me in a way I never thought possible. He pulls me on top of him again, and now that we're really doing this, I don't restrain myself. I grind my hips against his erection, teasing him until he groans against my lips. My borrowed T-shirt has bunched up, and the only barrier now between our bodies is the thin layers of our underwear.

His hands find their way to my hips, and with his fingers digging deep into my exposed skin, he takes control, setting the pace. The friction is hitting me in the right spot, making me see stars already.

"This is going to end really fast for me," I murmur against his lips.

"Fuck."

He rolls on top of me and drags his lips down my chin and neck while he plays with my tits through the T-shirt. I arch my back, an invitation for him to explore further. He pushes the fabric all the way up until my breasts are exposed.

"God, Sadie. You're so beautiful." He covers one of my nipples with his mouth, using his tongue to tease my sensitive bud mercilessly.

Moaning, I thread my fingers through his soft curls, something I've wanted to do since the first time I met him.

"Confess. You've been dreaming about my boobs for a while, haven't you?"

He releases my nipple with a soft pop, then runs his tongue over it, leaving a trail of goose bumps over my skin.

"I only got a peek, but yeah, I've wanted to do this—" He bites me lightly. "—for a while."

I take his hand and guide it between my legs. "Feel how wet I am, Danny. This is what you do to me."

He forgets my tits for a moment and stares into my eyes

while his fingers slide under my knickers and then find my clit. I gasp loudly.

"It's your time to confess, Sadie. Have you fantasized about me doing this to you?" He sweeps his finger over my clit again, making my toes curl from pleasure.

"Yes."

"What else have you fantasized about?" He places an openmouthed kiss on my neck.

"Your mouth everywhere on my body, your tongue inside me, claiming me."

He makes a guttural sound in the back of his throat and leans back. "I want this gone."

I lift my arms, allowing him to get rid of my T-shirt. Still maintaining eye contact, I trace the line of his boxers.

"You know what else I dreamed about?"

"What?" he asks in a low tone, thick with desire.

I push his underwear down, freeing his erection. He hisses when I curl my fingers around his shaft.

"I want to make a lollipop out of you, lick you clean."

He reaches behind my head and grabs a handful of my hair to pull me to him. His lips crash over mine, furious and hungry. While he devours my mouth, I work his cock, sliding my hand up and down, feeling it grow even larger under my touch.

He ends the kiss abruptly and rests his forehead against mine, breathing heavily. "Sadie, I'm about to explode here. Tell me what you want."

I might have fantasized about this moment, but I really didn't plan a play-by-play scenario. Do I want Danny to come in my hand, my mouth, or inside me? Hmm, he can probably recover fast.

I lean forward and whisper in his ear, "I want to sixty-nine."

I've never seen a guy react as fast as Danny does. He flips us over, so now he's under me. I laugh at his enthusiasm.

"Shh. We don't want to wake up the entire house." He laughs.

"Sorry, I forgot."

I jump off the bed to shimmy out of my knickers. Danny gets rid of his boxers equally fast.

"Damn, you're gorgeous," I say in awe.

"No, you are." He reaches over, taking my hand. "Come here."

I kneel next to him on the mattress, lean down, and kiss him softly on the lips—or try to. We're both too horny for sweet kisses. Reluctantly, I ease back and straddle Danny, facing away from his mouth. I'm glad it's dark and I'm a little tipsy, because this position always made me self-conscious in the past.

But awkwardness has no place tonight. I'm too comfortable around Danny for that. He grips my hips, bringing my pussy closer to his face. I lick his shaft from bottom to top at the same time his tongue sweeps over my clit, making me moan like a kitten. Holding the base, I bring his length into my mouth, not stopping until the head hits the back of my throat. Danny sucks me harder in retaliation, and soon it becomes clear this is a competition to see who can make the other come first.

Bring it on, babe.

I alternate deep-throating him and licking the top of his cock while pumping him up and down with my hand. With a grunt, he sucks my clit into his mouth, making me lose my focus for a second. The bastard laughs, which only spurs me on. I double my efforts, counting on victory when he grows harder in my mouth. I didn't bank on him bringing his game up to eleven. When he penetrates me with his tongue, it shatters through the control I had over my own body.

The orgasm comes so swiftly and strongly that I have to stop what I'm doing and focus on keeping my legs from giving out. I let go of his erection and press my cheek against his thigh, curling my fingers around the sheet as the wave of the most intense orgasm I've ever had levels me to the ground.

Only when the tremors subside do I remember about Danny.

But when I look, his dick is hanging half limp, and there's a whole mess of jizz around it.

Fuck. He came? When?

I roll over to the side and, leaning on my elbow, look at him. His eyes are closed, and there's a stupid grin on his face. It still feels like I fucked up.

"I'm sorry," I say.

He opens one eye. "About what?"

"I didn't finish you off properly."

He runs his fingers over the back of my legs. "I disagree."

Of course he would. He's a guy. He climaxed. He'd be happy about that. But I'm too much of a perfectionist to be satisfied with my performance.

I get out of bed and head for the bathroom, already thinking how I'm going to make up for it.

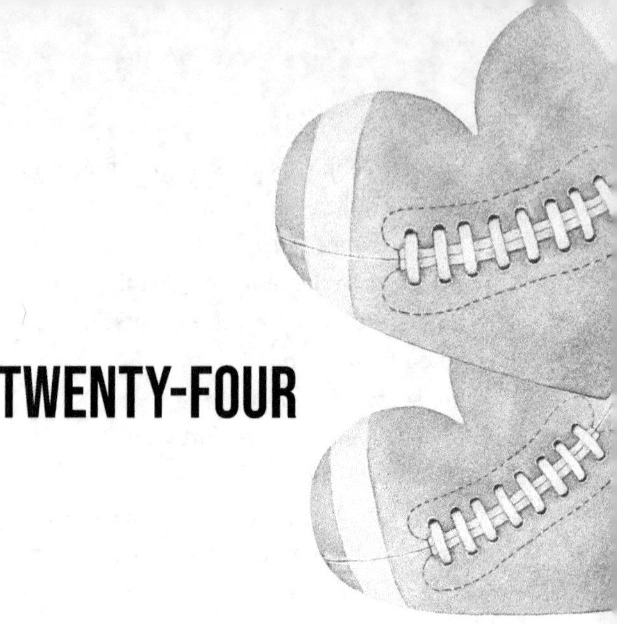

TWENTY-FOUR

DANNY

In my current post-sex state of mind, I can't find it in me to worry about what Sadie and I just did. We crossed a line that was already blurred to begin with, and right now, I have zero regrets. And I also know I want more, probably tonight if she's game.

She returns to the room a moment later, carrying a towel.

I lean on my elbows. "You didn't have to do that. I can clean myself."

"The reason the mess is there is because of me. It's the least I can do."

She wetted the towel with warm water, and as she runs it over my crotch and legs, my cock hardens again, getting ready for round two.

"I'm beginning to think you didn't do it only to be nice."

Her luscious lips split into a radiant smile. "It was totally self-serving. I also brought this." She shows me the condom wrapper I didn't notice before.

My heart is thundering now, and my entire being is yearning to touch her again. Yet I ask, "Are you sure?"

She nods. "More than anything."

I watch as she rips the foil packet open with her teeth, then rolls the condom down my length. God, I'm so turned on that I'm pretty sure it won't take much to push me off the edge again. I've gone too long without sex, and Sadie just puts me in overdrive.

Like a cat in a jungle, she crawls in my direction, but I'm done letting her set the pace. I'm too hungry for her, and I need to impale myself into her heat stat. I grab her by the waist and pull her up until her pussy is flush against my cock.

"Someone is eager." She laughs.

"I've been lusting after you for too long."

"You have?" She tilts her head to the side. "How long?"

"Honestly, since the night at the Red Barn party, only I was too angry to realize it then."

"You also made quite an impression on me that night."

She gyrates her hips, and the tip slides right in. She's so wet, I can sheathe myself in her with a single thrust.

"I think I'm done with talking, Sadie." I skim my hands down to her hips, keeping her in place as I jerk upward.

She moans loudly.

As I predicted, I slide in with ease. She feels too good though, so to avoid a quick-draw move, I wait for a couple of beats, hoping I can get used to her tightness.

Leaning forward, she flattens her palms on my chest and closes her eyes. "Hell, this is.... God, I can't even form a sentence."

"I haven't done anything yet." I chuckle. "I'm trying not to explode too soon."

"Think of unsexy things." She moves her hips, spurring me into action.

"I don't think that'd help much," I breathe as we both begin to move faster.

Right now, I don't know who is fucking whom. All I know is my head is getting lighter, probably because all my blood has converged to my junk. But as much as I love the view of Sadie's tits bouncing as she rides me, I need more. I need to be closer, to go deeper.

I flip us around, managing to stay inside her.

"There. Much better." I silence her protest with my lips, sucking her tongue into my mouth as I pound into her without mercy.

She brings her knees up, locking her legs behind me. My cock seems to grow larger, or maybe Sadie's pussy is squeezing me more. I don't know. I've lost the ability to think straight as tendrils of desire curl at the base of my spine. The release is near; my balls are tight as hell. But I want to prolong this moment for as long as I can. I want to make Sadie come again before I surrender myself to oblivion.

She moans against my lips, becoming tense around me. The tremors come and she screams quietly, the sound of her climax muffled by my mouth. Her nails scratch my back, and the pain mixes with the built-up pleasure. I can't fight it any longer, so I don't. Grunting, I piston in and out of her, milking my release to the max. I could fuck her for eternity, if that was possible. I've never had a pussy as sweet as hers.

I don't stop moving until I sense Sadie relax under me. Resting on my elbows, careful not to crush her, I lean back. Her eyes are hooded, and she has a happy, lazy smile that I want to believe only I have the privilege of witnessing.

"Hey," I say.

"Hi." Her grin widens. "That was amazing."

"Yeah, it was."

"So worth all the yearning and sexual tension."

I bring my lips to hers for a kiss because I can't resist her. In fact, I don't know how I was able to keep my distance all this time.

"Hmm, Danny?" she whispers against my lips.

"That's my name, don't wear it out."

She smacks my arm, laughing. "You and your movie quotes."

"Come on, you gave me the perfect opening."

"I can't believe you know *Grease*. I thought only girls watched musicals."

"Remember, I was raised by a single mom. Besides, I only watched it when I was a kid, and that quote stuck in my head. I used it on my mother all the time. It drove her nuts."

"I bet. Anyway, what I wanted to say is that you should probably get rid of the condom before there's a leakage."

"Oh, right."

I pull out and immediately know we have a problem. It's wet down below.

Sadie tenses and sits up.

"Oh my God. Where did the condom go?"

I stare at my dick like a moron—my very bare dick. All that's left of the condom is a rubber ring at the base.

"Shit. It broke."

"How? Ugh. Never mind." Sadie pushes me out of her way and jumps off the bed.

She rushes to the bathroom, closing the door with a bang. I stand too and get rid of what's left of the condom. I still can't believe it broke. It's a brand-new package.

Sadie comes out a minute later, clearly not happy, and begins to get dressed.

"Are you okay?" I ask her. "I'm clean if you're worried about that."

She whirls around, looking possessed. "No, I'm not okay, Danny. I'm not on the pill!"

I wince at her outburst. "Calm down."

"Don't tell me to calm down. If I end up knocked up, it only ruins my life, not yours."

"I'd never walk out on you if you were pregnant."

"You don't get it. But how could you? You're a guy. If I get pregnant, I'm off the team. I can say goodbye to any chance of playing professionally. Nothing changes in your life."

I understand she's freaking out, but I'm beginning to get

angry just the same. "That's an unfair statement. Besides, it's not the end of the world. We can get a morning-after pill."

"Just shut up, Danny. You're only making it worse. And why in God's name did you have to buy such cheap condoms?"

"That condom wasn't cheap. Maybe your vagina has thorns." The moment those words leave my mouth, I regret them. "I'm sorry, Sadie. I didn't mean it."

"Ugh! I knew I should have kept my distance from you. This is all my fault for letting hormones take control."

She's already dressed and ready to burst out of my room.

"Do you think I wanted this to happen?"

She gives me an irate look. "I'm pretty sure your dick was more than on board, and now I have a legion of your little swimmers going up to my womb as we speak."

"You're being overdramatic. Come on, I'll take you to a pharmacy so we can buy the morning-after pill."

"I'm not going anywhere with you. You've done enough."

She walks out of my room in a huff, and I follow, naturally, not caring that I'm butt naked. I can't let her get behind the wheel like this. I know she's no longer drunk, but I'd consider raving mad just as dangerous.

"Sadie, come on. You're acting crazy."

"I swear to God, Danny, if you don't stop talking, I'm going to punch you in the throat."

"Just let me put some clothes on and I'll go with you."

"I said no."

"Why are you being so stubborn? This isn't only your mistake, it's mine too."

Her eyes turn rounder, and there's a tightness in her features that looks different than anger. She seems hurt, but I didn't say anything that she hadn't already said to me.

"Dude? What's with all the noise?" Andy complains from the hallway.

I turn around. "Go back to bed, Andy."

No surprise, he does the opposite and walks over. "Why are you naked? Oh…."

The sound of the door banging shut makes me turn. Sadie ran out.

Damn it. I can't follow her like this. By the time I put some pants on, she'll be long gone.

"What happened? Why did Sadie leave like that?"

I return to my room without saying a word. Andy follows. After I find my boxers, I sit on the edge of my bed and rest my head in my hands.

"I fucked up."

"How?"

"We hooked up and the condom broke. Sadie freaked out, and you saw the rest."

Andy sits next to me. "Damn. She's not taking any type of birth control, is she?"

"No."

"The morning-after pill is super effective though, especially if she takes it right away."

"That's what I said, but she was beyond listening to me."

"Well, bitches be crazy. Now that you fucked her out of your system, it's all good. You can move on."

I let out a heavy sigh. That's what I should do, but the idea of simply forgetting her brings a sudden ache to my chest.

"What if I can't move on?"

Andy doesn't speak for a few beats, and then he lets out a whistle. "Damn, you've fallen for her, Danny-boy."

"Maybe."

He snickers. "'Maybe,' he says. Sure. Well, if you said anything you shouldn't to her tonight, there's always tomorrow to grovel."

"I suggested her vagina had thorns when she complained about the quality of the condom."

I don't know why I felt the need to give Andy more ammunition to torment me.

He throws his head back and laughs.

"I think for that one, you'll require more than one day of groveling. Probably a week."

I groan at the thought. "I know."

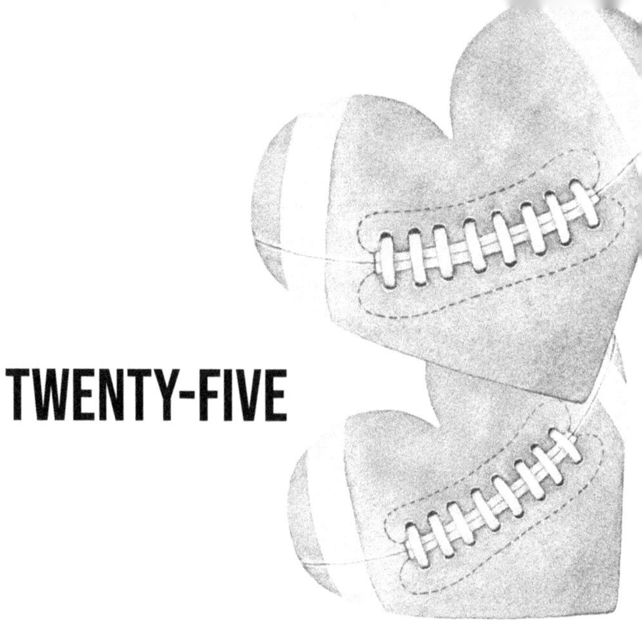

TWENTY-FIVE

SADIE

I ran out of Danny's apartment so fast, I almost tripped on my way down the stairs. I couldn't slow down and give him the chance to put on clothes and come after me. I'm too furious, and he should stay the hell away from me. I've already said too many things no sane person would have. I've gone berserk, and I need to calm the fuck down before I can make sense of everything.

The adrenaline cleared any remaining vestiges of alcohol in my blood. I'm painfully sober as I drive away from Danny's building. I don't know the direction of any pharmacy that's open now, but it doesn't matter. I don't think I can face the pharmacist alone. I should have let Danny come with me, but somehow, his presence would only make things more humiliating.

It's not his fault the condom broke. And I'm the one who gambled and decided to trust a rubber barrier that's not one hundred percent foolproof. I have no one to blame for this mess but me. I took out my frustration and anger on Danny, and I already regret it so much.

My hands are shaking when I call Vanessa. It's past midnight, and I'm sure she's asleep, but I have no one else to call. I can't tell Katrina; she's too much of a gossiper, and I don't consider her my friend anyway.

The phone rings four times before Vanessa's sleepy voice comes through. "Hello?"

"Hey, Vanessa. Sorry to call you so late."

"No worries, Sadie. Are you okay?"

"No. Can I come over? I need a favor. It's an emergency of sorts."

"Yeah, of course. I'll text you the address."

"Thank you."

I have to park first before I can copy the address on Google maps; I can't multitask while driving, and even if I could, I shouldn't. I'm relieved when the automated voice says I'm eight minutes away from her house. I put the car in drive and veer back onto the empty street. A minute later, Danny calls. I press the decline button. Does he seriously think I can talk to him right now? If I wanted to have a conversation, I wouldn't have left his apartment.

The ping on my phone lets me know he left a voice mail. Not satisfied, he also texts me several times. Glancing at my phone screen, I see the notifications pop up one after the other. My guilt doubles. I was horrible to him, and here he is, trying to reach out.

Finally, the robotic lady tells me I've arrived at my destination. I park in front of a small house with a cute front yard and a porch. The light outside is on, and when I exit the car, I catch Vanessa peeking from the window. She has the door open for me before I reach the front steps. She's in pj's, making me feel guiltier that I decided to bother her.

"Hey, are you okay?" She watches me intently.

I walk in and survey the small living room to make sure we're alone.

Maybe guessing my train of thought, she says, "Heather is asleep."

"Oh, I didn't know you lived with your sister."

"I couldn't talk my parents out of that one. It's okay. We both have busy schedules and don't see each other much."

"I miss my brother, but I don't think I could live with him, at least not without a referee to intervene."

"Sometimes I feel like that's what I need. But quit stalling. You woke me from a pleasant dream, tell me why."

I can't hold her gaze, so I choose to stare at the floor instead. "Can you come with me to the pharmacy? I need a morning-after pill."

Vanessa touches my shoulder. "What happened? Did someone—"

"I wasn't raped. I just couldn't deal going with the guy. He offered."

"Was it Danny?"

Blush rushes to my cheeks. "Yes, how did you know?"

"You two have been pussyfooting around each other since the Red Barn party. I never bought your friendship. I knew there was more."

I sigh. "Well, now there's nothing. I totally lost it and acted like a deranged psycho. He's probably never going to speak to me again, which is fine. This awful situation just worked as a reminder of why I didn't want to date anyone in the first place."

"I get that. Soccer is also my number one priority. There's no room in my life for boys. Too much drama, you know?"

"Yep, don't I?"

"Do you want something to drink?" she offers.

"No, I'm good, thanks."

"Okay, well, make yourself at home while I go change."

"All right."

Vanessa disappears down the corridor, and I start to browse through the picture frames she has on the bookshelf in the living room. It's mostly pictures of her with her family. In one of them, they're standing in front of the huge statue of Christ the Redeemer in Rio de Janeiro. I barely have time to look at them all before she returns wearing a pair of jeans and shoes. She kept her pajama top.

"Ready?" she asks.

"Yep. Let's go."

During the short drive, Vanessa doesn't try to get more information about the fight with Danny, and for that, I'm glad. As I'm parking the car in front of the pharmacy, another text message from him comes through. It's short and shows completely on the notification.

> I'm really sorry. Please text me back. I'm worried.

Vanessa's gaze is also down, so she must have read the message too.

"You should text him back, Sadie."

"I will. After I buy this bloody pill."

"You'll be fine. I've taken the morning-after pill before. It works."

"Deep down I know it will, but my brain acts like an arsehole sometimes. If something has a 0.1 percent chance of going bad, that's what my mind gets stuck on."

"I hear ya. Well, there's nothing for it but to go in, get the pill, and hope you're not carrying a mini Danny in your womb already."

My eyes widen. "What the fuck, Vanessa? Is that supposed to make me obsess less about this situation?"

"I was joking, but you have to admit, you and Danny would make adorable babies. Oh, what if it's twins? Can I be the godmother of one? But it has to be the smart one. I definitely don't want to get stuck with a Heather version of your baby."

My mouth is hanging open as I stare at Vanessa. "You've lost your mind."

"Hey, I'm just helping out your asshole brain. I'm sure it hadn't thought of the twin angle yet."

"It had not. But now it's taken it a step further and is showing the possibility of triplets."

"Jesus, I didn't know Danny had super sperm." She scoffs.

"Well, he had a super cock. It managed to break the condom."

"Or maybe you have a super vagina. Have you thought about that?" She raises an eyebrow.

I snort. "Danny accused my vagina of having thorns."

Vanessa laughs. "He said that? Oh my God, I'm learning a whole new side of Danny all thanks to you."

"Should we go in now? I think you've taken the piss enough already."

"Sure, but did it work? Are you feeling less anxious?"

I want to say no, that she only made it worse, but that'd be a lie. I *am* feeling better. I guess by coming up with all those crazy scenarios, she helped me realize I was creating a storm inside a glass of water.

"Yeah. Thanks for your help." I look at the pharmacy building and let out a heavy sigh. "Let's get this humiliation over with."

TWENTY-SIX

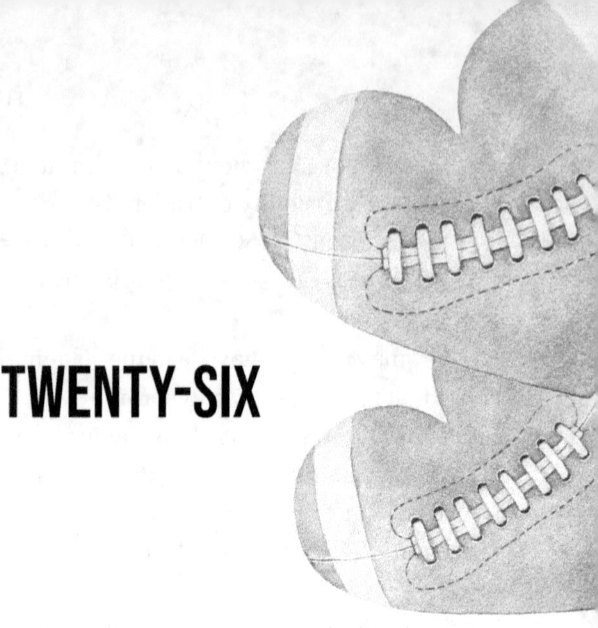

DANNY

An hour after my last message, Sadie finally texted me back to tell me she was home. She didn't mention the morning-after pill, but I assumed she got it. I didn't sleep at all last night. Instead, I kept replaying our fight and dissecting what I should have said instead of what came out of my mouth.

Restless and tired as hell, I'm in a foul mood when I finally give up sleeping and get out of bed. Everyone is still in snooze town—no surprise, since it's only five past six. I drink a glass of orange juice and stare into space for a minute.

"Fuck. It's groveling time."

I get dressed quickly and head to Sadie's dorm, hoping she's there. I have no way of getting inside her building, and judging by her radio silence, I have zero hope she'll answer my call this morning. So I wait in front of the door until someone walks out.

Ten minutes later, a dude who looks like he barely got any sleep steps out, and I slip in before the door shuts again. My heart is hammering loudly as I take the stairs two steps at a time.

I have no idea what I'm going to tell Sadie, but our story can't end like this because of a fucking broken condom.

In front of her door, I knock softly at first. When I don't hear any sound inside, I pound harder and call her name.

"Hold on," a female voice says, irritated.

Not Sadie. Shit. It must be her roommate.

A disheveled short girl opens the door a sliver. Her makeup is smeared, and I can smell her rancid breath from where I stand.

"Who are you?"

"I'm Danny. Is Sadie in?"

"No. She didn't come home last night."

Fuck. I rub my chin in frustration as I wonder where she could have possibly spent the night.

"Do you know where she might be?" I ask.

"No. We don't keep tabs on each other. Can I go back to sleep now?"

"Sure. Sorry to bother."

She shuts the door in my face without another word. I can't even complain about her rudeness. I did come in at an ungodly hour. I pull up my phone and call Andy, hoping he picks up. He does so after the fifth ring.

"Danny, you'd better be dying in your room to be calling me this early."

"I'm not home. I came to see Sadie and grovel like you suggested, but she didn't spend the night in her dorm. Do you have any idea where she could have gone?"

"Maybe she went to her dad's."

There's no way she'd have gone to him.

"Probably not."

"Then I'd start calling her teammates. Start with Vanessa since she's the captain."

Duh. I'm an idiot. I don't know why I didn't think about that before.

"Do you happen to have her number?" I ask.

"Yeah. I'll text you. Good luck, bro."

He ends the call, but a minute later, he comes through with Vanessa's number. I wait until I'm back in my car to place the call; in case she does pick up the phone, I don't want anyone eavesdropping on my conversation, even if campus is currently a ghost town at this hour.

To my surprise, Vanessa answers after the second ring.

"Hello?"

"Hey, Vanessa. It's Danny. Sorry to bother you so early. I was wondering if—"

"Yeah, she's here. Sleeping now. Do you need my address?"

Wow. That was easy.

"Sure."

"I'll text you."

Before she hangs up, I ask, "How angry is she still?"

"Honestly, I don't think she was ever mad at you. But you definitely should talk. I'd suggest you stop on your way to grab coffee and some unhealthy breakfast. And since I'm being so helpful, you'd better bring me some too."

I chuckle. "Sure. I can do that. Thank you, Vanessa."

"No problem."

Thirty minutes later, I'm standing in front of Vanessa's house. It's not far from where Troy and Charlie used to live. Last year, there was a moment when Andy considered moving into their place while they were traveling, but in the end, he decided to stay put and avoid the hassle. Jane has a room there, but she spends most of her time at our place.

I realize I'm stalling, which means the coffee is getting cold. I'm about to get out of the car when Heather, Vanessa's twin sister, walks out dressed in workout clothes. She has her sunglasses on and doesn't seem to notice me parked in front of her house. She heads straight to her car on the other side of the road. I wait until she's gone to step out. The fewer people who know about what happened between Sadie and me, the better. I hate being the subject of gossip and Sadie does too.

I text Vanessa, letting her know I'm outside. I could knock or ring the doorbell, but just in case Sadie is up already, I don't want her to ask Vanessa not to let me in. I'm banking on surprise, which could backfire. It's not like I have a lot of options though.

Vanessa opens the door and tells me Sadie just got up. She'll be out in a second, and she doesn't know I'm here.

"Thanks."

She takes the greasy bag and tray with coffee and sets them on the kitchen counter. I remain standing in the middle of her living room, feeling awkward. She grabs a random cup from the tray and takes a sip.

"They're all the same. Coffee and milk. No sugar."

"Perfect. Just how I like it."

"Do I smell coffee?" Sadie asks from the hallway, but she halts when she sees I'm in the house. "How did you find me?"

"A hunch."

She narrows her eyes and turns to Vanessa. "Did you call him?"

"No. He called me. I wasn't going to lie and say you weren't around."

"Traitor."

"You need to talk. I'm just going to drink my coffee in my room. Have fun, kids. And please don't break anything."

Sadie crosses her arms and watches her friend leave.

"I'm sorry," I blurt out. "I said a bunch of things last night that I shouldn't have. I don't believe for a second that your vagina has thorns."

Her eyes widen a fraction right before she shakes her head. "I'm not angry about that comment anymore. I know you didn't mean it. I acted crazy, I know, and I'm sorry."

My heart fills with hope, and with that sentiment spreading through my chest, I dare move closer to her.

"Please tell me we're good, Sadie."

She drops her gaze to the counter and sighs loudly. "This isn't about the fight anymore, Danny. It's about what I want—what we both want."

"What do you know about what I want?" I ask, wary now.

She glances at me. "You want to play for the NFL. You don't want drama, and last night was nothing but drama."

"True, but it was an extenuating circumstance. I like being around you. I didn't plan on it. I didn't expect to meet someone I could potentially fa—"

"Don't say it. Please." She sounds pained, and it drives a screwdriver through my chest.

"Sadie…."

She rubs her forehead, shaking her head again. God, if that isn't a sign that I'm about to receive the biggest turndown in the history of turndowns, I don't know what is.

"I can't do this. I can't start a relationship with you, or anyone, for that matter. Yesterday, it was a condom that broke. Tomorrow, it will be a cheerleader who gets too friendly with you. I just can't deal with the drama of dating someone so visible, so popular."

"Are you kidding me? You don't want to date me because I'm popular?"

"It's not only that. Please, Danny, don't make this any harder than it already is."

I'm trembling from anger and frustration. After I swore off getting involved with someone, I had to go and fall for a girl who's more stubborn and unattainable than I thought I was.

"So that's it, then. We pretend nothing ever happened between us and we go back to being just friends."

She watches me with regret in her eyes. "I don't think staying friends is possible for us anymore. We tried, Danny, and it backfired. We should just go our separate ways."

Andy told me to grovel, and I was prepared to do that. But I can't do it. I can't humiliate myself when it's clear that what I'm feeling is one-sided.

"Message received loud and clear. I'll stay out of your way and won't bother you anymore."

I turn around and walk out, fighting the urge to look back. I don't expect Sadie to change her mind, but there's a small part of me that wonders if this end is killing her as much as it's killing me. I can't risk a peek though. If I find nothing in her gaze that shows she cares, then it will be even worse for me.

TWENTY-SEVEN

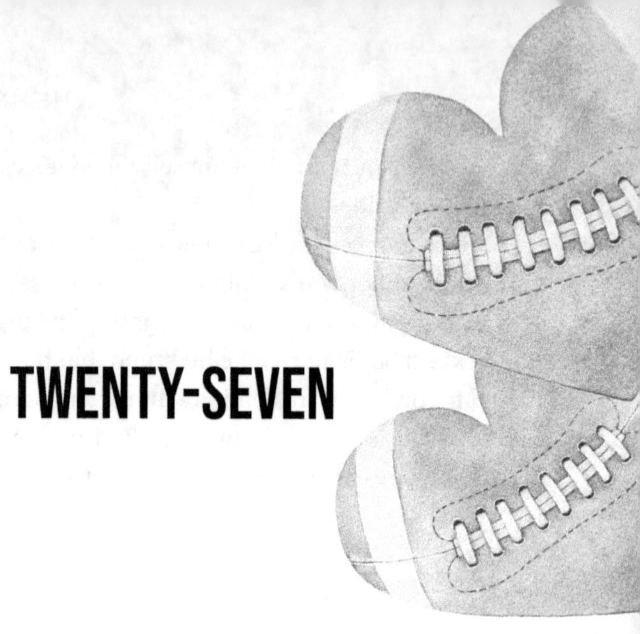

DANNY – FOUR WEEKS LATER

I didn't expect the first game of the season, with me being the official starting quarterback, to be as intense and challenging as this one is. We're tied, and it's now down to this last play. Andy is in position, ready to run long when I make the pass. The crowd is clamoring. My pulse is drumming loudly in my ears, but my focus is sharp.

When the time comes, it's like everything happens in slow motion, even though only seconds go by. I throw the ball hard as Andy flies across the field. He catches it in midair and lands in the end zone.

I yell, throwing my fists up in the air. There isn't enough time left on the clock to allow the other team a chance to even the score again. It's over.

I'm jostled to the side when my teammates jump on me in celebration. Howls, whistles, and claps on the back are exchanged as we walk to the sideline. The Rushmore band plays our victory song, and it feels surreal. I'm a happy motherfucker, and yet I feel something is missing.

Not something. *Someone.*

I remove my helmet, and, like an idiot, I look at the stands, hoping in vain to see her face in the crowd, even though I know she wouldn't be there even if we were still friends. She has a game herself in a couple of hours.

Andy throws his arm over my padded shoulders. "Who are you looking for, Danny-boy?"

"No one." I push him off me.

He laughs and then sprays water from the plastic bottle all over his face.

Coach Clarkson walks over, grinning, which is not something I see frequently. He's a serious man, always with a poker face on.

He shakes my hand. "Good job, son."

"Thanks, Coach," I reply in a daze. "It was a close one. I'm sorry."

"Why are you apologizing? You played a heck of a game. You should be proud."

"I *am* proud."

"Good."

"The Ravens are playing later. Are you going?" I ask out of the blue, catching Coach by surprise.

"Yeah. I wouldn't miss it."

"I'm sure Sadie will do great."

He tilts his head to the side, watching me with renewed interest. Crap.

"Do you know my daughter?"

"I met her at a mixer at the beginning of preseason training."

"Ah, of course. I haven't really talked to her much. When it comes to soccer, Sadie has a one-track mind. I'd be concerned if I wasn't the same when it comes to football." His eyes shine with pride, which makes me sad and a little envious too.

Sadie is so busy holding on to her anger about her parents' divorce that she doesn't see how much her father cares about her. She also doesn't know how much I wish I had a father who appreciated me like that. Fuck, I'd be happy just to know who he is.

"We should head back to the locker room. Don't want to make you late for her game."

Coach claps my back and smiles.

A minute later, Andy catches up with me. "I can't believe you were digging for intel about Sadie from her father. You're hopeless, Danny."

"Piss off, Andy. I was not trying to get intel."

"You don't have to lie to me, buddy. Maybe we should check out her game, show our support for the girls."

I give him a droll look. "You're out of your mind. Nothing against the Ravens, but I'm not going to show up at Sadie's game after our last conversation."

"Sorry for suggesting. In that case, let's go out and celebrate in style. We earned it, man."

I grin. "Fuck. We sure did."

SADIE

Excited energy surrounds me as I gather around in the locker room with my teammates, all wearing our Ravens uniform and ready to kick some butt. In my case, I'm hoping I'll be allowed to touch the ball today. As hard as I trained, it wasn't enough to convince Coach Lauda to bench Melody or Joanne in my favor. I didn't want to replace Joanne because she's become one of my closest friends. Melody is another story. It isn't that I don't like her, but she is my competition, which means she must be destroyed. Yeah, it doesn't make sense. She's on my team, and this is her last year. My brain can be scary sometimes.

If my relentless focus didn't earn me a starting position, at least it helped me ignore the hole in my chest. I knew I was getting close to Danny, but I didn't realize how deep those feelings went until I cut him out of my life. Now there's an ache in my chest that won't go away, and every time I see my dad's name flash on my phone when he calls, it reminds me of Danny.

Before coming here, I checked his game score. I couldn't bring myself to actually watch the game on TV. That'd be too painful. They won by a close margin. I almost broke down and texted Danny to congratulate him but wised up at the last second and didn't. He'd probably think my text was to rub it in that they almost lost.

Coach Lauda is finishing up giving her pregame speech. I missed most of it thinking about Danny. A few more sentences and we're off to the field. I'm one of the last ones in the line out of the locker room. The crowd gathered is modest, and that's saying something. Half the stands are empty. I'm sure the football stadium was bursting at the seams. It's so unfair how some sports get all the attention and others don't, especially the ones played by women. The National Women's Soccer team winning the last World Cup worked wonders to bring more attention to us, but it still pales in comparison to male-dominated sports.

Gah, why am I so bitter? This is nothing new to me.

As I head for the bench, I hear louder shouts coming from nearby. I look up and see a small group of people, all wearing Ravens team shirts with Vanessa's number. Their faces are painted with the Brazilian flag.

"Your family?" I ask her.

She looks up. "Yeah. They're big supporters. Never miss any of my games, much to Heather's chagrin."

"Why would she care that your family comes to your games?"

"Sometimes it clashes with football, so you know, they can't see her shake her pom-poms."

Grinning, I say, "Well, cheerleading is a hard sport."

"I'm not saying it isn't. I know Heather works her butt off, but it's wasted. I mean, her entire job is to look pretty and cheer for a bunch of guys who don't need cheering. They have their fans."

"Would you feel differently if the cheerleaders were assigned to support the chess tournament? Or the debate team?"

"Those aren't sports."

"Fine. You win. Table tennis, then. Or better yet, cricket."

Vanessa wrinkles her nose. "They probably could use some cheerleaders. That sport is so boring."

"Not as boring as baseball."

She covers my mouth with her hand. "Shhh, woman. That's America's favorite pastime. We can think these things, but don't say them out loud."

The assistant coach signals for her to get ready, so she steps back, releasing me. Not much later, the game begins. I park my ass on the bench with two of the Three Musketeers, Charlotte and Phoebe. Like I predicted, Steff is where she belongs, guarding the goal. I've never sat on the bench before, and to say it's nerve-racking is an understatement. I want to shout, pace, do anything to get rid of this jittery energy. It's quite maddening. Forty-five minutes never took so long to pass, and by the time we roll into the halftime break, we're losing one to zero.

Morale is low inside the locker room, and there's no indication from Couch Lauda that she plans on using me in the second half. If we were winning, that'd be another story.

When we head back out, my mood is down to the sewers. I wanted to play today more than anything because I need the reminder that sacrificing Danny was worth it. If we lose and I don't get the chance to show my skills, it'll be a real pisser.

Dejected, I sit on the bench next to Felicia Hopkins, the goalie Steff replaced.

"Why are you so sour, Clarkson? It's not like you got shoved aside for new blood." She laughs.

"I just want to play. I can't believe you're not bitter."

"I don't have anything to prove or any aspiration of playing pro. My goal was to get a free ride at college, which the Ravens gave me. I'm a happy camper."

"I guess it's good to have low ambitions."

"Uh, thanks?" She chuckles. "Although I don't think that was a compliment."

"I'm sorry. I'm such a bitch when I'm not happy."

"Aren't we all?"

My legs are bouncing up and down as I watch the game. When the opposing team almost scores again, I jump and yell, frustrated. Couch Lauda gives me a glower in warning and then starts to shout instructions to Vanessa. A minute later, someone cuts off Melody as she's getting near the goal, hitting her leg instead of the ball. She falls hard, crying out.

"Fuck!" I run to the sideline and watch her clutch her leg while her face is scrunched in pain.

The referee pauses the game, and then our medical staff rushes to the field to check on her. A moment later, she needs to be helped off the field because she can't walk without assistance.

Couch Lauda turns to me. "Sadie, warm up."

"Yes, Coach."

I start running along the sideline while the game resumes. We're playing at a disadvantage with one less member, but I can't jump in without a proper warm-up or I'll end up pulling a muscle. It doesn't help with my nerves though.

Finally, after what feels like forever, I join my teammates on the field. There's no time for a quick convo with Vanessa because the other team has the ball and they're advancing toward our goal. Joanne has taken Melody's place as the first striker, so I fall back a little. Our defense manages to steal the ball back, and then it's counterattack time. Vanessa dribbles past one, two players, and I know she plans to kick the ball to Joanne, but she'll get swarmed by the other team's defense in a few seconds while I'm wide open with more room to work a play.

I run ahead of Vanessa, careful to stay behind at least one defensive player to avoid an offside.

"Vanessa! Over here!" I shout.

She seems to ignore me, maintaining her intention to pass the ball to Joanne, when, at the last second, she kicks the ball with her heel in my direction. I don't hesitate when I have control of the ball and kick it even though I'm outside the goal line. The ball makes a curve, going over the defense and right into the corner of the goal. Their goalkeeper had no chance.

"Yes!" I jump so high, I could have been mistaken for a gymnast.

Vanessa and Joanne run to hug me, and then we wave at the small crowd. Vanessa's family goes crazy, making so much noise that it compensates for the half-empty bleachers and the lack of a band.

My heart is beating loud as fuck, and it feels like it's going to burst out of my chest. This high, this feeling is pure gold, and for a moment, it makes all the sacrifices worthwhile.

The game isn't over yet, and I give it my all through the rest of it. In my mind, it's win or nothing. We score again, this time thanks to my assist, Vanessa sending a bazooka to the goal that not even Steff, our Wall, could have stopped.

Minutes after the game is over, I'm still riding on the euphoria of the win as I laugh and get hydrated near the bench. I'm in mid-swallow when I feel a tap on my shoulder. I turn and find Dad standing there, smiling proudly at me.

"Congratulations, honey. You were amazing out there."

"Thanks. I didn't know you were coming."

"It won't be possible every time, but I'm glad my schedule didn't conflict with yours. I'll be here whenever I can."

Shit. I don't know what to say. Dad is the reason I got interested in sports to begin with. I didn't start to play football until I moved to England, and my reason for starting in the first place was to fill the void he left in my life.

"I'm okay with that."

He beams. For once, it seems I said the right thing, and it's like a huge weight is lifted off my chest.

TWENTY-EIGHT

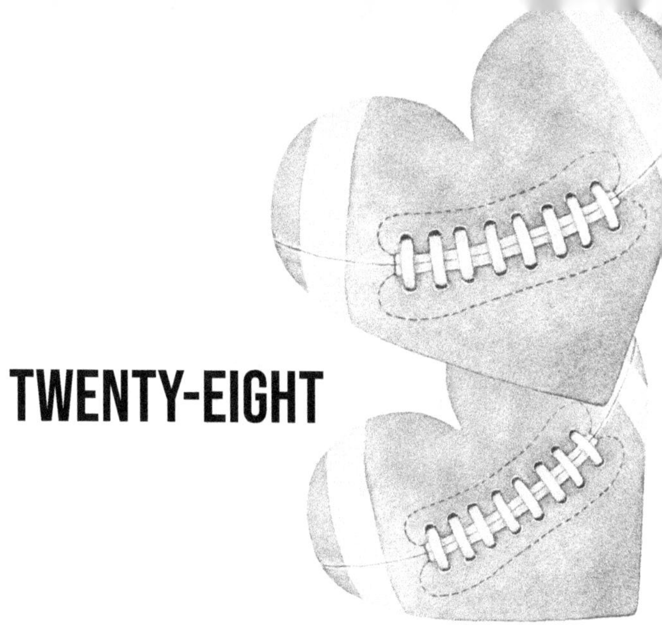

DANNY

Our celebration is at full swing at Tailgaters, a popular college hangout not far from the stadium, when the Ravens show up. Half of the people here are underage, but since this isn't technically a bar, no one gets carded on the way in. It's the easiest thing to get a fake ID if you have the right connections and enough money though. Andy got mine as a birthday present.

Despite my commitment to not party too hard—which I didn't during preseason training—I reckon I deserve to let loose a bit. I wasn't expecting to see Sadie here though, and that immediately puts a damper on my good mood. I toss my head back and gulp down the last of my beer, trying my hardest to ignore her presence.

"Ah hell. It seems the Ravens had the same idea we did," Andy pipes up. "Are you going to be okay, Danny-boy?"

"Bite me, Andy. I can hang out with them."

But I'm hoping Sadie will give me a wide berth. She's been in my head for too long, and I'm just beginning to get over her.

Paris joins us at the high-top table, carrying more drinks. I twist the cap off my beer bottle and gulp down half in one go.

"Whoa. Easy there, buddy," Paris says.

"He's trying to drown his sorrows in alcohol. Let him be," Andy replies.

I set the bottle back on the table with a loud thud and wipe my mouth with the back of my hand. "What sorrows? You're delusional."

My eyes catch Vanessa's from across the room, and with a smile, she heads our way. I no longer have a visual of Sadie, not that I was looking for her.

"Hey, boys. I heard about your win. Congratulations," she says.

"You too," Paris says. "Here, have a beer." He offers his, which still has the cap on.

"It's okay. I was heading to the bar. Who really needs a drink is our MVP." She looks around until she sees what she was looking for. Waving, she says, "Sadie, over here!"

Ah hell. Why, Vanessa? Why?

I take another sip of my beer, and when Sadie joins us, I look at everything but her.

"Hey, what's up?" she says in greeting.

"Sadie, what do you want to drink?" Vanessa asks.

"Oh, I don't think I should be drinking. Bad memories from the last time I got trollied."

I stiffen my back and finally look at her. No, not look. Glare. *Is she for real?*

"Is that so?" I ask, not hiding my annoyance.

She widens her eyes as surprise shines in them. "Are you mental? I wasn't talking about *that* night."

Shame washes over me and I look away, finishing my beer as I do so. Fuck. Maybe I should just go home. I can't keep my cool when I'm around her, and I don't want to make a fool of myself.

A loud ruckus by the entrance of the bar draws my attention.

Sadie and Vanessa turn to investigate the noise as well. A second later, I spot the cause, and if I thought the evening couldn't get any worse, I was wrong. Nick Fowler and his sycophants are here.

"Son of a bitch. Why can't we get rid of that pest?" Vanessa mumbles angrily.

"Didn't they lose their game?" Paris asks.

"Yeah, they did, which means Nick will be more obnoxious than usual."

"Let him. I hope he gives me another chance to smash his balls," Sadie replies, earning an angry glance from Vanessa.

"Don't even think about it. With Melody out of commission, we need you. I won't let you get a suspension because of that weasel." She turns to look at us. "That includes the three of you too."

"You're not my captain," Paris retorts angrily.

"No, but I am, and Vanessa is right," Andy cuts in. "As much as I'd love to teach Fowler a lesson, I won't jeopardize the team. Let's just ignore him."

"Too bad he doesn't seem like he wants to ignore us. Asshole is coming our way," I say.

I shift closer to Sadie, an automatic move. I don't know if she noticed, but if she did, at least she didn't step away.

"Well, well, if it isn't the football players trying to pluck the flowers from my garden," Nick slurs.

"What the fuck are you talking about?" Vanessa glowers. "And what's that awful smell? Did you take a dive in a cesspool before coming here?"

He shoots her an angry glance, but he's too drunk to hold the stare for too long.

"I'm saying football players have their cheerleaders. They don't need to fuck around with our girls."

"Your girls? Aren't you a delusional wanker?" Sadie retorts angrily. "Just piss off already. You're stinking up the place."

Nick takes a step toward her. "Listen here, you little b—"

I push him back. "Back off, Nick. No one wants you around. You're an embarrassment to this school's sports department."

Suddenly, Nick is yanked back by his friend. "Sorry, guys."

"Let go of me, Leonard." He tries to break free, but he's too drunk for that.

"Nick, we're leaving. If Coach finds out you were drunk and creating trouble again, you'll be benched."

"You should let him get benched. It's not like he's doing much for your team anyway," Andy chimes in.

I see the remark doesn't sit well with Leonard, but he swallows his anger and drags Nick out.

"Okay, I definitely need a drink after interacting with that mongrel," Vanessa declares.

"Blimey. Me too. He's a fucking prat." Sadie replies absentmindedly.

I notice she's touching the place where her scar is. I never found out how she got that, and now I probably never will. The thought that we've gotten so close and then so far apart in such a short span of time does my head in and also makes me unbearably depressed.

"You know what? I think I'm just going to call it a night," I declare.

Andy's eyebrows shoot up. "Really?"

"How many beers did you have?" Sadie asks, surprising the hell out of me.

"Plenty, but I'm not driving."

I leave it at that and walk away. Let her think whatever she wants. She wanted me out of her life; she doesn't get to know anything about mine.

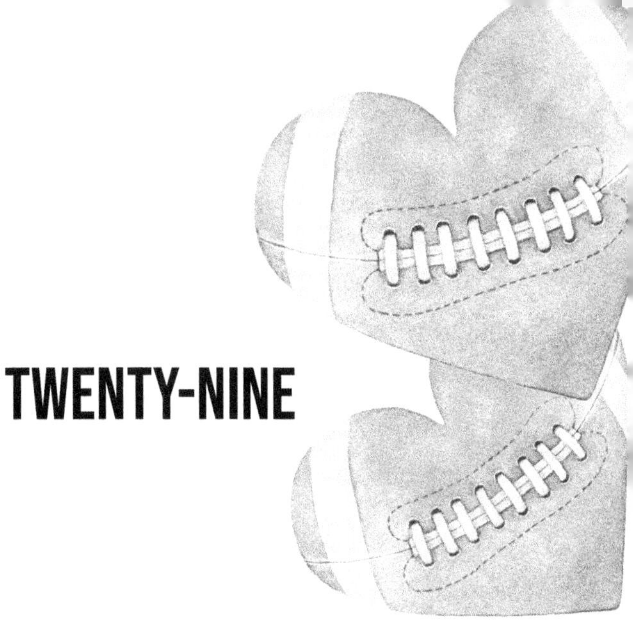

TWENTY-NINE

SADIE

The celebration last Saturday after the game was a total bust. I knew it would be hard. Anything that resembles a pub isn't really my scene anymore. Places like Tailgaters remind me of my attack, and then Nick had to show up. The arsehole who knifed me was someone like him. Drunk out of his mind.

But the main reason my evening was rubbish was because of Danny. I thought I could handle seeing him again. I was wrong. He wasn't happy to see me either. That much I could tell. Then he just left, and I spent the rest of the evening wondering how he got home. Did he Uber or have a jersey chaser lined up to give him a ride and later *ride* him?

I acted like a total psycho and stalked him on social media just to see if he hooked up with anyone after Tailgaters. Which was stupid as fuck. The whole point of ending whatever I had with him before it developed into more was to avoid drama and the heartache. But it didn't work out that way. I was blindly jealous and couldn't concentrate on anything on Sunday. Not even my one-hour run helped.

Monday morning, I head to class still feeling like shite. I'm glad it's an easy-breezy one, an elective about The Beatles. It boggles my mind that we're required to take classes that have nothing to do with our degree, but I've gotten a free ride, so I shouldn't complain.

No sooner do I sit down than I sense the obvious stares of my male classmates. They know I play football, so at first, I think they're just staring because I was brilliant last Saturday. But then the snickers follow, and I realize those stares aren't of appreciation. They're leery and mocking.

I get up from my seat and march up to the closest wanker to me. "What are you staring at?"

"Nothing." He hides his phone quickly, looking guilty as hell.

"Rubbish. Let me see your phone."

He leans back. "No way."

"They were looking at a list that popped up this morning on social media," a girl three rows down from us chimes in.

"What list?"

"It ranks all female athletes. Best ass, best tits, most likely to have a threesome, most fuckable, and so on. It's disgusting."

"What?" My voice rises to a shriek. "Who posted that?"

"No one knows. It's been shared a lot though. You were voted heavily in a few categories."

"Bloody hell." I turn and storm out of class. I need to get to the bottom of this.

In the hallway, I call Vanessa to ask if she's heard about it already.

"Yeah, I've seen it," she says before I even open my mouth.

"Do you know who posted it, because I'm going to kill whoever did."

"No, but I have my suspicions."

"Nick motherfucking Fowler," I grit out, trying my hardest to contain the red-hot rage going through my veins. And I haven't even seen the list yet. I'm sure I'll explode like the Tasmanian Devil when I do.

"He's one of my suspects, but there are more assholes on campus. I wouldn't put it past one of the frat boys either. They aren't saints."

"That's disgusting. We need to do something about it."

"Have you seen the list?"

I shake my head. "No. The wanker looking at it in class didn't want to show me. Probably a wise decision. I might have taken my anger out on him."

"He probably deserved it if he was reading it. I'm calling Coach Lauda, because this is something that requires bringing in the big guns. It's not only offensive but disrespectful to all women busting their asses to be the best athletes they can be. I'm sick of being sexually objectified."

Her mention of Coach makes me think about my dad. He has influence here, but I don't want him getting involved. Asking a man to help solve our problems doesn't feel right. Fuck the patriarchy.

"Let's meet after you talk to Coach. If we can't find out who created the list in the first place, we can't make the culprit pay."

"Oh, we *are* going to discover who the motherfucker is. And then I'm going to destroy him. I promise you that. Talk later, and try not to kill anyone before class is over for the day."

I can't make such a promise, but I don't tell Vanessa that, so I lie. "Sure. I'll be on my best behavior."

I return to the classroom, still fuming. None of the tossers who were staring before dare to look in my direction. I know I'm giving off crazy psycho vibes, and I'm not going to tone it down. But what was a pleasant class before becomes unbearable. I can't sit there and analyze a fucking Beatles love song when I want to murder someone.

My next class proves to be just as painful, and by the time lunch rolls around, I'm coming out of my skin. I made plans to meet Joanne and Vanessa at the main cafeteria, but destiny would have it that I cross paths with Danny and Andy first. I know by the way they look at me that they've seen the list.

"Sadie, are you okay?" Danny asks in his usual knight-in-shining-armor manner, melting a little of my anger.

I don't know if it was the idea that he could have gone home with another girl last Saturday that's making my chest feel like it's bleeding out or that I simply just miss him so damn much.

God, I don't need to feel all mushy when some wanker on this campus needs an arse whooping.

"Not really. Do you know who posted that list?" I ask.

His blue eyes turn stormy. "No, but when I find out, he'd better run fast."

I shake my head. "Stay out of it, Danny. This isn't your problem."

"The hell it isn't!"

I wince at his outburst. Vanessa was definitely wrong when she thought Danny didn't have a temper. He's just better than most at keeping it in check.

"This isn't only your problem, Sadie," Andy butts in. "This jackass has disrespected our friends. Do you seriously think we'll just stand on the sidelines and do nothing?"

"He attacked us, not you. He didn't make a list asking people to vote for who has the biggest schlong or who is the ugliest football player on campus. I'm sorry if I don't see this as a general problem. It's an attack against female athletes, and it should be handled by us."

"So you're saying we aren't allowed to be your allies?" Danny asks angrily.

I can see that I'll never be able to get my point across, so to avoid an argument in front of the entire cafeteria, I back down.

"You know what? Do what you want." I spot Vanessa, Joanna, and Melody across the room and use it as my escape route. "I have to go."

DANNY

"That was pleasant," Andy states dryly as soon as Sadie is out of earshot.

"It could have been worse. She reined in her anger."

"You sure didn't." Andy stares at me knowingly.

"That list was all kinds of fucked up. Of course I didn't. I don't care about what Sadie said, I'm getting involved."

"Don't be stupid now, Danny-boy. What are you going to do if you find out the person responsible for it is Nick Fowler?"

"Then he's dead meat."

"That's the whole problem, and I get why Sadie doesn't want you to meddle. If you touch Nick, even if it's justified, you'll get expelled, and there goes your dream of playing for the NFL."

I grind my teeth in frustration, knowing he's right.

"What if that list mentioned Jane. Would you be levelheaded then?"

"Hell to the fucking no. But again, my future doesn't depend on me graduating. Yours does."

"Your point is moot until we have a culprit. Who are we going to pressure to give up the intel?"

"Not Leo. He's too smart to blab." Andy pulls his cell phone out. "Ricky Montana it is."

I raise an eyebrow. "Do you think he knows?"

"Possibly. He has his ears to the ground. He deals in gossip."

Ricky Montana was in one of Andy's classes last year, and thanks to an exchange of favors, Andy took him under his wing for a while. But then shit happened, Jane came into the picture, and now Andy is no longer the king of parties on campus, so we haven't seen Ricky in a while.

Andy puts the call on speaker so I can hear it.

"Andy, my man. Long time no hear," Ricky's cheery voice comes through.

"Hey, Ricky, what are you doing right now?"

"I was about to grab some grub. Why?"

"Can you meet me at the main cafeteria? It's important."

"Sure can, homie. See you in ten."

Andy and I look for a free table, but it's prime lunchtime and the place is packed. While I'm looking for one, I spot Sadie playing with her food but not making a motion to eat any. I'm distracted and end up bumping into someone.

"Ouch, Danny. Look where you're going," Gwen says, followed by a giggle.

"Sorry. I didn't see you."

"Clearly."

I'm still looking in Sadie's direction like an idiot.

"You're probably wondering if what that list is saying is true."

Her comment makes me snap my attention to her. "What are you talking about?"

"You know, if the new Raven striker has had that many orgies. I mean, she's from England, and you know how European girls are."

I glower. "No, Gwen, I don't know how they are. My advice is to stop spreading rumors. It's a nasty habit, one I'm sure your sorority sisters would frown upon."

"I'm not spreading anything. Just making a comment. You're so touchy, Danny."

"Yo, Danny-boy. Are you coming?" Andy waves me over. He's found a table.

"Yeah."

I walk around Gwen, asking in my head for the thousandth time how I was able to date that girl. She's rotten.

I'm about to sit when my phone vibrates in my pocket. It's my mother. She never calls in the middle of the day unless it's important.

"Hey, Mom."

"Danny, sorry to bother you. Do you think you can swing by the apartment for dinner tonight?"

With everything that's going on, I really don't feel like paying her a visit. That thought makes me feel guilty as hell though.

"I'm a bit busy. Can I come later in the week?"

"I really need to speak to you in person, honey. It can't wait."

Shit. That puts me on high alert. A bunch of terrible scenarios rush through my head.

"Okay, I'll come over. Is everything okay with you, Mom?"

"Oh, I'm fine, honey. I'll see you at seven, okay?"

"Yep. I'll be there."

"Is everything okay, Danny?" Andy asks as soon as I put my phone away.

"I'm not sure. Mom wants me to come over for dinner tonight. She said it couldn't wait."

"Hmm, and you're worried it could be something serious, like she's sick or something."

"That's the first thought that crossed my mind. But she said she's fine."

"Maybe she's met someone." He wiggles his eyebrows up and down.

"Why do you have to do that?"

"Do what?"

"You know, let me know you're thinking dirty thoughts about my mother."

He scoffs. "I did no such thing. You're the one with a filthy mind."

"I'm getting food." I stand up.

"Grab me a burger, will ya?"

Usually I'd tell him to buy his own food, but once again I'm distracted. At least this time, I don't bump into anyone as I head to the food line.

THIRTY

"Mom, I'm home," I call as I enter the apartment.

She appears in the living room a second later, wiping her hands on her apron.

"Hi, honey. You got here early."

"I didn't want to be late." I walk over and plant a kiss on her cheek. "Do you need help with dinner?"

"Oh no. I've got everything all set. I'm making ham and cheese lasagna."

"My favorite."

Mom returns to the kitchen, and I follow her, too anxious to find out what she wanted to talk to me about. I pull up a stool while she chops vegetables for the salad.

"So, I'm here. What did you want to tell me?"

She doesn't answer for a couple of beats, but I notice the new rigidness around her mouth.

"Mom? You're making me worried."

With a sigh, she stops chopping and looks at me. "It's about your father. He got in touch."

Suddenly, it feels like my world has gone off-kilter. I'm glad I'm sitting because I might have collapsed otherwise.

"I see. Why?"

A long time ago, Mom told me the truth about my conception and why my father wasn't in the picture. I pretended for her sake that I didn't care, but what eight-year-old wouldn't care that their father would rather he'd never been born?

"He's sick, and I guess he wants to make amends."

I laugh bitterly. "Oh, that's rich. So he only wants to connect with his son because he's on his deathbed?"

Her eyes fill with tears. "Honey, I know this is hard for you. It's not easy for me either. I almost fell off my chair when he showed up at Dr. Francis's office."

"What? He came by your place of work? The nerve!"

"He figured I wouldn't take his call. He was right. After I recovered from the shock of seeing him in the flesh after all these years, I wanted to toss him out. Of course, I couldn't cause a scene in the office."

"The bastard was counting on that."

"Yeah. He cornered me, and I had no choice but to hear what he had to say." She sighs. "Long story short, he wants to meet you."

"I don't care that he's dying. I want nothing to do with the man." I stand suddenly as all my years of suppressed anger come to the surface.

"I'll be behind any decision you make. I won't push you to meet him. But I also couldn't not let you know about it."

I pull my hair back, yanking at the strands. "I-I can't be here, Mom. I have to go."

"What about dinner?"

"Freeze it, will you?"

Her expression falls, but I don't want her to witness me wrestle with my conflicted feelings. I head out, forgetting to kiss her goodbye. My mind is going a hundred miles an hour, trying to reconcile the fact that I've always wanted to know my father and the truth that he only wants to meet me because he's dying.

The drive back to campus is torment. The radio is on, but no song that comes through helps with my dark mood. Traffic is brutal, and for once, I don't have the patience for it. I honk and curse, getting dangerously close to having a road rage episode.

This is hell.

After an eternity, I finally turn onto my street. But when I park in front of my building, I don't get out of the car right away. I'm not sure who is home, but I know I'm not in the mood to see or talk to anyone. I can't just sit here though.

Decision made, I get out and go for a jog. My head is full of thoughts, so I let my feet take me wherever they want. I run until my breathing comes out in bursts and sweat dots my skin. When I finally stop, I brace my hands on my knees to catch my breath. I have no idea where I am until I look up and see I'm in front of the library building. This is where Sadie and I used to meet every day for our morning runs.

I'm not sure why my subconscious decided to bring me here, but being reminded of what I lost is just adding insult to injury. I turn around, determined to get the hell out of here as fast as possible, even though my legs are beginning to protest. I stop when I see a familiar figure running in my direction, her blonde ponytail swishing with the rhythm of her pace.

She sees me and slows down, coming to a stop in front of me. She must have just started her run because she looks fresh out of the shower.

"Hey, I didn't expect to see you here," she says.

"Same."

She furrows her brow. "What's wrong? Did something happen?"

Am I that transparent?

"Why do you ask?"

"You don't look happy."

I rub my face, not knowing how to respond to that, then look out in the distance. "I went to see my mom today."

She steps closer and touches my arm. "Is everything okay?"

I try to ignore the goose bumps that form on my arm thanks to her hand there.

"No. But you probably don't want to hear me cry about my problems."

"Danny, you can talk to me."

I raise an eyebrow. "Can I? I remember vividly the last time we spoke. You didn't want anything to do with me. Friendship was off the table."

"I was wrong."

I want to yell at her, say she can take her friendship card and shove it where the sun doesn't shine, but I don't do any of that. That proves how low my self-esteem is that I'm willing to accept her crumbs. Pathetic.

Bone-tired, suddenly, I head for the steps leading to the library building and sit down. Sadie follows and drops next to me.

"My father contacted my mother. Showed up at her work."

"Without more context, I'm going to assume that's a bad thing."

I bring my knees up and hug my legs. "Sorry. I should probably explain why I never met him before."

"You don't have to, but I'm all ears if you do."

After our fight, Sadie should be the last person I'd want to unload my family drama to. But even after all these weeks without speaking, the feeling that I can tell her everything hasn't gone away.

"When he and my mother were dating, he neglected to tell her he was married. She only discovered after she got pregnant and he freaked out. Told her he wanted nothing to do with me and gave her money to have an abortion."

She touches my arm and squeezes. "I'm so sorry, Danny. That's total rubbish."

"Yep. And now he's sick, probably dying, and he wants to meet me."

"You must be feeling all sorts of conflicted emotions, aren't you?"

I nod once. "I am, and that's the problem. Why am I feeling guilty for saying I don't want to meet the son of a bitch? He told my mother to get rid of me. He never once in nineteen years reached out to ask how we were doing. And suddenly I'm supposed to meet him to make him feel better about his guilty conscience?"

"You're feeling guilty because you're not a horrible person like he is. You shouldn't though. You're probably going to think even less of me for saying this, but as far as I'm concerned, he's not your father. He's just a sperm donor, and you shouldn't feel an ounce of remorse for saying no to him."

"I don't think ill of you, Sadie."

She withdraws her hand from my arm, and I miss the contact.

"Why not? You should. I was a real bitch to you."

"A little."

"Not a little. Major cunt-ness. I think...." She pauses and sighs. "I think the reason I lost it was because I let you get too close. I never felt that way about anyone before, and I became overwhelmed and frightened."

My traitorous heart is racing as I turn to her. "What are you saying, Sadie? Did you fall for me?"

"Bugger. I shouldn't have said anything." It's her turn to hug her knees and look away.

"Too late now. You can't unsay it."

She faces me, glaring now. "It doesn't matter, does it? I fucked up royally, and right now, I'm just trying to do the right thing and be a good friend, but I'm already messing it up again. Clearly I suck at relationships of any kind."

"Yeah, you're horrible. You can't even do a love declaration properly."

She opens her mouth, twisting her face into an expression of indignation. "Danny Hudson, you're such a concei—"

I reach for the back of her head, keeping her in place while I crush my lips to hers, ceasing her protest. She tenses for a split second before she returns the kiss with the same fervor. Damn it, I missed her taste, and the way being close to her makes me feel. This could be another mistake, but hell, there's no turning back now.

We break apart after a minute, and when I see Sadie's hooded eyes, my face splits into a smile.

"Why did you stop?" she asks.

"Because we're making out in front of the library."

"I don't care if people see us."

"You don't?"

"I want to kiss you whenever I feel like it. That is, if you want me to kiss you often."

I cup her cheek and run my thumb over it. "Damn straight I do. But I have one condition."

"What?" She leans back.

"No more friends-with-benefit BS."

Her eyebrows shoot up. "Wait. You want to date me?"

I chuckle. "Why do you sound surprised?"

"Because… well, in case you haven't noticed, I have issues."

"Who doesn't? I like you, Sadie. More than I thought I could like anyone again."

"What about us keeping our focus on our careers?"

"I say we were wrong about the whole thing. Being apart didn't help with my concentration."

She scrunches her nose in the cutest way possible, making me want to kiss her again. But I restrain myself.

"No, it sucked actually," she replies. "There's only a tiny issue."

"What is it?"

"How do you think my father will react when he learns you're sleeping with his daughter?"

Ah hell. I forgot about Coach Clarkson. But since I'm a guy, that's not what my mind focuses on.

"Are you saying sex is back on the menu?" I grin.

She narrows her eyes. "Based on your response to what I just said, maybe we should hold off on that for a little bit."

"Okay, okay. So let's stress about Coach Clarkson, then. That's way more fun."

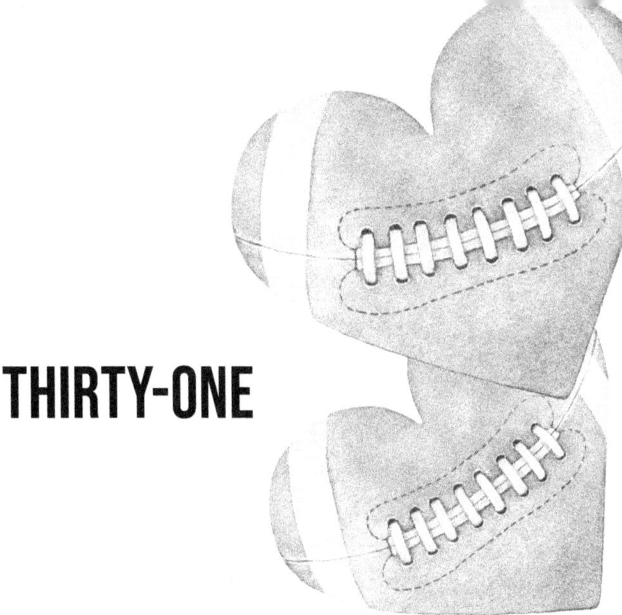

THIRTY-ONE

SADIE

My heart is beating like a drum, audible and fast as Danny and I walk side by side back to my car, his hand firmly clasping mine. When he said he ran all the way here from his apartment, I thought he was mental. Now I get to give him a lift back home, and I'm glad he felt the need to exert himself until he forgot his problems.

I'm giddy like a schoolgirl, and the butterflies in my belly are having a dancing competition. When we're both inside the car, it's like the air becomes supercharged with electricity. The sun has set, and the only illumination is coming from the streetlights.

Instead of turning on the engine, I turn to him. A second later, we meet in the middle for another hot kiss that sets fire to my body and melts my bones. His hand is resting on my waist, and mine has found its way into his hair. I twist my fingers around a strand as I tilt my head to the side, deepening the kiss.

I love the way his tongue dances with mine, taking and giving control. I can't believe I was stupid enough to walk away from this, from him. My body tingles all over as desire spreads through me like wildfire. I regret saying I want to take things slowly, because I'd love nothing more than to straddle Danny and ride him into oblivion.

But I don't want to mess things up again, so taking it slower —not slow—is the safest bet for us.

Danny bites my lower lip and then places open kisses across my jaw and neck. I arch my back, offering my throat for him to feast on. His hand has slid lower, and now his fingers dig deep into my hip. Would he think less of me if I begged him to move his hand between my legs? I'm so turned on that I'm beginning to lose my mind.

Breathless, I say, "I think I should take you home now."

"Yeah, I think you should," he whispers in my ear but makes no move to let go of me.

His mouth returns to mine, and it's another minute before I find the strength to ease off and keep him from following.

"If we don't stop now, I won't be able to drive at all."

He chuckles. "You know how hard it is for me not to make a sarcastic comment?"

"If you know what's best for you, you won't."

Still grinning, he rubs his thumb over my swollen lips. "Sometimes I don't, Sadie. You'd better keep me straight."

My core throbs as my dirty mind conjures up all kinds of kinky scenarios where I could keep Danny straight. And one of them involves taking our make-out session to the back seat of the car.

Reluctantly, I return to my side of the vehicle and turn the engine on. No surprise, all the windows are foggy. We've been kissing for a while.

I'm self-conscious when I pull out of the parking spot. Danny won't take his eyes off me.

"Uh, Sadie?" he says.

"Yeah."

"You forgot to turn the headlights on."

Ah, fuck. How can I get mad at him for making fun of my driving skills when I keep giving him ammunition?

"Stop distracting me."

"How am I distracting you?" I hear the hint of amusement in his tone.

"You're sitting next to me. That's plenty distracting."

"I'm not sure how I can solve that problem for you. Would you like me to move to the back seat?"

"And make me look like an Uber driver? No, thanks. Stay where you are."

He laughs. "Okay, babe."

"Babe? Is that going to be your nickname for me now?"

"You don't like it?"

"It's a bit generic."

"What would you like me to call you, then? Darling? Sweetheart? Sugarplum?"

I snort. "Sugarplum? I don't think I've ever heard that one before."

"Then it's settled. Sugarplum it is."

I peel my eyes off the road for a split second to glower at him. "You're acting sassy already and we've only been dating for a hot minute."

He gives me a boyish shrug. "What can I say? You rubbed off on me."

I open my mouth to reply, but Danny's phone interrupts. He fishes it out of his pocket and answers.

"Hey, Andy."

"Where are you?" he asks loud enough that I can hear from my side of the car.

"I'm on my way back home. Why?"

"I saw your car parked in front of the building and I was wondering. How was your dinner with your mom?"

"I'll tell you when I get home," he replies without the levity from before.

Curse Andy for reminding Danny of his shitty day. I know it's wrong to be annoyed with his roommate, but I'm a lioness when it comes to protecting the people I love.

I grip the steering wheel tighter. *Holy shit. Is that what I feel for Danny? I love him?* I knew I cared about him, and our fallout hurt me more than I thought it would. But I didn't realize I had fallen so hard already.

You'd better not say anything to him, Sadie, or he'll think you're a veritable psycho.

My thoughts are suddenly too loud, and I miss the next thing Andy says. All I know is that by the time I park close to Danny's building, he's gripping his phone in a viselike hold and staring out the window with his jaw clenched.

"What happened?" I ask.

He turns to me, looking too grim for my liking.

"We know who uploaded the list."

My spine becomes taut in a flash. "Who?"

"A freshman named Gary Hanson. Do you know him?"

"Never heard the name before. So not Nick Fowler?"

I can't help the disappointment. I wanted the dick to be responsible, so I'd have a reason to make his life miserable.

"As far as Andy knows, neither Nick nor anyone on the men's soccer team was involved."

"How did Andy discover who it was?"

Danny's eyes flash with guilt. "I know you told me to stay out of it, but I just couldn't, Sadie. We know a guy who's into every bit of gossip on campus. He asked around, and that's how we got to Gary."

"Do you think he could be covering for someone?"

"I don't know. Anyway, Andy passed the information to the school's administration and the coaches."

I squint. "When you say coaches, do you also mean my father?"

"I think so."

I turn away, leaning my head back. "Bollocks. I really wanted to keep my father from finding out or getting involved. I hate this."

Danny covers my hand with his. "Why are you so intent on keeping him out of your life, Sadie?"

I close my eyes, hating that his question makes my eyes prick with tears. "Because he let me down when I needed him the most."

"Come here." He reaches over, sliding his hand behind my neck and pulling me to him.

His lips are soft over mine, and the kiss is sweet and lazy. There's still the underlying raw need in it, but Danny isn't trying to sex me up right now. I can sense the emotion, his feelings in the way he worships my mouth. I melt into him, letting him erase the sadness from my heart.

He breaks the kiss too quickly, though, and presses his forehead against mine. "Come up?"

"I'm not sure I should," I breathe out.

"I promise to be on my best behavior."

"You're not the problem. I am."

"Come on, sugarplum. Are you saying you can't resist my charms?" He grins.

"No, I can't. You're my weakness, Danny Hudson."

"I'm not sure if I should take that as a compliment."

I capture his face between my hands and flatten my lips to his, no tongue this time. Then I push him back. "Get out before my knickers disappear."

He shakes his head, laughing. "You're one bossy woman. I'll call you later, okay?"

"Okay."

He gets out, and I watch him leave, unashamed to check his fine tush as he walks away. The boy is so pretty it hurts. I can't believe I almost let him slide through my fingers. I was definitely dead from the neck up for the past four weeks.

No more. I'm gonna have my cake and eat it too.

My heart is soaring as I drive off. I plug in Anika's Spotify list and sing out loud to Spice Girls' "Wannabe."

Irrefutable proof that I've fallen head over heels for Danny.

DANNY

I have a stupid grin on my face when I walk through the door. Andy is in the kitchen baking something. Jane is sitting at the dining room table, typing away on her laptop, and Lorenzo is nowhere to be seen. My guess, he's in his bedroom.

Andy looks up and notices my happy expression, which prompts him to raise an eyebrow in question.

"What's with the I-just-got-my-dick-sucked face?" he asks.

Jane whips her head toward Andy, frowning. "I thought we talked about those comments. You're giving Lorenzo a bad example."

"He's not around, sweet cheeks." He winks at her, making her blush.

"This is not my post-BJ face," I reply good-naturedly.

"Something happened though. You were looking gloomy when you left for your mom's."

"Yeah. The conversation with her wasn't pleasant, but then I decided to go for a run, and I feel much better."

I wonder how long I'll be able to evade Andy's probing questions. I don't want to hide from him that I'm dating Sadie, but not telling him right away will surely drive him mad. I can't pass up the opportunity to yank his chain.

"What did she want to tell you?" Jane asks.

"Guess who decided to show up after nineteen years wanting to meet me?"

Andy stops whisking his mixture and stares bug-eyed. "Shut up. Your father?"

I nod, crossing my arms and leaning against the kitchen counter. "Yep. He's dying, and he wants to make peace with his shitty conscience or whatever."

"That's horrible. I mean, that he's dying," Jane says.

"Sure, maybe to the people he didn't abandon. I couldn't care less."

"So you're not going to meet him?" Andy asks, watching me intently.

"Nope."

"Danny, are you sure? This might be your only chance to get to know him," Jane replies kindly, but her words fuel the guilt I'm already feeling.

I like Sadie's reaction much better, and that's why I'm in love with her.

I stand straighter as the realization solidifies in my head. I suspected it, but after today, I know.

"So what if Danny never gets to know the douche? You can't miss what you never had," Andy retorts.

He's wrong about that. I can miss something I've never had. I realize it's not a real person I'm missing though but the idealization of a father figure.

"It doesn't matter. I told my mother I don't want to meet him, and that's that."

I turn around and head for my room.

"You still haven't told us why you looked like you were on cloud nine when you came in," Andy pipes up.

"Ah yeah. I was making out with Sadie in her car. Talk to you tomorrow."

"Wait, what?" he shouts. "You can't simply tell us that and leave."

Not stopping or looking back, I say, "Watch me."

Like the pest he is, Andy follows me. "Dude, you're with Sadie now? For real?"

I fall back in my bed and lace my fingers behind my head. "Yep. I bumped into her during my run, we talked, and, well... we decided to give dating a try."

"Do you think that's a smart idea considering what happened a month ago?"

I frown. "Why are you playing devil's advocate now? I thought you were Team Sadie."

"I'm Team Danny. I just want to make sure you're not jumping into a relationship because of the deal with your dad."

I'm torn between feeling moved by Andy's concern and annoyed that he'd think I'd use Sadie to forget my problems.

"That's not what this is about." I sit up, no longer relaxed.

Andy stares at me for a few seconds without saying a word. Then he grins a little. "I get it now. Well, welcome to the club, buddy."

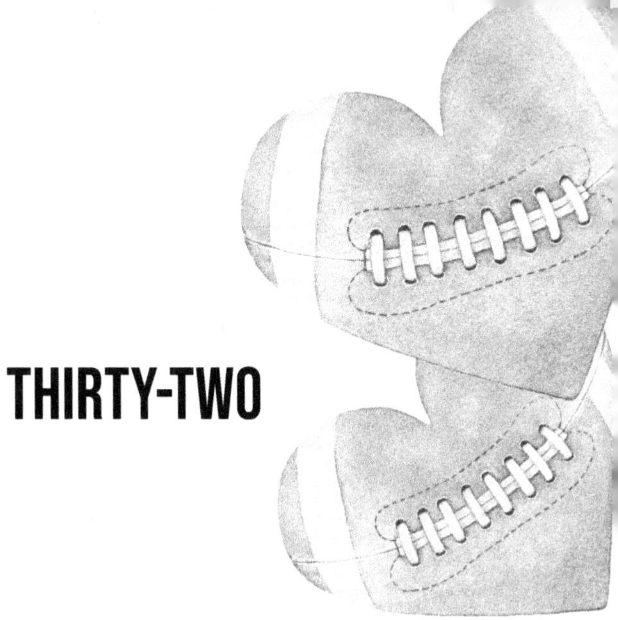

THIRTY-TWO

SADIE

Even though I'm officially dating Danny, and we spent a couple hours on the phone last night, we didn't make any plans to meet today. So when Vanessa texted me, wanting to meet up for lunch, I said yes. The main cafeteria is always packed at lunchtime, but I don't have any trouble finding her in the sea of students. She's snagged a big table, and almost the entire team is there.

I head toward the buffet to grab lunch first, narrowing my eyes as I try to read today's specials from afar. Distracted, it's no surprise that when Danny throws his arm over my shoulders, I let out a yell and jump, startled.

He howls like a fiend.

"Bloody hell. You almost gave me a heart attack," I say, pressing my hand over my chest.

"Sorry, sugarplum. I couldn't resist. You were making love with your eyes at that menu board, and I got jealous."

My eyebrows arch. "You were jealous of food?"

He pulls me into an embrace, leaning down to kiss me softly on the lips. In the middle of the cafeteria. In front of everyone.

Be still my heart. We are really doing this.

When he pulls back, he's smiling from ear to ear, and his eyes have a pleased twinkle in them. As for me, I'm dangerously close to combusting on the spot.

"Hey," he says lazily.

"Hi." My lips curl into a grin.

"Please stop making fuck-me eyes at each other. We're in the middle of the cafeteria for crying out loud," Andy complains.

I hadn't realized he was nearby. That's the effect Danny has on me. He makes me forget the world exists, which is a little scary. I'm not used to being so wrapped up in someone like that.

Danny glowers in his direction. "Like you and Jane are any different."

Andy tries to hold on to his annoyance, but the corners of his lips twitch upward. "Touché."

He gets in line, and Danny and I follow him. We're holding hands, and now everyone is staring, including Danny's ex, who's sitting not far from where we are. If looks could kill, I'd be dead on the spot. She doesn't care that I caught her staring. She maintains her hateful eyes on us. I do the only thing suitable in this situation: I step even closer to Danny and rest my head against his shoulder.

Eat your heart out, bitch.

"I didn't know you'd be here today. I made plans to sit with Vanessa and the girls," I tell Danny with regret. I wouldn't mind having lunch with him.

"That's okay. I'm not the possessive and controlling kind of boyfriend."

I lean back and look up. "What kind of boyfriend are you?"

He smirks. "The best kind."

"God," Andy groans. "*Stawp it.*"

Before either of us can reply, we're interrupted by a tall and lanky guy. "Hey, dudes. What's up? Oh, hello, dudette. I didn't see you there with Danny blocking the view."

"Hey, Ricky," Danny replies. "This is my girlfriend, Sadie."

"Nice to meet you, girlie. Hey, you were on that list."

Any goodwill toward Ricky evaporates into thin air. "So?"

"Such crappy bullshit. I'm glad I could help find the dickwad who uploaded it."

"Oh, it was you?" I asked, surprised, not connecting the dots until now.

Ricky nods. "Yep."

"Mr. Montana here is a master of digging up dirty on everyone," Danny pipes up.

"But anyway, I'm stoked that I bumped into you." He looks at Danny. "I got more news on that front."

Danny squeezes my hand a little tighter as his entire body becomes tense. Mine is too.

"What news?"

"Sadie, there you are." Vanessa joins us, interrupting the conversation. She spares a glance in Ricky's direction, and I notice the guy is now staring at her with open admiration.

The line moves, and we're forced to step forward too.

"Ricky was about to tell us more about that nasty list," I say.

"That's why I came here to get you. Gary fessed up about the whole thing after he was threatened with expulsion. It turns out he wasn't responsible for creating the list. The assholes from the soccer team did it, and that list was shared with all the fraternity houses for voting."

"Son of a bitch. I'm going to kill him," Danny grits out.

I pull on his arm, forcing him to look at me. "You're not getting involved. Let school administration handle it."

"Really? Are you saying you're not going to do anything yourself?"

"Of course she isn't," Vanessa butts in. "Right, Sadie?" She gives me a meaningful look.

"As much as I'd like to rip his nut sack off, I won't touch Nick as long as he's punished accordingly."

"He will be," Danny says with conviction.

His comment doesn't give me comfort though. He made it sound like Nick would get his punishment one way or another.

DANNY

We don't hear anything about Nick and the other nimrods responsible for the list for the rest of the day. Gossip about the situation didn't even spread through campus, which, to me, doesn't bode well. It meant school administration was trying to salvage the situation, perhaps give Nick a mild punishment such as academic probation instead of expulsion.

I tried to keep my frustration bottled up during practice, but I messed up a few passes and got yelled at by Coach Clarkson. It took everything in me not to seek him out afterward and ask if he knew anything about Nick, but I didn't want to make him suspicious of my interest. I was afraid he'd guess about Sadie and me. The fear itself was ludicrous. We weren't hiding from anyone on campus that we were dating; it wouldn't take long for the gossip to reach Coach's ears.

It's not until after dinner that my suspicions are confirmed by a text from Sadie.

> Nick and his wanker friends aren't off the soccer team!!!! I'm going to murder someone.

I call her instead of replying via text.

"What happened?" I ask.

"I don't know. All I know is the arsehole will only miss a few games and that's it. That's complete rubbish. What kind of message is the school sending? I want to break things."

My hands have already curled into fists. I'm with Sadie on the breaking things ideas, but mine is more specific. I want to break Nick's face.

"Do you want me to come over?" I ask.

"As much as I'd love to see you, I'm heading to Vanessa's place. We need to strategize and think of a way to convince whoever needs to be convinced that the only acceptable punishment for Nick Fowler and everyone involved is expulsion."

"Anything I can do to help?"

She lets out a heavy sigh. "Just… don't do anything to Nick, okay?"

"Why would you say that?"

"Because apparently, I'm the only one who knows about your temper when provoked. Everyone else thinks you're a levelheaded bloke." She chuckles.

Another person saying this might have pissed me off, but coming from Sadie, it's amusing.

"Are you accusing me of being a hothead?" I ask, not fighting the grin.

"No, just stating a fact. And that's one of the things I love about you."

My heart stops beating for a second, only to hammer against my rib cage in the next. A stretch of silence follows. I don't know how to respond to that. Did she mean to say she loves me, or should I take it as a meaningless expression?

"So you love things about me?" I ask finally.

She mutters a curse under her breath, and it sounds distant. She must have pulled the phone away from her face.

"Sadie?"

"Bloody hell. Yes, Danny. I love things about you. Don't let that go to your head."

"Too late now."

"You can be such a bellend sometimes."

"I bet that's one of the things you love about me," I tease.

"You're flirting with danger by taking the piss when I'm in a bad mood."

"All right, all right. I won't say another word, except that…."

I pause, not knowing if I should confess what's on the tip of my tongue.

"Except what?" she asks, her voice softer, uncertain.

"Except that I love things about you too."

She doesn't reply right away, but her breathing has changed, turned shallow. With the way my heart is beating faster and my lungs are squeezing tight, I'm betting I sound the same.

"If you wanted me to turn into melted butter, you succeeded, Danny Hudson. I'll talk to you tomorrow."

The line goes dead before I can reply. It doesn't matter. I keep staring at my phone with a goofy grin. But then I remember the reason I called Sadie in the first place, and my amusement is replaced by anger.

I'm not going after Nick and getting myself expelled. I'm not a dumbass. But that doesn't mean I can't get involved. Practice is in the morning tomorrow, and I plan to arrive early to have a real talk with Coach Clarkson. If there's anyone who can apply pressure and force school administration to do more, it's him.

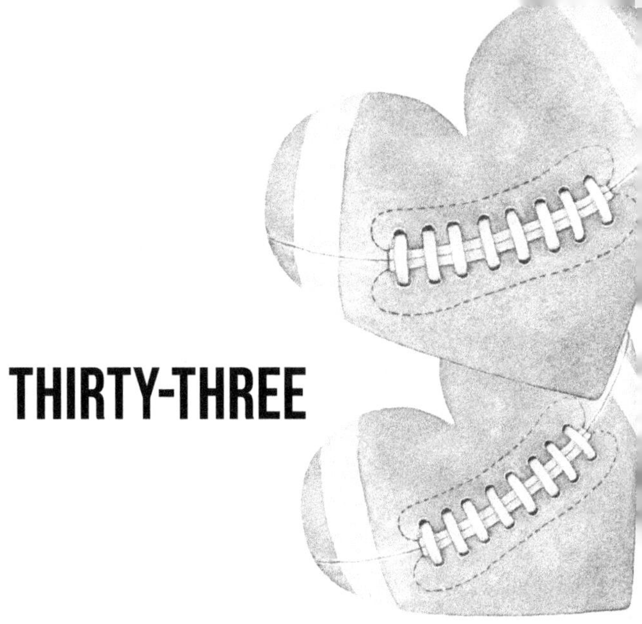

THIRTY-THREE

DANNY

When I arrive at the Rebels headquarters, the parking lot is empty save for Coach Clarkson's car and a brand-new beamer SUV I don't recognize. It's not unheard of for boosters to meet with Coach, so I don't think much about it as I head inside.

His office door is closed, but he kept the blinds open, allowing me to see that he's in fact meeting with someone. I sigh, regretting not calling him last night to ask for a time to talk. I veer to my locker to change into practice gear, hoping whoever is with him doesn't stay long.

It takes me all of two minutes to change. I could try to study while I wait, but I'm antsy and can't concentrate. I move closer to Coach's office instead, curious to see who is meeting with him this early. I can't see the visitor's face from my position, and if I step closer, Coach will spot me there, spying. However, I have a clear view of Coach's face, and his serious countenance makes me suspect whatever the topic of the conversation is, it's not pleasing him at all.

They aren't speaking now, just locked in a staring contest. If they were, I'd be able to eavesdrop since the walls and door are paper thin.

Finally, Coach shakes his head and says, "I can't help you with that. If he doesn't want to meet you, that's his decision, and I'll stand behind him."

A sense of dread drips down my spine. My chest constricts, and my heart begins to beat in a staccato rhythm.

"I'm sorry you feel this way, but I appreciate your time. If you change your mind, let me know."

The man stands, and Coach does the same. They shake hands, and when the man turns, I recognize him. It's Josh Fitzpatrick, an NFL legend. My stomach bottoms out, and I can't move a muscle. Shock prevents me from retreating. When he walks out, he catches me standing there, paralyzed like a statue.

"Danny," he says, clearly surprised.

I can't look away while my mind tries to process that this top athlete who filled our cheap TV screen while I was growing up is my father. Denial would be easier, but now that he's standing so close to me, I can see myself in his face. We have the same chin, the same eye shape and color. My hair coloring and curls, I got from my mother.

No, this can't be. This man, wealthy beyond reason, wouldn't let his son live in near poverty.

Coach walks out of the office and clears his throat. I shift my attention to him, and our eyes lock. The anguish in his gaze confirms what the bit of conversation hinted at. I take a step back.

"What are you doing here?" I force the words out, looking at my father again.

"Danny, please. I just want to talk to you."

My body is suddenly shaking with fury. I ball my hands into fists, clenching my jaw so tight it hurts.

"Who the fuck do you think you are to ambush everyone in my life? First at my mother's office, and now here?"

"I want a chance—"

"A chance for what? You had nineteen years!" I yell.

"You need to leave," Coach Clarkson tells him.

Josh gives him a scathing glare that tells me he's not used to people ordering him about.

"Very well. I'll go." He heads toward the exit but pauses next to me. "This isn't how I wanted our first meeting to go, son."

"I'm not your son," I grit out, taking a step to the side while fighting the sickness in my stomach.

My pulse is pounding in my ears, and for a while, it's all I can hear. I'm trapped in a personal nightmare, unaware of my surroundings. Then I feel a hand on my shoulder, which snaps me back to the here and now.

"Are you all right, Danny?" Coach asks me.

"What did that asshole want?"

Coach steps back and rubs his face. "He wanted my help to convince you to sit down with him."

"Did he tell you why?"

My stomach is twisted in knots. The idea that my father would air this secret to Coach Clarkson is mortifying. I feel dirty, unworthy, and I don't know why. I'm not the bastard who abandoned his kid.

"Yes, he did. Do you want to come in and talk?" He points at his office.

I shake my head. "No. I-I need to go."

Faster than lightning, I turn around and leave the locker room. I don't head to the parking lot though, counting on my father to be waiting outside to corner me again. Instead, I veer for the field, and then, I run.

SADIE

I wake up to the shrill sound of my phone ringing. Katrina moans from her side of the room and begs me to answer it.

With my eyes still closed, I blindly search for it on my nightstand. When I finally have it in my hand, I open one eye and see it's my father calling. A week ago, that'd be an automatic send to voice mail, but today, I press the green button.

"Dad. Why are you calling me so bloody early?"

"Sorry, hon. It's about Danny."

As if a jolt of electricity went through my body, I sit up on high alert.

"What happened to him?" I ask, ignoring the fact that Dad knew to call me about Danny.

"He met someone he wasn't ready to this morning, and he didn't react well."

My stomach clenches painfully as an awful suspicion crawls into my brain. I don't voice it out loud though. I can't assume he knows about Danny's drama with his father. I won't betray his trust.

"Where is he now?"

"I don't know. He bailed before I could stop him. His car is still parked in front of the building. Wherever he went, he's on foot."

I jump out of bed and search for a pair of pants. "I'm coming over. Have you tried calling Andy?"

"Yes, he's also looking for him. I figured I'd try you as well since you and Danny have gotten so… close."

"He's my boyfriend, Dad."

Maybe the confession is ill timed, but he obviously suspected it already. Might as well let him know it's not a fling.

"We can talk about that later. Let me know when you have news."

"Sure. I'll keep you posted."

"What's going on?" Katrina asks in a drowsy tone.

"Nothing. Go back to sleep."

"Did something happen to Danny?"

Like I'd say anything so she can run her mouth and tell her

sorority sisters about it. Fat chance of that. I walk out without bothering to reply.

In the hallway, there's a flutter of activity already. I may have been asleep, but the campus is wide awake. It's already past eight in the morning, and not everyone didn't have class early like me. I pull my cell phone out and call Danny, but it rings until it goes to voice mail. Either he doesn't have his phone on him or he's ignoring my calls too.

When I walk outside the building, I see Andy pulling in. *Shite.* If he's here, then he doesn't have a bloody clue about where Danny could be.

"Any word from him?" we both ask at the same time.

Andy curses. "No. I've looked everywhere I could think of."

"Dad said he left on foot. How far could he have gone?"

"If he was running, pretty far. I hate to do this, but we need to call for reinforcements," he says with his phone already in his hand.

"Who?"

"Puck and Paris for now. I wouldn't dare ask anyone else and risk gossip. Jane is out looking for him too. We'll split up to cover more ground."

"Good plan. Call me if you hear anything," I tell him as I head to my car.

"You do the same."

With my heart stuck in my throat, I get behind the steering wheel. I don't leave the car park right away; instead, I try to put myself in Danny's shoes. Where would I go if I wanted to disappear for a few hours? In the end, I drive to the place where he was last seen, the Rebels' headquarters. I spot Danny's car parked in front of the building. I get out, but instead of going in, I walk over to the wired fence that surrounds the training field. On the other side is the tree line and, hidden by the small forest, the Red Barn.

The entrance to the field is unlocked. No one is practicing outside now, which works for me. I run, covering its length in record time, barely breaking a sweat by the time I reach the other end. I slow down once I get to the forest track. The ground is uneven, and I can't risk spraining an ankle.

My heart is thudding loudly inside my chest as I approach the Red Barn. It looks sad and forlorn in the silence of morning. The door's unlocked, and when I push it open, the hinges creak loudly. I stop by the threshold and scan the open room. It's dim inside, but I can still see Danny sitting on the floor at the far end of the room, hugging his legs. His head is down, hanging between his shoulders.

"How did you find me?" he asks without lifting his gaze to mine.

"A hunch."

I walk over at a normal pace, which is hard when all I want to do is rush to him and pull him into my arms. When I'm near, I simply drop next to him and wait.

"Who told you?"

"Dad."

He glances up then. "Coach Clarkson called you? Why?"

"He knew we were close, and now, well, he knows we're together. I told him. I'm sorry."

His eyebrows furrow. "Why are you apologizing?"

"Because maybe you wanted to tell him yourself. He's your coach, after all."

"That was my plan when I went to see him this morning, but then…." He looks away.

"Your father was there." I finish the sentence for him.

"Yes. The son of a bitch wanted Coach's help."

"I'm so sorry, Danny."

"Did Coach tell you who he is?"

"He didn't say anything, only that you met someone you weren't keen to."

"My father is Josh Fitzpatrick."

The name sounds familiar, but it takes me a second to associate it with the person. When I do, I'm assaulted by a wave of anger. I'm mad at the man for not wanting to have Danny in his life until now, but I'm also angry at his mother for never telling him who his father was. It doesn't take a genius to figure out Danny's life was filled with hardships. He could have grown up like a king.

"Why didn't your mother ever tell you about him?" I ask.

"I don't know. Maybe because he wanted her to have an abortion. He wasn't a famous player when they were together."

Unable to keep my distance any longer, I place my hand on his arm. "Oh, Danny."

"Don't feel sorry for me."

His eyes are hard as they gaze into mine.

"I'm not sorry for you. I'm angry on your behalf. I want to punch your piece-of-shite father in the throat. I want to make you stop hurting so much."

He reaches over, cupping my cheek. "You being here is already helping me."

His fingers slide to the back of my head, tangling with a handful of my hair. He nudges me forward, leaning in to meet me in the middle. When he kisses me, it's soft and tender. It's a brush of lips that spells heartache. I let him set the pace, even though my entire body is yearning for more. I want to show him in any way I can how much he means to me. How much I love him.

He breaks the kiss before it deepens, then leans his forehead against mine. "I'm sorry I got everyone worried. That wasn't my intention."

"I know it wasn't. You wanted to be alone, to process what happened on your own terms without anyone interfering. And I ruined it for you."

"You didn't ruin anything, Sadie. I'm glad you were the one who found me."

I trace his full lips with the tips of my fingers, then his jaw. "You're the most beautiful man I've ever met. It's almost unfair."

He chuckles. "Have you looked at yourself in the mirror lately?"

Shaking my head, I say, "I'm not only talking about the exterior." I flatten my palm against his chest, feeling how fast it's beating. "Your beauty comes from within. Your face and body might have made it difficult to keep things platonic in the beginning, but it was your heart that won me over. I love you, Danny Hudson."

His beautiful blue eyes stay glued to mine, almost as if he's searching for the truth. Does he find it hard to believe I could love him?

His lips slowly curl into a grin as he reaches for my face again. "I'm going to kiss you now, Sadie. *Properly.*"

When he says properly, he truly means business. I don't have time to be a little upset that he didn't say he loves me back because his possessive mouth has already made it impossible for me to think straight. The small distance between our bodies vanishes. We're both twisted in a way that brings our chests together, but soon I move to straddle him instead. I just need to be as close to him as possible.

Danny moves his feverish kisses to my neck, leaving goose bumps on my skin as his tongue brands me. I throw my head back, letting out a contended sigh. My fingers are in his hair, twisting and pulling as a manner to ground me somehow. It's impossible though. The warm feeling in my chest has turned me as light as a feather, and now I'm soaring high.

"Danny?"

"Hmm?" he hums in my ear.

"I'm done taking things slowly."

He leans back and looks into my eyes. "Are you sure? We don't need to put sex back on the table yet. I'm fine with waiting."

"I'm not. I said that because...." I lower my gaze, insecure suddenly. "Because I was afraid. I should know better than anyone that life is short and it can end at a moment's notice."

Danny runs his hand down to where my scar is. "Are you talking about this?"

I nod. "I was out celebrating with my teammates in London one evening. My friend and I were followed once we left the pub. The arseholes wanted to harm her, so I jumped in front of a knife to protect her."

His expression is one of wonder. He doesn't say anything for a couple of beats before he captures my face between his hands. "You're the most amazing person I've ever met. I love you so much, Sadie. So damn much."

I didn't tell the story behind my scar to get a love declaration from him, but damn if I'm not basking in it just the same. In an instant, we're kissing again, and then our clothes become superfluous. I don't care that we're in a public space. I just want to be with Danny again.

I pull my T-shirt off, making him freeze for a second.

"What?"

"You're not wearing a bra."

I glance down and then back at him. "I slept in this. When my father called me, I only worried about putting pants and shoes on."

"I really don't want to talk about Coach right now."

He shuts off my reply with his mouth while his hands find my tits. With expert fingers, he teases my nipples, turning them hard in an instant. I straddle him again, even though my sweatpants and his shorts are still in the way. I need the friction to ease the throbbing between my legs.

"Sadie… this is… fuck. We can't keep doing this or this party will be over before it starts."

"Fine."

I get off him and then jump to my feet.

"I didn't mean for you to get away from me."

"God. Blokes do live in hope and die in despair, don't they? Relax. I just need room to do this." I pull my sweatpants and knickers down my legs, then quickly step out of them.

Danny only freezes for half a second before he stands as well and gets rid of the rest of his clothes. He barely has a chance to remove his boxers before I'm on him like a bum on a hot dog. I run my nails across the expanse of his chest while I kiss the hollow of his throat. He makes a sound that's all male when my hand curls around his shaft. His mouth is on my neck now, licking and kissing as I have my fun with him below.

"Sadie, did you bring protection?"

"No. I'm on the pill now."

Unexpectedly, he lifts me and presses me against the wall. I wrap my legs around his hips, bringing my core flush against his erection. His lips slant over mine possessively, and with a precise thrust, he's inside me. I moan against his lips, not expecting the swift wave of pleasure that rolls down my spine.

We don't talk, too busy savoring each other. Our kisses are fiery and urgent, and they match the tempo of Danny's hips pumping in and out of me. This is the hottest thing I've ever done in my life. It's no surprise when I can't keep the climax at bay.

I bite his lower lip as I come hard, the feeling intensified by the increase of Danny's pace. He grows harder inside me, and then his entire frame is shaking. He groans loudly as he empties himself in me. I hold on to him for dear life, digging my nails in his shoulders. He doesn't seem to mind.

He keeps moving in and out even when his tremors subside. I lose track of time, but eventually we both still, and nothing can be heard save for our labored breathing.

Until the front door creaks again and a familiar voice says, "What the hell?"

Danny and I both turn into statues.

My father is here.

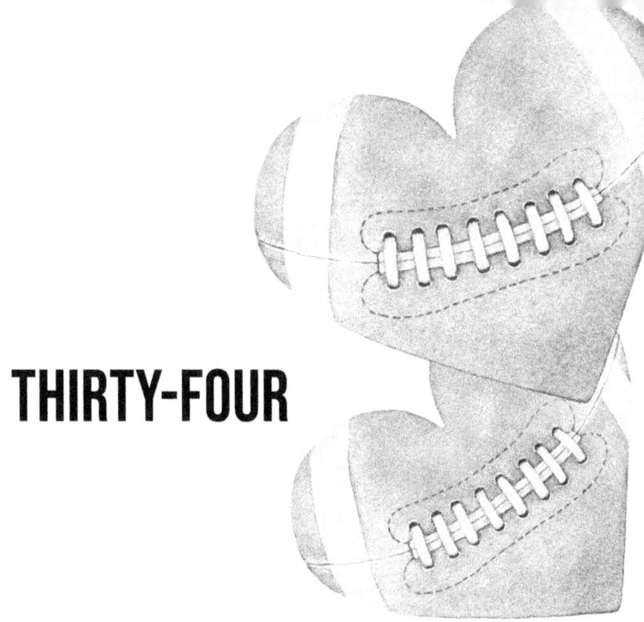

THIRTY-FOUR

DANNY

*S*hit. *Shit. Shit. What the hell am I going to do?*

I stare at Sadie, seeing my panic mirrored in her eyes. Her face is pale too. Coach Clarkson just caught me in the most compromising position with his daughter, and the only thing I can do is pretend I'm made out of stone. My cock is still inside her, for fuck's sake. I just want a hole to open and swallow Sadie and me. Not even in my wildest nightmares had I pictured this. He's going to have my balls.

"Get dressed, you two, and meet me outside," he says.

The door bangs shut, and only then do I dare to look over my shoulder. He's gone.

"Bloody hell," she blurts out, unlatching from me.

I step back, still reeling from being busted. Quickly, Sadie gets dressed, and that spurs me into action as well.

"I'm so dead," I say.

"*You're* dead?" she shrieks. "What about me? This is so mortifying."

She shoves her arms through her T-shirt sleeves and then pulls the fabric down with a jerky movement. Then she searches for her shoes. We finish getting dressed at the same time and then face each other.

"We'd better go before he comes back in here and drags us out by our ears."

"Has he ever done that to you?" I ask.

"No. But I think he's raving mad enough to do it."

"Great. Well, then, you'd better fix your shirt. It's inside out."

She glances down and curses. "Hell."

A minute later, we leave the Red Barn together, holding hands. A united front seemed like a good idea, but when Coach Clarkson's furious gaze lands on our interlaced fingers, I realize it was an error in judgment. But Sadie squeezes my hand tighter, signaling me to stay strong.

"Well, are you going to yell at us now?" she asks.

"Damn straight I will. What were you thinking? I called you to help me find my quarterback, not fuck him in public!"

I wince. "Sir, it was my fault. I wasn't thinking."

"No shit, you weren't thinking." He puts his hands on his hips and glares at us. "Do you have any idea what would have happened to your reputation if someone else had caught you instead of me? And in the wake of that horrible list, Sadie. Really?"

"Surprise, surprise. Only *my* reputation would have been smeared, right? Not Danny's."

Coach sighs. "You know the world we live in. It took me threatening to cancel football season to get Nick Fowler and everyone else involved with that list punished accordingly. Do you think the dean would have followed through if he found out about your tryst in the woods?"

"That's not fair," she replies, but without the usual spunk.

"Like I said, sir, it was my fault," I cut in. "Please don't yell at your daughter."

She pulls her hand from my grasp. "What the hell, Danny! I don't need you to take the fall for me. I can speak for myself."

I look at her, feeling way out of my depth now. *Shit.*

"Sadie, I didn't mean it like that."

Her gaze softens, but she won't take her words back. Instead, she glances at Coach. "We're both at fault. Blame it on hormones. We knew it was risky, and we went for it anyway. I'm sorry you had to see it, but I'm not sorry we did it. I have no regrets."

Coach stares at Sadie, motionless, but his eyes are shining with outrage. Damn, I've never seen him so incensed in my life.

Finally, he shakes his head. "What's done is done. I just wish I could bleach my eyes and unsee that."

Heat rushes to my cheeks. Mortification doesn't seem to cover what I'm feeling. I don't think I'll ever be able to look Coach in the eye again.

"Great. Can we go now?" Sadie asks.

"Let's." He turns around and heads down the path back to the training field.

Sadie and I give him a head start before we follow him. But now our united front is broken. Her arms are crossed in front of her chest, and she's pouting.

"I'm sorry," I whisper.

"For what?"

"For acting like a typical guy and forgetting you're more than capable of defending yourself."

"You did act a bit Neanderthalic."

"I know."

She gives me a side-glance. "I'm sorry I yelled at you. I know you had good intentions."

"When it comes to you, only the best."

She quirks an eyebrow. "Even when they're naughty?"

I glance at Coach walking ahead of us with tension in his shoulders. He's still pissed, but hell, it can't get any worse. I step closer to Sadie and throw my arm over her shoulders.

"Especially the naughty ones."

When we approach the training building, Coach turns to us. "I'd like to see you in my office, Danny."

My stomach bottoms out. I thought yelling in the woods

was it. I should have known better. Not only had I skipped practice, but I was caught railing his daughter in an empty building.

Yeah, I'm screwed.

"Yes, Coach."

I watch him disappear inside the building, then glance at Sadie. She gives me an encouraging smile.

"He won't be too hard on you."

"You don't know that."

"He likes you. I think he's just embarrassed that he saw us together."

My face feels warm again. "He's not more embarrassed than I am."

She grins. "You know, that'd be a fantastic story to tell our grandkids."

Despite my predicament, I smile in return, my chest expanding with emotion. I step closer and circle her waist with my arms.

"Grandkids, huh? I like that."

I lean down and nuzzle her neck. She shivers under my caress, moaning softly.

"You'd better go before he comes back out," she whispers without conviction.

"Right." I place a soft kiss below her ear and then step back. "Wish me luck."

She wrinkles her nose. "I don't think luck will help you at all. I'll pray for a miracle."

"Sadie!"

She laughs, skipping away. "Kidding. Call me later."

I watch her leave, and only once she steps through the wired fence gate do I go into the building. The locker room is empty, which is strange because practice was supposed to last a few hours in the morning. Guilt makes my insides feel like jelly. I'm queasy, dreading this meeting with Coach.

He left the door to his office open, but I knock on it anyway.

He keeps his gaze glued to the computer screen as he waves me in.

"Shut the door," he says.

I swallow the huge lump in my throat and do as he told me. The click of the door shutting feels too loud and ominous. It's like I'm heading to the gallows.

I pull up a chair and sit down, keeping my gaze glued to his desk.

"I can't tell you how disappointed I am, Danny."

"I know, sir. I am truly sorry you had to see… that."

"No sorrier than I am."

I lift my gaze to his. "I want you to know that it wasn't a casual hookup. I'm in love with your daughter."

His eyes widen a fraction, but he quickly schools his emotions again.

"I see. This isn't an ideal situation. My reputation is based on me treating all my players with impartiality. You dating Sadie changes things."

"It doesn't have to. I'm still committed to the game, sir. I want to play in the NFL."

Coach regards me in silence for a couple of beats. "I wouldn't be doing my job if I didn't point out that your father being an NFL legend could open more doors for you."

His comment catches me completely by surprise.

"You said I had a chance before you knew about my father."

"And I wasn't lying. But I'm a big believer on taking responsibility, and if he's finally willing to shoulder his—"

"No! I don't want anything to do with that man. I don't need his handouts. If I make it to the NFL, it will be by my own merit."

"Fair enough. I won't mention him again. Now back to the subject of my daughter. I can't forbid you to date her, but I won't tolerate PDA of any form in front of me. Is that understood?"

Like I'd want to poke the beast with a short stick.

"Yes, Coach."

"I also expect no more meltdowns from you. I need to be able to count on my quarterback."

Shame washes over me, and the urge to avoid his gaze is immense. But I know Coach wouldn't appreciate cowardness.

"You can, sir. There won't be a repeat of what happened this morning."

When he narrows his eyes, I know he's not only thinking about me bailing after meeting my father. His mind is in the Red Barn again.

Shit.

"Good. You can leave now."

I jump out of my chair as if I was electrocuted. This has been the most excruciating talk of my life.

When I return to the locker room, I find Andy waiting for me, sitting in front of my locker.

"What are you doing here?" I ask.

"Making sure Coach left you intact." His eyes drop to my crotch. "I see he didn't rip your nut sack off."

I immediately put a protective hand over my junk. "What?"

Andy grins like a fiend. "I can't believe he caught you with Sadie. Classic, bro."

"How did you know?"

He quirks an eyebrow. "How do you think?"

"She told you?"

"She didn't mean to do it. I think she was a bit distraught. Don't worry, Danny-boy. Your secret is safe with me."

"It'd better be. No one can know, Andy. I'm serious."

"I know. My lips are sealed. However, I can't promise I won't tease you to no end."

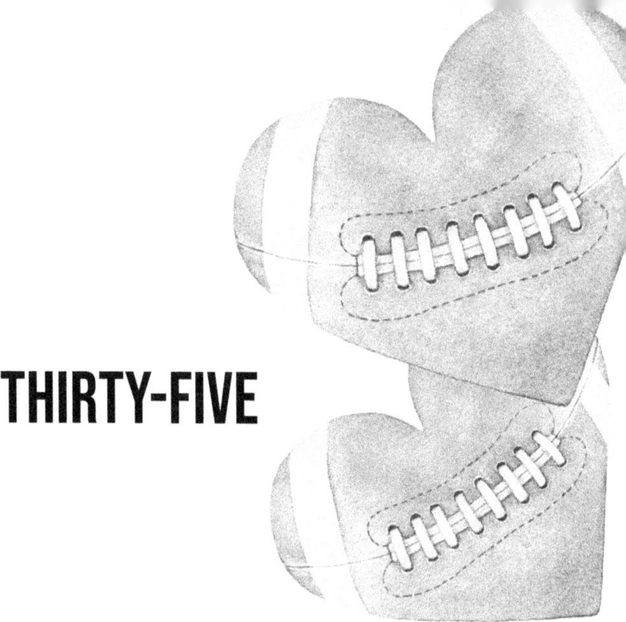

THIRTY-FIVE

SADIE

Once practice is over, I can barely walk. Coach Lauda trained us harder than before. It was drill after drill, and now my legs are mush.

"Bloody hell. Do you think Coach was trying to compensate for something?" I ask Vanessa on our way out of the locker room.

"I think she's peeved that it took pressure from Coach Clarkson to get Nick Fowler dealt with."

"Yeah, I'm not happy about that either. Why couldn't the school do it from the get-go? It's bloody aggravating."

"Do you think he got involved because he's your dad?"

I clench my jaw tight, not knowing how to answer that. When I don't reply right away, Vanessa continues.

"Sorry. I didn't mean to put you on the spot."

"It's okay. I don't know. I…. We aren't close anymore."

"Shit. I had no idea, Sadie."

"It's okay."

My mood has definitely taken a swing downward. Dad meddling in the Nick situation, plus what happened this morning is doing my head in. I don't know how to feel about him.

Vanessa, probably sensing the switch in my disposition, doesn't say another word. We continue the trek down the hallway in silence until we're out of the building and she nudges my arm.

"That ought to cheer you up," she says.

My head had been elsewhere, so I didn't see Danny standing in front of his car waiting for me. He's leaning against the door with his legs crossed and hands in his pockets in a casual stance. The pose has pushed his jeans lower, showing a hint of golden skin.

Damn it, now I'm drooling.

I was never one prone to big displays of affection in public, but I find myself running in his direction. He straightens before I jump into his arms and seal my lips to his. Laughing, he kisses me back with a whole lot of enthusiasm. We only break apart when Vanessa and my other teammates start wolf-whistling and making crude remarks in jest.

"Hi," he says, smiling from ear to ear.

"Hi. I didn't expect to see you here."

"I wanted to surprise you."

"I see you survived the meeting with Dad in one piece." I press my hip against his crotch.

"Barely."

"Was it that awful?"

"It could have been worse."

"What did he say to you?"

"He hasn't forbidden us to date, but he doesn't want to see any PDA in front of him."

I twist my face into a grimace. "Like I'd want to do that."

"I hope you aren't busy. I want to take you out on a proper date." He reaches for a strand of my hair and rolls it around his finger in a distracted motion.

"I'd love to, but can this date be for takeout we get to eat in bed? I'm knackered. Coach worked us hard today."

"In bed, huh? I think that can be arranged." He kisses the corner of my mouth, making me melt on the spot.

"Get a room, you two," Vanessa hollers.

I step back from Danny's embrace and glower in her direction. "Piss off, Castro."

Danny laces his fingers with mine and tugs my arm. "Come on. I'll walk you to your car."

"Maybe drive me to it?"

He quirks an eyebrow. "Really? You can't walk? I thought you were a top athlete."

I hit his chest playfully. "Shut up. I was five minutes late today, so I had to park all the way in the back. And didn't you hear me when I said Coach Lauda destroyed us?"

He laughs. "I'm just teasing you, sugarplum. Come on."

It literally takes less than a minute to drive to where my car is parked. I get out quickly before I get too comfortable and decide I don't need to drive today at all. Danny waits so I can follow him. I blow him a kiss, and I'm still smiling when I face the side of my car and get the shock of my life.

The window is busted, and someone spray-painted "Cunt, you will pay."

The blood in my veins grows cold, and my entire body is paralyzed. I hear Danny's door open, but I can't take my eyes off those awful words.

"Sadie?" he calls, then says, "What the fuck?"

"I-I can't believe someone would do this," I say, disheartened.

"I'm going to kill him," he grits out.

His statement snaps me out of my shock. I look at him wide-eyed. "You don't think Nick Fowler did this, do you?"

"Who else, Sadie? You shot him down multiple times, and your dad got him expelled."

I shake my head, still in denial. "You won't do anything. Promise me, Danny."

His face is beet red, and the fury shining in his eyes tells me he has murder on his mind. I can't let him go after Nick and destroy his career. I grab him by the arms and shake him a little.

"Danny, please. If you love me, you won't go after Nick."

"How can you ask me that? He's threatening you."

"Let the authorities deal with him."

"Do you know how impossible your request is?"

"Fine. I'm calling on my favor, then."

His jaw drops, and the look in his eyes tells me he didn't expect that. "Are you serious?"

"Dead serious."

My heart is thundering in my chest now. I hadn't considered the implications of the words sprayed on my car until Danny pointed it out. I try to control the fear that's constricting my chest, but the familiar panic is rising. I let go of him and hug my middle.

He pulls me into his arms and hugs me tightly. "I won't let anything happen to you, Sadie. I promise you."

I bury my face in his chest, curling my fingers around his T-shirt while I try to force my heart to slow down. Being surrounded by Danny's strong arms does help to keep my fear at bay. I want him to take me away, but not until we deal with this situation properly.

"We need to call campus security," I say.

A car pulls up behind Danny's. It's Vanessa. She lowers her window and sticks her head out.

"What's going on?"

I ease out of his embrace to reply, "Someone vandalized my car."

"What?" she shrieks.

She's out of the car in the next second and staring at the damage.

"Son of a bitch. Do you think this is Nick Fowler's doing?" she asks.

"Who else?" Danny replies angrily.

Vanessa has her phone out and glued to her ear before we can say anything else. She calls Coach Lauda first, then campus security. I let Danny steer me to his car and wait for everyone to arrive at the scene inside and away from prying eyes.

My teammates are the first ones to see the damage, but then Coach Lauda appears with my father in tow. Great. I hadn't considered that she would call him too. Both stare at my car for a brief moment before they exchange words in hushed whispers.

"I'm going to talk to them," Danny tells me.

"Okay." I sink deeper in the seat, crossing my arms in front of my chest.

I should be the one speaking to them, but I'm still reeling from the ugliness of the situation. I know once I'm over the shock, anger is going to take control, and the thirst for retaliation is going to light my veins on fire.

I probably spaced out, because I get spooked when Dad knocks on the window. Clenching my jaw, I lower the barrier.

"What?"

"Are you okay, honey?"

"I'm fine."

He frowns, obviously not believing the lie.

"Do you want to stay at my place for a few days?"

I swallow the huge lump in my throat. I don't know why his offer makes me want to cry. It's like I've reverted to my six-year-old self who would love nothing more than to let her father protect her.

"I want to stay with Danny," I reply.

Dad's jaw clench tells me he's not happy about my answer, but what can he do?

"All right. We'll get to the bottom of this, sweetheart. You don't have to worry, okay?"

"I'm not worried."

It takes another fifteen minutes to be done with the circus. I have to answer the campus security questions, but my testimony isn't that helpful. Sure, we all suspect Nick Fowler, but without eyewitnesses, there's nothing they can do.

On the way to Danny's place, my mood switches from stunned to aggravated. When he parks in front of his building, I want to smash things. My hands are balled into fists, and my nails are digging into my palms' soft flesh.

"We're here." Danny covers my hand with his.

"I know."

"Tell me what I can do to help."

I look at him and wrestle to find the right answer. I don't want him to pick up on my murderous vibe. It took a while to calm him down and dissuade him of the idea of kicking Nick's ass.

"How about that date?"

He stares at me as if trying to read my thoughts. "Anything you want."

I touch his face. "I want tacos, a silly movie, and you."

He takes my wrist, turning my hand around to place a kiss on my palm. "That can be arranged."

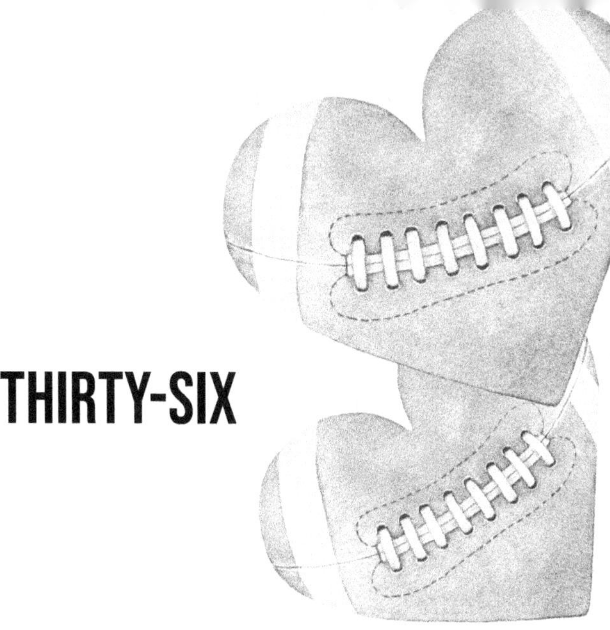

THIRTY-SIX

DANNY

We're lucky that we have the apartment to ourselves. Lorenzo has a school function, which will buy Sadie and me a few hours of privacy. Andy must have his phone in silent mode or he would have blown mine up already, just like Puck and Paris have. News about what happened to Sadie's car has already spread like wildfire through campus.

"Do you have any preference where you want to order tacos from?" I ask.

"I thought maybe we could make them ourselves."

I rub my neck. "I'm sure we have taco shells and salsa, but I'm not really good in the kitchen."

She smirks. "Lucky for you, tacos are my specialty."

Unable to resist, I pull her closer, caging her in against my body. "Oh yeah? Are you trying to win me over through my stomach?"

"Isn't that how it's done?" Her smile broadens.

"It's a perk, but I'd be yours even if you were the worst cook in the world."

She blinks fast, and I swear her eyes seem brighter. I lean forward, ready to steal a kiss, but she steps back, breaking free from my embrace.

"I'm famished. I'd better get started before you meet my hangry version."

"Is it worse than your angry version?"

"Of course, dude. It's a compound feeling."

I make the sign of the cross in jest. "Then no, I don't want to see that side of yours."

Sadie shakes her head before she turns around and veers for the fridge. "I hope you have some type of protein."

"Andy always has meat handy. He and Lorenzo are carnivores."

"Me too. How about you?" She pulls a tray of ground beef from the fridge.

"I eat meat, but I won't die if I go a couple of days without it."

She gives me a scathing glance. "You'd better not be a closet vegetarian, Danny. That would seriously not work in your favor."

"Oh, so you're saying if I'm not ravenous for blood and rotten flesh, I'm not good for you?"

She twists her nose, making her look more adorable than what's fair. It's hard to stay on my side of the kitchen island.

"Who's eating rotten flesh?"

I point at the tray of meat in her hand. "That's rotten flesh right there."

"Gross. Stop putting images in my head."

I pull up a stool and sit down. "All right. I'll stop."

"Where do you keep the taco shells?"

"I think there's some in the pantry. I'll get them."

I stand again and go look for the dry ingredients to make dinner. In the pantry, I also find a margarita mixer bottle. It's the middle of the week, but hell, after what happened today, we both could use a drink. I bring everything to the kitchen and set it on the counter. Sadie eyes the margarita mixer and raises an eyebrow at me.

"Are you trying to get me drunk, Danny?"

"Not at all. But we can't have tacos without margaritas. That's against the law."

She chuckles. "Is that so?"

"Yep."

"Are you even old enough to drink?"

My jaw drops. "How dare you bring up that pesky detail?"

She shrugs. "Don't you know this already? Antagonizing people is my favorite pastime."

I circle around the island and walk over until she has nowhere to go. I place my hands on each side of the counter to cage her in.

"Do you want to know what my favorite pastime is?"

She lifts her chin and looks into my eyes. "Flirting with danger?"

I grin. "Flirt? Nah, I've moved on to making sweet love to danger."

My mouth covers hers before she can get another sassy remark in. I keep my hands on the counter, trying my best not to invade her space. I just want to savor her lips for now. But Sadie is a wicked little thing. She hooks her fingers around my belt loops and tugs me forward. My hands immediately find her face, and what was meant to be a sweet kiss becomes hotter than tamales in a split second.

Her hands are in my hair now, pulling hard enough to toy with the line between pain and pleasure. I lift her onto the counter, nudging her legs apart to press my hips against hers. We break apart to help each other out of our shirts. Sadie is wearing a sports bra though, which is a fucking pain in the ass to deal with.

"Why couldn't you be a feminist and refuse to wear these contraptions?" I ask as I attempt to unclasp the hindrance.

"Try to run while your tits are bouncing left and right and

come back to me on that."

She runs her tongue down my neck while her nails scratch my chest. Desire shoots down my spine, and my patience leaves the building.

"Fuck, I give up." I forget the clasp and curl my fingers around Sadie's waistband. "These need to go."

"Here? Your roommates can come in at any moment."

"They won't."

I tug her pants down, and unlike her sports bra, they come off easily, even with her sitting on the counter. I'm on my knees and between her legs in the next second, dying for a taste. I lick her through the thin layer of her underwear first, making her jerk forward. Letting out a loud moan, she grabs a lock of my hair and twists it around her fingers.

Spurred on by the sexy sounds she's making, I slide her panties to the side and sweep my tongue over her clit, loving her sweet taste.

"Danny, oh my God." She yanks my hair back, making it hurt a little.

Pain mixes with desire, creating a potent cocktail that makes my cock grow harder. Damn it, I can't come in my pants. That would be unacceptable. I clench my butt cheeks, trying my hardest to ignore the tightness of my balls. This is all about Sadie. I want her to fall apart on my tongue first.

I focus on how she reacts to each of my caresses. She likes when I circle my tongue around her bundle of nerves, and when I suck her clit into my mouth, she jerks forward again. I grab her hips to keep her in place, digging my fingers into her skin as I begin to fuck her pussy with my tongue. Her little moans turn louder, and then she screams my name and trembles under my touch. I insert two fingers inside her and milk her orgasm until her body relaxes and she grows quieter.

Her hand is still in my hair, but she's no longer pulling at the strands. Now she's running her fingers through my curls, sending ripples of pleasure throughout my body. I look up, finding her leaning her head against the cupboard. Her eyes are closed, and her breathing is a little uneven.

I uncurl from my kneeling position and kiss the hollow of her throat.

"Only you could distract me from tacos," she says.

"I hope you're not hangry yet." I bite her earlobe softly.

"Not hangry. Only hungry… for you."

Our gazes lock, and the heat I see in her eyes is almost enough to make me lose the tight control I have over my body. I pick her up, earning a little squeak from her, and then run to my bedroom.

"Danny, what are you doing?" she asks through a laugh.

I drop her on the mattress and get rid of my jeans as fast as I can. She's still giggling when I join her in bed.

"Stop laughing, woman. This is a serious matter." I kiss her neck while grinding my hips against hers.

She opens her legs for me, hooking them behind my ass. "Yes, very serious," she whispers against my lips.

I claim her mouth as I thrust forward, sheathing myself in her. There's no going slow because she already drove me to the point of no return in the kitchen. I can't think of anything besides pounding into her and making her scream my name again. I was ready to explode a minute ago, and it takes less than that for me to lose it and climax inside her. Another minute goes by before I stop moving and collapse half on top of her.

"Holy shit," she says. "You were really on the verge."

I glance at her. "Did you…?"

She smiles. "Not this time. I couldn't keep up with you."

Not what I wanted to hear. "I'm sorry."

She touches my face. "Danny, don't apologize. You made me come in the kitchen, and that was hot as hell."

"Give me a moment and I'll make it up to you."

She leans on her elbows. "There's nothing to make up for, silly boy. But you can have your way with me *after* dinner."

I kiss her arm softly. "Fine. After dinner, then."

THIRTY-SEVEN

DANNY

Mission accomplished. I think. When I drop Sadie at her dorm the next morning, she no longer has the haunted look in her eyes. I'm not an idiot to believe she isn't worried about the threat anymore. Hell, it was hard for me to pretend I wasn't thinking about it while I was with her.

But I can't let her worry about me on top of everything else. I promised I wouldn't take matters into my own hands, and I won't break my vow. Keeping Sadie's trust is more important than revenge, but that doesn't mean I'll let my guard down.

Vanessa volunteered to drive her to practice, and since I can't skip training twice in a row, I had to accept that I can't be around Sadie twenty-four seven.

I'm determined to not think about how much I want to hurt Nick Fowler for putting fear in Sadie's heart. There's no doubt in my mind that he wrote those disgusting words on her car. Thinking about football helps a little, but when Coach asks to talk to me before we head to the field, my concentration evaporates into thin air.

I didn't expect to have another one-on-one meeting with him, but here I am, once again, in his office.

"What happened now?" I ask, not trying to hide my irritation.

His grim expression doesn't comfort me.

"Nick Fowler wasn't responsible for the vandalism to Sadie's car."

"The hell it wasn't him," I blurt out. "Who else would have the motivation to do something like that?"

"We don't know. The investigation is still in progress. Nick, however, isn't the culprit. He was already in Alabama when the vandalism happened."

"Then maybe it was one of his former teammates."

Coach clenches his jaw. "All soccer players were accounted for when it happened. It wasn't a retaliation."

I rub my face. "If those assholes didn't do it, who is trying to harm Sadie?"

"I don't know. Maybe she pissed someone off. You know my daughter has a temper."

I shake my head. "She hasn't mentioned anything."

Coach sighs, leaning against the back of his chair. "When you look at me, it's probably difficult for you to picture me as anything other than your coach. But I was once a young football player like you, and even back in my time, girls were vicious trying to catch our attention. Could the attack be attributed to an envious girl you dissed in favor of Sadie?"

My spine goes rigid in an instant. "You think this was motivated by petty jealousy?"

"I can't rule out anything."

I pass a hand over my face. "I haven't led anyone on. Sadie is the only girl I've ever wanted to date since I got here."

The moment the words leave my mouth, my stomach coils tightly. I hadn't dated anyone at Rushmore before Sadie, but my past has caught up with me. Gwen has given enough proof that she isn't over me like she claimed. I can't tell Coach about my suspicion though. He's already unhappy that I'm dating Sadie. If he thinks our relationship is putting his daughter in danger, he'll order me to stay away.

"Well, it goes without saying that I need to make sure Sadie is safe, Danny. She won't let me protect her, but she trusts you, which means I have to trust you too."

"Sir, I won't let anything happen to her. You have my word."

He nods. "Good. You can join the team on the field now. I'll be there shortly."

I put my game face on and head out. I can't let him see the guilt that's now swirling in my chest. I barely see anything in front of me. My mind is still stuck on the possibility that I'm responsible for the target on Sadie's back.

It's no surprise that I play like shit, getting sacked more times than I can count and making erroneous passes. At one point, Andy has to pull me aside for words.

"What the hell is wrong with you?" he asks.

"I'm worried, okay?"

"I get that, but you can't allow your personal problems to interfere with the game. Nothing is going to happen to Sadie."

I shake my head. "You don't know that."

"Yes, I do. Coach Clarkson would never let anything happen to his daughter. You don't think he has campus security following her around?"

"She'd hate it if that was true."

"Well, she can't hate it if she doesn't know about it." He shrugs.

"She's going to stay with me until we find out who's responsible."

"I know that, dumbass. And I wouldn't have it any other way. Now can you please focus? We need to win this week's game."

My blood freezes when I realize we aren't playing at home this weekend.

"What's with that horrified look?" Andy asks.

"We have an away game."

His eyebrows arch. "Ah, fuck. Well, I'm sure the girls aren't playing at home either this weekend."

I press a closed fist against my chest, trying to ease the sudden tightness there. I have to figure out who vandalized Sadie's car before the weekend or I'll go nuts.

"Yeah, probably," I reply, distracted.

He claps my back. "Come on. Let's see that golden arm shine."

SADIE

I can't say learning from Couch Lauda that Nick Fowler wasn't the douche who vandalized my car didn't affect me. I was sure it was him. Now I have no clue. But there's nothing I can do besides try to move past that.

The referee's whistle stops the game, and it takes me a second to realize it was because of me. Charlotte is lying flat on her back after I fouled her.

"Are you all right?" I offer her my hand.

Grimacing, she lets me help her up. "I hope so. But what the hell was that?"

"I'm sorry."

"Sadie!" Couch Lauda calls.

"Bollocks," I mutter and then run to the sideline. "Yes, Coach?"

"What were you thinking? You bulldozed Charlotte."

"I'm sorry. I didn't mean to."

"Is this about the incident yesterday?"

I want to deny it, but I don't think lying will help me. "In a way. I'm really mad that the only suspect has an airtight alibi."

"There's nothing we can do about that. I'm relieved that Nick Fowler isn't behind it. It's possible this was a bad-taste prank."

I bite my tongue, not wanting to dig a bigger hole for myself. "Yes, probably."

"I should bench you until you cool off, but we can't really afford that. Our next game will be tough. I need my best players sharp, Sadie. Can I count on you?"

I nod. "Yes you can, ma'am."

"Good. Now get back there and try not to maim your teammates."

Being chewed out by Coach Lauda helps. I hadn't realized before that I let my anger take control. I'm still aggressive, but I'm careful not to hurt anyone. By the end of practice, Coach is no longer watching me with disapproval. No surprise, considering I scored two goals against Steff.

In the locker room, Vanessa stops next to me. "Do you have any plans tonight?"

"I'm going back to Danny's."

"Really? You two went from zero to a hundred faster than a Tesla."

I smirk. "I can't deny that. I'd be on cloud nine if it weren't for that bloody graffiti on my car. I'm annoyed that we're back to square one."

Vanessa leans against the locker, crossing her arms over her chest. "It's possible some jealous bitch did that."

I frown. "Seriously? That's extreme."

She shrugs. "Bitches be crazy. You're the hot freshman who snagged the most eligible bachelor on campus. I know a bunch of girls who are eating their hearts out now."

"Any of them psychos?"

"Possibly. I'd have to ask my sister if any of her cheerleader friends have a crush on Danny."

"Do you think she'd tell you?"

"I think she would, but to be honest, I don't think this was done by a cheerleader. Doesn't Danny have a jealous ex?"

I groan. "Fuck me. I didn't even consider her. I was too focused on blaming Nick."

Joanne walks over. "What are you talking about?"

"We're trying to discover who trashed Sadie's car. We may have found a new suspect."

Joanne arches her eyebrows. "Oh, that crazy sorority chick. What's her name again? Gwen?"

"How do you know she's crazy?" I ask.

Joanne's face turns a shade redder. She rubs her neck, looking sheepish. "Uh, well, I was hanging out with one of her sisters at their house and overheard a conversation."

At first, I don't get why Joanne would be embarrassed about that until it dawns on me. "Oh."

"What did you hear?" Vanessa asks.

"I heard her saying that Danny deserved better than European trash."

"What the fuck?" I snap. "Man, I knew she was a cunt."

"Yeah, I got into her face and got kicked out," Joanne adds.

"Why didn't you tell me?"

"I didn't want to upset you."

Right. She didn't want me going berserk on Gwen's ass. But I can't fault her for thinking I would. I did kick Nick in the balls, after all.

"I'm glad you told us now, Jo," Vanessa chimes in. "Gwen does sound like a person who would threaten Sadie because of a guy."

"But how do we prove she did it?" I ask.

"The ChiO and Theta houses are having a joint charity event party on Thursday," Joanne replies. "We should crash it and try to get information then. You know how trashed people get at those parties."

Or drugged.

I shake my head, trying to forget my bad experience. "Count me in. If this bitch Gwen is responsible for my car, then she needs to pay."

"Sadie...," Vanessa starts.

"In the right way. I'm not touching her. I'll let the school handle it."

"Are you gonna tell Danny about your suspicion?" Joanne asks.

"Not without proof."

"Good idea. He may think you're picking on Gwen because you're jealous of her," Vanessa says.

I glare at her. "Like I'd be jealous of that girl."

Vanessa lifts both hands in a sign of peace. "Sorry. Forget I said anything."

I look away, pretending to be very interested in the contents of my locker. Anything to hide the fact that I am suffering from major retroactive jealousy. Danny did date the bitch, despite her odious personality. Everyone has a past, but that particular one is hard to swallow.

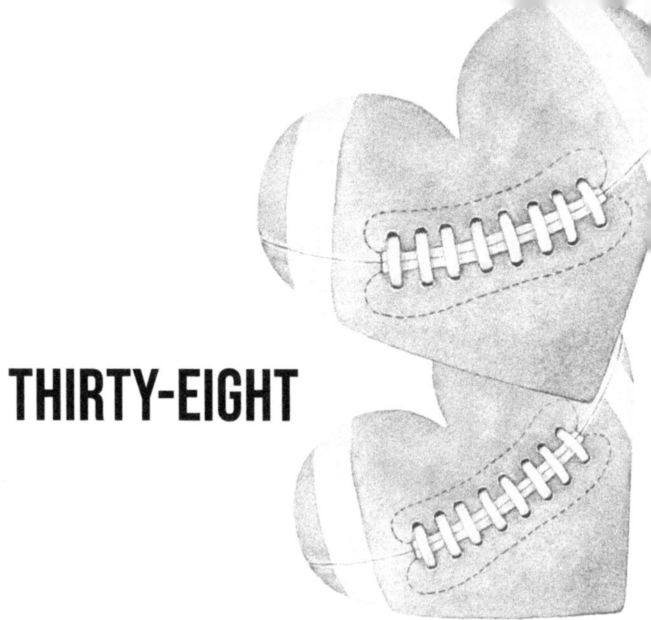

THIRTY-EIGHT

SADIE

Vanessa drove to the sorority party, and now we're standing on the corner of Greek row, waiting for the rest of the gang to arrive—Joanne, Charlotte, Steff, Phoebe, and Felicia. I'm surprised when Melody approaches us, still using crutches to move around.

"What are you doing here?" Vanessa asks.

"Do you seriously think I'd pass up the opportunity to mess with those Greek whores?"

"Whoa. I didn't know you drank the Greek hatorade too," I say.

"Melody pledged to ChiO. She didn't make it." Vanessa smirks, earning Melody's death glare.

"I only pledged because I'm legacy and I was trying to please my mother," she grits out.

"I'm sorry. That sucks," I say, trying to keep the peace.

If Melody wants to help bring Gwen down, I won't send her away.

A moment later, Joanne walks over with Charlotte, Steff, and Phoebe, and Felicia in tow.

"All right, what's the plan?" Joanne asks.

"We should split up. Some of us can mingle and try to fish for information from the drunks while I head to Gwen's room and try to find incriminating proof," I reply.

"What kind of proof are you hoping to find?" Charlotte asks.

I shrug. "I don't know. Something useful."

"I know which room is Gwen's, but please don't get caught," Joanne pipes up.

I pull a half-empty bottle of tequila from my purse. "Don't worry. I came prepared. If I get caught, I can always claim I was drunk out of my mind and got lost."

Vanessa shakes her head. "Why I'm allowing you to do this is beyond me. We could get in serious trouble."

I toss my arm over her shoulders. "You're doing it because some skank trashed my car, and family sticks together."

She sighs. "Of course you would remember that."

"We're looking too suspicious standing here. Let's go already," Melody says, irritated.

We let her hop ahead of us. Vanessa and I fall behind the group, and when the noise from the party gets loud enough, I say, "You don't need to stick with me. I'll go snoop in Gwen's room alone."

"No way. I'm coming with you. If we fall, we fall together."

A warm feeling spreads through my chest. I didn't expect to find friendship here at Rushmore so quickly, especially considering how awful I can be. The fact that my teammates are willing to risk punishment to help me fills me with emotion.

God, I think I'm getting choked up. For fuck's sake.

We're swarmed by people the moment we step inside. I didn't expect the place to be so packed on a Thursday, but I guess the weekend does start earlier on most college campuses.

Joanne turns to me. "Gwen's room is the third door to your left. I hope it's not too late and it's occupied."

Melody's gaze sweeps the room. "If it's occupied, it's not by her. She's over there." She nods in Gwen's direction. "We should go before she sees you, Sadie."

"Wait, you're coming with me?"

She gives me a droll look. "I can't be seen here. There's a reason why I didn't make it through pledge week."

Shit. Now I really need to know what Melody did. However, now is not the time to satisfy my curiosity.

We head to the stairs, hoping no one will notice three non-sorority girls going up to the second floor. We're lucky no one pays attention to us. As we move down the hallway, we hear giggles from some of the rooms we pass.

"I guess some bimbos already found their dicks for the night," Melody mumbles.

"You really don't like them, do you?" I ask.

She looks over her shoulder, frowning. "What's to like?"

I know better than to answer that. Besides, we've reached Gwen's room, and all my focus is now on the search.

"Damn, what's that smell?" Vanessa wrinkles her nose.

"Eau de bitch?" I reply. "Okay, I'll take the closet. Someone take the room and...." I push a third door open. "And the bathroom. Wow. I didn't know these girls had en suites."

"ChiO is the biggest sorority in the country, which means a lot of wealthy alumni," Melody replies.

Inside the closet, the sickly sweet smell of Gwen's perfume is strong enough to make me gag. I search through her clothes quickly, sticking my hand in pockets and looking inside her purses. I also touch the back of the wall, hoping to find a secret compartment. I lose track of time, but I know I've spent too much in here.

"Girls, I found something," Melody calls from the bathroom.

"Me too," Vanessa says.

Since Vanessa is closer, I go see what she found first. She has a huge box on Gwen's bed, and inside are several pictures of Gwen with Danny and mementos of their relationship.

Jealousy and nausea hit me at the same time.

"Oh God. I think I'm going to be sick," I say.

"Man, if she's holding on to all this crap, then she definitely isn't over Danny," Vanessa observes, picking up a homemade Valentine's Day card that says "Gwen and Danny forever" in glitter letters.

The door opens suddenly, and in comes the fucking bitch and the last person I'd expect to see with her: Danny.

DANNY

"You didn't tell Sadie where you were going tonight?" Andy asks from shotgun.

"Nope. She has plans with her teammates, and I don't plan to linger at the party."

"Bro, she *will* find out."

I clench my jaw tight. "I know. I'm not trying to keep this a secret, but I figured telling her after the fact is better. Do you seriously think Sadie would agree to let me come here without her?"

"If she can't trust you…."

I rub my face. "It has nothing to do with trust. I wouldn't be happy if she went to a frat party without me either."

Andy chuckles. "Relax, Danny-boy. I'm just teasing you. I'm like that too. Territorial as fuck."

"Don't I know it? Besides, the whole point of coming tonight is to find out the truth. Gwen won't confess if I show up at her sorority party with Sadie on my arm."

Andy shakes his head. "It's your funeral."

"Can you please be a little more supportive?"

"I *am* supportive, and that's why I'm telling you your grand idea is stupid as hell."

I park on the street parallel to Greek row and get out of the car. I'm aware of the risks, but I have to find out if Gwen is the one threatening Sadie. It's my job to make sure she's safe, especially if the danger is my ex.

Andy follows me but keeps his piehole shut as we stride side by side to the ChiO house. The bulk of people in attendance are Greeks, but because it's a charity event, the crowd is more varied than usual. People I barely know turn to me to shake my hand or clap me on the back as if we're old friends. I follow along with the charade, pretending not to be bothered that strangers are so familiar with me.

In the entry foyer, I stretch my neck and look for Gwen. I find her in the middle of an open room to our right, chatting with her sisters, red Solo cup already in hand.

My stomach twists. Now comes the hardest part—playing nice with her. Sadie once told me I was a terrible actor. I hope she's wrong.

"Found her. Wish me luck," I tell Andy.

I make a beeline to Gwen, conscious of all the stares following me through the party. When she notices my approach, she walks away from her group of friends, beaming from ear to ear.

"Danny, what are you doing here?" she asks.

"This is a party for charity, isn't it? You know I'm a sucker for good causes." I force a smile, hoping I don't look like a deranged psycho.

"I'm glad you came." She looks over my shoulder. "Are you alone?"

"Nah, Andy is here somewhere."

My reply makes her smile harder. She steps closer, touching my arm. I have to fight the urge to increase the distance between us.

"Can I get you something to drink?"

I take the cup from her hand and drink from it, making sure I keep my eyes on hers as I do so. It's cranberry juice and vodka, Gwen's favorite. It could have been something worse. As flirtation goes, I think I'm doing a good job. Her eyes sparkle with delight, and her smile is still firmly in place.

I don't finish her drink, returning the cup to her after a couple of sips.

"I think I'm okay for now," I tell her.

"You always liked to share red Solos."

"Yeah, and you didn't forget."

She moves closer, making it harder to not take a whiff of her drunken breath.

Okay, I'm officially queasy.

"Oh, Danny. You know I'd never forget anything about you, about us."

Unable to endure her closeness, I step back. But to keep up the pretense, I take her hand and say, "I want to talk to you in private."

"Let's go to my room, then. No one will bother us there."

Fuck me. This will look bad. I can already picture Sadie receiving a text with a picture of me and Gwen. This act better deliver results.

I let Gwen steer me through the party and up the stairs. On the way there, I spot a couple of Sadie's teammates. I lock gazes with Joanne Barnes. Her murderous expression tells me she came to the worst possible conclusion. I shake my head, hoping to convey that this is not what it looks like.

Surprisingly, she doesn't make a move to stop me. Then I see Andy heading her way. There's nothing I can do but hope he can explain to Joanne what I'm up to and that she'll believe him.

A sliver of dread drips down my spine as I walk down the corridor. How am I going to keep Gwen's hands off me long enough to get a confession from her? I really didn't think things through. I'm such an idiot.

Still lost in my thoughts, I don't see the situation I'm stepping into until Gwen opens her bedroom door and my gaze connects with Sadie's.

Fucking hell.

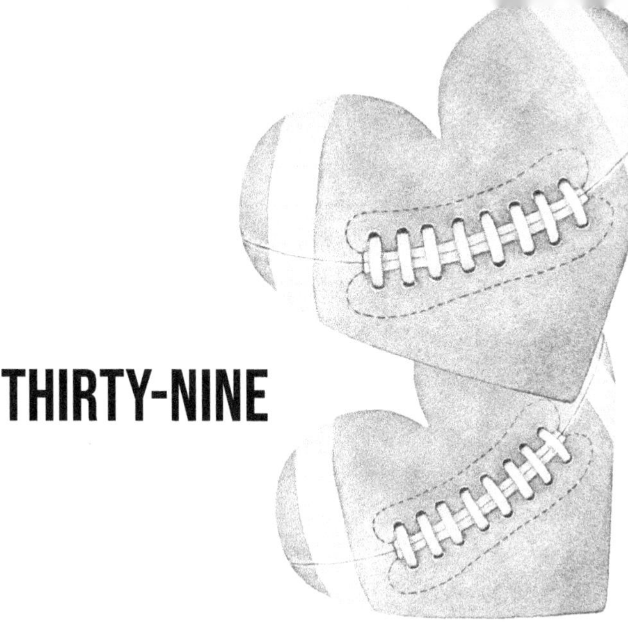

THIRTY-NINE

I t takes a moment for the rest of my body to catch up with what my eyes are seeing. At first comes the sharp pain in my chest, the ache of betrayal. Then comes the anger surging through me like a tidal wave.

"What the hell are you doing in my room?" Gwen shrieks.

Despite the shitstorm that's coming from her, I can't take my eyes off Danny.

"Sadie… it's not what it looks like," he says.

"I'm calling the cops," the bitch continues. "This is home invasion."

Melody rushes out of the bathroom, holding something in her hand. "Go ahead. Call them. I'm sure they'd love to know about the stash of Rohypnol I found hidden inside your toilet tank."

She waves a clear plastic bag with small glass vials inside.

"What the hell!" Danny takes the bag from Melody and stares at its contents.

"That's not mine!" Gwen's eyes widen in fear.

Suddenly, the truth about the night I was drugged comes

rushing through me. We'd never thought to turn our suspicions to a female party.

"Did you spike Sadie's drink at the Pike party?" Danny takes a step toward his ex, looking possessed.

My anger at him diminishes. Maybe he had a valid reason for coming to Gwen's room. I can't jump to conclusions, not when it comes to him.

"How dare you accuse me of something that despicable?" Gwen retorts.

Melody takes the bag from Danny. "I bet we'll find your fingerprints all over these vials."

"You bitch. Give me that." She jumps on Melody, surprising everyone.

Melody loses her balance and ends up falling with Gwen on top of her. The act of violence triggers something in me. I react on impulse and shove Gwen off Melody. She lashes out like a feral animal, scratches my face with her nails, and we become tangled in a catfight. She pulls my hair and tries to bite my hand.

For fuck's sake. This is insane.

Despite the situation, I hold back. I could do some serious damage to her, but if I break her nose with a punch, it'll be hard to explain to Coach Lauda.

Vanessa and Danny manage to break us apart. Vanessa is the one holding me, but I don't offer resistance. Danny, on the other hand, has to put some muscle into restraining his ex. Man, she's a total psycho.

"Let me go!" She tries to shake free.

"Stop it, Gwen," he demands.

We must have made too much noise, because the room quickly fills with more people. I see Andy and Joanne. The other newcomers all seem to be Gwen's sorority sisters.

"What's going on?" one of the girls asks.

"I found these bitches in my room," Gwen accuses us.

A tall brunette takes a step forward, looking directly at Melody. "*You*. I told you you weren't welcome at ChiO house."

"I wouldn't be here if one of your sisters hadn't threatened a Raven."

The girl looks at Gwen. "What's she talking about, little sister?"

Ugh. Do they seriously call each other that? Barf.

"She's lying. They're all here because Danny ditched their friend for me."

Danny's expression contorts in disgust.

My hands ball into fists. "You lying cunt. We're here to find proof you vandalized my car, but instead we discovered you drugged me at the Pike party."

"What?" Joanne says. "She's the one who spiked your drink?"

"Son of a bitch." Andy passes a hand over his face.

"All lies!" Gwen shrieks again.

"Settle down, Gwen. It's over," Danny tells her.

"You need to leave now. This is a matter for the ChiO," the brunette says.

"Fine. We'll go. But we're taking the proof with us." Melody shows everyone the bag with the drugs.

"That's not mine, Caroline. I swear. The bitch must have planted it in my bathroom," Gwen whines.

Melody shrugs. "They won't find my fingerprints on them, that's for sure."

Caroline pinches the bridge of her nose, sighing loudly. "Whatever. Just go, and take your proof with you."

Danny finally releases Gwen and shortens the distance to me. She sits on the edge of her bed, hugging herself, and starts to cry in earnest. Crocodile tears.

"Are you okay?" he asks me.

"Yeah."

He touches my face where Gwen scratched me. "You're bleeding a little."

"I'll probably need rabies shots."

He shakes his head and then pulls me into a hug. "You're

crazy, girl. What were you doing here?"

"What I said I was. Looking for proof that your ex trashed my car."

His body becomes tense against mine. He pulls back and looks into my eyes, ready to reply, when Andy taps him on the shoulder and motions us to follow him out. Yeah, we shouldn't linger here in case Gwen decides to pounce on me. Fucking crazy cunt.

Danny takes my hand, and we don't stop moving until we're outside the ChiO house and away from the front door.

Then I stop and force him to look at me. "What were you doing with that bitch?"

"Same thing as you were. I figured if I led her on, I could get her to confess she damaged your car."

I pull my hand from his and cross my arms. "So you flirted with her?"

"A little."

He didn't even need to reply. His eyes look guilty as hell.

I bite my tongue. Getting into a fight because of Gwen would be giving her too much power over our relationship.

"You're not going to say anything?" he asks.

"Not right now."

I can see he has words lodged in his throat, but our friends walk over, so whatever they are will have to wait.

"What are we going to do now?" Vanessa asks.

"We need to hand this over to the police." Melody shakes the plastic bag.

"Damn. I can't believe Danny's psycho ex was the one who drugged you, Sadie," Andy pipes up.

"Yeah, me neither. It makes me wonder what her endgame was." I hug myself, hating that because of her, Nick motherfucking Fowler got his hands on me.

"Guys, I don't want to be the one to rain on your parade, but most likely, the police won't be able to do anything with that evidence," Joanne butts in.

"What do you mean?" I ask.

"They could only use it against Gwen if they had been the ones who found those drugs."

"Hell, you're right," Andy replies.

"So we can't do anything against her? She'll just walk away free?" I ask.

When no one replies, I have my answer. All this drama and humiliation for nothing.

I throw my hands in the air. "That's just spit-on-your-neck fantastic, innit?"

"Maybe she'll get kicked out of her sorority?" Charlotte suggests.

"That would be a heavy blow to her ego," Danny replies.

I glare at him. "Yeah, because that punishment is severe enough for drugging me and almost getting me sexually assaulted by Nick Fowler."

Danny winces at my remark, right before his gaze turns murderous. "Don't remind me of that."

"Why the hell not? It's the truth."

"Sadie…," Vanessa starts.

"Don't 'Sadie' me. I have to go." I turn around and stride away from the ChiO house.

"Sadie, wait up," Danny calls after me.

That makes me walk faster.

He jogs to catch up and then blocks my path. "Stop, please."

"Why, Danny? What do you want from me?"

He runs his fingers through his hair, sighing in frustration. "I don't want you to leave angry with me. I'm sorry I didn't tell you what I had in mind beforehand. When Coach Clarkson asked me if a jealous girl could have been responsible for your car, I only had one suspect in mind."

"And you thought seducing the information out of her was the way to go?"

He frowns. "Are you telling me your way was better?"

"At least it didn't involve getting near an arsehole and pretending to like them."

"I'm sorry, okay? I couldn't think about anything besides making sure you were safe." He takes me by the shoulders and steps into my space. "I love you so damn much, Sadie. I'd do anything for you."

Suddenly, my eyes prickle. What the hell? I never cry. But here I am, on the precipice of bawling my eyes out.

"You're an idiot." I grab his shirt and pull his mouth to mine.

His arms slide to my back, pulling me closer while his tongue takes possession of mine. My cheeks become hot and wet, and I curse whatever broke in me that turned me into a puddle of emotions.

He pulls back, cradling my face in his hands. "You're crying."

"You'd better get a good look at it, because this is a rare sight."

He wipes the moisture from my cheeks with his thumbs. "Did you drive here?"

"No."

"Good. Let's get home, then."

FORTY

DANNY

"**I** love this." Sadie sighs in my arms.

"Me too." I kiss the top of her head and then hug her tighter.

She's snuggled nicely against my chest, and our legs are tangled together. Our breathing has finally returned to normal after our "good morning" sex marathon.

"I wish we could stay like this forever." She kisses my chest, then rests her cheek against me.

"I don't want you to go back to your dorm."

"And you think I do?" She chuckles. "But I can't simply stay here indefinitely. This apartment is already a full house."

I open my mouth to suggest we look for our own place but then bite my tongue. It might be too soon to suggest that. We just started dating, after all. I can't help the way I feel about her though. The idea of not waking up next to her every day is grim. But besides the fact that I don't want to rush things and scare her, I'll never be able to find a rental as cheap as what Andy charges me. And I can't ask him to let Sadie move in with me. This apartment *is* already at full capacity.

Both our alarms go off at the same time.

I groan. "Peace broken. The world intrudes."

She leans on her elbow and reaches for her phone on the nightstand. "We missed our morning run."

I pull her against me and nuzzle her neck. "I prefer the type of cardio we did."

She giggles, and it's like music to my ears.

"So do I. But I don't think doing the horizontal tango will help us win games." She sits up, throwing her legs to the side of the bed. "Coach Lauda wants us in top shape for Saturday's game."

"I got the same speech from Coach Clarkson."

"I think I'm going back to my dorm today," she says on the way to the bathroom.

I get up suddenly. "What? Why?"

She stops and looks over her shoulder. "We know who trashed my car. I don't think your psycho ex will do anything to me now that everyone knows she was behind it."

My chest becomes tight. Drugging Sadie and leaving a threatening note on the side of her car are the craziest stunts Gwen has ever pulled. I can't help but to be concerned. Unhinged people don't care about consequences.

"Just because we know she did it doesn't mean we should let our guard down."

Sadie furrows her brow. "I'm not going to live in fear, Danny. If I let her get into my head, she wins."

I walk over and stop in front of her, placing my hands on her arms. "Just promise me you'll be careful."

"Of course I will. That applies to you too." She rises on her tiptoes and gives me a quick peck on the lips. "I'm going to shower now. Stop worrying so much."

"I'll try. Want company?"

"Tempting, but no. I can't be late for class."

I drop my hands and watch her disappear inside the bathroom.

The feeling of doom is still swirling in my chest despite my promise to not worry. I won't have peace of mind until Gwen is gone from Rushmore and this city.

***

SADIE

Telling someone I won't let a deranged person get me rattled is easier said than done. I didn't want Danny to stress about me too much, so I had to put on a brave face. But my stomach has been coiled tight the whole morning. I'm not sure if it's because of Gwen or that her despicable acts simply triggered my PTSD again.

I'm so jumpy that when someone taps me on the shoulder while I'm in line to buy a snack, I jerk back.

"Relax, Sadie. It's just me," Jane says.

"Blimey, girl. You almost gave me a heart attack."

"I heard about what happened yesterday. How are you?"

"Jittery as fuck, as you just witnessed," I blurt out, and then regret it. "Please don't tell Danny I said that. I don't want him to freak out."

"He's already concerned."

"I know."

"But I think everything will be all right. A girl in one of my classes is a ChiO. Danny's ex was kicked out of the sorority, and school administration is investigating the claims against her."

"They are? We didn't tell anyone what we found in her bedroom."

Jane shrugs. "Someone did. Anyway, I thought you'd be happy to know."

"I'd be happier if she had been expelled already."

"I know. It's possible she'll only get academic probation. Better than nothing, right?"

"Not really" is on the tip of my tongue, but I keep my retort bottled in. Jane has been nothing but kind to me. I shouldn't bite her head off because I don't like her news. Don't shoot the messenger and all that.

I plaster a fake smile on my face and say, "Sure."

"It's your turn now." She nods toward the counter. "I have to run to my next class. See you later."

"Yeah, see ya."

I buy an orange juice and a protein bar, then rush out of the cafeteria. I lost track of time, and now I only have five minutes to cross the park and get to the Humanities building. I'm about to break into a run when someone yanks my arm.

"Hey!" I turn, coming face-to-face with the psycho. "What the hell? Let go of me."

"You think you won this war, don't you?" she asks, still clutching my arm in a vise grip. "You're sorely mistaken. Danny and I are meant to be together, and no one will come between us, least of all some European trash like you."

Goddamn it. The crazy in her eyes is real. My heart is racing as I pull my arm free from her grasp.

"You're delusional and belong in a psych ward."

My words have no impact on her as she continues her tirade. "This is your final warning. Stay away from Danny or you'll regret it."

She whirls around and walks away while all I do is stare at her gobsmacked. My pulse is pounding loudly in my ears, and my chest is tight.

For fuck's sake. She did not just put me in a state of panic. I should have done something, but save for punching the bitch in her throat, there was nothing I could do. My speech to Danny this morning flashes in my mind mockingly. I told him I doubted she'd do anything to me now that everyone knows what she did to my car. What a fucking joke. No one can predict what deranged people will do.

I pull my cell phone out and look at the time. I'm already late for class, but hell, I'm in no condition to sit through a lecture.

If Gwen thinks she can simply threaten me and get away with it, she's mistaken. It's time I speak with the dean's representative. If he can't help me, then I'll use every resource I have.

That crazy fucker needs to go.

FORTY-ONE

DANNY

This whole deal with Gwen has taken up too much space in my head. The first thing I do when I return to the locker room is check my phone for messages from Sadie. There's only one, and it's just a bunch of goofy emojis. It brings a smile to my face, which is erased in the next minute when an email notification pops up on my screen. It's from the dean's office.

My mood turns bitter after I read the message. The dean would like to speak to me about Gwen at my earliest convenience. It doesn't come as a surprise, but I know if I want him to take the matter seriously, I have to tell him everything about my past with her.

With a deep sigh, I send a quick reply with my availability. The sooner I get this over with, the quicker they'll act. At least, I hope so.

On my way out the building, I call Sadie. It rings until it goes to voice mail. I'm hoping I can convince her to stay another night at my place. My gaze is down as I leave her a quick voice message.

"Danny Hudson?" a male voice asks.

I look up and find a teenager standing in front of the building.

"Yeah."

He doesn't say anything for a couple of beats, but his stare is unnerving.

"Can I help you?" I ask.

He shoves his hands in his pockets. "I'm sorry. I didn't expect this to be so hard."

Chills run down my spine. I look at the kid closely. *Do I know him?*

"You lost me," I say.

"You look a lot like him."

A sudden lump forms in my throat, and my stomach feels like it turned into lead. I finally figure out why he looks familiar. He resembles the jerk who fathered me.

That means....

"My name is Josh Fitzpatrick, Jr. I'm your—"

"Brother. You're my brother."

He nods. "I'm sorry to show up like this out of the blue. I wouldn't have come if it wasn't important."

His face is solemn, and suddenly I realize he's hating having to be here. He didn't come to meet his half brother; he came to plead for his father. The knowledge should make me angry, but all I'm feeling in this moment is sadness.

He's as much a victim in all this as I am. I won't send him away like I did his dad.

"If you want to talk, walk with me."

I head to my car, not bothering to wait for his reply. He does follow me, but he doesn't say a word until I stop next to my vehicle.

"You must be wondering why I came here," he says.

"I'm fairly certain I know why."

He watches me through slits. "I didn't know you existed until a month ago."

"Somehow I don't think that would change anything between us. You wouldn't have sought me out before you felt you had no choice."

He lifts his chin. "That's right. I wouldn't. I hate the fact that you exist."

I try not to wince at his words, but only a cold-blooded person wouldn't react to that statement.

"I have no interest in pursuing a relationship with your old man. I don't want any of his money either."

His eyebrows shoot up to the heavens. "Do you think I hate you because I'm afraid you'll make a dent in my inheritance? I don't care about the money. All I care about is my mother, and your existence is a constant source of pain to her."

Ah shit. Way to make me feel bad about something I didn't do.

"I can't help that. I know you didn't come here to wish me gone, so go on, say what you want and leave."

His nostrils flare, and his hard swallow is audible.

"I know my—*our* father isn't the best person in the world. But for some twisted reason, my mother loves him more than life itself. I don't know what will happen to her if he dies. So I'm here to ask you to help him, not for him but for my mom."

"Help him how?"

My question seems to catch him by surprise. "You don't know?"

"I never gave him the chance to say a word. I only know he's sick."

Josh passes a hand over his face. "He has leukemia. I'm not a match, so we're hoping you are."

Clarity rushes over me. My father didn't come to reconnect with me because he's dying. He came because he had no choice. That makes me feel ten thousand times worse.

"I see." I look out in the distance, seeing nothing.

"The doctors say it's a long shot, but will you at least find out if you're a match?"

There's so much sadness and resentment in my brother's voice that it makes my chest constrict. Bitterness washes over me. I'll never be able to have a relationship with him. I think if the situation wasn't so wrapped in hurt, we could have been friends.

I glance at him again. "Of course I will. I didn't know that's what he wanted. I'm not a heartless bastard."

His lips curl upward, dispelling the animosity for a moment. "You didn't take after him, then."

"No. And my guess is you didn't either."

He shakes his head. "The jury is still out on that. I'll let his assistant know you're willing to help. He'll handle everything."

"Sounds good."

He nods and then walks away.

SADIE

I left the meeting with the dean's assistant feeling discouraged. He was dismissive as fuck about my concerns. He obviously never watched *Fatal Attraction*.

Women can be psychos too, buddy.

His assurance that he'd look into the Gwen matter felt hollow to my ears. Since I'm not going to sit around and wait for her to come at me with a knife, I decide to use the last trump card I have up my sleeve.

I drive straight to the Rebels' headquarters. Danny messaged me an hour ago, so I know practice is over for the day. It means Dad will be in his office, watching tapes until past dinnertime—that is, if his habits haven't changed.

The car park is almost empty, but his car is there. Not willing to take risks, I dig in my purse and fish out the can of pepper spray I bought after the encounter with Gwen. I'm on edge as I stride across the car park, paying close attention to my surroundings. I hate that the bitch did this to me.

My heart is racing when I enter the building, and it doesn't slow down until I see Dad in his office. A wave of relief washes over me. Deep down, I know he'll never let anything happen to me. I don't fight the feeling like I would have a couple of months ago. My resentment with him has lessened considerably, and I think Danny is responsible, in part, for it.

His door is open, but he's facing away from it, watching the TV screen. A football game is on. Most people would notice someone lurking behind them, but not Dad when he's in the zone.

I knock on the doorframe. "Hey, Dad. Got a minute?"

He turns so fast that he almost falls out of his chair.

"Sadie. What are you doing here?"

I enter and then shut the door. "I need to ask you a favor."

He gets up and drags his chair back to behind his desk.

"If it's anything within my ability, I'll be glad to help."

I pull up the chair opposite his and sit down. He follows suit. Immediately, an uncomfortable silence descends.

For fuck's sake. This is horrible. And I know I'm to blame for it.

"I'm not sure you're aware that a sophomore transfer was responsible for trashing my car."

His eyebrows furrow. "I'm aware. She wasn't simply a random student. Danny told me it was his ex."

"He did? I didn't know he had."

Dad nods. "He told me before practice. Even though I appreciate his transparency on the matter, I can't say I'm happy about it."

Oh boy. He's not going to like what I have to say, then.

"Please don't blame him for the actions of his psychotic ex."

"I'm not blaming him, but I can't help thinking if you hadn't gotten involved with Danny in the first place, none of this would have happened."

I take deep breaths, trying to control my temper. "If he hadn't come into my life, I wouldn't be here talking to you."

Dad's eyes narrow, but I don't give him the chance to offer a rebuff.

"Danny is the best thing that's happened to me since I discovered football. He's helped me so much, Dad."

He leans against his chair. "You really love him, don't you?"

"Yeah, I do. So I need you to promise me not to get angry with him once I tell you what happened."

"If your news is anything along the lines of Madonna's 'Papa Don't Preach,' you can forget me not getting angry."

I choke on my saliva. "God, Dad. I'm not pregnant!"

Relief is evident on his face. "For heaven's sake, Sadie. Don't scare me like that."

Glowering, I cross my arms over my chest. "You scared yourself by jumping to conclusions."

He rubs his face. "Fair enough. What's the favor you want to ask me, then?"

"Gwen accosted me earlier today."

He sits straighter. "What did she do?"

"She spewed garbage. Talked a bunch of nonsense about Danny belonging to her and told me I'd regret it if I stayed in her way."

"She threatened you?"

"Pretty much. I had a meeting with the dean's assistant, but I don't think he took me seriously."

"That guy is a moron. I'll go straight to the dean. He *will* take this matter seriously. You have my word."

"Thanks, Dad. That's all I need from you."

He nods. "Of course, honey. I wish you'd have come to me as soon as it happened though."

"I wanted to go through the proper channels and not pull the 'I'm the coach's daughter' card."

"But you *are* the coach's daughter. There's nothing wrong with using your connections to keep you *and* Danny safe."

His comment drops like a ball of glass shards in my stomach. I had been so concerned about Gwen coming after me that I didn't consider she might hurt Danny too.

"I think her beef is only with me," I reply without conviction.

"Are you back in your dorm? I don't like the idea of you staying there while this woman is still around campus. Maybe you should stay with me for a few days."

The refusal is on the tip of my tongue, but then I think about Danny. What if by staying with him, I'm painting a target on his back too? If I stay with Dad for a few days, she'll think her threats scared me.

"I can do that."

His eyebrows shoot to his hairline. "Really?"

I smirk. "You were expecting me to say no, right?"

He rubs the back of his neck and looks at his computer screen. "Absolutely. But I'm glad you said yes. It'll be like old times."

My smile wilts a fraction. I'm not sure it will ever be like the old times between us, but I don't tell him that.

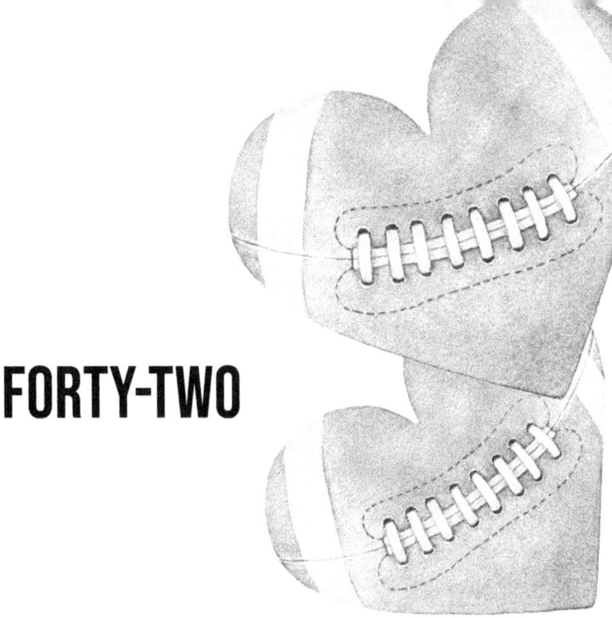

FORTY-TWO

SADIE

No sooner do I step foot inside my father's house than my phone pings with a message. I check right away, guessing it's from Danny. I missed his call earlier, but I didn't want to talk to him before I had taken care of the Gwen situation.

> I need to talk in person. Can I come over?

My stomach coils tightly as worry consumes me.

> I'm at my dad's.

> When will you be home?

I bite my lower lip. Maybe I should just call him.

"Sadie, what type of food do you feel like? Italian, Mexican, Chinese?" Dad asks me from the kitchen.

"Anything you want. Hey, can Danny come over?"

He joins me in the living room, frowning. "Did something happen?"

"I'm not sure. He says he needs to talk in person."

Immediately, Dad's expression darkens, but not in a way that makes me think he's unhappy about my request. I think he's worried about Danny too.

"He can come over, honey. As long as you don't...."

"Get within six feet of each other?" I raise an eyebrow.

He shakes his head. "If he's coming over, I'm ordering Chinese *and* Mexican. That boy can eat."

My smile broadens. "Really? I've never seen him pig out. He's super conscious about his diet."

Dad gives me a droll look. "You haven't seen him after a game."

"You've got me curious."

I text Danny back, still smiling.

I'm spending the night. Come over for dinner? We're ordering Chinese and Mexican.

Are you sure it's okay?

Yup.

Okay, see you in ten.

DANNY

During the short ride to Coach's house, I almost changed my mind several times. Having dinner with him and Sadie has the makings of a terrible idea. But I do need to talk to her about meeting my half brother today and what I agreed to do. Since I have to disclose that decision to Coach too, might as well kill two birds with one stone.

The thought doesn't give me comfort though. I'm a nervous wreck as I ring the doorbell. This is the first time Sadie, Coach, and I will be together under one roof after he caught us in the Red Barn.

Thankfully, Sadie is the one who opens the door.

"Hey." She smiles, rescuing my mood from the pits of despair.

I step closer and lean down to kiss her on the lips but change my mind at the last second and kiss her on the cheek instead.

"What was that?" she asks.

I look over her shoulder to make sure Coach isn't in the vicinity, then whisper in her ear. "Can't risk igniting your father's wrath again."

Shaking her head, she laughs. "He's not going to bite your head off if you kiss me on the lips."

"Don't count on that," Coach grumbles, coming into the living room with a mug in his hand.

I jump away from Sadie, my body as rigid as a board. "Good evening, sir."

He takes a seat on the couch and brings the mug to his lips while staring at me. That's not the man I got to know on the field. That's a pissed-off father who knows I'm sleeping with his daughter.

Hell. I shouldn't have come.

"Would you like something to drink?" Sadie asks me.

"Water, please."

She walks toward the kitchen, leaving me alone to deal with her dad.

Great.

"Have a seat, son. I won't bite."

"Are you sure? You're looking pretty feral to me, sir."

My stupid reply only makes Coach Clarkson glare harder.

Fuck me.

Sadie returns with a glass of water in hand but stops in her tracks when she notices my stiff stance and her father's angry expression.

"Blimey. You promised you wouldn't do that, Dad."

He looks at her innocently. "Do what?"

"Act like Danny is the devil."

With a semi-guilty face, he turns to me. "I'm sorry, son. Please sit down. I'll try to behave."

I take a seat on the opposite chair, and when Sadie hands me the glass of water, I drain the whole thing in a few gulps. Nervousness made my throat dry.

She joins her dad on the couch, and now both are looking at me expectantly.

"What's on your mind, Danny?" Coach asks.

"I met my half brother today."

"What?" Sadie sits straighter. "When? Where?"

"After practice. He was waiting for me outside the building."

"What did he want?"

"To ask for my help. I never gave my father the chance to talk. It turns out he has leukemia, and I'm his last chance to find a donor in the family."

"Wow. That's awful," Sadie replies. "What did you say to him?"

"That I'd do the test to see if I'm a match."

"That's very noble of you, son," Coach says.

I drop my gaze to the coffee table in front of me. "I still don't want anything to do with the man, but I'm not going to turn my back on him like he did to me."

Sadie gets up and, to my surprise, sits on my lap, looping her arms around my neck.

Jesus. What is she doing? Her dad is sitting right there.

"You're a wonderful person, Danny."

She hugs me, resting her cheek on my shoulder. I look at Coach, panicked. His eyes are narrowed, but he doesn't seem as pissed as I thought he'd be.

"What's the recovery time if you're a match?" he asks.

"I don't know. I haven't really looked into it yet. I guess I'll take one step at a time."

Sadie leans back and, thankfully, gets off my lap. "No need to worry before we get the results back. When are you taking the test?"

"It's just a blood test. Tomorrow morning."

Coach stands. "We *do* need to worry about it, Sadie. I'm sure donating stem cells isn't a simple procedure. We have to account for Danny's recovery time. It might take weeks."

Shit. I haven't considered that possibility. Guilt makes me gloomy again.

She puts her hands on her hips. "Dad, can I talk to you in the kitchen?"

I sink farther into the couch and barely notice when they leave the room. I don't want to disappoint Coach Clarkson or let the team down. But I also can't tell my father's cancer to wait until it's a convenient time for me.

The doorbell rings, pulling me back to the here and now. Since Sadie and Coach are still in the kitchen, I answer the door. It's a delivery man with a food order. I take the bags from him and apologize for not having any tip on me.

"It's cool, man. The tip was included in the online payment. Good luck in Saturday's game."

"Thanks."

And just like that, my guilt doubles. I hadn't considered the Rebels' fans.

"Is that the food?" Sadie returns to the living room.

"Yeah."

"Which one?" She looks inside the generic bag.

"No clue."

"Mexican," she says after a couple of seconds. "Come on, we can dig in while we wait for the Chinese delivery."

I follow Sadie to the dining room, where there are plates and utensils set up already. A minute later, the doorbell rings again, and Coach goes to answer it.

"What did you tell your father?" I ask in a low tone.

"Nothing."

"Sadie… I don't want to antagonize Coach Clarkson more than my presence here is already doing."

"You're not. Trust me. Dad gets tunnel vision when it comes to football. I was just reminding him that his players aren't robots and that personal problems shouldn't be dismissed. If you have to take weeks off to recover, so be it."

"It's not that simple."

She glares. "It *is* that simple. The world won't end if you miss a couple of games."

I watch her through slitted eyes. "Oh yeah? Was that your attitude when—"

Ah hell. I can't believe I was about to mention her attack. Sadie's face blanches. I didn't stop soon enough, and she got where I was going.

She swallows hard. "No, but I learned from it."

"I'm sorry."

She shakes her head. "It's fine. Let's eat."

Coach joins us and seems oblivious to the sudden tension in the air. We eat in silence. I have to force down the food because my appetite is gone.

I never thought I'd pray for time to go faster while in Sadie's company, but I can't wait to leave. The thought makes me guilty. It's not her fault I'm so damn conflicted about my decision.

"Well, since the mood is absolutely rubbish, I might as well hammer the nail in the coffin," Sadie announces.

I frown. "Did something else happen?"

She exchanges a meaningful glance with her father, which makes me even leerier.

"Gwen threatened me again."

"What?" I grit out.

"She found me on campus today and told me to stay away from you or I'd regret it."

My hands curl into fists while rage runs free through my veins. I knew she wouldn't simply go away quietly. She's a fucking nutjob.

"You have to tell the dean. She can't be allowed to stay at Rushmore."

"I have a meeting with him first thing in the morning," Coach replies. "But I've asked Sadie to stay here until the matter is resolved."

I feel partial relief, but that's quickly replaced by a sharp pain. I turn to her. "You could have stayed with me."

Remorse seems to shine in her eyes. "I know, but I felt like a mooch. Besides, I haven't really spent any time with Dad since I moved to California."

Now I feel like a jerk. *Way to go, Danny.*

I rub the back of my neck and stare at my plate. "Yeah, I get that. Forget what I said."

Coach clears his throat. "Anyone want dessert? I have ice cream."

I shake my head, getting up. "None for me. I'll help with the dishes."

"I'll join you," Sadie says.

Together, we clear the table and then head to the kitchen. Coach doesn't follow us. I set all the dirty dishes in the sink, and when Sadie finishes disposing of the trash, I pull her into my arms and hug her tightly.

"I'm sorry this was so weird," I say.

"Me too. I should have told you earlier why I was staying at Dad's."

I ease back and look into her eyes. "Why didn't you tell me about Gwen earlier?"

"Because I didn't want you getting involved."

"Sadie, I *am* involved. She's going after you because of me."

"Exactly. I knew if I told you, you'd seek her out. I don't want her near you. That bitch is crazy. I wouldn't put it past her to kidnap you."

I want to tell Sadie she's exaggerating, but that'd be a lie. In truth, I don't know how far Gwen would go.

"I wish I could do a better job of protecting you."

She smirks. "You're doing a fine job, mister. I promise I'll come over after my game Saturday."

"You know we aren't playing at home, right? We won't get back until late."

She loops her arms around my waist and rises on her tiptoes.

"And I'll be waiting for you. In your bed. Naked."

A loud groan makes her jump back. We turn to see Coach Clarkson perform the quickest pivot of all time and walk away.

"Do you think he heard me?" Sadie asks.

"Oh, he heard you."

And he's going to flay me alive tomorrow at practice. Fucking great.

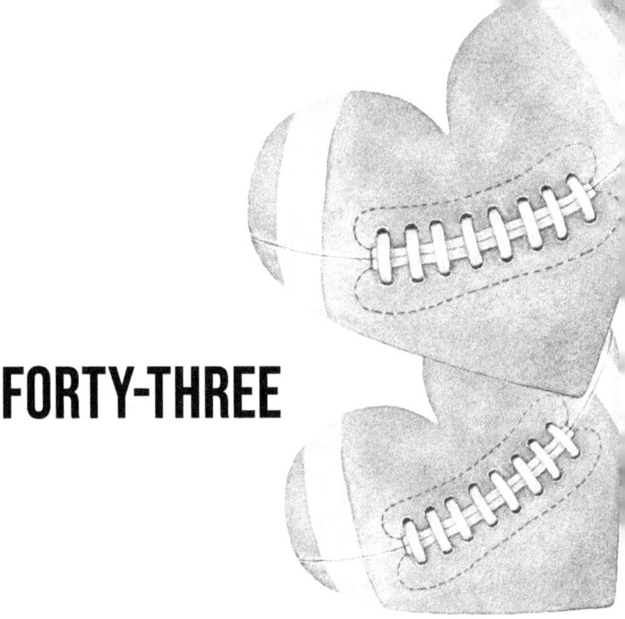

FORTY-THREE

"Thanks for letting me tag along to say goodbye to Danny, Dad."

He scoffs. "I didn't think I had a choice."

"You're not wrong." I laugh.

"Jesus, you've only been apart for a few days."

"So?" I take a large sip of my iced chai latte.

Those days were hard. I thought staying at Dad's until the Gwen situation got resolved was a good idea at the time. I didn't think about the practicality of it. With school, practice, and Dad suddenly expecting me to be home in time for dinner, I barely saw Danny.

"Nothing," he grumbles, clutching the steering wheel tighter until his knuckles turn white.

"Anyway, I appreciate you forgetting for a second that you don't like the idea of me dating one of your players."

He sighs. "It'll take me longer than a week to get used to it, Sadie. It's not because Danny is one of my players."

"Oh?" I raise an eyebrow.

He passes a hand over his face. "I haven't seen you grow

up, honey, and it kills me that I've missed so much. I know you're a young woman now, but to me, you're still my little girl."

My eyes prickle, filling with tears as I become overwhelmed with emotion that seems to overflow my tight chest. Crossing my arms, I look out the window, hiding any rogue tear that I don't manage to keep from escaping.

"Did you ever regret not asking for custody of Dom and me?" I ask through the lump in my throat.

"Every single day, Sadie. Giving you up was the hardest thing I've ever had to do in my life."

"Why did you, then?"

He doesn't answer for a couple of beats. "It wasn't an easy decision. Your mom loves you and Dom very much, sweetie. She wouldn't have been able to handle being apart from you."

"But you could? How is that fair?"

"She wasn't well."

"What do you mean?"

He grows quiet, and I fear I already know the answer to my own question.

"She was depressed, wasn't she?"

"Yeah. I didn't want to give her a reason to…. Well, I thought it was best for everyone if I didn't ask to share custody."

A lonely tear escapes the corner of my eye, and I hastily wipe it away. "All this time I thought you simply didn't love me enough."

"Honey, how could you think that?"

There's so much hurt in his question that it's almost impossible to keep from bawling like a little girl.

This is ridiculous. I never cry, for fuck's sake.

"I wasn't a very smart six-year-old. Besides, I was hurting too much with the separation. I needed to blame someone."

"No, I think you were too smart. You sensed your mother couldn't cope with more grief, so you chose me to channel your anger."

I sink farther in my seat, feeling so small that I might have turned into Frodo.

We finally pull into the car park in front of the Rebels' headquarters, where the team's buses are waiting. Some of the players and cheerleaders have arrived, including Danny, Andy, and Heather, Vanessa's twin. I'm glad the cheerleaders and the players aren't interacting—*yet*.

This is the first time Danny is playing an away game since we became official, and I'm getting a little jealous that the cheerleaders get to tag along and I can't. It's damn stupid since the reason I'm unable to attend Danny's game is because I also have to play today.

Is being love-drunk making me stupid too? God, I hope not.

Once Dad parks his car, I turn to him. "Okay, I'm going to say hello to my boyfriend now. It will involve major PDA."

Twisting his face into a grimace, he says, "I'll look the other way."

I smirk, then get out of the car. Danny doesn't know I planned to come to see him off, so he doesn't look in my direction until I'm almost on top of him.

His eyes widen. "Sadie?"

"That's my name, don't wear it out."

I jump in his arms, needing to soak up his essence as much as I can. He hugs me tight, nuzzling my neck in the process. Bollocks. He really shouldn't have done that. Now I want to take him inside the locker room for a quickie.

Must not entertain these thoughts.

"I had to come and wish you good luck in person," I say.

"We don't need luck," Andy chimes in.

"Ignore him," Danny tells me, then leans down to kiss me. He stops suddenly, then glances over my head. "Where's Coach?"

I curl my fingers around his shirt. "Relax. I've warned him already. He's not going to look." Then I pull him the rest of the distance until our lips collide.

He kisses me hard and deep, much to Andy's chagrin, who is pretty vocal about his annoyance. We ignore him and snog like the two horny teenagers we are.

"Coach is coming," Andy warns us, and we jump apart, only to discover the bellend lied.

"Dude, you suck," Danny tells him.

He shrugs. "I'm not even a little bit sorry."

More people start to arrive, so Danny and I refrain from kissing, but we remain attached at the hips until Dad does make an appearance and tells everyone to get into the buses. Danny gives me a quick peck on the lips and jogs after Andy. Since I came with Dad, I'm taking his car back to the house. I don't have to be at the stadium until later.

I remain standing in front of the Rebels' headquarters until all buses depart. I can't help the morose feeling that sweeps over me.

Ugh, get a grip, Sadie.

My phone rings, and I thank heavens for the timely distraction. It's Vanessa.

"Hey, girlie. What's cracking?" I ask.

"Have you heard?"

"Heard about what?"

"That psycho bitch. I was with Couch Lauda when the dean called half an hour ago to let her know Gwen has been expelled."

"Shut your face. For real?"

"Yep. I thought you should know as soon as possible."

I pump my fist into the air. "Fuck yeah. Thanks for letting me know. The dean must have called my father too, but he already left with the team."

"I'm sure he did."

The sound of a car accelerating draws my attention to the street. I turn and see a black sedan coming straight at me. What the hell?

There's no time to do anything besides jump to the side,

hoping to not be turned into roadkill. I roll as I hit the ground, glad for my hoodie's protection.

The car misses me by a couple of inches, but it keeps barreling straight ahead without slowing until it hits the wired fence, punching through it. It finally comes to a halt, but that doesn't give me comfort. Whoever is behind the wheel wanted to kill me.

"What the hell was that?" Vanessa asks, and I realize I'm still holding my phone.

"Someone just tried to run me over with a car," I shout through the fear that's made my heart beat loudly in my chest.

My pulse is drumming in my ears as I get up on shaky legs. I have to get out of here.

"What? Oh my God. Are you okay?"

"N-No."

My panic is rising, the devastating emotion taking control of my muscles. The driver gets out, and there's no surprise on my part when I see Gwen, bleeding from a cut on her forehead, her deranged eyes set on me.

"Sadie, are you there? Sadie!" Vanessa shouts. "Shit. I'm coming over."

I should run, should tell Vanessa that Gwen was the one who tried to kill me. But terror already took my ability to think, to speak. I'm trapped by my own mind at the mercy of a psychopath.

"You fucking bitch. Did you think you'd get rid of me that easily?" she taunts me, slowly walking over.

It's like she knows I can't move. Or maybe she wants me to run so she can chase me like in those slasher movies.

"I bided my time, waited patiently for Danny to finally see that I'm the only one for him. Then you had to come along and ruin everything I've worked for."

For fuck's sake. I can take her now that she isn't inside a three-thousand-pound car coming at me at sixty miles an hour. That is until she flips open a switchblade. Nausea takes over me.

Shakes wreak havoc throughout my body. My scar throbs as if my body remembers the pain of a similar blade piercing my skin.

No. No. No.

This is a nightmare.

I have to run.

The mental command finally breaks through my paralysis. I take off toward Dad's car, and Gwen comes after me.

"Where do you think you're going, Eurotrash?"

I don't look back. I just need to focus on running as fast as the wind.

I'm able to cross the car park in the blink of an eye. She won't catch me before I'm safe inside my vehicle, but when I try the driver's door, it's locked. I glance over my shoulder. She's almost on me. I won't have time to check the other doors. *Fuck.* I dash between the cars, hitting the side mirror of one in the process. I barely notice the pain.

The sound of an engine approaching distracts me. I glance at the street and see one of the buses came back. That second of distraction costs me, and now she's right behind me. I turn, raising my arms to deter her attack. The knife slashes my palm open, and I cry out in pain. She pulls her arm back to stab me again.

"Gwen! Stop!" Danny screams.

It was his bus that returned. My heart soars with hope and then plummets in despair in the next second when she turns her murderous attention to him.

"You betrayed me! You promised we would be together forever!" she shouts like a maniac, waving the blood-coated knife.

I should get out of her range now that she's distracted, but sudden anger overrides my survival instincts. I reach for her wrist and try to wrestle the weapon from her. My hand is burning as if acid was poured over it, but I push through the pain, fueled by adrenaline.

She's taller than me though, and freakishly strong, which works to her advantage. With a shove, she breaks from my hold. I stagger back, colliding with a parked car. She intends to finish me off, witnesses be damned.

Suddenly Danny and my father are there, restraining her. Dad applies pressure to her wrist, and the knife falls to the ground. He kicks it away for good measure.

Shock is quickly taking over again. My breathing is erratic, my pulse beating too fast. But when Danny pulls me into his arms, the wave of panic that was rising slowly recedes. He's my fortress. He's home.

I bury my face against his chest and finally allow myself to cry.

FORTY-FOUR

SADIE

I've been sitting in Dad's office for over an hour. The police were called, and Gwen was arrested. I gave my statement to them, and to the dean, who came personally to see how I was doing. Now I'm clutching my second cup of coffee while Danny rubs my back in a soothing way. Dad is talking to the dean outside, and even though the door is open and I can hear the conversation, I'm not paying attention to what they're saying.

"Are you sure I can't get you anything to eat, sweetheart?" Danny asks.

I shake my head. "No, I'm okay. You should get going or you'll miss your game."

"The bus left half an hour ago. I spoke to Coach. I'm sitting this game out."

I whip my face to his. "What? You have to play."

"I don't. Do you think I can concentrate after what happened? My fucking ex almost killed you in front of me."

My chest becomes even tighter. I was only thinking about my trauma and didn't stop to consider Danny's.

I touch his cheek. "I'm so sorry. Do you want to talk about it?"

He gives a pained look. "God, no. You're the victim. I'm the one who should be offering you comfort, not the other way around."

"Danny… come on. That monster put us both through the wringer. I'm not made out of paper, you know. I can be your rock too."

"You are my rock." He leans forward and kisses me gently.

A knock on the door interrupts our moment. Couch Lauda is there.

"How are you feeling, Sadie?" she asks.

"Better than an hour ago."

She nods. "That's good. I just want you to know that if you want to sit today's game out, it's okay."

I jump out of my chair. "Are you benching me? I can play. I *wanna* play."

Her eyebrows shoot up. "You just experienced a traumatic event. No one will judge you if you miss one game."

"You don't understand. I need to play. It's the only thing I can control right now. Please, don't make me sit on the bench."

Coach Lauda's expression is filled with doubt. I don't know what else I can say to convince her that I'm not going to fuck up if I play.

"If Sadie says she can play, she can play," Danny pipes up.

She turns to him. "You aren't playing today."

"No, but I'm not Sadie."

I glance at him. Is he saying I'm stronger than he is?

Coach Lauda sighs. "If that's what you want, then I'm not going to stand in your way. But if I suspect at any point that you aren't well, I *will* bench you. Understood?"

"Yes, ma'am."

She leaves, and a minute later, Dad comes in. "How are you, kiddo?"

"I'm okay. My hand is throbbing a little, but thank goodness I'm not a goalie."

"Coach Lauda told me you're playing today."

I frown. "Please don't try to change my mind."

He rests his hands on his hips and stares me down. "I'm not, but I wouldn't be doing a good job as a parent if I didn't ask if you're sure."

"I am."

His lips form a thin flat line while we engage in a staring contest. After a moment, he sighs. "All right. I'm heading to San Diego in a few. I wish I could stay but—"

"The team can't lose their QB and coach at the same time," I finish for him.

He nods. "Right."

"I'll take care of Sadie, sir. I promise," Danny says.

"I know you will, son."

Vanessa, Joanne, and Melody crowd the entrance to Dad's office. They've been here a while, but with the aftermath, we didn't have a chance to speak yet.

Dad looks over his shoulder and says, "I guess I should let your friends talk to you now. I'm done being on the receiving end of their death glares."

He walks out, and then they come in.

"How are you feeling, Sadie?" Joanne asks first.

"Bloody awful, but I told Coach I want to play."

Vanessa and Joanne trade a worried glance, but Melody watches me through narrowed eyes. "How angry are you right now that you let that bitch bleed you?"

"Melody!" Vanessa exclaims.

I smirk. "Fit to be tied."

"What's that?" Vanessa cocks her head to the side.

"It means I'm bloody pissed off."

"I feel sorry for the other team. This game is going to be epic." Melody smiles from ear to ear.

DANNY

I wasn't sure if Sadie would be able to handle the pressure of a game after this morning, but I kept my worries hidden for her benefit. In the end, my concerns were all in my head because she kicked ass. Melody's earlier comment was spot on. Sadie was able to funnel her anger toward decimating their opponents. She scored two goals and assisted on the third.

Seeing her thrive in the field softened the guilt I had been feeling for bailing on my team today. It was the right decision for me though. I wouldn't have been able to focus, and maybe the Rebels would have lost by a landslide and not the four-point difference. It sucks that we didn't win, but it's the beginning of the season. We can recover.

The highlight of staying behind was being on the sideline when the whistle announced the end of the game, and Sadie ran into my arms. Best thing ever.

I couldn't follow her into the locker room, but I'm waiting for her in front of the building when she gets out.

She says goodbye to her teammates and walks over, beaming. I take the duffel bag from her shoulder, and surprisingly, she doesn't put up a fight.

"You're so gentlemanly today."

"Only today?" I raise an eyebrow.

She shrugs, smiling in the sassy way I love.

"*You* are quite amenable," I add.

She loops her arm around my waist, hugging me sideways. "What can I say? Sometimes I like having a strong man doing manly things for me."

"Uh-huh. I smell a trap here."

"No trap. I just want to be taken care of for a change."

I turn her around to look in her eyes. "I'll always take care of you, sugarplum, even when you tell me to go to hell."

Silently, she rises on her tiptoes and kisses me. I pull her closer, deepening the kiss and quickly running the risk of devouring her out in public. My pulse quickens, and chills of desire roll down my spine. I pull back, already breathing hard.

"If you need me to do manly things to you, I have a few ideas in mind."

She bites her lower lip, tempting me even more.

"We'd better crack on, then."

FORTY-FIVE

SADIE

Monday morning after the attack was strange. Lots of staring and gossiping. By Tuesday, no one gave a crap that I almost became another blonde casualty in a horror movie. Gwen is still behind bars. It's likely her lawyer will plead insanity. As long as she's locked up, I don't care where she winds up. Prison, psych ward—it's all the same to me.

I'm finishing a paper in the library when Danny finds me. He drops into the seat next to mine and kisses me soundly on the cheek.

"Hey, sugarplum. Are you done?" he asks.

"Nearly. I need another minute."

"What's the paper about?"

"An analysis of the lyrics of 'Julia' by The Beatles."

"I don't think I know that one."

"It's less popular for sure. It's the only one in their entire catalog recorded by John Lennon alone. It's supposed to be an ode to his mother."

"Ah, gotcha."

I'm just about to hit the Save button when Danny's phone pings. A few seconds later, I see from my periphery the sudden tension on his face.

"What's wrong?" I turn to him.

"I just got the test results from the lab." He looks up. "I'm not a match."

Hell. With everything that happened, I forgot about the bloody test. Judging by the stunned glint in Danny's eyes, the results were not what he was expecting.

"We knew it was a long shot," I say. "How do you feel about it though?"

"I'm not sure." He runs his fingers through his hair and looks away. "He's a piece of shit for what he's done to my mother and his wife, but after meeting my half brother, hearing his plea, I feel bad that I can't help the douche."

I cover Danny's hand with mine. "At least you tried. Maybe they'll be able to find another donor."

"Yeah, maybe." He stands suddenly. "I need to see my mother."

"Isn't she working today?"

He shakes his head. "She has Tuesdays off."

"Do you want me to come with you?"

His forehead crinkles. "Don't you have class after lunch?"

I close my laptop and get up too. "Eh, I'm still too traumatized. I can't be arsed."

Danny's furrow deepens, and I guess he didn't get my joke.

"Oh, for fuck's sake. I was taking the piss. What I meant to say is that you're more important than some stupid lecture."

He cracks a tiny smile. "Oh, okay, then. And yes, of course I want you to come."

I collect my things, and we leave the library together. His arm is around my shoulders, possessively, and I confess it feels so bloody nice. I don't care about feminism when it comes to him. I love being claimed by Danny.

He texts his mother as we walk to the car, getting an immediate reply.

"She's asking what you'd like to eat for lunch."

"Anything, really. I'm not that picky, but ask if she has cookies."

He chuckles. "Don't worry. She'll have cookies."

"Oh, I almost forgot to tell you. I spoke to my mother before class this morning. She and Dominic are coming to visit me at the end of the month."

"That's great. You must miss them a lot."

I bob my head up and down. "I do. You know Mum was frantic when she learned about Saturday's incident. It was hell convincing her that she didn't need to drop everything to come see me."

"I think you've told me that story a few times, babe."

I hit his chest with the back of my hand playfully. "Bellend."

He laughs, making it hard to pretend to be angry at him.

"Who will be hardest to impress, your mother or your brother?"

I snort. "You'll have Mum wrapped around your finger in a second. Dom will be a bit trickier, but the worst of the lot is definitely Dad."

"Hopefully I'll return to his good graces once we give him grandkids."

A fuzzy and warm feeling spreads through my chest. I love hearing Danny talk about our future. Getting married and having kids were never part of my vision board. It's crazy how one person can make you see the world in a different light. Now I can't imagine my life where he's not in it.

I glance at him and notice that, despite our easy banter, there's tension around his mouth. His arsehole father must be still weighing heavily on him. To take his mind off the wanker during the ride, I purposely keep the chat light. We talk about our favorite shows, movies, and songs. We rank Will Ferrell's movies from best to worst, then disagree about Hermione and Ron's pairing in *Harry Potter*. He thinks she should have ended up with Harry, and I'm a total shipper of Hermione and Draco. I earn an "are you mad?" look from him for that one. In fact, the discussion lasts until we arrive at his mother's.

The delicious scent of freshly baked cookies reaches us out in the hallway. My stomach grumbles loudly in appreciation. It's already past one, and I only had an apple for breakfast.

"You're not going to judge me if I go straight for dessert, right?" I ask.

"Are you kidding? I'll totally judge you."

He opens the door and calls for his mother. She appears in the living room, holding a tray of cookies.

"Hello, darlings. I hope you're hungry."

"Famished," I say, following the tray with greedy eyes.

She sets them on the coffee table and says, "Lunch is ready. Go wash your hands."

"What are we having, Mom?" Danny asks.

"Pasta carbonara. I hope it's okay, Sadie."

I grin. "Oh yeah. I love Italian food."

She beams and then heads to the kitchen.

Danny veers off the corridor, and no sooner does he give me his back, I step closer to the cookies.

"Don't even think about it. Wash your filthy hands first, piggy," he says without looking over his shoulder.

"Joy killer," I mumble.

I follow him into the bathroom in the hallway. He washes his hands first, then watches me with keen attention as I wash mine. I glare at him through the reflection.

"You'll pay for this, *Potter*," I say in my best Draco impression.

He spins me around before I get the chance to dry my hands and kisses me so passionately that I forget why I was annoyed with him in the first place. The temperature is rising at alarming speed, and if we don't stop, we'll both need a cold shower before we can face his mum.

As if I summoned her with my thoughts, she calls us from the living room. Danny ignores her and deepens the kiss, pressing his erection against my belly.

Bloody hell. What is he trying to do here? With regret, I push him back.

"Danny, stop it."

His eyes are at half-mast, eating me up. "Sorry, I couldn't resist."

"Please don't say my Draco impression caused this."

Twisting his face into a scowl, he steps back. "You had to ruin the moment."

With a smug grin, I walk out of the bathroom and quickly make my way back into the living room. I can smell the pasta now, but I still throw a longing glance at the cookie tray.

"Come on now, Cookie Monster." Danny throws his arm over my shoulders and steers me to the kitchen.

The apartment is small and doesn't have a formal dining room. The table is tucked into a corner, and the food is served on the kitchen counter. There's a big bowl of steaming pasta, plus garlic bread and salad.

"Go on. Grab a plate. It's self-service here," she tells me.

We all fill our plates and head to the table. I moan loudly after the first bite. Danny's mum smiles proudly while Danny raises an eyebrow.

"That good, huh?" he asks.

"It's so, so good."

He smirks. "Aren't you glad you didn't stuff your face with cookies?"

I nod, since I just took a huge bite of garlic bread. Not ideal for kissing later though. Oh well.

We eat in silence for a few minutes, and only when Danny is about done does his mum speak.

"What's on your mind, Danny?"

He sets his utensils down and glances at her. "I'm not a match."

Her brows shoot up, and then sadness sweeps over her eyes. "Oh, honey. I'm sorry."

"Don't be sorry. It is what it is."

"Don't try to downplay how the news is affecting you, Danny. You're my son. I know you better than yourself."

"Yeah, yeah." He picks his piece of garlic bread apart.

"At least you've met your half brother," I chime in, trying to be helpful.

"I don't think he wants to get to know me."

I shrug. "His bloody loss, innit?"

"I didn't expect the news to affect me so much. I mean, I was resigned that he would die, and I didn't care. Then my brother showed up, and it changed my perspective of things. Now that I can't really do anything, I feel helpless."

"Why do you feel helpless, honey?" his mum asks. "We knew the chances you'd be a match weren't great."

Eyes downcast, he replies, "I know."

"Maybe he'll find another donor and you can develop some kind of relationship with him," his mother adds.

Danny's spine goes rigid. "I still don't want anything to do with him. I haven't changed my mind about that."

"All right." She gets up and turns to me. "Are you all done?"

"Oh, I can take my plate to the sink," I protest.

"Nonsense, sweetie. You're a guest. You go get your cookie while I clean up and take Danny with you. He needs something sweet to wash off that sourness."

"I'm not sour," he retorts.

I nudge his arm with my elbow. "Come on, sourpuss. Let's get some well-deserved sugar."

Danny trudges behind me, and he doesn't crack a smile even when I feed him a cookie.

"I thought coming here was supposed to make you feel better," I say.

"Yeah. I guess not even my mother's cooking can get me out of my funk."

"Anything *I* can do?"

There's a slight upturn of his lips. "Yeah." He steps closer, invading my personal space. "We can go wash our hands again."

"Danny Hudson, you're horrible. Your mum is right there." I point at the kitchen.

He kisses me below my ear, sending shivers down my spine. "She knows I'm not a virgin anymore."

I shake my head despite the desire that's weakening my resolve. "I'm not going to shag you in your mother's bathroom," I grit out.

"Fine. Wanna come see my old room?"

I narrow my eyes. "Is that a trick?"

He widens his eyes, playing the innocence card. "I'd never trick you, babe."

He's definitely up to something, but I *am* curious about his bedroom. "Okay."

His face splits into a radiant smile that could light up an entire stadium. He glances over my shoulder and hollers, "Mom, I'm showing Sadie my room."

"Okay."

He takes my hand, looking too pleased with himself.

Yeah, super dodgy behavior there, mate.

I expect him to jump on me as soon as we're alone, but he doesn't. Instead, he watches me as I take his room in.

When I don't say anything for a whole minute, he asks, "What? No comment?"

I look at him, smiling. "You've always been a hopeless romantic, haven't you?"

"What makes you say that?"

I point at the *Howl's Moving Castle* poster on the wall. "Dead giveaway."

He reaches for my hair and tucks a strand behind my ear. "I'm not ashamed of that."

I throw my arms around his neck. "You shouldn't be. It's sexy as hell."

His eyes twinkle with delight as he curls his lips into a crooked smile. "I'd like to point out that you're the one who's starting it this time."

"I know. Does your door lock?"

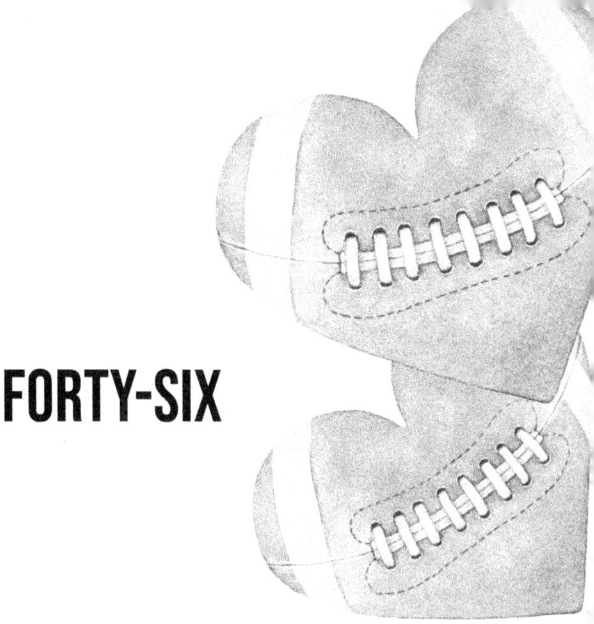

FORTY-SIX

DANNY – THREE YEARS LATER

I've been sitting in my car for the past ten minutes, trying to gather the courage to ask Coach Clarkson the most important question of my life. My hands are clammy, and it feels like I've swallowed a dozen bees that are now buzzing in my stomach.

A text message distracts me from my rising panic. I glance at the phone. It's from Josh, my half brother, congratulating me for my NFL contract with the Tampa Bay Buccaneers, which was announced yesterday. We kept in touch despite our rocky beginnings. Despising the same man bonded us.

The prick found a bone marrow donor after his plea in the media and made a full recovery. He never tried to reach out to me again. It was clear that he only contacted me out of desperation. It took me a long time to accept that he would never be anything besides a sperm donor, and that wasting time feeling sorry because the piece of shit didn't want to be part of my life was pointless.

I text Josh back, thanking him for his message, and then get out of the car. My pulse accelerates, and my body tingles all over with anticipation. It's akin to pregame jitters, but the stakes are much higher. I force one leg in front of the other, not stopping until I'm standing outside Coach's office. The door is closed, so I take a steadying breath before knocking.

"Come in," he says.

"Hey, Coach. Do you have a minute?"

His face splits into a grin as he waves me over. "Of course, son. Come in."

I shut the door and pull up a chair. He's watching me expectantly, almost as if he knows why I'm here. I suppose he could have guessed. I've been dating Sadie for three years, and I've never hidden from anyone that she was the one for me. Eventually, Coach Clarkson got over his annoyance with me dating her. But now that I'm standing in front of him, seeking the ultimate approval, I feel puny, almost unworthy.

"Well," he probes, "what can I do for you, Danny?"

I clear my throat. "Sir, you know how I feel about your daughter. I'm crazy about her."

He nods. "I know."

"Well, now that my future is settled, I'm ready to take the next step in our relationship."

He leans back, lacing his fingers together and resting them over his stomach. "Go on."

"I'd like your blessing to ask Sadie to marry me."

His expression reveals nothing. His face could have been made of marble. I swallow the huge lump in my throat while I endure his stare. I can't flinch, can't show that I'm terrified he'll say no.

Finally, after what feels like an eternity, he cracks a smile. "Of course you have my blessing, son. I couldn't have hoped for a better match for my daughter than you."

A wave of relief washes over me, and I sink lower in my chair, releasing the breath I was holding.

"Thanks, sir."

"I planned to torture you longer, but you were looking a little green there, and I didn't want you throwing up in my office."

"Now I know where Sadie gets her mean streak from."

He shakes his head, laughing. "Oh no, Sadie is a whole new level."

"Well, I'd better get going." I stand up.

"Do you know already how you're going to pop the question?"

I grin. "Yeah."

SADIE

"Did you eat that entire Ben & Jerry's carton already?" Vanessa asks with her hands on her hips.

I lick the spoon and then answer, "I did. And don't give me that look. These containers are tiny."

"Tiny but loaded with calories. Are you sure you want to pudge up now that your beau is moving across the country?"

I glower. "Bloody hell. Don't remind me of that, okay? Why do you think I inhaled all that ice cream?"

She takes the empty carton from my hand and sets it on the coffee table. "Get up. We're going for a ride."

Like a petulant child, I cross my arms. "Why? I'm perfectly fine sitting here on your couch."

"Because I'm already sick of you moping around."

"I've only been here for two hours!"

"Long enough. Come on. You need to burn all those calories you consumed. Let's go for a run."

She's right, I shouldn't drown my sorrows in food. I'm beyond happy that Danny achieved his goal, but I'm also terribly sad that we'll be apart in only a few months. I've been trying not to think about it or show it in front of him. I don't want to put a damper on his excitement.

"Fine."

Vanessa turns on the radio, and when "Hips Don't Lie" by Shakira comes up, she sings along too loudly for my ears.

"Oh God." I pinch the bridge of my nose for a second. "You're determined to annoy me today."

After a few minutes on the road, it occurs to me to ask where we're going.

"You'll see." She smirks.

"You're acting super dodgy. What's going on?"

"I'm not acting dodgy."

I narrow my eyes. "Right."

After another ten minutes, we arrive at the Rebels' training field.

"Why are we here?" I look out the window and search for Danny's car in the parking lot, but I don't see it.

She shrugs. "I figured we could run on the boys' turf for a change. Come on. I'll race you to the Red Barn. The last one there buys dinner."

The pest gets out of the car before I can protest her stupid bet. We're well matched in speed, so what will determine the winner is whoever has a head start. I run to catch up because she doesn't wait for me once she hits the grass. Bitch.

She speeds ahead, and as hard as I pump my legs, I can't take over the lead. All that ice cream I ate is sitting heavily in my stomach, and it's slowing me down. Bollocks. She laughs as she reaches the door of the Red Barn, then disappears inside.

A few seconds later, I follow her and stop. Danny is standing in the middle of the room, wearing his best jeans and my favorite T-shirt, and holding a little box in his hand. My heart leapfrogs to my throat, getting stuck there. Suddenly, "A Picture of You" blasts from the speakers. It's the song that was playing when I gave him a ride to Ikea. That was when I began to fall for him.

I walk over, extremely aware of how fast my heart is beating now. My throat is tight, and I can't believe I'm actually shaking.

"Danny, what is this?" I choke out.

"Sadie, you came into my life like a thunderstorm. Loud, fierce, and so damn beautiful. I couldn't help being enthralled by you, even though I wasn't looking for love."

"Danny...."

My nose burns as tears slowly fill my eyes. I'm still not a crier, but I'm not made of stone either.

He drops to one knee and opens the box, revealing a beautiful diamond ring. "You're the best thing that's happened to my life, sugarplum. Please say you'll marry me."

Unable to speak, I simply nod.

"Is that a yes?" he asks.

"Of course it's a yes. Now get off your knees and kiss me already."

"Hold on. He needs to put the ring on first," Vanessa pipes up from behind the bar.

I look over my shoulder. "How long have you known about this?"

"Nearly three years!" She laughs. "I called it, didn't I?"

Danny takes my hand, and I forget Vanessa. He slides the ring on my finger and then finally pulls me into his arms to kiss me like he did the first time.

***** THE END *****

Thank you for reading *Heart Starter*! Curious to know what's the deal between Paris and Vanessa? Read their story in *Heart Smasher*.

HEART SMASHER

REBELS OF RUSHMORE BOOK FOUR

I thought my last year at Rushmore was going to be epic. The Ravens were kicking butt and taking names. As the captain of the team, I took special pride in that.

Until one wrong decision sent me spiraling down a dark void. I didn't think I'd ever find the way out.

Then he came along. The last person on earth I thought would help me, Paris Andino, a linebacker for the Rushmore Rebels.

We've never gotten along before, mainly because he had a girlfriend who hated my guts.

Now he's single and determined to make up for all the times he acted like a jerk.
The last thing I need is a knight in shining armor with a guilt conscience—especially one who can smash my heart into pieces.

ONE

A nudge on my arm startles me awake. I sit straighter and try to focus on what Father Medina is saying. *Try* being the key word here. Maybe I shouldn't have had a big lunch, but it's hard to resist my grandmother's *feijoada*. Beans, rice, and meat will put anyone to sleep. Pair that up with an unusually hot afternoon for California in March, and I'd need caffeine injected straight into my veins in order to stay awake. My friends from school think I'm crazy for drinking coffee, and their parents think *my* folks are crazy for letting Heather and me drink it. It's a cultural thing.

Why is the church so stuffy today? Its stucco walls are supposed to keep the heat out. Unlike most Catholic churches, this one isn't rich in decorations and frills—probably because the building is new.

I wipe my clammy forehead with the back of my hand and mutter, "Why is it so hot in here? Is Father Medina trying to turn us into stew?"

"Maybe only you. You shouldn't have eaten like a pig earlier," Heather retorts.

Jerk.

Someone snickers behind me, and I look over my shoulder to glower. It's Paris Andino, which means I can't really hold on to my annoyance for more than a second. I've known him for like forever. We always hang out at the Morales Country Club, and there's church. The boy is my kryptonite. How could he not be, with his tanned skin, dark hair, and the bluest pair of eyes I've ever seen, framed by ridiculously long lashes?

I don't realize I'm staring at him like an idiot until Heather elbows me again, giving me a new direction for my glare. *"What?"* I whisper-shout.

"Can you at least pretend to pay attention to the sermon?"

"It's not my fault Father Medina's voice is so monotonous." A yawn sneaks up on me.

"It *is* your fault for staying up late watching old soccer games," she retorts.

"I'm not going to apologize for having an interest in a worthwhile activity. Unlike you."

"You mean an obsession, right? Besides, I do plenty of worthwhile stuff."

"Preening in front of the mirror doesn't count, sis." I smirk.

Paris chuckles again, and this time, Heather is the one who looks over her shoulder. "Can it, Andino."

Father Medina clears his throat, scowling. At least, for once, his annoyance isn't directed at me. Heather faces forward again and slouches. As the twin who never gets in trouble, she hates being scolded. Her face is now redder than a tomato.

The sermon continues for another fifteen minutes without any more interruptions, which is a miracle considering the audience is all teenagers who, like me, were probably strong-armed into going through confirmation. I manage to stay awake, thanks to the knowledge that Paris is right behind me. My tummy is filled with crazy butterflies.

We're supposed to break into groups now and discuss the lesson given during the sermon, but I have to pee badly, so first I head to the secondary building where the restrooms are. Mercifully, Heather doesn't come with me. No doubt she would take the opportunity to lay all the blame for what happened earlier on me.

I'm distracted when I walk out of the restroom, so when Paris's voice echoes in the hallway, I jump back, startled.

I press a hand to my chest. "Jeez, you almost gave me a heart attack."

"Sorry. I didn't mean to scare you." He smiles, revealing his adorable dimples.

A blush creeps onto my cheeks while my heart speeds up like a midfielder who just snagged the ball from the opposing team and has a clear path to the goal.

Keep it cool, Vanessa. Keep it cool.

"Are you waiting for someone?"

"Yeah. You."

My idiotic heart skips a beat. I croak, "Me? Why?"

"On a scale of one to ten, how mad is Heather right now?"

Disappointment floods through me. Did Paris just corner me to ask about my sister? I'm used to Heather getting all the attention from boys at school. She's blonde, beautiful, and has already developed all her assets, unlike me. I seem destined to have an athletic frame, which usually works for me. Right now, however, jealousy is coursing through me.

I cross my arms and frown. "Why do you care?"

Paris's smile wilts a fraction. "I don't care. I mean, I thought maybe you needed a break from her, if she's acting like a total dragon."

My irritation dissipates like magic. I was already getting a break from her, but he doesn't know that.

"What do you have in mind?" I ask.

His lips curl into a mischievous grin. "I can't tell you. It's top secret."

"So… what? Am I supposed to just follow you blindly?"

"Yeah. I promise it'll be cool."

Little does he know I'd follow him even if he was planning to open the gates of Hell.

God. That was dramatic. I think Heather's antics are rubbing off on me.

Waving my hand in a carefree way, I reply, "Fine. Lead the way."

His grin widens into a broad smile that makes my heart skip a beat. He doesn't say anything else, just veers in the opposite direction of where the group meetings are taking place. He has long legs, so I follow a bit behind him, which allows me to check him out. Unlike other thirteen-year-olds, Paris isn't scrawny. That's probably because of football. I've heard he's already the most popular boy at All Saints, the private middle school he goes to. We're in the same grade, but Heather and I attend public school.

I'm lost in admiring his tush and don't notice that he's led me out of the secondary building and to the back of the church. Cory, his older brother, is standing near a sycamore tree, looking hella suspicious.

"Did you get it?" Paris asks.

"Mathias hasn't come out yet."

"Uh, get what?" I butt in.

No sooner do I ask than Cory's friend walks out the back door, holding a bottle of red wine. *Crap.*

"You're joking, right?" I blurt out.

"Aw, come on, Vanessa. Don't tell me you're Miss Goody Two-shoes like your sister," Mathias pipes up.

"Please. I'm nothing like Heather." I turn to Paris. "You said this was gonna be cool."

His face falls, and I regret my words.

"You don't need to drink any," Mathias says before pulling the cork free with his teeth.

I've never tasted wine before, and I *am* a little curious. But the idea also makes me leery. The image of Aunt Marietta drunk at every family gathering has made me less keen to try alcohol.

Mathias takes a big chug of the wine and then passes the bottle to Cory, who follows his friend's example. I'm surprised to see him breaking the rules. I always pegged him as the responsible older brother. He drinks way more than Mathias, as if he wants to get wasted at any cost. When he finally lowers the bottle, I wonder if there's anything left. He wipes his mouth with the back of his hand but doesn't make a motion to return the bottle to his friend.

"Did you leave any for us?" Paris takes the bottle from Cory.

"Yeah, yeah, little bro. Still plenty for you and your girlfriend."

I gasp, and Paris replies quickly, "She's not my girlfriend."

My face is burning up, and I'm glad I don't blush as obviously as Heather does.

"Yeah, that'd be gross," I say.

Cory and Mathias laugh. I don't dare glance at Paris to see his reaction, so I look at my shoes instead. After a moment, Paris nudges my arm, forcing me to turn to him.

"Want some?" He offers me the bottle.

I wasn't planning to drink, but to recover from embarrassment, I accept the offer and bring the bottle's rim to my lips. The first sip almost makes me gag. I force it down, not wanting to increase my humiliation. The second gulp is larger and, as the alcohol goes down my throat, I begin to relax. I can't possibly be getting drunk already, can I?

"Hey! What are you kids doing back there?" someone yells in the distance.

I pivot on the spot, hiding the bottle of wine behind my back.

"Shit! That's one of the coordinators," Mathias blurts out. "Scram."

He and Cory take off toward the midsize public park next to the church grounds. I'm frozen, not knowing what to do. If the coordinator catches me with the wine, I'm screwed. My parents will flay me alive.

Paris takes my hand and tugs it. "Come on. We have to get out of here."

I let him steer me in the direction of the park. We run side by side, and I'm glad that, thanks to soccer, I can keep up with him and his extremely long legs. We've lost Cory and Mathias already, but we don't stop running until we reach the old tree house, deep in the forest. We don't go up, as it might fall apart at any moment. No one comes here save for teenagers looking for trouble.

Oh, that's us.

"Jesus! That was close." Paris drops my hand and then rests both of his on his knees as he catches his breath.

I'm not as winded as he is, and that fills my chest with pride. "At least we got the wine," I say.

He grins. "Hand it over. I'm parched."

I pass the bottle to him, but not before I take another sip. It doesn't taste as bad now. For a few minutes, we keep taking turns until the bottle is empty.

"I'm still thirsty," I say.

"Yeah, I don't think alcohol really helps with that."

"How long do you think we should stay hidden?" I glance at the sky, noticing it's already turning orange.

"We have to get back before our parents come to pick us up."

I shove my hands in my pockets. "Do you think the coordinator recognized us?"

His face twists into a grimace. "It's possible."

"Crap." I look away, thinking about what my punishment will be for ditching Bible study and getting drunk. My stomach feels queasy with the possibility that my parents might take soccer away from me.

Paris touches my shoulder. "Don't worry. If you get in trouble, I'll take full responsibility."

"That's not fair. No one forced me to skip class and drink wine."

He steps closer to me, making my breath hitch. "True, but I had ulterior motives for inviting you to tag along."

"What ulterior motives?" I whisper.

"Uh, getting you alone."

My brows shoot to the heavens. "You're not planning to kill me, are you?"

"What? No." He rubs the back of his neck. "I'm making a mess of things, and I don't think it has anything to do with the wine."

"You're not making any sense."

"I like you, Vanessa."

My jaw drops. Paris Andino *likes* me? Am I dreaming? Or maybe I'm having a drunken vision.

He steps toward me, his expression already falling. "I'm sorry. It was stupid of m—"

I jump into his space and throw my arms around his neck… and then I kiss him on the lips. He tenses, but then his arms wrap around my waist. That's as far as my drunken impulsiveness goes, though. I've never kissed anyone in my life, and I have no idea what to do next. I begin to pull back, but Paris frames my face with his hands and then teases my lips open with his tongue. Holy *shit*. I'm French kissing Paris Andino. Someone pinch me. I have no idea what I'm doing, but thanks to the wine, I'm not freaking out too much about it.

"Vanessa Cristine Castro!" My mother's shrill voice cuts through the air.

Paris and I jump apart and turn. My parents are standing not too far from us, and with them, Paris's parents and Cory. *Oh my god*. I want a hole to open and swallow me. Mom's shrewd gaze zeroes in on the discarded wine bottle at our feet, and then it's freaking Armageddon.

That's it. I'll be grounded for life.

TWO

"I can't believe you two!" my father yells from behind his desk. "I can't tell you how disappointed I am in your behavior."

I wince in my chair, trying to appear smaller, something that's almost impossible when I'm already almost five foot nine. Our father is mostly a calm person, but when he loses his temper, he *loses his temper*. Sadly, that's been happening more frequently, and Cory is often the target of his wrath.

"It was my idea, Dad. Just punish me," my brother says.

I shake my head, not willing to let him take the fall alone. "I drank the wine too."

Dad slams his open palm on the mahogany desk, shaking the two picture frames on it. "Enough! Both of you are grounded for a month. It's school and home."

"What about football?" I ask.

"You're the star of the team, I'm not going to screw over Coach Smith because you acted like an idiot. You can still play, but that's it. No going out for pizza with your teammates after a game."

That's going to suck, but at least I can still play.

I slouch in my chair, and reply meekly, "Okay."

"Will that also apply to my extracurricular activities?" Cory asks.

There's an edge to his tone, which means I might witness another argument between him and Dad. They've been at odds since he told us he wasn't playing football in high school. He wanted to pursue other interests. I believe Dad would have been okay with that—he isn't a crazy sports fan—if Cory's new interest wasn't art. He wants to pursue painting, and according to my parents, that's not a career.

"No. Your canvases and paint brushes will survive not being used for a month."

"I have a field trip to New York in two weeks. It's paid for."

Dad leans back in his plush leather chair. "You should have thought about that before you decided to steal Father Medina's wine."

"That's bullshit!" Cory jumps to his feet, almost sending his own chair tumbling back.

Dad's spine goes taut as he points a finger at Cory. "You just earned another week of punishment."

"Whatever." He stalks out of the office and bangs the door shut.

I'm not sure what to do. Cory used to be the role model for the perfect son. He never raised his voice and always did what he was told. But ever since he started high school, it's like he turned into a different person. Or a switch was flipped.

Dad pinches the bridge of his nose. "What's going on with your brother, Paris?"

"I don't know."

He picks up a framed photo of Cory and me. "I hardly recognize my own son."

"Maybe you could let him go to New York, I mean, since you're letting me play—"

"No, absolutely not." He sets the picture frame down. "He's

out of control. What I need to do is tighten the leash."

"I think he's just angry that you're not being supportive of his new interests. I mean, artists can make a lot of money, and he might change his mind later."

"That's the problem, son. Your brother went from being an *A* student to someone who doesn't care about anything besides getting into trouble. You'd tell me if your brother was taking drugs, wouldn't you?"

I swallow the lump in my throat. I refuse to believe Cory would be involved with drugs. "I don't think he is, Dad. Truly."

"It's a good thing you're still at All Saints. I knew we should have kept Cory in private school."

I have no comment to that. The only private school in Littleton that goes through high school is as expensive as an Ivy League college. My parents have money, but not that kind of money.

"How long do you think Mom will stay mad at the Castros?" I ask to change the subject, and also because I want to know if it'd be safe to ask Vanessa to be my girlfriend.

She doesn't go to All Saints, and the only chance I get to see her is at church. But if my parents aren't on speaking terms with hers, getting her alone again will be hard. I was kicked out of the youth program—not that I cared about confirmation anyway.

Dad gives me a droll look. "Have you met your mother? The Castros will stay on her blacklist until she dies."

Great.

"May I be excused?" I ask.

He waves his hand. "Yes. And Paris, please don't go looking for more trouble, okay? I can't deal with two rebel sons."

"I won't," I lie.

There's no chance I'm going to give up on Vanessa. But before I contact her, I should probably wait until the dust settles. She doesn't have a cell phone, and she isn't on social media. I have no choice but to wait for another opportunity to get her alone.

THREE

I haven't seen or heard from Paris in two weeks. He and Cory didn't attend service the Sunday following the wine incident, so I had to bear all the judgmental glances alone. I'm glad that the gossip in my school lasted only a couple of days, and it wasn't bad. Mostly the girls wanted to know what kissing Paris Andino was like. Yeah, he's popular in my school too.

Maybe the kiss didn't mean anything to him, or I sucked at it. Schoolwork and soccer practice keep me busy though, and the days begin to blend together. I can't say that I don't think about him, and on occasion, my mother will bring up Paris's mother during dinner by calling her that "horrible woman," and one of those instances is now.

"I saw her at the supermarket today. She has an assistant to help her with groceries. An assistant!" She gestures wildly with her hands.

"Maybe she was buying a lot of things, honey," Dad replies calmly.

It's an English-only day in our house, which means Mom's

tirade won't be as colorful as it would if she were speaking Portuguese. My parents moved from Rio de Janeiro to California just after they got married, because Dad received an amazing job offer. Heather and I were born in California, and we went through a phase growing up when we refused to speak Portuguese even though we had other family members living nearby. I guess a lot of bilingual kids go through that. But now that we speak both languages fluently, my parents decided it would be good for Mom to practice her English more, since she's less exposed to it—most of her friends speak either Portuguese or Spanish.

"She has two sons. Why can't they help her? It's in poor taste, I tell you."

"I heard they're still grounded," Heather pipes up.

I whip around to her. "Who told you that?"

"Tara Carmichael. Her parents are friends with one of the Andinos' neighbors. The Andinos were at the party but without Paris and Cory."

"Maybe they didn't want to go to the party."

"Well, the hosts' daughter, some girl named Lydia, goes to All Saints as well, and she confirmed that Paris is only allowed to leave the house for school and football."

Mom snorts. "That's the least punishment that pervert should get for trying to corrupt Vanessa."

My face heats in a flash. I drop my gaze to my plate and cease asking questions about Paris. But Heather seems determined to keep talking about him.

While Mom continues to talk about her day, Heather leans close and whispers in my ear. "You have competition, sis. Tara told me this Lydia chick all but implied she's Paris's girlfriend."

I clutch the fork and knife tighter. "Whatever. I don't care."

"Right. Well, it's good if you don't. He's cute and all, but he isn't the last cookie in the package."

The food tastes like ashes now, and I can barely swallow.

Not much later, the doorbell rings several times in a row, and when we don't get to the door yet, the knocking comes.

"Oh my god. What now?" Mom gets up in a huff and strides toward the front of the house.

Since I've lost my appetite, I follow her to see what the commotion's about.

Aunt Marietta storms in like a freaking hurricane, carrying several shopping bags. She's my mother's cousin, but Heather and I call her aunt. I'm not sure why she brought all the bags into the house instead of leaving them in her car, until I realize she probably came by taxi so she could drink during her shopping spree.

"What are you doing here, Marietta?" Mom asks.

"*Prima, babado fortíssimo pra te contar,*" she starts in Portuguese.

Mom doesn't really care for her, and with a scowl firmly in place, she replies, "In English, please."

"Fine! Well, I was doing some shopping downtown when I heard the most awful news. One of the Andino boys is dead."

My blood freezes in my veins, and it feels like I'm falling into the hole that opened underneath my feet.

"Oh my god. Which one?" Mom asks, pressing a hand against her chest. Like she cares.

"I think the oldest. Dreadful thing. Apparently he killed himself and the younger one found the body." She makes the sign of the cross as if she were a religious person. I feel like yelling at her, demanding more information, but I can't find my voice.

Heather pulls me into a side hug. I didn't notice her walking over.

"That's terrible news," Dad says.

"I need to see Paris," I blurt out.

Everyone looks at me as if I just sprouted a second head.

"You're not leaving this house, young lady," Mom retorts.

"Mom, please. Now is not the time for pettiness," I beg.

She widens her eyes. "I'm not being petty. It's not appropriate, Vanessa."

"Your mother is right, honey. We don't know when this happened, and I'm pretty sure everyone is still in shock. You should wait until tomorrow."

My vision is blurry with unshed tears. I turn around and run upstairs before they can see me cry my eyes out. I dive onto my bed and hide my face under a pillow. My heart is breaking for Paris and his family. I didn't spend as much time with Cory as I did with Paris, but he was always nice to me. Why would he kill himself? He was always in a good mood, always had a smile on his face.

Heather comes in and sits on the edge of my mattress. "It's going to be okay, Nessa."

She never calls me by that nickname unless I'm hurt, like when I get injured playing soccer. I'd trade physical pain for this agony burning in my chest any time.

"He lost his brother, Heather. How can that be okay?"

"It won't be for a long time, but eventually, it will get better."

I turn around, wiping the moisture from my cheeks. "I need to see Paris tonight."

"Are you sure? Maybe you should wait until tomorrow, like Dad said."

Determined now, I sit up. "No. I'm going tonight. Will you cover for me?"

"How do you plan to get there?"

"By bike. It's not that far."

"Do you remember the way?"

I went to Paris's house once last year, before our folks became mortal enemies.

I nod. "I think so."

She studies me for a couple seconds before she replies, "Okay."

I don't waste a minute. I put on a hoodie and then a pair of sneakers before Heather and I tiptoe down the stairs. Aunt

Marietta is still talking nonstop. Everyone is in the living room, leaving the path to the garage door clear. It's torture, walking slowly to avoid making noise, but eventually I get to the garage.

"I'll tell everyone you're not feeling well," Heather says before I take off.

"Thank you. I owe you one."

"Yes, you do. I hope you get to see Paris. If you do, tell him I'm sorry too."

Her words make me choke, and almost reignite the tears. But I can't cry, not now when I need clear vision.

I pedal as fast as I can, hoping not to get lost. I remember a few landmarks that help guide me, but it's already dark, and I'm afraid I might miss a turn. I sharpen my focus, and just when I think I've gone too far, I see a familiar car signal to turn right. It's Father Medina's car. He must be going to Paris's house.

It turns out he was heading to the same destination, because when I get there, he's already parked and left the car. But I recognize the neighborhood and the house's brick exterior and red door.

My heart is about to leap out of my throat and my breaths come in bursts. I remove my helmet and stride toward Paris's front door. I'm shaking, suddenly afraid that my presence will only make things worse.

I finally gather the courage to ring the doorbell, and then I wait on pins and needles. I expect Paris's mother to answer the door, or perhaps her assistant, but instead it's a girl my age.

"Whatever you're selling, now is not a good time," she says with an air of arrogance.

Who the hell is she?

"I'm not selling anything. I'm Paris's friend. I came to see him."

Her eyes narrow as if what I said offended her. "Well, he can't see anyone right now."

"You don't know that," I retort, not willing to be sent away by this annoying stranger.

"Lydia, who is it?" a female voice asks from inside the house.

Hell, this is the neighbor who claims she's Paris's girlfriend.

Maybe she is. Why else would she be here?

She looks over her shoulder, and replies, "Some girl who wants to see Paris. I told her he can't see anyone right now."

A woman in her fifties bearing a strong resemblance to Paris's mother joins the obnoxious girl blocking my way. Her eyes are red and puffy. "I'm sorry, dear, but he's not in any shape to see anyone at the moment. I'll tell him you stopped by, okay? What's your name?"

"It's Vanessa Castro. When do you think I can talk to him?"

Her face crumples, and I think she's on the verge of crying. "It's hard to say. Why don't you call the house first before dropping by?"

"Okay. I'll do that."

She shuts the door in my face before I have a chance to step back. Now I'm heartbroken and jealous as hell. With heavy feet and an even heavier heart, I trudge back to my bike. A sense of numbness washes over me. I ignore the thunder and lightning that sparks in the sky, and the rain that drenches me in a matter of seconds. I take a sharp curve going too fast and lose control.

The last things I remember are approaching headlights and the sound of tires screeching.

FOUR

The John Rushmore main cafeteria is as busy as ever, despite the time of the day. There are smaller dining halls in different buildings, but this is the one most of the student body prefers, mainly because the jocks and Greeks prefer it and are here at all hours. I come here because the food is better. It's way past lunchtime and I don't know what all these people are still doing here. Today, I'm not in the mood to brave the crowds, though. Honestly, I'd have gone to a fast-food joint, but Coach Lauda has put all of us on a healthy diet, so I have to set the example for the girls. After all, I'm team captain.

Joanne is the last to join us at the table, and her tray has enough food for at least three football players.

"What's all that?" Steff, our keeper, asks.

"I'm trying to eat things I've never had before," she grumbles.

"And you decided to eat them all at once?" I ask through a chuckle.

"I'm pretty sure I'll hate eighty percent of what I got, and I really don't want to stand in that huge line again. Why is it still so busy?"

"Who knows? Maybe the football gods are making an appearance," Steff replies without hiding her sarcasm.

I don't have anything against the Rebels, save for one particular player. Paris Andino and I have a history—something no one on my team knows, and I plan to keep it that way. I'd die of embarrassment if they found out he was my first kiss and that, later, he pretended I didn't exist.

Jackass.

I inspect Joanne's tray carefully, noticing her selection is not that eclectic. I see an egg salad sandwich, a falafel, a pyro with Greek salad, and a regular ham and cheese sub.

"Why do you think you need to change how you eat?" Phoebe asks, tossing her multicolored hair over her shoulder.

"I've been told I'm a picky eater."

I trade a glance with Steff. Could the person who said that be Joanne's mysterious girlfriend?

"Where's Sadie?" Charlotte chimes in. "I thought she was joining us."

"Didn't you see her message in the group chat?" Joanne asks.

When Charlotte gives her a blank stare, I add, "She was running late, which is code for she got busy with Danny."

"Those crazy kids have been going at each other like two horny rabbits. It's a miracle they have any energy left for sports," Steff pipes up, right before she shoves a piece of chocolate in her mouth.

"Hey, what's that?" I glower.

Her eyes widen innocently, but the corners of her mouth twitch up. "What?"

"I saw that piece of chocolate, Steff. We're all supposed to be eating healthier during the week," I retort, more angrily than is warranted.

I want a piece of chocolate, damn it. I'm about the get my period, and the craving is bad. I'm pretty sure I'll cave at home, because now that I saw her eat some, my mouth is watering. I stare at my fruit salad and feel depressed. I so don't want to eat that right now.

The chat continues, but I notice Phoebe is staring at her plate of food with a downcast expression. She seems paler too.

I reach across the table and touch her hand. "Hey, are you okay?"

She looks up. "Yeah. I think I need some orange juice to wash down my sandwich."

She gets up before I can offer to tag along. I keep my eyes trained on her though. She looked like she was about to pass out. Once she's out of the area with all the tables, she seems to trip over something and staggers forward, right into the arms of Paris.

Hell. I knew something was off. I jump out of my seat and make a beeline toward her. But an entire table decides to vacate just then, and several people end up blocking my way. It takes me a few extra seconds to reach them, and by the time I do, Lydia is there, yelling at poor Phoebe.

Son of a bitch.

"What's going on here?" I ask, not hiding my aggravation.

Phoebe puts her hand on her forehead and sways a little. Shit. She *is* sick. I step next to her and take her arm, steadying her.

"It's nothing," Paris replies.

"Nothing my ass," Lydia shrieks. "That girl was all over your space, Paris."

"I tripped," Phoebe replies feebly.

"Are you okay, hon?" I ask her, ignoring Lydia Bitch Face.

"I need to use the restroom."

"Okay. Let's go."

"Keep your players away from Paris, Vanessa," Lydia sneers.

I whip my face in her direction. "Fuck off, Lydia."

"Hey, that wasn't necessary." Paris comes to his girlfriend's defense, making my blood boil.

I switch my death glare to him. "Keep a leash on your bitchy girlfriend, Paris. You may be a pussy when it comes to her, but no one else is."

PARIS

I swallow the retort that bubbles up my throat as I watch Vanessa steer her teammate away from us. Her long dark hair is pulled back into a high ponytail, and it sways back and forth in a hypnotic way. I should look away, but I can't. She's always had that power over me. I don't know who I'm more angry at right now—Vanessa or myself. I should aim my annoyance at Lydia, but she's out of control like that because I let her get away with shit. Her antics are getting old and making it much harder to remember why I put up with them in the first place.

"I can't believe you let that bitch talk to us like that," Lydia complains.

"What did you want me to do? Curse at them, start a fight? You're the one who caused the drama." I turn around and head for the cafeteria's exit.

I sense several pairs of eyes staring at us. As usual, Lydia created a circus, and I'm once again the clown in her show.

"She had her hands all over you. I'm sick and tired of bimbos coming on to you."

I push the door open with excessive force and increase my pace. Lydia has to run to keep up with me.

"She tripped. I just happened to be in her way," I grit out.

"Whatever. I don't buy it."

I stop suddenly and whirl around. We're now in the middle of the quad, and there are fewer people around. "You need to stop with this nonsense, Lydia."

Her doe eyes widen and become brighter. Damn it. Here come the waterworks.

"I can't stop it. Every girl on campus wants to take you away from me. No one cares that you have a girlfriend. How do you think that makes me feel?"

"I can't help what other people do. I'm with you, and you need to trust me. I never give you any reason to be jealous."

The tears roll down her cheeks. Any other time, I'd pull her into a hug and console her. But I'm finally beginning to see her behavior as pure manipulation. Still, I hesitate. There's a part of me that fears her over-the-top reaction is out of her control. I remember that horrible day when I found Cory unresponsive. My stomach twists into painful knots.

Lydia wipes her tears with a jerky swipe of her fingers and then gives her back to me. Her entire body is shaking.

Hell.

I walk over and pull her back to my chest. "Please don't cry."

"I can't help it. I've been under so much stress. Do you know how hard it is to get into a good medical program?"

"Uh, I'm premed too, remember?" I turn her around in my arms and tuck a loose strand of hair behind her ear.

Her expression softens, and then she rises on her tiptoes and presses her lips to mine.

There was a time when her kisses would spread warmth through my chest. Now, my heart constricts painfully. I know it's over, but how do I tell her when she's already spiraling?

Cory's death might not have been my fault, but if I end things with Lydia now and she does something drastic, I'll never forgive myself.

FIVE

As I walk across the Morales Country Club parking lot, I tug down the hem of my dress. The fabric itches and I hate the color—a burnt orange that makes me look like a pumpkin—but I can't complain. If I had gone shopping with Mom and Heather in Littleton last month, I would have been able to choose something more my style. Our hometown isn't far from LA, where John Rushmore University is located, but when it comes to my family, the notion of a quick visit doesn't exist.

"Stop fidgeting, Vanessa. You look like you have fleas," Mom complains.

Heather snickers. "Maybe she does."

"Shut your face, Heather."

"Girls, can you please not bicker tonight?" Dad asks in his patient voice.

"What's this dress made of? Pine needles?" I turn to my mother.

She rolls her eyes. "It's gorgeous. Just stand straighter and think about how much fun you'll have tonight."

Unlikely. Coming to these stuffy parties at my parents' club is a pain in my ass. Not even Heather seems to enjoy them anymore—probably because she already dated all the cute guys from the club throughout high school. And most of them won't be back home for this anyway, since many went to out-of-state colleges. Heather and I both got scholarships to attend Rushmore—I got one for soccer, and Heather for cheerleading—so going there was a no-brainer. Besides, Rushmore is an excellent school. The only drawback is its closeness to Littleton.

Inside the main building, we follow the herd of new arrivals to the reception area, where high tables have been strategically distributed and waiters are serving canapés and glasses of champagne. Heather and I each take a glass, and while our folks are distracted greeting old friends, we go in different directions and blend in with the crowd. I find a corner where no one can disturb me and pull out my cell phone.

The Ravens group chat is quiet tonight, and I think that has to do with the gruesome training session we had today. My legs aren't *too* sore yet, but tomorrow is going to be murder.

> VANESSA: How is everyone tonight?

> SADIE: I want to die.

> JOANNE: Same. I can't feel my legs.

> STEFF: You guys are a bunch of whiny babies.
> I'm fine.

I see that Sadie starts typing a reply but decides not to send the message in the end. A grin tugs the corners of my lips. I bet she was typing something sassy and thought better of it. I take a sip of my drink and type my response.

> VANESSA: Make sure you rest tonight,
> especially you, Sadie.

> SADIE: Bloody hell. Why are you singling me out?

> STEFF: Maybe because of your bedroom activities. 🥒

> SADIE: Don't be haters because you aren't getting any. Besides, Danny is great with his tongue.

> JOANNE: Whoa. TMI, sister.

A bubble of laughter goes up my throat. I knew chatting with the girls would lift my spirits.

"What's so funny?" a male voice asks.

I tense, knowing who I'm going to find standing in front of me. Paris fucking Andino.

"None of your business." I swipe away the group-chat screen and lower my phone.

"You're mad at me. Is it because of the cafeteria incident?" he asks, seeming unfazed by my harsh reply.

Ignoring his asinine question, I ask one of my own. "Where's your girlfriend? Am I going to be called a tramp because you're talking to me?"

Guilt seems to shine in his eyes. It was the same look he gave me when we got caught making out in the forest after drinking all that wine. "She's not here." His voice is tight and cold.

"Pity. I was looking forward to another lovely conversation with her."

"I didn't come here to argue with you. Yeah, what Lydia said was shitty, but—"

"There's no *but*, Paris. Your girlfriend is a heinous bitch, and I don't know what's more pathetic—the fact that you put up with it, or that you actually defend her actions."

He runs his fingers through his hair and sighs. "You don't

know what's going on, okay? I'm trying my best to do the right thing."

His confession gives me pause. "Why? What kind of hold does Lydia have over you?"

He swallows hard, making his Adam's apple bob up and down. "For starters, she was there for me when I needed it most."

My stomach drops through the earth. He must be referring to when he lost his brother. I touch the scar near my elbow, remembering that day.

"That's hardly a reason to stay with someone," I reply.

Paris's hard gaze stays on my face as he clenches his jaw. I want to know what he's thinking, but the moment is interrupted by his phone's ringtone. I can guess who's calling him.

He answers the call with a "Hey baby," and that's my cue to leave. I can't handle listening to his conversation. It's puke inducing.

I don't go far before Heather finds me.

"What did Paris want?" she asks.

"I have no clue."

"Riiight." She narrows her eyes. "Tell me, sis. Why do you dislike his girlfriend so much? Is it because she's a bitch, or because she's dating the guy you like?"

"Do you seriously think I care who Paris dates? He was just a stupid crush when I was thirteen."

She gives me a droll look. "Come on, you disobeyed our parents and rode off on your bike during a downpour to get to that boy. You even got a scar as a result. He was more than a crush, and you aren't over him yet."

Heather walks away before I can refute her theory. There's no point though. She isn't wrong. I don't think I'm over Paris, which is crazy. It's been *nine years*, for crying out loud. A first kiss shouldn't carry that much weight. I thought focusing on soccer would be enough to make me forget about him, but apparently not. To get over someone, you need to get under someone else. Which means…

I need a boyfriend.

***

PARIS

I should have known Lydia wouldn't allow me to enjoy an evening without her. She couldn't attend the charity gala with me and my parents tonight because she has to study. I could have given them an excuse and not come, but I was hoping Vanessa would be here. Like me, she often gets roped into family events. I wasn't wrong, but as usual, our conversation went south fast.

I'm annoyed—or rather, conflicted as hell—about my motives for being at this party. Dealing with Lydia on top of everything is not what I want. She calls, citing a panic attack, and she's alone in her dorm room. I'm already feeling guilty. I went to talk to Vanessa with the excuse of apologizing, but the truth is, I just wanted to be near her. I'm not sure what it is about her, but every time we interact—meaning argue—it brings back feelings I thought I had buried a long time ago. She was my first crush, my first kiss, and truth be told, I've never gotten over her.

Hence why I walk out of the party without telling my folks I'm leaving. We didn't come together, which allows me to sneak out.

No sooner do I get behind the steering wheel of my truck than heavy rain begins to fall, creating a curtain of water around me. I drive carefully, especially since I've had a few drinks already.

Shit. This wasn't a smart move, Paris.

I decide to park and wait for the rain to lessen. As I look for a safe place to pull over, something darts in front of my truck, and in a knee-jerk reaction, I turn the wheel sharply to my right to avoid running over whatever it is. The tires lose traction, and the truck spins out of control. My pulse skyrockets as I attempt to stop what's happening, which is pointless. The truck crashes against something solid, and pain explodes all over my face thanks to the airbag.

My breath comes in bursts, and it takes a moment for my heart to stop trying to jump out of my chest. When the shock begins to dissipate, the sound of an approaching siren makes me tense. Hell. If the cops ask me to take a breathalyzer test, I'm screwed. I throw my head against the headrest, close my eyes, and think about how I put myself in this situation.

Vanessa's parting words come to the forefront of my mind. Being with Lydia because she helped me through tough times is not an excuse to stay with her. It's been a while since she cared about anything other than herself.

The siren stops, and a car door opens. Johnny Law is here. I open my eyes and, a moment later, he's standing just outside my window.

"Are you okay there, son?"

I lower the window and face my doom. "I've had better evenings."

"The ambulance is on its way." He narrows his eyes. "You're on the Rebels football team, aren't you? Paris Andino?"

I know there are quite a number of Rebels fans in Littleton, but I'm a bit surprised the cop is one of them.

"Yes, sir."

He rubs his face, looking worried. "Can you move your legs and arms?"

"I don't think I broke anything."

"Good. Good. Don't worry, son. We'll get you out of here in one piece."

He doesn't even ask if I've been drinking. I can't believe my luck. I close my eyes and send a little prayer to whatever is out there. It seems my ill-fated decision will not ruin my life after all. But it definitely brought much-needed clarity.

This accident might not end my career, but it'll definitely be the end of something else.

SIX

PARIS - SIX MONTHS LATER

My phone vibrates in my pocket. It's the only reason I notice it's ringing. The bar is too crowded and loud. Not surprising, considering Tailgaters has a two-for-one special tonight. I check my phone, and when I see who's calling, I shove it right back in. Lydia has been blowing it up ever since she returned from her retreat in Colorado, and after a peaceful summer of being single and drama-free, I'm not keen to let her back into my life. Our breakup was not an easy one. There were tears, and suicide threats. I had to get her parents involved, because I was done carrying the burden alone. I feel some remorse over it, but I have to put myself first. It's the first week of my senior year at Rushmore, and I want to enjoy it.

"Your pants are shaking, bro," Andreas pipes up.

I take a sip of my beer before replying. "I know. It's Lydia again."

"Oh shit. She's back from Colorado, right?" Danny asks.

"Yep."

"I don't blame you for avoiding her. I know too well what it's like to be in a toxic relationship." Danny shudders.

My teammates never hid that they didn't like my ex very much. Andreas was the most vocal about his dislike. Danny tried to be more diplomatic. But since I broke up with Lydia, everyone stopped walking on eggshells when the topic was her.

"Well, you have Sadie now," I say, genuinely happy for him.

"Yeah." His face splits into a goofy grin, making him look younger than he is. He just turned twenty-one, but I still see him as the baby of the team.

All my friends have awesome girlfriends, and I'm not the least bit jealous. Truth be told, I don't want to jump into another serious relationship until I'm thirty and my parents start to get on my nerves about settling down. I want to know what it's like to live without worrying about someone else.

Andreas throws his arm over Danny's shoulder. "We got the golden ticket, Danny Boy." He looks sheepishly at me. "Ah, sorry, dude. You're going to find your special girl too. Don't worry."

I open my mouth to say I'm in no hurry when I catch sight of Vanessa Castro across the room. She's with her loser boyfriend, and I'm not sure why, but seeing them together puts me in a foul mood.

"What are you staring at?" Andreas asks, following my line of vision. "Ah, maybe Paris has already found his target."

I glower. "Shut your mouth, Rossi."

His eyes widen. "Jesus, will you relax? I was just kidding. I know you two are like cats and dogs."

"But sometimes that's the attraction, isn't it? Enemies to lovers and all," Danny chimes in.

"Come again?" Andreas raises an eyebrow. "Are you reading Sadie's romance novels?"

Danny scoffs. "Sadie doesn't read romance, but so you know, enemies to lovers is a universal trope found in other genres outside of romance."

"Sure, sure." Andreas laughs.

"Don't listen to him. Everyone knows Rossi is an uncultured swine."

"What the fuck, Andino," Andreas retorts.

I finish the rest of my beer and tell them I'm getting another round. Then I make my way to the bar. After I catch the bartender's attention, my gaze wanders to Vanessa and her boyfriend on the other side of it. She seems tense, and the douche looks unhappy about something. It looks like they're having an argument, but it's impossible to hear anything over the loud music blasting from the speakers.

I shouldn't stare. Couples fight. It's normal. But something seems off. It's only when the bartender returns with my drinks that I peel my gaze away from them.

"Thanks," I tell him.

Unable to resist, I glance in Vanessa's direction again, but she's gone.

VANESSA

I walk out of the crowded bar and take a deep breath of the cool evening air. It's the end of August, and finally summer has begun to lose its grip on the weather. I'm a fall girl through and through.

I hoped Ryan wouldn't follow me, but he comes right out.

"So that's it? You're just going to walk away from me?" he says.

"That was the idea, but it seems you won't let me do that either."

"Excuse me for not wanting my girlfriend to spend the weekend in Vegas with a bunch of hos."

I whip my face to his. "Hos? So my cousins and my sister are whores to you?"

Ryan sneers, turning his beautiful-in-a-preppy-way face into an ugly mask. "I've seen the way they dress."

"Unbelievable. You know what, Ryan? I don't give a fuck what you think. We're done."

I stride away, fuming. I can't believe I wasted six months of my life with this asshole. That's what I get for breaking my rules about dating. I always swore I wouldn't date a frat boy because, in my book, they're all fuckers. Ryan proved me right.

"Don't you dare walk away from me."

"Watch me." Without looking back, I raise my hand and flip him off.

He drove, which sucks, but the bar isn't far from my place, so I'm fine with walking. I hear Ryan run after me, which I ignore. That is, until he grabs my arm and yanks me back.

"I told you not to walk away from me," he grits out.

"Let me go!" I try to break free from his grasp, but he sinks his fingers deeper into my arm.

"I don't think so, sugar. You see, *I'm* the one who decides when this relationship ends, and I'm not done with you yet."

He pulls me toward him, snaking his free arm around my waist, and then forces his mouth on me. I clamp my lips shut as I try to push him off. I can't budge him, and that makes me even madder. I'm not a helpless chick—I should be able to fight him off. He pushes me against the side of a random car and nudges my legs apart with one thigh. Fucking hell. Is he seriously assaulting me?

Adrenaline shoots through my veins. I refuse to be the victim. He's stronger than I am, so I use the only weapon at my disposal. My teeth. I bite his lower lip until I taste blood.

He pulls his head back, touching the cut. "You bit me," he says, as if he's surprised.

His body is still blocking me, but there's a gap between us now, so I use that to my advantage. I shove him back with my free hand, hoping he'll release me. No such luck. His eyes turn murderous, and in the next second, his hand is wrapped around my neck and he's choking me.

"You fucking bitch. Who do you think you are?"

"I may be a bitch, but not your bitch, asshole."

"We'll see about that." He squeezes my throat tighter, and then traps my arm between our bodies before he releases my wrist and thrusts his hand up my skirt.

Angry tears gather in my eyes. I can't scream, and I can't free my arm to punch the side of his face. His fingers are already inside of me, rough and invasive. But the most concerning part is that I can't breathe, and black dots are forming in my vision. He's going to kill me before he has the chance to rape me. Or maybe that's his goal—to fuck my corpse.

"Get off her!" someone yells.

Ryan is yanked back in the next second, and as I gasp for air, I see that my savior is none other than Paris.

Ryan staggers back and then tries to punch Paris, but he's no match for the Rebels' linebacker. Paris blocks his punch and delivers one of his own, sending Ryan to the ground.

"You asshole! You broke my nose," Ryan whines a moment later.

"Oh, I plan to break way more than that, motherfucker." He steps toward him, but I finally snap out of my paralysis and grab the back of Paris's jacket.

"No. He's not worth it." My voice sounds hoarse.

He looks over his shoulder, confusion etched on his face. "He assaulted you."

His words feel like a punch to my throat. I know what Ryan did, but hearing it out loud gives it more meaning, more weight.

"And he's going to get what he deserves, but not from you."

"Say goodbye to football, fucker. I'll make sure you never play again," Ryan retorts, already back on his feet.

The fact that he thinks he can issue threats after what he did to me makes my blood boil. I walk around Paris, and before Ryan knows what's coming for him, I kick his family jewels with all my strength.

He howls, bending forward while he cradles his junk. "You

crazy bitch," he wheezes.

Paris gets between Ryan and me and asks, "Are you okay?"

"I'm shaken, but okay."

He keeps staring at me as if he wants to peer into my thoughts and check if I'm telling the truth. Finally, he asks, "Do you want to call the cops?"

I'm still riding the anger and adrenaline, yet the idea of rehashing what happened with a bunch of strangers makes me queasy. Hell, and what about my parents? If the police get involved, they'll know, and then my entire family will know. The story will follow me for the rest of my life. I'll cease to be Vanessa, the kickass soccer player, and become the Castro girl who was almost raped by her douche ex.

"No," I say. "Hopefully, I ended his ability to procreate tonight."

Paris narrows his eyes and clenches his jaw so hard, I can almost hear his teeth grinding together. He's judging my decision, like he always does. I shouldn't expect any less from him.

The sound of a car peeling out of the parking lot draws my attention to where Ryan had been a minute ago. The weasel took advantage of our moment of distraction and ran away.

Paris curses under his breath, aggravating me further.

"Why are you upset? I'm the one who was attacked."

He opens and shuts his mouth without saying a word, and then shakes his head. "I'm not upset, I'm angry as fuck."

"Me too." I cross my arms, feeling cold and vulnerable.

It seems the effects of the adrenaline are gone and the reality of what happened tonight has finally sunk in fully.

"I'll take you home," he says softly, which only makes matters worse.

I'm on the verge of crying now, but hell if I'll let the tears fall in front of him. He saved me from a horrible situation tonight, but that hasn't erased all the occasions he acted like a jerk toward me.

I follow him to his truck in silence, and the nonverbal streak continues all the way to my place. Only when he parks in front of my house does it dawn on me that I never gave him my address. I live near campus in a rental my parents got for Heather and me after our freshman year. Quite a few students rent in this neighborhood, but there are also young families. Our house isn't new, and we've had a few plumbing issues, but I love that the neighborhood is quiet and safe.

"How do you know where I live?"

"I've been here before."

My brows arch. "You have? When?"

"I don't know. Last year? Heather threw a party when you were at an away game."

That information should make me angry again. Heather never told me about any party. We have a deal that parties need to be agreed upon by both of us beforehand. But I've spent all my rage, and all that's left is sadness.

"Well, thanks for giving me a ride home." I reach for the door handle.

"Are you going to be okay? Is your sister home?"

"I don't think she's home, but I'll be fine," I lie.

Paris, being the nosy person he is, doesn't buy my bullshit. "I'll wait with you until she gets home. You shouldn't be alone."

I'd fight him, because he's not the boss of me, but the truth is, he's right. I could call Sadie, or any of my other teammates, but then I'd have to tell them what's wrong, and I don't want anyone to know. I suppose Paris will have to do.

"Okay. You can come in."

Tilting his head, he stares at me. "Good. I was expecting you to be difficult."

"No. I've run out of sass." I get out of the truck and don't wait for Paris to follow me.

By the time I reach the front door, tears are rolling down my cheeks, and I pray he doesn't see them.

SEVEN

I almost said the wrong thing to Vanessa back in that parking lot. I couldn't believe she didn't want to call the cops. But clarity came to me before I could put my foot in my mouth. Who am I to judge her decision in that situation? I'm glad she let me come into her house, but now I don't know what to do.

As soon as she opened the front door, she bolted down the hallway. I glance around, noticing that everything is immaculate and organized. Even the picture frames on the bookshelf are placed in chronological order. I spend some time looking at them, but when I see a picture of our old youth group at church, I have to look away. Cory and I are in that picture.

I wonder why it's on display and who put it there. Vanessa didn't seem to care much about my family back then. She never called or came to see me after Cory died. And then she acted surprised when I didn't want anything to do with her when we met again in high school.

I shake my head, refusing to dwell on the past, and make myself comfortable on her couch. But as much as I don't want to think about our younger years, I can't help it. I was a mess, and even if she didn't want to be my girlfriend, I could have used a friend.

Time slips by, and when I finally return to the present, I see that a half hour has passed and Vanessa is still in her room. I'm all for respecting people's privacy, but I'm worried sick she might do something foolish. I have to check on her.

Mind made up, I take a few steps toward the hall, but I freeze when I hear a door open at the end. I debate running back to the couch, but this house is too small, and she'd catch me. A few seconds later, she returns to the living area and finds me there, rooted to the spot like a damn tree.

Her eyes widen a fraction. "Were you coming to check on me?"

I rub the back of my neck. "Yeah."

"I had to take a very long shower."

It's then that I notice her hair is damp. I also see the red mark that asshole left on her neck. The anger from before returns with a vengeance. "Is your throat bothering you?"

She covers the mark with her hand. "A little."

"I can make you tea with honey." I veer for the open kitchen without waiting for her reply.

"It's my house, Paris."

I look over my shoulder and take note of her standing there, a frown on her face and her hands on her hips. Something stirs in my mind, and my pulse accelerates. It's an old memory of her, looking at me just like that before everything went to hell. Despite the current situation, I grin. That pissed-off look is better than the dead look in her eyes from before. "I know it's your house, but I want to help."

"Aren't you the gentleman?" She crosses her arms.

"Sarcasm noted. For your information, I *am* a gentleman."

She snorts. "I guess for a select few."

"Are you still mad about last semester's incident?"

"That's just your most recent offense. You took your

girlfriend's side as usual, even though you knew she was being a fucking bitch."

I wince. Vanessa isn't wrong. I've acted like a total jerk many times because of Lydia.

"I'm sorry. I had my reasons. Besides, she's no longer my girlfriend. I thought you knew that."

She scoffs, rolling her eyes. "It took you long enough. I bet your teammates let out a collective sigh of relief."

She's not holding back, but everything coming out of her mouth is a reminder of the firecracker girl who stole my heart when I was thirteen. I smirk. "Andy set off fireworks to celebrate."

Surprisingly, she returns the grin. "That tracks."

We don't speak for a couple of beats. I don't know why she's staring at me in silence, but I know why I'm staring back. My heart is beating faster, the same way it did all those years ago when we were alone in the park and I confessed I liked her.

"You said you'd make tea?" she asks, breaking the spell.

I blink fast, and then look at everything but her. "Yeah. Just point me in the right direction."

She walks around me and proceeds to open cabinets. "Heather and I aren't huge tea drinkers, but I know I saw chamomile here somewhere."

After she empties most of the cupboard, she finally locates the tea box, which she sets on the counter next to two coffee mugs and a jar of honey.

"There. Now you have everything you need to make tea."

"Uh, where's your kettle?"

"Don't have one. Just stick the mug in the microwave." She's grinning when she heads to the living room. I suppose there isn't much to making tea, and she did half the job by getting the supplies ready.

Well, there's nothing for it but to make the tea.

Vanessa turns on the TV, and when I join her carrying two

steamy cups of tea with honey, I see she has *The Fellowship of the Ring* on the wide screen.

"I didn't know you were a *Lord of the Rings* fan." I set one mug in front of her on the coffee table.

She pulls a pillow over her lap and crosses her legs. "I don't trust anyone who isn't a fan."

My lips twitch upward. "That's a good qualifier to judge one's character."

I bet that motherfucker ex of hers didn't like *Lord of the Rings*.

"Ryan hated it," she says as if reading my mind. "I should have dumped his sorry ass when I found out."

She reaches for her mug and blows on the liquid before taking a tentative sip.

"I never understood why you went out with that loser in the first place."

Her expression closes off. "You're one to talk."

"Touché. But in my defense, Lydia wasn't always difficult. I wouldn't have fallen in love with her otherwise."

I don't know why I said that to Vanessa. Maybe I'm trying to salvage my reputation for being such a pussy. I'm not even sure I ever truly loved Lydia. I try my tea, burning my tongue in the process. I should have blown on it first. I chance a peek at Vanessa, wondering if she noticed my grimace. Her gaze is glued to the TV screen, and her jaw is set in a hard line. Hell. I don't know what to make of that expression.

"What's wrong?"

"Nothing."

The sound of a key makes me sit up straighter. I turn my attention to the front door, belatedly remembering I don't have an excuse for being here with Vanessa. It's either the truth, or Heather will think we were about to hook up.

Vanessa's twin stops short when she finds me sitting like a damn statue on her couch. She cuts her eyes to Vanessa, and I can guess the direction of her thoughts.

"Hey. I thought you were going to stay at Ryan's tonight," she says.

"Change of plans," Vanessa replies curtly.

"Oh." She turns to me. "Are *you* spending the night, then?" I open my mouth to deny it, but Heather continues. "If you are, please make sure you lower the toilet seat after you use it."

"He's not spending the night, Heather," Vanessa grits out. "We're just watching a movie."

"Fine. Make sure you keep the volume low, please. I have to wake up early tomorrow for cheer practice." She strides down the hallway and a moment later, a door bangs shut.

"Do we have to worry about your sister spreading rumors about us?" I ask.

Vanessa looks at me. "Why, Paris? Are you afraid Lydia is going to find out and come after your balls?"

My nostrils flare, but I don't fall for her baiting. She's mad about something I said earlier. Maybe it was my comment about Lydia not being a bad girlfriend in the beginning. Whatever the reason, I have to maintain my cool. Vanessa just went through an ordeal no one should have to experience. If she wants to use me as her punching bag, so be it. I plan to stay until she kicks me out.

"No. I'm thinking about you."

"Right, because it's okay for guys to dump their girlfriends and jump in bed with another chick thirty seconds later. But if a girl does it, she's a whore."

"I don't make the rules."

"The rules are garbage. I'm sick and tired of the double standards."

Ah hell. I can't believe the conversation has devolved to this topic. This would be dangerous territory on any occasion, but with Vanessa ready to blow, it's definitely not a place I want to linger.

"That's why my favorite character in the *Lord of the Rings* franchise is Éowyn," I say, keeping my face glued to the TV.

I can sense Vanessa's gaze burning a hole through my face.

"For real?" she asks after a moment.

I look at her then. "For real."

She clamps her jaw while her sharp gaze remains glued to my face. Then, begrudgingly, she says, "Well, Paris. You're not a total lost cause."

I grin and face the TV again, trying to ignore how her comment lightened my heart.

EIGHT

VANESSA

I wake up with a beefy arm wrapped around me. My head is resting against the shoulder attached to said arm. Shit. Paris spent the night? The light coming from the partially closed shades tells me he did.

Careful not to wake him, I dislodge his arm and scooch to the side. We're still in the living room, wearing all our clothes. Relief washes over me. I didn't try to fix a mistake by making a bigger one.

Paris fidgets and then makes a sound in the back of his throat that's pure male. For a moment, I get carried away and imagine what it would be like waking up in his arms after I rode him to exhaustion. He's always been so handsome, but now, with all his muscles and insane tattoos, he just oozes sex appeal.

He opens his beautiful blue eyes then and catches me staring. Busted. Do I have a lust-infused gaze? Was I drooling? His first reaction is to reward me with a lazy smile that turns my insides into jelly. It's unfair how gorgeous he is even after sleeping on the couch in an awkward position. I probably look like a witch.

"Hey," he says in a rough voice that's seriously impairing my ability to think straight.

"You spent the night."

And just like that, the grin vanishes from his face, and he sits straighter on the couch. "Yeah. I'm sorry. I must have fallen asleep."

Ah hell. Me and my big mouth. "I didn't mean to accuse you of anything. It wasn't my intention." I spring to my feet. "Coffee?"

Paris follows my example, but heads for the door instead. "Nah. I'd better get going. I think I overstayed my welcome."

Disappointment floods through me, and I don't know why. I didn't even want Paris to come in last night. Why am I bummed out that he's leaving?

"Thanks for staying with me last night."

He turns, and a hint of a smile teases his lips. "You're welcome."

His hand reaches for the door handle, but he pauses and stares at it for a couple of beats. I hold my breath as hummingbirds flutter in my chest.

"Can I text you later?" he asks.

My heart skips a beat. Why am I reacting to Paris like I'm thirteen again?

"Sure. Do you have my number?"

He shoves one hand in a pocket, lowering the waistband of his jeans enough to reveal a patch of tanned, taut skin, and then pulls out his phone. My eyes zero in and remain glued to that peekaboo show for a second too long.

"Here. You can type it in."

I jerk my head up again, mortified that he caught me staring like an idiot twice in a row.

Our fingers brush in the exchange. I try not to think too much about it. *There were no electric sparks, Vanessa. It's all in your head.* Maybe this is a belated reaction to last night's ordeal. It cannot be lingering feelings from my stupid crush of nine years ago. My mind must need a distraction, and Paris Andino fits the bill.

My hands are shaking, though, as I type my digits into his phone. When I return the device to him, I do my best to not touch him again.

He types something before putting the phone away. "There. I sent you a text. Now you have my number too."

I'm curious to read his message, but I control my impulse to check. He finally opens the door, squinting as the morning sun hits his face.

"It's going to be another gorgeous day in Cali." He shields his eyes with his hand and glances at the sky. "Do you have any plans?"

Plans? I scramble my brain, trying to remember. I know something is going on today.

Paris laughs. "I just asked if you had plans, I didn't give you a math equation to solve."

"Why did you say that?"

"Your face…" He shakes his head. "Never mind. Don't worry. My question was innocent. No ulterior motives this time."

A blush spreads through my cheeks. I can't believe he just referred to our first-kiss moment.

He clears his throat. "Anyway, I'd better go. I'll check on you later."

I watch his wide, strong back as he walks to his truck, my brain working furiously in the background, trying to remember what I was supposed to do today. I'm drawing a blank. No surprise there. I'm operating without my caffeine fix.

My phone vibrates in my hand—it's a calendar reminder for a hair appointment.

"Fuck!" I run back to the house.

Now I remember my plans for today. My cousin Lorena's wedding. I can't believe I forgot. And now I have to deal with my family and pretend I wasn't almost raped in a parking lot by Ryan last night. Hell and damn.

***

PARIS

I wish I didn't have to leave Vanessa's place in a hurry. Spending the night wasn't in the plan, and I have a million things to do before going to my folks' place later. The first is heading over to Andreas's place for another tasting fest. He decided to pursue a career in baking, and he loves to use us as his guinea pigs. Not that I'm complaining. He's a talented motherfucker.

I'm already late, but there's no way in hell I can show up at his apartment wearing the same clothes I wore yesterday. He'll demand to know where I spent the night—meaning, who I slept with—because besides being obsessed with cooking, he's also a fucking busybody. He loves to know all the juicy gossip so he can tease us to no end. And since he was firmly in the I-hate-Lydia camp, he's been trying to help me out in the romance—*hookup*—department.

The music on the radio gets cut off by an incoming call. I press the accept button right away. "Hey, Dad."

"Good morning, son. Where are you?"

"Uh, on my way home. Why?"

"Hold on." I hear the sound of his footsteps, and then the *snick* of a door shutting. "Lydia is downstairs with your mother. She's in tears."

"What? Why? What happened?" I fire off those questions automatically, but then I remember she's no longer my girlfriend and I shouldn't let her theatrics control me anymore.

"Something to do with you ignoring her phone calls and not spending the night at your place."

My stomach coils tightly. How the hell does she know I was gone all night? She either waited for me outside my building like a psycho, or she cornered one of my roommates. Both are terrible scenarios.

"I'm ignoring her calls to send a message that we're over. I thought she was getting better."

"That girl has severe mental issues, son. I can't tell you enough how glad your mother and I are that you put an end to it. We never liked her."

That's total BS. They loved Lydia in the beginning, because she comes from a respectable family. I love my parents, but they put too much value on appearances and status. For instance, when they saw my first tat, my father yelled at me for hours and my mother didn't talk to me for weeks. *No patient will want to be operated on by a surgeon who looks like he belongs to a motorcycle club.* Those were my father's words.

They calmed down only when they saw that it was a tribute to Cory. They probably thought I wouldn't get more ink done. Now I'm covered in tattoos, and there's not a damn thing they can do about it.

"What do you want me to do about Lydia?"

"Your mother wants you to come over and deal with her."

The idea makes my skin crawl. If I show up now, I'll never make it to Andreas's place.

"Can't. I'm already late for an important appointment."

"She's your girlfriend, Paris," Dad replies, sounding frustrated.

"My ex-girlfriend," I retort. "You know what's going to happen if I cave to her emotional blackmail. She'll think she can get me back, and I can't return to that bullshit."

He sighs. "We definitely don't want to encourage her. I'll make up an excuse. Don't worry."

"Thanks, Dad."

"What's the appointment? If it's important, you shouldn't be late."

I groan in my head. I shouldn't have expected Dad to let that one slide. He's a stickler for rules and manners. People being late is one of his pet peeves, which is ironic, because he sometimes makes his patients wait for up to an hour before he sees them. In his mind, in-demand doctors shouldn't be readily available. If they're running on time, it means they aren't good.

His view of the world is seriously messed up.

"I'm meeting Coach Clarkson for breakfast," I lie. "If I hurry, I'll be there just in time."

He grumbles. "You definitely don't want to upset your coach. And you'd better be here on time. Only the bride is allowed to be late to a wedding."

Hell. I'd forgotten where I'm supposed to be later today.

"Do I really need to come to this thing?"

"Yes, Paris. You do. Especially after leaving your mother and I alone to deal with your crazy ex. I'll see you later."

He ends the call abruptly, something he always does when he's pissed. Shit. If going to a stupid wedding wasn't already bad enough, now I have to deal with my aggravated folks. It's going to be a hella fun party.

NINE

VANESSA

I thought today was going to be hard. I was never good at pretending, but it turns out, the chaos of being in the midst of a wedding party is exactly what my mind needed to not dwell in darkness. My family never met Ryan—today was going to be the day of formal introductions. But everyone is busy freaking out over nothing, so no one has asked me about him yet. It was providential that he decided to show his true colors before more damage was done.

Heather—bless her vanity—has been too preoccupied with her hair, makeup, and clothes to bother me. I'm sure eventually she's going to corner me and ask what Paris was doing in our house last night. Maybe I should tell her about Ryan. I know she won't tell a soul if I ask her to keep it a secret. But I'm not ready for that conversation yet.

"What are you doing sitting down, child?" Aunt Lorena marches in my direction, her arms moving wildly.

"I was resting my feet."

She grabs my arm and forces me to stand. "Your dress is all wrinkled now."

I step away from her and smooth the offending lines. "It's not."

"Amateur," Heather sighs from across the room.

She found a mirror and has been preening in front of it for God knows how long. She's only a bridesmaid. I can't imagine what it's going to be like when she's the bride. One word flashes in my mind. *Bridezilla.*

My cousin Lorena—yeah, she was named after her mom—finally makes her grand entrance into the room designated for her wedding party. I try to keep my face from showing how much I detest her dress. It's simple and, dare I say, prudish. If I ever get married—which I don't think is going to happen—I'd probably go for a modern style too, but what she's wearing is a snooze. I bet it cost a pretty penny, though.

I glance at Heather who, unlike me, is not hiding what she thinks. Her face is twisted into a scowl. I hurry to her side before the Lorenas can see her expression. If Mom finds out Heather was acting like… well, like Heather, she'd give us both an earful. In her infinite wisdom, Mom believes twin sisters are supposed to keep each other in line.

"Reset your face to factory settings, Heather," I tell her.

She blinks fast. "What?"

"You know, the usual resting bitch face."

My teasing does the trick. She focuses her displeasure on me. "You're hilarious, Vanessa."

"I know." I smirk.

"What do you want?"

I lean closer to whisper in her ear. "Your face showed how much you luuuve Lorena's dress. I came to run interference."

She rolls her eyes. "Thanks for the save."

"You're welcome."

She looks over her shoulder for a moment, and then it's her turn to lean in. "You have to agree with me. She looks like shit. I wouldn't be caught dead wearing that nineteenth-century nightgown."

I fight the urge to laugh. "Well, maybe if you were a ghost, you'd wear it."

She wrinkles her nose. "Nuh-uh. If I ever come back to haunt you, I'll be wearing something glorious designed by Alexander McQueen."

"Why would you haunt *me*?"

"Because you're a pain in my ass."

"I'm deeply hurt." I fake a distraught expression and press my hand against my chest. "I'm pretty sure there are other people you could haunt instead. Maybe one of your ex-husbands, who you caught cheating on you with his secretary."

Instead of being offended by my remark, she smiles. "Yeah, I'd haunt his ass too."

"Girls, the ceremony is about to start." Mom waves maniacally at us. "Come on."

"Oh goody," I murmur.

As Lorena and Aunt Lorena leave the room, beckoning all of us to follow, Heather glances at my wrinkled dress. "Shit. Mom is gonna have a cow when she notices those lines."

"Well, go in front of me, then."

"It's not gonna work," Heather singsongs.

She does walk ahead of me though, and I stay glued to her back, but like an eagle, Mom manages to notice what I was trying to hide. She grabs my arm and forces me to stop.

"What did you do to your dress?"

"Nothing." I step back, running my hands over the skirt.

"She sat down," Heather, the traitor, replies.

Mom pinches the bridge of her nose. "*Meu Deus, joguei pedra na cruz.*"

Shit. She's speaking in Portuguese, which means she's pissed.

"No one told me I wasn't supposed to sit down."

"It's a taffeta dress, of course you can't sit down."

"Yeah, Vanessa. That's like Fashion 101," Heather chimes in.

I glare at her through narrowed eyes. It's a promise of

retaliation, and she'd better believe it'll come sooner rather than later.

"Nothing to do about that now. Everyone is waiting," Mom replies.

She pushes me through the door, and we all go down the stairs of the Malibu megamansion Lorena's parents rented for the joyous occasion. I can't even begin to imagine how much it cost.

Aunt Lorena is pacing at the bottom, blowing smoke through her nose like she's Daenerys's dragon about to melt the Iron Throne. "What took you so long?" she asks. "Get outside and in line already."

Mom hurries out the door to find Dad in the family seating area at the head of the aisle, and Heather veers for her spot in the line. The processional music starts, and Aunt Lorena makes her entrance. Since I'm the last of the bridesmaids to walk down the aisle before the maid of honor, I don't go very far. Cousin Lorena gives me a death glare, as if I made her wait for hours and not a couple of minutes. With that sour puss, either she'll either make it rain on her wedding day, or the groom will run away.

A friend of Aunt Lorena who's acting like a glorified wedding planner shoves a small bouquet of flowers into my hands and practically pushes me forward when I don't start walking on my cue. Not expecting the "help" and unused to having my leg movements restricted, I stagger forward, almost losing my balance completely. That would have been a scene-stealing moment, to fall flat on my face just before the bride goes down the aisle.

I manage a save and regain my balance, but as I do so, my gaze darts to my right and collides with Paris's amused one.

You have got to be kidding me.

PARIS

After being roped into coming to the wedding of someone I hardly know because my parents want to parade me around, I was prepared to be bored out of my mind. They love to boast that I play for the Rebels and I'm headed to med school next year, as if those are their accomplishments, not mine. Sure, they helped along the way by paying for all those football camps and extra classes. That doesn't make me feel any less like a show pony.

Thanks to the Lydia drama earlier, the possibility that Vanessa might be here wasn't on my radar. I didn't connect the dots until I saw her. The bride is her cousin, something I should have known, considering we used to attend the same church every Sunday until the great scandal of my thirteenth year— a.k.a. when Cory's friend stole Father Medina's wine.

Now I can't help the thrill of excitement that rushes through me as I watch her walk down the aisle, wearing a formfitting dress that accentuates all her assets. I drown out the rest of the circus, because my attention is now solely on the most beautiful bridesmaid I've ever seen. The lavender color of her dress looks great against her tanned skin. And I don't know what they did to her hair, but it looks luscious and soft. I'd give anything to run my hands through the strands.

She's always had a nice ass, but now… damn. The sight is giving me a boner, which is awfully inconvenient and inappropriate, considering my mother and father are sitting next to me. I need to stop imagining things that aren't going to happen. I adjust my pants and force my eyes away from Vanessa's curves. Mercifully, she finishes her walk fast, removing the temptation.

Perhaps I should pay attention to the ceremony.

I do try, but my eyes have a will of their own and keep wandering back to Vanessa. During one of those moments, she looks in my direction, as if sensing my stare. I should look away, pretend it isn't her I'm watching, but I hold her gaze instead. She's too far away, and I can't begin to guess what she's thinking.

I'm not sure what's happening to me. For the longest time, I was able to pretend I had moved on. Before I fell for her, she was one of my best friends, a constant in my life. We didn't go to the same middle school, but I used to see her every weekend at the country club and at church. So when I lost Cory and she vanished from my life, it was a blow I couldn't recover from. I held on to my rancor, shut her out, and allowed Lydia to feed my animosity toward her. Vanessa never explained why she didn't contact me after I lost my brother. Maybe I should have asked her.

The connection breaks when the priest declares the couple husband and wife. After the kiss, the crowd erupts into cheers and applause. The newly married couple walk down the aisle side by side, followed by their wedding party. Vanessa is the only one who doesn't follow the procession train. The groomsman she would have been paired with walks alone, looking confused.

I look for her, but she's gone. Everyone begins to stand up, and I follow suit. But as I move into the aisle, I can't help but look over my shoulder and search for her.

Damn it. Where did she go?

TEN

VANESSA

Paris didn't take his eyes off me during the entire ceremony, and I want to know why. I can't believe Aunt Lorena invited the Andinos, knowing how my mother feels about them.

Actually, I can. Mom and Aunt Lorena are stepsisters and never truly got along. Their relationship makes mine with Heather look like rainbows and cupcakes. Heather gets on my nerves, and I get on hers, but that's mostly because we're super different. We aren't besties, but I know she has my back and I have hers.

Just as Lorena and her new husband—I already forgot his name, because I'm that bad at remembering details that don't interest me—are declared married, I notice Granduncle Walter looking a little pale. While everyone else pays attention to the newlyweds as they return down the aisle together, I check on him.

"*Tio*, are you okay?"

"*Que?*" he leans closer, cupping his right ear.

"I asked if you're okay," I shout.

"*Ta muito calor. Muito calor.*" He yanks at his tie, trying to loosen it as he complains about the heat.

It's not even that hot out here, but maybe he's taking some medication that makes him flush, or his jacket is too thick. It does look like it's made of a heavy material.

"I'll get you some water," I say, and receive a blank stare in return.

He understands and speaks perfect English, but I repeat it in Portuguese just the same, and then use a shortcut to get to the reception's nearest bar. When I'm halfway there, it occurs to me that I should have helped him into some shade. But I'm pretty sure if I return without the water, he's going to be unhappy, and he'll let me know it. He's famous for his sharp tongue. I hike up my skirt and quicken my steps. The heels of my sandals sink into the grass, making my progression slower than I would have liked. As long as I don't trip again, I'll be fine.

The bartender looks bored when I reach him, but his face splits into a fake smile a second later.

"Hi, can I get some water, please?" I ask.

"Of course."

I grab the water and thank him. Urgency makes me turn around too fast, and I end up colliding with the person who was right behind me.

"Oops. Sor—oh, it's you."

Paris was the solid chest I collided with, and now my face is in flames. He looks too damn fine in a suit.

"You sound disappointed," he says through a smirk.

"Just surprised."

"I thought you saw me earlier."

"I did." God, I'm wasting time making a fool of myself while Granduncle Walter is withering under the sun. "I'm sorry. I have to get this water back to my granduncle. He isn't feeling well."

In a flash, the mirth vanishes from Paris's eyes and his serious mode activates. "What's the matter with him?"

"I don't know. He was complaining about being too hot. He's probably just dehydrated, right?"

"Where is he?"

"He's sitting in the front row."

"Let's get back to him, then."

Unbidden, he laces his arm with mine and steers me back through the grass path. I'm not sure if he's doing it because he saw me walking with difficulty earlier or if there's another reason. All I know is that my heart is beating much faster now, and I'm too aware of the feel of his strong arm against mine. Mercifully, we find Granduncle Walter alive and well.

I uncap the bottle and hand it to him. "Here's your water, *tio* Walter."

"*Ah, muito obrigado, querida.*" He takes a few sips and then lets out a satisfied sigh. Then his sharp gaze takes in Paris standing next to me. "*E esse rapaz, quem é?*"

I open my mouth to translate, but Paris extends his hand. "I'm Paris Andino. Nice to meet you, sir."

A spark of recognition lights up his eyes as they shake hands. "Ah, you're Dr. Andino's kid."

"That's correct. Are you feeling better now?"

"Yes. Much better. But I could use some assistance getting back inside."

"Of course." Paris steps forward and helps Granduncle Walter from his chair.

Instead of taking my shortcut, he leads him down the aisle, leaving me no choice but to follow the duo. It's a short walk, but Paris maintains a slow pace. He seems content chatting with my granduncle, and I'm shocked that the old man is giving him the time of day. He's a grumpy son of a bitch.

Is there anyone in the universe who doesn't fall prey to Paris's charms?

I get my answer not much later. As Paris leads Granduncle Walter through the double doors of the beachfront mansion, Mom comes out of nowhere and stops me from following them.

"What were you doing with that Andino boy, Vanessa?"

I fight the urge to roll my eyes. Mom has never forgotten about the wine-and-kiss incident. After they busted us, there was a huge argument between my parents and Paris's folks, which resulted in a fallout. Soon after, the Andinos changed parishes.

"He's a guest here, Mom."

"So? Do you plan to socialize with every single person at the reception?"

"He goes to the same school I do, or have you forgotten? We run in the same circles."

Her spine goes taut. "I'd prefer if you didn't. That boy got you drunk and took advantage of you. God only knows what would have happened if we hadn't found you. I can't believe Lorena had the audacity to invite his family."

Myriad emotions rush through me, and I don't know which one is strongest. I'm angry at my mother for making a big deal about something that happened eons ago, and distraught thanks to the reminder that what she feared could happen then *did* actually happen yesterday—or almost did. And the boy she mistrusts so much is the one who saved me.

"I heard it was Vanessa who attacked Paris that day," Heather says as she joins us.

I'd tell her to suck a lemon, but her interruption is much appreciated.

Mom strikes faster than a cobra. "Those rumors were spread by that awful woman."

By *awful woman*, she means Mrs. Nora Andino, Paris's mother. It's been only an hour since this event started, and already the drama level is high. I need a drink stat if I hope to survive the rest of the day *and* evening.

Now that Mom is distracted by Heather, I slink away into the house and head to the busiest area inside, which, conveniently, is near one of the bars.

Unfortunately, my path gets blocked by another pissed-off parent—Paris's mother.

"Hello, Mrs. Andino. Long time no see," I say in a sugary tone.

Her eyes narrow as she gives me a head-to-toe appraising glance. "You haven't changed much, have you?"

I'm ninety-nine percent sure that was meant as an insult, but I play along. "I disagree. I'm taller, and now I have these." I grab my breasts, pushing them higher. It took a while, but I finally caught up with Heather in the curves department.

Mrs. Andino's eyes bug out before they narrow to slits. "Crass as always. And I'm the bad guy for telling everyone you weren't the victim."

Fuck. Why is everyone hell-bent on reminding me of that day? It rubs raw a wound that's still bleeding. I bet if she knew what happened last night, she'd blame me for that as well.

"A pleasure as always, Mrs. Andino." I walk around her, hating that my eyes are now burning. I'm not going to cry over her cheap insult.

The bar is busy, and I need more than a glass of wine to calm my nerves. I spy a waiter going to the kitchen, so I follow him. No one pays me any attention as I search for the stash of booze. I finally locate a closet where there are several cases of wine, whiskey, gin, and other spirits. Picking something strong would be the smart choice, but I don't want to get drunk too fast. I choose a red wine, glad it's one of those bottles with a twist cap.

I can't return to the party holding my prize, so I veer for the door that leads out the side of the house where several white catering vans are parked. I want solitude, so I keep walking until I find the gate that leads to the beach. Since high-heeled sandals and sand don't mesh well, I get rid of my shoes and leave them by the gate before continuing my trek.

The moment my bare feet touch the sand, a sense of peace washes over me. I take deep breaths and stare at the ocean. The feelings of impotence and unworthiness slowly leave my body. Can I spend the entire reception here?

I'm supposed to be taking official pictures right now, but fuck that. I don't want to capture how dreadful I feel for eternity. No one will care that I'm not in them anyway. I was never close to Lorena—I was asked to be in the wedding party only because they felt they had to include me as family. Lorena will probably be thankful I'm not in the pictures. Plus, I'm already considered the black sheep of the family—might as well live up to my reputation.

Before I take a sip of wine, I walk around a natural bend in the beach to where a tall stone wall conceals me from any wedding guest onlookers. Feeling dejected, I sit on a small boulder and unscrew the bottle cap. The first swig is a large one, but the next swallows are not even mouthfuls. Drinking the wine too fast would mean I'd have to get another bottle soon.

"Care for company?" Paris's smooth voice reaches me through the wind.

I glance at him, noticing he took off his shoes as well. His tie is gone, and the first two buttons of his shirt are unfastened.

"I'd ask how you found me, but it seems following my trail has become your specialty."

One corner of his lips twitches up. "I saw you take the stairs to the beach from my vantage point. Your granduncle is fine by the way."

The jerkface is trying to make me feel bad for not asking, so I shrug and pretend his comment doesn't bother me. "He's a tough one. I wasn't concerned."

"Sure, sure."

"We have a saying in Brazil—*vaso ruim não quebra*," I continue, and then take another sip.

"I suppose you're not going to translate that for me." He sits next to me on the boulder—uninvited—brushing his shoulder against mine.

"The literal translation is bad vase doesn't break, but the meaning is nasty people live long. I thought you spoke Portuguese, or at least understood it."

"What Walter said was easy enough to guess."

"Walter, is it?" I raise an eyebrow, giving him a side-glance. "I didn't know you were already buddies."

"What can I say? We clicked." He meets my stare, his blue eyes dancing with mirth.

I look away in a rush before I drown in them. Then I bring the bottle to my lips, wishing the alcohol would start working already and melt away this new tension caused by Paris's presence. I can't deal with all the emotions his nearness is stirring in me. It's clearer than ever that he is my weakness.

"Can I have some of that?" he asks.

"Sure." I pass the bottle to him without looking, and then force my eyes to stay focused on the waves crashing against the shore.

We remain quiet for a while, and because I'm wrestling with my heart, I don't ask for the wine back. That'd mean talking to Paris some more.

He breaks the silence. "I'm sorry if my mother said something that upset you."

"She didn't say anything she hasn't before." Since he forced me to talk, I reclaim the wine, and this time, I drink a big gulp.

"Easy. There's more where that came from."

Like the classy girl I'm not, I wipe my mouth with the back of my hand. "I don't want to go back too soon. In fact, I want to stay out here for as long as I can."

He doesn't offer a comment for a while, and I begin to relax. Or maybe it's the wine finally kicking in.

"I'm in awe that you're here to begin with," he murmurs.

"Why would you say that?" I snap. "Did you expect me to curl up into a ball and cry my eyes out instead?"

"I... well, no. But... are you okay?"

I turn so he can see my scowl, and I realize my mistake a second later when I'm blasted by his charged stare. There are so many emotions swimming in his gaze, I can't possibly decipher them.

"Yes," I hiss and jump to my feet to put much-needed distance between us.

"You don't need to pretend with me, Vanessa. I don't expect you to have gotten over what that motherfucker did that fast."

"Shut up, Paris. You know nothing about me."

He runs past me and blocks my way. "You're right, I don't. I'd like to change that though."

His confession feels like whiplash. I step back. "Why?"

He clenches his jaw, keeping his penetrating gaze locked with mine. It brings back memories I buried deep in my mind a long time ago. He looked like this when I finally saw him again a few months after Cory's death. We bumped into each other at the country club. His cold demeanor that day broke my heart, and that wasn't the only time he hurt me since then.

"You know what? Never mind." I whirl around and stride away, but I move too fast and don't watch my step. My right foot sinks into a hole, and I lose my balance and fall at an odd angle, getting red wine all over the front of my dress. Pain flares around my ankle, making me see stars. "Fuck!"

"Are you okay?" Paris crouches next to me, looking all worried and shit. Meanwhile, I'm trying not to cry.

"No," I whimper.

"Let me see your foot." He wraps his strong hands around my calf and lifts my leg from the hole. I'd take pleasure in his touch if I wasn't in so much agony.

"How bad does it hurt?"

"Pretty fucking bad. God, I don't need this."

"It might not be as serious as you think. It's probably only a sprained ankle."

"A sprained ankle will keep me on the bench for too long."

He hooks his arm with mine and helps me up. "Come on. Let's get you back to the house. Can you walk?"

I try putting weight on my right foot and let out a pitiful cry. "No."

Before I can stop him, he sweeps me off my feet and into his arms. "Paris, put me down."

"You can't walk. It's better if you don't put weight on your foot before we know what's wrong. It could do more damage."

That thought alone stops any further protest I might have. I'm still cradling the wine bottle as we come into full view of anyone standing on the balcony. It's my luck that my parents are the ones who see me first.

"Vanessa!" Mom yells and then vanishes from my view.

She's probably running to meet us halfway.

Here we go again.

ELEVEN

PARIS

"I'm sorry," I tell Vanessa as I walk back to the reception.

"For what? My bad luck?"

"If I hadn't followed you to the beach, you wouldn't have twisted your ankle, and we wouldn't be about to get yelled at for hours."

"That's true. And why the hell am I still holding on to this bottle of wine?"

"You didn't want to litter?" My reply is meant as a joke, but it doesn't remove the frown lines between her brows. "It won't be as bad as the first time. We're adults now."

She snorts. "Have you met my mother?"

No sooner does she speak than the woman in question arrives at the gate. *"Vanessa, minha filha. O que aconteceu? O que este moleque fez?"*

I'm completely lost as to what she's saying, but I don't miss the death glare she aims my way.

"It's nothing, Mom. I wasn't paying attention and twisted my ankle. Paris is just helping me get back to the house."

"What happened?" Vanessa's father joins the scene, looking more worried than angry.

I see more people coming down the stairs, and brace for the onslaught of angry Brazilians, talking a mile a minute. My hope is that my folks aren't aware of the commotion. They'd only add fuel to the fire, and we'd have a repeat of the stolen wine scene. And now I don't have Cory to help me out. A sharp pang flares up in my chest, but I don't have time to dwell on it, not when I have to explain myself to Vanessa's family.

"Paris thinks I might have sprained my ankle," Vanessa answers her father.

"What does he know?" her mom sneers. "He's not a doctor yet, is he?"

"I've seen my fair share of injuries, ma'am. But you're right, I'm not a doctor. We need to take Vanessa to the ER to get her ankle X-rayed."

"*We?*" Her voice rises to a shriek. "You've done enough."

Damn it. I misspoke, and that wasn't my intention. I don't know why I included myself in the trip to the hospital. I have no business going with Vanessa anywhere, even though I wouldn't mind tagging along to make sure she's all right.

"Will you quit, Mom? Paris is only helping. Now could you please move out of the way so we can get up the stairs? I'm not exactly a lightweight, you know?"

Her parents and other curious people who came to snoop move out of the way to allow me to pass. I take the steps two at a time, mainly to put distance between us and them fast.

"You weigh nothing by the way," I tell Vanessa.

"Now you're just showing off. I'm packed with muscle."

Her reply makes me chuckle, despite the situation. "Your sass is back. I hope that means your ankle isn't as painful as before."

"Nah, I'm finally drunk enough that I can't feel it as much. With my luck, I'm sure I got hurt terribly and I'll have to forget the entire soccer season."

"Stop being so pessimistic. I'm sure it's not too serious."

When I reach the landing, there's a small crowd waiting for us. I spot Heather front and center, sporting a smirk. She takes a sip of her champagne, unfazed that I'm carrying her sister. Jesus, doesn't she care to know what happened to Vanessa?

"Paris, what in the world?" Mom's shrill voice catches my attention.

Hell. So much for hoping my folks wouldn't notice the tumult.

"Your son once again tried to corrupt my daughter." Vanessa's mother joins the scene, and I get a flashback of their fight of nine years ago.

"My son did no such thing!" Mother's eyes bug out.

"Do you think they'll come to blows this time?" Vanessa whispers.

"Hopefully not."

Her mother and mine begin their back-and-forth argument. The mother of the bride joins them and tries in vain to calm them down, which incenses Vanessa's mother more. If they weren't arguing about us, I'd record the confrontation and post it all over the internet. This is gold. Not one of them is paying attention to us now.

"If I tell you I can sneak us out and take you to the hospital, would you let me?"

"Do you see an opening for a swift escape?" Her eyebrows arch.

I mince to the side until we're not in the center of the circle, but we still have to get away without anyone noticing.

Heather appears out of nowhere. "Do you plan on carrying my sister for the entire reception, Andino?"

"She can't walk," I retort.

"Yes, Heather. I twisted my ankle, thanks for asking."

"Sure, and neither of you dislikes this arrangement." She finishes her drink and walks away.

Shit. Am I that transparent? But more important, why did she add Vanessa to her statement?

"Your sister is a piece of work," I mutter.

"Ignore her. I do most of the time. If you want to get out of here, it has to be now. Sooner rather than later our parents will notice we're not watching their shit show, and they'll come looking for us. I really don't want to deal with more yelling today."

I look over the heads of a few guests trying to stay clear of the argument. I don't mind having to special-order my shoes because of my size when I can see over any crowd. Being tall definitely has more perks than hindrances, and being able to find an escape route right now is one of them.

"I think I got it."

I make my move, striding away from the reception area via the path that leads to the side of the house. Soon I see all the white vans parked there, but most importantly, no guests.

"Did you drive?" she asks.

"Yeah. I don't attend events with my folks anymore without having a way to fly the coop."

"Smart. Unfortunately, I didn't have a choice about coming with my parents today."

"It's okay. I got you."

Surprisingly, she rests her cheek against my chest, making me feel all kinds of crazy shit. The scent of vanilla reaches my nose, igniting a little fire in the pit of my stomach. It's an aroma that's embedded in my memory. She must still use the same brand of shampoo as she did nine years ago. My heartbeat accelerates to a hundred, and the desire to hug her tighter is almost overwhelming. It seems all the emotions I suppressed when I was barely a teen are coming back to the surface like a volcanic eruption.

"Thanks, Andino. I almost don't mind that you're the reason I need to go to the ER."

There's no accusation in her tone. She must be buzzing.

"Hey, now. Your clumsiness is what caused your accident. Don't go spreading rumors." I stop next to the passenger side of my truck. "Can you stand for a second? I need to open the door for you."

"Yep."

I let her slide out of my arms. She braces a hand against the truck, standing on one foot. That's when I notice she isn't wearing her sandals.

"Shit, we forgot your shoes," I say.

She drops her gaze to the ground. "You too, buddy."

I look down as well, and then shrug. "It's okay. I can get them later. Besides, I have a pair of sneakers in the truck."

"Are you going to open the door for me, or are we waiting to get busted?"

"Oops, sorry."

When I unlock the door, the truck alarm beeps, making me wince a little. It's paranoia. No way anyone can hear it from the house.

I attempt to help Vanessa slide into the truck, but she puts her arm up. "It's okay, Paris. I got it."

She sets the almost empty bottle of wine in front of her seat and turns, facing me. Then she braces her hands against the doorframe, bending her knee in preparation for a little jump. Yeah, not gonna happen.

"Nope." I wrap my hands around her tiny waist and lift her onto the seat without effort. "There."

She watches me through narrowed eyes. "I could have gotten in without your help."

"I'm sure you could, and it'd probably have been pretty entertaining to watch, but we're trying to get out of here in a hurry, remember?"

I can see her mind working to come up with a clever retort, but in the end, she simply swings her legs into the cab and shuts the door. I run around the front and, when I get behind the steering wheel, she's sporting a frown and her arms are crossed. Man, I wish I had the ability to read her thoughts. I could ask, and I plan to, but first, I need to get us out of here.

It's not prudent to drive without shoes on, so I twist my body to reach behind my seat. I know I threw a pair of sneakers somewhere in the back.

"What are you doing? I thought you were in a hurry to leave."

My fingers brush against one shoe. I snatch it and show it to her. "Looking for the other one."

"Ew, gross. Get that away from me." She pushes my arm back.

Ignoring her, I resume my search, but my movements are constricted thanks to the suit jacket. I dive farther between our seats and finally get a visual of the missing shoe. Stretching my arm to the max, I manage to grab it, but the noise of tearing fabric follows.

"You just ripped your jacket," Vanessa tells me.

"Noticed it." I return to my seat and, grumpily, put the shoes on, wincing that I didn't have the foresight to wipe off the sand first.

"You don't need to bite my head off."

"I didn't. You'd know if I did."

Annoyed, I put the truck in drive and head out of the parking area slowly to avoid making more noise than needed.

She snorts. "I think I can tell when you're being a jerk. Been there, done that."

My cheeks hollow as I work my jaw. A retort is on the tip of my tongue, but I can't fault her for that jab.

"Are you going to be mad at me the entire trip to the hospital?" I ask instead.

"Yes."

"I just wanted to help."

"I know. It's your knight-in-shining-armor complex at work."

I hold the steering wheel tighter. "I don't have a knight-in-shining-armor complex. But if I see a friend struggling, of course I'm going to help."

"So we're friends now?" I feel her stare on my face.

Curious, I peel my gaze off the road for a second to look at her. The distrust shining in her eyes kills me.

"For my part," I reply, wondering if she'll get the reference.

She blinks fast, and then faces the road. "Nice one, Frodo."

A smile tugs at the corners of my mouth, making me forget my ripped jacket and the family feud we probably reignited today.

TWELVE

VANESSA

As Paris guessed, I have a sprained ankle, and I have to wear a brace until the Ravens' trainer checks me and gives her diagnosis Monday morning. I called Coach Lauda on the way home to get it over with, thinking she'd be mad as hell. She was only concerned about my well-being, which surprised me. I'm feeling dejected just the same. My shoulders slump as I stare at my phone.

"What's wrong?" Paris asks.

"I'm not sure. I thought I was gonna get my ass chewed by Coach Lauda."

"Why would you think that? What happened was an accident."

I shrug. "I don't know. Maybe because I know it could have been avoided. If I hadn't been drinking, and if I hadn't let you get under my skin, I'd have seen the hole in the sand."

"I got under your skin?"

Shit. I can't believe I let that confession roll off my tongue.

I let out an exasperated sigh and look out the window. "Yes, Paris. You did. Are you happy now?"

His calloused hand covers mine and squeezes, sending a zing of pleasure up my arm. My heart takes off, chasing the butterflies that spring from my stomach. I glance at him, nervous all of a sudden.

"I'd be happier if you'd forgive me for all the crappy stuff I did to you in the past," he says.

A huge lump gets lodged in my throat. I want to believe him so badly, but can I? There were many occasions where Paris acted like a jerk, especially throughout high school.

Unbidden, the prom night humiliation scene comes to the forefront of my mind. Paris and I were elected prom king and queen, but when it came to the official dance, he left me standing alone in the middle of the ballroom like an idiot and danced with Lydia instead.

"The list is a mile long."

He quirks an eyebrow. "Only a mile? I can deal with that."

My heart skips a beat. Damn it. I won't be able to keep my crush hidden if he keeps slinging his charm my way. Is that his intention? No, he's probably trying to clear his guilty conscience. That's all.

I realize I've been staring for far too long without saying a word.

My phone's ringtone breaks the spell. Unfortunately, it's my mother calling again. I've ignored her calls since we escaped the wedding, texting her only to let the family know I was on the way to the ER, but I didn't say which one.

"Are you going to keep blowing off your folks? It's only gonna get worse."

"I know, but if I tell them I'm home, they'll come running, and all I want to do right now is take a nap." I reach for the door handle, ready to hop out of his truck. We've been parked in front of my house a while now and there's no need to prolong the awkwardness.

"Hold on. I'll help you." He's out of the truck before I can protest.

My rebellious side wants to jump out before he has the chance to walk around the vehicle, but my stupid heart is looking forward to Paris's help. I want his hands on my body again. They felt too damn good. Man, I'm in trouble. I can't allow him to linger, or I'll end up doing something regrettable.

I do open the door myself and swing my legs to the side of the seat. He steps forward but stops suddenly, frowning.

"What's wrong? I don't think I gained a hundred pounds on the ride from the hospital. You can still lift me as if I weigh nothing."

With a shake of his head, he replies, "I... that's not it. I don't want to be handsy like before. It wasn't cool."

I roll my eyes. "For fuck's sake, Paris. I know you didn't mean anything dirty by it."

I wholeheartedly believe my statement until I catch a flash of guilt in his eyes. Maybe his mind was in the gutter when he touched me. Now I really want him to touch me again. I'm actually dying for him to pick me up caveman style. I can't even blame my crazy thoughts on painkillers, since I refused them. Maybe I'm still drunk.

"Do you want me to carry you to the front door?" he asks.

"Sure, if you don't mind."

And I'm in his arms again. Anyone seeing us wearing our fine clothing would think we're newlyweds. A bubble of laughter goes up my throat.

"What's so funny?"

I shake my head. "Nothing."

"Come on, Vanessa. You're going to make me self-conscious. Am I not carrying you right?"

"You're fine. Let me get the key from my bag. You can put me down."

He does so and waits nearby while I fish the small object from my tiny purse. I'm glad I kept it with me when I decided to hide from everyone at the beach.

"Do you want to come in?" I ask as I open the door.

"I thought you wanted to take a nap."

Damn it. He caught me.

"I do, but... I don't know. I think I should offer you a beverage for your troubles."

He narrows his eyes. "I will come in on the condition you tell me what you were laughing about."

"Oh my god, Paris. Why do you care?"

"My pride is at stake here. Laughter is not what I expect when I'm carrying beautiful women in my arms."

My heart swells and then shrivels. He thinks I'm beautiful, and yet jealousy pierces my chest, even though the upturn of his lips tells me he's joking. Why did he have to use the word in plural? I hop on one foot into the house, leaving the door wide open for him to follow. I must look ridiculous, but they didn't have crutches for me at the hospital. I need to get some tomorrow.

"It's silly," I say, and wait until he closes the door behind him to continue. "It just occurred to me that we looked like we just got married."

I didn't expect the confession to bring a blush to my cheeks, but here we are. I'm glad that I don't turn red like Heather does. Yippee-ki-yay for my tanned skin.

Paris chuckles. "What kind of ceremony did we have that I ended up with a ripped jacket and you have red wine stains all over your dress?"

"Uh, the fun kind?" I smirk.

His face splits into a radiant grin, and I neglect to breathe. I forgot how beautiful he is when he smiles.

"You're right. You *are* a silly girl. But it's good to hear your laughter. I've missed it."

Okay, now I forget how to do *all* the basic stuff. I don't move, I don't blink, I just stare at him like an idiot. Finally, I croak, "You've missed my laughter?"

He maintains my stare, and the intensity in his gaze turns up several notches. "I've missed you, Vanessa."

"I… I don't know what to say."

And clearly that isn't what he was expecting to hear, judging by how his face seems to crumble.

"It's okay, you don't have to say anything. I just wanted you to know." He glances at the kitchen. "How about that beverage?"

I swallow the lemon-sized lump in my throat and say, "Make yourself at home. I have to sit down." I head for the couch and plop there. Ideally, I should get out of this binding dress, but I don't want to leave his company just yet.

"Do you want anything? Tea with honey again?" he asks.

"God no. I need something stronger, please. There's tequila in the cupboard above the sink."

"Can you handle the burn?"

I give him a droll look. "I've drunk tequila before, Paris."

"I know, what I meant was…" He shakes his head. "Jesus, why can't I get my thoughts straight when I'm around you?"

"Uh, that sounds like a trick question."

"I never asked you how your throat was. It seems you didn't bruise after all."

Oh, and here I thought there was more to his statement. I touch my neck. "The wonders of makeup."

Instead of veering into the kitchen, he sits next to me on the couch. "How bad is it?"

Now it's my turn to get my thoughts in a jam. His nearness is doing in my head. "I… not that bad."

"If you hadn't stopped me last night, I would have bashed his face in with my fists."

"I know. That's precisely why I stopped you. He's not worth getting arrested. He's a weasel, a vermin who doesn't deserve the air he breathes."

I can't believe I let Ryan fool me with his good-guy persona. My ego was bruised, and I needed someone who treated me well, which Ryan did in the beginning. Then his true colors started to show.

Paris nods, then gets up. "So, let's have some tequila."

"Are you drinking too?" My eyebrows arch.

"One shot won't hinder me."

"Well, you can always stay." Holy shit. Did I seriously say that out loud? "I mean, on the couch like last night."

He laughs. "I got your meaning the first time. I think you're trying to use me as a buffer against your parents."

Relief washes over me that his train of thought went in that direction. "You wouldn't be a buffer—on the contrary. You'd be gasoline poured over fire."

"True."

I watch him grab the tequila and then get out two shot glasses without having to look for them. I wonder for a moment how he guessed their location. Maybe he already knows where we keep them from the last time he was here, partying with my sister. I'm not bitter *at all* about that. I wonder if he brought his bitchy ex with him. They were still dating at the time, so there's a high chance that he did.

He returns to my side and fills up the glasses. Then he hands me one and lifts his for a toast. "To your speedy recovery."

"*Tim tim*," I reply in the Brazilian way, then I toss my head back and swallow the shot.

It burns down my throat in a good way.

Paris shakes his head and shudders. "I haven't had tequila in ages."

"You could have grabbed lemon and salt."

"Nah, that's for amateurs." He picks up the bottle. "Another?"

"Yes, please." He fills my glass again, but his own remains empty. "So, I'm to drink alone from now on?"

Looking sheepish, he rubs the back of his neck. "As much as I'd love to keep drinking, I can't. I have to drive home eventually."

"Right." I gulp the second shot, slam the glass onto the table, and melt against the back of the couch. My body is tingling and as light as a feather. I'm getting a good buzz.

"You look tired. Maybe I should go."

I grab his arm without thinking. "Don't go just yet."

His gaze bounces between my eyes as if he's searching for something. I don't know if he'll find what he's looking for in them, but I'm certainly getting pulled into his orbit. I lean forward, dropping my own gaze to his full lips, which are partially open.

"Vanessa…" He says my name like a caress.

I press a hand to his chest, loving how warm his skin is under his shirt. "Your heart is beating so fast."

He cups my cheek and rubs his thumb over my lower lip. "I know."

Our mouths are getting closer and closer… we're seconds away from making that regrettable mistake I shouldn't want, but really do.

The sound of a key turning pulls Paris away from me as if he was yanked backward by an elastic band stretched to the max. He jumps off the couch just as Heather walks in.

Fucking great.

"So, you're home already. Thanks for letting us know." She bangs the door shut and trudges into the kitchen.

"I *just* got home," I say.

"If you don't call Mom, she's gonna have an aneurysm."

"I will."

"I should go," Paris announces

I want him to stay, but now that Heather's home, it's better if he leaves.

"Yeah, you definitely should," she pipes up. "If you want to keep your nut sack attached to the rest of your body."

"What the hell, Heather!"

She gives an *I'm just telling the truth* shrug before she uncaps the water bottle she got from the fridge. "Mom is convinced Paris is up to no good. *Again.*"

If a person could die of embarrassment, I'd be in extreme danger of biting the dust.

"Message received," Paris replies. He glances at me. "I'll text you tomorrow, okay?"

"Yeah, sure. Drive safe. And thanks for the ride."

"Anytime."

No sooner does he walk out the door than Heather takes his place on the couch. "All right. I could have bought that you were just hanging out last night, but after today, that excuse won't fly anymore. What the hell is going on with you and Paris?"

"Nothing."

"Bullshit."

"I'm not lying!" I grab a pillow and hug it to my chest. My pitiful shield against my sister's inquisition. "And you'd better not start spreading rumors about us."

She gets up in a huff. "Please. With the way you two are behaving around each other, I won't need to say a word. The rumor mill will turn into a damn factory."

THIRTEEN

PARIS

Like an idiot, I blew up Vanessa's phone yesterday, so it's no surprise that she ignored me save for the first reply. Maybe it's better if I let her be. We almost kissed after the wedding, and she's not someone I can simply make out with and move on. She has a hold on me whether I want it or not, and if I'm to stay away from complicated relationships from now on, I have to keep my distance from her.

School and football, those are the only two things I'll focus on. It's a good thing the season is starting this weekend with our kickoff game, and my classes this semester are extreme. Whenever I'm not practicing, my ass will be glued to a chair in the library.

As I walk to my next lecture, my head is pounding with the amount of information the biochemistry professor dumped on us this morning. I have ten minutes to spare, but the building for my next class is on the opposite side of campus, which means I have to haul ass if I'm gonna make it there on time.

A vibration in my pocket alerts me to a text message. It's fucking stupid that my heart lurches with the possibility that

Vanessa might have texted me back. I fight the urge to check but lose the battle pretty quickly. To my disappointment, it's a stupid joke Puck, the goofball on our team, sent to the Rebels group chat.

"Paris!" a female voice yells from behind me.

I grind my teeth. I should have known Lydia would corner me at some point during this week. I was hoping it would take her longer to track me down. I put on my headphones and pretend I don't hear her as I keep walking toward my next class.

Something yanks on my backpack to make me stop.

Annoyed, I pull my headphones off and turn to…yep. Lydia. "What the hell!"

"You wouldn't stop," she replies, out of breath.

"Maybe because I didn't hear you."

"You've been avoiding me."

Ah, straight to the point. She was never one to beat around the bush.

"I've been busy." I move to keep walking, but she blocks my path.

"You said we could be friends. Was it all bullshit?" Her eyes fill with tears, a move I fell for so many times before, it's not even funny.

"What was so important that you had to go see my folks, Lydia?"

She bites her lower lip and drops her gaze to her shoes. "I needed you. I've been so lonely lately, and I have no one to talk to. You're the only person who gets me, Paris."

"I'm sorry, Lydia. I can't be your go-to person anymore."

She whips her face up to mine, her eyes now flashing with anger. "So that's it? Our years together mean nothing to you anymore. All the times I was there for you when you needed it most, forgotten."

Her raised voice starts to draw attention. *Great.* She's causing a scene again, and worse, she's going to make me late for class.

I lift my hand. "Stop right there. This is not going to work anymore."

"This what?" she shrieks.

"The guilt trip. I haven't forgotten the time we were together or how you helped me in my darkest hour, but it's in the past, Lydia. You have to move on. We both do. We're not good for each other."

Her hands ball into fists and her body is shaking now. *Hell.* I thought we were past this. It's been six months since we broke up. She's been to therapy, went to the fucking retreat in Colorado, but she's regressed to the same state she was in when I ended things.

A small crowd has gathered around us, and sadly some of the vultures are recording the scene. I need to end this before it gets worse. From the corner of my eye, a pair of crutches catches my attention. I turn, my stomach falling through the earth when I see Vanessa standing there. *Fuck.* That's the one witness I don't need.

I must have stared at her for too long, because Lydia sneers. "Oh, I get it now. *You* have moved on."

I return my attention to her, trying to hide the truth. "What are you talking about?"

"You're such a jerk. She's the reason you broke up with me, isn't she? That fucking Raven whore!"

Anger rises in the pit of my stomach. Lydia can call me names all she wants, but I won't tolerate insults toward Vanessa. Not anymore.

"Enough, Lydia," I grit out. "We're done here."

I walk away before I say something I'll regret. As I do, I glance around. Vanessa is no longer in the crowd, but I wonder if she stayed long enough to hear Lydia's insult.

A nimrod is still pointing his stupid camera at me, so I push his phone down none too gently as I walk past him. "Show's over, jackass."

Once I break through the ring of people, I search for Vanessa.

She shouldn't have gotten far on crutches. Apparently she did, though, because I don't see her anywhere.

My phone pings again, but I ignore it this time. There's zero chance it's a text from her, and I have no fucks to give about anyone else.

***

VANESSA

"God, that wasn't pleasant, was it?" Sadie pipes up on the way to the humanities building.

"No," I grumble.

"I thought Paris broke up with that hag ages ago."

"He did. Six months ago."

"Blimey. Poor lad. It was painful to watch, but I couldn't look away."

"Yeah, she's a train wreck." I stop in front of the door, and since I don't see a button to open it, I ask, "Do you mind getting that?"

"Duh, obviously. Man, I'm gutted about your injury."

"It's okay. The trainer said I can return to practice in a couple of weeks. It sucks that I can't play for our first game though."

I'm glad we changed the subject, despite the new topic being my inability to play soccer for a while. I so didn't want to keep talking about Paris. Yesterday, I had a moment of clarity. As much as I'm into Paris, I can't allow myself to follow that path. It'll only lead to heartache and stress. So I replied to one of his texts to avoid being a total cow, but I ignored the rest. Witnessing his argument with his ex just served to reinforce my decision.

"That's brilliant! God, who do you think Coach Lauda is going to sub in your place?"

"I'm not sure," I reply absentmindedly. "Ginny Sanders maybe." Then I notice who is walking down the corridor toward us and freeze.

Ryan.

"Oh, your boyfriend is coming."

Shit. I never told anyone I broke up with him. Last weekend felt like I was caught in a tornado, like Dorothy in the *Wizard of Oz*. If I landed in Oz, then Lydia is definitely the Wicked Witch of the West. But who the fuck is Ryan in this scenario? I can't think of a character evil enough to represent him.

"He's *not* my boyfriend anymore," I reply through clenched teeth while my fingers curl tighter around my crutches.

Sadie doesn't have a chance to get another word in before the asshole is standing in front of us. My only solace is that Paris's handiwork still shows on Ryan's face.

"Good morning, ladies." He smiles despite his busted nose.

"What happened to your face?" Sadie asks, erasing the son of a bitch's smirk in a flash. God, I love her bluntness.

"Nothing. What happened to your friend?" He nods toward my crutches.

"Why do you care?" I snap. "Run along, Ryan."

He sneers. "I hope it's broken. It's exactly what you deserve."

Sadie jumps in front of me, body poised to strike. "What the fuck did you just say to her?"

Ignoring her aggressive stance, he walks backward with the odious smirk in place, the venom in his eyes aimed solely at me. "Karma is a bitch, babe."

Sadie makes a motion to go after him, but I use one of my crutches to stop her. "Don't. He just wants to get a reaction from me. He didn't take the breakup well."

"That's no excuse. He acted like a total wanker."

"He *is* a wanker."

She glances at me. "When did you end things?"

"Last Friday."

Her eyes widen. "And you didn't tell me?"

Guilt sneaks its way into my heart. I could have told her that I had broken up with the douche without giving her all the nasty details.

"I'm sorry. I had a busy weekend with my family, and then the accident. It slipped my mind."

Pouting, she crosses her arms. "I'm still mad at you. I tell you everything."

"I know. I feel awful now that I didn't update anyone about my new single status."

Her expression softens. "You don't need to feel bad. And if I'm totally honest, I'm relieved you tossed that bellend to the curb. I never liked him."

I stare into the distance, thinking about what led me to start dating Ryan in the first place.

"Yeah, he was a bad decision. Proof that you shouldn't jump into a relationship as an attempt to mend a broken heart."

"Wait—what? Who's the arsehole I need to punch for breaking your heart?"

I blink fast, regretting my confession. "No one you know."

She narrows her eyes, and I can tell she's trying to see if I'm lying. "Lucky him then."

I give her a pitiful smile. "Come on. Let's get to class."

FOURTEEN

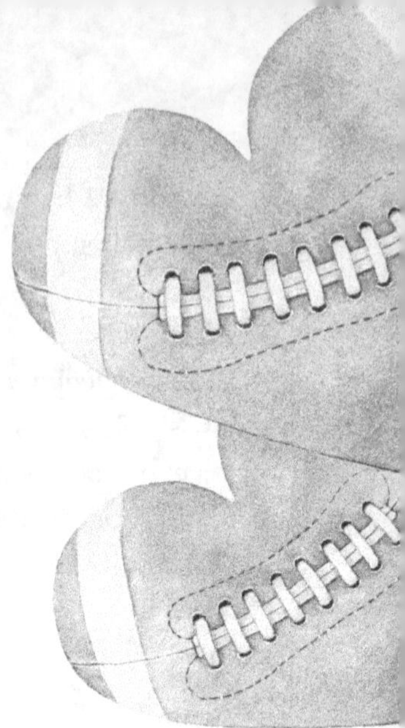

I should take the hint that Vanessa doesn't want anything to do with me. And after the scene she witnessed earlier today, I can't fault her for her decision. I spend the entire day trying to get my mind off her, but nothing works.

During practice, I play like shit. My concentration is shot. I get chewed out by Coach Harrison *and* Coach Clarkson. I can't blame them. We're playing our biggest rival this weekend, and we need a sharp defense.

In the locker room, Danny finds me. "Is everything okay with you, man?"

I stuff things in my duffel bag, avoiding eye contact. "Yeah, I'm fine."

He rests his foot on the bench next to my bag and leans forward. "Bullshit. Don't lie to me, Andino."

Damn it. He's not going to let this go. I raise my head to look at him. "I have personal shit going on. But I'm working on it."

"Are you referring to the argument you had earlier with Lydia?"

I straighten my spine, annoyed that the story has gotten around. "How did you hear about it?"

His cheeks hollow before he replies, "Sadie told me."

"Wait, who told *her*?"

"She saw you guys."

Shit. I only had eyes for Vanessa and didn't even notice the blonde firecracker standing next to her.

"Well, it wasn't pleasant, but that's not my only problem."

He claps my shoulder. "Do you want to have a drink after this so you can fill me in?"

"I appreciate the offer, but I can't tonight. I'm heading to the library to study."

"All right, but the offer stands if you change your mind."

"Thanks, bro."

In hindsight, maybe I should have accepted Danny's offer instead of keeping my original plan. But then again, he has a reputation for playing matchmaker. If he gets a whiff of my interest in Vanessa, I'm doomed. I should be thankful Andreas graduated already and they can't gang up on me.

I grab something from a vending machine and head to the main library. I see some familiar faces—mostly people in the premed program. I stand out in the library, not only because of my size, but because this isn't a place jocks typically hang out.

I head for my usual spot, a table in a corner by a large window, but it's occupied by none other than Vanessa. Electric surprise rushes through me. I quicken my steps until I'm standing right in front of her.

"I never pegged you as a library type of girl," I say.

She glances up from the old book she has in front of her, eyes round. "What are you doing here?"

I chuckle. "I'm a regular. I usually sit at this table."

"Oh. I didn't realize they were reserved. I'll leave." She begins to collect her things.

"I'm not asking you to go. It's big enough for both of us. We can share."

She stares at me like a deer in headlights. "I… well, as long as we don't distract each other. I really need to study."

I pull up the chair across from her. "Yeah, same here. What's your major? I don't think I've ever asked."

Her brows furrow. "How could you, when the only times you've spoken to me in the last nine years have been to antagonize me?"

Shame makes my face hot. I do feel horrible about the way I behaved, even though I believed I was right to act in that manner. I don't think that anymore.

"Psychology," she replies.

"Oh," I blurt out. I don't know why her answer surprises me.

"What? Don't tell me you disagree with that choice."

"No, of course not. I was just caught by surprise. I thought you wanted to play soccer professionally."

"That would be cool, but I still need to graduate with a degree, and psychology has always interested me."

I nod. "It's a good career path."

Still watching me, she taps her pen nervously against her notebook.

"What's wrong?" I ask.

She shakes her head and returns her attention to the old tome in front of her. "Nothing."

Despite almost messing things up, I'm smiling like an idiot as I pull out my laptop and log on to the school's website. I manage to keep my mouth shut for maybe a minute before I ask, "What class are you studying for?"

"Oh, medieval literature. It's an elective."

"Yikes, that sounds… brutal."

"Yeah, I'm regretting my life choices right now."

I can't help but think her statement has a double meaning. I should leave things well alone. I did promise I wouldn't distract her, but I'm too fucking curious.

"That asshole's not bothering you, is he?"

Her eyebrows shoot to the heavens. "Uh…no."

I sense the lie as soon as it rolls off her tongue. I know her too well. "He came looking for you today, didn't he?"

She leans back and crosses her arms. "We bumped into each other. It seems neither of us can shake off our past so easily."

I mimic her stance. "No, it seems we can't. But I won't let the past dictate my future."

"Me neither."

"Are you sure about that?" I raise an eyebrow.

"What do you mean?"

"Why did you ignore my texts, Vanessa?"

Man, I'm acting like a total creeper by putting her on the spot like this.

She opens and shuts her mouth, but no answer comes forth. To save the situation, I continue. "I just wanted to make sure your mother isn't distributing Wanted, Dead or Alive posters with my face on them."

My ruse works. She cracks a smile.

"No posters yet. But you never know with her."

"I'll give her a wide berth, then."

I force my eyes away from her gorgeous face and try to focus on the words in front of me. It takes me a while, but eventually, I get absorbed by the assignment and almost forget I'm sitting across from the girl of my dreams.

The moment the idea crosses my mind, I stop typing. I never thought about her in those terms. I had a major crush on her when we were younger, but I guess I was too immature to think like that. I glance at her again and immediately become ensnared by the way her luscious dark hair falls across her cheek, and how the soft light from the desk lamp turns her skin golden. She looks like a sun goddess, and I want to worship her.

She lifts her eyes, catching me staring. "What?"

"Nothing."

"Hmm, okay." Her stomach grumbles, and she makes a face. "Sorry about that. I forgot to eat before coming here."

I give her one of the snack bars I got earlier. "Here."

She looks around in a cagey manner. "I thought we weren't allowed to eat in the library."

"You can if you're sneaky about it."

Her luscious lips split into a grin before she snatches the snack from my hand. "Look at you, still breaking all the rules."

"Some rules are meant to be broken."

She nods and then attacks the food. I should look away, but my gaze drops to her lips and stays glued there long enough that she notices.

"Whuh?" she asks with her mouth full.

"You have crumbs all over your face."

She swallows and wipes the corners of her mouth. "Are they gone?"

"You missed some." I reach over and rub a spot under her lower lip.

She lets out a soft gasp and leans back a little. An apology is at the tip of my tongue, but when I see how hooded her eyes have become, I refrain.

I clear my throat. "There. All gone."

"Thanks."

"No problem."

My phone vibrates on the table. It's a text from a classmate. He's telling me to look to my right. I do so and find him waving me over.

"Who's that?"

"A fellow premed student. I think he needs my help with something. I'll be right back."

I could have asked him via text what he wants, but I need to put distance between Vanessa and me. The atmosphere was getting charged with sexual tension, and I was a moment away from sitting next to her and finishing what we started at her house.

This isn't how I planned for my first months of freedom to go. I wanted to be myself, figure things out on my own.

Now all I want is to make up for lost time with the girl I never forgot.

VANESSA

A gale of relief whooshes out of me as soon as Paris walks away to talk to his friend. I knew sharing a desk with him was a mistake when my intention in coming to the library was to have a distraction-free study session. If I'd known he'd be here, I'd have steered clear.

I watch him from afar, unable to resist getting my fill. There's a sudden ache in my chest, and I try in vain to massage it away with my fist.

This is not good, Vanessa. You can't jump off the edge when it comes to Paris.

I can't stay here. When he disappears down an aisle with his friend, it's my chance to leave without having to explain why I'm bailing, or worse, him insisting on giving me a lift. Because of my sprained ankle, I can't drive, and Heather is busy with cheer practice. The plan was to get in a couple of hours of solid study and grab an Uber.

I shove my belongings into my backpack as fast as I can and pray that he won't return before I can trudge my way out of the building. Speed walking with crutches is a challenge, but I manage to escape unseen. I move away from the library as fast as I can, just in case Paris decides to look for me before I request a car.

The loud boom of thunder is the only warning I get before the sky falls on me like a waterfall. I search for cover, but the closest awning is the damn library building. I keep moving toward the nearest street corner instead as the cold droplets of rain quickly drench my clothes. My phone is getting wet too, so I try my best to shield it, but the crutches get in the way, and the damn thing slips through my wet fingers.

"Fucking hell."

I drop them so I can bend down and rescue the device before it's ruined. I'm completely soaked now, and what's worse, the app says there aren't any cars available.

"Vanessa!" Paris's loud voice travels through the roar of the storm.

Shit.

I turn around and watch the maniac run after me in the downpour. "What?"

"You left."

"Yeah, I decided to go home."

When he stops mere inches from invading my personal space, I can see that he's not amused.

"Is my company so unbearable that you had to run away in the rain?"

"I wasn't run—"

"Bullshit. You were."

Car headlights illuminate his face, highlighting all his sharp angles and the hard set of his jaw. Man, he's *pissed.*

"If you're so certain, then why did you come after me? That's stalker behavior."

"Stalker..." He rubs his face. "I came after you because I was worried. It's late, raining cats and dogs, and I know you can't drive with a sprained ankle. If that makes me a stalker, then fuck, I guess I am."

Guilt makes me wince. I'm acting like a total bitch because I'm terrified of my feelings and how they're impairing my judgment.

"I was about to order an Uber," I reply meekly.

"No." His voice is hard, leaving no room for argument.

Remorse gives way to irritation. "What do you mean, *no?*"

"I'm taking you home. If after that you want to delete my

phone number, block me, and never speak to me again, then fine."

That would remove all the temptation and solve my problem, but it isn't what I want. I should just accept his offer, but that's not what comes out of my mouth.

"You're not the boss of me."

Why am I even fighting him? There aren't any rides available anyway. But his attitude is making me so damn angry. I don't like being told what to do, even if the one doing the telling is the guy I can't stop thinking about.

"You're lucky I'm not your boss." He grabs my crutches from the ground with one hand and then takes my arm with the other. "Come on. I have to get my stuff from the library first."

I plant my feet, refusing to budge. "I'll wait here."

"Yeah, nice try, honey."

"I'm not your *honey*, jackass."

I jerk my arm back, not really expecting to break free of his hold. But we're wet, and he wasn't gripping me too tight. I lose my balance with the momentum, and on reflex, put all my weight on my right foot, which is a monumental mistake. Not only does it not stop my fall, it also hurts like a mother. A yelp escapes my lips.

My back doesn't meet the ground though. Paris catches me, wrapping my body in his arms and pulling me against him. My pulse skyrockets, and any coherent thought flies out of my head. I'm wide eyed when I look up and meet his stare. We don't speak as we drink each other in. Then comes the certainty that if we don't break apart, I might attack his mouth.

"Why are you so difficult?" he whispers, inching closer.

"I'm not." I drop my gaze to his lips for a second, and then go back to his eyes.

"Don't look at me like that," he grumbles.

"Like what?"

He cups my cheek, making me shiver. "Like you want me to kiss you."

"What if I do?"

"Well, then."

His hand finds the back of my head as his lips claim mine. Clutching his biceps, I surrender to his sweet invasion, regretting I didn't succumb to him sooner. The first swipe of his tongue against mine destroys the dam that was keeping all my feelings trapped. They burst through in a violent and devastating flood. I was a fool for believing I could ever move on from him.

He curls his fingers around a strand of my hair and tilts my head to the side as he deepens the kiss. It was fireworks kissing him the first time. Now, it's a comet zooming across the sky, and I can't get enough. If I couldn't forget him then, there's absolutely no chance I'll be able to now.

"Get a room!" someone yells in the distance.

We both ease back, but his arm is still around me, and his hand is in my hair. He rests his forehead against mine, and says, "You have no idea how long I've waited to kiss you again."

"If you say nine years, I'm gonna kick you in the shin," I joke.

He pulls back. "Okay, I won't say nine years then."

I narrow my eyes to slits. "Is that how long?"

Now he really puts distance between us by releasing me. "I kinda don't want to answer now."

I'm back to being mad at him. He gave me the cold shoulder after Cory died, ignored me completely, never even mentioned the heartfelt poem and note I left in his mailbox when I couldn't see him, and in high school, continued his streak of being a total jerk. And now he's claiming he's been into me since then? He was my first crush and first heartbreak.

I cross my arms. "You just did. Let's go get your stuff."

"Okay." He retrieves my discarded crutches and hands them over. "Are you angry with me?"

"No," I reply and then head toward the library.

He matches my pace and walks by my side, but he doesn't utter another word. There's a palpable tension between us now, and I hate it. I wish I could forget how much he hurt me in the past. I understood his silence immediately after his brother's death. He was grieving. And I could ascribe his later cruelty to being young and immature, but then he continued to be a complete tool toward me for most of college.

I know lowering my defenses around him will come back to bite me in the ass. And yet, my lips still tingle from his kiss, and I still yearn for more.

FIFTEEN

PARIS

The looks I get as I stride back into the library, dripping water, would have been comical if I were in a mood to appreciate them. I can't wrap my mind around what Vanessa wants. She was as into that kiss as I was, but then, bam, an innocent comment has her pulling a one-eighty on me.

She said she'd wait in the lobby, but I wonder if she plans to ditch me again. If she does, I should just let her go, but I can't in good conscience allow her to wander alone at night when it's pouring and she can't defend herself properly.

The visual of her son-of-a-bitch ex assaulting her has been burned into my memory. He's lucky he hasn't crossed my path.

I'm surprised when I find her in the same spot. She's shivering, so I don't think twice before pulling a hoodie from my backpack and offering it to her.

"Here. You can wear this."

She eyes the bunched-up piece of clothing but doesn't take it. "It's gonna get soaked as well. I'll put it on when I'm in your truck."

"Right." I stuff the hoodie back in my bag. "Wait here. I'll get the truck."

"Leave your backpack with me then. It will get totally wet otherwise."

Man, what's wrong with me? It's like being in her presence has taken away my ability to think. "Good call."

I sprint toward the parking lot. The rain doesn't look like it's going to ease up anytime soon. I don't mind the cold or the wetness, but driving wearing drenched clothes will be hell. I jump in the back seat first and find my gym bag. Unfortunately, the clothes aren't clean. I normally wouldn't give a damn, but I don't want to smell like a rotten egg with Vanessa in my truck. I end up taking the towel and covering the driver's seat instead.

Vanessa walks out of the building the moment I pull up, moving fucking fast for someone on crutches. I get out to help her with those, and that's the only thing she allows me to do. She manages to get into my truck without any help. Better this way. I shouldn't touch her or get near her when she keeps giving me mixed signals.

When I return to my side of the truck and open the door, I find her in her bra. I freeze. "What are you doing?"

"Changing out of my wet shirt. You said I could borrow your hoodie."

I clench my teeth and slide behind the steering wheel, then shut the door hard. What the hell is she trying to do to me? Drive me insane? Fine. Two can play at this game. I remove my wet shirt and toss it to the back of the truck before putting my seat belt on.

"Really, Paris? You're going to drive like that?"

"I don't have a spare, and you're wearing my only dry piece of clothing."

She falls silent, so I dare a peek. It's a big mistake. She looks perfect wearing my clothes, sexy as hell, with her long, tousled damp hair and a pout that only makes me want to kiss her again. I force my gaze back on the road.

"Are you going to tell me why you got angry with me back there?" I ask, because I'm obviously a glutton for punishment.

"If you don't know, I'm not going to tell you," she grumbles.

"That's just fucking dumb. In case you don't already know, men are dense. You have to spell things out for us."

I expect her to pile on to what I just said, but instead, she asks, "Do you remember what happened after our parents caught us kissing?"

"Yeah. They yelled for an eternity and became mortal enemies," I joke, even though that's pretty much what happened.

"No, after that. You stopped talking to me."

I grip the steering wheel tighter. "I was waiting for the dust to settle."

She snorts. "The dust didn't take nine fucking years to settle, Paris."

"I didn't wait *that* long. A week."

"What are you talking about?"

A traffic light turns red, which is providential, because I need to look at her when I say this. "I came looking for you at your soccer practice. I thought I was being sneaky, but your mother saw me and told me that if I didn't leave you alone, she'd send you to live with your grandparents in Brazil."

"What? That's ridiculous. She'd never do that."

"Well, she sounded pretty believable. I didn't want you to get punished because of me, so I decided to wait longer and then..." I look away.

"And then Cory."

"Yeah." My voice is thick, and the knot in my chest tightens.

She doesn't speak for a moment, and I find that I can't say anything else either. The light turns green, and as usual, I wait a couple of seconds before driving. I don't accelerate, and that saves me from colliding with the asshole who runs a red light. He speeds in front of my truck, missing it by a hair. I stomp on the brake hard, and my body lurches forward. The seat belt digs into my bare chest, burning—that's why one shouldn't drive without a shirt on.

"Motherfucker! He could have hit us," Vanessa blurts out.

"Yeah." I slip my hand under the seat belt and rub the chaffed spot.

"Are you okay?"

"I'm fine," I say, sounding harsher than I intended.

Speaking about my brother put me in a funk, and now I just want to get Vanessa home and be alone for a while.

A heavy silence drops over us like a thick blanket, smothering and unyielding. I could turn on the radio but I'm not in the mood to be entertained. I shouldn't let the darkness drag me under again, but I can't find an ounce of motivation to stop it.

When I park in front of Vanessa's house, I say without looking at her, "We're here. You can return my hoodie later."

She exits without a word. I keep my gaze glued to the windshield even when she opens the back door to grab her crutches. A second later, my face gets hit by a ball of fabric.

"Here's your hoodie now. Thanks for the ride." She slams the door shut and trudges to the front door without a shirt on.

Son of a bitch.

I get out of the truck and sprint to catch up with her. "Vanessa, wait."

"Just leave, Paris." She leans one of her crutches against the wall and shoves her now free hand inside her huge bag.

"I planned to, but I can't go without clearing the air between us."

She whips her face to mine while her hand remains buried deep in her bag. "There's nothing to clear. You believed some bullshit lie my mother told you, and then life happened. You picked Lydia, and then decided to match her horrid personality."

The neighbor's front door opens, and on instinct, I step in

front of Vanessa, bracing my right arm against the wall behind her, and hiding her from view.

"What are you doing?" she grits out.

"You're half-naked."

"So?"

The neighbor doesn't acknowledge us as he proceeds to take his dog for a night walk. Yet, I don't move, and she doesn't either. One moment we're locked in a battle of stares, the next, I'm claiming her mouth, and pressing my body against hers. Her back meets the front door and she drops the crutches. The air is chilly, but I'm on fire, burning from the inside out for her.

Her fingers thread through my hair, yanking at the strands. "Paris," she murmurs.

I ease back. "Do you want me to leave?"

Her hooded eyes stay locked on my lips. "No, I want to find the damn key in my bag."

I step back, giving her room to rummage through the accessory that seems meant to hide things. She finally fishes out the key with an air of triumph. I don't follow her inside immediately, needing to know she really wants me there.

She looks over her shoulder, and asks, "Are you coming?"

I almost leap inside, pulling her into my arms while I push the door closed with my foot. My mouth finds hers again and, like magic, the darkness that consumed me during the trip here vanishes into thin air. All I needed was my girl.

SIXTEEN

VANESSA

It's futile to hold on to my grudge, to fight the hurricane of feelings that I kept bottled inside for so long. Paris was an idiot for believing my mother, but he was only thirteen. Then he lost his brother, and that viper Lydia swooped in when I couldn't, thanks to fate fucking up my life.

Or maybe we needed the gap. How many love stories start at the cusp of teenagehood and last more than a few months?

I don't want to think about the past. The moment is now. I'm with Paris, and he's kissing me like he wants to drown in me. I want to touch him everywhere, explore the hard planes of his body, feel the smoothness of his soft skin against my fingertips.

But Heather could come home at any moment, and I don't want her to interrupt us again. Pulling back just a little, I say, "Let's go to my room and get you out of those wet jeans."

Paris's heavy-lidded gaze bounces between my eyes, searching. "Are you sure?"

"Yes. More than anything in the world."

He kisses me hard as he lifts me off the floor. My legs

immediately wrap around his hips. Our mouths are fused together when he strides down the hallway.

I pull back suddenly, even though I don't want to interrupt the toe-curling kiss. "Wait. Do you know where we're going?"

"I was waiting for you to tell me." He rubs the space between my eyebrows. "Get rid of this frown, beautiful. I never went exploring at that party last year, save for using the restroom."

"How did you know what I was thinking?"

He kisses the corner of my mouth, and then whispers in my ear. "Because I know you too well."

Desire travels down my back and curls at the base of my spine while goose bumps prickle over my arms. "It's the door to your left."

Without missing a beat, Paris holds me with one arm so he can open the door. He doesn't move farther into the room after he shuts us inside though.

"What is it?" I ask.

He turns half away and glances at the knob. "Your door doesn't lock?"

"Sadly, no. Don't worry. Heather never comes into my room."

His lips split into a devilish grin. "Good. I don't want to hold back for fear of getting caught."

I reciprocate the smile. "Put me down? I want to get rid of these jeans."

"As you wish." He lowers me gently and then drops to his knees in front of me. "Let me help you."

My breath catches when he unzips them and runs his tongue dangerously close to where I desperately want his mouth to be. I thread my fingers through his hair and watch as he pulls the damp fabric down my hips and rolls the jeans off me. Even though it's tricky getting rid of wet pants, he does so easily, and this moment is so hot, I might combust on the spot just watching him.

"God, you're beautiful," he says, right before he kisses my sex through my panties.

Anticipation and lust are making me shake from head to toe, something Paris notices. "I can stop if you want."

"No," I croak. "Please don't."

He skims his hands up and down the sides of my legs. "Are you nervous, kitten?"

A shaky laugh bubbles up my throat, giving me away. "No."

He narrows his heated gaze. "There's no reason to be. Remember, it's me."

I blink fast as I process his words. Doesn't he know I'm a jumble of nerves for that very reason? Or maybe he thinks my reaction is connected to my assault. If anything, I need Paris to erase every memory I have of Ryan.

"I know it's you. I trust you." I cup his cheek.

He turns his face and kisses my palm before looking up again. "I'll make you feel good, gorgeous."

"You already are."

His smile lights up the room and makes my heart soar. This is the point of no return for me. I'm jumping off the edge and I don't care if there's solid ground below or not. I've broken the dam, now I can't pretend anymore I'm not in love with him, always have been.

He pushes my panties aside and licks my clit with a sensuous stroke of his expert tongue, making me see stars. I hold on to his shoulders because I'm turning to putty in his hands.

With a groan, he grips my hips harder, digging his fingers into my skin. His tongue is merciless and is quickly turning me into stardust. I buckle forward when the first wave of orgasm hits me, glad that he has a firm hold on me. He pulls back when I'm still in the throes of it, but before I can complain, he replaces his mouth with his hand. His thumb flicks my clit left and right while he penetrates me with two fingers.

"That's it, kitten. Come for me."

Nothing comes out of my mouth save for incoherent sounds. I'm breathless and boneless when the wave recedes.

I don't realize I have turned my hands into claws until I see the marks my long nails leave on his shoulder. "I'm so sorry."

Chuckling, he unfurls from his crouch. "Don't be. I didn't feel a thing."

Keeping my eyes glued to his, I rub his erection through his jeans. "We have to remedy that."

He groans, then captures my face between his hands and kisses me while I tease him through his clothes. It's not enough though.

I pull back and whisper against his lips, "Watch me."

It's my turn to kneel before him, a veritable Greek god, and help his cock out of its briefs. I drop my jaw when I see his size. Paris is big *everywhere*. Before he takes my hesitation the wrong way, I wrap my fingers around the base, and lick its length from bottom to top.

"Oh my god, Vanessa." His fingers snake through my hair.

Loving how he says my name like he's dying a little, I bring the soft tip into my mouth and spend a moment playing with the sensitive skin. His grip on my hair increases. He has a thick strand twisted in his fist, and the little bit of pain spurs me on. I swallow his entire length until it hits the back of my throat. I've never deep-throated anyone before, but I'll do anything to drive Paris wild.

"Oh yeah, babe. Just like that." He begins to move his hips, an early attempt to fuck my mouth.

I want him to do it, but not yet. I'm having too much fun exploring, learning what he likes. I pull back just enough to keep my lips around the head while I work him with my hand. My fingers glide up and down easily, and he seems to grow larger with each stroke.

"I want all the way in your filthy mouth again, kitten," he says in a voice that's tight with need.

I suck him again, loving his taste, the feel of his cock against my tongue.

"That's it, babe. Suck me harder."

He thrusts his hips forward, and this time, I do let him take control. His grunts of pleasure and his dirty mouth are making my clit throb again. I might come just from listening to him.

He's rough and demanding, but I can take it. I can take all of him. He's pulling my hair harder now, and I don't think he realizes it yet, but it feels so damn good.

"Fuck! I'm gonna come."

He tries to pull out, but I grab his butt cheeks and keep him where he is. His cock throbs against my tongue as his release fills my mouth. I drink it all, and when it's all gone, I'm sad there isn't more. He goes perfectly still for a moment, and the grip he has on my hair lessens. I ease back, releasing him with a wet pop, and let my knees fold until I'm sitting on the balls of my feet.

His expression is soft as he looks at me, but it changes in a flash to something close to remorse. He drops into a crouch in front of me and asks, "Did I hurt you, babe?"

"Uh, what? No."

He watches me closely. "Are you sure?"

I nod. "Yeah. I never knew you had such a dirty mouth."

His lips twitch as if he can't decide if he should smile or continue to worry. "I never talked like that before, but with you…" He picks up a lock of my hair and lets it run through his fingers. "You drive me crazy, kitten."

Pure elation spreads through my chest. I'm insanely happy that his ex never got to see this side of him.

"I want more of you, Paris." I get back on my feet, pulling him with me.

He quirks an eyebrow. "How much more?"

Making sure I don't put any weight on my right foot, I rise on my tiptoes and kiss his jaw. "Everything."

He slants his lips over mine, kissing me hard and fast before stepping back. He yanks his jeans and underwear all the way down and then steps out of them. He makes a motion in my direction, but I raise my hand, halting him.

"Hold on for just a second. Let me take a moment to appreciate the view."

He gives me a crooked smile. "Fine, but only if you get rid of that." He points at my bra.

"I suppose that's fair." I reach behind my back and release the clasp.

I don't break eye contact as I lower each strap individually and finally let the bra fall at my feet.

Paris's Adam's apple bobs up and down as he swallows hard. "Damn it. You're breathtaking."

I drop my gaze to his ripped chest and abs and try to make out all the ink he has there. "So are you. When did you start getting those?"

"Two years after Cory died." He touches a spot on his left pec. "I got this one for him."

I look closer so I can read the quote. My heart lurches in my chest when I recognize the words. It's a quote from the poem I wrote him. *In the darkness, I shall remember how your gaze brightened everything.*

"I... I didn't think you cared about that."

He frowns. "Do you know where this is from?"

His question takes me aback. "Of course I do. I wrote it."

He stares at me without blinking, without breathing. "*You* wrote it?" He gets the words out as if he's having a hard time processing them.

"Yes. I wrote you a letter, and the poem. I stuck the envelope in your mailbox the day after Cory died."

Paris's face becomes paler. He shuffles back until he sits on the edge of my mattress, holding his head in his hands. "I can't believe this."

"Can't believe what?"

He looks up. "Lydia gave me that poem. She said she wrote it."

My stomach clenches painfully. And then comes the rage.

"That lying *bitch*. She must have stolen the letter and copied the poem."

His blue eyes become glassy as he holds my stare. "I had no idea. This poem meant so much to me. Now I feel a million times worse for all the things I did to you. Especially that ridiculous stunt at prom."

I'm angry as fuck that Lydia lied to him, that she drove us apart, but I also hate hearing the sadness in his voice. I close the distance between us and capture his face between my hands. "I don't want to think about the past, or all the moments that snake stole from us. I just want to be with you."

He reaches for my face and rubs my cheek. "Same, kitten."

Our mouths meet as we drop onto the mattress. The kiss is unhurried at first, but the fire between us can't be contained. I fall on my back with Paris on top of me. His cock presses against my belly, already rock hard.

I open my legs wide for him, lifting my knees. He releases my lips to continue his torture down my neck and then my chest. His large hand covers one of my breasts while his tongue teases my other nipple to the point that I'm begging for another release. I've had fun in the bedroom before, but never in my life has a guy turned me on so much that I could orgasm without penetration or clit stimulation. I didn't even think it was possible until now.

"Paris, I need more."

He lifts his sexed-up face to look at me. "Me too, gorgeous. Where do you keep your condoms?"

"Nightstand."

He doesn't even need to move to reach the drawer. He pulls the box out and flips it over. Only one packet falls from it. We both don't speak for a long stretch. Is he thinking about how often Ryan and I had sex?

"Well…" He picks up the condom. "I guess we have to make this last a really long time."

"Fine by me. There's no limit to how many times I can climax during one fuck."

He watches me through narrowed eyes as he rips the packet open. "It's okay, kitten. I have good stamina."

My gaze inevitably drops to his erection, and a sliver of nervousness returns to my chest. We're really doing this. I never allowed myself to fantasize about sleeping with Paris, because I never thought it would happen. I sincerely believed I had lost him to that leech forever. Now I'm terrified I'm going to suck.

He rolls the condom down his length and returns to his position between my legs. But before he lowers his body to mine completely, he rests his forearms on each side of my shoulders and really looks at me.

"What?" I ask.

"I'm giving you the chance to change your mind."

"Paris..."

"I don't want to mess things up between us anymore. I'm done hurting you without realizing it."

My heart skips a beat. Here he is being one-hundred-percent Paris, something I thought I hated, and yet the butterflies in my stomach say otherwise. "The only way you can screw things up is if you don't shut up and fuck me already."

His eyes widen a fraction, and then he leans back and lifts one of my legs, setting it over his shoulder. His fingers wrap around his shaft, then he pumps it a couple of times, not breaking eye contact. The visual makes me hornier, so much so, that I bring my fingers to my pussy and play with myself too.

A groan comes from deep in his throat. He places his cock right at my entrance, and says, "If getting railed by me is what you want, kitten...."

In one powerful move, he sheathes himself in me, making me cry out. He's filling me completely, stretching me to the max. This isn't my first time, but it feels like it could be. He rotates his hips without pulling back, letting me get used to his girth.

"How does it feel, babe?"

"Do you really want to know?" I peer at him through half-open eyes.

He reaches over and rubs his thumb over my lower lip. "Yes."

"I'm not sure. Move your hips again." I give him a wicked grin.

Instead of gyrating his pelvis like before, he pulls back halfway and then slowly fills me once more. "Like that?"

I close my eyes and hum. "Yeah, like that. It feels good, really good."

He slides his hand down my chest and grabs one of my breasts, kneading it as he proceeds to fuck me properly. Man, this is even better. I can't concentrate anymore.

"Now it's your turn," I breathe out. "Confess."

"I love fucking your tight pussy, babe," he grunts. "Never had anything better."

A shadow of doubt crosses my mind. Is he telling me the truth, or is that just dirty talk?

"I can tell by your face that you don't believe me." He leans forward, keeping my leg firmly resting over his shoulder. I'm lucky that I'm flexible, because he's stretching me in more ways than one like this. "I'm not lying, kitten. I swear to God." He kisses me slowly, matching the tempo of his thrusts. I throw my arms around his neck, needing him closer as I melt into the mattress.

There's a sudden shift between us. The pace increases, our tongues dancing together with more fury, more passion. The headboard bangs loudly against the wall, mixing with the creaking of the bed. We might end up breaking it, but I don't care. The world could end, and I wouldn't make him stop.

It's fortunate our mouths are fused together when I climax, because it's violent and earth shattering, and I'd have screamed at the top of my lungs otherwise.

"I'm sorry, babe," he says a moment later against my lips.

"Why are you apologizing?"

"Because I'm… motherfucker," he groans, and pounds into me faster and faster. His cock thickens, grows harder, and pulses inside of me.

He slows down and rests his forehead against mine. His breathing is coming out in bursts when he says, "I couldn't hold on any longer. That's why I was apologizing."

His confession makes me laugh. "Dude, you gave me the best orgasms of my life."

He leans back and studies me. "Did I? For real?"

I nod. "Now get off me before you make the condom pointless."

He kisses my nose first. "You're cute when you're bossy."

My leg hurts a little from being in that awkward position for so long, but I try to hide that from Paris. He slides off me and gets out of bed. It's only then that I think of a reply.

Leaning on my elbows, I say, "So that means I'm always cute."

He looks over his shoulder, and smiles. "You're gorgeous."

A blush creeps up my cheeks. Luckily, Paris heads into the bathroom to dispose of the condom, and I don't have to hide my reaction from him. I collapse on the bed and stare at the ceiling while sporting a grin that I'm sure is the goofiest ever.

Paris returns a moment later, and I have to force the smile from my face. I get off the bed and veer to the bathroom to freshen up, kind of dreading the post-sex talk. But when I return to the room, he's out.

I guess we don't need to talk tonight. I slide in next to him and fall asleep so fast, I don't have time to worry about tomorrow.

SEVENTEEN

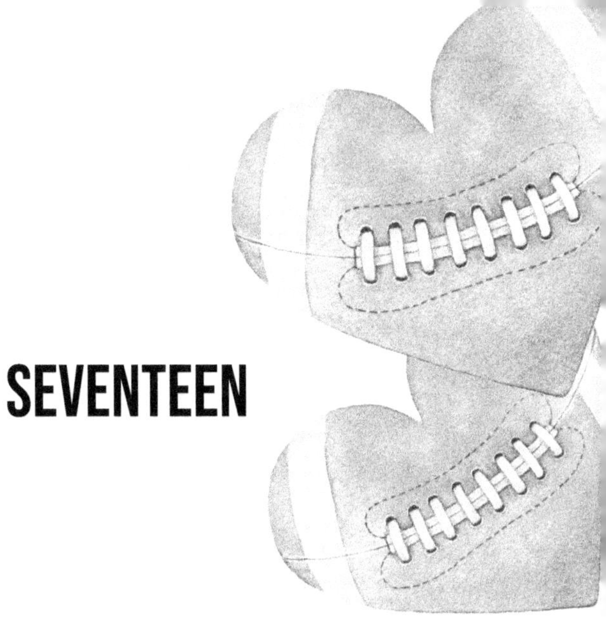

I wake up with someone kissing my shoulder. At first, I think I'm dreaming, but then the last vestiges of sleep ebb away. The solid chest pressed against my back reminds me this isn't a dream. I slept with Paris, and he ended up spending the night. I wait for apprehension to hit me. He's my first love and heartbreak, and I've been wrestling with my feelings—lust, longing, and fear—for a while. But the anxiety doesn't come, maybe because, not satisfied with kissing me, he runs his fingers down my stomach.

Letting out a sigh, I snuggle closer. "Hmm, I could get used to waking up like this."

"Me too." He bites my shoulder gently as his fingers glide between my legs, finding my folds already slick with desire.

He slides down the bed and turns me on my back at the same time. The sheet is partially covering us, and before he disappears underneath it, he locks his heated gaze with mine, making it difficult to breathe.

"Have I told you how glorious you look in the morning?" he asks and places an open-mouth kiss below my belly button.

I shiver. "No, and it'd be a lie anyway."

"Not from where I am. Now let's find out if you taste as sweet as last night."

He moves farther south, disappearing from view. Instead of peppering a trail of kisses down my belly, he slides his warm tongue all the way to my center and, when he gets to my clit, he licks my bundle of nerves nice and slow.

I twist my fingers around the sheet beneath me, arching my back as a desperate moan escapes my lips. "Oh, Paris. *Yes.*"

He alternates between licking and sucking my clit into his mouth. My toes are already curling, and he's only just begun. This proves that last night's performance wasn't a fluke. He's not only a feast for the eyes, he's also a god in bed. In less than a minute, he has me panting. He nudges my legs farther apart, and then flattens his palm on my pubic bone and eats my pussy as if it's the best thing he's ever had. I can already feel the telltale signs that an orgasm isn't far. My nipples are as hard as little pebbles. Closing my eyes, I play with them, heightening my pleasure.

The hinges of my bedroom door creak loudly a second before Heather says, "Hey, have you… oh my god."

My eyes fly open, and I'd have jumped into a sitting position if Paris wasn't between my legs. "Heather! What the hell!"

"Sorry! I didn't know you made up with Ryan." She begins to back away, but then Paris's head pops from under the sheet.

"She did *not* make up with that asshole," he growls.

If I wasn't dying of mortification, I'd take pleasure in Heather's reaction. Her eyes bug out of her skull cartoon style. Then she squints. "I *knew* there was something going on between you two."

"Get out!" I toss my pillow at her.

She finally does, shutting the door. I close my eyes and pinch my nose. "Kill me now."

"And you said she would never barge in here." He laughs.

I open my eyes and glare. "This has *never* happened before. Maybe she knew you were here and wanted to catch us."

Paris folds his arms over my tummy and rests his chin on top of them. "My truck *is* parked right out front."

"Ugh! One more reason to kill her."

"Do you want to do that after I get you off?" He wiggles his eyebrows up and down.

I don't know if I should laugh or yell. "No. She killed the mood." I push him off me and get up.

"Yeah, I should get going anyway. I don't want to be a witness to murder. That could hinder my chances of getting into a good med school."

"You're making fun of me, and I don't appreciate it." I grab a pair of clean undies from the chest of drawers and put them on hastily.

Paris finds his jeans and wrinkles his nose. "Damn. I should have hung these in the bathroom to dry."

Remorse dampens my anger a little. "Crap. I totally forgot about it too. Are they still super wet?"

"Damp, but hell, nothing for it now."

He gets dressed and I simply watch. Never mind that I'm still wearing only a pair of panties.

He notices, and with a sexy smile, walks over. "I think that maybe you *do* want me to finish what I started." He circles my waist with his strong arms.

"The issue is that I'll want more, and we're out of condoms."

He twists his face into an exaggerated frown. "True. I'll stop by the drugstore later. We won't want for condoms, kitten."

And here comes the dreaded morning-after talk.

"About that… what exactly are we doing?"

He grows serious and it's not an act now. "Honestly, I wasn't planning on jumping into another serious relationship."

Disappointment floods through me. I should be on the same page—I just got out of a relationship. But it's Paris, and I'm in love with him.

"Yeah, same." I try to pull away, but he holds me against him.

"You didn't let me finish. It wasn't the plan, because I never thought you'd give me the time of day."

"Oh."

He traces my hairline with the tips of his fingers. "I won't lose you again, babe."

My heart overflows with emotion, and if I'm not careful, I might blurt out the truth and surely scare the crap out of him. Who says the *L* word after one hookup? Crazy people. I don't want him to think I'm from the same psycho town as Lydia.

"What are you saying, Paris? Do you want to date me?"

"I do." He kisses my neck, making my eyes flutter. "But I think we should keep things on the down-low for now."

I pull back and look him in the eye. "Why?"

Letting out a sigh, he steps back, releasing me. I miss the contact immediately. "Well, there's the issue of our families. I want to date you without the drama."

I cross my arms. "We can't avoid our parents forever. But it's more than that, isn't it?"

He pinches his lips together, and his eyes look hella guilty now. "Yeah, there's the Lydia factor. We are one-hundred-percent over, at least on my part, but you saw her on the quad. She's clearly not ready to let me go. And after what you told me about the stolen poem...."

"What? You don't believe she did that?"

"That's not what I'm saying at all. I believe you. But knowing what she did... it just proves that she isn't a stable person."

"That's too fucking bad. Paris, you can't make life decisions around her moods."

His expression is pained, which makes me want to scream.

"I know. I'm trying to spare you."

"I don't need your protection. I can handle any shade she throws my way. Don't use her as an excuse to keep this quiet because you're afraid to hurt Lydia's precious feelings."

"I don't care about her feelings." Rubbing his jaw, he glances away. "I think I've already fucked this up. I should go."

My stomach drops through the earth. That's it? He's just going to walk away because I don't agree with his idiotic thought process?

"Yeah, I guess you should."

"I'll call you later."

I almost say *don't bother*, but that would be childish. I end up not saying a word, but I don't miss the fact that he walks out of my room without kissing me goodbye.

I turn away from the door as tears gather in my eyes. I *knew* this was too good to be true. I trusted Paris, and he once again smashed my heart to pieces.

Ugh. I'm so fucking stupid. Maybe I shouldn't have lost my temper so quickly and tried to see it from his side.

The door opens again, and I'm ready to tell Heather to get lost, but arms hug me from behind, and Paris's mouth kisses my shoulder.

"I'm sorry, kitten. I'm an idiot."

The anger swirling in my chest is quickly replaced by relief. He came back, and I can't help melting into his body. "Yes, you are."

"You're right. I can't keep my happiness on hold because other people are miserable, or in her case, insane." He turns me around in his arms. "I want to be with you."

I search his eyes and find nothing but honesty in them. It makes me feel guilty that I was quick to judge his motivation. If I'd been in his shoes and found out my ex had been lying to me for years, I'd go nuclear on his ass. But Paris isn't like me. Raging jealousy made me react that way. I don't want Lydia taking up any more space in his mind than she already did. I have to trust him, or this will never work.

"I want to be with you too. And maybe it wouldn't be the end of the world if we don't broadcast that we're together yet. I'm not saying that to spare Lydia—I actually want her to rot in hell. But it'd be nice to get to know you without the world intruding."

"Are you saying you want to date me in secret?"

I shrug. "Why not? It could be fun sneaking around. And major bonus points for avoiding parental drama."

"Yeah, but can Heather keep a secret?" He arches an eyebrow.

"Oh, I've been saving up dirt on her for a long time. She'll keep mine if I keep hers."

"Now I'm curious."

"If I tell you, then I'll lose my bargaining chip."

He cradles my face between his hands and claims my lips. This should be a see-you-later kiss, not the fire-starter kind. I'm regretting not letting him finish his tongue play after Heather barged in.

As if reading my mind, he says, "Sit on my face, kitten."

"What about you?"

He bites my earlobe softly, then whispers in my ear, "Oh, don't worry, I'm gonna enjoy myself thoroughly."

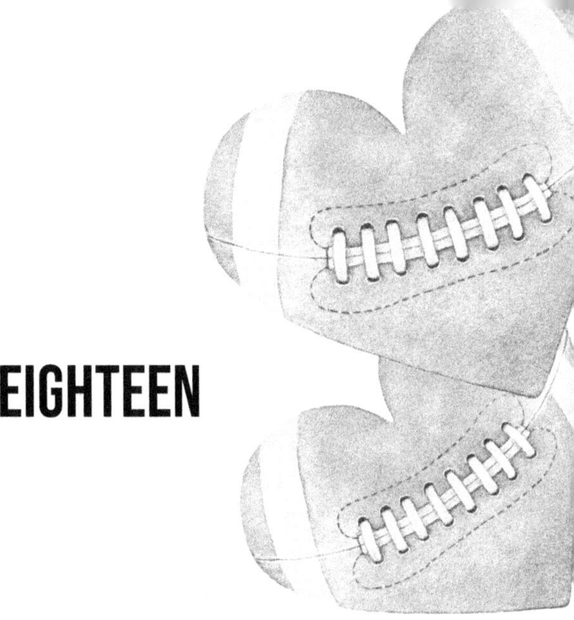

EIGHTEEN

PARIS

I've been walking around campus with the biggest smile, so it's no surprise that when I meet up with Danny and Puck at Zuko's Diner to grab a quick lunch, I can't wipe it off my face. Perhaps I should tone it down. It's not my MO to be this chipper, but hell, I don't want to. Not even the knowledge of Lydia's lies is going to bring me down. I'll deal with her later.

"What's up, boys?" I ask as I slide into Puck's side of the booth seat. "Did you order already?"

"Nah, we just got here," Puck replies. "We were waiting for you and Rossi."

"Oh, I didn't know Andy was coming." I reach for the menu.

"Yeah, apparently Puck has news he'd like to share with all of us in person." Danny gives Puck a meaningful glance.

"I hope he's not late as usual. I'm starving. I could eat everything they have here," I say.

Someone whacks me upside the head with a menu. "I'm not always late, jackass."

Andreas sits across from me and pushes his aviator

sunglasses onto his head. I rub the spot where he hit me, but not even his antics are going to sour my mood.

I notice his leather jacket, and say, "Tom Cruise called and wants his *Top Gun* outfit back."

"Well, he can sit and wait." Andreas smirks, not falling for my bait. I chuckle nonetheless, making him frown. "Wait. Did I just hear Paris laugh? Did I miss something?"

"If you did, we all did. I have no idea what's gotten into him," Puck replies.

"He probably got laid," Danny chimes in.

The menu becomes very interesting all of a sudden. I keep my gaze down, pretending to scan the offerings when I already know what I want.

"Holy shit! He totally did." Andreas smacks his hand on the table, rattling the condiments tray. "All right. Spill. We want a name."

"I'm not going to kiss and tell."

"That's right, Paris. Those things should remain private," Puck pipes up.

As the most religious dude in our group, it makes sense that he believes that. I grew up in a churchgoing family too, but my folks are only superzealous when it suits their interests. As for me, I just follow along to avoid headaches.

"Of course you believe that." Andreas shakes his head and glances at the menu. "How's that chastity vow working out for you?"

"It's going great. Now can we stop focusing on Andino's love life for a second so I can tell you why I wanted you here?"

"Hooray to that," I say.

"You have our undivided attention, Puck," Danny replies.

"Hold on. I got to make a call first." He pulls out his phone and presses the video chat button. A moment later, Troy's face appears on the scream. The former quarterback for the Rebels, he's been living in London with his girlfriend since he graduated a year ago, and I haven't seen him since.

"Hey, Puck. What's up, man? Long time."

"I know. The whole gang is here." He turns his camera so Troy can get a visual of all of us.

We all wave at the camera and say hello before Puck sets his phone against the window and Troy has a view of the entire table.

"I'm dying here, man," Troy says. "What's going on that you need all of us together?"

"Duh, can't you guess?" Andreas answers before Puck can. "He's getting married."

I kick him under the table. "Dude. Shut up!"

"Ouch," he complains.

"Never mind Rossi, Paris. He loves to be a dick." Puck laughs. "But anyway, that's exactly why I wanted you all here. Mia and I are getting married next month, and I want you guys to be my groomsmen."

"In a month?" My brows arch. "What's the hurry?"

"Oh my god, Andino. Are you thick? It's a shotgun wedding." Andreas laughs.

Danny scowls. "You don't know that."

Puck rubs the back of his neck. "Actually, that's why. Mia is pregnant."

That only makes Andreas laugh harder. "Chastity vow my ass."

"Wow, congratulations, man." Troy interrupts Andy's antics. "Count me in."

"Yeah, me too. And congrats," I add.

"Same," Danny says, "And you are happy about it, right?"

Considering he grew up without knowing who his father was and then later found out the man was a total douche, I don't find it strange that he's asking.

"I couldn't be happier. I've always known Mia was the one."

"But what happened to the chastity vow? I thought you were dead serious about that," Andreas asks without mirth. I guess he's done making fun of Puck.

"Yes, we were, but after Mia's cousin passed away unexpectedly, we decided that life was unpredictable."

A shadow drops over me. I know too well what the sudden death of a loved one can do. In my case, I jumped into a toxic relationship. Puck's outcome is far better than mine was.

"Since you guys are all there, I might as well tell you my news too," Troy pipes up.

Andreas sits straighter and his brows arch as he says, "Don't fucking tell me you proposed to Charlie without telling me beforehand."

Troy rolls his eyes. "I wouldn't dream of doing that to you."

Danny and I chuckle. Since I'm sitting across from Andreas, I get the full blast of his glare.

"What's the news?" Danny brings the conversation on track.

"We're moving back to California. Charlie and I both got offered jobs in LA."

We all take turns congratulating Troy on his move, and then he says he needs to run errands. We're ready to order when the bell chime draws my attention to the diner's entrance.

Ryan walks in with one of his douchey friends, and my entire body tenses. "That motherfucker," I say under my breath.

"Who are you talking about?" Andreas turns to look, and so does Danny.

"Who's that?" Puck asks.

"A frat-boy asshole," Andreas replies.

My tight grip on the edge of the table is the only thing keeping my ass on the booth seat. Ryan doesn't glance in our direction, and he should thank his lucky stars that he doesn't get assigned a booth on our side of the diner.

"What did he ever do to you?" Danny asks.

I'm seething as I try to control my rage, so I don't answer right away.

"Shit. He must have done something awful. Paris is about to blow," Andreas replies.

My appetite is gone, and I know that if I stay a moment longer, I won't be able to contain myself. I'll march to that fuckwad and do what I should have done the night he attacked Vanessa.

I get up suddenly. "I can't be here."

"Bro, wait up," Andreas says, but I don't listen.

I stride toward the exit, trying my best to not look toward Ryan. My hand is on the knob when I hear his laughter. I turn and see he's at the farthest booth from the front. My body is already moving to head that way when a hand on my shoulder stops me.

"Whatever he did, you're in no condition to confront him now," Andreas tells me.

"Bullshit," I say, even though he's right.

"Bullshit my ass. You have murder in your eyes, Andino. Come on, let's get out of here." He opens the door and practically has to shove me out, because I'm rooted to the floor.

My rage doesn't simmer down once I'm in the parking lot. I'm filled to the max with it. Puck and Danny also followed and are crowding me now. They're blocking me from running back inside.

"Are you going to tell us why seeing Ryan Watergate made you go berserk?" Andreas asks.

"I can't tell you." I begin to pace. "Fuck! I want to kill that asshole."

"Let's get out of here then, before you have the chance," Andreas says.

"I came with Puck, so I'll ride with Paris," Danny says, as if I'm not there.

I turn around to glare at the trio. "I don't need a fucking babysitter."

"No offense, bro, but you do," Puck replies. "Go on, Danny. Take Paris away before he explodes."

Danny presses his hand against my back and nudges me

toward my truck. He wouldn't be able to move me if I put up a fight, but the sane part of my brain is slowly regaining control. I get behind the steering wheel and take a couple of deep breaths while I wait for Danny to get in.

"Are you okay to drive?" he asks as soon as he shuts the door.

"Yep." I put the truck in gear and accelerate too fast, burning rubber.

"Jesus, take it easy, man."

I ease off the gas pedal, managing to maintain the speed limit.

Danny lets me stew for a few minutes before he opens his mouth. "You don't need to tell me why you wanted to pummel Ryan, but is it something you can get over, or do I need to worry about it?"

I clutch the steering wheel tighter, clenching my jaw. "I'm not sure I can get over it."

Danny rubs his face and curses. "What can we do then, to avoid you getting in trouble if you decide to punish the bastard?"

"Keep him away from me."

"Yeah, that's not gonna work. We aren't attached to your hip, or his. Maybe if you told me why you hate his guts, then it'd be easier to help you fight the urge to annihilate him."

"I hear what you're saying, but unfortunately, I'd be betraying someone's trust if I told you."

"Can't you tell me what he's done without revealing your friend's name?"

I'm fucking torn. I'm bound to cross paths with Ryan again, and if today was any indication, I will *end* him. Then what? Get kicked off the team, expulsion, arrest? Maybe telling Danny would help, but even if I don't reveal Vanessa's name, I still feel like I'm betraying her trust.

"This stays between us, all right? No one can know, not even Andy or Sadie."

"Bro, you can trust me."

"I caught Ryan sexually assaulting someone outside of Tailgaters one night. I stopped him, but the victim didn't want to press charges. Which... I get it. But I'm still fucking mad that the motherfucker did that and wasn't punished for it."

"Man, that's fucked up. Now I get why you wanted to go savage on him. I'd probably have the same reaction."

I laugh without humor. "No, you wouldn't. You're the most chill guy I know."

"Not when someone I care about is involved. Sadie was attacked in London before she moved to LA. I can tell you now because she's fine with people knowing."

"No shit. I'm sorry, man."

"Yeah, she got stabbed trying to protect a friend from some drunks. Sometimes when I see her scar, I get a burst of anger. If the guy who did that to her crossed my path, I'd probably destroy him."

"Thanks for telling me, man. I don't know if it will help contain my anger, but I'm glad I'm not the only one who's protective of the ones they love."

"So, this is about Lydia, then?"

Shit. I can't believe I let that fucking comment slip. I can't let Danny believe Lydia was attacked. That wouldn't be right.

"No, Lydia wasn't the victim."

It takes a couple of beats for the coin to drop. "Oh shit. It was the girl who put that smile on your face earlier. I didn't know it was already that serious. I thought it was just a hookup."

"It wasn't just a hookup, and that's all I'm going to say."

"Fair. I'm done prying."

Vanessa's identity is a secret, but for how long? We don't plan to hide that we're dating forever. When we come out, Danny will know she was the girl Ryan attacked. Then my betrayal will be complete.

I'm so fucking consumed by my guilt that it's not until I drop Danny off that it dawns on me... I not only gave him too many clues about Vanessa, but I also confessed that I love her. I knew before last night that my feelings for her were deep, but I didn't think I was already in love with her.

I guess now I know.

NINETEEN

I spend an hour getting ready for my first stay-in date with Paris. Since we want to keep our relationship a secret, not going out in public is a must. So we agreed to takeout and a movie at home. I'm probably overdressed for it. I'm wearing my favorite pair of jeans, the ones that make my ass look fucking amazing, and a pretty top with a low neckline to show off my cleavage. I'd be wearing heels too, if it weren't for my sprained ankle.

I asked Heather if she could spend the night at her boyfriend Leo's place, so when I find her in the kitchen eating instant noodles, my disposition sours.

"What are you still doing here?"

"Relax. I'm leaving as soon as I finish dinner."

"You couldn't eat at Leo's?"

"I'm hungry now."

Glowering, I cross my arms. "You'd better not be here when Paris arrives."

"And if I am, so what? I've already seen everything." She smirks.

"I still think you knew he was in my room when you barged in."

Unfazed, she swallows a mouthful of noodles. "Think whatever you want. I don't get why you want to date him in secret though. You guys have been into each other for a long time. Anyone with a pair of eyes could see that."

"That's such bullshit. Paris and I barely interacted with each other at Rushmore unless he was defending his ex."

"If you say so." She shrugs.

"I do. Anyway, family drama and that fucking bitch drove us apart the first time. We want to date in peace for a while."

"Oh please. You were only thirteen. There's no chance a relationship then would have lasted more than a few months."

She couldn't be more wrong, and the thought makes my stomach coil tightly.

"Right, then explain to me why Paris dated Lydia for so long."

Heather sets down her bowl and grows serious. "Lydia is a conniving snake. She took advantage of Paris's grief to sink her claws into him. And didn't you just find out that she stole your poem and claimed she wrote it?"

I grimace. I told Heather the story this morning. "Don't remind me. I want to punch her in the throat for that one alone."

"But you can't do it because of your position on the Ravens. I get it. Maybe I can get revenge for you." She smiles in a chilling way.

I narrow my eyes. "You've been watching too much Netflix."

"So? Do you want to know why Paris put up with all her bullshit?"

My spine goes taut as my interest piques. It seems Heather knows more about the details of Paris and Lydia's relationship than I do.

I wave my hand. "Go on. You're going to tell me anyway."

"Every time she wanted to manipulate Paris into doing something, she threatened to kill herself."

My blood turns cold, and a new knot forms in my chest. "How do you know that?"

She shrugs. "I can't remember where I heard the story, but it didn't come from only one source. You can't tell me it doesn't fit her personality to pull shit like that. Can you imagine what that was like for Paris? I mean, he lost his brother to suicide."

I hug my middle, feeling wretched. "He probably felt he couldn't let that happen again."

"Exactly." She rinses her bowl and sticks it in the dishwasher. "Anyway, I'd better go. I don't want to make Paris uncomfortable with my presence."

In a daze, I veer for the couch. It takes a couple minutes for Heather to leave, but I know she does when the front door bangs shut. I'm reeling from what she told me, sad beyond measure that Paris had to deal with that fucker for so long. I really should beat the shit out of her for all the suffering she caused. I don't realize I'm crying until I feel moisture on my cheeks. Damn it. There goes my makeup.

I jump from the couch, ready to run—more like hop—to my bathroom to check the damage, but a knock on the front door stops me short. Shit. It must be Paris. I don't want to make him wait outside. I change direction, but before I open the door for him, I look at my reflection in the mirror and wipe the corners of my eyes. The smudging was minimal.

I open the door with a smile that's a little forced. It changes into something genuinely radiant when I see Paris standing there in all his six-foot-four glory, holding a bouquet of pink roses along with the take-out containers. My heart does a somersault in my chest as tingles of excitement ripple through my body.

"Hi," I say.

"Hello, kitten."

I step back to allow him in, and then close the door. The smell of delicious Chinese food invades the space, but even though I was hungry before, food is now the last thing on my mind.

"Are those for me?" I eye the roses when all he does is stare at me with a grin.

"Ah, yes." He hands over the bouquet. "I was a little distracted."

I bring the flowers to my nose before I thank him for them. "They're beautiful."

"Not as beautiful as you."

I laugh, making Paris blush. He rubs the back of his neck. "Sorry. That was corny."

Stepping into his space, I kiss his cheek. "Lucky for you, I love corny."

His free arm snakes around my waist, pulling me flush against his body. His mouth finds mine next, and I melt into his embrace. If I could, I'd never stop kissing him. Happiness should be the only thing pumping into my heart, but instead, overwhelming sadness breaks through. I could have had him like this for much longer if Lydia hadn't interfered.

Reluctantly, I pull back. "I'd better put these in a vase."

I sense him watching me as I limp to the kitchen. I don't care to use the crutches in the house, so moving around is a little slow.

He follows me and sits on a high stool by the kitchen counter, setting the food there. "Is something wrong?"

I whip my face in his direction. "What? No. Why are you asking?"

His gaze narrows. "Kitten, don't lie to me. You look sad. Did something happen?"

Giving my attention to the flowers, I don't answer him. I don't know what to say without bringing up Lydia, and I really don't want to remind Paris of his ex.

"Vanessa…"

I let out a heavy sigh and look into his eyes again. "I want to tell you something."

He sits straighter in his chair. "Okay."

"I didn't abandon you when you lost your brother. When I

found out what happened, I begged my parents to take me to see you. They didn't think it was a good idea, despite my pleas. I went anyway on my bike. But when I got there, Lydia answered the door, and she wouldn't let me through. Then another woman showed up—I think she was your aunt. I mean, she looked a bit like your mother. Anyway, she told me you weren't in any condition to see anyone. I left, and it started to rain heavily." I touch the faint scar near my elbow.

"What happened?"

"I was almost hit by a car, ended up falling off my bike and breaking my arm. That's why I didn't see you. I wound up in the ER, and after that, my parents grounded me. I did convince my father to drive me to your house the next day to deliver the letter. But when my parents finally eased off my punishment, you were..." I drop my gaze to the counter. "It didn't look like you needed me anymore."

"She was just a friend then. She didn't become my girlfriend until freshman year of high school."

"Well, same difference."

He walks around the counter and pulls me into his arms. "I'm glad you told me. I'm also a bit mad that you could have gotten really hurt because of me."

"I was heartbroken for you. I wanted to be there."

He caresses my cheek with the back of his hand. "But is that why you're sad? It's in the past, kitten. All that matters is that we're together now."

I lower my gaze to the hollow of his throat, trying to hide the truth. It's probably pointless. He must see it in my eyes. I don't want to reveal what Heather told me though.

"I was sad because, thanks to my parents being stubborn mules, the accident, and Lydia acting like a soap opera villain, you got stuck in an unhealthy relationship."

He pinches my chin with his forefinger and thumb and lifts my face. "Maybe I had to go through that to appreciate what I have now."

He's right. I'm acting like a Debbie Downer.

I lift my right foot and then rise on the tip of my toes with my left so I can reach Paris's mouth. We don't waste time with small kisses. Our mouths crash together hungrily, impatient, and I know dinner will be forgotten for a while. He picks me up and goes straight to my room. I don't notice the plastic bag in his hand until he sets me down on the bed and empties it over the mattress. Three large boxes of condoms bounce off.

"Oh my god. Did you get a month's supply?"

"One month? Are you insane? That won't last a week." He grabs the hem of his T-shirt and peels it off.

His pecs and arms flex, making my mouth water. I know exactly what I'm doing to him first. I stand up and push him onto the bed.

"What are you doing, kitten?" he asks through a smile.

"I'm taking charge." I flatten my palms against his solid chest and nudge him back. "Lie down and let me have my fun."

His eyes turn smoldering in a flash. He cups the back of my head and pulls me to him for another gloriously hot kiss. Desire pools between my legs, making my clit throb. Maybe I shouldn't have worn jeans.

Before Paris decides to take control, I pull back and push off him so I can get rid of my clothes. He leans up on his elbows and watches me through hooded eyes. I take off my pants first but leave my underwear on. My long top covers them. Paris doesn't seem to mind. His attention is on my thighs, and his heated gaze feels like a caress.

"I love what soccer does for you, babe."

My lips curl into a grin. "I bet you do, but these have nothing to do with sports." I pull my top off and lob it to the side. I'm not wearing a bra, so instantly, Paris's gaze fixes on my breasts.

He stretches out an arm. "Come here, kitten. Let me feast on your lovely tits."

I wag my forefinger. "Oh no, sir. I said I was in charge, and I want to feast on *you*."

I straddle his thighs and then lower my mouth to his chest, licking the area around his nipple. He hisses, and then curls his fingers around a strand of my hair. I tease him a bit before biting softly, then I switch to the other side. While my tongue is busy, I run my fingers up and down his washboard abs, stopping my caress when my fingers reach the waistband of his pants.

"Vanessa, babe, what are you doing to me?" he asks in a raspy whisper.

"I'm exploring."

I pepper open kisses down his stomach, loving how he responds to me. His breathing is shallow, and his erection is straining against the fabric of his jeans.

"I want to explore too."

"Soon."

I unbutton his pants, and then open his fly slowly. Paris, impatient man that he is, lifts his ass and pushes the fabric as low as he can.

"Hey, I was going to do that," I complain halfheartedly.

"I'll let you peel them off my legs—just please get rid of them."

I was planning on tasting him, but I can't say no when he sounds like he's about to die.

I should have known it was a ruse. I need to slide off him to remove his jeans, and no sooner are they gone than he tackles me, flipping me over on the mattress so he's on top.

"Hey, that's not fair. I call foul play."

"Sorry, kitten. You weren't playing fair either." He thrusts his hips forward, rubbing his hard cock against my core.

We're both still wearing our underwear, but the friction alone is making me light-headed. Or maybe it's the skillful way he mingles his tongue with mine, taking and giving in equal measure. I forget my original plan and surrender to him. He's in no hurry to fuck me though. Instead, he mimics what's to come, grinding his pelvis against mine. My panties are soaked through when I climax out of the blue. I usually know when it's about to happen. Not this time.

"Oh my god, Paris. Don't stop," I beg him between feverish kisses.

He grunts in response, making me wonder why he isn't as chatty as the last time. I miss his filthy mouth, but I don't mind what his tongue is doing one bit. My body relaxes against the mattress as the wave of my release subsides.

He pulls back, resting his forearms on the mattress. "How are you feeling, kitten?"

"Pretty good." I smile.

"Do you know what I want to do now?" He runs his fingers over my collarbone.

"Eat dinner?"

He rewards me with a crooked smile. "Close." He brings his mouth to my ear and whispers, "I want to eat your pussy."

"Hmm. Only if I get to taste you at the same time."

"Deal."

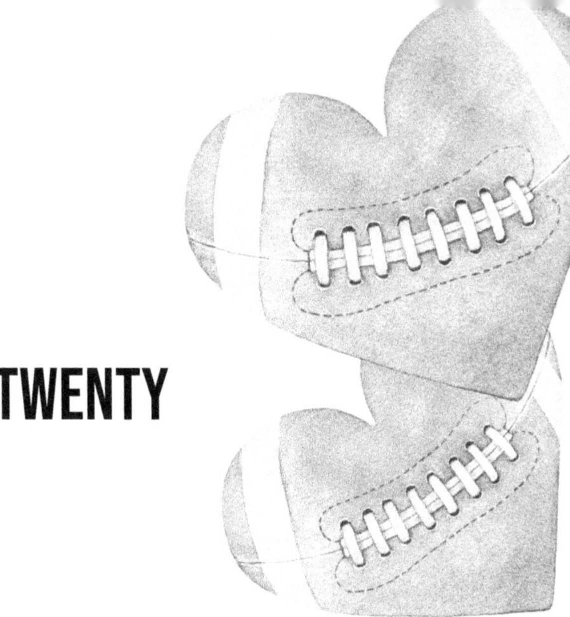

TWENTY

PARIS

I've never gotten into position so fast as I do with Vanessa. I lie on my back and grab her hips while she hovers above me. Like any guy, I love a sixty-nine, but I can't say I had many of those during my too-fucking-long previous relationship.

I lick her pussy before she can even get her hand around my cock. I pay attention to her reaction, testing things out to see what she likes best. Her legs begin to shake, telling me I'm doing something right. But when her luscious mouth wraps around me, I forget all about technique and let instinct take over.

I'm wild, out of control. My mind is scrambled. I can't think properly when her mouth feels like I'm actually fucking her pussy. Damn it. My girl is good. My balls are tight, ready to explode. I want to prolong this sweet agony, but Vanessa is merciless. She sucks me harder while massaging my balls, and that's my undoing. I come hard, thrusting my cock deeper into her mouth and grunting against her pussy.

She hasn't climaxed yet, and that's something I have to fix ASAP. I dig my fingers deeper into her hips and alternate between fucking her with my tongue and flicking her clit. She releases my cock and rests her cheek against my hip. Sexy moans escape her lips, and it's not long before she's screaming my name at the top of her lungs. I keep going, stopping only when her legs give out and she collapses next to me.

"Okay, I'm done for now, and we didn't even need the condoms." She laughs.

"Give me a few minutes."

She rolls onto her side and props her head on her hand, elbow on the mattress. "The night is young, and our food is getting cold. There's no hurry."

"True, but any minute that I'm not touching you is a waste."

"You're sweet." She walks her fingers over my thigh, getting closer to my dick.

It begins hardening again. "What did I tell you?"

"Well, if you insist." She sits up and reaches for the one box of condoms that didn't get pushed to the floor.

I link my hands behind my head and watch her get out one foil packet and rip it open. Her gaze meets mine, and a devious grin unfurls on her lips.

"What's up, kitten?" I ask.

She rolls the condom down my shaft and then straddles me. "I'm riding you, cowboy."

I grab her by the hips, positioning her better, but she's the one who guides my cock to her entrance. Even with me wearing protection, her pussy feels fucking amazing. I'm already addicted to my girl, and we've only just begun.

Flattening one hand on my shoulder, she gyrates her pelvis slowly, torturing me in the best possible way. I want to control her movements, make her go faster, but at the same time, I like watching her take charge.

I cup one breast instead and tease her nipple with my thumb. She closes her eyes and moans while moving her hips faster.

"You like that, babe?" I ask.

"Yes," she hisses.

Her pleasure makes me grow harder. She leans forward, bracing both hands on my shoulders while she rises as high as she can before slamming back into me. She's too far from me though. I want to taste her. I reach for the back of her head and bring her closer so I can claim her mouth. She can't move as fast in this position, but I don't care. I need to kiss her.

She leans back a little and looks into my eyes. My heart beats faster, and it has nothing to do with what we're doing in bed. It feels like it's going to burst out of my chest from pure joy. I cup her cheek, and her eyes go soft.

"What?" she asks.

"Nothing. Just drinking you in."

She caresses my lips with her thumb, which proves to be too much temptation for me. I grab her wrist and suck her finger into my mouth. A shuddering breath whooshes from her open lips, and she tightens around me. We begin to move again—I can't help but piston in and out of her, even though she's on top. The rules are out the window. When it comes to making my girl feel good, I won't play fair.

We're both taken over by desire, lost in a fog of lust as we chase our orgasms. I don't know anymore where I end and she begins. At one point, I flip her over so I can fuck her hard while kissing her senseless. She bites my lower lip before she gasps in pleasure. I follow her a moment later, shaking from head to toe as the release overcomes me.

I'll never get tired of this. Never.

It goes without saying that the take-out food I brought is already cold. To be fair, I could skip dinner and the movie and spend the whole damn night in bed with Vanessa, finding new ways to make her come.

She decides to use her crutches in the house again, after I offered to carry her everywhere. An offer that was self-serving, because I'll take any opportunity to touch her. It seems that, now that I've allowed my feelings for her to come to the surface, I want to compensate for all the years I pretended they weren't there.

In the kitchen her attention zeroes in on the food containers, but I nudge her toward the high stool. "You sit your pretty tush there while I warm up dinner, honey."

"How housewifey of you, darling." She smirks.

She still has the glow of someone who was properly fucked, and my plan is for her to always have that post-O-town look. It's crazy how I went from wanting to remain unattached for years after Lydia to thinking of ways I could see Vanessa every day. We both have crazy schedules, so the likelihood of that being possible is slim.

"Do you need anything?" she asks, bringing me back to the here and now.

"What?"

"You have a dazed look on your face, as if you're lost. The plates are in the cupboard behind you."

Shit. I didn't realize I spaced out. "Yeah, plates would be helpful."

I focus on getting the food ready and try not to let my mind wander again. There's no point worrying about things that we can figure out as we go.

"This is surreal," she pipes up.

I glance at her with an eyebrow raised. "What is?"

"You standing half-naked in the middle of my kitchen, prepping dinner."

My lips curl into a crooked smile. "I'm only half-naked because you made me put on my jeans."

"And that was me compromising. Do you know how tempting it is to watch you move around without a shirt on?"

I face her and give her an unobstructed view of the goods. Her eyelids drop a little as fire crackles to life in her gaze. The attention makes me grow hard again, and I forget about dinner.

"If you keep looking at me like that, I'll bend you over that counter and have my way with you."

She stretches her arms over the hard surface and bends forward like a cat, giving me a better view of her glorious tits. "Is that so?"

"Don't tempt me, kitten," I growl.

"Oh, I'm not tempting you. I'm daring you."

I set the plate in my hand near the sink and reach her in three long strides. She lets out a little squeak when I pick her up from the stool and do exactly what I promised—bend her over the counter. Keeping one hand flat against her back, I unzip my jeans.

"I shouldn't have let you convince me to put these back on," I tell her.

"The important thing here is that *I* didn't."

I spread her legs before shoving my hand under her long T-shirt. *Motherfucker*. She's not wearing underwear. I lean forward, pressing my chest against her back, while I bring my lips to her ear and my fingers play with her wet pussy.

"You're one filthy kitten," I whisper.

She moans, "If I'm filthy, it's your fault."

Her reply is like a shot of libido down my cock. I like the idea that I'm the only one who turns her on like this. I shove my hand in my front pocket and fish out the condom I put in there, then ease back so I can get it on as fast as I can.

Vanessa looks over her shoulder and laughs. "You have a condom?"

"It pays to be prepared, babe." I roll the protection down my shaft, and then make her lie flat over the counter once more. "About your dare—last chance to change your mind."

"Never."

"That's my girl." I slam into her, sheathing myself to the hilt, and the world ceases to exist again.

TWENTY-ONE

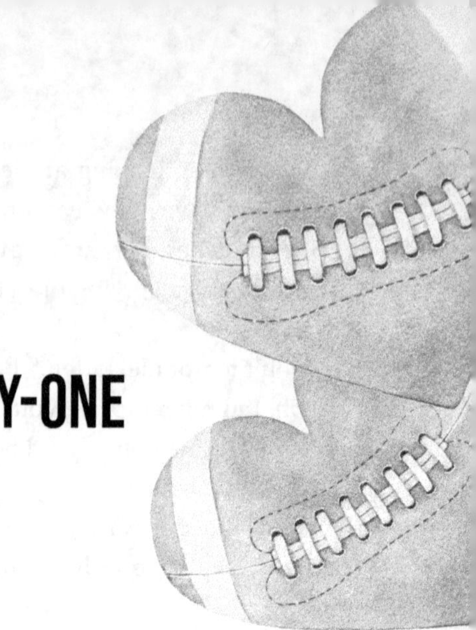

VANESSA

Even if I hadn't sprained my ankle, I still wouldn't be able to walk properly. Paris fucked me so good last night that my legs and hips hurt. I even got a bruise, which had never happened before. He wasn't happy about that. I, however, don't care one bit. The little ache is worth all the mind-blowing orgasms he gave me.

Letting him walk out of the house this morning was hard. He looked so delicious, and one morning quickie wasn't enough. Unfortunately, we can't live in our bubble forever.

Paris offered me a ride to campus, but since no one is supposed to know we're dating, I refused. Besides, with the way we can't keep our hands off each other, we were bound to stop halfway to fuck in the back seat of his truck.

I'm showered and ready to go, but the text I sent Heather earlier asking if she'd be able to drive me went unanswered. I'm going to be late if I don't get moving, so I pull up the Uber app. I hate depending on people for anything—especially my sister. She collects favors and loves to cash in at the most inconvenient times. I'm one second away from requesting a ride when she walks in.

I lift my face from the phone, ready to bitch about her radio silence, when I notice her expression. Her eyes are puffy and red. Heather never cries about anything, so her look *could* be attributed to allergies. But...

"What happened to you?" I ask.

"Nothing." Her reply is clipped, and she doesn't meet my stare.

Hell, maybe she's upset. She continues toward her room, still avoiding eye contact.

"Did you and Leo have a fight?"

She stops and looks over her shoulder. "No. Stop being so nosy."

I sigh. "Fine. Don't tell me. Can you give me a ride to school, or should I call an Uber?"

She turns to me, putting her hands on her hips. "Why can't your boyfriend drive you?"

"Because we don't want people to know we're dating. Did we not have this conversation already?"

She purses her lips before replying. "What time do you have to be on campus?"

"In half an hour."

"Yeah, whatever, I'll drive you. I just need a quick shower." She disappears down the hallway, leaving me perplexed. Since when can Heather get ready in less than half an hour?

I should tell her I'll request a car, but now I'm curious about what's going on with her. And a little concerned.

A ping on my phone alerts me to an incoming message. It's Paris, saying he misses me already. A broad smile blossoms on my lips, but it's erased just as quickly when another message pops up, this one from Ryan, asking if we can grab lunch today.

My blood runs cold from just thinking about the idea of spending any time with the asshole. But then rage erupts in the pit of my stomach, leaving me shaking. How dare he contact me? I type back furiously.

Not in this lifetime, or next.

When I see the three dots appear, my stomach twists into knots, making me queasy. I block him before he can send his message through. Then I set the phone on the counter, and I fucking lose it. Tears roll down my cheeks, and I can't stop the flood. I didn't react this poorly when I bumped into him, so why does a simple text have this effect on me?

"Vanessa? Why are you crying?" Heather asks as she comes into the kitchen.

Shit. I so didn't want her to see me like this.

I wipe the moisture off my face. "Nothing."

"Bullshit. You wouldn't be bawling your eyes out like that for no reason. Did something happen with Paris? Did he dump you?"

"What?" I squeak. "No. Why would you say that?"

"Because I can't think of any other bad news that would put you in that pitiful state."

I open my mouth to offer an angry retort, but she's not wrong. If Paris dumped me, I'd be devastated. Which is crazy because, until we're out in the open, I don't feel like I'm his girlfriend. That thought makes me sad. In a strange way, it distracts me from the reason I was crying.

"Well, you're wrong."

She crosses her arms and gives me the *I'm going to beat the truth out of you no matter what* look. "Then what happened?"

I was determined to keep Ryan's assault a secret, but maybe my reaction has to do with the fact that no one save Paris knows. I don't want to tell any of my friends on the team, because I feel ashamed that it happened. I'm their captain—I'm supposed to be their role model, the strongest Raven. I definitely don't want to be reminded that Paris witnessed the whole thing. It's a source of immense mortification for me.

I know it's crazy to think like that. Why am I embarrassed about something that was done *to* me? What a great psychologist I'll be one day. That weasel Ryan is the one who should be ashamed. Instead, he's walking around campus with the same arrogant air. He's texting me as if nothing happened.

"Ryan tried to rape me after I broke up with him," I blurt out.

Heather stands there like a statue for a couple of beats. No blinking, no widening of her eyes, no reaction whatsoever. It's no wonder her nickname since high school is Ice Queen.

"When?" she asks finally.

"The day before Lorena's wedding."

Her eyebrows furrow. "That's when Paris came over."

Unable to withstand her detached stare, I look away. "Yeah. He stopped Ryan. Would have beat the shit out of him if I hadn't intervened."

"Why?" Her voice rises an octave.

"Why what?"

"Why did you stop Paris?"

"Because I didn't want him to get in trouble because of that asshole. He wanted to kill Ryan."

"And with reason!" She throws her hands in the air. "I think I'd have killed him myself."

Her admission shocks me. "You would?"

"Why are you surprised? In fact, I'm curious why you didn't rip Ryan's nut sack off yourself."

I blink as I process her words. "No ripping, but I kicked him there. Hard."

"That's something. Did you report him to the police?"

My shoulders sag as I let out a heavy sigh. I shake my head. "I don't want to be known as the girl who was almost raped by her boyfriend."

Glowering, Heather puts her hands on her hips. "You'd

rather let a rapist walk free so he can do the same to another girl? Most likely there won't be a Paris around to save them."

Hell. Heather is making me feel like shit. No wonder I didn't want to tell anyone.

"I wasn't thinking about anyone but myself, okay? Yes, that makes me selfish, but fuck, I was just trying to survive," I retort angrily.

"Survive?" Her eyebrows arch. "You've been acting like nothing happened, happy as can be with your new boyfriend."

"Who are you to judge me? You have no idea what it was like for me, how hard it still is. Until you've been in my shoes—"

"I've been in your shoes!" she yells, turning red and sounding out of breath.

My heart skips a beat and then jams hard against my rib cage. "What?"

Her eyes widen as she realizes she blurted out a confession she probably didn't mean to. "Never mind." She begins to turn, but I jump off my high stool and grab her arm.

"Heather." I take a deep breath and loosen my hold. "When were you assaulted?"

She won't look at me, but I can feel her arm tremble.

"It happened a long time ago. It doesn't matter now."

My stomach coils tightly, making me want to hurl. "How long ago?" I whisper.

"Freshman year of high school." She wipes the corners of her eyes.

I release her arm then and stand in front of her. "Who?"

She finally meets my stare. "I don't know. I went to a party, and someone spiked my drink. I woke up alone in a strange bed, my underwear was gone, and there were bloodstains on my inner thighs. So you see, I *couldn't* bring the asshole who raped me to justice, because I don't know who he was. But you can make sure Ryan never pulls that shit again, and you're choosing to let him walk free."

I'm crying again as my heart shatters into a million pieces. "You never told anyone what happened?"

"I told Mom, and she urged me to keep it a secret. You know, for the same bullshit reason you just gave me. She didn't want me to carry the stigma of being a rape victim like it was a scarlet letter."

"I'm so sorry."

I feel like an idiot for saying that. Ryan didn't succeed, and he still made me feel dirty and unworthy. Heather was actually violated, and all I have to say to her is *sorry*.

"Yeah, me too. You know what, I think you should call that Uber after all." She veers toward the hallway.

"I don't need to go. I can stay with you."

"No. You're the last person I want around me right now."

Her comment feels like a punch to my chest. I want to curl into a ball and cry some more. But I have to respect Heather's wish to be alone. She gave me the house so I could spend time with Paris. The least I can do is offer her the same courtesy.

TWENTY-TWO

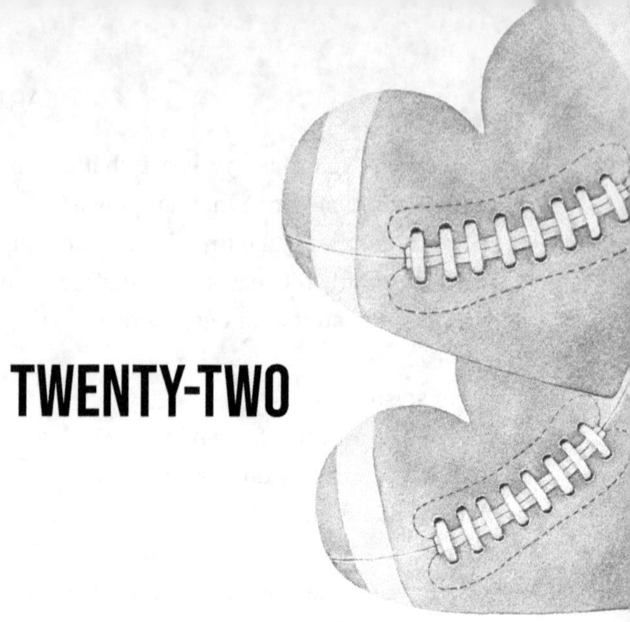

VANESSA

I should have asked the Uber driver to take me anywhere but campus. Going to class was pointless. I couldn't concentrate, couldn't hold a conversation for more than a few seconds before I spaced out. I kept replaying Heather's confession in my head, and the guilt in my chest festered like a disease. I can't believe I never noticed anything in high school. Was I so caught up in my own drama with Paris that I failed to see what she was going through? She's my twin. I should have sensed that something terrible had happened to her.

The morning goes by in a blur, and by the time lunch rolls around, I'm ready to get the fuck out of there. I have no idea where I'm going, but it's definitely better than staying and pretending I'm not falling apart.

It's not until I pull my phone out to call an Uber that I see all the missed text messages and a couple of phone calls from Paris. There are also messages from Sadie, and a few other team members. Hell. I don't want to talk to anyone, not even through texting.

What I need is to gather the courage to report Ryan, but every time I think about it, the fear that no one will believe me keeps me in a choke hold. Paris would need to testify, a whole circus would form, and the personal details of my life would be cut open and dissected. I don't think I can solve this one alone. I probably should make an appointment to talk to a therapist. I *will* make one.

That decision makes me feel a little bit better. As for my teammates, I can blow them off for a few more hours, but I don't want to do that to Paris. What we have is too new, and he could mistake my radio silence as a sign that I'm no longer interested in dating him. I don't want to lose him again.

I scroll through his texts. They're sweet at first, but then, they grow worried. He didn't leave me any voice messages though. I stop near a bench and prop my crutches against it, then start a reply.

I don't get further than a couple of words before my phone is yanked from my hands. "What the fu—" The swear word gets lodged in my throat when I see it's Ryan who fucking stole my phone.

"Who are you texting, darling?"

"Give me my phone back, asshole." I step forward and wince when I put all my weight on my bad foot. At this rate, I'll never get cleared to play soccer.

I don't get the phone back, and I can tell from Ryan's furious expression that he's read most of the texts Paris sent me.

"That's why you fucking blocked me, bitch? You're screwing that meathead? How long has it been going on?"

"Fuck you, Ryan. I don't owe you any explanations. Give me my damn phone!" I reach for his hand and try to yank it free, but he shoves me so hard that I stagger back and, thanks to having only one good foot, I fall and hit my face against the metal bench.

White-hot pain flares across my cheek, and for a dizzying

moment the world flickers to black. My ears are ringing, but I can still hear the sound of shouting.

A moment later, a stranger drops into a crouch in front of me. "Are you okay?"

"I don't know." I touch my cheek and find it wet.

"You have a cut there," he says. "Here, I got your phone back."

"Thanks."

"Can you stand up?"

I wish I could say yes, but I'm light-headed as fuck. Now that I've regained focus, I look over his shoulder and search for Ryan. He's gone, which is too bad, because he deserves to be punched in the throat.

"I may need assistance," I tell him.

He pulls me up and immediately steps back. I appreciate his effort to make sure he doesn't overstep. I pay attention to him. He's young, probably a freshman, and on the scrawny side. I wonder if he was the one who yelled at Ryan.

"Thanks for intervening," I say.

"Of course. I thought he was your friend at first, acting like an idiot, or I would have butted in sooner."

"He's an asshole. I'm surprised he didn't start anything with you."

"Too many witnesses." He nods his head toward a spot behind me.

I turn and see the crowd that's beginning to disperse. "And yet, you were the only one who helped."

"I think someone else would have, too. I was just the fastest."

"Well, thank you for the assist. I'm not usually this pathetic, but I'm not in top shape currently." I point at my foot.

"Yeah, which makes his actions even worse. You probably should take care of that cut. I can walk with you to the medical building."

As much as I appreciate the offer, I don't want him to witness me having another meltdown. I was barely holding it together already, and Ryan had to show up to fuck me up even more.

I search for a tissue in my backpack, and then dab the wound. "It's okay. I can get there on my own. What's your name?"

"Philip Meester. You're Vanessa Castro, right? The Ravens' midfielder."

God, I wish he hadn't recognized me. "Yup. Nice to meet you, Philip. I'd better get going."

"Uh, do you want to report Ryan Watergate to campus police? What he did wasn't cool."

My eyebrows shoot to the heavens. "You know Ryan?"

Philip looks a little guilty, and I don't understand his reaction. "Yeah. I met him during rush week. I ended up joining the Pikes, though."

Shit. That means he knows Leo, Heather's boyfriend, since Leo's the president of that fraternity. That also means Philip probably knows that Ryan is my ex.

"I'll deal with Ryan later," I say.

He stares at me a beat too long and then says, "I hope you do. I'll back you up if needed. Take care, Vanessa."

I watch him leave, and I wonder if there is a hidden meaning behind his comment. It's almost as if he knows more stuff about Ryan than what he witnessed a moment ago.

The sting on my face snaps me out of my musings, and it also serves as a wake-up call. I have to report Ryan. Not to the campus police though. They'll involve the school administration, and *they'll* do anything they can to smooth things over and avoid a scandal. The school's reputation took a hit when Nick Fowler, a former soccer player at Rushmore, posted a sexist list that included all female athletes.

The sting from the cut doesn't burn as much, but even if it's superficial, it's bleeding a lot. Instead of going to see a nurse, I head into the first restroom I come across and try to stop the blood flow. The cut is minimal, but my cheek is swollen from the impact.

I think about what Heather told me, and how our mother reacted. Would she have told Heather to keep quiet if she knew who her rapist was? It's hard to tell with Mom. She's so focused on appearances though, hence why she created all that drama after the stolen wine incident. She wanted to make sure there was no doubt Paris was the one who tried to corrupt me.

Shit. Paris. I never texted him back. How am I going to explain my messed-up face? I don't know how he'll react, even if I say I'm ready to report Ryan. He might do something to that bastard first.

Maybe I should just tell him I fell. It's a miracle he hasn't gone after Ryan yet. If he knows how I got my new injury, he might do something that for sure will fuck up his future. I can't have that on my conscience.

I clean up the blood and then grab a new paper towel and dry off my face. I go through several until I'm confident I don't look like an extra from a slasher movie, and then I head out.

It's just my luck that the man I need but should avoid right now finds me before I can get the cut taken care of. Paris's face is closed off at first—a sign that he was already thinking the worst about my silence. But when his attention shifts to the cut on my cheek, he goes from serious to concerned in zero point one second.

He reaches me in a couple of long strides, stopping short of invading my space completely. "Kitten, what happened?"

"I... uh, I fell." The lie feels bitter on my tongue, but I'm doing this to protect him.

"You fell? How?"

"I'm not really sure. I tripped and hit my face on a bench. I'm on my way to the infirmary."

He's watching me closely, almost as if he doesn't believe me. I never lie, so it's no surprise I'm terrible at it. My body is trembling, and my heart is beating so fast, it's hard to believe he can't hear the thumping.

Before he can see the deception on my face, I say, "I'm sorry I never replied to you. It's been nonstop for me this morning, and when I finally had a break, this happened." I point at my cheek.

His expression softens. "I was a little worried, if I'm honest. I did blow up your phone. I thought that maybe you..." He rubs the back of his neck, looking sheepish.

The adorable expression makes me feel even guiltier about lying to him. I want to kiss him and forget that I'm being a total bitch for not telling him the truth. But he was the one who wanted to keep our relationship a secret for now, so I don't dare any PDA.

Although... Ryan already knows I'm dating Paris. Pretty soon the news will be across the entire campus and, knowing that piece of shit, he's going to spin a story that will make me look bad. He was already insinuating that I was screwing Paris before I broke up with him. I'm running out of time. I need to go to the police, but I don't think I can bring Paris with me. No, I have to do this on my own.

"You thought that I what?" I ask.

"That you changed your mind about us."

A knot forms in my chest. The vulnerability in his tone makes me want to be truthful with him about something at least, even if it's going to blow up in my face.

"I won't change my mind. I've been in love with you since we were thirteen."

He doesn't speak for a beat, just stares at me. But then laughter bubbles up his throat. He shakes his head, and I feel like an idiot.

"Okay, then. I'd better go now and find a hole to hide in." I make a motion to circle around him, but he raises his arm, and blocks my path.

"You're not going anywhere, kitten." He steps into my space, snaking his strong arms around my waist. "Not until I kiss you." He leans down and presses his lips softly against mine.

I melt into his embrace, wanting more than an innocent peck on the lips, but Paris eases off before I can attack his mouth. "Come on. Let's get that boo-boo taken care of."

"Okay," I reply dreamily, forgetting for a moment that we aren't thirteen anymore.

I wish that we were.

TWENTY-THREE

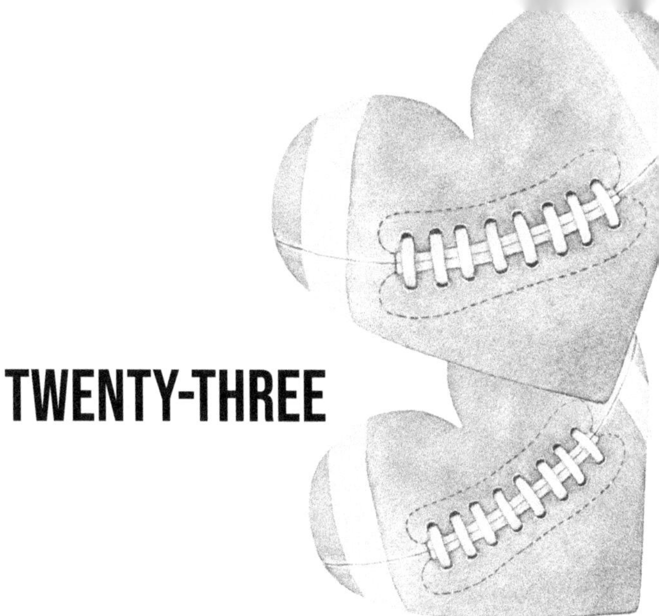

PARIS

"Ugh, I look hideous." Vanessa touches the bandage on her cheek.

I peel my eyes away from the road to glance at her. "You look as beautiful as always, kitten."

"How can you say that? The right side of my face is twice as big as the left."

"You'd look gorgeous even if your entire head was a giant watermelon."

She twists her expression into an exaggerated scowl, making me laugh. It sucks that she got hurt, but I'm still riding the high of her confession. She said she's been in love with me since we were kids—pretty much as long as I've been in love with her. I have yet to confess though, and as much as I wanted to say the words right then, it didn't feel right professing my love when she had a bleeding cut on her face.

"You're just saying that to get laid."

"I'm not!" I retort, fighting the urge to laugh again.

She grows quiet, making me curious. I chance another look and find her facing the window.

I cover her hand with mine. "What's wrong, kitten?"

"Nothing. Can we go to your place instead of mine? I mean, if that's okay?"

"Of course it's okay. Although, I have to head to practice in an hour."

"Shit. I forgot you have a life besides coming to my rescue."

I bring our joined hands to my lips and kiss the top of hers. "Being your knight in shining armor is my number one priority, sweetheart."

Her eyebrows furrow. "I'm not a damsel in distress."

Damn, and here I thought I was being romantic with my comment. I didn't realize how sexist it was.

"I know you aren't. You're a fierce warrior, but even the most badass heroes can use help from time to time."

She narrows her eyes. "Nice save."

"So, why can't you go home? I mean, not that I don't love the idea of you in my bed, but I live with three loud and messy dudes."

"Yeah, I'm aware of that. Heather asked for the house. Since she did me a solid yesterday, I can't deny her the favor. But if you don't want your roommates to know about us, I can call one of my teammates."

"Are you crazy? You're staying with me. I thought I made my point when I kissed you in front of everyone earlier."

"Well, there weren't a lot of people around us then."

"Trust me, all it takes is one person for the rest of Rushmore to know."

"Why? Because you're on the football team?"

This sounds like a trap, so I'd better tread carefully. I know the Ravens aren't happy that the football team gets tons of perks from the school administration while they have to fight for everything, even though they're one of the best college soccer teams in the country.

"Well, yeah. And I'm not saying that because I'm cocky."

"I know you aren't."

"Do you need to stop by your house to pack an overnight bag?" I change the subject before we plunge deeper into a topic that's political and unpleasant.

"Nah, I can sleep in one of your T-shirts."

"Or you can sleep wearing nothing at all." I wink.

She runs a hand through her hair and pulls a section over her face to hide the bandage. "I have a better idea. I can wear your T-shirt over my head so you don't have to look at this hideousness."

"Hmm. I think you're fishing for compliments, kitten."

"Now you're confusing me with my twin."

A random song comes through the speakers, and Vanessa reaches for the volume dial. "I love this one."

"Who sings this?" I ask. "Justin Timberlake?"

"Oh my god. Who *are* you? How can you not know 'I Want It That Way'? It's a Backstreet Boys classic!"

"You expect me to know songs by a nineties boy band? I wasn't even born."

"Okay, fine. This song came out in 1999. But it was featured in one of my favorite shows of all time."

"I'm going out on a limb here and saying it's not a fantasy series." I smirk.

"Duh. *Brooklyn 99*. It's a hilarious cop show."

"I think I've heard of it. You can introduce it to me when I get back from practice. Although I might have other things in mind." I run a hand up her thigh, but she bats it away before I reach her pussy.

"I don't feel sexy, so Jake Peralta will have to be your consolation prize."

I wrinkle my nose. "Yeah, like I want a dude replacing my hot-as-sin girlfriend."

"I'm your girlfriend?" The surprise in her voice is authentic, but it shouldn't be. Hell, maybe I didn't make myself clear yesterday.

I'm glad I have to stop at a red light so I can reply to her while looking into her eyes. "Yes. Did you have any doubt about that?"

"I wasn't sure." She shrugs. "Maybe it has to do with the fact we weren't broadcasting our relationship to the world yet."

Guilt pierces my chest like an iron spear, making me regret ever asking her to keep us a secret. She didn't want to do it at first, and now I know she changed her mind because she loves me.

"I'm sorry. I was an idiot for wanting to hide that you're my girl."

A blaring car horn warns me I'm holding up traffic. Reluctantly, I switch my attention to the road and miss her reaction to my statement.

A moment passes before she says, "I never thought I'd confess this, but I love hearing you call me *your girl*. It's even better than being your girlfriend."

"Get used to it then, kitten. You were always my girl. I just lost sight of you for a while."

She doesn't reply, and I'm afraid I said something wrong. In my peripheral vision, I see her wipe the corner of her eye.

"Babe, are you crying?"

"What? No." She looks out the window as she sinks into the truck seat.

I turn on the blinker and park in the first spot I find, which is in front of an empty store with a For Rent sign.

"Is this where you live?" she asks.

"No." I unbuckle my seat belt and pinch her chin to turn her face to mine. "You know you don't need to hide anything from me, right, kitten?"

Her eyes go rounder. "I'm not hiding anything."

"I made you cry. I'm sorry."

She shakes her head. "It's nothing. I'm just overly emotional these days. It's probably PMS."

"You have reason to be, even if it's not PMS." I cup her cheek. "I'm here for you. Always. I love you."

Her breathing hitches. Then her eyes become brighter and rounder. She looks away, covering her face with her hands. Her body starts to shake, so I free her from the constraints of her seat belt and pull her into a hug. A ragged sob escapes her lips, but I refrain from saying a word. I let her cry for as long as she needs, her face pressed against my chest.

I suspected she was putting on a brave face in front of me, and like an idiot, I pretended she was fine. But she isn't, not by any stretch of the imagination, and I'm certain it all comes back to the evening she was attacked. I need to do something. That son of a bitch can't remain unpunished. But using brute force isn't the way to go, even if I'd love nothing more than to give him the ass kicking of his life.

I need to find another way to make him pay.

TWENTY-FOUR

VANESSA

Paris's roommates aren't home when we finally make it there. His apartment is on campus, not far from where Andreas and Danny live. The building is similar, with its red brick exterior and modern industrial style. The apartment itself is spacious, with a big open kitchen and living room. There's even an area where they managed to fit a foosball table. Any other day, I'd want to play.

"Welcome to *minha casa*," he says.

Despite feeling wretched, I crack a smile. "Are you learning to speak Portuguese?"

He pulls me into his arms and kisses me on the cheek. "I'd do anything for you, kitten."

"I know. I feel the same way about you. So… should I learn to speak Greek?"

He eases off and when I look up, I catch his exaggerated scowl. "You know I don't speak Greek, right?"

"What? The smartest kid in All Saints never learned the language of his people?"

"Mock me all you want. Unlike your folks, my parents didn't make Cory and me learn. They were too concerned about what the neighbors would say if they heard us speaking a foreign language."

"That's too bad. I can't wait to speak Portuguese with you in front of them. Your mother will have a cow." I laugh.

"Probably, if she doesn't die of a heart attack when you come to my game on Saturday."

Oh crap. His first game of the season. I forgot about it. I must make a face, because his eyebrows furrow.

"You're coming, right?" he asks.

"I… I don't know. The Ravens also play on Saturday, and I need to be there."

He closes his eyes for a moment and shakes his head. "Of course. I'm an idiot. Don't mind me."

"Let me know the time. Maybe I can make it to both."

"All right." An alarm beeps, and it's coming from his pocket. He pulls his cell phone out and curses. "Shit. I have to go, kitten. Are you going to be okay?"

"Yeah. Don't worry about me."

"There's food in the fridge. Help yourself to anything you want."

I nod. "I'll be all right. Go. I don't want you to be late because of me."

"Hold on, let me give you a tour of the apartment first."

He takes my hand and veers toward the hallway. "The first door to your right is James Parker's room. He's one of the Rebels' new recruits."

"Yeah, I've seen him around."

"Nice guy, but messy as hell. Don't go in there if chaos makes your skin crawl."

I wrinkle my nose. "How bad is it?"

"Bad." He laughs, and then points at the door to our left. "This is Mark and Doug Ronson's room."

"Brothers?"

"Cousins. One is premed like me, and the other is studying computer science."

"Gotcha. Brainiacs like you."

"I'm not a brainiac," he grumbles.

I snort. "Sure you aren't."

"Anyway, this is my room." He opens the last door at the end of the hallway.

It's a big space with a massive wall-to-wall window that offers a great view of campus. The king-size bed is set against a black wall with chalk scribbles all over it.

"What's that?"

"Oh, that's my brainstorm wall. I turned it into a blackboard so I can doodle, write notes..."

I squint, "Draw dick pics..."

"What?" He walks closer and curses. "Those Ronson fuckers." He tries to wipe off the drawing with his fingers, but all that does is make it blurry.

"Was that supposed to be a picture of *your* dick? Because if it was, they got the size seriously wrong."

He looks at me and smirks. "That they did."

His dimples make an appearance, and I melt. I love when he smiles at me like that. He walks over and pulls me against his solid chest. Then he kisses me quickly on the lips before stepping back. "Hell, I wish I didn't have to go to practice."

"Yeah, me too. I'll be here when you get back though."

"That's something to look forward to." He kisses me again and then almost bolts out the door, taking all the happiness with him.

My heart becomes heavy again, as if it's made of steel. I'm suddenly bone tired, so I just stay in his bedroom. I was supposed to see the team's trainer today, but I told her I wasn't feeling well and rescheduled for tomorrow. There's no chance I'll make it to the police station today either. I haven't changed my mind, but I have to be stronger mentally to face something I know will be brutal to my mental health.

I'm a mess, a veritable yarn ball of guilt. I'm letting my team down by not showing up for my checkup, by not answering their messages. I thought I was stronger. I thought I could forget about what Ryan did to me and move on with my life. But things aren't that simple. Whether I like it or not, that bastard left a permanent mark on my soul. Heather's confession didn't help either. My guilt for not reporting him has doubled, despite the fact I've decided to rectify that.

Alone in Paris's bedroom, I cry again. It seems that's all I can do today. I've taken enough psychology classes to know that crying is part of the healing process, but all it does is make me feel weak and pathetic. I thought I was a badass, but maybe I'm a meek damsel in distress after all.

I end up falling asleep, and when I wake up, I see that it's past seven p.m. I stay curled up in Paris's bed though, not having the energy to move. I bring my nose to his pillow because it smells like him, a mix of nutmeg, sandalwood, and leather. It does give me some comfort, but my chest feels hollow, and it seems I'll never be happy again. God, now I'm having emo thoughts. What's wrong with me?

The front door opens, and male voices warn me that two of Paris's roommates are home. I knew that the new guy on the team was rooming with him, but I had no clue who the other two were. It isn't like I kept tabs on who was in Paris's life. I was aware mostly of his relationship with Lydia, and as much as I tried to tell myself I didn't care, the sight of them together always made my heart bleed slowly and steadily.

Since I'm no longer alone in the apartment, there's zero chance I'm going to venture into the living room. I'm glad that Paris has an en suite and I don't need to go out there to use the restroom. My stomach feels empty, but I can survive without eating. I'm not sure I can keep anything down anyway.

I look at my phone just as a message flashes on the screen. It's Sadie, asking if I'm okay. I type a quick reply, partially lying once again. Then I flip my phone down so I can't see her answer and feel worse about my deceit.

I force myself out of bed to use the bathroom. It's spotless, which is a relief. Guys can be pigs. When I catch my reflection in the mirror, I wince. It's no surprise that I look like a witch, with tangled hair and dark circles under my eyes. The swelling on my face has lessened, but the area is bruising. I can't wait too long to report Ryan. I need the evidence that he hurt me. And Paris will find out I lied to him today.

God, what a fucking mess I made. My eyes prickle as the urge to cry renews.

I bite the inside of my cheek to try to stop the waterworks, and then I search for a hairbrush.

Instead, I find a pink hair band. I step back, shoving the drawer shut fast, as if there were a snake in there. What else has Lydia left behind? I don't want to succumb to retroactive jealousy, but that's exactly what's happening now.

"Kitten?" Paris calls from the room.

Shit. He's back, and I'm on the verge of losing my mind again. He already saw me fall apart once today. I don't want him to think I'm breakable.

"I'll be right out." I finger-comb my hair, since I didn't find a brush. It's not much of an improvement, but better than nothing.

When I walk out of the bathroom, he's sitting on the edge of the bed. His face splits into a broad smile, making my heart beat a little faster. The darkness swirling in my chest loses strength.

"How are you feeling?" he asks.

"Much better now."

I walk over with the intention of sitting next to him. But he pulls me onto his lap and kisses me so sweetly that I might develop an addiction. Who am I kidding? I'm already addicted to him. I melt into his embrace, taking solace in his warmth and strength.

"I missed you," he whispers against my lips.

"I missed you too."

He eases back and looks into my eyes. "I'm going to sound cheesy as hell, but I can't believe that you're actually here. It feels like a dream."

Hearing the man I love tell me that, it's impossible not to melt. But at the same time, this moment feels bittersweet. There's a burden in my chest, the lie I told him weighing heavily on my conscience.

Before he can read my soul's torment in my gaze, I pinch his arm playfully.

"Ouch. What was that for?" he asks.

"To prove you aren't dreaming."

He narrows his eyes. "Oh, you're playing with fire, kitten."

In a blur, I go from sitting on his lap to flat on my back with Paris on top of me.

"What are you doing?" I ask through a laugh.

"There are other less painful ways to prove that I'm not dreaming." He nuzzles my neck, sending goose bumps down my arm.

"You're one horny dude, aren't you?"

Resting on his forearms, he leans back. "That's what happens when I have a girlfriend who looks like you. I can't help myself."

I knit my brows together. "Your girlfriend doesn't look too hot right now."

"Tell that to my cock." He gyrates his hips, pressing his erection against my core.

Humming, I close my eyes. "Okay, I'll pretend I believe you."

"Believe me, kitten. No one has ever put my libido into overdrive like you do."

"Like you have so many to compare with me," I blurt out, then regret my words immediately when I see the constricted look on his face.

He rolls off me onto his back and stares at the ceiling. Shit. I should have kept my mouth shut.

Leaning on my elbow, I say, "I shouldn't have said that. I'm sorry."

"I'm actually glad that you did." He looks at me. "I didn't know how else to talk about it without sounding like an ass."

"I don't follow."

He sighs. "Lydia wasn't my first."

"Oh." Several emotions compete to take over my heart. I'm jealous of whoever "initiated" him, but I'm also glad it wasn't that manipulative bitch.

"Yeah. I knew she wanted to be more than friends, and I wasn't sure if that was what I wanted. The summer before freshman year, I went to visit my family in Greece, and that's when I lost my virginity to some random girl I met at a party."

"Do you even remember her name?"

He grimaces. "Will you think less of me if I say that I don't?"

"Uh, yes and no. I mean, I'm glad you don't remember, because it means she doesn't have any hold on you."

He caresses my cheek with the back of his hand. "Kitten, only you have a hold on me."

"Good. So does that mean you only slept with two girls besides me?"

"Ehhh…"

My jaw drops. "You dog! How many girls did you screw in Greece?"

"Oh, just the one, and only once. The others came later."

My heart constricts painfully. He started dating Lydia at the beginning of freshman year. That memory is imprinted on my mind, because the sight of them holding hands obliterated me. I never pegged Paris as the unfaithful type, and even if he cheated on that viper, it doesn't sit well with me.

"Don't give me that look. I didn't cheat on Lydia."

Relief washes over me, but more questions pop into my head. "You've been inseparable since you started dating."

"Not exactly. We were getting too serious too fast, and I freaked out. On spring break that year, I broke up with her. That's when the other girls came into the picture, but before you call me a dog again, there were only two."

"And then you went right back to that witch."

"Yeah. Not the smartest decision I ever made."

I rub the space between his brows, trying to smooth the lines there. "It's over now. She'll never come near you again if I have anything to say about it."

He cracks a smile, and his eyes dance with glee. "Oh, what are you going to do, kitten? Fight over me?"

"If it comes to that, hell yes. You're mine, Andino." I straddle him. "Don't forget that."

"Hmm, I think you'd better remind me with actions."

I lean forward, touching his nose with mine. "Are you daring me?"

"You betcha."

TWENTY-FIVE

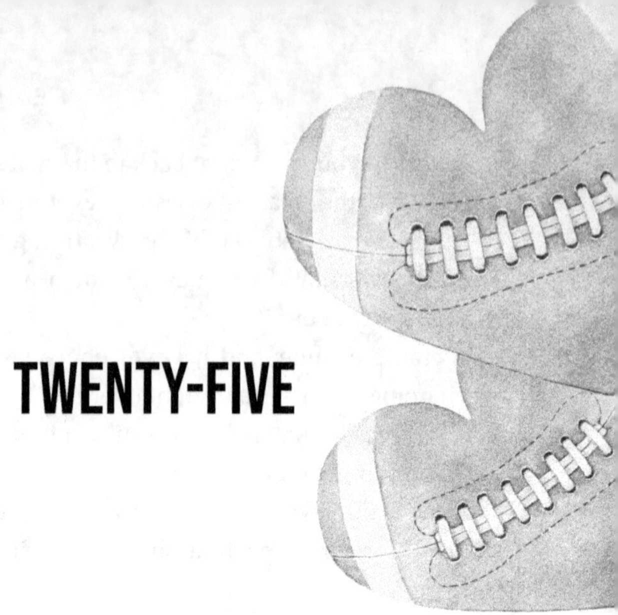

PARIS

I wish I could have played chauffeur for Vanessa this morning, but Coach Clarkson wanted us on the field bright and early, so I dropped her off at her place before heading to practice. At least I was able to keep my mind on the game, but that didn't mean I wasn't counting the minutes until I got to see her again.

I've never felt impatient like this before. Lydia was my only previous serious girlfriend, and truth be told, she never made me feel this way. I thought I loved her, but now that I'm out of that relationship, I'm realizing I mistook gratitude for love, and then it morphed into guilt.

"Good practice today, Andino," Danny says, running a hand over his long hair. "I'm glad to see your mind was one hundred percent in the game."

"Yes. I'm back, bro."

Most of the guys have left the locker room, something I notice when Danny grows serious.

My spine becomes taut, and I have an idea why he waited

until we were practically alone to come talk to me. "You have something on your mind."

"Am I that transparent?"

"Yeah, don't ever play poker."

He chuckles. "You aren't the first person to tell me that. Anyway, it's about Vanessa. She's the mystery girl, isn't she?"

I'm surprised it took him until today to figure out I'm dating her. "Yes."

"You don't have to worry. I won't say a word about what you told me. But… hell, now I want to punch the shit out of that son of a bitch even more."

His comment ignites the fury that's been simmering in my gut since I was denied the same. "Join the club, bro."

"If doing something to him wouldn't mess up your life, I wouldn't stand in your way."

I clap his shoulder. "Thanks, man. Coming from you, that's pretty fucking huge."

He squints. "I'm beginning to hate this reputation I have that I don't lose my temper."

"I'm just saying, you don't act on impulse. That's why you're a badass quarterback."

He crosses his arms. "I suppose that's true. But there are exceptions, and if I were in your shoes, I wouldn't stop to think about the consequences."

"What are you trying to say, Hudson? Do you *want* me to go after Ryan?"

His eyes widen. "No, that's not what I'm saying at all." He shakes his head. "Please don't do anything stupid. Catch you later for lunch?"

"I'm meeting Vanessa at noon in the main cafeteria. You and Sadie are more than welcome to join us."

"Sounds good. Just be warned—I don't think Sadie knows about you and Vanessa yet."

My eyebrows furrow. "How did you hear about it, then?"

"Conrad made a comment earlier. Didn't she spend the night at your place?"

Mental head slap. I'm such an idiot. Conrad is one of my roommates, and he was around when Vanessa and I came out of the bedroom this morning.

"Ah, yeah. I completely forgot I introduced them."

"What happened with not wanting to come out in public yet?"

"I don't want to pretend around her."

I don't get into the specifics about Lydia stealing Vanessa's poem. It's not that I want to keep it a secret, but until I talk to Lydia, it's best if my friends don't know.

He nods. "Do you think Lydia will be a problem?"

"Yeah. But I don't care."

VANESSA

My phone vibrates in my pocket, sending my heart aflutter. Sadly, it isn't a message from Paris, but a text from Sadie, whom I've been neglecting.

> You're a sucky friend. I hate you.

Ah damn. I'd better call her back to find out if she's angry about my silence, or if it's something else.

She answers on the first ring. "Oh, look who's alive."

"I'm sorry. My life has been hectic." Not a lie.

"Yeah, hectic in *Paris's bed.* How could you not tell me you were dating him?" she yells, forcing me to pull the phone away from my ear to avoid hearing damage.

"We decided to keep it on the down-low to avoid drama."

"Since when am I drama? You know I'd have kept your secret!"

Way to make me feel shitty about it, Sadie. My excuse is lame, I know. I was afraid that she'd make me explain how I got together with Paris, and I still can't talk to her about my attack, but for different reasons. She's going to find out after I report Ryan, but hopefully not before the game on Saturday. It's the first of the season, and I need the girls' focus to stay sharp, especially with me out of commission. I can't fuck up our season by dumping my situation on them.

"I'm sorry, okay? It's all so new and unexpected. I wanted to enjoy Paris without the world knowing about us."

"Talk about unexpected. I didn't think you cared much for the guy."

"Well... I've known him since we were kids."

"Shut your face. How come I didn't know that? Oh yeah, because you're an arsehole who tells me nothing."

Shaking my head, I sigh. "How long are you going to stay mad at me?"

"It depends on your groveling. Buuut... you know I can be easily bribed." She laughs.

And just like that, I know that we're good. "A round of drinks on me the next time we go out?"

"Yeah, that should do it. Anyway, when you said you wanted to avoid drama, were you referring to his ex, or yours?"

I snort. Like I care about what that asshole thinks. "Mostly her. How did you find out about Paris anyway?"

"Not from Danny. He'd better not have known before me, or he'll be sorry. He won't get off easily like you did."

I roll my eyes. Sadie and Danny couldn't be more different in terms of personality, and yet, they're perfect for each other. Even her father, Danny's coach, has accepted their relationship as endgame. I know in the beginning it was hard for him to forget that his QB was screwing his daughter, especially after he caught them in a compromising position.

"If he does know, he probably only learned about it recently.

Please don't go savage on him. He might not have had the chance to tell you."

"Don't worry. I'm not going to castrate the boy. I like his dick too much to do that to him."

A bubble of laughter goes up my throat. "I bet you do. So, who told you?"

"Eh, you're not going to like it."

I'm about to enter the main building on campus, where the cafeteria is. I'm meeting Paris there in ten minutes, but I decide to finish the conversation with Sadie away from eavesdropping ears.

"Hold on." I tuck my crutches under one arm so I can move and hold the phone at the same time. Then I change course and trudge to a nearby tree. "Why?"

"It seems your douche ex posted a video on TikTok accusing you of cheating on him with Paris. It's gone semiviral."

"That *motherfucker*," I say through clenched teeth.

"Yeah. I blocked his ass after that encounter the other day, but the girls on the team didn't. I don't think they even know you broke up with him."

"I blocked him too, and yeah, I should have sent an update on the group chat."

"But how did that wanker find out?"

I pinch the bridge of my nose, regretting now keeping my friends in the dark for so long. "I had another confrontation with the bastard yesterday."

"You have got to be kidding me. What did he do?"

My stomach clenches painfully, making me sick. I don't want to tell Sadie that he hurt me for the same reason I don't want her to know about the assault. Damn it. I'm sick and tired of Ryan fucking with my life.

"Vanessa? Are you still there?" she asks when I take too long to reply. "If that bellend did something to you, I'm going to rip his nut sack off."

"He—"

"You fucking whore!" a woman screams behind me, and I practically jump out of my skin.

I turn to see Lydia marching toward me with murderous intentions flashing in her crazy eyes.

Hell.

"Who's that?" Sadie asks.

"The drama I was trying to avoid. I'll call you later." I put my phone away before Sadie can reply. I need my hands free in case the she-devil wants to get physical. I hope she tries something. If she throws the first punch, I'll have no choice but to defend myself. No one will be able to accuse me of breaking the student code of conduct, and I'll get my revenge. The lying bitch deserves an ass kicking.

Forcing a fake smile, I reply, "Lydia, always a pleasure."

"I *knew* you were trying to take Paris away from me."

My eyebrows shoot to the heavens. "*I* was trying to take Paris from you? Isn't that what you did to me? You know that plagiarism is a crime, right?"

Her eyes bug out. "What are you talking about?"

"Quit the innocent act, honey. Paris and I know that you stole my letter, copied my poem, and claimed you wrote it."

"That's a lie. You're just making up shit to take him from me! I watched the video your ex posted on TikTok. You've been screwing my boyfriend behind my back all this time."

Is this bitch for real?

"*Ex*-boyfriend. And are you really going to stand there and deny you stole my poem?" I laugh in derision. "You are one crazy bitch. I'm glad that Paris is finally aware of how awful you are."

She's not taking my bait, and I'm sick of this conversation. I might end up throwing the first punch if I don't leave. I try to walk around her, but unfortunately, I'm still wearing the ankle brace, and I'm too slow to move.

My only warning that she's snapped is a deranged yell before she tackles me to the ground. The grass softens my fall, but one of the crutches ends up underneath me and pokes into my back. The most dangerous thing is Lydia and her long nails, though. She tries to scratch my face and ends up pulling the bandage off my cut before I can grab her wrists and push her back.

"Get off me!" I yell.

Like a rabid dog, she comes at me again with bared teeth. I barely have time to sit up, much less to pull my arm back to punch her ugly face.

"Lydia, what the hell!" Paris is suddenly there, dragging his ex off me. "Are you insane?"

"Don't touch me!" She struggles against his hold.

Meanwhile, someone else drops into a crouch by my side. "Are you okay?"

It's the freshman who helped me yesterday. Philip Meester. Why is he always around when I'm in distress? Maybe he's a stalker posing as a Good Samaritan. That would be my luck.

"Uh, no."

He helps me up, even though I wish I didn't need his assistance. But I don't think I could get up on my own, even if my ankle wasn't sprained. I'm shaking from head to toe, adrenaline making my heart thump fast inside my chest. I'm pissed that I didn't get a chance to do some damage to Lydia like I wanted to.

Paris is no longer holding her, but she's far from calm. "How could you *do* this to me? I thought you loved me!" she whines.

Oh my god. She's still playing the victim card, even though I told her we know she lied.

"Do *what* to you? We've been broken up for six months, Lydia."

"Don't play dumb with me. I know you were screwing that cunt way before we broke up."

He takes a step forward, pointing a finger in her direction. "You watch your mouth when you talk about Vanessa. The only person here who deserves to be called that awful name is you."

Lydia's face turns bright red, and her jaw drops. "I—I can't believe you said that to me! Do you want me to k—"

He takes a step back, raising his palm. "Don't you *dare* say that. I will *not* fall prey to your manipulations anymore. I cannot be responsible for your actions."

"So you don't care if I die?"

Fuck. Can I punch her now? I can't believe she's doing this to Paris in front of all these witnesses. Of course a bunch of the assholes are recording the scene. I bet someone is broadcasting it live. I fucking hate how social media gives power to scum.

"I'll be sad, but I'm not your therapist or your parent."

Crocodile tears run down her cheeks. "You'll regret your words one day, Paris." She turns and runs away, shoving some onlookers out of her path.

"Wow," Philip says, drawing Paris's attention to him.

His eyebrows furrow, maybe because he doesn't like how close the guy is to me. "Who are you?"

The kid's cheeks flush. "I... uh, my name is Philip Meester."

"How do you know Vanessa?" Paris walks over and draws me closer to him and away from Philip.

Man, it seems this altercation with Lydia dialed up his protective mode to the max.

"I helped her the other day when her ex was giving her trouble."

Oh hell. Shut up, Philip.

Paris tenses. "What did he do?" His hold around my waist tightens.

"He stole her phone, and when she tried to get it back, he pushed her onto a bench. That's how she got that cut." He gestures to my cheek.

Paris turns me around and gazes into my eyes. His own are swimming with the hurt of betrayal. "You said you tripped."

"I'm sorry. I didn't want you to go after Ryan before I had the chance to report him to the police."

Rubbing his face, Paris stares into the distance.

"Paris? Please, look at me."

He does so, and I'm surprised that his eyes aren't brimming with anger as I expected. I lied to him, after all.

The hurt is still there, though.

He pulls me into a tight hug, hiding his face in the crook of my neck. "I'm sorry I wasn't there to protect you from him. I'm sorry that I didn't go after him and make him pay for hurting you the first time."

"Don't apologize. What happened to me wasn't your fault."

"Not the first time, but everything he's done since *is* my fault. I'll make it right, kitten. I promise."

I pull back and capture his gaze. "You're not going after him. Please tell me that isn't what you're planning to do."

He caresses my cheek gently, then gives me a peck on the lips. "Don't worry about it, kitten. Let's go home."

TWENTY-SIX

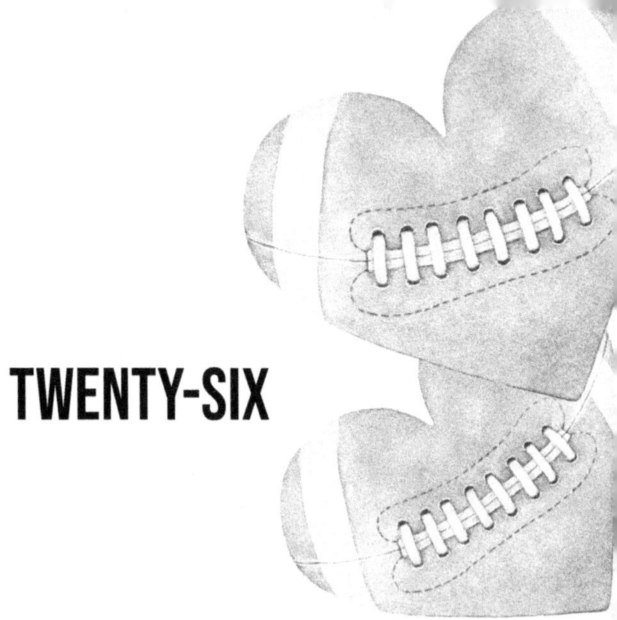

Paris drops me off at my place, but he doesn't linger, not even after I beg him to come inside. I look out the window and watch him leave with tears in my eyes. He swore he wasn't angry with me for lying, but my heart tells me otherwise. I didn't trust him. Now the guilt is consuming me.

Heather walks into the living room. "What happened this time?"

Wiping my cheeks, I turn around. "Fucking Ryan happened."

Her face is a cold mask as she studies me. "Are you talking about the TikTok video?"

"You've seen it?"

"I don't think there's a soul on campus that hasn't seen it. What happened to your face?"

Shit, I forgot that Heather didn't see me yesterday. I touch the cut, which, mercifully, Lydia didn't rip open again. "Ryan."

Heather's blue eyes turn as dark as a stormy sky. "He did that to you? When?"

"Yesterday. He stole my phone while I was texting Paris and

found out about us. When I tried to get my phone back, he pushed me. I fell and hit my face on a bench."

"And you still didn't report him?" Heather's voice rises, and I wince.

"I didn't have a chance, okay? I'm going to, but I was a fucking mess yesterday, and then Paris showed up. I couldn't tell him what happened. He'd probably have flipped and committed murder."

Heather puts her hands on her hips and glowers. "Now Ryan has that TikTok video. Anything you do will seem like a revenge plot."

"That's probably why he did it—to discredit me. But there were a few people around when he pushed me, and one guy helped me get rid of him."

"Good. Will the guy confirm your story?"

"I think so. You might know him. He's a Pike pledge."

Her eyebrows shoot up. "What's his name?"

"Philip Meester."

She squints as if she's thinking hard about it. "God, I don't know if I remember him. But if he hopes to become a Pike, he *will* cooperate."

Heather has been dating Leo for a long time. I don't really get the sense that they're crazy in love like Paris and I are, but whatever they have going on seems to work for them.

"Okay, get ready. I'm taking you to the police station now."

"What?" My eyes bug out while my heart leaps into my throat and gets stuck.

"You said you were going to report Ryan. The longer we wait, the harder it will be to prove he did anything. Time is not your friend now that Paris knows he hurt you again."

She's right. Paris will do something stupid. I know it deep in my bones. Nausea hits me suddenly and so violently that I don't have time to run to the bathroom or the kitchen sink. I puke into the vase that holds the flowers Paris gave me. There isn't much to spew, since, thanks to the altercation with Lydia, I didn't eat lunch.

When I'm done emptying the contents of my stomach, Heather offers me a napkin.

I wipe my mouth, and then say, "I know what I have to do. I'm just afraid no one will believe me."

She narrows her eyes. "Do you seriously think you were Ryan's first victim? Trust me, the moment you report him, more girls will come out of hiding and do the same. I know at least two that I suspect were victimized by him."

I blink fast as I process her words. "How would you know that?"

"I'm head cheerleader, and I'm dating the president of a fraternity. I run in different circles than you, and drunk girls talk."

"Okay, but since when do you have information that Ryan is a bastard?"

Her shoulders sag as she sighs. "Don't hate me, but I heard those rumors while you were dating him."

"Why didn't you *tell* me?" I shriek.

"A few reasons. I didn't know if they were true, and Ryan seemed to treat you well. And you needed to get over Paris."

I cover my face with my hands. "I had to go and pick the worst sort of distraction from him."

"I don't blame you for going for Ryan. He's the exact opposite of Paris—clean-cut and attractive in a cold way. In hindsight, he has the looks of a serial killer. But enough stalling. Go take a shower and get ready so we can nail that son of a bitch."

"Okay."

I head to my room, and when I'm alone, I call Paris. Maybe if he knows I'm going to report Ryan right now, it'll stop him from doing something stupid.

He doesn't answer my call, and the invisible knife stabbing my chest moves deeper. I sit on my bed, barely able to breathe as

I type a message to him. My hands are shaking, and I have to retype words several times to get rid of the typos. By the time I set down my phone and stare at the bedroom's closed door, I'm spent. The desire to curl up in a fetal position again and not move for hours is overwhelming. But I have to find the strength to do the right thing. Ryan must be stopped.

I 'm a bundle of nerves as I sit across from the police officer taking my statement. It's a woman, but still, I feel like she's judging me and not believing a word that comes out of my mouth.

"Tell me again why you didn't report the assault as soon as it happened?"

"How many times are you going to ask my sister that?" Heather butts in. "Honestly, it's no surprise victims of sexual assault don't report it."

"I didn't want the stigma," I answer the cop before she decides to arrest Heather. "I know it's not a good excuse, but that's what I was thinking at the time."

"And then you encountered your ex twice after he allegedly assaulted you."

She keeps using that word—*allegedly*—and it's setting my teeth on edge. It takes all my willpower not to lash out at her like Heather is doing.

"Yes. The first time I was with my teammate, Sadie Clarkson, and the second time was when he caused this." I point at the cut on my face.

"And you said Philip Meester witnessed the altercation?"

"That's correct."

"We're going to need his contact details to confirm the story."

"Isn't part of your job getting his information?" Heather asks, not hiding her annoyance.

The lady cop gives her a nasty look but mercifully doesn't offer a retort.

"There's something else you should know," I cut in. "Ryan recently posted a TikTok video making accusations about me."

That piques the cop's interest. She sits straighter and arches one of her brows. "What kind of accusations?"

"He said that I cheated on him with Paris Andino, the guy who stopped the assault, and that it's been going on for years. That's a lie. I didn't start dating Paris until after I broke up with Ryan."

"I see." She switches her gaze to her desktop and types away. "Does he have any proof that he's telling the truth?"

"How could he have proof?" My voice rises an octave. "He's lying."

"I have to ask the tough questions, Miss Castro. Since the Me Too movement started, there's been a rise in reports of sexual assault, but unfortunately, some of those claims have been false."

"Oh, so we now have to blame a good initiative for that?" Heather chimes in. "Watch Ryan come back to say he's the victim."

"He's already doing that by claiming I cheated on him," I grumble.

"I think I have everything I need on my end," the cop says. "I'm going to ask you to follow my colleague, who's going to take pictures of your injury."

"Okay, and then what?"

"Then we're going to interview your witnesses, although I have to say, Paris Andino's testimony might not hold a lot of weight, since he's in a relationship with you."

"That's bullshit," Heather blurts out.

The cop gives her another stern look. I'm surprised she didn't have Heather arrested yet. She's really pushing this cop's buttons.

"I also agree that it isn't fair," I say. "I wasn't dating Paris when Ryan decided that raping me was the way to handle our breakup. If Paris hadn't been there, Ryan would have succeeded."

"I understand your frustration. However, there isn't any physical evidence of the first assault, so it will be your and Paris's word against Ryan's." She links her hands and leans forward. "As horrible as it sounds, that cut on your face is the only solid proof we have that your ex has been abusive—that is, provided that your witness confirms your story."

"So, I'm lying until a stranger says I'm not?"

"You could have tripped on your own and decided to use the accident to get back at your ex for the video," the cop says matter-of-factly, like just being here wasn't already difficult.

"Okay, but when you get the statement from the witness, are you going to arrest Ryan?"

"We'll bring him in for questioning, but I have to say, I don't think he'll even warm the bench in a cell."

"Has anyone ever told you how *great* you are at making victims feel safe and heard?" Heather pipes up.

"Lying is not in my job description. Ryan Watergate is from a prestigious family. Do you know how many guys like him stay in prison for any significant amount of time?"

"Maybe if the police did a better job collecting evidence, they would stay in prison," Heather retorts.

The cop stands and signals someone behind us. That's it. Heather has gone and done it. She's getting arrested for pissing off a cop.

To my surprise, though, the cop didn't call for backup. She's called over the person who's going to take my picture.

Before I follow the second cop, I turn to Heather. "Please try to keep your thoughts to yourself while I'm gone."

"Don't worry. I'm done wasting my time."

Not exactly the answer I wanted, but when it comes to Heather, it's the best I'll get.

I follow the second cop—a short and chubby guy in his forties—down a narrow corridor and into a small room where there's a backdrop and a professional camera already set up on a tripod.

"This won't take long, sweetheart," he says, sporting a kind smile.

I thought giving my statement to a female cop would make the process easier, but she turned out to be a mean witch. This guy is already much better. And he's right—taking the pictures goes fast.

When we're done, he asks, "Does it still hurt a lot?"

"Just a little."

"And your ankle? Did you also hurt that when you fell?"

I shake my head. "No, that one was on me. Although, it was probably the reason I couldn't avoid hitting my face on that bench when my ex pushed me."

"We're going to get him, sweetheart. Don't worry."

I tilt my head. "That isn't what your colleague said."

"Don't listen to Officer Sanchez. She's a bitter old hag."

His comment makes me laugh. "Thanks for saying that."

He shrugs. "Well, someone has to say it. But don't tell anyone I did. She'll have my balls if she finds out."

"Your secret is safe with me. What happens next?" I ask again, because I'd like to hear *his* answer.

"You'll be assigned a detective who's going to call you again to set up an interview. You'll have to answer the same questions you already did, on top of more detailed ones."

"Great. I can't wait."

"Don't worry. The detective assigned to you will have experience dealing with your type of case."

"That's good to know."

Fifteen minutes later, Heather and I walk out of the precinct. Despite the second cop's assurances, I feel flat and depressed.

In a rare display of affection, Heather tosses her arm around my shoulders. "We'll get him, sis. I promise you."

"I wish I was as optimistic as you are. You heard that first cop. She didn't believe a word I said. And if Ryan is arrested, I bet his lawyers will use the same arguments that she did."

"Then we'll find another way to get evidence against him."

"Unless we catch him on camera, I don't see how. I have zero faith anyone else will report him if I become a laughingstock at school."

"We'll think about it tomorrow. There's another matter we have to take care of."

"What?"

"We need to cut a bitch."

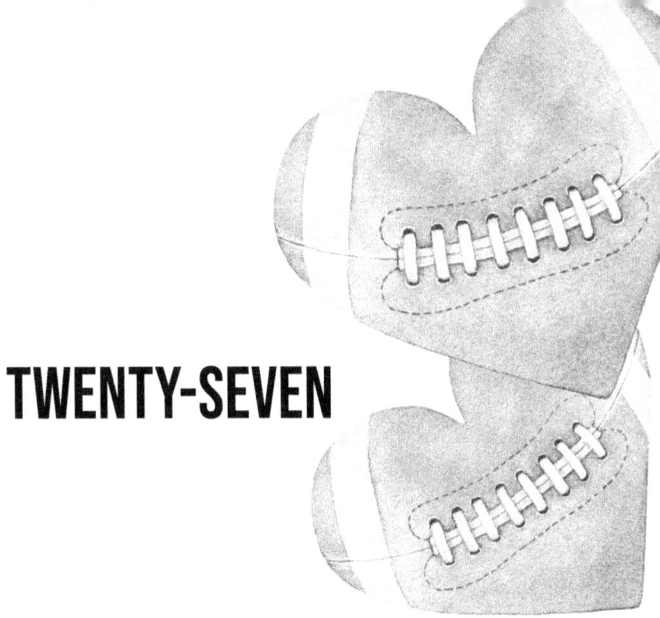

TWENTY-SEVEN

PARIS

It took every ounce of self-control to hide the rage brewing inside me from Vanessa. I didn't want her to be frightened or concerned. But that meant dropping her off at her place and leaving right away. It killed me that I had to go even though she begged me to stay. The latch keeping the beast contained had already begun to loosen.

My foot is heavy on the gas pedal and I'm gripping the steering wheel so tight, my knuckles are white. I'm driving way past the speed limit. Maybe my subconscious wants me to be stopped by a cop, because what I have in mind will for sure fuck up my life.

Ryan is a dead man walking.

The music from the radio gets cut off by an incoming call. It's Vanessa. I can't answer—not when I've allowed fury to consume me whole. A moment after the call stops, a ping on my phone alerts me to a text message. I don't peek. I'm almost to my destination: Greek Row.

I should slow down, but I continue at almost the same speed. When a delivery van backs out of one of the driveways, I almost collide with it. I stomp on the brakes, making the tires screech. The seat belt digs into my chest as momentum sends me forward. It hurts, but I ignore the pain.

A guy yells outside. From the corner of my eye, I see him running toward my truck. He's not Ryan, but I'm past the point of caring. If he wants to start a fight, I'm game. The van is still blocking me, so I get out of the truck with the intention of continuing on foot.

"What the hell is your problem?" the guy asks.

He's close now, and that's when I recognize him. It's Leo Stine, Heather's boyfriend.

"If you know what's good for you, you'll back the fuck off." I start to circle around the van.

"Where are you going, Andino?" The pest follows me.

"None of your business," I grit out. "Get lost."

"Does this have anything to do with Vanessa?"

I stop suddenly and turn around. "What do you know about Vanessa?"

I'm sure I look like the devil incarnate, but my aggressive stance doesn't seem to intimidate him. He lifts his chin and holds my stare. "I know more than you think."

I'm beyond thinking straight. In a split second, I'm holding him by his shirt and off the ground. "Then you'd better tell me, motherfucker, before I use you for practice."

He loses his arrogant air. His eyes go round, and his face turns pasty. "What the fuck are you doing, man? Put me down."

"Not until you tell me what you know."

"I just know that Ryan is a piece of shit, that's all."

I shake him roughly. "Try again."

More shouts in the vicinity warn me of incoming interference. Yet I don't break eye contact.

"Let me go, Andino." He grabs my wrists and tries to make me release him. Fat chance of that happening.

"Not until you tell me what you know about Ryan and

Vanessa. And if you think your frat friends can help you, you're mistaken. I can turn your face into pulp before they reach us."

He glances to the right and then back at me. "Fine. I know what Ryan did to Vanessa in the parking lot of Tailgaters."

All my blood seems to freeze in my veins. "How do you know that?" I grit out.

"Put me down, and I'll tell you."

As much as I want to keep putting the fear of God in Leo, I have to remember he isn't Ryan. I set him down and release him. He steps back and runs his hands over his shirt, trying to smooth the wrinkles I put there. His friends finally join us and form a shield around him.

"Are you okay, Leo?" one of them asks.

"I'm fine."

I keep my eyes on him. I might no longer have him in my grasp, but I can still break his fucking nose despite his bodyguards.

"I'm waiting for an answer, Leo," I growl.

"Let's talk inside. This isn't a conversation for the middle of the street."

"Wait. Are you inviting him in?" a second idiot asks.

"Yes, Blake. Do you have a problem with that?" Leo snaps.

The guy shakes his head. "No, not at all."

This is not how I envisioned my day turning out. I was dead set on ending Ryan, but I can't not follow Leo inside the Pike house and learn what he knows. I can destroy Ryan later.

I've been here before, but not during the day. The house looks different when there aren't disco lights flashing and loud music pouring from the speakers. The walls in the living area are a dark-gray-brown color, and all the furniture follows the same neutral palette. The best colors to hide dirt. There's a faint smell of beer and cigarettes under the fake scent of pine in the air. No amount of air freshener can mask that combo.

Leo heads for a black leather couch and drops onto it like a sack of potatoes. He points at the couch next to his. "Take a seat, Andino."

"I'm fine standing."

The two friends who came to the rescue linger nearby. Leo looks at them, "You can go now."

"Are you sure?" one of them asks, giving me a cagey side-glance.

"Fucking leave or I'll rearrange your face," I snap.

They glance at their president again for reassurance, which they get through a nod, as if he's a damn mafia boss. Once they're gone, Leo types a message on his phone before switching his attention to me.

"Start talking, jackass," I say.

"On the night Vanessa was attacked, one of my pledges saw part of it and caught the incident on his phone."

Just when I thought I couldn't get more furious, Leo's confession proves me wrong.

"Are you telling me that instead of helping her, he decided to record the assault?" I grit out while my hands curl into fists.

"I didn't know what was happening at first," a guy replies from behind me.

I turn around and see Philip Meester, the freshman who told me what Ryan did to Vanessa yesterday.

"You!" I'm on him in the blink of an eye, pushing him against the wall and wrapping my fingers around his neck.

"Paris, wait! It's not what you *think*." Leo jumps up from the couch.

Philip's face is already getting redder, and he can't talk with the way I'm squeezing his throat.

"You watched Vanessa almost get raped by that piece of shit and you *recorded* it?" I shout in his face.

His brown eyes are round and fearful. He can't answer with words, and he tries to shake his head.

"Paris! For fuck's sake. You'll end up killing him." Leo grabs the back of my shirt and yanks.

In a knee-jerk reaction, I kick back, hitting his leg.

"Motherfucker!" he blurts out. "If you don't let him explain, I'm calling campus police on your ass. Then it's goodbye football season."

I glare at him for a second, and then I release his friend, but only because now I'm going to punch Leo instead.

He walks back with his hands raised in a sign of peace. "Don't do something you'll regret, Andino."

"I was going to help," Philip wheezes, halting me and saving Leo from a broken nose. "But you showed up before I could."

"And you expect me to believe that?"

"I swear to God. I was in the middle of shooting a video for my YouTube channel when I heard the commotion. If you look at the footage, you'll see that I wasn't near them. I ran toward them when I realized the situation was serious, but you got there first."

"I've seen the video, he's not lying," Leo chimes in.

I turn to him. "Why didn't you say anything to me or Vanessa?"

"Because she didn't want to report Ryan." Leo throws his hands in the air. "I heard her loud and clear in the video."

I rub my face as I try to calm the fuck down. "Who else has seen this video?"

"I only showed it to Leo," Philip replies.

"And you still have it?"

He nods. "Yeah. Did she change her mind?"

A nagging suspicion comes to the forefront of my mind. Squinting, I ask, "Were you following Vanessa when Ryan pushed her?"

"No. I was following *him*. I bumped into him by chance in the humanities building and overheard him on the phone saying he'd be late to a meeting because his girlfriend was being difficult."

His girlfriend. I can't believe that asshole is still referring to Vanessa as such.

"Did you also film that?" I ask, not hiding my anger.

"No. I didn't think he was going to hurt her when there were so many people around. I was wrong."

"And earlier today? Did you 'just happen' to bump into Vanessa by chance?"

His face becomes bright red, and guilt flashes in his eyes. He drops his chin. "No. I was actually following her today."

My protective instinct flares up, and the desire to hurt him returns with a vengeance. I never pegged myself as a jealous caveman, but I never loved anyone so intensely and completely as I love Vanessa.

"You'd better have a good reason for that, besides being a fucking stalker."

"Philip is not a stalker," Leo butts in. "He's a nice guy who was worried."

"Vanessa doesn't need a bodyguard," I growl.

He quirks an eyebrow. "Why? Because she has you?"

The comment was meant to hurt, and it does the job. I dropped the ball when it came time to keep my girl safe.

"What's going to happen now? Is she ready to report Ryan?" Philip asks. "I can testify about yesterday's incident, and the police can have the footage from the assault."

I don't want to keep talking about Vanessa's personal life with these two, so I just reply, "We'll be in touch."

"Where are you going now?" Leo asks, his body tense again.

"Don't worry. I'm not going after Ryan. That was my intention earlier, but sending him to prison will be far more satisfying than breaking his bones."

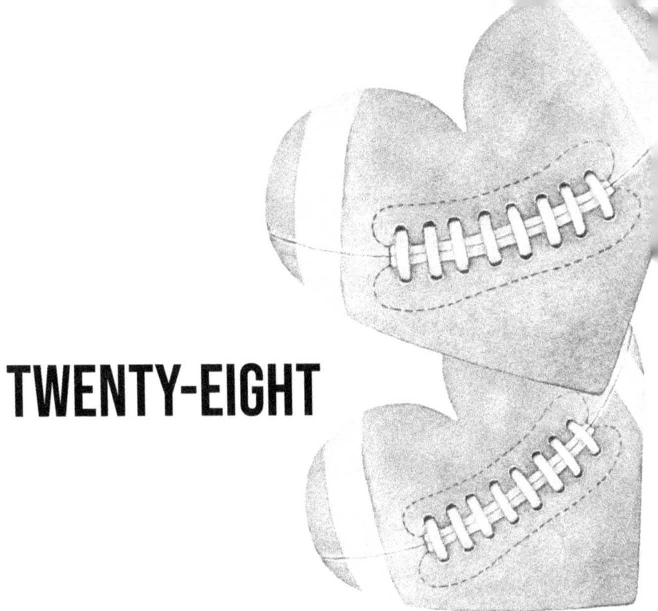

TWENTY-EIGHT

VANESSA

The police station is at the corner of a busy intersection, and it takes forever for the pedestrian light to turn to WALK. As much as I'd like to share Heather's enthusiasm about going after Lydia, I can't find an ounce of motivation now. She hurt me deeply, lied to Paris, and drove us apart. But she isn't the only reason we stayed that way for so long. That girl is awful, but I can't lay all the blame on her. If Paris and I had talked instead of bickering, we would have found out about her deception before now.

"It's not worth getting revenge on her," I say.

"I disagree, but she kicked your ass, not mine." Heather shrugs. "I can still blacklist her from all social activities on campus, and you can't stop me from doing that."

"She didn't kick my ass," I retort. "I would have fought back if Paris hadn't interrupted us."

"Right, your knight in shining armor. Speaking of which, there he is."

"What?"

I stop in my tracks, which happens to be in the middle of the road, and follow her line of vision. Paris's truck is parked on the other side and he's standing next to it, leaning against the door with his arms crossed in front of his wide chest. The air is already getting cold, but he's not wearing a jacket, so his impressive muscles and beautiful tats are on full display. I'd run to him if I could.

"Go on." Heather nudges me. "I know you'd rather ride back home with him than me."

Before I take another step, I turn around and hug her. "Thank you for coming with me today."

"You don't need to thank me. I'm just glad that you did report him."

When we break apart, Heather's blue eyes are brighter. She turns away fast, maybe to hide the emotion in them. I continue toward Paris, who is now walking over. Before I can take more than two steps forward, he reaches me and hugs me tightly.

"How did it go?" he asks.

I melt against his chest and sigh. "It was rough. I'll tell you everything on the way home." Pulling back, I tilt my face up and look into his eyes. "I'm so happy to see you though. You're like a balm for my tired soul."

He cups my cheek gently. "I'm sorry I missed your call. I... I wasn't in the right frame of mind to talk to anyone. After I calmed down, I read your text. I wasn't sure if you wanted me here, but I had to make sure you were okay."

"How did you know where I was?"

"This is the closest police station to campus. It wasn't hard to guess."

"I'm glad you found me. And I'm sorry I didn't ask you to come with me." I drop my gaze to the hollow of his throat.

"The important thing is that you decided to report him to the police, and you weren't alone."

I look up again, smirking. "You should have seen Heather. She gave the cop so much shit, I'm shocked she's not behind bars."

He steps back, leaving enough room for me to maneuver my crutches. "Come on. You can tell me all about it in the truck."

"I can't wait to get rid of these," I grumble.

"When's your next appointment?"

"Tomorrow."

He opens the door for me, and then takes the crutches from my hands and tosses them in the back. I wait for him to help me into the truck simply because I want his hands on me.

He quirks an eyebrow. "I thought you didn't like it when I assisted you."

"That was then, this is now."

Twisting his lips into a crooked grin, he wraps his hands around my waist and lifts me effortlessly onto the seat. Before he can step back, I throw my arms around his neck and cross my legs at the ankles behind his legs, caging him in.

"What are you doing, kitten?" he asks through a laugh.

"You owe me a kiss."

"Is that so?"

"Yes. From you, a kiss is the only acceptable form of greeting."

"I'm fine with that." He slants his lips over mine and coaxes them open with his tongue.

I pull him closer, needing everything he can give me and more. I'm needy and hungry for my guy. Perhaps this isn't the best place to attack his mouth, but after the day I've had, getting lost in Paris is exactly what I need.

He pulls back, breaking the kiss but not moving away. He rests his forehead against mine and whispers, "I love you so damn much, kitten. You have no idea."

"Oh, I think I do. Probably as much as I love you."

He steps back, smiling from ear to ear. I toss my legs inside the vehicle and wait for Paris to shut the door. The butterflies in my stomach are wide awake now, all thanks to that smile. My depression can't fight the effect Paris has on me.

As soon as he drives off, he reaches for my hand and laces

our fingers together. We don't speak for several minutes. I'm happy to bask in his presence and his touch.

"Am I taking you home?" He breaks the silence.

"Yeah. What time is practice for you today?"

"In a couple of hours."

I nibble on my lower lip. That's not a lot of time to really talk about everything that happened. "You don't have class before that?"

"I did, but I'm calling in sick." He smirks.

My brows furrow. "I hate that I've become a distraction."

"Kitten, don't say that. You're the best thing that's happened to me in a very long time."

My eyes prickle, and I keep them focused on the road. "I can say the same about you. I can't wait until this ordeal with Ryan is over."

He squeezes my hand. "About that… I have news."

My heart tightens. "You didn't hurt him, did you?"

"No. I wanted to, and I went looking for him on Greek Row, but I ended up having a chat with Leo Stine and Philip Meester instead."

"Oh? What about?"

"Philip caught your assault on camera."

I take a sharp breath as I process his words. "How?"

"He was shooting a video for his YouTube channel when you and Ryan came into the shot. He wasn't near, but it seems he managed to record it. I didn't watch the video, so I'm taking his word for it."

I blink fast, fighting the tears that are threatening to spill at any moment. "There's evidence that Ryan…" A lump prevents me from continuing. I look out the window, pressing a fist against my lips as I try to hold myself together.

"Hell, I should have waited until we were home to tell you. I thought you would be—"

"Happy?" I turn toward him.

The truck slows down until it comes to a complete stop. He

puts it in park and looks at me. I don't even know if he found a place to park or if we're at a red light. My attention is solely on him.

"No, not exactly happy. Relieved? Now that bastard can't lie and say the assault never happened. You can send him to jail."

"Knowing that there's a video of the lowest moment of my life, and that it will be seen by many strangers until this is all over, makes me feel violated."

His anguished expression only worsens with my confession. "Kitten…"

"Maybe one day I'll be glad that Philip was there, but I'll feel relief only when Ryan is behind bars."

He reaches for my face and gently runs his fingers over my hairline. "I'll be there for you, kitten, every day, and in every way you need me."

TWENTY-NINE

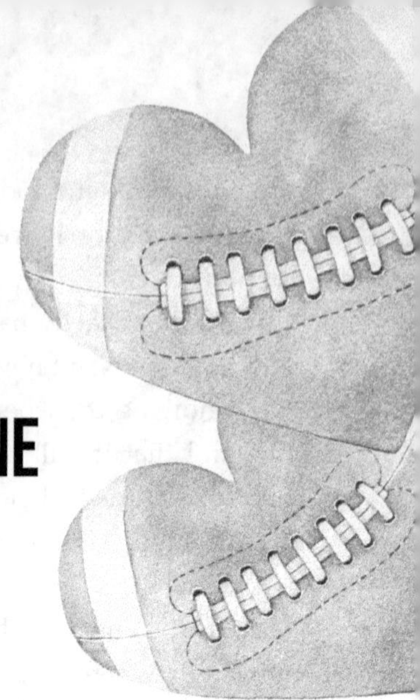

VANESSA

A phone rings somewhere in the distance, waking me before I'm ready. I don't move from my current position, though. I'm too comfortable, resting my head against Paris's warm chest. His arm tightens around my shoulder.

"Who's calling at this ungodly hour?" he grumbles.

"It's not my phone."

"I know. That's my father's ringtone."

The shrill stops finally, but the damage is done. I'm awake, but so is Paris—all of him. I run my fingers down his abs until I reach the tip of his erection.

"Since we're up…" I say before I slide down his body.

"Hmm, that's a much better way to wake up."

Unfortunately, I don't make it to my destination before his phone rings again. It's a different ringtone this time, meaning someone else is calling him. That's never a good sign in my book, and considering everything that's happening in our lives, we can't ignore it.

I prop myself up. "Maybe you should answer it."

He spares a couple seconds staring at me before he sighs, "You're right." His brows furrow when he sees the number. "It's Danny." He puts the call on speaker. "Hey, man. Why are you calling so early?"

"I take it you haven't seen it yet."

"Seen what?" He sits up fast, his entire body tense, as if he's bracing for a storm.

"Lydia posted a video last night on TikTok. It's bad, bro. You need to watch it."

"It's rubbish," Sadie pipes up in the background. "Anyone with a brain could tell her tears were fake."

Shit. I *knew* that snake wouldn't leave things alone. I grab my phone and open the app. "What's her account handle?"

A second later, I receive a text from Sadie with the link.

Paris and I watch it on my phone together while he keeps Danny on the line. Honestly, I think he forgot he was on a call. The video is three minutes long, and she spends half the time talking about her mental health issues—a.k.a. building sympathy—and the other half talking trash about Paris and blaming him for her relapse. She ends the video saying she doesn't know if she'll be able to survive that betrayal.

"I can't believe she's done that after what you went through with Cory. She can't be that evil, right?"

"She's totally pulling a *13 Reasons Why* move," Sadie replies to my outburst.

Paris rests his head in his hands. "She might actually hurt herself."

I throw my arm around his shoulders and pull him closer to me. "Maybe. But you can't let her make you feel guilty about her decisions. The video she posted on TikTok was malicious, but it's also a cry for help—and she needs a professional, not you. She wants everyone to hate you, and that's not the move of a stable person."

"I have to call my dad back."

"Okay, man. Keep us posted," Danny says before he ends the call.

I drop my arm from Paris's shoulder and move to give him some space, but he reaches for my hand and stops me from going too far as he returns his father's call.

"Hey, Dad."

"I don't know what happened, son, but you need to help us find Lydia."

"What do you mean, find her?"

"She's missing. Her parents just left our house after yelling at us for half an hour. They're blaming you for her meltdown. Were you seriously cheating on her with that Castro girl?"

I bristle. Paris's hold on my hand tightens.

"I *never* cheated on Lydia," he grits out. "And stop calling Vanessa 'that Castro girl.' She's my girlfriend, Dad, and I love her."

My heart swells with emotion despite the shitty situation.

"Oh. Well, don't tell your mother yet. She isn't in any state to receive that news. Despite your current relationship situation, you must find Lydia. You need to salvage your reputation somehow."

He swallows hard. "So that's what this is all about. You're concerned about my reputation."

"I don't want anything to happen to the girl, but you're my son—my priority is to make sure *you* are okay. I don't believe for a second you're responsible for whatever's going on with her. But I've read some of the comments people left on her video. They hate you, son."

We purposely avoided the comments, but I imagine they're vile. I loathe people sometimes. Keyboard warriors and their digital pitchforks can rot in hell.

"How do they know she's gone? Couldn't she be avoiding their calls?"

"Maybe. But they're worried. You know more about her habits than they do. Do you know where she could be?"

I watch Paris closely, hating how this conversation is affecting him. His face is pinched, and the hard set of his jaw tells me he's wrestling with a guilt he shouldn't feel.

"I'm not sure. I have to get my head on straight. I'll call if I have news."

"Okay, son. I'll do the same if I hear anything."

Paris ends the call. His shoulders sag, and he stares at his phone without moving. There's a knot in my chest now. I don't know how to help him, and I'm afraid anything I say will sound insincere or self-serving. I hate Lydia for what she's doing to us, but I don't want her to die.

"Do you have any idea where she would go?" I ask softly.

He turns to me, revealing bright, anguished eyes. "No. Isn't that terrible? I dated her for years, and I don't fucking know where she would go."

The loud noise of a door banging shut prevents me from saying something that would only make things worse.

"Vanessa?" Heather calls out. "Are you decent?"

"Just a second." I jump out of bed and get dressed quickly.

When Paris doesn't make a move to at least put on his underwear, I toss his boxers at him. "Get dressed, unless you want to give Heather a peep show."

He blinks fast, and then replies, "Uh, no to that."

"I'm coming in," Heather announces a second before she opens the door.

"What's going on?" I ask, noticing she's still wearing the same outfit as yesterday. She has clothes at Leo's, so if she spent the night there, she'd have changed.

"What's going on is that I was right to follow my instincts. You can thank me later."

I lift my hands. "Thank you for what exactly?"

"I wasn't happy with your attitude about not giving that snake some sort of punishment, so I decided to take matters into my own hands."

"Oh my god, Heather. What did you do?" I ask, worried that she's responsible for Lydia's disappearance.

Paris is standing now, a giant who's tenser than before.

Heather waves a hand dismissively. "Oh relax. I didn't kill the bitch. I had a feeling she was going to pull one final stunt to destroy you and Paris, so I stalked her place and all her social media accounts. Then she posted that TikTok video." She shakes her head. "Classic manipulator move."

"Cut to the chase, Heather," Paris butts in. "Do you know where she is?"

"Sure do." She lifts her phone and presses play on the video already loaded on her screen.

A grainy but recognizable video of Lydia riding a mechanical bull at some bar plays for us as a crowd of drunks cheers her on.

"I followed her to a dive bar off campus, can't remember the name now. She was partying without a care in the world. I have more videos like this, including one where she's making out with some random dude."

"That just proves she didn't harm herself, but people can argue she was acting out because she was depressed," I say.

Heather smiles like a fiend. "I got close enough to capture part of her conversation. I got a confession, sis. She fully admitted to the dude she was with that she ruined her ex's life."

"Can I see that video?" Paris asks, his voice cold and tight.

She plays it for him. It's only a snippet, but it does contain her confession.

Paris's cheeks hollow as he watches it, and by then, his jaw is locked tight. "Thanks." He returns Heather's phone. "What are you planning to do with it?"

"It's up to you. I have a TikTok video in my drafts, ready to go. Just say the word."

His eyes narrow a fraction before he replies, "Load it up."

THIRTY

VANESSA

The fire Lydia started by posting that bullshit TikTok was quickly put out once Heather posted her video of Lydia confessing to lying about the whole thing. That bitch's plan to make people hate Paris backfired, and she ended up earning all the hate herself.

However, the next few days aren't blissful. I'm a stressed-out mess, thanks to waiting for an update on my case against Ryan. The day after I reported that scumbag, Paris and I returned to the station so he could give his statement. I also wanted the cops to know about Philip's video.

Because Ryan hasn't been arrested yet, I maintain my decision to keep my assault a secret from the team. I don't want any distractions. This is an important game for us. We're playing our biggest rival, and I feel guilty enough that I'm warming the bench instead of leading them on the field.

Paris's game started earlier, but I didn't go. As much as I'd love to support him, my team needs me more than he does.

There are five minutes left on the clock in the second half, and we have yet to score. We're tied at 0–0. My replacement is a talented freshman, Ginny Sanders, without much experience. She hasn't yet jelled with the team—Sadie already yelled at her a few times for losing the ball to our adversaries while attempting to pass. Charlotte, our second midfielder, is doing everything she can to compensate.

Despite my promise to Paris to take it easy today, I'm on my feet, shouting encouragement to the team. The Ravens are on the attack, Ginny has the ball, and Sadie is positioned perfectly to receive the pass and score. But Ginny touches the ball wrong, sending it directly to the only defensive player between Sadie and the goal. The defensive player deflects the shot, earning us a corner kick at least.

Sadie's face is red, and not because she's been running. She's ready to go off on the poor girl again, but arguing among ourselves won't help us win the game.

"Sadie!" I shout, trying to draw her attention to me.

She turns in my direction. I signal quickly with my hands, urging her to calm down. In a typical Sadie move, she looks up at the sky and groans, before running toward the goal to get in position.

Joanne, our second striker, doesn't waste any time and sprints toward the corner to make the kick. My heart is pounding fast and hard against my rib cage, and I don't dare breathe. This is our chance to score. Sadie and Charlotte are in position, but Sadie, the tallest, has the better chance of touching the ball.

The whistle blows, and then Joanne fires the ball toward the goal box in a perfect arch. I hold my breath, gripping my crutches tight. Several players jump all at once, but it's Sadie's blonde head that connects with the ball and sends it straight toward the goal. The keeper tries to block, stretching her arms to the max to no avail.

The ball touches the net, and a yell rips out of my throat. It's swallowed by thousands more from the crowd. Sadie and Charlotte run to the sideline to celebrate with me, almost knocking me down with their enthusiasm. The game isn't over yet, and now the opposing team will be more aggressive than before.

I wish I could run along the sideline to keep up with the players. It takes a herculean effort to remain in one spot. My gaze is glued to the field, my attention solely on the game, and for that reason, I don't notice anyone approach me from behind. Strong arms snake around my waist and pull me against a solid body, making me yelp.

"How's it going, kitten?" Paris asks close to my ear.

"Oh my god. You scared me," I reply through a laugh.

He chuckles. "Didn't mean to."

"Did you guys just score?" Danny stops next to me.

"Yeah. Didn't you see?"

"We literally just stepped onto the field when the crowd went wild," Paris replies.

"It was awesome. Sadie scored."

"Ah man. And I missed that?" Danny looks crestfallen.

"I'm sure you can watch the replay," I say. "How was your game?"

Paris releases me but only to switch positions and stand next to me. He keeps one of his arms wrapped around my waist. "You didn't keep up with the score?"

My face becomes hotter as shame surges through me. "No. I'm sorry. I've been too absorbed in this game."

The corners of his lips twitch upward. "I know. I was just yanking your chain. We won by a landslide, 27 to 3."

"That's awesome." I rise on my tiptoes and pull his face to mine for a kiss.

Like always, it's electrifying and makes my entire body tingle with desire. For that reason alone, I ease back quickly. Attacking his mouth while the Ravens are still playing isn't a good example for the team.

I return my full attention to the girls. As I predicted, the opposing team becomes more aggressive, but our defense holds.

I relax only when the referee whistles to signify the end of the game.

Danny runs to Sadie and scoops her into his arms. A lazy smile blossoms on my face. They're so adorable together.

Paris kisses the side of my forehead. "In a few weeks, that'll be us celebrating."

I turn to him, beaming from ear to ear. "I can't wait."

It takes a few minutes for our celebration on the field to end. Per tradition, the MVP of the game—Sadie—gets soaked in what's left of the icy water. Because she's a fiend, she pulls me to her side while the dunking is happening, meaning I get drenched as well. I'm caught between cursing at her and laughing from the belly up.

During all this, there's a moment when my gaze connects with Paris, who's hanging with Danny far from the splash zone. His lips are turned slightly upward, as if he's trying not to laugh, but his amused eyes give him away.

I break away from the girls and walk over. "What are you smiling at?"

"You."

"Oh yeah?" I drop the crutches and jump into his arms, getting him wet too.

He picks me up and slants his mouth over mine. His kiss is demanding, hungry, and possessive, making me forget there are thousands of witnesses. A throat clearing nearby interrupts our moment. I pull back but hold Paris's heated gaze.

"I hope you're ready to do some explaining," Heather says.

Wait. My *sister* came to a Ravens game?

I slide off Paris and turn to her. "Wow, you're here, and I'm not even playing today."

She smirks. "When I heard Paris was coming, I knew I had to be here."

Leeriness takes hold. "Why?"

She hikes her thumb and points at a spot in the stands. Our parents are there, in their usual seats near the field, but unlike any other day, they aren't happy. I can see their frowns from where I stand.

"Hell, I didn't know they were still planning to come despite me being on the bench."

"Your surprise is amusing. Of course they came. They're the Ravens' biggest fans. Duh."

"I didn't know," Paris pipes up. "You could have given *me* the heads-up. I would have refrained from making out with Vanessa in front of them."

Heather laughs. "Why would I do that? The main reason I came was to watch my folks go apeshit on your asses."

"I hate you," I grumble. "Remember, sis. Payback is a bitch."

THIRTY-ONE

PARIS

I should have known Heather was up to no good when she said she'd come to the Ravens game. She's always had a penchant for making things go up in flames while she watches the mayhem calmly with a wicked grin on her face.

If I'd known their parents would be in attendance, I'd have behaved better. Surprisingly, when I go to say hello to them, they don't bite my head off. Maybe they don't want to make a scene in front of an audience.

When Vanessa invites me to come to dinner with them, her parents' death glares intensify up to eleven. If looks could kill, I'd be dead. But I'm unable to deny any request she makes—she has me wrapped around her finger good, and I'm totally fine with it.

That's how I find myself at Trattoria La Nonna, sitting across from Mr. Castro, who can't stop glaring at me. I've never been more uncomfortable in my life. Vanessa is next to me, but not even her warm hand on my thigh is helping me relax. Maybe it's doing the opposite.

"So, you're really determined to piss off everyone to be together," he says.

"Dad, come on. Why should we cater to the whims of others? Paris makes me happy."

Her mother shakes her head. "Every time he comes into your life, you get hurt, *filha*. You can't blame us for being concerned."

"I never meant for Vanessa to get hurt, Mrs. Castro. I love her with all my heart," I reply.

Vanessa squeezes my leg in response, making me turn to look at her. I can't help the smile that tugs at the corners of my lips. I'm under fire here, and she still makes me grin like a fool.

"*Love* her…" Her father snorts. "You just started going out. How can you make such a claim?"

My smile vanishes, but I'm not angry. I'm dead serious when I lock gazes with him. "I've loved her since we were kids, Mr. Castro. Sure, life and other people got in the way, but my feelings for her never faded. They were just dormant."

"What about that awful girl you dated for years? Did you forget her just like that?" Vanessa's mother snaps her fingers.

"She's an easy one to forget," Heather pipes up. "Lydia doesn't have an interesting bone in her body. No wonder she had to resort to deceit and manipulation to hold on to Paris for so long."

I don't want to talk about Lydia. I don't know yet how I feel about her. It was upsetting to learn she lied to me, but I can't ignore the fact that she's not healthy and needs medical attention. I definitely don't hate her, but I do pity her, and I want her to be well.

"Lydia is not an issue, Mom. But there is something I'd like to tell you." Vanessa tenses.

There's only one topic that would make her react like that. I cover her hand with mine and squeeze, hoping it will give her some support. This won't be an easy conversation.

Her parents sit straighter in their chairs.

"What is it, honey?" her dad asks.

"I never told you why Ryan wasn't at Lorena's wedding. I broke up with him the night before, and…" She drops her chin, letting out a heavy exhale.

I don't know what else to do except keep holding her hand. It breaks my heart to watch the love of my life struggle to tell her parents about that nightmarish evening.

"And what?" her mom probes.

"He attacked me."

Mr. Castro's eyes go round, and his face contorts into an expression of pure rage in the blink of an eye. "What do you mean he *attacked* you?" he grits out.

"He tried to…" Vanessa wipes the corners of her eyes.

"Say no more," her mother cuts in.

"You're not going to even let her finish?" Heather retorts, her voice rising an octave.

Hell, is she going to cause a scene? I hope not.

"That's not what I'm doing," Mrs. Castro replies. "Look at your poor sister. I know what she wants to say, and I'm sparing her."

"He tried to rape me," Vanessa finally blurts out.

A long stretch of silence follows. Her parents don't blink, don't move.

"That son of a bitch," her father says in a voice that's dangerously low. "Did you report him, honey? I hope you did, because I have half a mind to make sure he won't be able to take a piss standing."

Whoa. I had no idea Mr. Castro had a dark side. I thought he was the level-headed one in her parents' relationship.

"I came close to it," I chime in.

Mr. Castro's expression of pure rage morphs into something else, and maybe I'm reading too much into it, but it seems his opinion of me might be changing a bit.

"Paris stopped Ryan, and he'd have killed him if I'd let him," Vanessa adds.

"Really?" Mrs. Castro's eyebrows arch. "You'd ruin your future to avenge our daughter?"

"Yes, ma'am. I would. In a heartbeat."

"Oh my god. From what century are you guys?" Heather throws her hands in the air.

"Anyway… to answer your question, Dad, I did report Ryan. We're waiting to hear back from the detective investigating the case."

"He hasn't been arrested yet?" he asks.

"Because Vanessa didn't report him right away, there's more red tape now," Heather replies.

"They have enough evidence against him, though. His arrest is imminent," I say with more confidence than I feel. The police are taking their sweet time to go after that bastard.

Someone's phone rings, and everyone at the table checks their devices, including me. It's Vanessa's, but she doesn't answer right away.

She glances at me instead, her eyes a little rounder than before. "It's the detective."

"Oh my god. Answer them," Heather tells her.

Vanessa presses the green button but doesn't put the call on speaker. "Hello?"

I can't hear what the caller is saying, so I settle for watching Vanessa closely. The muscles around her mouth are tense, and she looks a little paler than before. Those fuckers had better not be calling to say Ryan is going to walk.

"Okay. Thanks for letting me know."

She sets the phone down in silence. Her gaze is focused on nothing. It's like she's in a daze.

"What happened?" her mother and Heather ask at the same time.

"Ryan was arrested an hour ago."

Relief cuts through the chains that were squeezing my chest tight. I toss my arm over her shoulders and kiss the side of her head. "Thank fuck."

Instead of chastising me for cursing, Mr. Castro adds, "Amen to that. I hope that bastard rots in jail."

"Yeah, let's hope so," Vanessa replies.

"And if he doesn't..." Heather waves her steak knife. "It's bye-bye, birdie."

VANESSA

I lift my legs and cross them at the ankles behind Paris's back, allowing him to penetrate me deeper. He groans against my lips and increases the pace, flattening me against the mattress. My headboard creaks loudly, and I'm sure at any moment Heather is going to complain about the noise. It's the first time Paris and I have banged while she's been in the house.

After dinner with my folks, we came back to my place. Heather went straight to her room, claiming a headache. I didn't have the heart to encourage her to go see Leo. I don't think she's happy with him, after learning he knew about Philip's video and didn't tell her.

"Shh. Take it easy, babe," I whisper against his lips.

"I'm trying. But your pussy feels so damn good, kitten."

"Maybe we should put the mattress on the floor."

"Next time. I can't stop now."

I can feel him swell inside me. The pressure is building for me as well. I don't want to stop. Instead, I capture his face between my hands and kiss him hard. It's a smart move, because in the next second, I come, and I can't climax quietly when Paris is fucking me into oblivion. Although with the racket my bed is making, I doubt Heather can hear me screaming anyway.

"Oh my god, kitten," Paris mutters before his body convulses with the power of his release.

I clench my internal walls, milking him to the max. He loves when I do that, but it's amazing for me too. Case in point, I come a second time, and the sensation is more bone melting than the first. Paris doesn't stop moving until a couple of minutes later, and by then, I'm pudding.

He rolls off me but keeps half his body covering mine. We're slick with sweat, our breaths coming in bursts. I'm in recovery mode, but I snuggle closer, wanting to meld myself into him.

"Thanks for coming to dinner tonight. I don't think I'd have been able to tell my folks about Ryan if you hadn't been there," I say.

"Yes, you would." He draws lazy circles over my arm, giving me goose bumps.

"I just want this to be over, but I know it will be a long process."

"And I'll be with you, kitten, every step of the way."

Like a real cat, I rub my cheek against his chest. "Thank you. I guess I need a knight in shining armor after all."

He laughs, and the sound is a delicious rumble that I feel deep in my core.

"I don't think you do, babe. You're my Éowyn. I'm just thankful that you let me fight by your side."

My heart swells with emotion. I didn't believe I could love Paris more, and here he is, proving me wrong again. I raise my head and look into his eyes, a smile tugging at the corners of my lips. "Are you saying you're my Merry, then?"

He matches my grin and cups my pussy. "I think I'd rather be your Faramir."

THIRTY-TWO

Puck's wedding day has finally arrived. The ceremony isn't taking place in a church, like I originally thought, but at a beautiful location in Oak Glen, which is a couple hours away from LA. Puck told us he couldn't get a date soon enough in their church, but a family friend who works at the Oak Glen venue told him there had been a cancellation. It's in the mountains, and the views couldn't be more spectacular. I'd say they lucked out. The sun is out, but the weather is mercifully cool.

I fidget with my suit while Vanessa stares at me, grinning. She looks stunning as always. Her dress is a deep-burgundy shade that looks amazing against her tanned skin, but the best feature is how it hugs her curves perfectly. It's taking a lot of effort on my part to keep my hands to myself.

My brows arch. "What's up, kitten? Like what you see?"

"Always. But why are you yanking at your clothes like a five-year-old boy?" She steps into my space and fixes my tie.

"This doesn't fit right. It's too tight." I move my arms, feeling the fabric's tension around my guns when I do so.

"Stop doing that, or you'll end up with another torn jacket."

I grimace, stopping at once. "Right. I think I need to buy the next size up."

She curls her luscious lips into a devilish grin, and her eyes dance with mirth. "You're getting bigger."

Like the devil she is, she moves even closer, pressing her body to mine. Immediately, my dick stirs in my pants.

I narrow my eyes. "What are you doing, kitten?"

"Nothing." She rises on her toes and brings her mouth close to my ear. "The ceremony won't start for another half hour though."

I loop my arms around her waist. "What do you have in mind?"

"Whatever you fools are planning, forget it." Danny butts in, making me groan.

"We aren't planning anything," I retort, annoyed that he's interrupting my fun.

"Sure, that's why you're holding Vanessa in front of you like a shield." Sadie smirks.

Vanessa begins to laugh, hiding her face against my chest. "She got us there, babe."

"Since when have you turned into a cockblocker, Danny Boy?" I grumble.

He shakes his head. "I'm not trying to be a party pooper, but whatever idea you guys had, Andy had it first."

"What's Andy up to now?" Troy asks as he joins us with his girlfriend, Charlie. "Where are he and Jane, by the way?" He glances around, looking for his best friend and his sister.

Danny and Sadie trade a guilty look, and I connect the dots. That horny idiot. Troy might have come to accept that his little sister is dating Andreas, but that doesn't mean he wants to have a front-row seat to their sex life.

"Are you guys looking for me?" The man in question walks toward us, and it doesn't take a genius to know what he has been up to. Messy hair, wrinkled clothes, loose tie. Jane is more put together, but her face is a little red.

"Are you fucking kidding me?" Troy puts his hands on his hips and glares at the duo.

"Stop staring at us like that," Jane retorts, finger-combing her long blonde hair.

"You're not going to fight, are you?" Danny takes a step forward, ready to jump between them.

Charlie links her arm with Troy's and pulls him back. "No one is fighting. Come on, Troy. Leave them alone."

"Aw, man. I was hoping for a kerfuffle," Sadie jokes.

"Kerfuffle?" Vanessa raises a brow. "Even I know that word doesn't belong to this century, even in the UK."

Sadie laughs. "It doesn't, but it's fun to say it out loud, innit?"

I look over her head and spot a very tall and colorful woman coming our way—the wedding planner, a.k.a. Puck's older sister, Raquel. Her '70s-print dress is bright, and it hurts my eyes if I stare at it too long.

"There you are," she says, a little out of breath. "The ceremony is about to start, and I need my groomsmen. Come on, come on." She urges us toward the cluster of chicks wearing light-blue dresses.

I kiss Vanessa on the cheek. "I'll be right back. Don't go running away with a bottle of wine and spraining your ankle again."

She wrinkles her nose. "Never again. I'll watch where I step this time."

I scoff. "Oh, so wine stealing isn't off the menu?"

"Mr. Paris Andino, get your butt out there before I forget you're a grown man and smack you upside the head." Raquel points in the direction I should have gone already.

"Yes, ma'am." I sprint toward my friends, but I don't miss the laughter coming from Vanessa and the other girls.

I already know they are going to tease me about being scolded by Raquel mercilessly today.

VANESSA

While Paris goes to the nearest bar to get us fresh drinks, I walk to the edge of the reception area, where it's much quieter and I can admire the view without interruptions. The sun set a while ago, and since we're far from the city, the stars are shining in the clear midnight-blue sky. I take a deep breath and let a sense of peace wash over me.

Puck's wedding is much better than the last one I attended. For starters, I have no family around to create drama, and I'm not dealing with a recent trauma. To be fair, it hasn't been that long since Ryan assaulted me, but I'm in a much better place mentally, thanks to the support I've received from my family, friends, and most important, Paris. He's been my rock, and the best boyfriend I could have wished for.

Ryan is free right now, waiting for his trial. I was a mess when he was released from jail, but thanks to a huge campaign on social media spearheaded by Heather, we managed to get the asshole expelled from Rushmore. It's going to be a while before the case goes to court, but at least I don't run the risk of bumping into him at school.

"A penny for your thoughts." Paris returns to my side, holding two glasses of champagne.

I turn around and take one of the flutes from him. "I was just thinking about life in general and how lucky I am that you're in mine."

"No, *I'm* the lucky one because you gave me a second chance."

"We were always meant to be together. Fate was just waiting for the right place and time to intervene."

His brows furrow. "I'd have preferred to come back to you in a way where you didn't have to suffer."

"Hey, turn that frown upside down. Everything happens for a reason. If I had to go through Hell to get to you, then it was worth it."

He sets his glass on the fence separating us from the twelve-foot drop and pulls me against his body. "I promise you'll never have to go through it again, kitten."

We both know that's an impossible promise to keep. The road ahead of us isn't yet clear of obstacles or monsters. I don't call him on it, though.

I cup his cheek. "Even if another detour into Hell is in my future, it won't be as daunting, because I know you'll be with me. And even if, for whatever reason, you aren't… in the darkness, I shall remember how your gaze brightened everything."

Paris stares at me without saying a word. Yes, I quoted the poem I wrote for Cory, because it expresses exactly how I feel right now.

He captures my face between his hands and presses his forehead to mine.

"And I won't be afraid, for I know you're with me." He recites the second verse, choking me up. "I love you, kitten. Always have, and always will."

I kiss him then, while tears roll down my cheeks. Typical Paris, always making me bawl my eyes out.

He pulls back gently and wipes the moisture from my face. "Don't cry, kitten."

I look into those beautiful blue eyes and see the promise of a beautiful life together. "These are good tears, babe. Very good tears."

Life won't always be easy, but I know Paris will be there for me, come rain or shine. He was many of my firsts, and he's now my forever.

**** THE END ****

Thank you for reading *Heart Smasher*!

**If you're looking for another second chance romance from me,
Wonderwall is your book. And guess what? The main
characters are from the same hometown as Paris and Vanessa!**

SEBASTIAN

If there's one thing I've learned in my life it's that fate is a f*cking
bitch. So don't get too comfortable, my friends. Don't think that
just because you are happy now, your life is going to be an
eternal parade of pink unicorns and sunshine. Once upon a time,
I had everything a person could hope for—great parents, loyal
friends, and Liv. She was everything to me, my best friend, the
girl of my dreams, my kingdom come. And then bam! I had
nothing. Sure, now it seems like I'm the king of the world. I have
fame, an endless supply of beautiful women at my feet, and
more money than I can spend in my lifetime. It's all meaningless

without the girl I can't forget. So when I see her in the last place I expect, I don't think twice, I vow to get her back.

LIV

They say you never forget your first love, but I wish I could. Sebastian was the boy next door, the one who stole my heart, only to give it back bruised and broken. I've tried my best to move on, to erase him from my mind, but how can I do that when he is literally everywhere? There's no escape when your ex-boyfriend is on the cover of every magazine when his music won't stop playing on the radio. Was it a stupid decision to move across the ocean to the same city he calls home? Maybe. I was only following my dream. I didn't expect Sebastian to crash back into my life. He is different from the boy I once knew, darker, and much more dangerous to my heart. Resisting him would be the smart choice. I just don't know if I'm strong enough.

FREE NOVELLA

CATCH YOU

Do you want another swoony romance? Then **scan the QR code** to get your free copy of *Catch You*.

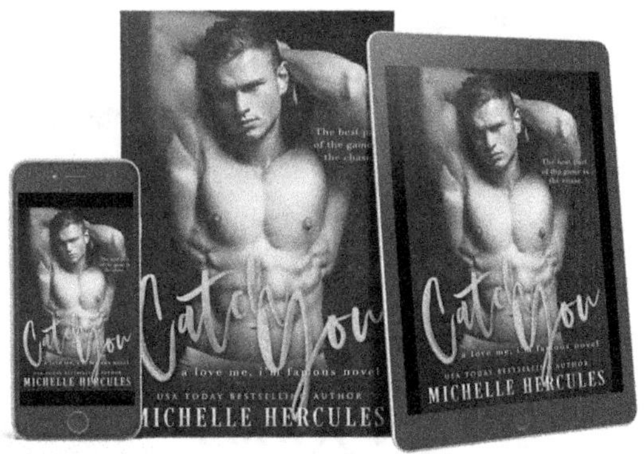

Pride and Prejudice meets Veronica Mars in this enemy-to-lovers romance.

Kimberly
I had always thought Owen Whitfield fit the mold of the

brainless jock perfectly. Group of idiot friends? Check. Vapid girlfriend? Check. Ego bigger than the moon? Check. As long as he stayed out of my way, coexisting with his kind was doable. Until one day our worlds collided, changing everything. He pissed me off so badly that I had no choice but to give him a taste of his own medicine. Little did I know that my act of revenge would come back to bite me in the ass. How was I supposed to know Owen would turn out to be the best partner in crime I could hope for?

Owen

I never paid much attention to Kimberly Dawson, but I knew who she was. Ice Queen was what we called her. She was gorgeous, no one could deny that. But she was also a condescending bitch, which was enough reason for me to stay the hell away from her. She thought I was a dumb jock, and that was okay until she came crashing into my life. Against my better judgment, I let her embroil me in her shenanigans, forcing us to spend too much time together. It was my doom. She got under my skin. She was all I could think about. I never thought I would be the knight in shining armor to anyone, not until she came along.

Scan the QR code to get your FREE copy!

ABOUT THE AUTHOR

USA Today Bestselling Author Michelle Hercules always knew creative arts were her calling but not in a million years did she think she would become an author. With a background in fashion design she thought she would follow that path. But one day, out of the blue, she had an idea for a book. One page turned into ten pages, ten pages turned into a hundred, and before she knew it, her first novel, The Prophecy of Arcadia, was born.

Michelle Hercules resides in Florida with her husband and daughter. She is currently working on the *Blueblood Vampires* series and the *Filthy Gods* series.

Sign-up for Michelle Hercules' Newsletter:

Join Michelle Hercules' Readers Group:
https://www.facebook.com/groups/mhsoars

Connect with Michelle Hercules:
www.michellehercules.com
books@mhsoars.com

facebook.com/michelleherculesauthor
instagram.com/michelleherculesauthor
amazon.com/Michelle-Hercules/e/B075652M8M
bookbub.com/authors/michelle-hercules
tiktok.com/@michelleherculesauthor?
youtube.com/@MichelleHerculesAuthor